Anton Chekhov
SHORT STORIES

Anton Chekhov

SHORT STORIES

Edited and introduced by
Gordon McVay

Foreword by
Zinovy Zinik

Illustrated by
Debra McFarlane

THE FOLIO SOCIETY
London 2001

Contents

Foreword   ix
Introduction   xiii

The Death of a Civil Servant
(*Translated by Patrick Miles and Harvey Pitcher*)   1

Fat and Thin (*Translated by Patrick Miles and Harvey Pitcher*)   4

The Huntsman (*Translated by Patrick Miles and Harvey Pitcher*)   6

Sergeant Prishibeyev
(*Translated by Patrick Miles and Harvey Pitcher*)   10

Misery (*Translated by Constance Garnett*)   14

Easter Night (*Translated by Patrick Miles and Harvey Pitcher*)   19

Romance with Double-Bass
(*Translated by Patrick Miles and Harvey Pitcher*)   29

Vanka (*Translated by Patrick Miles and Harvey Pitcher*)   35

The Reed-Pipe (*Translated by Patrick Miles and Harvey Pitcher*)   39

Boys (*Translated by Harvey Pitcher*)   47

Kashtanka (*Translated by Harvey Pitcher*)   53

A Lady's Story (*Translated by Constance Garnett*)   71

No Comment (*Translated by Patrick Miles and Harvey Pitcher*)   75

The Beauties (*Translated by Constance Garnett*)   79

A Dreary Story (*Translated by Constance Garnett*)   87

Gusev (*Translated by Constance Garnett*)   139

The Grasshopper (*Translated by Constance Garnett*)   152

In Exile (*Translated by Constance Garnett*)   175

Ward No. 6 (*Translated by Constance Garnett*)   184

The Black Monk (*Translated by Constance Garnett*)   234

Rothschild's Fiddle (*Translated by Constance Garnett*)   263

The Student (*Translated by Gordon McVay*)   272

The House with the Mezzanine (*Translated by Constance Garnett*)   276

Peasants (*Translated by Constance Garnett*)   292

Ionych (*Translated by Constance Garnett*)   322

Encased (*Translated by Harvey Pitcher*)   339

Gooseberries (*Translated by Constance Garnett*)   351

About Love (*Translated by Constance Garnett*)   361

A Doctor's Visit (*Translated by Constance Garnett*)   369

On Official Duty (*Translated by Constance Garnett*)   379

The Darling (*Translated by Harvey Pitcher*)   394

The Lady with the Dog (*Translated by Constance Garnett*)   405

In the Ravine (*Translated by Constance Garnett*)   420

The Bishop (*Translated by Constance Garnett*)   456

Notes   471

Illustrations

Everyone called her simply 'the lady with the dog' (page 405) *frontis*

Leaning against a dripping birch-tree, stood an old shepherd,
gaunt, bare-headed (page 39) *f.p.* 41

He had just reached a very high note when someone way up in the
gods uttered a loud gasp (page 69) 56

I opened the window, and fancied I was dreaming (page 132) 137

Ryabovsky, evidently much embarrassed, held out both hands to
her, as though surprised at her arrival (page 168) 152

In every dark poplar, in every grave, one felt the presence of a
mystery, promising a life which was gentle, beautiful, eternal 328

But at the very moment when he was tumbling down, Varenka
came in with two ladies (page 347) 345

In those unblinking eyes, and in that little head on the long neck,
and in her slenderness there was something snake-like (page 431) 441

In the twilight of the church the crowd swayed like the sea 456

vii

Foreword

What is the secret of Chekhov's popularity outside Russia? This hackneyed question immediately prompts another one: with which image of Chekhov is the Western world most familiar? One might note at the outset that the 'true' image of Chekhov is scarcely any clearer to his native readers in Russia than it is to his foreign admirers.

There is, of course, a stereotypically melancholic image of Chekhov, as a shy and diffident figure, a stoic dressed in black and constantly coughing, nostalgic for the old world of decaying country estates, brooding on the relentless passage of time, and lamenting the loss of human decency. This pseudo-aristocratic invention coexists with another image of Chekhov, the idol of die-hard sceptics, a man of astringent temperament, who would dismiss with sharp irony any notion of social progress as utopian nonsense dreamt up by the three sisters of Uncle Vanya in a cherry orchard, with cries of seagulls and ladies with their dogs in the background—Chekhov seen as a precursor of the Beckettian theatre of the absurd. To balance the pessimistic nature of the latter, there was also a lesser known typecasting of Chekhov, presented to students in old Soviet school textbooks—as an enthusiast of the proletarian work ethic, a moralist and educationalist, the godfather of Soviet socialist realism.

This schizophrenic multiple personality of Chekhov is further complicated by a reading of his letters, from which he emerges as a gregarious man, a womaniser and gourmand, who loved to entertain and be entertained, practical and clever with money, witty in his earthly wisdom, who managed to build two estates (in Melikhovo and in Yalta) by writing funny short stories and plays, and all his life supported his family of hapless brothers, sister, defenceless ailing mother and tyrannical heartless father. The grandson of a serf, Chekhov grew up to become the most European amongst Russian writers of his times.

And yet, in each of the parodies of the 'true' Chekhov there is a grain of truth. Moreover, the melancholic image of Chekhov, so dear to the older generation in Britain, was enhanced in his later years when, as his tuberculosis progressed, he did indeed become increasingly reclusive, shunning great public events, concentrating on life's routine, ironical towards modern political trends, while sorting out the backlog of his own past. Perhaps it was his demonstrative suspiciousness towards grand metaphysical ideas and his rejection of party ideologies, coupled with his love of gardening, that made him so attractive to the British reader, especially when it became clear that his apolitical stance, his scepticism and ostensible indifference towards 'big issues' was a cover-up for his deeply hidden romanticism. This ideological evasiveness, his instinct for self-parody and irony is, to my mind, crucial for understanding Chekhov's temperament and his work. It requires some clarification.

In a letter of February 1898 to his publisher and friend, A. S. Suvorin, Chekhov remarked that 'major writers and artists should engage in politics only enough to protect themselves from it'. Chekhov's anti-political stance was an existential necessity: for him, there was no other way to preserve one's integrity and clarity of mind in a country that, since the time of Ivan the Terrible, had been divided into a ruthless autocratic élite and a faceless populace, unevenly spread across the huge territory of Russia, treated as sub-human, and kneaded and cowed into submission by the iron-fisted administrative apparatus of a tyrannical government. In between these two dark forces, there was always a small minority of well-educated and creative intelligentsia, of writers, poets and journalists, a chattering, debating class who, in return for some protection and privileges, often allowed themselves to be used by Russia's rulers as a propaganda tool to manipulate the ignorant masses.

This vicious circle seems to be endlessly self-repeating, as if authors in Russia are forever doomed to face two choices: either to become political operators subservient to the Government, or to assume the mantle of prophets (most commonly of the Cassandra type), indulging in Tolstoyan moral invective or gloomy Dostoyevskian denunciations of liberalism. Both these alternatives were appalling to Chekhov, who defended his own rejectionist stance with irony and manifest disdain.

In reality, his attitude to the political involvement of the writer was much more complicated. One of Chekhov's early masterpieces is a sketch entitled 'The Malefactor' or 'The Wrecker' (*Zloumyshlennik*)—the story of a dim-witted villager who regularly unscrews nuts and bolts off the local railway line for use as home-made fishing tackle, and who in his innocence does not comprehend the simple fact that his actions cause the constant derailment of local trains.

This story could serve as a model for a main preoccupation of the mature Chekhov: namely, that people's immediate actions rarely correspond with their aspirations—that there is an abyss between a person's words and his deeds. And, more generally, that grandiose ideals (whether it is the Future Happiness of Mankind or the Radiant Future of the Railways) are often expressed to conceal a mediocre and unhappy mind that takes refuge in face-saving rhetoric. Unlike his characters, the author tactfully encourages us to try to survive without such 'lofty ideas'—be these the ecclesiastical mysticism of Dostoyevsky or the dialectical materialism of Marx. His characters, in his later stories as well as in his plays, demonstrate that it is very easy in our age to become a party demagogue or a persecuted intellectual, but very difficult to opt for loneliness and integrity.

But Chekhov also knew that without a profound sense of belonging to something larger than our egotistical self, man dies. The befuddled simpleton who is capable of dismantling an entire railway line for his angling equipment is not very far in his bewilderment from a character created by the later Chekhov, Professor Kovrin in the story 'The Black Monk'. In this fable of lost aspirations, the gigantic fleeting shadow of the Black Monk is a figment of the Professor's diseased imagination, an apparition of his haunted self, a token of a megalomaniac's delirium: but the moment this apparition disappears, Kovrin loses any sense of the uniqueness of his gifts, ambitions and desires, he becomes a nobody and recognises his own mediocrity. Should we cling to our deliriums (utopian ideologies, religious obsessions) or should we wake up to so-called reality, whatever the cost and means?

Chekhov (like some of his characters) had an occasional dream of falling asleep with the hope of waking up from the nightmare of the present into the radiant light of a future forty or more years on. A comparison of the related dates shows that he might have woken up in the heyday of the Stalinist purges, in which the typically Chekhovian exhortation to work had been transcribed to fit the regulations of a Soviet labour camp. Yet, had this happened, Chekhov would have been well equipped to preserve his moral integrity in such an atmosphere of the ideological manipulation of words. He was not against political involvement as such, but against the demagogical abuse of words in political life, and in exposing this abuse he saw the precise political role of the writer.

At the time of the Dreyfus trial in 1898 Chekhov was in Nice, where he closely followed the turmoil caused by Émile Zola's 'J'Accuse', an open letter to the French authorities which split the French intellectual world down the middle*. Chekhov admired Zola's courageous stand, and became convinced of Dreyfus's innocence. However, among those who sided with the French establishment against its victim was Chekhov's friend, A. S. Suvorin, editor of the influential conservative newspaper, *New Times*. In his letter to Suvorin, already mentioned above, Chekhov described the political atmosphere in France at the time of the Dreyfus trial—the insincerity, prejudice and anti-Semitism. Chekhov maintained:

> Even if Dreyfus were guilty Zola would still be right, for the writer's task is not to accuse or persecute, but to stand up even for the guilty once they have been condemned and are suffering punishment. People will retort: what about politics and the interests of the State? But major writers and artists should engage in politics only enough to protect themselves from it. There are enough accusers, public prosecutors and gendarmes without writers joining in, and in any case the role of Paul is more becoming for writers than is the role of Saul.

In his cautious approach to democracy, Chekhov always sides with individuals, not political causes. Unexpectedly for a Russian, Chekhov has faith in us regardless of our political affiliations or social status. We love him because he loves us, even though we no longer love ourselves. Chekhov firmly believes that in the most wretched of human beings there is an explosive element of unpredictability, a potential for change. This change of personal fate is sometimes invisible to the outside world, sometimes not comprehended even by the person undergoing change; but in any case, according to Chekhov, it is not conditioned simply by the proverbial cast-iron Russian political alternatives of bloody tyranny versus religious mysticism. And Chekhov's promise of such an inner change gives us all an equal chance of salvation, at least in the realm of the author's imagination. It had happened to Professor Kovrin with his Black Monk and it happened to the philanderer Gurov and his Lady with the Dog. It happens to us, too, each time we read that elusive writer Anton Chekhov, and try to define his true image.

ZINOVY ZINIK

* Alfred Dreyfus was a captain of Jewish origin in the French army accused, court-martialled and sentenced to life imprisonment on Devil's Island on a false charge of espionage, in order to cover up the corruption and conspiracy amongst the highest ranks of the French military.

Introduction

I

Chekhov's art reflects the man—elusive, subtle, and understated, humane, modest, and undogmatic. Biographies and investigations abound, yet critics remain perplexed by the enigma of his personality and of his works. Reserve and 'objectivity' evoke a multiplicity of response.*

In Britain Chekhov is best known for the great dramatic quartet—*The Seagull, Uncle Vanya, Three Sisters*, and *The Cherry Orchard*. These mysteriously ambiguous plays, with their 'subtext' and 'undercurrents', their characteristic blend of triviality and profundity, relevance and irrelevance, laughter and tears, require for performance a selfless ensemble and the most delicate orchestration.

Desmond MacCarthy noted, over sixty years ago, that 'the themes of personal despair and universal hope are interwoven':

> Chekov is the dramatist of good-byes . . . ; good-byes to hopes, possessions and ambitions, good-byes to love . . . Yet out of this conception of life, which the practical optimist would label 'depressing', and the Communist regard as sociologically symptomatic, Chekov makes a work of art which exalts like a beautiful piece of music. It is not in a mood of depression one leaves the theatre after seeing *The Three Sisters*, the best of all his plays . . .†

Yet Chekhov's greatest plays were all composed in his last decade, when they were scrupulously, if at times over-fussily, staged by Stanislavsky and Nemirovich-Danchenko at the newly founded Moscow Arts Theatre. Throughout his brief life, Chekhov was regarded as primarily a writer of short stories.

The self-deprecating author once famously declared: 'Medicine is my

---

* For a brief biographical sketch of Chekhov, see the Notes, p. 471.
† Desmond MacCarthy, *The New Statesman and Nation*, 5 February 1938, p. 206. MacCarthy here spells the writer's name as Chekov. Others have preferred Checkov, Chehov, Chekoff, Tchechov, Tchehov, Tchekhof, etc.

lawful wife, and literature is my mistress.'* However, within the artistic sphere, he felt more at ease with the short story: 'Prose writing is an unhurried and sacred undertaking. The narrative form is a lawful wife, whereas the dramatic form is a gaudy, loud-mouthed, brazen and tiresome mistress.'†

Although universal in theme and mood, Chekhov's plays present a limited cross-section of Russian society—mainly the educated middle class or gentry (landowners, doctors, teachers, writers, actresses, soldiers)—set alongside a sprinkling of servants. Yet his imagination was restless, and his experience wide, from the Ukrainian steppes to the Siberian wastes, from the literary world of Moscow and Petersburg to the life of country doctors and peasants in Melikhovo and beyond. He wrote to Aleksey Suvorin on 27 October 1888: 'In this head of mine there's a whole army of people longing to be let out and waiting for my command . . .'

It was in his short stories that this 'army' was released. Korney Chukovsky eloquently observed:

> If all the people portrayed in the many-volumed collection of Chekhov's *Short Stories*—all his policemen, midwives, actors, tailors, prisoners, cooks, religious devotees, teachers, prostitutes, landowners, bishops, circus performers, functionaries of all ranks and departments, peasants from northern and from southern regions, generals, bathhouse attendants, engineers, horse-thieves, monastery novices, merchants, singers, soldiers, match-makers, piano-tuners, firemen, examining judges, deacons, professors, shepherds, lawyers—if all of these could, in some miraculous way, come streaming forth from his books out into a Moscow street, what a terrific mob they would make!—even the largest square could not hold such a crowd.‡

It would be a travesty to depict the mature Chekhov as an exuberantly cheerful writer, or a boisterously extrovert person, but Chukovsky's

* Letter to A. S. Suvorin, Moscow, 11 September 1888. This comment is varied in letters of 17 January 1887, 11 February 1893 and 15 March 1896. All quotations from his letters are from *Chekhov: A Life in Letters* (London: The Folio Society, 1994)
† Letter to A. N. Pleshcheyev, Moscow, 15 January 1889.
‡ Kornei [Korney] Chukovsky, *Chekhov the Man*, translated from the Russian by Pauline Rose (London: Hutchinson, 1945), p. 8.

point is well made. Chekhov, indeed, began his career as a purveyor of carefree bagatelles for the humorous, light-weight journals of Moscow and Petersburg. When studying medicine at Moscow University (1879–84), he composed and published hundreds of comic short stories, often under the pseudonym Antosha Chekhonte. The pressure of deadlines and word-limits helped to teach him the art of conciseness.

From late 1885 he found himself fêted by celebrated authors such as Dmitry Grigorovich, and by the editor Aleksey Suvorin. He attracted the attention of serious, 'thick' journals, publishing his long stories 'The Steppe' in 1888 and 'A Dreary Story' in 1889, as well as various collections. Several plays were performed, including popular one-acters such as *The Bear* and *The Proposal*, and more complex full-length dramas such as *Ivanov* and *The Wood Demon*.

While professing a streak of south Russian indolence, Chekhov toiled unremittingly. Ill-health and fastidiousness reduced the quantity of his output, and its quality soared. After 1890 he achieved many of his finest stories, including 'Ward No. 6', 'The Student', 'The House with the Mezzanine', 'Peasants', 'Ionych', 'Encased', 'The Lady with the Dog', 'In the Ravine', and 'The Bishop'. In 1895 his scientific and humanitarian treatise *The Island of Sakhalin* eventually appeared in book form.

Painstakingly and unostentatiously, Chekhov illumined everyday, mundane material, to illustrate his perpetual themes—the elusiveness of love, the fragility of marriage, the near-impossibility and even undesirability of personal (and hence selfish) happiness, the pervasiveness of human waste, loneliness, and frustration, the ubiquity of *poshlost* ' (vulgar, trite banality), the gulf between aspiration and achievement, the inexorable passage of time, and yet also mankind's indomitable longing for meaning, freedom, the ideal. Chekhov's mature short stories, like his plays, are distinguished by their subtlety of 'mood', unobtrusive musicality, and inconclusive conclusions, and by episodes of 'epiphany', when the present moment opens unexpectedly into eternity.*

Chekhov's gloomy reputation is, perhaps, hardly surprising. Death,

---

* These moments of transfiguration or heightened awareness (when the present reaches out into the past and the future) may be experienced by the characters themselves or the narrator, in visions, dreams, memories, reflections, upon dying or thinking of death. At such moments—for instance, in 'Gusev', 'The Student', 'The House with the Mezzanine', 'Ionych', 'Gooseberries', 'The Lady with the Dog', 'In the Ravine', and 'The Bishop'—the sensitive reader responds in sympathy.

misery, mediocrity and folly pervade his greatest stories. Stunted lives, misplaced goals, such a yearning for love—and such lovelessness. Peggy Ashcroft remarked in 1989: 'You can't be black and white when you talk about Chekhov . . . I think he was a bit of a pessimist really. He was a pretty sad man himself . . . When I say he's a pessimist, I mean that he doesn't think that suddenly it's going to be all lovely for any of the characters. He knows that it's going to go on being very, very difficult.'*

NB.

Peggy Ashcroft understood that the categories of 'optimism' and 'pessimism' (or 'comedy' and 'tragedy') are inadequate and almost irrelevant when applied to Anton Chekhov. Hence critics have tentatively called his plays 'tragi-comedies', and his outlook on life 'optimo-pessimism'.† His best works, such as *Three Sisters* and 'The Bishop', capture the beauty and the brevity of human life, the blessing and the bewilderment.

In 1923 William Gerhardie pondered:

Chehov was neither pessimist nor optimist. To him life is neither horrible nor happy, but unique, strange, fleeting, beautiful and awful . . .
. . . All the time he works on real life. But in his hands it becomes more than real life; and, after Chehov has done with it, it is still real life . . . There is behind it all a quite exceptional gift of love and sympathy . . . And there is that sense of the temporary nature of our existence on this earth at all events, that he seems never able to forget, through which human beings, scenery, and even the very shallowness of things, are transfigured with a sense of disquieting importance . . . It is as if his people hastened to express their worthless individualities, since that is all they have, and were aghast that they should have so little in them to express: since the expression of it is all there is. And life is at once too long and too short to be endured.‡

Chekhov's sensitive characters seek, yet seldom find. The professor (in 'A Dreary Story') and Bishop Pyotr (in 'The Bishop') realise that something most important is missing from their lives. At the end of 'The

* See Gordon McVay, 'Peggy Ashcroft and Chekhov', in *Chekhov on the British Stage*, ed. Patrick Miles (Cambridge: Cambridge University Press, 1993), p. 84.
† S. N. Bulgakov, *Chekhov, kak myslitel'* [*Chekhov as a Thinker*] (Moscow: 'Literaturnyi kruzhok imeni A. P. Chekhova', 1910), p. 31.
‡ William Gerhardi [Gerhardie], *Anton Chehov: A Critical Study* (London: Richard Cobden-Sanderson, 1923), pp. 22, 153.

Lady with the Dog', Gurov and Anna still strive for openness and free-dom. Exceptionally, Ivan Velikopolsky (in 'The Student') is granted an insight into the abiding power of truth and beauty.

Beyond the picture of life as it is Chekhov shows a dream of life as it might be. In him the lure of cynicism is countered by the fire of idealism. Vladimir Lakshin described Chekhov as an 'advocate of inner freedom': 'His path was that of the lonely, conscientious quest for truth. The path of patience and tolerance. Of justice and compassion for others.'*

Chekhov's attitude to religion is ambivalent. Although his letters con-tain several avowals of disbelief, the spiritual values and moral code of Christianity were ingrained in him since childhood.† Thus, he could see himself as a kind of secular monk, and advocate a solitary search for faith, 'all alone with one's conscience'.‡ Such stories as 'Easter Night', 'The Student', and 'The Bishop' show a sympathetic understanding of the religious mentality.

Mikhail Gromov maintained that Chekhov possessed the quality of 'being civilised in a Christian manner': 'He was not a religious person, but he liked this stylistic ambience of solitude, pensiveness, silence.' From early in life he had become accustomed to the loneliness, the almost monastic austerity, and the patient concentration of literary work.§

In one of his notebooks Chekhov wrote:

Between 'God exists' and 'there is no God' there lies an entire vast field which a true sage traverses with great difficulty. A Russian knows

---

* V. Ya. Lakshin, in the volume *Chekhoviana: Chekhov v kul'ture XX veka* [*Chekhov-iana: Chekhov in Twentieth-Century Culture*], ed. V. Ya. Lakshin *et al.* (Moscow: 'Nauka', 1993), p. 4.

† Chekhov wrote: 'I have no religion now' (to I. L. Leontyev, Melikhovo, 9 March 1892); 'I'm a non-believer' (to M. O. Menshikov, Yalta, 28 January 1900); 'I lost my faith long ago' (to S. P. Diaghilev, Yalta, 12 July 1903). Yet the values he esteemed most highly coincide with those of Christianity—freedom, justice, goodness, truth, conscience, mercy, forgiveness, duty, patience, harmony, beauty, a quest for purpose and noble meaning.

‡ 'If non-religious people were allowed to live in monasteries and were excused from prayer, then I would become a monk' (to A. S. Suvorin, Melikhovo, 1 December 1895); 'One ought to believe in God, but, if faith is absent, one shouldn't replace it by idle sensationalism, but instead seek and seek, seek all by oneself, all alone with one's conscience' (to V. S. Mirolyubov, Yalta, 17 December 1901).

§ Mikhail Gromov, *Chekhov* (Moscow: 'Molodaya gvardiya', 1993), pp. 163, 59, 40.

only one of these two extremes, but he finds the middle ground between them uninteresting, and he usually knows nothing or very little.*

Chekhov's greatest work, so complex in its simplicity and so profound in its ordinariness, explores the middle ground between sense and senselessness, love and loneliness, belief and disbelief, joy and grief, freedom and restriction, involvement and indifference, civilisation and barbarity, truth and falsehood, health and ill-health, light and dark, life and death.

His reputation has fluctuated during the past hundred years, but is now firmly established. The essential ambiguity of his tragi-comic art has led some to view him as a wistful, autumnal pessimist, a killer of human hopes, while others perceive him as fundamentally a humorist, ironic, absurdist, or detached. Chekhov combines compassion with irony, the absence of illusion with a yearning for faith, something close to despair with something akin to hope. He helps us to endure.

In a letter of 1888 Chekhov made his most famous pronouncement on freedom and truth:

> I'm afraid of people who try to read between the lines to find my 'tendency' and who will insist on viewing me as a liberal or conservative. I'm not a liberal, or a conservative, or a gradualist, or a monk, or an indifferentist. I should like to be a free artist and that's all, and I regret that God has not given me the strength to be one. I hate lies and violence of all kinds . . . I regard signs and labels as mere prejudice. My holy of holies is the human body, health, intelligence, talent, inspiration, love and the most absolute freedom imaginable, freedom from violence and lies, no matter what form these may take. That is the programme I would adhere to if I were a great artist . . .†

It seems particularly apt that the man who loathed labels succeeds so triumphantly in evading categorisation.

---

* Quoted, for instance, in Gordon McVay, *Chekhov's 'Three Sisters'* (London: Bristol Classical Press, 1995), pp. 81–2 (similarly, in a diary note of 1897).
† Letter to A. N. Pleshcheyev, Moscow, 4 October 1888.

II

As Chekhov's fame increased towards the end of the 1880s, a number of critics (mainly journalists of a utilitarian, socially committed hue) began to assail him for his apparent failure to propound aims, ideals, opinions, and 'solutions' in his works. In response to such attacks, Chekhov gradually formulated his own concept of the dispassionate, objective, non-judgemental author. As a point of principle, he not only disclaimed authorial omniscience and the right or duty to moralise, but actually professed the positive value of disclosing one's own ignorance. He emphasised that the writer's task was to pose a question correctly, but not to offer solutions.

Yet, although his scientific training and habitual scepticism inclined him towards non-didactic objectivity, Chekhov remained deeply aware of the importance of 'aims' for an author, and of the aimlessness which he deemed characteristic of himself and the writers of his generation.*

Moreover, despite his air of aloofness, Chekhov was never a totally neutral and impartial observer. He selected his material carefully, inviting the readers to act as jury. He aspired to truthfulness, brevity, originality, and sincerity, cultivating 'indifference' and 'coldness' as a deliberate artistic device, to intensify the emotional effectiveness of his writing. For all his restraint and seeming inscrutability, he valued culture, civilisation, charity, and sensitivity. He was never a proponent of 'amoral' art.

Chekhov's letters illuminate his literary aims and methods:

It seems to me that one shouldn't expect writers to solve such questions as God, pessimism, and so on. The writer's task is simply to

* 'Remember that the writers we call eternal or merely good, and who intoxicate us, possess one extremely important feature in common: they are going somewhere and summon you to follow them, and you can sense with your entire being, not only with your mind, that they have a definite aim . . . The best writers among them are realistic and describe life as it is, but because every line is saturated with a conscious aim, you can feel, apart from life as it is, also life as it should be, and this captivates you. But what about us? . . . We have neither immediate nor distant aims, and our souls are quite empty. We have no politics, we don't believe in revolution, there's no God, we're not afraid of ghosts, and I personally do not fear even death or blindness. A person who desires nothing, hopes for nothing and fears nothing cannot be an artist' (letter to A. S. Suvorin, Melikhovo, 25 November 1892).

record how and in what circumstances somebody spoke or thought about God or pessimism. The artist should not be the judge of his characters and of what they say, but only an impartial witness. I heard a confused, totally inconclusive conversation of two Russians about pessimism and my duty is to convey this conversation exactly as I heard it, whereas the people to evaluate the conversation are the jury, that is, the readers. My only task is to be talented, that is, to know how to distinguish important evidence from the unimportant, to know how to illuminate characters and speak in their language . . . It's high time for writers, especially artists, to admit that in this world one can't understand anything, as Socrates once admitted, and Voltaire . . .*

An artist observes, selects, conjectures, arranges—and these very acts presuppose as their starting-point a question—for if from the start he's not set himself a question, there would be nothing to conjecture or select . . .

In demanding that an artist should have a conscious attitude towards his work you are right, but you are confusing two concepts: *solving a question* and *posing a question correctly*. Only the latter is obligatory for an artist . . .†

Chekhov knew the value of laconicism and restraint, and cherished the expressive, polished detail. He wrote to his brother Aleksandr: 'Brevity is the sister of talent' (Moscow, 11 April 1889); 'Beware of precious language. Language should be simple and elegant' (Sumy, 8 May 1889).

He advocated self-control, not self-indulgence, and shunned sentimentality:

I wrote to you once that one has to be indifferent when writing sad stories. You didn't understand what I meant. One can weep and groan as one writes, and suffer along with one's heroes, but I think one must do so without the reader noticing. It makes a more powerful impression the more objective one is. That's what I meant . . .‡

* Letter to A. S. Suvorin, Sumy, 30 May 1888.
† Letter to A. S. Suvorin, Moscow, 27 October 1888.
‡ Letter to L. A. Avilova, Melikhovo, 29 April 1892.

Allow me to repeat my advice—write more coldly. The more emotional a scene is, the more coldly one should write, and the more powerful will be the emotional effect. One shouldn't coat things in sugar . . .*

Chekhov encouraged Maksim Gorky, the autodidact from Nizhny Novgorod, who had become a national celebrity in 1898 after publishing two volumes of stories:

Your only shortcoming is a lack of restraint, a lack of grace. Grace is when a person spends the minimum of energy to achieve a particular effect. Your expenditure is patently excessive.

Your descriptions of nature are artistic; you're a genuine landscape painter. But the frequent comparisons with human beings (anthropomorphism), when the sea breathes, the sky gazes, the steppe basks, nature whispers, speaks, grieves, etc.—such comparisons make the descriptions rather monotonous, sometimes sugary, sometimes vague. Vividness and expressiveness in nature descriptions can be achieved only by simplicity, by such simple phrases as 'the sun set', 'it turned dark', 'it started to rain' and so on—and you possess this simplicity to a high degree, unlike most writers . . .†

Here's another piece of advice: when you're reading proofs, strike out, wherever possible, words qualifying nouns and verbs. You have so many qualifying words that the reader's attention becomes confused and wearied. It's quite clear when I write: 'A man sat down on the grass.' It's clear because it's simple and doesn't hold up one's attention. On the contrary, it's obscure and hard on the brain if I write: 'A tall, narrow-chested, red-bearded man of medium height sat down on the green grass, which had already been trampled underfoot, sat down noiselessly, glancing round timidly and fearfully.' That doesn't sink in immediately, and yet fiction *has* to sink in immediately, in one second . . .‡

---

* Letter to L. A. Avilova, Moscow, 1 March 1893.
† Letter to M. Gorky, Yalta, 3 January 1899.
‡ Letter to M. Gorky, Yalta, 3 September 1899.

III

The thirty-four stories in this Folio edition are arranged chronologically, spanning from 1883 to 1902.* These stories, chosen for their artistic excellence and thematic variety, demonstrate Chekhov's 'exquisite' sense, 'amounting to genius, of what must be said and what can be left out, of a setting, an atmosphere, a situation, a character, all presented in the fewest possible strokes'.†

Throughout the volume, the Russian system of names has been preserved. In full, this consists of a first or Christian name, followed by a patronymic (son or daughter of the father) and surname. Characters are often described formally by their Christian name and patronymic alone (without the surname); women's names have feminine endings; diminutives are used to express familiarity, endearment, etc. Thus, Ivan Dmitrich (son of Dmitry) Gromov, in 'Ward No. 6', is usually referred to politely as Ivan Dmitrich; his affectionate first name is Vanya.

It was difficult to decide which stories to omit. A second volume, scarcely inferior, might be compiled, to include such longer works as 'The Steppe', 'The Duel', and 'My Life', and shorter pieces such as 'Enemies', 'The Kiss', 'Neighbours', 'The Teacher of Literature' ['The Russian Master'], 'Anna on the Neck', 'The Bride', and many, many more.

The music-loving Chekhov was very conscious of the 'musicality' of prose. 'I usually put the finishing touches to a story in proof-form, and correct it, so to speak, from the musical point of view.'‡ 'A sentence has to be made—that's what art is. Anything superfluous must be discarded . . . You have to pay attention to its musicality and not tolerate "came" and "became" almost side by side in the same sentence.'§

For all his love of brevity and simplicity, Chekhov wrote, quite often, in long, flowing, unhurried sentences, which contain musical cadences

* See the Textual Notes, pp. 472–80 for Russian titles, details of first publication, etc.
† J. B. Priestley, *Anton Chekhov* (London: International Profiles [International Textbook Company Limited], 1970), p. 84.
‡ Letter to V. M. Sobolevsky, Nice, 20 November [2 December] 1897.
§ Letter to L. A. Avilova, Nice, 3 [15] November 1897. Writing to R. F. Vashchuk on 28 March 1897 he stressed the importance of correct, literary punctuation, 'because in a work of art punctuation often plays the part of musical notation'.

(threefold groupings of verbs, nouns or adjectives) and a distinct, if subdued, lyricism. Many recent translators misguidedly 'modernise' Chekhov, transposing his vocabulary, phraseology and sensibility into an alien, brisk, crude, vulgarly hearty key. The result, at times, is as if an Impressionist painting had been overpainted in Expressionist style—the original colours and contours are barely discernible.

Of current translations, those by Patrick Miles and Harvey Pitcher are outstanding, in their accuracy and in their fidelity to Chekhov's true voice. Their versions required little, or no, emendation for this Folio selection.

In Britain a unique position is occupied by Constance Garnett (1861–1946), whose pioneering translations of Chekhov's stories appeared in thirteen volumes, from 1916 to 1922. Garnett's versions are generally accurate, and particularly felicitous in conveying the rhythm and texture of Chekhov's prose, and his descriptions of nature and people. Her dialogue, however, is often stilted, and she frequently fails to capture Chekhov's deliberate repetition of significant words and phrases. Accordingly, I have revised Constance Garnett's translations for this edition, in the hope of bringing them even closer to the spirit and letter of Chekhov's text.*

For their help and encouragement in preparing this book, and in translating 'The Student', I am especially grateful to my wife Kathy, my son Martin, my daughter Mary, Patrick Miles, Harvey Pitcher, Kit Shepherd, Lucy Smith and Emily Thwaite.

* No rendition of a Chekhov story can be wholly adequate or definitive. 'The Student', for instance, is written in unobtrusively rhythmical prose, embodying an intricate pattern of echoes and associations. In the Biblical narrative, direct quotations from the Gospels are interwoven with colloquial speech; past and present are linked by numerous parallels (woodcock, thrush, cock; light, fire, flames; workmen, cold, torment; supper, Last Supper; the widows' allotments, the Garden of Gethsemane; [non-]recognising and remembering). Both Peter and the student warm themselves, Jesus and Lukerya are hit, Peter and Vasilisa start weeping, Peter and Lukerya are troubled. Words and images recur, forming minor leitmotivs—darkness, gloom, night, evening; desert, deserted; the wind, blowing; dull, still; spring, winter; east, west; face, expression; shuddered, quivered, flickered, stirred, trembled; all around, afar off, close; could be heard, happened, continued, unbroken; it seemed, he thought, reflected, evidently, probably, apparently; home, mother, earth, death, life, soul. The story progresses from denial to recognition, from a feeling of oppression to a feeling of youth, health, strength. He was only twenty-two years old . . .

Vladimir Lakshin once remarked that Chekhov's quiet voice can best be heard, 'not in ceremonial halls or upon a crowded square, but in the silence of one's home, the snugness of a railway compartment, on the terrace of a *dacha* [country cottage], when sitting by lamplight'.*

Chekhov's stories are to be savoured in tranquillity.

GORDON McVAY

* V. Ya. Lakshin, in the volume *Chekhoviana: Chekhov v kul'ture XX veka*, p. 5.

The Death of a Civil Servant

One fine evening, a no less fine office factotum, Ivan Dmitrich Kreepikov, was sitting in the second row of the stalls and watching *The Chimes of
Normandy* through opera-glasses. He watched, and felt on top of the
world. But suddenly . . . You often come across this 'But suddenly . . .' in
short stories. And authors are right: life is so full of surprises! But suddenly, then, his face puckered, his eyes rolled upwards, his breathing
ceased—he lowered his opera-glasses, bent forward, and . . . atchoo!!!
Sneezed, in other words. Now sneezing isn't prohibited to anyone or in
any place. Peasants sneeze, chiefs of police sneeze, and sometimes even
Number 3s in the Civil Service. Everyone sneezes. Kreepikov did not
feel embarrassed at all, he simply wiped his nose with his handkerchief
and, being a polite kind of person, looked about him to see if he had
disturbed anyone by sneezing. But then he did have cause for embarrassment. He saw that the little old gentleman sitting in front of him, in the
first row, was carefully wiping his pate and the back of his neck with his
glove, and muttering something. And in the elderly gentleman Kreepikov recognised General Shpritsalov, a Number 2 in the Ministry of
Communications.

'I spattered him!' thought Kreepikov. 'He's not my chief, it's true, but
even so, it's awkward. I'll have to apologise.'

So he gave a cough, bent respectfully forward, and whispered in the
General's ear:

'Please excuse me, Your Excellency, for spattering you . . . it was quite
unintentional . . .'

'That's all right, that's all right . . .'

'Please, please forgive me. I—I didn't mean to!'

'Oh do sit down, please, I can't hear the opera!'

Disconcerted by this, Kreepikov gave a stupid grin, sat down, and
began to watch the stage again. He watched, but no longer did he feel on
top of the world. He began to feel pangs of worry. In the interval he went
over to Shpritsalov, sidled along with him, and, conquering his timidity,
stammered:

'I spattered you, Your Excellency . . . Please forgive me . . . I—it
wasn't that—'

'Oh for goodness' sake . . . I'd already forgotten, so why keep on about it!' said the General, and twitched his lower lip impatiently.

'Hm, he says he's forgotten,' thought Kreepikov, eyeing the General mistrustfully, 'but looks as nasty as you make 'em. He won't even talk about it. I'll have to explain that I didn't want—that sneezing's a law of nature . . . Otherwise he may think I meant to *spit* at him. And if he doesn't now, he may later! . . .'

When he got home, Kreepikov told his wife about his breach of good manners. His wife, he felt, treated the incident much too lightly: at first she had quite a fright, but as soon as she learned that Shpritsalov was 'someone else's' chief, she calmed down again.

'Even so, you go along and apologise,' she said. 'Otherwise he'll think you don't know how to behave in public!'

'That's right! I did apologise to him, but he acted sort of strangely . . . I couldn't get a word of sense out of him. There wasn't time to discuss it, either.'

Next day, Kreepikov put on his new uniform, had his hair trimmed, and went to Shpritsalov to explain . . . As he entered the General's audience-room, he saw a throng of people there, and in their midst the General himself, who had just begun hearing petitions. After dealing with several petitioners, the General looked up in Kreepikov's direction.

'Yesterday at the Arcadia Theatre, Your Excellency, if you recall,' the little clerk began his speech, 'I sneezed, sir, and—inadvertently spattered . . . Forg—'

'Drivel, sir! . . . You're wasting my time. Next!' said the General, turning to another petitioner.

'He won't even talk about it!' thought Kreepikov, going pale. 'He must be angry, then . . . No, I can't leave it at that . . . I must explain to him . . .'

When the General had finished interviewing the last petitioner and was on his way back to the inner recesses of the department, Kreepikov strode after him and mumbled:

'Your Excellency! If I make so bold as to bother Your Excellency, it is only from a sense of—of deep repentance, so to speak! . . . I'm not doing it on purpose, sir, you must believe me!'

The General pulled an agonised face and brushed him aside.

'Are you trying to be funny, sir?' he said, and vanished behind a door.

'Funny?' thought Kreepikov. 'Of course I'm not trying to be funny! Calls himself a general and can't understand! Well, if he's going to be so snooty about it, I'm not going to apologise any more! To hell with him! I don't mind writing him a letter, but I'm not coming all the way over here again. Oh no!'

Such were Kreepikov's thoughts as he made his way home. He did not write to the General, though. He thought and thought, but just could not think what to say. So next morning he had to go to explain in person.

'Yesterday I came and disturbed Your Excellency,' he started stammering, when the General raised his eyes questioningly at him, 'not to try and be funny, as you so kindly put it. I came to apologise for sneezing and spattering you, sir—it never occurred to me to try and be funny. How could I dare to laugh?! If we all went about laughing at people, there'd be no respect for persons, er, left in the world—'

'Clear out!!' bellowed the General suddenly, turning purple and trembling with rage.

'Wha-what?' Kreepikov asked in a whisper, swooning with terror.

'Clear out!!' the General repeated, stamping his feet.

Something snapped in Kreepikov's stomach. Without seeing anything, without hearing anything, he staggered backwards to the door, reached the street, and wandered off . . . He entered his home mechanically, without taking off his uniform lay down on the sofa, and . . . died.

Fat and Thin

Two friends bumped into each other at the Nikolayevsky railway station: one was fat, the other thin. The fat man had just dined in the station restaurant and his lips were still coated with grease and gleamed like ripe cherries. He smelt of sherry and *fleurs d'oranger*. The thin man had just got out of a carriage and was loaded down with suitcases, bundles and bandboxes. He smelt of boiled ham and coffee-grounds. Peeping out from behind his back was a lean woman with a long chin—his wife, and a lanky schoolboy with a drooping eyelid—his son.

'Porfiry!' exclaimed the fat man, on seeing the thin. 'Is it you? My dear chap! I haven't seen you for ages!'

'Good Lord!' cried the thin in astonishment. 'It's Misha! My old schoolmate! Fancy meeting you here!'

The two friends kissed and hugged three times and stood gazing at each other with tears in their eyes. It was a pleasant shock for both of them.

'My dear old chap!' began Thin after they had finished kissing. 'Who would have guessed! Well what a surprise! Let's have a good look at you! Yes, as smart and handsome as ever! You always were a bit of a dandy, a bit of a lad, eh? Well I never! And how are you? Rich? Married? I'm married, as you see . . . This is my wife Luise, née Wanzenbach . . . er, of the Lutheran persuasion . . . And this is my son Nathaniel—he's in the third form. Misha was my childhood companion, Nat! We were at grammar school together!'

Nathaniel thought for a moment, then removed his cap.

'Yes, we were at grammar school together!' Thin continued. 'Remember how we used to tease you and call you "Herostratos", because you once burned a hole in your school textbook with a cigarette? And they called me "Ephialtes", because I was always sneaking on people. Ho-ho . . . What lads we were! Don't be shy, Nat! Come a bit closer . . . And this is my wife, née Wanzenbach . . . er, Lutheran.'

Nathaniel thought for a moment, then took refuge behind his father's back.

'Well, how are you doing, old chap?' asked Fat, looking at his friend quite enraptured. 'In the Service, are you? On your way up?'

'Yes, old boy, I've had my Grade 8 two years now—and I've got my St

Stanislas. The pay's bad, but, well, so what! The wife gives music lessons and I make wooden cigarette-cases on the side—good ones, too! I sell them at a rouble a time, and if you buy ten or more then I give a discount. We manage. First, you know, I worked in one of the Ministry's departments, now I've been transferred here as head of a sub-office . . . So I'll be working here. And what about yourself? You must be a 5 now, eh?'

'No, try a bit higher, old chap,' said Fat. 'Actually I'm a Number 3 . . . I've got my two stars.'

Thin suddenly went pale, turned to stone; but then his whole face twisted itself into an enormous grin, and sparks seemed to shoot from his eyes and face. He himself shrank, bent double, grew even thinner . . . And all his cases, bundles and bandboxes shrank and shrivelled, too . . . His wife's long chin grew even longer, Nathaniel sprang to attention and did up all the buttons on his uniform . . .

'Your Excellency, I—This is indeed an honour! The companion, so to speak, of my childhood, and all of a sudden become such an important personage! Hee-hee-hee . . .'

'Come now, Porfiry!' frowned Fat. 'Why this change of tone? You and I have known each other since we were children—rank has no place between us!'

'But sir . . . How can you—' giggled Thin, shrinking even smaller. 'The gracious attention of Your Excellency is as—as manna from on high to . . . This, Your Excellency, is my son Nathaniel . . . and this is my wife Luise, Lutheran so to speak . . .'

Fat was about to object, but such awe, such unction and such abject servility were written on Thin's face that the Number 3's stomach heaved. He took a step back and offered Thin his hand.

Thin took his middle three fingers, bent double over them, and giggled 'Hee-hee-hee' like a Chinaman. His wife beamed. Nathaniel clicked his heels and dropped his cap. It was a pleasant shock for all three of them.

The Huntsman

It is midday, hot and close. Not a puff of cloud in the sky . . . The sun-parched grass looks at you sullenly, despairingly: even a downpour won't turn it green now . . . The forest stands there silent and still, as if gazing somewhere with the tops of its trees, or waiting for something.

Along the edge of the scrub ambles a tall, narrow-shouldered man of about forty with a lazy, rolling gait and wearing a red shirt, patched trousers that were his master's cast-offs, and big boots. He is ambling along the road. To his right is the green of the scrub, to his left a golden sea of ripe rye stretching to the very horizon . . . He is red in the face and sweating. Perched jauntily on his handsome, flaxen head is a small white cap with a stiff jockey peak to it—evidently a present from some young gentleman in a fit of generosity. He has a shooting-bag over his shoulder, with a rumpled black grouse hanging out of it. The man is holding a cocked twelve-bore in his hands and keeping a weather eye on his lean old dog, who has run ahead and is sniffing round the bushes. All is completely quiet, not a sound in the air . . . Every living thing has hidden away from the heat.

'Yegor Vlasych!' the sportsman suddenly hears a soft voice say.

He starts, looks round, and frowns. Right beside him, as though she had just sprung out of the ground, stands a pale-faced peasant woman of about thirty, with a sickle in her hand. She tries to look into his face, and smiles at him bashfully.

'Oh, it's you, Pelageya!' says the sportsman, stopping and slowly uncocking his gun. 'Hm! . . . What brings you to these parts?'

'The girls from our village are working here, so I've come over with them . . . As a labourer, Yegor Vlasych.'

'Uhuh . . .' grunts Yegor Vlasych, and slowly continues on his way.

Pelageya follows him. They walk about twenty paces in silence.

'It's a long time since I saw you last, Yegor Vlasych . . .' says Pelageya, looking fondly at the rippling motion of his shoulders. 'Not since you came into our hut for a drink of water at Eastertide—that was the last time we saw you . . . Yes, you came inside for a minute at Easter, and Lord knows the state you were in—under the influence, you were . . . You just swore at us, beat me and went off again . . . And I've been wait-ing and waiting—I've worn my eyes out looking for you to come . . . Ah,

6

Yegor Vlasych, Yegor Vlasych! You could have called in once, just once!'

'To do what?'

'Not to do anything, of course, but . . . it is your household, after all . . . Just to see how everything is . . . You are the head . . . Oh, you've shot a little grouse. Ye-gor Vlasych! Why not sit down and have a rest—'

As she says all this, Pelageya keeps laughing like a simpleton and looking up at Yegor's face . . . Her own face positively breathes happiness . . .

'All right, I'll sit down for a bit . . .' Yegor says nonchalantly, choosing a spot between two fir-trees growing side by side. 'What are you standing up for? You sit down too!'

Pelageya sits a little way off in the sun and, ashamed to show how happy she is, keeps covering her smiling mouth with her hand. A couple of minutes pass in silence.

'You could have called in just once,' Pelageya says quietly.

'What for?' sighs Yegor, taking off his cap and mopping his ruddy brow with his sleeve. 'What's the point? Calling in for an hour or two's just a bother, it just gets you worked up, and as for living in the village all the time—my soul couldn't take it . . . You know yourself I've been mollycoddled . . . I need a bed to sleep in, good tea to drink, fine conversations . . . I need everything to be just right . . . and all you've got there in the village is poverty and grime . . . I couldn't stick it for a day. Supposing they even made a decree, saying I had to live with thee come what may, I'd either burn the hut down, or I'd lay hands on myself. I've loved the easy life since I was a kid, you won't change me.'

'And where are you living nowadays?'

'At the master's, Dmitry Ivanych's, as one of his shooters. I provide game for his table, but really . . . he just likes having me around.'

'It's not a proper way of life, that, Yegor Vlasych . . . For other people that's their leisure, but it's as though you've made it your trade . . . like a real job . . .'

'You're stupid, you don't understand anything,' says Yegor, gazing dreamily at the sky. 'Never in all your born days have you understood what kind of a man I am, nor will you . . . You think I'm crazy, I've ruined my life, but to those as knows, I'm the top shot in the whole district. The gents know that all right, and they've even written about me in a magazine. There's not a man can compare with me when it comes to hunting . . . And I don't despise your village jobs because I'm spoilt or proud. You know I never done anything else since I was small than shooting and keeping a dog, don't you? If they took my gun away, I'd

7

use my line, if they took my line away, I'd catch things with my hands. I did a bit of horse-dealing, too, I went the round of the fairs when I had money, and you know yourself that once a peasant's joined the huntsmen and horse-dealers, it's goodbye to the plough. Once that free spirit's got into a man, there's no winkling it out. Just like when a gent goes off with the players, or one of them other arts, he can't work in an office or be a squire again. You're a woman, you don't understand, but you got to.'

'I do understand, Yegor Vlasych . . .'

'You can't do, if you're going to cry about it . . .'

'I—I'm not crying . . .' says Pelageya, turning away. 'It's a sin, Yegor Vlasych! You could at least have some pity and spend a day with me. It's twelve years now since I married you, and . . . and there's never once been *love* between us! . . . I'm not crying . . .'

'Love . . .' mumbles Yegor, scratching the back of his hand. 'There can't be any love. We're man and wife in name only, we're not really, are we? To you I'm a wild man, and to me you're just a simple girl who doesn't understand anything. Call that a match? I'm free, I'm mollycoddled, I come and go as I please, and you're a working-girl, you trudge around in bast shoes all day, you live in dirt, your back's always bent. The way I see myself, when it comes to hunting I'm number one, but when you look at me you just feel pity . . . What kind of a match is that?'

'But we were married in church, Yegor Vlasych!' Pelageya sobs loudly.

'Not freely we weren't . . . You haven't forgotten, have you? You can thank the Count, Sergey Pavlych, for that—and yourself. Because he was so jealous I could shoot better'n him, the Count got me drunk on wine for a month, and when a man's drunk you can make him change his religion, never mind get married. He went and married me off drunk to you, to get his own back . . . A huntsman to a cowherd! You could see I was drunk, so why did you marry me? You're not a serf, you could have gone against his will! 'Course, it's a great thing for a cowherd, marrying a huntsman, but why didn't you stop and think first? Now it's nothing but tears and tribulation. The Count has his laugh, and you're left crying . . . banging your head against a wall . . .'

They fall silent. Three mallard fly in above the scrub. Yegor looks up and stares after them until they turn into three barely visible points, and come down far beyond the forest.

'What do you do for money?' he asks, turning back to Pelageya.

'Nowadays I work in the fields, but in winter I take in a little baby

8

from the orphanage and feed him with a bottle. I get a rouble and a half a month for it.'

'Uhuh . . .'

Once more there is silence. Over in the cut rye, someone begins softly singing, but breaks off almost immediately. It's too hot to sing . . .

'I hear you've put up a new hut for Akulina,' says Pelageya.

Yegor does not reply.

'So she must be to your liking.'

'That's how it is, such is life!' says the sportsman, stretching. 'Have patience, orphan. I must be going, though, I've been chatting too long . . . I've got to be in Boltovo by nightfall . . .'

Yegor rises, stretches again, and slings his gun over his shoulder. Pelageya stands up.

'So when will you be coming to the village?' she asks quietly.

'No point. I'll never come sober, and a drunk's not much use to you. I get mad when I'm drunk . . . Goodbye, then!'

'Goodbye, Yegor Vlasych . . .'

Yegor sticks his cap on the back of his head, calls his dog over with a tweet of the lips, and continues on his way. Pelageya stays where she is and watches him go . . . She can see his shoulder-blades rippling, the rakish set of his cap, his lazy, casual walk, and her eyes fill with sadness and a deep tenderness . . . Her gaze runs all over the slim, tall figure of her husband and caresses and strokes him . . . He stops, as if feeling this gaze, and looks round . . . He says nothing, but from his face and hunched-up shoulders, Pelageya can tell that he wants to say something to her. She goes up timidly to him and looks at him with pleading eyes.

'Here!' he says, turning aside.

He hands her a very worn rouble note and moves quickly away.

'Goodbye, Yegor Vlasych!' she says, mechanically taking the rouble.

He walks off down the road, which is as long and straight as a taut thong . . . Pale and still, she stands there like a statue, and her eyes devour every stride he takes. But now the red of his shirt merges with the dark of his trousers, his strides become invisible, his dog cannot be distinguished from his boots. Only his little cap can be seen; then . . . suddenly Yegor turns off sharply to the right into the scrub and his cap disappears among the green.

'Goodbye, Yegor Vlasych!' whispers Pelageya, and rises on tiptoe to try and catch a last glimpse of his little white cap.

9

Sergeant Prishibeyev

'Staff-Sergeant Prishibeyev! You are accused of using insulting language and behaviour on the third of September of this year towards Police Officer Zappsky, District Elder Berkin, Police Constable Yefimov, Official Witnesses Ivanov and Gavrilov, and six other peasants; whereof the first three aforenamed were insulted by you in the performance of their duties. Do you plead guilty?'

Prishibeyev, a shrivelled little sergeant with a crabbed face, squares his shoulders and answers in a stifled, croaky voice, clipping his words as though on the parade ground:

'Your Honour Mr Justice of the Peace—sir! What it says in the law is: every statement can be mutually contested. I'm not guilty—it's them lot. This all came about because of a dead corpse, God rest his soul. I was walking along on the third—quiet and respectable like—with my wife Anfisa, when suddenly I spy this mob of varied persons standing on the river-bank. "What perfect right has that mob got to be assembled there?" I ask myself. "What do they think they're up to? Where's it written down that common folk can go around in droves?" So I shout, "Hey, you lot—disperse!" I started shoving them, to get them to go indoors, I ordered the constable to lay into them, and—'

'Just one moment. You're not a police officer or elder: is it your business to be breaking up crowds?'

'No, it ain't! It ain't!' voices cry from different corners of the courtroom. 'He's the bane of our lives, yeronner! Fifteen years we've put up with him! Ever since he gave up work and came back here the village ain't been worth living in. He's driving us mad!'

'It's quite true, yeronner,' says the elder who is one of the witnesses. 'The whole village complains of him. He's impossible to live with. Whether we're taking the icons round the village, or there's a wedding, or some do on, say, he's out there shouting at us, kicking up a row and calling for order. He goes about pulling the kids' ears, he spies on our womenfolk to see they're not up to something, like he was their own father-in-law . . . The other day he went round the huts ordering everyone to stop singing and put all their lights out. "There's no law permitting you to sing songs," he says.'

'All right, you'll have time to give evidence later,' says the magistrate.

'At the moment let's hear what else Prishibeyev has to say. Go on, Prishibeyev.'

'Yessir!' croaks the sergeant. 'You were pleased to observe, Your Honour, that it's not my business to be breaking up crowds . . . Very good, sir . . . But what if there's a disturbance? We can't allow them to run riot, can we? Where's it written down that the lower orders can do what they like? I can't let them get away with that, sir. And if I don't tell them to break up, and give them what for, who will? No one round here knows what proper discipline is, you might say I'm the only one, Your Honour, as knows how to deal with the lower orders, and, Your Honour, I know what I'm talking about. I'm not a peasant, I'm a non-commissioned officer, a Q.M.S. retired, I served in Warsaw as a staff-sergeant, sir, after I got an honourable discharge I worked in the fire-brigade, sir, then I had to give up the fire-brigade by virtue of health and worked for the next two years as janitor in an independent classical school for young gentlemen . . . So I know all about discipline, sir. But a peasant's just a simple fellow, he doesn't know any better, so he must do what I tell him—'cause it's for his own good. Take this business, for example. I break up the crowd and there lying in the sand on the river-bank is the drownded corpse of a dead man. On what possible grounds can he be lying there, I ask myself. Do you call that law and order? Why's the officer just standing there? "Hey, officer," I say, "why aren't you informing your superiors? Maybe this drownded corpse drowned himself, or maybe it smacks of Siberia—maybe it's a case of criminal homicide . . ." But Officer Zappsky doesn't give a damn, he just goes on smoking his cigarette. "Who's this bloke giving orders?" he says. "Is he one of yours? Where'd he spring from? Does he think we don't know what to do without his advice?" he says. "Well you can't do, can you, dimwit," says I, "if you're just standing there and don't give a damn." "I informed the inspector yesterday," he says. "Why the inspector?" I ask him. "According to which article of the code? In cases like this, of people being drowned or strangulated and suchlike and so forth, what can the inspector do? It's a capital offence," I says, "a case for the courts . . . You'd better send a despatch to His Honour the examining magistrate and the justices straight away," I says. "And first of all," I says, "you must draw up a document and send it to His Honour the Justice of the Peace." But the officer, he just listens to me and laughs. And the peasants the same. They were all laughing, Your Honour. I'll testify to that on oath. That one there laughed—and this one—and Zappsky, he laughed too. "What are you all grinning at?" I says. Then the officer says: "Such matters", he says, "are nothing to do with the JP." Well, the blood rushed to my head when I heard him say that. That is what you said, isn't it, Officer?' the sergeant asks, turning to Zappsky.

'That's what I said.'

'Everyone heard you say them words, for all the common people to hear. "Such matters are nothing to do with the JP"—everyone heard you say them words . . . Well, the blood rushed to my head, Your Honour, I went quite weak at the knees. "Repeat to me," says I, "repeat, you . . . so-and-so, what you just said!" He comes out with them same words again . . . I goes up to him. "How dare you say such things", says I, "about His Honour the Justice of the Peace? A police officer and you're against authority—eh? Do you know", I says, "that if he likes, His Honour the Justice of the Peace can have you sent to the provincial gendarmerie for saying them words and proving unreliable? Do you realise," says I, "where His Honour the Justice of the Peace can pack you off to for political words like that?" Then the elder butts in: "The JP", he says, "can't deal with anything outside his powers. He only handles minor cases." That's what he said, everyone heard him . . . "How dare you", says I, "belittle authority? Don't you come that game with me, son," I says, "or you'll find yourself in hot water." When I was in Warsaw, or when I was janitor at the independent classical school for young gentlemen, soon as I heard any words as shouldn't be said I'd look out on the street for a gendarme and shout, "Step in here a minute, will you, soldier?"—and report it all to him. But who can you tell things to out here in the country? . . . It made me wild. It really got me, to think of the common people of today indulging in licence and insubordination like that, so I let fly and—not hard of course, just lightly like, just proper, so's he wouldn't dare say such things about Your Honour again . . . The officer sided with the elder. So I gave the officer one, too . . . And that's how it started . . . I got worked up, Your Honour. But you can't get anywhere without a few clouts, can you? If you don't clout a stupid man, it's a sin on your own head. Especially if there's good reason for it—if he's been causing a disturbance . . .'

'But there are other people appointed to keep public order! That's what the officer, the elder and the constable are there for—'

'Ah, but the officer can't keep an eye on everybody, and he don't understand what I do . . .'

'Well understand now that it's none of your business!'

'Not my business, sir? How do you make that out? That's queer . . . People behave improperly and it's none of my business? What am I supposed to do—cheer them on? They've just been complaining to you that I won't let them sing songs . . . And what good is there in songs, I'd like to know? Instead of getting on with something useful, they sing songs . . . Then they've got a new craze for sitting up late with a light burning. They ought to be in bed asleep, but all you hear is laughing and talking. I've got it all written down!'

'You've got what written down?'

'Who sits up burning a light.'

Prishibeyev takes a greasy slip of paper from his pocket, puts his spectacles on, and reads:

'Peasants what sit up burning a light: Ivan Prokhorov, Savva Mikiforov, Pyotr Petrov. The soldier's widow Shustrova is living in illicit union with Semyon Kislov. Ignat Sverchok dabbles in black magic, and his wife Mavra is a witch, she goes around at night milking other people's cows.'

'That's enough!' says the magistrate and turns to examining the witnesses.

Sergeant Prishibeyev pushes his glasses on to his forehead and stares in amazement at the JP—who is evidently not on his side. His eyes gleam and start out of his head, and his nose turns bright red. He looks from the JP to the witnesses and simply cannot understand why the magistrate should be so het up and why from every corner of the courtroom comes a mixture of angry murmurs and suppressed laughter. The sentence is equally incomprehensible to him: one month in custody!

'For what?!' he asks, throwing up his arms in disbelief. 'By what law?'

And he realises that the world is a changed place, a place impossible to live in. Dark, gloomy thoughts possess him. But when he comes out of the courtroom he sees some peasants huddled together talking about something and by force of a habit which he can no longer control, he squares his shoulders and bawls in a hoarse, irate voice:

'You lot—break it up! Move along! Diss-perse!'

13

Misery

'To whom shall I convey my grief?'

The twilight of evening. Big flakes of wet snow are whirling lazily about the street-lamps, which have just been lit, and settling in a thin soft layer on roofs, horses' backs, shoulders, caps. Iona Potapov, the sledge-driver, is all white like a ghost. He sits on the box without stirring, bent as double as the living body can be bent. If a regular snowdrift fell on him it seems as though even then he would not think it necessary to shake it off . . . His little mare is white and motionless too. Her stillness, the angularity of her lines, and the stick-like straightness of her legs, make her look like a halfpenny gingerbread horse. She is probably lost in thought. Anyone who has been torn away from the plough, from the familiar grey landscapes, and cast into this slough, full of monstrous lights, of unceasing uproar and scurrying people, is bound to think.

It is a long time since Iona and his nag have budged. They came out of the yard before dinner-time, and not a single fare yet. But now the shades of evening are falling on the town. The pale light of the street-lamps changes to a vivid colour, and the bustle of the street grows noisier.

'Sledge to Vyborgskaya!' Iona hears. 'Sledge!'

Iona starts, and through his snow-plastered eyelashes sees an officer in a military overcoat with a hood over his head.

'To Vyborgskaya,' repeats the officer. 'Are you asleep? To Vyborgskaya!'

In token of assent Iona gives a tug at the reins which sends cakes of snow flying from the horse's back and from his own shoulders. The officer gets into the sledge. The sledge-driver clicks to the horse, cranes his neck like a swan, rises in his seat, and more from habit than necessity brandishes his whip. The mare cranes her neck, too, crooks her stick-like legs, and hesitatingly sets off . . .

'Where are you shoving, you devil?' Iona immediately hears shouts from the dark mass shifting to and fro before him. 'Where the devil are you going? Keep to the r-right!'

'You don't know how to drive! Keep to the right,' says the officer angrily.

A coachman driving a carriage swears at him; a pedestrian crossing the road and brushing the horse's nose with his shoulder looks at him venomously and shakes the snow off his sleeve. Iona fidgets on the box as though he were sitting on thorns, jerks his elbows, and turns his eyes about like one possessed, as though he did not know where he was or why he was there.

'What rascals they all are!' says the officer jocosely. 'They keep on trying to run up against you or fall under the horse's feet. They must be doing it on purpose.'

Iona looks at his fare and moves his lips . . . Apparently he means to say something, but nothing comes but a sniff.

'What?' enquires the officer.

Iona gives a wry smile and, straining his throat, brings out huskily:

'My son . . . er . . . my son died this week, sir.'

'Hm! What did he die of?'

Iona turns his whole body round to his fare, and says:

'Who can tell! It must have been from fever . . . He lay three days in the hospital and then he died . . . God's will.'

'Turn round, you devil!' comes out of the darkness. 'Have you gone mad, you old dog? Look where you are going!'

'Drive on! drive on! . . .' says the officer. 'We shan't get there till tomorrow going on like this. Hurry up!'

The sledge-driver cranes his neck again, rises in his seat, and with heavy grace swings his whip. Several times he looks round at the officer, but the latter keeps his eyes shut and is apparently disinclined to listen. Putting his fare down at Vyborgskaya, Iona stops by a restaurant, and again sits huddled up on the box . . . Again the wet snow paints him and his horse white. One hour passes, and then another . . .

Three young men, two tall and thin, one short and hunchbacked, come up, railing at each other and loudly stamping on the pavement with their galoshes.

'Cabby, to the Police Bridge!' the hunchback cries in a cracked voice. 'The three of us . . . twenty kopecks!'

Iona tugs at the reins and clicks to his horse. Twenty kopecks is not a fair price, but he has no thoughts for that. Whether it is a rouble or whether it is five kopecks does not matter to him now so long as he has a fare . . . The three young men, shoving each other and using bad language, go up to the sledge, and all three try to sit down at once. The question remains to be settled: which are to sit down and which one is to stand? After a long altercation, ill-temper, and abuse, they come to the conclusion that the hunchback must stand because he is the shortest.

'Well, drive on,' says the hunchback in his cracked voice, settling himself and breathing down Iona's neck. 'Cut along! What a cap you've got, my friend! You wouldn't find a worse one in all Petersburg . . .'

'Hee-hee! . . . hee-hee! . . .' laughs Iona. 'It's nothing to boast of!'

'Well, then, nothing to boast of, drive on! Are you going to drive like this all the way? Eh? Shall I give you one in the neck?'

'My head aches,' says one of the tall ones. 'At the Dukmasovs' yesterday Vaska and I drank four bottles of brandy between us.'

'I can't make out why you talk such stuff,' says the other tall one angrily. 'You lie like a brute.'

'Strike me dead, it's the truth! . . .'

'It's about as true as that a louse coughs.'

'Hee-hee!' grins Iona. 'Me-er-ry gentlemen!'

'Tfoo! the devil take you!' cries the hunchback indignantly. 'Will you get on, you old plague, or won't you? Is that the way to drive? Give her one with the whip. Hang it all! give it to her!'

Iona feels behind his back the jolting person and quivering voice of the hunchback. He hears abuse addressed to him, he sees people, and the feeling of loneliness begins little by little to be less heavy on his heart. The hunchback swears at him, till he chokes over some elaborately whimsical string of epithets and is overpowered by his cough. His tall companions begin talking of a certain Nadezhda Petrovna. Iona looks round at them. Waiting till there is a brief pause, he looks round once more and says:

'This week . . . er . . . my . . . er . . . son died!'

'We shall all die . . .' says the hunchback with a sigh, wiping his lips after coughing. 'Come, drive on! drive on! My friends, I simply cannot stand crawling like this! When will he get us there?'

'Well, you give him a little encouragement . . . one in the neck!'

'Do you hear, you old plague? I'll make you smart. If one stands on ceremony with fellows like you one may as well walk. Do you hear, you old dragon? Or don't you care a hang what we say?'

And Iona hears rather than feels a slap on the back of his neck.

'Hee-hee! . . .' he laughs. 'Merry gentlemen . . . God give you health!'

'Cabman, are you married?' asks one of the tall ones.

'I? Hee-hee! Me-er-ry gentlemen. The only wife for me now is the damp earth . . . Hee-ho-ho! . . . The grave that is! . . . Here my son's dead and I am alive . . . It's a strange thing, death came in at the wrong door . . . Instead of coming for me it went for my son . . .'

16

And Iona turns round to tell them how his son died, but at that point the hunchback gives a faint sigh and announces that, thank God! they have arrived at last. After taking his twenty kopecks, Iona gazes for a long while after the revellers, who disappear into a dark entry. Again he is alone and again there is silence for him . . . The misery which has been for a brief space eased comes back again and tears his heart more cruelly than ever. With a look of anxiety and suffering Iona's eyes stray restlessly among the crowds moving to and fro on both sides of the street: can he not find among those thousands someone who will listen to him? But the crowds flit by heedless of him and his misery . . . His misery is immense, beyond all bounds. If Iona's heart were to burst and his misery to flow out, it would flood the whole world, it seems, but yet it is not seen. It has found a hiding-place in such an insignificant shell that one would not have found it with a candle by daylight . . .

Iona sees a house-porter with a parcel and makes up his mind to address him.

'What time will it be, friend?' he asks.

'Going on for ten . . . Why have you stopped here? Drive on!'

Iona drives a few paces away, bends himself double, and gives himself up to his misery. He feels it is no good to appeal to people. But before five minutes have passed he draws himself up, shakes his head as though he feels a sharp pain, and tugs at the reins . . . He can bear it no longer.

'Back to the yard!' he thinks. 'To the yard!'

And his little mare, as though she knew his thoughts, falls to trotting. An hour and a half later Iona is sitting by a big dirty stove. On the stove, on the floor, and on the benches are people snoring. The air is full of smells and stuffiness. Iona looks at the sleeping figures, scratches himself, and regrets that he has come home so early . . .

'I have not earned enough to pay for the oats, even,' he thinks. 'That's why I am so miserable. A man who knows how to do his work, . . . who has had enough to eat, and whose horse has had enough to eat, is always at ease . . .'

In one of the corners a young cabman gets up, clears his throat sleepily, and makes for the water-bucket.

'Want a drink?' Iona asks him.

'Seems so.'

'May it do you good . . . But my son is dead, mate . . . Do you hear? This week in the hospital . . . It's a strange business . . .'

Iona looks to see the effect produced by his words, but he sees nothing.

17

The young man has covered his head over and is already asleep. The old man sighs and scratches himself . . . Just as the young man had been thirsty for water, so he thirsts for speech. His son will soon have been dead a week, and he has not really talked to anybody yet . . . He wants to talk of it properly, with deliberation . . . He wants to tell how his son was taken ill, how he suffered, what he said before he died, how he died . . . He wants to describe the funeral, and how he went to the hospital to get his son's clothes. He still has his daughter Anisya in the country . . . And he wants to talk about her too . . . Yes, he has plenty to talk about now. His listener ought to sigh and exclaim and lament . . . It would be even better to talk to women. Though they are silly creatures, they blubber at the first word.

'Let's go out and have a look at the mare,' Iona thinks. 'There is always time for sleep . . . You'll have sleep enough, no fear . . .'

He puts on his coat and goes into the stables where his mare is standing. He thinks about oats, about hay, about the weather . . . He cannot think about his son when he is alone . . . To talk about him with someone is possible, but to think of him and picture him is insufferable anguish . . .

'Are you munching?' Iona asks his mare, seeing her shining eyes. 'There, munch away, munch away . . . Since we have not earned enough for oats, we will eat hay . . . Yes . . . I have grown too old to drive . . . My son ought to be driving, not I . . . He was a real cabman . . . He ought to have lived . . .'

Iona is silent for a while, and then he goes on:

'That's how it is, old girl . . . Kuzma Ionych is gone . . . He said goodbye to me . . . He went and died for no reason . . . Now, suppose you had a little colt, and you were own mother to that little colt . . . And all at once that same little colt went and died . . . You'd be sorry, wouldn't you? . . .'

The little mare munches, listens, and breathes on her master's hands. Iona is carried away and tells her all about it . . .

18

Easter Night

I was standing on the bank of the Goltva, waiting for the ferry to come over from the other side. At normal times the Goltva is a river of no great pretensions, taciturn and pensive, glinting meekly from behind thick rushes; now, a whole lake lay spread before me. The rampant spring waters had swept over both banks and flooded large areas on either side, capturing marshes, hayfields and vegetable plots, so that it was quite common to encounter on the surface lone poplars and bushes sticking out like grim crags in the darkness.

The weather struck me as magnificent. It was dark, yet even so I could see the trees, the water, and human beings . . . The world was lit by stars, bestrewing every corner of the sky. I don't think I have ever seen so many stars. Literally, you couldn't have stuck a pin between them. There were ones as big as goose eggs and others as tiny as hempseed . . . Each and every one of them, from great to small, had come out to parade for the festival, washed, refurbished and jubilant, and each and every one was quietly twinkling. The sky lay reflected in the water; the stars bathed in its dark depths and trembled with the faint ripples on the surface. The air was warm and still . . . Far away on the other bank, in impenetrable dark, several bright red fires were blazing furiously . . .

Close by me stood the dark silhouette of a peasant in a tall hat and holding a short, knobbly staff.

'The ferry's taking a long time, isn't it?' I said.

'Yes, about time it was here,' the silhouette answered.

'Are you waiting for the ferry too?'

'No . . .' yawned the peasant, 'I'm just waiting for the luminations. I'd go, but I ain't got the five kopecks for the ferry.'

'I'll give you them.'

'Thank you kindly sir, but I'd rather you put up a candle for me there in the monastery, with those five kopecks . . . That'll be more interesting, with me standing here. Where's that ferry got to—has it vanished or something?'

The peasant went down to the water's edge, seized the ferry rope, and yelled:

'Ieronim! Ieron-i-m!'

As though in answer to his shout, a long peal from a great bell came to us from the other bank. The peal was rich and deep, like the thickest string on a double-bass: it was as though the darkness itself had given a hoarse cough. Immediately a shot rang out from a cannon. It rolled away in the darkness and petered out somewhere far behind me. The peasant took off his hat and crossed himself.

'Christ is Risen!' he said.

Hardly had the waves from the first peal of the bell died on the air, when a second one resounded, hard on it a third, and suddenly the darkness was filled with a continuous, vibrant din. Beside the red fires new ones blazed up, and they all started moving together and flickering restlessly.

'Ieroni-m!' came a long echoing cry.

'They're shouting for him from the other bank,' said the peasant. 'So the ferry's not there either. He's fallen asleep, our Ieronim.'

The fires and the velvety tolling of the bell were calling me . . . I was beginning to get impatient and fidgety. Finally, though, peering into the dark distance, I saw the silhouette of something very similar to a gallows. It was the long-awaited ferry. It was approaching with such slowness that had it not been for the gradual sharpening of its outlines, one might have thought it was standing still, or, indeed, going towards the other bank.

'Come on, Ieronim!' shouted my peasant. 'There's a gentleman waiting!'

The ferry crept up to the bank, lurched, and creaked to a halt. On it, holding the rope, stood a tall man in a monk's cassock and a conical cap.

'What kept you?' I asked him, leaping on to the ferry.

'Forgive me for the Lord's sake,' replied Ieronim quietly. 'Anyone else?'

'No, just me . . .'

Ieronim grasped the rope with both hands, bent himself into the shape of a question mark, and let out a groan. The ferry creaked and lurched. The silhouette of the peasant in the tall hat began slowly to recede from me: so the ferry was under way. Soon Ieronim straightened up and began to work the rope with one hand. We gazed silently at the bank towards which we were floating. There the 'luminations' the peasant was waiting for had already begun. At the water's edge barrels of tar were blazing like enormous bonfires. Their reflections, as ruddy as a rising moon, crept out towards us in long wide strips. The burning barrels lit up their own smoke and the long shadows of people flitting about by the fires, but the area to either side of the barrels and beyond them, whence came the velvety tolling of the bell, was all dense black gloom still. Suddenly, slashing the darkness, a rocket shot up to the sky in a golden streamer; it described an arc, and as if smashing against the sky disintegrated in a crackle of sparks. A roar went up from the bank, like a distant 'hurrah'.

'Beautiful!' I said.

'Yes, beautiful beyond words!' sighed Ieronim. 'It's that kind of night, sir! Another time and we wouldn't even pay any attention to rockets, but tonight we rejoice at every vain thing. And where might you be from?'

I told him.

'Mmm . . . it's a joyful day today . . .' continued Ieronim in a sighing little high-pitched voice like that of someone recovering from an illness. 'The sky rejoices, and the earth, and all that is under the earth. All creation is celebrating. Only tell me, good sir: why is it that even in the midst of great rejoicing a man cannot forget his sorrows?'

I was afraid that this unexpected question was inviting me to join in one of those protracted, uplifting discussions that monks who are idle and bored are so partial to. I was not much disposed to conversation, so I merely asked:

'What sorrows do you have, Father?'

'Usually the same as everyone else's, Your Honour, good sir, but this day a particular sorrow has befallen the monastery: at the liturgy itself, during the lessons, Nikolay the monk died . . .'

'Well, it's God will!' I said, affecting the monastic tone. 'We all must die. Shouldn't you rather be rejoicing? . . . They say that anyone who dies at Easter, or during Eastertide, is sure to go to the kingdom of heaven.'

'That's true.'

We fell silent. The silhouette of the tall-hatted peasant merged with the features of the bank. The tar barrels blazed higher and higher.

'The scriptures make clear to us the vanity of sorrow, as does contemplation,' Ieronim broke the silence. 'But why will the soul still grieve and not listen to reason? Why does one want to weep so bitterly?'

Ieronim shrugged his shoulders, turned to me, and spoke rapidly:

'If it was me had died, or someone else, perhaps no one would have so much as noticed, but it was Nikolay who died! Nikolay, of all people! It's hard to believe, even, that he's no longer in the world! I stand here on the ferry and I keep thinking to myself that his voice is going to call out to me from the bank. So that I wouldn't be scared on my own on the ferry, he would always come down to the river-bank and hail me. He would get out

21

of bed every night specially. A kind soul he was! God knows, how kind and considerate! Many a mother's not as kind to her own children as Nikolay was to me! The Lord save his soul!'

Ieronim took hold of the rope, but immediately turned to me again.

'Oh, and what a brilliant mind, Your Honour!' he said liltingly. 'What sweet and melodious speech! It was just as they'll be singing soon at the Mass: "O how loving-kind! O most sweet is Thy voice!" And apart from all his other human qualities, he had an extraordinary gift!'

'What was that?' I asked.

The monk eyed me carefully, then, as if persuaded that I could be trusted with a secret, he chuckled.

'He had the gift of writing canticles . . .' he said. 'It was a miracle, sir, no less! You'll scarcely believe it if I tell you. Reverend Father, our archimandrite, is from Moscow, our Father Vicar graduated from the Kazan Academy, and we have learned monks in orders here, and elders, but let me assure you, sir, there isn't one of them who could write things himself—yet Nikolay, a simple monk, a mere deacon, who hadn't studied anywhere and was nothing at all to look at, he could! It was a miracle, a veritable miracle!'

Ieronim clasped his hands and, forgetting all about the rope, continued excitedly:

'Our Father Vicar finds it difficult putting sermons together, when he was writing the history of our monastery he made our lives a misery and had to drive into town a dozen times. Nikolay, though, could write canticles! Canticles! That's a different matter from a sermon or a history!'

'Are canticles so hard to write, then?' I asked.

'V-ery hard . . .' said Ieronim with a roll of the head. 'It doesn't matter how wise or saintly you are, if God hasn't given you the gift. Monks who don't know what they're talking about reckon all you have to do is know the life of the saint you're writing it to, and model it on all the other canticles. But that's not correct, sir. Of course, anyone who writes a canticle has to know the saint's life inside out, down to the last minutest detail. He must consult the other canticles, too, to know how to begin and what to write about. To give you an example, the first collect-hymn always begins with the words "Most High Elect" or "The Chosen One" . . . The first *ikos* must always begin with an angel. I don't know if you're interested, but in the canticle to Jesus the Most Sweet the *ikos* begins like this: "Angels' Creator and Lord of Hosts!", in the canticle to the Most Holy Mother of God it's "An Angel was sent down from the Heavens to be a

Messenger", and to St Nicholas the Miracle-Worker—"Angel in form, though in substance an Earthly Being", and so on. It always begins with an angel. Of course, you do have to consult the other canticles, but it isn't the saint's life or how the canticle compares with other ones that matters—it's the beauty and sweetness of the thing. Everything in it must be graceful, brief, and pregnant with meaning. Every tiny line must breathe a softness, a gentleness, a tenderness; there mustn't be a single word that's coarse, harsh, or out of place. You must write in such a way that the worshipper rejoices in his heart and weeps, and his mind is shaken and he's all a-tremble. In the canticle to the Holy Mother of God there are the words: "Rejoice, O Thou too high for the mind of man to scale; rejoice, O Thou too deep for the eyes of Angels to fathom!" Elsewhere in the same canticle it says: "Rejoice, O Tree of fairest Fruit that nourishest the faithful; rejoice, O Tree of benign Canopy that shelterest the multitudes!" '

As though taking fright at something, or suddenly overcome with shame, Ieronim covered his face with his hands and rocked his head from side to side.

'Tree of fairest Fruit . . . Tree of benign Canopy . . .' he muttered to himself. 'To find such words! Only the Lord bestows such a power! For brevity he'd link several words and thoughts together—and how smooth and pregnant he succeeds in making them! "Thou art a light-enduing Beacon to the people . . ." it says in the canticle to Jesus the Most Sweet. "Light-enduing"! You won't find that word in conversation or in books— yet he managed to think it up, to find it in his own mind! As well as smoothness and felicitousness, sir, every line must also be adorned in divers ways—with flowers and lightning and wind and sun and all the objects of the visible world. And you have to compose every exclamation so that it falls smoothly and easily on the ear. "Rejoice, thou Lily that dwellest in the heavens!" it says in the canticle to St Nicholas the Miracle-Worker. Not just "Lily of heaven", but "Lily that *dwellest* in the heavens!" That way it's smoother and sweeter on the ear. And that's how Nikolay used to write, too! Just like that! Oh, I can't begin to tell you how he used to write!'

'Well, in that case it's a pity he's died,' I said. 'But let's carry on across, Father, or we shall be late . . .'

Ieronim started out of his thoughts and scurried to the rope. On the bank all the bells were beginning to peal out. Probably the procession was already under way near the monastery, for the whole of the dark area beyond the tar barrels was now dotted with moving lights.

23

'Did Nikolay have his canticles printed?' I asked Ieronim.

'How could he?' he sighed. 'And it would have seemed strange, too. For what purpose? No one in our monastery's interested in that sort of thing. They don't approve. They knew that Nikolay wrote them, but they ignored them. Nowadays, sir, no one thinks very highly of new writings!'

'They're prejudiced against them?'

'That's right. If Nikolay had been an elder, well then perhaps the brotherhood would have taken some interest, but he wasn't yet forty. There were those that laughed at his writing, and even held it a sin.'

'Why did he write, then?'

'Well, more for his own consolation. Of all the brotherhood I was the only one who actually read his canticles. I'd slip along to him without letting the others see and he'd be so glad that I took an interest. He would hug me, stroke my head, and call me affectionate names, as though I were a little child. He would shut up his cell, sit me down next to him, and we'd read away . . .'

Ieronim left the rope and came up to me.

'He and I were like friends, somehow,' he whispered, looking at me with gleaming eyes. 'Wherever he went, I went too. When I wasn't there, he would miss me. And he loved me more than anyone else, and all because I used to weep over the canticles he wrote. It's touching to think of! Now I feel just like an orphan or a widow. You see, they're all good, kind, devout people in our monastery, but . . . none of them has that softness and gentility, they're more like commonfolk. They all talk loudly and clump their feet, they make a lot of noise and are always clearing their throats, whereas Nikolay always spoke quietly, affectionately, and if he noticed that someone was sleeping or praying, then he would creep past as though he were a little fly, or a gnat. And his face was loving and compassionate . . .'

Ieronim gave a deep sigh and took up the rope again. By now we were approaching the bank. We were drifting out of the darkness and the stillness of the river straight into an enchanted realm full of choking smoke, crackling light and uproar. Round the tar barrels one could now clearly see people moving. The flickering of the fire gave their red faces and forms a strange, almost fantastic, appearance. Occasionally among the heads and faces one glimpsed the muzzles of horses, as motionless as if cast in red copper.

'They'll be singing the Easter Canon in a moment . . .' said Ieronim,

24

'but Nikolay isn't there, so there's no one to really take it in . . . Nothing that was written was sweeter to him than that canon. He would enter into every word of it! You're going to be there, sir, so you listen closely to what they sing: it'll take your breath away!'

'Aren't you going to be in the church yourself?'

'I can't, sir . . . I've got to work the ferry . . .'

'But can't someone take over from you?'

'I don't know . . . Someone should have relieved me at eight, but they haven't, as you see! . . . And I must confess, I'd like to be in church . . .'

'You are a monk?'

'Yes . . . that is, I'm a lay brother.'

The ferry ran into the bank and stopped. I thrust a five-kopeck piece into Ieronim's hand and jumped ashore. Immediately, a cart with a little boy and a sleeping peasant woman in it trundled creakily on to the ferry. Ieronim, who was lit faintly by the fires, took up the rope, bent himself double, and set the ferry in motion . . .

I took a few steps through mud, then was able to walk on a soft, freshly trodden path. This footpath led to the dark, cavern-like gates of the monastery through clouds of smoke and a jumbled mass of people, unharnessed horses, carts and britchkas. The whole assortment was creaking, snorting and laughing, and over it all played a ruddy light and the billowy shadows of the smoke . . . It was utter chaos! And to think that in this crush they could still find room to load a small cannon and to sell gingerbreads!

On the other side of the wall, in the precinct, no less of a commotion was going on, but there was a greater sense of order and dignity. The air smelt of juniper leaves and benzoin incense. People talked loudly, but there was no sound of laughter or horses' snorting. Around the tomb-stones and crosses huddled people with Easter cakes and bundles. Evidently many of them had come from far away to have their Easter cakes blessed, and were now weary. Young lay brothers scampered to and fro over the cast-iron slabs that lay in a solid strip from the gates to the church door, their boots ringing on the metal. In the belfry, too, they were bustling about and shouting.

'What a night of turmoil!' I thought. 'How superb!'

It was tempting to see the same turmoil and sleeplessness in every-thing around, from the night dark to the iron slabs, the crosses on the graves and the trees beneath which people were bustling. But nowhere were the excitement and turmoil so evident as inside the church. At the

25

entrance a ceaseless struggle was going on between the ebb and the flow. Some were going in, others coming out and shortly returning, only to stand for a while and move off again. People were darting aimlessly all over the place, apparently looking for something. A wave would start from the entrance and travel the length of the church, unsettling even the front rows where the solid, respectable people were standing. There could be no question of concentrated prayer. There were no prayers at all, only sheer, spontaneous childlike joy seeking a pretext to burst out and express itself in any form of movement, be it only the non-stop roaming and jostling.

The same extraordinary activity strikes you in the Easter service itself. The sanctuary gates are wide open in all the side-chapels, and dense clouds of incense float about the chandelier in the nave; all around you are lights and the blaze and crackle of candles . . . There is no provision for readings; the singing goes on briskly and cheerfully to the very end of the service; after each hymn of the canon, the clergy change their vestments and come out to cense, and this is repeated nearly every ten minutes.

I had just squeezed in, when a wave surged up from the front and hurled me back. Before me passed a tall, portly deacon holding a long red candle; behind him hurried the archimandrite, grey-haired, wearing a gold mitre, and swinging his censer. Once they had disappeared, the crowd pushed me back to my previous place. But in less than ten minutes another wave surged and again the deacon appeared. This time he was followed by the Father Vicar, the very one whom Ieronim had described as writing the history of the monastery.

Merging with the crowd and infected by the universal jubilation and excitement, I felt unbearable pity for Ieronim. Why would no one relieve him? Why couldn't someone less feeling and less impressionable be sent to the ferry?

'Cast thine eyes about thee, O Zion, and behold!' they were singing in the choir. 'For lo! from the West and from the North, and from the Sea and from the East, as to a light by God illumined, have thy children assembled unto thee . . .'

I looked at the faces. They were all radiant with triumph; but not a single person was listening to and taking in what was being sung, and none of them was feeling his 'breath taken away'. Why would no one relieve Ieronim? I could imagine this Ieronim standing humbly somewhere by the wall, hunched up and snatching greedily at the beauty of each sacred phrase. All that was now glancing past the ears of those

26

standing about me, he would have drunk in thirstily with his sensitive soul, he would have drunk himself into ecstasies—till his breath was taken away—and there would not have been a happier man in the whole building. Now, though, he was plying back and forth on the dark river and grieving for his dead brother and friend.

Behind me another wave surged forward. A stout, smiling monk fiddling with a rosary and looking over his shoulder squeezed past me sideways, clearing the way for a lady in a hat and velvet cloak. Behind the lady, holding a chair above our heads, hurried a monastery servant.

I came out of the church. I wanted to have a look at the dead Nikolay, the unacclaimed writer of canticles. I strolled round the precinct, where a row of monks' cells stretched along the monastery wall, I looked in through several windows, and, seeing nothing, turned back. Now I do not regret not having seen Nikolay; goodness knows, perhaps if I had seen him I should have lost the image that my imagination now paints of him. I picture this attractive, poetical man who would come out at night to call to Ieronim, who besprinkled his canticles with flowers, stars and sunbeams, and was completely alone and not understood, as shy, pale, with soft, meek and sad features. As well as intelligence, his eyes surely glowed with affection and that barely restrainable childlike rapture that I had heard in Ieronim's voice, when he quoted to me pieces from the canticles.

When we emerged from the church after Mass, the night was already gone. Morning was breaking. The stars had faded and the sky was now a sombre greyish-blue. The cast-iron slabs, the tombstones and the buds on the trees were coated with dew. It was distinctly fresh. Beyond the monastery wall there was no longer the animation that I had seen at night. The horses and people looked weary, sleepy, they scarcely moved, whilst all that was left of the tar barrels was a few heaps of black ash. When a person feels weary and wants to sleep, he thinks that nature is experiencing the same state. It seemed to me that the trees and the young grass were sleeping. It seemed that even the bells were not ringing so loudly and cheerfully as in the night. The turmoil was over and of the excitement only a pleasant languor remained, a craving for warmth and sleep.

Now I could see the river and both its banks. Above it, here and there, drifted humps of thin mist. A grim chill wafted from the river. When I jumped on to the ferry, someone's britchka was already standing on it, and a couple of dozen men and women. The rope, which was damp and, it seemed to me, sleepy, stretched away far across the broad river and disappeared in places in the white mist.

27

'Christ is Risen! Anyone else?' asked a quiet voice.

I recognised Ieronim's voice. Now the darkness of the night no longer prevented me from making out the monk's appearance. He was a tall, narrow-shouldered man of about thirty-five, with large rounded features, half-closed, listlessly peering eyes, and an unkempt little spade beard. He looked extremely sad and weary.

'Haven't they relieved you yet?' I asked in surprise.

'Me?' he asked back, turning his numbed, dew-covered face to me, and smiling. 'There's no one to take my place now till morn. They'll all be going to the father archimandrite soon to break the fast.'

He and a strange little peasant in an orange fur hat resembling one of the limewood tubs they sell honey in, applied themselves to the rope, gave a groan in unison, and the ferry moved off.

We floated across, disturbing on our way the lazily rising mist. Everyone was silent. Ieronim worked the rope mechanically with one hand. For a long time his meek, bleary eyes roamed all over us, then he brought his gaze to rest on the rosy, black-browed face of a young merchant's wife, who was standing on the ferry next to me, hunched up silently in the enveloping mist. He did not take his eyes off her face the whole way.

There was little that was masculine in that prolonged gaze. In the woman's face I feel Ieronim was searching for the soft and loving features of his late-lamented friend.

Romance with Double-Bass

Pitsikatoff was making his way on foot from town to Prince Bibuloff's country villa where 'a musical evening with dancing' was to take place in celebration of the engagement of the Prince's daughter. A gigantic double-bass in a leather case reposed on Pitsikatoff's back. He was walking along the bank of a river whose cooling waters rolled on if not majestically, then at least most poetically.

'How about a dip?' he thought.

In the twinkling of an eye he had taken off his clothes and immersed his body in the cooling stream. It was a glorious evening, and Pitsikatoff's poetic soul began to attune itself to the harmony of its surroundings. And imagine what sweet emotions filled his spirit when, swimming a few yards upstream, he beheld a beautiful young woman sitting on the steep bank fishing! A mixture of feelings welled up and made him stop and catch his breath: memories of childhood, regret for the past, awakening love . . . Love? But was he not convinced that for him love was no longer possible? Once he had lost his faith in humanity (his beloved wife having run off with his best friend, Sobarkin the bassoon), a sense of emptiness had filled his breast and he had become a misanthrope. More than once he had asked himself: 'What is life? What is it all for? Life is a myth, a dream . . . mere ventriloquy . . .'

But now, standing before this sleeping beauty (there could be no doubt she was asleep), suddenly, against his will, he felt stirring in his breast something akin to love. He stood a long time before her, devouring her with his gaze . . .

Then, sighing deeply, he said to himself: 'Enough! Farewell, sweet vision! It's time I was on my way to His Excellency's ball . . .'

He took one more look at the fair one and was just about to swim back when an idea flashed into his mind.

'I'll leave her a token!' he thought. 'I'll tie something to her line . . . It'll be a surprise—"from an unknown admirer".'

Pitsikatoff quietly swam to the bank, culled a large bouquet of wild flowers and water-lilies, bound them together with goosefoot and attached them to the end of the line.

The bouquet sank to the bottom, pulling the gaily painted float after it.

Good sense, the laws of nature and the social station of my hero would seem to demand that the romance should come to an end at this point, but (alas!) the author's destiny is inexorable: because of circumstances beyond the author's control the romance did not end with the bouquet. In defiance of common sense and the entire natural order, our poor and plebeian Pitsikatoff was fated to play an important role in the life of a rich and beautiful young gentlewoman.

On reaching the bank, Pitsikatoff got a shock. His clothes were gone. Stolen . . . While he had been gazing in admiration at the fair one, anonymous villains had pinched everything except his double-bass and his top-hat.

'Accursed Fate!' he exclaimed. 'Oh Man, thou generation of vipers! It is not so much the deprivation of my garments that perturbs me (for clothing is but vanity), as the thought of having to go naked and thereby offending against public morality.'

He sat down on his instrument case and began to think how he was going to get out of this dreadful situation. 'I can't go to Prince Bibuloff's without any clothes,' he mused. 'There will be ladies present. What is more, the thieves have stolen not only my trousers, but also the rosin I had in my trouser pocket!'

He thought long and painfully, until his head ached.

'Aha!'—at last he'd got it—'not far from here there's a little bridge surrounded by bushes. I can sit under there till nightfall and then make my way in the dark to the nearest cottage . . .'

And so, having adopted this plan, Pitsikatoff put on his top-hat, swung the double-bass on to his back and padded off towards the bushes. Naked, with his musical instrument slung over his shoulders, he resembled some ancient mythological demigod.

But now, gentle reader, while our hero sits moping under the bridge, let us leave him for a while and turn to the young lady who was fishing. What has become of her? When the fair creature awoke and could see no sign of her float she hurriedly tugged on the line. The line tautened, but neither float nor hook appeared. Presumably Pitsikatoff's bouquet had become waterlogged and turned into a dead weight.

'Either I've caught a big fish,' thought the girl, 'or the line has got entangled.'

After another couple of tugs she decided it was the latter.

'What a pity!' she thought. 'They bite so much better towards dusk. What shall I do?'

In the twinkling of an eye the eccentric young lady had cast aside her diaphanous garments and immersed her beauteous person in the cooling stream right up to her marble-white shoulders. The line was all tangled up in the bouquet, and it was no easy matter extricating the hook, but perseverance triumphed in the end, and some fifteen minutes later our lovely heroine emerged from the water all glowing and happy, holding the hook in her hand.

But a malevolent fate had been watching out for her too: the wretches who had stolen Pitsikatoff's clothing had removed hers as well, leaving behind only her jar of bait.

'What am I to do?' she wept. 'Go home in this state? No, never! I would rather die! I shall wait until nightfall, then walk as far as old Agatha's cottage in the dark and send her to the house for some clothes . . . And in the mean time I'll go and hide under the little bridge.'

Our heroine scuttled off in that direction, bending low and keeping to where the grass was longest. She crept in under the bridge, saw a naked man there with artistic mane and hairy chest, screamed, and fell down in a swoon.

Pitsikatoff got a fright too. At first he took the girl for a naiad.

'Perhaps 'tis a water-sprite,' he thought, 'come to lure me away?', and felt flattered by the notion, since he had always had a high opinion of his appearance. 'But if it is not a sprite but a human being, how is this strange metamorphosis to be explained? What is she doing here under the bridge, and what has befallen her?'

As he pondered these questions the fair one recovered consciousness.

'Do not kill me!' she whispered. 'I am the Princess Bibuloff. I beseech you! They'll give you lots of money! I was disentangling my fishing-hook just now and some thieves stole my new dress and shoes and everything!'

'Mademoiselle,' Pitsikatoff replied plaintively, 'they've stolen my clothes too—*and* the rosin I had in my trouser pocket!'

Usually people who play the double-bass or the trombone are not very inventive, but Pitsikatoff was a pleasant exception.

'Mademoiselle,' he said after a pause, 'I see that my appearance embarrasses you. You must agree, though, that there is just as good reason for me to stay under here as for you. But I have had an idea: how would it be if you were to get into the case of my double-bass and close the lid? Then you wouldn't see me . . .'

So saying, Pitsikatoff dragged the double-bass out of its case. Just for a moment he wondered whether he might be profaning Art by using his case thus, but his hesitation did not last long. The fair one lay down in the case and curled up in a ball, while he fastened the straps with a feeling of pleasure that nature had endowed him with such intelligence.

'Now, Mademoiselle, you cannot see me,' he said. 'You can lie there and relax, and when it gets dark I shall carry you to your parents' house. I can come back here for the double-bass afterwards.'

When darkness fell Pitsikatoff heaved the case with the fair one inside on to his shoulders and padded off towards Bibuloff's villa. His plan was that he should walk as he was to the nearest cottage, get some clothing there, and then go on . . .

'It's an ill wind that blows nobody good . . .' he thought, bending under his burden and stirring up the dust with his bare feet. 'No doubt Bibuloff will reward me handsomely for the deep concern that I have shown over his daughter's fate.'

'I trust you are comfortable, Mademoiselle?' he enquired with a note of gallantry in his voice like that of a gentleman inviting a lady to dance a quadrille. 'Please don't stand on ceremony. Do make yourself at home in there.'

Suddenly the gallant Pitsikatoff thought he saw ahead of him two figures shrouded in darkness. Peering more closely he assured himself that it was not an optical illusion: there really were two figures walking ahead and—they were carrying bundles of some kind . . .

'The thieves!' it flashed through his mind. 'I bet that's who it is! And they're carrying something—must be our clothes!'

Pitsikatoff put the case down at the side of the road and chased after the figures.

'Stop!' he shouted. 'Stop thief!'

The figures looked round, and seeing they were pursued, took to their heels. The Princess continued to hear the sound of rapid footsteps and cries of 'Stop, stop!' for a long time, then all was quiet.

Pitsikatoff was quite carried away by the chase, and no doubt the fair one would have been lying out there at the roadside for a long time to come, had it not been for a lucky chance. It so happened that Pitsikatoff's two colleagues, Dronin the flute and Flamboisky the clarinet, were making their way along the road at that same time. Tripping over the double-bass case, they looked at each other with expressions of surprise and puzzlement.

'A double-bass!' said Dronin. 'Why, it's old Pitsikatoff's! How could it have got here?'

'Something must have happened to him,' Flamboisky decided. 'Either he's got drunk or he's been robbed . . . Anyway we can't leave his instrument lying here. Let's take it with us.'

Dronin heaved the case on to his back and the musicians walked on.

'What a ruddy weight!' the flautist kept groaning all the way. 'I wouldn't play a monster like this for all the tea in China . . . Phew!'

When they arrived at Prince Bibuloff's villa they deposited the case at the place reserved for the orchestra and went off to the buffet.

By now the chandeliers and candelabras were being lit. Princess Bibuloff's fiancé, Counsellor Sikofantoff, a nice handsome official from the Ministry of Communications, was standing in the drawing-room with his hands in his pockets, chatting to Count Tipplovitch. They were talking about music.

'You know, Count,' said Sikofantoff, 'in Naples I was personally acquainted with a violinist who could do absolute marvels. You'll hardly believe it, but he could get the most fantastic trills out of a double-bass—an ordinary double-bass—stupendous! He could play Strauss waltzes on the thing!'

'Come now, that's scarcely—' the Count objected.

'I assure you he could. He could even play Liszt's "Hungarian Rhapsody"! I shared a hotel room with him and to pass the time I got him to teach me Liszt's "Hungarian Rhapsody" on the double-bass.'

'Liszt's "Hungarian . . ."? Come now . . . you're pulling my leg.'

'Ah, you don't believe me?' laughed Sikofantoff. 'Then I'll prove it to you straight away. Let's get an instrument!'

Bibuloff's prospective son-in-law and the Count made for the orchestra. They went over to the double-bass, quickly undid the straps and . . . oh, calamity!

But at this point, while the reader gives free rein to his imagination in picturing the outcome of this musical debate, let us return to Pitsikatoff . . . The unfortunate musician, not having caught up with the thieves, went back to the spot where he had left his case but could see no sign of his precious burden. Lost in bewilderment, he walked up and down several times in vain, and decided he must be on the wrong road . . .

'How awful!' he thought, tearing his hair and feeling his blood run cold. 'She'll suffocate in that case. I've murdered her!'

Pitsikatoff tramped the roads till midnight in search of the case and then, exhausted, retired under the bridge.

'I'll look for it in the morning,' he decided.

But his dawn search proved equally fruitless, and he decided to stay under the bridge again until nightfall . . .

'I shall find her!' he muttered, taking off his top-hat and tearing his hair. 'Even if it takes me a whole year—I'll find her!'

And to this day the peasants who live in those parts will tell you that at night near the little bridge you can sometimes see a naked man all covered in hair and wearing a top-hat . . . and occasionally from beneath the bridge you can hear the melancholy groaning of a double-bass.

Vanka

Vanka Zhukov, a boy of nine apprenticed three months ago to Alyakhin the shoemaker, did not go to bed on Christmas Eve. He waited until his master and mistress and the older apprentices had left for the early morning service, then he fetched a little bottle of ink and a pen with a rusty nib from his master's cupboard, spread a crumpled sheet of paper in front of him, and began to write. Before forming the first letter, he looked round nervously several times at the doors and windows, glanced up at the dark icon, to left and right of which stretched shelves of lasts, and sighed brokenly. He was kneeling in front of a work-bench, on which lay his sheet of paper.

'Dear Grandad Konstantin Makarych,' he wrote. 'I'm writing you this letter. I wish you a Happy Christmas and all God's blessings. I have no father or mummy, you're the only person I have left.'

Vanka turned to look at the dark window, in which flickered the reflection of his candle, and vividly imagined to himself his grandfather Konstantin Makarych, who worked as a night-watchman on the Zhivaryovs' estate. He was a skinny little old man of about sixty-five, but amazingly lively and nimble, with a face that was always laughing and drunken eyes. During the daytime he slept in the servants' kitchen or played the fool with the cooks; at night, wrapped in his voluminous full-length sheepskin, he went the rounds of the estate beating with his watchman's clapper. Behind him, their heads hung low, walked old Kashtanka and Loacher, named after the fish on account of his dark back and long, weasel-like body. Loacher is an extremely deferential and affectionate dog, he gives the same adoring look to friend and stranger alike, but his reputation is nil. Behind that deference and docility there lurks the most Jesuitical cunning. No one knows better than he how to creep up and nip you in the leg, slip into the ice-house, or steal a peasant's chicken. Many is the time he has nearly had his back legs broken, a couple of times he has been strung up, and every week he is beaten within an inch of his life; but he always bounces back.

Now Grandfather was sure to be standing at the gates of the village church, squinting at its bright red windows, stamping up and down in his big felt boots, and fooling about with the servants. His watchman's clapper hangs at his belt. He waves his arms around, hugs himself to keep warm, and with an impish old chuckle keeps going up to the housemaids and cooks and pinching them.

'Why don't we have some snuff?' he says, offering the girls his snuffbox.

The girls take a pinch and sneeze. This sends Grandfather into indescribable raptures, he breaks into peals of merry laughter, and cries:

'Wipe the stuff off, it's freezing to you!'

They hold the box out to the dogs, as well. Kashtanka sneezes, shakes her muzzle about and walks away, offended. Loacher is too polite to sneeze and wags his tail instead. The weather is superb. The air is still, transparent, and crisp. It is a dark night, but the whole village can be seen clearly: the white roofs with plumes of smoke rising from their chimneys, the trees silvered with rime, the deep snowdrifts. The whole sky is strewn with gaily twinkling stars, and the Milky Way shines forth so clearly that you would think it had been washed and polished with snow for Christmas . . .

Vanka sighed, dipped his pen in the ink, and carried on writing:

'And yesterday I got a thrashing. The master dragged me out into the yard by my hair and walloped me with a strap, because I was rocking their baby in it's cradle and went and dropped off. And last week the mistress told me to gut a herring and I started from the tail so she took hold of the herring and wiped it's snout all over my mug. The older apprentices are always making fun of me they send me to the tavern for vodka and make me steal the master's gherkins and the master beats me with the first thing comes to hand. And there's nothing to eat here at all. They give me bread in the morning porridge for dinner and bread again for supper but the master and mistress they guzzle all the tea and cabbage soup. And they make me sleep in the passage and when their baby's crying I don't sleep at all but have to rock the cradle. Dear Grandad, for the Dear Lord's sake take me away from here take me home to the village I can't stand it any longer . . . I beg and beseech you and will pray for you always take me away from here or I'll die—'

Vanka's mouth trembled, he wiped his eyes with his grubby fist, and gave a sob.

'—I'll grind your snuff for you,' he continued, 'I'll pray to God for you, and if I do anything bad you can beat the hide off me. And if you're worried I won't have a job to do then I'll beg the steward to take Christian pity on me and let me clean boots or I'll take over from Fedka as shepherd-boy. Dear Grandpa, I can't stand it any longer its killing me. I

36

was going to run away to the village, but I don't have any boots and I'm scared of the frost. And when I grow up I'll look after you in return and won't let anyone harm you and when you die I'll pray for your soul just as I do for Pelageya my mummy.

'Moscow is a very big town. All the houses are gents' houses and there are lots of horses but no sheep and the dogs aren't fierce at all. The boys don't go about with the star here at Christmas and they won't let people go up and sing in the choir and once I saw some hooks for sale in a shop window with line on them and for all sorts of fish, very fine they were too and there was even one strong enough to hold a forty-pound wels. Also I've seen shops with all sorts of guns like the master's at home they'd be about a hundred roubles each I reckon . . . Also in the butcher's shops there are blackcock and hazel grouse and hares but where they shoot them the butchers don't say.

'Dear Grandad, when they have the Christmas tree with presents on at the big house get one of the gold walnuts for me will you and put it away in the green chest. Ask Miss Olga Ignatyevna, say its for Vanka.'

Vanka let out a deep sigh and once more gazed at the window-pane. He remembered that it was always his grandfather who went into the forest to get the Christmas tree for the big house, taking Vanka with him. Oh what fun that was! Grandfather crackled, the frost crackled, and looking at them Vanka crackled too. Before felling the tree, his grandfather would smoke a pipe, take his time over a pinch of snuff, and laugh at little Vanka shivering there . . . The young fir-trees clothed in rime stood motionless, waiting to see which of them was to die. Then, goodness knows where from, a hare shoots across the snowdrifts like an arrow . . . Grandfather can never resist shouting:

'Catch him, catch him! Catch the bob-tailed rascal!'

After cutting down the fir-tree, Grandfather would drag it off to the house. There they would set about decorating it . . . Miss Olga Ignatyevna, Vanka's favourite, bustled about most. When Vanka's mother Pelageya was still alive and worked for the Zhivaryovs as a house-maid, Olga Ignatyevna used to give Vanka sweets, and amused herself by teaching him to read, write, count to a hundred and even dance a quadrille. But when Pelageya died, the orphaned Vanka was packed off to his grandfather in the servants' kitchen, and thence to Moscow to Alyakhin the shoemaker . . .

'Come and fetch me dear Grandad,' Vanka continued. 'I beg you in Christ's name to take me away from here. Have pity on me a poor orphan

37

or they'll go on clouting me and I'm hungry all day long and I'm so miserable I can't tell you I cry all the time. And once the master hit me on the head with a last and I fell down and nearly didn't wake up. My life's so awful worse than any dog's . . . Please give my love also to Alyona One-Eyed Yegorka and the coachman and don't give my concertina away to anyone. I remain your grandson Ivan Zhukov. Dear Grandad come.'

Vanka folded the closely written sheet in four and put it into an envelope that he had bought for a kopeck the previous day . . . He thought for a moment, dipped his pen, and wrote down the address:

The Village. To Grandad.

Then he scratched his head, thought again, and added: '—Konstantin Makarych.' Pleased not to have been disturbed while writing, he grabbed his cap and without bothering to put a coat on over his shirt, dashed out into the street . . .

The men at the butcher's shop, in answer to his questions the day before, had told him that letters are dropped into post-boxes, then carried from the post-boxes to all the ends of the earth on mail troikas with drunken drivers and tinkling bells. Vanka ran up to the nearest post-box and pushed his precious letter through the opening . . .

An hour later, lulled by fond hopes, he was fast asleep. He dreamt he saw the stove. On it was sitting his grandfather, dangling his bare feet and reading the letter to the cooks . . . Round the stove walked Loacher, wagging his tail . . .

The Reed-Pipe

Stifled by the cloying air of the fir plantation and all covered in spiders'
webs and fir-needles, Meliton Shishkin, the bailiff from the Dementyevs'
farm, was slowly working his way to the edge of the wood, his shotgun in
his hand. His dog Lady, a cross between a mongrel and a setter, extremely
thin and heavy with young, was trailing along behind her master with her
wet tail between her legs, and doing her best not to get her nose pricked.
It was a dull, overcast morning. Great splashes of water fell from the
mist-shrouded trees and the bracken, and the damp wood exuded a pungent odour of decay.

Ahead, where the plantation came to an end, stood silver birches, and
between their trunks and branches the misty horizon could be seen.
Beyond the birches someone was playing on a shepherd's rustic pipe.
They were playing no more than five or six notes, drawing them out lazily
and making no effort to combine them into a tune, yet in the high-
pitched wail of the pipe there was something both sombre and singularly
mournful.

When the plantation began to thin out and the firs mingled with
young birch-trees, Meliton saw a herd. Cows, sheep and hobbled horses
were wandering among the bushes and snuffing the grass in the wood,
crackling branches underfoot. At the wood's edge, leaning against a dripping birch-tree, stood an old shepherd, gaunt, bare-headed and wearing
a coarse, tattered smock. He was staring at the ground, thinking about
something, and evidently playing the pipe quite mechanically.

'Morning, gaffer! God save you!' Meliton greeted him in a thin, husky
little voice that was completely out of keeping with his enormous stature
and fat, fleshy face. 'You've got the knack of that whistle! Whose herd is
that you're minding?'

'The Artamonovs',' replied the old man grudgingly, and put the pipe
away inside the front of his smock.

'So this must be their wood, too?' asked Meliton, looking around him.
'Well I never, so it is . . . I was nearly lost, I reckon. Scratched my face to
pieces on those firs.'

He sat down on the damp earth and began to roll a cigarette from a
scrap of newspaper.

Like his thin little voice, everything about this man was on a small scale—his smile, his beady eyes, his buttons and the little cap perched precariously on his greasy, shaven head—and seemed at variance with his height, his broadness, and his fleshy face. When he spoke and smiled, his smooth, pudgy face, and his whole appearance, seemed somehow womanish, timid and submissive.

'God help us, what weather!' he said with a roll of the head. 'They haven't got the oats in yet and this wretched rain looks as if it's hired itself out for the season.'

The shepherd glanced at the drizzling sky, the wood, and the bailiff's sodden clothes, pondered, and said nothing.

'It's been like this all summer . . .' sighed Meliton. 'Bad for the peasants, and no joy for the masters either.'

The shepherd glanced at the sky again, pondered, and said deliberately, as though chewing over every word:

'It's all heading one way . . . No good'll come of it.'

'What are things like here?' asked Meliton, lighting his cigarette. 'Seen any grouse coveys in the Artamonovs' scrub?'

The shepherd did not answer at once. Again he glanced at the sky and to left and right, pondered, and blinked . . . Evidently he attached no small importance to his words, and to lend them more weight endeavoured to deliver them slowly and with a certain solemnity. His face bore all the angularity and gravity of age, and because his nose had a deep, saddle-shaped bridge to it and his nostrils curled slightly upwards, its expression seemed sly and quizzical.

'No, I can't say as I have,' he answered. 'Our huntsman Yeryomka said he put up a covey on Elijah's Day, by Pustoshye, but I dare say he was lying. There aren't the birds about.'

'No, brother, there aren't . . . It's the same everywhere! When you come down to it, the hunting's paltry these days, a waste of time. There's no game at all, and what there is, isn't worth soiling your hands for—it's not even full grown! Such tiny stuff, you feel quite sorry for it.'

Meliton gave a contemptuous laugh.

'Yes, the way the world's going these days is downright daft! The birds don't know what they're doing, they sit on their eggs late and some of them, I swear, aren't off the nest by St Peter's Day!'

'It's all heading one way,' said the shepherd, raising his head. 'Past year there weren't much game about, this year there's even less, and mark my words, in another five there'll be none at all. As I see it, soon there won't be birds of any kind about, let alone game-birds.'

'Yes,' agreed Meliton after a moment's thought. 'You're right.'

The shepherd chuckled bitterly and shook his head.

'It beats me!' he said. 'Where've they all gone to? Twenty-odd years back, I remember, there were geese here, cranes, duck and black grouse—it was teeming with them! The gents would go out hunting and all you'd hear was "Bang-bang! Bang-bang!" There was no end to the woodcock, snipe and curlew, and as for teal and the little pipers, they were as common as starlings, or sparrows say—any number there were! And where've they all gone to? You don't even see a bird of prey these days. Eagles, falcons, the big eagle owls—they've all gone . . . There's less of every beast about. Nowadays, brother, you're lucky if you see a wolf or a fox, let alone a bear or a mink. And in the old days there were even elk! Forty years I've been giving an eye to the ways of God's world, year in, year out, and as I look at it, everything's heading one way.'

'One way?'

'To the bad, my boy. To ruination, I reckon . . . The days of God's world are numbered.'

The old man put on his cap and began to stare at the sky.

'It's a sad thing!' he sighed after a short silence. 'Dear God but it's sad! Of course, it's the will of God, it wasn't us made the world, but even so, brother, it's sad. If a single tree withers or, say, one of your cows dies, you feel sorry, don't you, so what will it be like, friend, to see the whole world go to rack and ruin? There's such goodness in it all, Lord Jesus Christ! The sun, the sky, the forests, the rivers, the animals—they've all been created, fashioned, fitted to each other, haven't they? Each has been allotted its task and knows its rightful place. And all this must come to naught!'

A melancholy smile flickered across the shepherd's face and his eyelids trembled.

'You say the earth is heading for ruin . . .' said Meliton, thinking. 'Perhaps you're right, the end of the world is nigh, but you can't judge just from the birds. You can hardly take the birds as an indication.'

'It's not just the birds,' said the shepherd. 'It's the beasts too, the cattle, the bees, the fish . . . If you don't believe me, ask the old men. They'll all tell you the fish aren't a bit like they used to be. Every year there are less and less of them—in the seas, in the lakes, in the rivers. Here in the Peschanka, I remember, you used to catch pike a good two foot long, and there were burbot, ide and bream, all decent-size fish too, but now you're grateful if you catch a jack-pike or a perch six inches long. You don't see a proper ruffe even. It's worse and worse with every year that passes, and in a little while there won't be any fish at all. Then take the rivers . . . *They're* all drying up!'

'That's true, they are.'

'To be sure they are. Each year they get shallower and shallower, and there are none of the good deep pools there used to be, brother. You see those bushes yonder?' asked the old man, pointing to one side. 'There's an old stream-bed behind them, called "the backwater". In my father's time, that's where the Peschanka flowed, but now look where the devil's led it! She keeps changing course and you see—she'll change it so much, in the end she'll dry up. Back of Kurgasovo there used to be ponds and marshes, but where are they now? And what's become of all the streams, eh? Here in this wood there used to be a running stream, and it was so full that the peasants would set their creels in it and catch pike, and the wild duck would winter by it; but now there's no water in it worthy the name even at the spring flood. Yes, my boy, everywhere you look things are bad. Everywhere!'

There was silence. Meliton stared before him in a reverie. He was trying to think of a single area of nature that had not yet been touched by the all-consuming disaster. Flecks of light glided over the mist and the slanting bands of rain, as though over opalescent glass, but immediately melted away: the rising sun was trying to break through the clouds and catch a glimpse of the earth.

'It's the same with the forests . . .' muttered Meliton.

'Same with them . . .' echoed the shepherd. 'They're all being felled, they keep catching fire, they dry up, and there's no new growth in their place. What does grow is straightway cut down again, it comes up one day and the next day people have cut it down—and so it'll go on, until nothing's left. I've been minding the village's herd, friend, since we got our freedom, before then I was a shepherd of the master's, and always in this same spot, and I can't remember a single summer day when I haven't been here. And all the time I give an eye to God's works. I've had time to watch them well, brother, in my life, and the way I look at it now, all things that grow are on the wane. Be it rye, or vegetables, or flowers of any sort, it's all heading one way.'

'People are better, though,' observed the bailiff.

'How, better?'

'They're cleverer.'

'Cleverer they may be, lad, true enough, but what's the good of that?

42

What fine use is cleverness to people on the verge of ruin? You don't need brains to perish. What's a hunter want brains for, if there's no game to shoot anyway? What I think is, God's made folk cleverer, but He's taken away their strength, that's what. Folks have become feeble, exceeding feeble. Now I know I'm not worth a groat, I'm the lowliest peasant in the whole village, but all the same, I've got strength, lad. You think: I'm in my sixties, but I mind the herd fair weather and foul, and I do night-watching for a couple of kopecks, and I don't fall asleep or feel the cold, but if you was to put my son, who's cleverer than me, in my place, why, next day he'd be asking for a rise, or going to the doctor. Ye-s . . . I eat nothing but bread—"give us this day our daily bread", it says—and my father ate nothing but bread, and my grandfather before him, but the peasants these days, they've got to have tea and vodka and white loaves, they've got to sleep from dusk till dawn, go to doctors, and be pampered in every way. And why? Because they've grown feeble, they haven't the strength to stick things out. They don't want to fall asleep, but their eyes start aching and that's that.'

'It's true,' Meliton agreed. 'The peasant's good for nothing these days.'

'Might as well admit it, we get worser every year. And take the gentry now—they've grown feebler than the peasants even. Gents these days have learnt everything, they know things they'd be better off not knowing—and what good does it do? They make you sorry to look on 'em . . . Skinny, weedy, like some Frenchie or Magyar, there's no presence to them, no dignity—they're only gents in name. Poor creatures, they've no place in the world, no work to do, you can't make out what they do want. Either they sit around with a rod catching fish, or they're flat on their backs reading books, or they're hanging about with the peasants trying to put ideas in their heads; and those as are starving take jobs as clerks. So they idle their time away and never think of getting down to a proper job of work. Half the gents in the old days were generals, but nowadays they're just—dross!'

'They're badly off these days,' Meliton said.

'And the reason is, God's taken their strength away. You can't go against God.'

Meliton stared fixedly before him again. After thinking awhile, he sighed the way staid, sober-minded people do, wagged his head, and said:

'And you know why all this is? Because we sin so much, we've forgotten God . . . so now the time's come for it all to end. You can't expect the world to last for ever anyway, can you? Enough's enough.'

The shepherd sighed and, as if to cut short a conversation that he found disagreeable, he moved away from the birch and began counting the cattle over silently.

'Hey-hey, halloo!' he shouted. 'Hey-hey! Damn you, where d'you think you're all going? What the devil's made them go into the firs? Halloa-loa-loa!'

He scowled and went over to the bushes to gather the herd together. Meliton rose and ambled quietly along the edge of the wood. As he walked, he stared at the ground beneath his feet: he was still trying to think of at least something that had not yet been touched by death. Again bright flecks crept over the slanting bands of rain; they danced into the tops of the trees, and melted away in their wet foliage. Lady discovered a hedgehog under a bush and tried to attract her master's attention to it by howling and barking.

'Have an eclipse recently, did you?' the shepherd called out from behind the bushes.

'We did!' replied Meliton.

'Thought as much, people everywhere are complaining there was one. So there's disorder in the heavens too, brother! And no wonder . . . Hey-hey! Hup!'

When he had driven the herd back out of the wood, the shepherd leant against a birch, looked up at the sky, calmly took his pipe out of his smock and started to play. As before, he played mechanically, producing no more than five or six notes; he might have been handling the pipe for the first time in his life, the sounds issued so uncertainly, haphazardly and tunelessly; but for Meliton, who was still thinking of the downfall of the world, his playing seemed to contain something desperately mournful and harrowing, which he would rather not have heard. The highest, shrillest notes, which trembled, then broke off abruptly, seemed to be sobbing inconsolably, as though the pipe were sick, or frightened; whilst the lowest reminded him for some reason of the mist itself, the forbidding trees and the grey sky. The music seemed to go with the weather, the old man, and what he had been talking about.

Meliton felt an urge to complain. He went over to the old man and, gazing at his sad, quizzical face and at the reed-pipe, mumbled:

'And life's got harder, too, old friend. Life's barely liveable, what with the bad harvests, the poverty . . . the cattle sickness all the time, illness . . . We're at the end of our tether.'

44

The bailiff's pudgy face flushed crimson and took on a woeful, womanish expression. He twiddled his fingers in the air as though groping for words to convey his indeterminate feelings, and continued:

'I've got eight children and a wife to support, my mother's still alive . . . and all I get is ten roubles a month without board. The poverty's made my wife a proper shrew . . . and I'm always hitting the bottle. Really I'm a steady, sober-minded sort of chap, I've had an education. I ought to be sitting in the quiet of my home, but all day I spend wandering about with my gun, like a stray dog, because I can't abide it, I loathe my own home!'

Realising that his tongue was babbling something totally different from what he had intended to tell the old man, the bailiff gave up and said with bitterness:

'If the world's going to perish, then the sooner the better! There's no point in hanging about and making people suffer for nothing . . .'

The old man took the pipe away from his lips and, screwing up one eye, looked down its small mouthpiece. His face was sad, and covered with large splashes like tears. He smiled and said:

'It's a pity though, brother! Oh Lord, the pity of it! The earth, the forest, the sky . . . animals—they've all been created and fashioned, haven't they, there's a sense running through it all. And it's all to come to naught. But it's the people I feel sorriest for.'

A heavy squall of rain rustled through the wood towards where they were standing. Meliton looked in the direction of the sound, did up all the buttons of his coat, and said:

'I'm off to the village. Cheerio, gaffer. What's your name?'

'Poor Luke.'

'Well, goodbye, Luke! Thanks for the conversation. Lady—*ici*!'

Meliton left the shepherd, sauntered along the edge of the wood and then down to a meadow, which gradually turned into marsh. The water squelched beneath his boots, and the russet-headed sedge, whose stems were still green and lush, bowed earthwards as though afraid of being trodden on. Beyond the marsh, on the banks of the Peschanka of which the old man had spoken, stood a line of willows, and beyond the willows the squire's threshing-barn showed blue through the mist. One could sense the proximity of that cheerless time which nothing can avert, when the fields become dark and the earth is muddy and chill; when the weeping willow seems to be sadder than ever and the tears trickle down her trunk; when only the cranes can flee from the all-pervading disaster and

45

even they, as though afraid of offending morose nature by declaring their happiness, fill the skies with mournful, melancholy song.

Meliton wandered towards the river and could hear the sounds of the pipe slowly dying away behind him. He still felt the urge to complain. Sadly he looked to right and left, and felt unbearably sorry for the sky, the earth, the sun, the forest, and his dog Lady; and when the pipe's top note suddenly pierced the air and hung there trembling, like the voice of a person weeping, he felt full of bitterness and resentment at the disorder manifest in nature.

The top note trembled, broke off, and the pipe fell silent.

Boys

'Volodya's here!' someone outside shouted.

'Master Volodya's here!' shrieked Natalya, running into the dining-room. 'Oh my goodness!'

All the members of the Korolyov family, who had been expecting their Volodya to arrive at any moment, rushed to the windows. A wide peasant sledge was standing by the entrance, and steam was rising in a dense cloud from the troika of white horses. The sledge was empty, because Volodya was already standing in the porch untying his hood, his fingers red and numb with cold. His school greatcoat and peaked cap, his over-shoes and the hair on his temples, were covered in rime, and the whole of him from head to foot was giving off such a delicious frosty smell that looking at him, you felt you wanted to hug yourself with cold and go 'brrr!' His mother and aunt rushed to embrace and kiss him, Natalya flung herself down at his feet and began pulling off his felt boots, his sisters started squealing, doors creaked and slammed, and Volodya's father ran into the entrance-hall in his shirt-sleeves, a pair of scissors in his hands, and shouted anxiously:

'We were expecting you yesterday! You got here all right? Safe journey? Oh come on, let him say hallo to his father! I am his father, for Heaven's sake!'

'Garf! Garf!' bayed the huge black dog Milord, thumping his tail against the walls and furniture.

Everything merged into one continuous joyful sound, which lasted a couple of minutes. When the first rush of joy was over, the Korolyovs noticed that in addition to Volodya the entrance-hall contained another young person, muffled up in scarves, shawls and hoods, and covered in rime. He was standing motionless in the corner, in the shadow cast by a large fox-fur coat.

'Volodya dear,' Mother whispered, 'who's your companion?'

'Oh sorry!' Volodya recollected himself. 'Allow me to introduce my friend Lentilov from second year. I've brought him to stay with us.'

'Delighted, you're most welcome!' Father said joyfully. 'I'm sorry I'm not properly dressed. Come on in! Natalya, help Mr Dentilov with his outdoor clothes! For Heaven's sake, can't anyone get rid of that damned dog?'

Not long afterwards, Volodya and his friend Lentilov, reeling from their noisy reception and still pink with cold, were sitting at the table drinking tea. A wintry sun penetrated the snow and tracery on the window-panes, played over the samovar and bathed its pure rays in the rinsing-bowl. The room was warm, and the boys felt a tickling sensation in their numbed bodies as the warmth and chill competed for supremacy.

'So, Christmas is almost upon us!' Father was intoning, rolling a cigarette from some dark reddish-brown tobacco. 'It seems no time since last summer, when your mother was in tears seeing you off, and lo and behold, you're back again. How time does fly! Before you can say knife, old age is upon you. Mr Reptilov, do help yourself to anything you want. We don't stand on ceremony.'

Volodya's three sisters, Katya, Sonya and Masha—Katya, the eldest, was eleven—sat at the table with their eyes fixed on the new acquaintance. Lentilov was the same age and height as Volodya, but where Volodya was plump and fair-skinned, he was thin, swarthy and covered in freckles. He had bristly hair, narrow eyes and thick lips, he was really very ugly, and but for his school jacket, you might have taken him from outward appearances for a cook's son. He was sullen, said nothing and did not once smile. Looking at him, the girls reckoned straight away that he must be very clever and learned. He was so preoccupied with his own thoughts that whenever he was asked something, he started, shook his head and asked for the question to be repeated.

The girls noticed that Volodya, who was always jolly and talkative, on this occasion likewise said little, never smiled and did not even seem pleased to be home. While they were having tea, he addressed his sisters only once, and even then his words were strange. Pointing at the samovar, he said:

'In California they don't drink tea, they drink gin.'

He too was preoccupied, and judging by the glances that he exchanged from time to time with his friend Lentilov, they shared the same thoughts.

After tea everyone went into the nursery. Father and the girls sat down at the table and took up the work that had been interrupted by the boys' arrival. They were making flowers and a fringe for the Christmas tree out of coloured paper. It was noisy, exciting work. The girls greeted each newly completed flower with cries of delight, even of horror, as if the flower had fallen from the sky. Papa was also in raptures and every so

48

often would throw the scissors down on the floor, complaining angrily that they were not sharp enough. Mamma would run into the nursery looking very worried and ask:

'Who's pinched my scissors? Ivan Nikolaich, have you pinched my scissors again?'

'For Heaven's sake, am I to be deprived of scissors?' Ivan Nikolaich replied in a tearful voice, leaning back on his chair and striking an offended pose, but a minute later he was in raptures again.

On previous arrivals Volodya had also helped to dress the Christmas tree or had run outside to see how the coachman and shepherd were getting on with the snow hill, but now he and Lentilov completely ignored the coloured paper and did not visit the stables even once; instead, they sat by the window and began whispering, then they opened up an atlas together and began studying a map.

'First get to Perm,' Lentilov said quietly. 'Next Tyumen . . . Tomsk . . . then on to . . . Kamchatka. From there the Samoyeds take you by boat across the Bering Straits, and that's it, you're in America. There are lots of fur-bearing animals in that area.'

'What about California?' Volodya asked.

'California's lower down. Once you're in America, California's no distance. Then we can earn a living by hunting and robbing.'

All day long Lentilov avoided the girls and glared at them, but after evening tea he happened to be left alone in their company for five minutes. It was awkward to remain silent. He coughed sternly, rubbed his left hand with his right palm, looked gloomily at Katya and asked:

'Have you read Mayne Reid?'

'No, I haven't . . . Tell me, can you skate?'

Absorbed in his own thoughts, Lentilov did not answer this question, but merely puffed out his cheeks and sighed as if he felt very hot. Looking up again at Katya, he said:

'When a herd of bison runs across the pampas, the whole earth shakes and the mustangs take fright and buck and neigh.'

Lentilov gave a sad smile and added:

'Then there are the Red Indians, they attack trains. But worst of all are the mosquitoes and termites.'

'Termites? What are they?'

'They're like little ants, only with wings. They've got a vicious bite. Do you know who I am?'

'You're Mr Lentilov.'

49

'No, I'm not, I'm Montihomo Hawk's Claw, Leader of the Unconquerables.'

Masha, the youngest girl, glanced at him, then at the window, where evening was already drawing in, and said dreamily:

'We had lentils for lunch yesterday.'

Lentilov's incomprehensible words, his constant whispering with Volodya, and Volodya being too preoccupied to play with them—all this was strange and mysterious, and the two older girls, Katya and Sonya, began to keep a close watch on the boys. That evening, when the boys went to bed, the girls crept up to their door and overheard their conversation. And what secrets they found out! The boys were planning to run away to somewhere in America to look for gold, and had already prepared everything for their journey: a pistol, two knives, some rusks, a magnifying glass to make fire with, a compass and four roubles in cash. They found out how the boys would have to cover several thousand versts on foot, fighting against tigers and savages along the way, then look for gold and ivory, kill their enemies, join some pirates, drink gin and finally marry beauties and cultivate plantations. Volodya and Lentilov were so carried away that they kept interrupting each other. Lentilov referred to himself as 'Montihomo Hawk's Claw' and to Volodya as 'my palefaced brother'.

'Whatever you do, don't tell Mamma,' Katya said to Sonya as they went back to bed. 'Volodya will bring us gold and ivory from America, but if you tell Mamma, they won't let him go.'

On the day before Christmas Eve Lentilov spent the whole time studying the map of Asia and making notes, while Volodya, looking languid and puffy, like someone stung by a bee, walked moodily about the house and ate nothing. Once he even stopped in front of the icon in the nursery, crossed himself and said:

'Oh Lord, forgive me my sins! Oh Lord, look after my poor unhappy Mamma!'

Towards evening he burst into tears. Before going to bed, he spent a long time embracing his father, mother and sisters. Katya and Sonya knew what it was all about, but Masha, the youngest, who hadn't the faintest idea what was going on, simply looked thoughtfully at Lentilov and said with a sigh:

'Nanny says, in Lent we should eat peas and lentils.'

Early on the morning of Christmas Eve Katya and Sonya climbed quietly out of bed and went to spy on the boys as they ran away to America. They crept up to the door.

'So you're not going?' Lentilov was asking angrily. 'Say it: you're not going?'

'Oh Lord!' Volodya was crying quietly. 'How can I go? I feel so sorry for Mamma.'

'My palefaced brother, please let's go! It was you said you were going and talked me into it, and now the time's come, you're in a funk.'

'I'm not in a funk, it's just . . . I'm sorry for Mamma.'

'Are you going or aren't you?'

'I am going, only . . . only not just now. I want to spend some time at home first.'

'In that case I'll go by myself!' Lentilov decided. 'I'll manage without you. And it was you said you wanted to hunt tigers and fight! In that case, give me back my pistol caps.'

Volodya began crying so bitterly that the sisters couldn't help crying quietly themselves. There was a silence.

'So you're not going?' Lentilov asked again.

'Oh . . . all right.'

'Get dressed then!'

To win Volodya over, Lentilov began praising America, roared like a tiger, described a steamboat, began swearing, and promised to let Volodya have all the ivory, and all the lion and tiger skins.

In the girls' eyes this thin little boy with the swarthy face, bristly hair and freckles was someone unusual, remarkable. He was a hero, a decisive, fearless individual, and he roared so convincingly that from outside the door it really did seem that there was a tiger or lion inside.

When the girls returned to their room and got dressed, Katya's eyes filled with tears and she said:

'Ooh, I do feel scared!'

Everything was quiet until two o'clock when they sat down to eat, but then it suddenly became clear that the boys were missing. They were sought in the servants' quarters, the stable and the steward's *fliegel*: they were not there. They were sought in the village: not there, either. Tea was drunk without them, and by the time supper was served, Mamma was extremely worried and even crying. That night they searched again in the village, and a party went to the river with lanterns. Heavens, what a hullabaloo!

Next morning the village constable arrived, and some document was being drawn up in the dining-room. Mamma was crying.

But now a wide peasant sleigh stops in front of the porch, and there's steam pouring off the troika of white horses.

'Volodya's here!' someone outside shouts.

'Master Volodya's here!' shrieks Natalya, running into the dining-room.

'Garf! Garf!' bays Milord.

It turned out that the boys had been detained in town in the shopping arcade (they'd been walking up and down asking everyone where they could buy gunpowder). As soon as he entered the hall, Volodya burst out sobbing and threw himself round his mother's neck. Trembling with horror at the thought of what was about to happen, the girls heard Papa take Volodya and Lentilov into his study and talk to them for a long time; Mamma was there, too, talking and crying.

'How *could* you do such a thing?' Papa was saying. 'Let's hope to goodness the school doesn't hear about it or you'll be expelled. Mr Lentilov, you should be ashamed of yourself! It was too bad, sir! You were the ringleader and I hope you'll be punished by your parents. How could you do such a thing? Where did you spend the night?'

'At the station!' Lentilov replied proudly.

Afterwards Volodya went to lie down with a towel soaked in vinegar pressed to his head. A telegram was sent off somewhere, and next day a lady arrived, Lentilov's mother, and took her son away.

On leaving, Lentilov's expression was stern and haughty, and when he was saying goodbye to the girls, he did not utter a single word, but took Katya's exercise book and wrote in it as a memento:

'Montihomo Hawk's Claw.'

Kashtanka

A TALE

I Behaving Badly

A young ginger-coloured bitch—a mixture of dachshund and mongrel, with a muzzle very reminiscent of a fox—was running up and down the pavement, throwing anxious glances to either side. Every so often she would stop and, whimpering, half-raise one frozen paw and then the other, trying to work out how she could possibly have managed to lose herself.

She remembered very clearly how she had spent the day, and how she had ended up on this unfamiliar pavement.

It began when her master, the joiner Luka Aleksandrych, put on his cap, placed some kind of wooden object, wrapped in a red cloth, under his arm, and shouted:

'Come on, Kashtanka!'

Hearing her name, the mixture of dachshund and mongrel came out from her sleeping-place on the shavings under the bench, had a nice stretch and ran after her master. Luka Aleksandrych's customers lived so terribly far away that, before calling on each of them, he needed to drop into several pubs to build up his strength. Kashtanka remembered that her behaviour on the way had been extremely improper. In her joy at being taken for a walk, she had pranced around, rushed out barking at the horse-drawn trams, dashed into courtyards and chased after dogs. The joiner was forever losing sight of her, stopping and shouting at her angrily. Once, with a voracious expression on his face, he had even got hold of her fox-like ear in his fist, pulled it and said very deliberately:

'Why don't you . . . just drop dead!'

After visiting his customers, Luka Aleksandrych called in briefly at his sister's, where he had a drink and something to eat, went on from his sister's to a bookbinder friend, from the bookbinder to the pub, from the pub to his old crony, and so on—with the result that by the time Kashtanka found herself on the unfamiliar pavement, evening was approaching and the joiner was as drunk as a lord. He was waving his arms about, sighing deeply and muttering:

'In her sins did my mother conceive me in my womb! Oh, sinner that I am! Here we are walking along the street looking at these little lamps, but once we die, we shall all burn in fiery Hyena . . .'

Or else he would assume a genial manner, call Kashtanka over and say:

'You, Kashtanka, are a little insect creature, nothing more. You fall as far short of a man as a carpenter does of a joiner . . .'

While he was talking to her like this, there suddenly came the sound of loud music. Kashtanka looked round and saw a regiment of soldiers advancing straight towards her. She could not bear music, as it set her nerves on edge, and started rushing about and howling. Much to her astonishment, the joiner, instead of taking fright, yelping and barking, smiled broadly, drew himself up to attention and gave a full salute. Seeing that her master was making no protest, Kashtanka began howling all the louder, and rushed distractedly across the road to the opposite pavement.

By the time she had collected herself, the music was no longer playing and the regiment had gone. She ran across the road to the spot where she had left her master, but alas!—the joiner was no longer there. She rushed this way and that, crossed the road again, but the joiner seemed to have disappeared from the face of the earth . . . Kashtanka began sniffing the pavement, hoping to find her master from the smell of his footprints, but some wretch had gone by earlier wearing new rubber galoshes, and now all the finer smells were mixed up with the pungent stench of rubber, so that it was impossible to make anything out.

While Kashtanka was running up and down looking in vain for her master, it grew dark. The lamps were lit on both sides of the street, and lights appeared in the windows of buildings. Large fluffy snowflakes were falling, making the roadway, the horses' backs and the coachmen's caps white, and the darker the atmosphere became, the whiter every object appeared. Unfamiliar customers were walking up and down past Kashtanka in a continuous stream, obscuring her field of vision and bumping into her. (Kashtanka divided the human race into two very unequal classes, masters and customers; between the two classes there was an essential difference: the former had the right to beat her, whereas she herself had the right to seize the latter by the calves.) The customers were hurrying somewhere and paid her no attention.

When it became completely dark, Kashtanka was overcome by a feeling of terror and despair. She huddled into a doorway and began crying bitterly. The day-long expedition with Luka Aleksandrych had worn her out, her ears and paws were frozen, and on top of that she was dreadfully hungry. During the whole day she had eaten only twice: at the book-

54

binder's she had had a little paste, and in one of the pubs she had found a sausage-skin near the counter—that was all. Had she been a human being, she would no doubt have thought to herself:

'No, life is intolerable, I must shoot myself!'

II The Mysterious Stranger

But she was not thinking of anything at all, only crying. When her head and back were completely covered by the soft fluffy snow and she had sunk into a heavy drowsiness from exhaustion, suddenly the entrance-door gave a click, creaked and struck her on the side. She jumped up. Through the open door came a man belonging to the customer class. Since Kashtanka had squealed and got under his feet, he could not fail to notice her. He bent down and asked:

'Where are you from, doggie? Did I hurt you? Poor little thing . . . Calm down now, calm down . . . It was my mistake.'

Kashtanka looked at the stranger through the snowflakes hanging on her eyelashes and saw in front of her a short fat little man with a plump clean-shaven face. He was wearing a top-hat and his fur coat was unbuttoned.

'What are you whining for?' he went on, knocking the snow off her back with his finger. 'Where's your master? You're lost, I suppose? Poor little doggie! What are we going to do with you then?'

Detecting a note of warmth and sincerity in the stranger's voice, Kashtanka licked his hand and began whining even more piteously.

'You're nice,' the stranger said, 'and comic, too. A proper little fox! Well, nothing else for it, you'll have to come along with me. Maybe you'll be good for something . . . Off we go, then!'

He smacked his lips and gestured to Kashtanka in a way that could mean one thing only: 'Let's go!' Kashtanka went.

Less than half an hour later she was sitting on the floor in a large bright room, head cocked to one side, gazing at the stranger with curiosity and a feeling of tenderness. He was sitting at a table having supper, and as he ate, he threw her scraps . . . First he gave her some bread and a green cheese-rind, then a piece of meat, half a pie, some chicken bones— but in her hunger she ate everything so fast she did not distinguish one taste from the next. The more she ate, the hungrier she felt.

'Your owners don't feed you much, do they?' said the stranger, observing the fierce greed with which she swallowed unchewed bits of food. 'And how thin you are! Just skin and bones . . .'

Kashtanka ate a great deal but was not satisfied, merely intoxicated by food. After supper she lay down in the middle of the room with her legs stretched out and, feeling a pleasant languor throughout her body, began wagging her tail. While her new master sprawled in an armchair smoking a cigar, she wagged her tail and tried to make up her mind which place was better: the stranger's or the joiner's? The stranger's set-up was poor and unattractive: apart from armchairs, a sofa, a lamp and carpets, he had nothing and his room seemed empty; whereas the whole of the joiner's lodging was chock-full of things: he had a table, a bench, a pile of shavings, planes, chisels, saws, a siskin in a cage, a tub . . . At the stranger's there were no smells at all, whereas at the joiner's the air was always thick and there was a wonderful smell of glue, varnish and shavings. But the stranger did have one very important advantage: he gave you plenty to eat and, to give him his full due, when Kashtanka was sitting in front of the table gazing at him tenderly, he did not once strike her, stamp his feet or shout: 'Clear off, damn you!'

After finishing his cigar, her new master went out and came back a minute later, carrying a small mattress.

'Hey, dog, come over here!' he said, putting the mattress down in a corner near the sofa. 'Lie down and go to sleep!'

Then he extinguished the lamp and left the room. Kashtanka stretched herself out on the mattress and closed her eyes. She heard barking from the street and was about to reply, when suddenly she was overcome by an unexpected feeling of sadness. She remembered Luka Aleksandrych, his son Fedyushka, her cosy little place under the bench . . . She remembered how on long winter evenings, when the joiner was planing wood or reading the paper out loud, Fedyushka was in the habit of playing with her . . . He would drag her by the hind legs from under the bench and play such tricks on her that everything went green before her eyes and all her joints ached. He made her walk on her hind legs, pretended she was a bell, i.e., tugged her so hard by the tail that she squealed and barked, gave her snuff to sniff . . . One trick was a special torture: Fedyushka would tie a piece of meat on a thread and give it to Kashtanka, then, when she had swallowed it, he would pull it back out of her stomach, laughing loudly. The more vivid her memories, the louder and more plaintively Kashtanka whined.

But soon warmth and exhaustion prevailed over sadness and she began to drop off. She could see dogs running about. One shaggy old poodle

she had seen in the street earlier that day, with a cataract on its eye and tufts of fur round its nose, ran past. Fedyushka, holding a chisel, chased after the poodle, then suddenly he himself was covered in shaggy fur, began barking merrily and was standing next to Kashtanka. He and Kashtanka sniffed each other's noses good-naturedly and ran into the street . . .

III A New and Very Pleasant Circle of Acquaintance

When Kashtanka woke up, it was already light, and the noise from the street was such that it could only be daytime. There wasn't a soul in the room. Kashtanka stretched and yawned, and began walking round the room in an angry, sullen mood. She sniffed the corners and the furniture, glanced into the hall and found nothing of interest. Apart from the one into the hall there was another door, and after some deliberation Kashtanka scratched with both paws, opened it, and went into the next room. Here a customer, whom she recognised as the stranger of yesterday, lay on a bed asleep, covered by a woollen blanket.

'Rrrr . . .' she began to growl, but, remembering yesterday's supper, wagged her tail and began sniffing.

On sniffing the stranger's clothing and boots, she discovered that they smelt strongly of horse. Another door, also closed, led off somewhere from the bedroom. By scratching and leaning her chest against it, Kashtanka opened this door and immediately became aware of a strange and very suspicious smell. Anticipating an unpleasant encounter, growling and looking round, Kashtanka entered a little room with dingy wallpaper, and started back in fright. Something unexpected and terrifying had met her eyes. A grey goose was advancing straight towards her, bending its neck and head towards the ground, spreading its wings wide and hissing. A little to one side of the goose a white cat lay on a small mattress. On seeing Kashtanka, it jumped up, arching its back, and with its tail sticking in the air and its fur standing on end, also began hissing. The dog was thoroughly scared, but in order not to betray her fear began barking loudly and rushed towards the cat . . . The cat arched its back even more, hissed and struck Kashtanka on the head with its paw. Kashtanka jumped back and, crouching on all fours, stretched her muzzle out towards the cat and broke into a loud shrill bark. At the same time the goose came up from behind and gave her a painful peck on the back. Kashtanka jumped up and rushed at the goose . . .

'What's going on?' a loud angry voice enquired, and the stranger came into the room in his dressing-gown, smoking a cigar. 'What's all this about? To your places!'

He went up to the cat, tapped him on his arched back and said:

'Fyodor Timofeich, what have you been up to? Starting a fight? You old rascal, you! Lie down!'

Turning to the goose, he shouted:

'Ivan Ivanych, to your place!'

The cat lay down obediently on his mattress and closed his eyes. Judging by the expression of his face and whiskers, he was annoyed with himself for losing his temper and getting into a fight. Kashtanka began whining with an offended air, while the goose stretched out his neck and began talking about something: he spoke rapidly, passionately and articulately, but was quite impossible to understand.

'All right, all right!' said the owner, yawning. 'You must all live in peace and harmony.' He stroked Kashtanka and went on: 'No need to be scared, Ginger . . . They're a good crowd, they won't harm you. Hang on, what are we going to call you? We can none of us do without a name.'

The stranger thought for a moment and said:

'I know . . . You'll be Auntie . . . Got it? Auntie!'

After repeating the word 'Auntie' several times, he went out. Kashtanka sat down and began to watch. The cat was sitting quite still on his mattress, pretending to be asleep. The goose continued to speak rapidly and passionately about something, stretching out his neck and marking time. He was evidently a very clever goose: after each long tirade he would step back in astonishment, pretending to admire his own speech . . . After listening to him and responding with a growl, Kashtanka set about sniffing the corners. In one of them stood a small trough containing soaked peas and soggy breadcrusts. She tried the peas but didn't like them, so she tried the crusts and began eating. The goose wasn't in the least offended that a strange dog should be eating his food, on the contrary, he began talking even more passionately and as a mark of confidence went up to the trough himself and ate a few peas.

IV Wonders Will Never Cease

Not long afterwards, the stranger came in again carrying a curious object, crudely knocked together out of wood and resembling a gate or frame. On its crossbar hung a bell and a pistol was fastened; strings stretched down from the tongue of the bell and the trigger of the pistol.

The stranger stood the frame in the middle of the room, spent a long time untying and tying something, then looked at the goose and said:

'Ivan Ivanych, if you please!'

The goose went up to him and stood there in an expectant pose.

'Right then,' said the stranger, 'let's start from the very beginning. First do your bow and curtsy. Quick!'

Ivan Ivanych stretched out his neck, nodded all round and scraped his foot.

'Well done . . . Now die!'

The goose lay on his back and stuck his feet in the air. After going through several other minor tricks of this kind, the stranger suddenly seized hold of his head, looking horror-struck, and shouted:

'Help! Fire! We're ablaze!'

Ivan Ivanych ran up to the frame, took the string in his beak and rang the bell.

The stranger was delighted by this. He stroked the goose on the neck and said:

'Well done, Ivan Ivanych! Now imagine you're a jeweller dealing in gold and diamonds. Imagine you arrive at your shop one day and disturb some thieves. How would you react in such a situation?'

Taking the other string in his beak, the goose pulled it and at once a deafening shot rang out. Kashtanka had loved the sound of the bell, but now the shot sent her into such transports of delight that she started running round the frame barking.

'Auntie, to your place!' the stranger shouted at her. 'Silence!'

Firing the pistol was not the end of Ivan Ivanych's work. For the next hour the stranger made him run round on a rope and cracked his whip, whereupon the goose had to jump over a hurdle and through a hoop, or rear, i.e., sit on his tail and wave his feet. Kashtanka, who could not take her eyes off Ivan Ivanych, howled with delight and on several occasions began running after him with a cheerful bark. Having exhausted the goose and himself, the stranger wiped the sweat off his brow and shouted:

'Marya, ask Piggie Ivanovna to step in, would you?'

A minute later grunting was heard . . . Kashtanka growled, put on a very brave face, and edged closer to the stranger to be on the safe side. The door opened and an old woman looked in, made some remark and ushered in a very ugly black pig. Ignoring Kashtanka's growls, the pig raised its little snout and grunted merrily. She was evidently very pleased to see her master, the cat and Ivan Ivanych. When she went up to the cat and gave him a little nudge in the stomach with her snout, and then began talking about something to the goose, you could tell from her movements, her voice and the way her little tail quivered that she was very good-natured. Kashtanka realised at once that there was no point in growling and barking at characters like that.

The master put away the frame and shouted:

'Fyodor Timofeich, if you please!'

The cat stood up, stretched lazily and walked over to the pig reluctantly, as if bestowing a favour.

'Right then, let's start with the Egyptian pyramid,' began the master.

He spent a long time explaining something, then gave the command: 'One . . . two . . . three!' At the word 'three' Ivan Ivanych flapped his wings and jumped on to the pig's back . . . Once the goose was firmly settled on the pig's bristly back, balancing himself with his wings and neck, Fyodor Timofeich, looking openly contemptuous, as if he despised his art and thought it not worth a kopeck, climbed with lazy half-heartedness on to the pig's back, from there clambered reluctantly on to the goose and stood on his hind legs. The result was what the stranger called the Egyptian pyramid. Kashtanka squealed with delight, but at that moment the old cat yawned, lost his balance and fell off the goose. Ivan Ivanych wobbled and also fell off. The stranger shouted, waved his arms and began another explanation. After spending a whole hour on the pyramid, the tireless master started teaching Ivan Ivanych to ride on top of the cat, then began teaching the cat to smoke, and so on.

Teaching ended when the stranger wiped the sweat off his brow and went out. Fyodor Timofeich gave a disdainful sniff, lay down on his mattress and closed his eyes, Ivan Ivanych went over to the trough, and the pig was led away by the old woman. Thanks to the mass of new impressions, Kashtanka had not noticed the day slip by, and that evening she and her mattress were already installed in the little room with the dingy wallpaper, where she spent the night in the company of Fyodor Timofeich and the goose.

V You've Got Talent!

A month had gone by.

Kashtanka was now used to receiving a nice meal every evening and being called Auntie. She had become used both to the stranger and her new fellow-residents. Life was running very smoothly.

Every day began the same way. Ivan Ivanych usually woke up first and went straight over to Auntie or the cat, arched his neck and began talking about something with passionate conviction, but as unintelligibly as ever. Sometimes he would raise his head and deliver long monologues. In the first days of their acquaintance Kashtanka imagined he talked so much because he was very clever, but within a short time she lost all respect for him; now when he came up to her with his long speeches, she no longer wagged her tail but dismissed him as a garrulous old bore preventing others from sleeping, and responded with an unceremonious growl.

Fyodor Timofeich, on the other hand, was a gentleman of a very different kind. This individual, on waking, did not utter a sound, did not stir, and did not even open his eyes. He would gladly not have woken up at all, for he was evidently not overfond of life. Nothing was of interest to him, he responded to everything with half-hearted indifference or contempt, and he even sniffed disdainfully when eating his nice supper.

Kashtanka, on waking, began walking round the rooms and sniffing the corners. Only she and the cat were allowed the run of the whole apartment, whereas the goose was not entitled to cross the threshold of the little room with the dingy wallpaper, and Piggie Ivanovna lived in a small shed outside somewhere and appeared only at lesson-time. The master woke up late, drank tea, and at once began working on his tricks. Every day the frame, the whip and the hoops were carried into the little room, and every day they went through almost the same routine. Teaching lasted three or four hours, so that sometimes Fyodor Timofeich in his exhaustion would be reeling about like a drunk, Ivan Ivanych panting with his beak wide open, and the master turning red in the face and forever wiping the sweat off his brow.

The days were made very interesting by the teaching and the meal, but evenings were rather tedious. Most evenings the master went out somewhere, taking the goose and the cat with him. Left on her own, Auntie lay down on her mattress and began to feel sad . . . This sadness crept up on her in an imperceptible kind of way and took possession of her gradually, as darkness did the room. It started with the dog losing all desire to bark, eat, run round the rooms and even look at things, then in her imagination two dim figures would appear, not quite dog, not quite human, with expressions that were kind and sympathetic, but hazy. Auntie wagged her tail when they appeared and felt she had seen them somewhere before and loved them . . . and each time as she fell asleep, she had the feeling that these figures smelt of glue, shavings and varnish.

When she was fully accustomed to her new life and had changed from a thin bony mongrel into a sleek well-fed dog, the master stroked her one day before teaching and said:

'Time you and I got down to business, Auntie. You've been kicking your heels long enough. I want to make an artist of you . . . Do you want to be an artist?'

And he began giving her various kinds of instruction. In the first lesson she learned to stand and walk on her hind legs, which gave her enormous pleasure. In the second lesson she had to jump on her hind legs for a piece of sugar held high above her head by the teacher. In subsequent lessons she danced, ran round on the end of the rope, howled to music, rang the bell and fired the pistol, and within a month she could already successfully replace Fyodor Timofeich in the Egyptian pyramid. She learned very eagerly and was pleased by her successes; running round on the rope with her tongue sticking out, jumping through the hoop and riding on old Fyodor Timofeich afforded her the greatest enjoyment. She would accompany each trick she mastered with a ringing, delighted bark, while her teacher would be amazed and delighted, too.

'You've got talent, talent!' he would say, rubbing his hands. 'Most definitely, talent! You're going to be a success all right!'

And Auntie became so used to the word 'talent' that each time the master said it, she would jump up and look round, as if it were her nickname.

VI A Troubled Night

Auntie had been having a dog's dream, in which the porter was chasing her with a broom, and woke up in a fright.

It was quiet, dark and very airless in the little room. The fleas were biting. Auntie had never been afraid of the dark before, but now for some reason she felt scared and wanted to bark. In the next room the master gave a deep sigh, a little later the pig grunted in her shed, then all was silent again. The thought of food lightens the heart, and Auntie began thinking of the chicken-leg she had stolen that day from Fyodor Timofeich and hidden in the sitting-room, in the space full of dust and cobwebs between the cupboard and the wall. It mightn't be a bad idea to go and see if it was still intact; very possibly the master had found it by now and eaten it. But the rule was that you mustn't leave the little room before morning. Auntie closed her eyes so as to fall asleep quickly, knowing from experience that the sooner you go to sleep, the sooner morning arrives. But suddenly an odd shriek rang out close by that made her start and jump to her feet. It was Ivan Ivanych, and this was not his usual earnest chatter, but a wild, piercing, unnatural shriek, like that of a creaking gate being opened. Unable to make out or understand anything in the dark, Auntie felt even more scared and growled:

'Rrrrr . . .'

A brief period elapsed, long enough to gnaw a good bone in, and the shriek was not repeated. Auntie gradually calmed down and dozed off. She had a dream about two large black dogs with tufts of last year's hair on their flanks and haunches; they were at a large tub greedily eating slops, which gave off a white steam and a very appetising smell, and every so often they would look round at Auntie, bare their teeth and growl: 'Don't think you're getting any!' But a peasant in a fur coat ran out of the house and chased them away with a whip; then Auntie went up to the tub and began eating, but no sooner had the peasant gone back through the gate than the two black dogs hurled themselves on her with growls, and suddenly the piercing shriek rang out again.

'Geek! G-g-geek!' cried Ivan Ivanych.

Auntie jumped up fully awake and, without leaving her mattress, broke into a howling bark. It was not Ivan Ivanych shrieking, she now felt, but someone else, an outsider. And for some reason the pig grunted once more in her shed.

But then came the shuffle of slippers, and the master entered the room in his dressing-gown, holding a candle. The flickering light danced over the dingy wallpaper and the ceiling, and chased the darkness away. Auntie could see that there was no one else in the room. Ivan Ivanych was sitting on the floor awake. His wings were spread wide and his beak was open, and he had a very exhausted, thirsty kind of look. Old Fyodor Timofeich was also awake. He, too, must have been woken by the shriek.

'Ivan Ivanych, what's the matter?' the master asked the goose. 'What are you shrieking for? Are you ill?'

The goose did not reply. The master touched his neck, stroked his back and said:

'You're a funny one. You can't sleep yourself, so you won't let anyone else.'

The master went out taking the light with him, and darkness returned. Auntie was terrified. The goose was not shrieking, but Auntie felt once again that a stranger was standing there in the darkness. What terrified her most was that this stranger could not be bitten, because he

63

was invisible and had no shape. And for some reason she imagined that something very dreadful was bound to happen that night. Fyodor Timofeich was restless, too. Auntie could hear him fidgeting about on his mattress, yawning and shaking his head.

From outside came the sound of knocking on a gate, and in her shed the pig grunted. Auntie began whining, stretching out her front paws and resting her head on them. The knocking on the gate, the grunting of the pig (why was she not asleep?), the darkness and the silence, seemed to her as melancholy and terrifying as Ivan Ivanych's shriek. Everything was in a state of anxiety and unrest, but why? Who was this invisible stranger? Then for a moment two dim little green sparks showed up by Auntie. It was the first time in their whole acquaintance that Fyodor Timofeich had come up to her. What did he want? Auntie licked his paw and without asking what he had come for, began howling softly and on various notes.

'Geek!' cried Ivan Ivanych. 'G-g-geek!'

The door opened again, and the master came in with his candle. The goose was sitting in his previous position, his beak open and his wings outspread. His eyes were closed.

'Ivan Ivanych!' called the master.

The goose did not stir. The master sat down on the floor in front of him, looked at him for a minute in silence and said:

'Ivan Ivanych! Whatever's the matter? Are you dying, is that it? Of course, I remember now!' he shouted, seizing his head in his hands. 'That's the explanation—the horse that trod on you today! Oh my God!'

Auntie did not know what the master was talking about, but could tell from his face that he, too, was expecting something terrible to happen. She stretched out her muzzle towards the dark window, through which she felt the stranger was looking, and howled.

'He's dying, Auntie!' said the master, with a gesture of despair. 'Dying! Death has visited your room. What are we going to do?'

Pale and agitated, the master returned to his bedroom, sighing and shaking his head. Scared of being left in the dark, Auntie followed him. He sat down on his bed and repeated several times:

'My God, what are we going to do?'

Auntie hovered round his legs. Not understanding why she felt so miserable and why everyone was so anxious, and trying to do so, she followed his every movement. Fyodor Timofeich, who rarely left his mattress, had also come into the master's bedroom and started rubbing against his legs. The cat was shaking his head, as if wanting to shake the gloomy thoughts out of it, and glancing suspiciously under the bed.

The master took a saucer, poured some water into it from the wash-basin and went back to the goose.

'Drink up, Ivan Ivanych!' he said gently, placing the saucer in front of him. 'Drink up, dear.'

But Ivan Ivanych did not stir and did not open his eyes. The master lowered the goose's head to the saucer and dipped his beak in the water, but he did not drink, only spread his wings still wider, while his head went on lying where it was.

'No, there's nothing more we can do!' sighed the master. 'It's all over. Ivan Ivanych is done for!'

And shining droplets trickled down his cheeks, like raindrops on a window-pane. Not understanding his feelings, Auntie and Fyodor Timofeich pressed close to him and looked at the goose in horror.

'Poor Ivan Ivanych!' said the master, sighing mournfully. 'And there was I dreaming we'd go to the datcha this spring and I'd take you for walks in the green grass. Dear creature, we worked so well together, and now you're no more! How ever am I going to manage without you?'

Auntie had the feeling that the same thing would happen to her, that for no apparent reason she, too, would close her eyes, stretch out her paws, open her mouth wide, and everyone would look at her in horror. The same thoughts were evidently passing through Fyodor Timofeich's mind. Never before had the old cat been so gloomy and sullen.

Dawn was breaking, and the invisible stranger who had frightened Auntie so much was no longer in the room. When it was completely light, the porter arrived, picked the goose up by the feet and took him off somewhere. Shortly afterwards, the old woman appeared and carried out the trough.

Auntie went into the sitting-room and looked behind the cupboard: the master hadn't eaten the chicken-leg, it was lying in the same place among the dust and cobwebs. But Auntie felt sad and miserable and wanted to cry. She didn't even sniff the leg, but settled herself under the sofa and began whining softly, in a thin little voice:

'Ooh-ooh-ooh . . .'

VII An Unsuccessful Début

One fine evening the master came into the little room with the dingy wallpaper, rubbed his hands and said:

'Right then . . .'

He was going to say more, but stopped and went out again. Auntie, who had studied his face and intonation very closely during lessons, decided that he was nervous and worried, and seemed to be cross. Shortly after, he came back and said:

'Today I'm taking Auntie and Fyodor Timofeich with me. Auntie, you'll take the place today of the late Ivan Ivanych in the Egyptian pyramid. What a mess! Nothing's ready, nothing's been learnt properly, we've had too few rehearsals! We'll disgrace ourselves, we'll be a flop!'

Then he went out again and returned a minute later in his fur coat and top-hat. Going up to the cat and taking hold of his front paws, he lifted him up and tucked him under his coat against his chest. Fyodor Timofeich responded with complete indifference and did not even bother to open his eyes. It evidently made absolutely no difference to him whether he was lying down, being lifted up, lolling on his mattress, or resting on his master's chest under the fur coat . . .

'Come on, Auntie,' said the master.

Not knowing what was going on and wagging her tail, Auntie followed him, and a minute later was sitting at his feet in a sledge. The master was hugging himself with cold and nervousness, and mumbling:

'We'll disgrace ourselves! We'll be a flop!'

The sledge stopped outside a strange big building like an inverted soup tureen. Its wide entrance had three glass doors and was lit by a dozen bright lamps. The doors opened with a clang and looked like mouths, gobbling up the crowds of people who bustled round the entrance. Horses, too, frequently galloped up to the entrance, but no dogs were to be seen.

The master picked Auntie up and put her under his coat against his chest with Fyodor Timofeich. It was dark and airless there, but warm. Two dim little green sparks showed up for a moment—the cat, disturbed by his neighbour's cold hard paws, had opened his eyes. Auntie licked his ear and, wanting to find the most comfortable position, shifted about restlessly, ruffled the cat's fur under her with her cold paws, and inadvertently poked her head out from under the coat, only to give an angry growl and dive back again immediately. She had seen what looked like a huge, badly lit room full of monsters; from behind the partitions and gratings which stretched along both sides of the room, terrifying faces looked out: horse faces, faces with horns or long ears, and one enormous fat face with a tail instead of a nose and two long bones, picked clean, sticking out of its mouth.

The cat mewed hoarsely under Auntie's paws, but at that moment the coat was flung open, the master said 'Hop!' and Fyodor Timofeich and Auntie jumped to the ground. They were now in a small room with grey plank walls; it contained no furniture apart from a small table with a mirror, a stool and some rags hanging in the corners, and instead of a lamp or candle a bright fan-shaped light was burning, attached to a small pipe fixed to the wall. Fyodor Timofeich licked the fur that Auntie had ruffled, and went to lie down under the stool. The master, still rubbing his hands nervously, began undressing . . . He undressed just as he did at home before lying down under his woollen blanket, that is, he took everything off except his underwear, then he sat down on the stool, looked in the mirror, and began doing the most astonishing things to himself. To begin with, he put a wig on his head with a parting and two tufts like horns, then he put a thick layer of something white on his face, and on top of the white drew in eyebrows, a moustache and red cheeks. But that wasn't the end of the business. After daubing his face and neck, he began to array himself in a strange, totally absurd outfit, the like of which Auntie had never seen before either indoors or out. Imagine very baggy trousers, made from the kind of crudely patterned floral chintz used in bourgeois homes for curtains and upholstery, and buttoning up right under the armpits, with one leg coloured brown and the other bright yellow. Swamped by these, the master then added a short chintz jacket with a large scalloped collar and a gold star on the back, different-coloured stockings and green shoes . . .

Auntie was dazzled and bewildered by the variety of colours. The white-faced, sack-like figure smelt of the master, it had the master's familiar voice, but there were moments of agonising doubt when Auntie was quite ready to run away from this colourful figure and bark. The new surroundings, the fan-shaped light, the smell, the master's transformation—all this evoked a vague dread and a feeling that she was bound to bump into some horror like the fat face with a tail instead of a nose. On top of this, somewhere in the distance hateful music was playing, and every so often there came an unintelligible roar. One thing alone helped

67

to calm her, and that was the imperturbability of Fyodor Timofeich. He was dozing very quietly under the stool and didn't even open his eyes when the stool was moved.

A man in tails and a white waistcoat glanced into the room and said: 'Miss Arabella's on. You're next.'

The master made no reply. He pulled a small suitcase out from under the table, and sat down to wait. Auntie saw from his lips and hands that he was nervous, and she could hear his uneven breathing.

'M. Georges, if you please!' someone outside shouted.

The master stood up and crossed himself three times, then got the cat out from under the stool and put him in the suitcase.

'Come here, Auntie!' he said quietly, holding out his hands.

Not knowing what was going on, Auntie went up to him. Kissing her on the head, he put her next to Fyodor Timofeich. Then darkness descended . . . Too terrified to utter a sound, Auntie trampled on the cat and scratched the sides of the suitcase, which rocked about like a boat and shuddered . . .

'It's me!' the master gave a loud shout. 'It's me!'

After this shout Auntie felt the suitcase strike something hard and stop rocking. Then came a loud deep-throated roar: someone was being clapped, and this someone, probably the character with a tail instead of a nose, was roaring and laughing so loudly that it made the locks on the suitcase shake. In response to the roar the master gave a shrill, piercing laugh such as he never did at home.

'What ho!' he shouted, trying to make himself heard above the roar. 'Ladies and gentlemen, your humble servant! I've just come from the station! Granny's kicked the bucket and left me a legacy! This suitcase feels very heavy—must be gold . . . Ho-ho! What if there's a million inside? Let's open it and have a look . . .'

The lock on the suitcase clicked. A brilliant light struck Auntie in the eyes; she sprang from the suitcase and, deafened by the roar, began racing at full speed round her master with ringing barks.

'Oh-ho!' shouted the master. 'If it isn't old Uncle Fyodor Timofeich! And dear old Auntie! My charming little relatives, blast you!'

He flopped down on the sand, grabbed hold of the cat and Auntie, and began hugging them. While she was being squeezed in his arms, Auntie caught a brief glimpse of the world to which fate had brought her, and was so struck by its magnificence that for a moment she was transfixed with delight and astonishment; then she broke free from her master's embrace and began spinning on the spot like a top, so vivid was the impression. This new world was vast and full of brilliant light; wherever you looked, everywhere, from floor to ceiling, all you could see were faces, more faces, and nothing but faces.

'Auntie, sit down, please!' shouted the master.

Remembering what that meant, Auntie jumped on to a chair and sat down. She looked at the master. His eyes had their usual kind, serious expression, but his face, especially his mouth and teeth, was distorted by a wide fixed grin. He himself was laughing, prancing about and twitching his shoulders, as if being in the presence of thousands of people made him feel very jolly. Believing in his jolly mood, Auntie suddenly had a feeling all over that these thousands of people were looking at her and, lifting up her fox-like muzzle, she began howling with joy.

'Stay there, Auntie,' the master said to her, 'while Uncle and I dance the Kamarinskaya.'

Fyodor Timofeich was looking round him with indifference, as he stood waiting to be made to do something silly. He danced in a languid, offhand, gloomy way, and you could tell from his movements, his tail and his whiskers that he was deeply contemptuous of the crowd, the brilliant light, his master and himself . . . Having done his share of dancing, he yawned and sat down.

'Right then, Auntie,' said the master, 'first you and I are going to sing and then we'll do some dancing. All right?'

Taking a small pipe out of his pocket, he started playing. Auntie, who could not bear music, moved about restlessly on her chair and began to howl. There was a roar of applause on all sides. The master took a bow, waited until the noise had subsided, and went on playing . . . He had just reached a very high note when someone way up in the gods uttered a loud gasp.

'Dad!' a child's voice shouted. 'Dad, it's Kashtanka!'

'You're right,' rasped a drunken tenor. 'It *is* Kashtanka! So help me, Fedyushka, that's Kashtanka! Here!'

Someone in the gallery whistled, and two voices, a child's and a man's, called out loudly:

'Kashtanka! Kashtanka!'

Auntie gave a start and looked in the direction of the shouts. Two faces—one hairy, drunken and grinning, the other chubby, rosy-cheeked and startled—struck her in the eyes, just as the brilliant light had done earlier . . . It all came back, she tumbled off the chair and dived into the sand, then jumped up and rushed towards the faces, squealing joyfully. The deafening roar that followed was penetrated by catcalls and the piercing cry of a child:

'Kashtanka! Kashtanka!'

Auntie leapt over the barrier, and then via someone's shoulder found herself in a box. To reach the next tier, she had to surmount a high wall. She took a leap, didn't make it, and slid back down. Then she was passed from hand to hand, licking people's hands and faces as she went, ascending higher and higher until finally she reached the gallery . . .

Half an hour later Kashtanka was walking along the street behind the people who smelt of glue and varnish. As he lurched along, Luka Aleksandrych tried instinctively, as experience had taught him, to keep a good distance between himself and the gutter.

'In the abyss of sin they wallow in my womb,' he mumbled. 'And you, Kashtanka, are a puzzlement. You fall as far short of a man as a carpenter does of a joiner.'

Fedyushka was striding alongside, wearing one of his father's old caps. Gazing at their backs, Kashtanka felt as if she had been following this pair for ages and was glad that her life had not been interrupted for a moment.

She still recalled the little room with the dingy wallpaper, the goose, Fyodor Timofeich, her nice meals, the lessons and the circus, but now it all seemed to her like a long, confusing, painful dream . . .

A Lady's Story

Nine years ago Pyotr Sergeich, the deputy prosecutor, and I were riding towards evening in haymaking time to fetch the letters from the station.

The weather was magnificent, but on our way back we heard a peal of thunder, and saw an angry black stormcloud which was coming straight towards us. The stormcloud was approaching us and we were approaching it.

Against that background our house and church looked white and the tall poplars shone like silver. There was a scent of rain and mown hay. My companion was in high spirits. He kept laughing and talking all sorts of nonsense. He said it would be nice if we could suddenly come upon a medieval castle with turreted towers, covered by moss and owls, where we could take shelter from the rain and in the end be killed by a thunderbolt . . .

Then the first wave raced through the rye and a field of oats, there was a gust of wind, and dust spiralled in the air. Pyotr Sergeich laughed and spurred on his horse.

'It's fine!' he cried. 'Quite splendid!'

Infected by his gaiety, I too began laughing at the thought that in a minute I should be drenched to the skin and might be struck by lightning.

Riding swiftly in a hurricane when one is breathless and feels like a bird, thrills one and puts one's heart in a flutter. By the time we rode into our courtyard the wind had gone down, and big drops of rain were pattering on the grass and on the roofs. There was not a soul near the stable.

Pyotr Sergeich himself took the bridles off, and led the horses to their stalls. I stood in the doorway waiting for him to finish, and watching the slanting streaks of rain; the sweetish, exciting scent of hay was even stronger here than in the fields; the stormclouds and the rain made it almost twilight.

'What a crash!' said Pyotr Sergeich, coming up to me after a very loud rolling peal of thunder when it seemed as though the sky were split in two. 'What do you say to that?'

He stood beside me in the doorway and, still breathless from his rapid ride, looked at me. I could see that he was admiring me.

'Natalya Vladimirovna,' he said, 'I would give anything just to stay here a little longer and look at you. You are lovely today.'

His eyes looked at me with delight and supplication, his face was pale. On his beard and moustache were glittering raindrops, and they, too, seemed to be looking at me with love.

'I love you,' he said. 'I love you, and I am happy at seeing you. I know you cannot be my wife, but I want nothing, I ask nothing; only know that I love you. Be silent, do not answer me, take no notice, but only know that you are dear to me and let me gaze at you.'

His rapture affected me too; I looked at his enthusiastic face, listened to his voice which mingled with the patter of the rain, and stood as though spellbound, unable to stir.

I longed to go on endlessly looking at his shining eyes and listening.

'You say nothing, and that is splendid,' said Pyotr Sergeich. 'Go on being silent.'

I felt happy. I laughed with delight and ran through the drenching rain to the house; he laughed too, and, leaping as he went, ran after me.

Both drenched, panting, noisily clattering up the stairs like children, we dashed into the room. My father and brother, who were not used to seeing me laughing and light-hearted, looked at me in surprise and began laughing too.

The stormclouds had passed over and the thunder had ceased, but the raindrops still glittered on Pyotr Sergeich's beard. The whole evening till supper-time he was singing, whistling, playing noisily with the dog and chasing it about the room, so that he nearly knocked over the servant with the samovar. And at supper he ate a great deal, talked nonsense, and maintained that when one eats fresh cucumbers in winter there is the fragrance of spring in one's mouth.

When I went to bed I lit a candle and threw my window wide open, and an undefined feeling took possession of my soul. I remembered that I was free and healthy, that I had rank and wealth, that I was loved; above all, that I had rank and wealth, rank and wealth, my God! how nice that was! . . . Then, huddling up in bed at a touch of cold which reached me from the garden with the dew, I tried to discover whether I loved Pyotr Sergeich or not . . . and fell asleep unable to reach any conclusion.

And when in the morning I saw quivering patches of sunlight and the shadows of the lime-trees on my bed, what had happened yesterday rose vividly in my memory. Life seemed to me rich, varied, full of charm. Humming, I dressed quickly and ran out into the garden . . .

And what happened afterwards? Why—nothing. In the winter when we lived in town Pyotr Sergeich came to see us from time to time. Country acquaintances are charming only in the country and in summer; in the town and in winter they lose half their charm. When you pour out tea for them in the town it seems as though they are wearing other people's coats, and as though they stirred their tea too long. In the town, too, Pyotr Sergeich spoke sometimes of love, but the effect was not at all the same as in the country. In the town we were more conscious of the wall that stood between us: I had rank and wealth, while he was poor and not even a nobleman, but only the son of a deacon and a deputy public prosecutor; we both of us—I through my youth and he for some unknown reason—thought of that wall as very high and thick, and when he was with us in the town he would criticise aristocratic society with a forced smile, and maintain a sullen silence when there was anyone else in the drawing-room. There is no wall that cannot be broken through, but the heroes of modern romance, so far as I know them, are too timid, spiritless, lazy, and oversensitive, and are too ready to resign themselves to the thought that they are failures, and that their personal life has disappointed them; instead of struggling they merely criticise, calling the world vulgar and forgetting that their criticism itself passes little by little into vulgarity.

I was loved, happiness was not far away, and seemed to be almost touching me; I went on living in careless ease without trying to understand myself, not knowing what I expected or what I wanted from life, and time went on and on . . . People passed by me with their love, bright days and warm nights flashed by, the nightingales sang, the hay smelt fragrant, and all this, sweet and overwhelming in remembrance, passed for me as for everyone rapidly, leaving no trace, was not prized, and vanished like mist . . . Where is it all now?

My father is dead, I have grown older; everything that delighted me, caressed me, gave me hope—the patter of rain, the rolling of thunder, thoughts of happiness, talk of love—all that has become nothing but a memory, and I see before me a flat desert distance; on the plain not one living soul, and out there on the horizon it is dark and terrible . . .

A ring at the bell . . . It is Pyotr Sergeich. When in the winter I see the trees and remember how green they were for me in the summer I whisper:

'Oh, my darlings!'

And when I see people with whom I spent my springtime, I feel sorrowful and warm and whisper the same thing.

Through my father's good offices he has long ago been transferred to town. He looks a little older, a little fallen away. He has long given up declaring his love, has stopped talking nonsense, dislikes his official work, is ill in some way and disillusioned; he has given up trying to get anything out of life, and takes no interest in living. Now he has sat down by the hearth and looks in silence at the fire . . .

Not knowing what to say I ask him:

'Well, what have you to tell me?'

'Nothing,' he answers.

And silence again. The red glow of the fire flickers upon his melancholy face.

I thought of the past, and all at once my shoulders began quivering, my head dropped, and I began weeping bitterly. I felt unbearably sorry for myself and for this man, and passionately longed for what had passed away and what life denied us now. And now I did not think about rank and wealth.

I broke into loud sobs, pressing my temples, and muttered:

'My God! my God! my life is wasted!'

And he sat and was silent, and did not say to me: 'Don't weep.' He understood that I must weep, and that the time for weeping had come.

I saw from his eyes that he was sorry for me; and I was sorry for him, too, and vexed with this timid, unsuccessful man who could not establish a life for me, nor for himself.

When I saw him to the door, he was, I fancied, purposely a long while putting on his coat. Twice he kissed my hand without a word, and looked a long while into my tear-stained face. I believe at that moment he recalled the storm, the streaks of rain, our laughter, my face that day; he longed to say something to me, and he would have been glad to say it; but he said nothing, he merely shook his head and pressed my hand. God help him!

After seeing him out, I went back to my study and again sat on the carpet before the fireplace; the red embers were covered with ash and began to grow dim. The frost tapped still more angrily at the windows, and the wind droned in the chimney.

The maid came in and, thinking I was asleep, called my name . . .

No Comment

In the fifth century, just as now, every morning the sun rose, and every evening it retired to rest. In the morning, as the first rays kissed the dew, the earth would come to life and the air be filled with sounds of joy, hope and delight, while in the evening the same earth would grow quiet again and be swallowed up in grim darkness. Each day, each night, was like the one before. Occasionally a dark cloud loomed up and thunder growled angrily from it, or a star would doze off and fall from the firmament, or a monk would run by, pale-faced, to tell the brethren that not far from the monastery he had seen a tiger—and that would be all, then once again each day, each night, would be just like the one before.

The monks toiled and prayed, while their Abbot played the organ, composed music and wrote verses in Latin. This wonderful old man had an extraordinary gift. Whenever he played the organ, he did so with such art that even the oldest monks, whose hearing had grown dull as they neared the end of their lives, could not restrain their tears when the sounds of the organ reached them from his cell. Whenever he spoke about something, even the most commonplace things, such as the trees, the wild beasts, or the sea, it was impossible to listen to him without a smile or a tear; it seemed that the same chords were sounding in his soul as in the organ. Whereas if he was moved by anger, or by great joy, or if he was talking about something terrible or sublime, a passionate inspiration would take hold of him, his eyes would flash and fill with tears, his face flush and his voice rumble like thunder, and as they listened to him the monks could feel this inspiration taking over their souls; in those magnificent, wonderful moments his power was limitless, and if he had ordered the fathers to throw themselves into the sea, then, to a man, they would all have rushed rapturously to carry out his will.

His music, his voice, and the verses in which he praised God, the heavens and the earth, were for the monks a source of constant joy. As life was so unvaried, there were times when spring and autumn, the flowers and the trees, began to pall on them, their ears tired of the sound of the sea, and the song of the birds became irksome; but the talents of the old Abbot were as vital to them as their daily bread.

Many years passed, and still each day, each night, was just like the one before. Apart from the wild birds and beasts, not a single living soul showed itself near the monastery. The nearest human habitation was far away, and to get to it from the monastery or vice versa, meant crossing a hundred versts or so of wilderness on foot. The only people who ventured to cross the wilderness were those who spurned life, had renounced it, and were going to the monastery as though to the grave.

Imagine the monks' astonishment, therefore, when one night a man knocked at their gates who, it transpired, came from the town and was the most ordinary of sinful mortals who love life. Before asking the Abbot's blessing and offering up a prayer, this man called for food and wine. When he was asked how he, a townsman, came to be in the wilderness, he answered with a long sportsman's yarn about how he had gone out hunting, had too much to drink, and lost his way. To the suggestion that he take the monastic vow and save his soul, he replied with a smile and the words: 'I'm no mate of yours.'

After he had eaten and drunk his fill, he looked around at the monks who had been waiting on him and, shaking his head reproachfully, he said:

'What a way to carry on! All you monks bother about is eating and drinking. Is that the way to save your souls? Just think, whilst you're sitting here in peace and quiet, eating, drinking, and dreaming of heavenly bliss, your fellow humans are perishing and going down to hell. Why don't you look at what's going on in the town! Some are dying of hunger there, others have more gold than they know what to do with, and wallow in debauchery till they die like flies stuck to honey. People have no faith or principles! Whose job is it to save them? To preach to them? Surely not mine, when I'm drunk from morning till night? Did God give you faith, a humble spirit and a loving heart just to sit around here within four walls twiddling your thumbs?'

Although the townsman's drunken words were insolent and profane, they had a strange effect upon the Abbot. The old man glanced round at his monks, paled, and said:

'Brothers, what he says is right! Through their folly and their frailty, those poor people are indeed perishing in sin and unbelief, whilst we sit back, as though it had nothing to do with us. Should I not be the one to go and recall them to Christ whom they have forgotten?'

The townsman's words had carried the old man away, and the very next morning he took his staff in his hand, bade the brethren farewell, and set off for the town. And the monks were left without his music, his verses, and his fine speeches.

A month of boredom went by, then another, and still the old man did not return. At last, after the third month, they heard the familiar tapping of his staff. The monks rushed to meet him and showered him with questions, but he, instead of being glad to see them again, broke into bitter tears and would not say a single word. The monks saw he had aged greatly and grown much thinner; his face was strained and full of a deep sorrow, and when he broke into tears he looked like a man who had been mortally offended.

The monks too burst into tears and began begging him to tell them why he was weeping, why he looked so downcast, but he would not say a word and locked himself away in his cell. Seven days he stayed there, would not eat or drink or play the organ, and just wept. When the monks knocked at his door and implored him to come out and share his grief with them, they were met with a profound silence.

At last he came out. Gathering all the monks about him, he began with a tear-stained face and an expression of sorrow and indignation to tell them what had happened to him in the past three months. His voice was calm and his eyes smiled while he described his journey from the monastery to the town. As he went along, he said, the birds had sung to him and the brooks babbled, and tender young hopes had stirred in his soul; as he walked, he felt like a soldier going into battle, confident of victory; and in his reverie he walked along composing hymns and verses and did not notice when his journey was over.

But his voice trembled, his eyes flashed, and his whole being burned with wrath when he started talking of the town and its people. Never in his life had he seen, never durst imagine, what confronted him when he entered the town. Only now, in his old age, had he seen and understood for the first time how mighty was the devil, how beautiful wickedness, and how feeble, cowardly and faint-hearted were human beings. As luck would have it, the first dwelling that he went into was a house of ill fame. Some fifty people with lots of money were eating and drinking immoderate quantities of wine. Intoxicated by the wine, they sang songs and bandied about terrible, disgusting words that no God-fearing person could ever bring himself to utter; completely uninhibited, boisterous and happy, they did not fear God, the devil or death, but said and did exactly as they wished, and went wherever their lusts impelled them. And the wine, as clear as amber and fizzing with gold, must have been unbearably sweet and fragrant, because everyone drinking it smiled blissfully and wanted to drink more. In response to men's smiles it smiled back, and

77

sparkled joyfully when it was drunk, as if it knew what devilish charm lurked in its sweetness.

More and more worked up and weeping with rage, the old man continued to describe what he had seen. On a table among the revellers, he said, stood a half-naked harlot. It would be difficult to imagine or to find in nature anything more lovely and captivating. This foul creature, young, with long hair, dusky skin, dark eyes and full lips, shameless and brazen, flashed her snow-white teeth and smiled as if to say: 'Look at me, how brazen I am and beautiful!' Silk and brocade hung down in graceful folds from her shoulders, but her beauty would not be hid, and like young shoots in the spring earth, eagerly thrust through the folds of her garments. The brazen woman drank wine, sang songs, and gave herself to anyone who wished.

Then the old man, waving his arms in anger, went on to describe the horse-races and bullfights, the theatres, and the artists' workshops where they made paintings and sculptures in clay of naked women. His speech was inspired, beautiful and melodious, as if he were playing on invisible chords, and the monks, rooted to the spot, devoured his every word and could scarcely breathe for excitement . . . When he had finished describing all the devil's charms, the beauty of wickedness and the captivating graces of the vile female body, the old man denounced the devil, turned back to his cell and closed the door behind him . . .

When he came out of his cell next morning, there was not a single monk left in the monastery. They had all run away to the town.

The Beauties

I

I remember, when I was a high-school boy in the fifth or sixth class, I was driving with my grandfather from the village of Bolshaya Krepkaya in the Don region to Rostov-on-the-Don. It was a sultry, languidly dreary August day. Our eyes were glued together and our mouths were parched from the heat and the dry burning wind which drove clouds of dust to meet us; one did not want to look or speak or think, and when our drowsy driver, a Little Russian called Karpo, swung his whip at the horses and lashed me on my cap, I did not protest or utter a sound, but only, rousing myself from half-slumber, gazed mildly and dejectedly into the distance to see whether there was a village visible through the dust. We stopped to feed the horses in a big Armenian village called Bakchi-Salakh, at a rich Armenian's whom my grandfather knew. Never in my life have I seen a greater caricature than that Armenian. Imagine a little shaven head with thick overhanging eyebrows, a beak of a nose, long grey moustaches, and a wide mouth with a long cherry-wood chibouk sticking out of it. This little head was clumsily attached to a lean hunchback carcass attired in a fantastic garb, a short red jacket, and full bright blue trousers. This figure walked straddling its legs and shuffling with its slippers, spoke without taking the chibouk out of its mouth, and behaved with truly Armenian dignity, not smiling, but staring with wide-open eyes and trying to take as little notice as possible of its guests.

There was neither wind nor dust in the Armenian's rooms, but it was just as unpleasant, stifling, and dreary as in the steppe and on the road. I remember, dusty and exhausted by the heat, I sat in the corner on a green box. The unpainted wooden walls, the furniture, and the floors coloured with yellow ochre, smelt of dry wood baked by the sun. Wherever I looked there were flies and flies and flies . . . Grandfather and the Armenian were talking about grazing, about manure, and about oats . . . I knew that they would be a good hour getting the samovar; that Grandfather would spend not less than an hour drinking his tea, and then would lie down to sleep for two or three hours; that I should waste a quarter of the day waiting, after which there would again be the heat, the dust, the jolting cart. I heard the muttering of the two voices, and I began to feel that I had been seeing the Armenian, the cupboard with the crockery, the flies, the windows with the burning sun beating on them, for ages and ages, and should only cease to see them in the far-off future, and I was seized with hatred for the steppe, the sun, the flies . . .

A Little Russian peasant woman in a kerchief brought in a tray of tea-things, then the samovar. The Armenian went slowly out into the passage and shouted: 'Mashya, come and pour out tea! Where are you, Mashya?'

Hurried footsteps were heard, and there came into the room a girl of sixteen in a simple cotton dress and a white kerchief. As she washed the crockery and poured out the tea, she was standing with her back to me, and all I could see was that she was of a slender figure, barefooted, and that her little bare heels were covered by long trousers.

The Armenian invited me to have tea. Sitting down to the table, I glanced at the girl, who was handing me a glass of tea, and felt all at once as though a wind had scurried across my soul and blown away all the impressions of the day with their dust and dreariness. I saw the bewitch-ing features of the most beautiful face I have ever met in real life or in my dreams. Before me stood a beauty, and I recognised this at the first glance as I should have recognised lightning.

I am ready to swear that Masha—or, as her father called her, Mashya—was a real beauty, but I don't know how to prove it. It some-times happens that clouds crowd together on the horizon, and the sun hiding behind them colours them and the sky with tints of every possible shade—crimson, orange, gold, lilac, muddy pink; one cloud is like a monk, another like a fish, a third like a Turk in a turban. The glow of sunset enveloping a third of the sky gleams on the cross of a church, flashes on the windows of the manor-house, is reflected in the river and the puddles, quivers on the trees; far, far away against the background of the sunset, a flock of wild ducks is flying homewards . . . And the boy herding the cows, and the surveyor driving in his chaise over the dam, and the gentlemen out for a walk, all gaze at the sunset, and every one of them finds it terribly beautiful, but no one knows or can say in what its beauty lies.

I was not the only one to find the Armenian girl beautiful. My grand-father, an old man of eighty, gruff and indifferent to women and the beauties of nature, looked caressingly at Masha for a full minute, and asked:

'Is that your daughter, Avet Nazarych?'

'Yes, she is my daughter,' the Armenian replied.

'A fine young lady,' said my grandfather approvingly.

An artist would have called the Armenian girl's beauty classical and severe; it was just that beauty, the contemplation of which—God knows why!—inspires in one the conviction that one is seeing correct features; that hair, eyes, nose, mouth, neck, bosom, and every movement of the young body all go together in one complete harmonious accord in which nature has not blundered over the smallest line. You fancy for some reason that the ideally beautiful woman must have such a nose as Masha's, straight and slightly aquiline, just such great dark eyes, such long lashes, such a languid glance; you fancy that her curly black hair and eyebrows go with the soft white tint of her brow and cheeks as the green reeds go with the quiet stream. Masha's white neck and her youthful bosom were not fully developed, but you fancy the sculptor would need a great creative genius to mould them. You gaze, and little by little the desire comes over you to say to Masha something extraordinarily pleasant, sincere and beautiful, as beautiful as she herself.

At first I felt hurt and abashed that Masha took no notice of me, but was all the time looking down; it seemed to me as though a peculiar atmosphere, proud and happy, separated her from me and jealously screened her from my eyes.

'That's because I am covered with dust,' I thought, 'because I'm sunburnt, and still a boy.'

But little by little I forgot myself, and gave myself up entirely to the consciousness of beauty. I thought no more now of the dreary steppe, of the dust, no longer heard the buzzing of flies, no longer tasted the tea, and felt nothing except that a beautiful girl was standing only the other side of the table.

I sensed this beauty rather strangely. It was not desire, nor ecstasy, nor enjoyment that Masha excited in me, but a painful though pleasant sadness. It was a sadness vague and undefined as a dream. For some reason I felt sorry for myself, for my grandfather and the Armenian, even for the girl herself, and I had a feeling as though all four of us had lost something important and essential to life which we should never find again. My grandfather, too, grew melancholy; he talked no more about manure or about oats, but sat silent, looking pensively at Masha.

After tea my grandfather lay down for a nap while I went out of the house into the porch. The house, like all the houses in the Armenian village, stood in the full sun; there was no tree, no awning, no shade. The Armenian's great courtyard, overgrown with goosefoot and wild mallows, was lively and full of gaiety in spite of the great heat. Threshing was going on behind one of the low fences which intersected the big yard here and there. Round a post stuck into the middle of the threshing-floor ran a dozen horses harnessed side by side, so that they formed one long radius. A Little Russian in a long waistcoat and full trousers was walking beside them, cracking a whip and shouting in a tone that sounded as though he were jeering at the horses and showing off his power over them.

'A—a—a, you damned brutes! . . . A—a—a, plague take you! Are you frightened?'

The horses, sorrel, white, and piebald, not understanding why they were made to run round in one place and to crush the wheat straw, ran unwillingly, as though with an effort, swinging their tails with an offended air. The wind raised up whole clouds of golden chaff from under their hoofs and carried it away far beyond the fencing. Near the tall fresh stacks peasant women were swarming with rakes, and carts were moving, and beyond the stacks in another yard another dozen similar horses were running round a post, and a similar Little Russian was cracking his whip and jeering at the horses.

The steps on which I was sitting were hot; on the thin rails and here and there on the window-frames sap was oozing out of the wood from the heat; red ladybirds were huddling together in the streaks of shadow under the steps and under the shutters. The sun was beating down on my head, my chest, and my back, but I did not notice it, and was conscious only of the thud of bare feet on the uneven floor in the passage and in the rooms behind me. After clearing away the tea-things, Mashya ran down the steps, fluttering the air as she passed, and like a bird flew into a little grimy outhouse—the kitchen, I suppose —from which came the smell of roast mutton and the sound of angry Armenian talk. She vanished into the dark doorway, and in her place there appeared on the threshold an old bent, red-faced Armenian woman wearing green trousers. The old woman was angry and was scolding someone. Soon afterwards Mashya appeared in the doorway, flushed with the heat of the kitchen and carrying a big black loaf on her shoulder; swaying gracefully under the weight of the bread, she ran across the yard to the threshing-floor, darted over the fence, and, wrapped in a cloud of golden chaff, vanished behind the carts. The Little Russian who was driving the horses lowered his whip, sank into silence, and gazed for a minute in the direction of the carts. Then when the Armenian girl darted again by the horses and leaped over the fence, he followed her with his eyes, and shouted to the horses in a tone as though he were greatly disappointed:

'Plague take you, unclean devils!'

And all the while I kept on hearing her bare feet, and seeing how she walked across the yard with a grave, preoccupied face. She ran now down the steps, swishing the air about me, now into the kitchen, now to the threshing-floor, now through the gate, and I could hardly turn my head quickly enough to watch her.

And the oftener she fluttered by me with her beauty, the more acute became my sadness. I felt sorry for myself and for her, and for the Little Russian who mournfully watched her every time she ran through the cloud of chaff to the carts. Whether it was envy of her beauty, or I regretted that the girl was not mine, and never would be, and that I was a stranger to her; or whether I vaguely felt that her rare beauty was accidental, unnecessary, and, like everything on earth, of short duration; or whether, perhaps, my sadness was that peculiar feeling which is excited in man by the contemplation of real beauty, God only knows.

The three hours of waiting passed unnoticed. It seemed to me that I had not had time to look properly at Masha when Karpo drove up to the river, bathed the horse, and began to put it in the shafts. The wet horse snorted with pleasure and kicked his hoofs against the shafts. Karpo shouted to it: 'Ba—ack!' My grandfather woke up. Mashya opened the creaking gates for us, we got into the chaise and drove out of the yard. We drove in silence as though we were angry with one another.

When, two or three hours later, Rostov and Nakhichevan appeared in the distance, Karpo, who had been silent the whole time, looked round quickly, and said:

'A fine wench, that at the Armenian's.'

And he lashed his horses.

II

Another time, after I had become a student, I was travelling by rail to the south. It was May. At one of the stations, I believe it was between Belgorod and Kharkov, I got out of the train to walk about the platform.

The shades of evening were already lying on the station garden, on the platform, and on the fields; the station screened off the sunset, but on the topmost clouds of smoke from the engine, which were tinged with rosy light, one could see the sun had not yet quite vanished.

As I walked up and down the platform I noticed that most

of the passengers were standing or walking near a second-class compartment, and that they looked as though some celebrated person were in that compartment. Among the curious whom I met near this compartment I saw, however, an artillery officer who had been my fellow-traveller, an intelligent, cordial, and sympathetic fellow—as people usually are whom we meet on our travels by chance and fleetingly.

'What are you looking at there?' I asked.

He made no answer, but only indicated with his eyes a feminine figure. It was a young girl of seventeen or eighteen, wearing a Russian dress, with her head bare and a little shawl flung carelessly on one shoulder; not a passenger, but I suppose a sister or daughter of the station-master. She was standing near the carriage window, talking to an elderly woman who was in the train. Before I had time to realise what I was seeing, I was suddenly overwhelmed by the feeling I had once experienced in the Armenian village.

The girl was remarkably beautiful, and that was unmistakable to me and to those who were looking at her as I was.

If one had to describe her appearance feature by feature, as the practice goes, then the only really lovely thing about her was her thick wavy fair hair, which hung loose with a black ribbon tied round her head; all the other features were either irregular or very ordinary. Either from a peculiar form of coquettishness, or from short-sightedness, her eyes were screwed up, her nose had an undecided tilt, her mouth was small, her profile was feebly and insipidly drawn, her shoulders were narrow and undeveloped for her age—and yet the girl made the impression of being really beautiful and, looking at her, I was able to feel convinced that a Russian face does not need strict regularity in order to be lovely; what is more, that if instead of her turned-up nose the girl had been given a different one, correct and plastically irreproachable like the Armenian girl's, I fancy her face would have lost all its charm from this change.

Standing at the window talking, shrugging at the evening damp, and continually looking round at us, the girl at one moment put her arms akimbo, at the next raised her hands to her head to straighten her hair, she talked, laughed, while her face at one moment wore an expression of wonder, the next of horror, and I don't remember a moment when her face and body were at rest. The whole secret and magic of her beauty lay just in these tiny, infinitely elegant movements, in her smile, in the play of her face, in her rapid glances at us, in the combination of the subtle grace of these movements with her youth, her freshness, the purity of her soul that sounded in her laugh and voice, and with that weakness we love so much in children, in birds, in fawns, and in young trees.

It was a butterfly's beauty so in keeping with waltzing, darting about the garden, laughter and gaiety, and incongruous with serious thought, grief, and repose; and it seemed as though a gust of wind blowing over the platform, or a fall of rain, would be enough to wither her fragile body and scatter its capricious beauty like the pollen of a flower.

'So—o! . . .' the officer muttered with a sigh when, after the second bell, we went back to our compartment.

And what that 'So—o' meant I will not undertake to decide.

Perhaps he was sad, and did not want to go away from the beauty and the spring evening into the stuffy train; or perhaps he, like me, was unaccountably sorry for the beauty, for himself, and for me, and for all the passengers, who were listlessly and reluctantly sauntering back to their compartments. As we passed the station window, at which a pale, red-haired telegraphist with upstanding curls and a faded, broad-cheeked face was sitting beside his apparatus, the officer heaved a sigh and said:

'I bet that telegraphist is in love with the pretty girl. To live out in the wilds under one roof with that ethereal creature and not fall in love is beyond the power of man. And what a calamity, my friend! what an ironical fate, to be stooping, unkempt, grey, a decent fellow and not a fool, and to fall in love with that pretty, stupid little girl who would never take a scrap of notice of you! Or worse still: imagine that telegraphist is in love, and at the same time married, and that his wife is as stooping, as unkempt, and as decent a person as himself . . . How awful!'

On the platform between our carriage and the next the guard was standing with his elbows on the railing, looking in the direction of the beautiful girl, and his battered, wrinkled, unpleasantly beefy face, exhausted by sleepless nights and the jolting of the train, wore a look of tenderness and of the deepest sadness, as though in that girl he saw happiness, his own youth, soberness, purity, wife, children; as though he were repenting and feeling in his whole being that this girl was not his, and that for him, with his premature old age, his uncouthness, and his beefy face, the ordinary human happiness of a passenger was as far away as heaven . . .

The third bell rang, the whistles sounded, and the train slowly moved off. First the guard, the station-master, then the garden, the beautiful girl with her exquisite, childishly sly smile, passed before our windows . . .

Putting my head out and looking back, I saw how, gazing after the train, she walked along the platform by the window where the telegraph clerk was sitting, smoothed her hair, and ran into the garden. The station no longer screened off the sunset, the plain lay open before us, but the sun had already set and the smoke lay in black clouds over the green, velvety young corn. There was a feeling of sadness in the spring air, and in the darkening sky, and in the railway carriage.

The familiar figure of the guard came into our carriage, and began to light the candles.

A Dreary Story

FROM THE NOTEBOOK OF AN OLD MAN

I

There is in Russia an emeritus Professor Nikolay Stepanovich, a chevalier and Privy Counsellor; he has so many Russian and foreign decorations that when he has occasion to put them on, the students nickname him 'The Iconstand'. His acquaintances are of the most aristocratic kind; for the last twenty-five or thirty years, at any rate, there has not been one single distinguished man of learning in Russia with whom he has not been intimately acquainted. There is no one for him to make friends with nowadays; but if we turn to the past, the long list of his famous friends winds up with such names as Pirogov, Kavelin, and the poet Nekrasov, all of whom bestowed upon him a warm and sincere affection. He is a member of all the Russian and of three foreign universities. And so on, and so forth. All that and a great deal more that might be said makes up what is called my 'name'.

This name of mine is renowned. In Russia it is known to every educated man, and abroad it is mentioned in the lecture-room with the addition 'honoured and distinguished'. It is one of those few fortunate names, where to abuse it or take it in vain, in public or in print, is considered a sign of bad taste. And that is as it should be. You see, my name is closely associated with the conception of a highly distinguished man of great gifts and unquestionable usefulness. I have the industry and endurance of a camel, and that is important, and I have talent, which is even more important. Moreover, while I am on this subject, I am a well-educated, modest, and honest fellow. I have never poked my nose into literature or politics; I have never sought popularity in polemics with the ignorant; I have never made speeches either at public dinners or at the funerals of my friends . . . In fact, there is no slur on my learned name, and there is no complaint one can make against it. My name is fortunate.

The bearer of this name, that is I, see myself as a man of sixty-two, with a bald head, with false teeth, and with an incurable tic douloureux. I am myself as dingy and unsightly as my name is brilliant and splendid. My head and hands tremble with weakness; my neck, as Turgenev says of one of his heroines, is like the handle of a double-bass; my chest is hollow; my shoulders narrow. When I talk or lecture, my mouth turns down at one corner; when I smile, my whole face is covered with aged-looking, deathly wrinkles. There is nothing impressive about my pitiful figure; only, perhaps, when I have an attack of tic douloureux my face wears a peculiar expression, the sight of which must arouse in everyone the grim and impressive thought, 'Evidently that man will soon be dead.'

I still, as in the past, lecture fairly well; I can still, as in the past, hold the attention of my listeners for a couple of hours. My fervour, the literary skill of my exposition, and my humour, almost efface the defects of my voice, though it is harsh, dry, and monotonous like that of a sanctimonious hypocrite. I write poorly. That bit of my brain which presides over the faculty of authorship refuses to work. My memory has grown weak; there is a lack of sequence in my ideas, and when I put them on paper it always seems to me that I have lost the instinct for their organic connection; the construction is monotonous; my phrasing is poor and timid. Often I write what I do not mean; I have forgotten the beginning when I am writing the end. Often I forget ordinary words, and I always have to waste a great deal of energy in avoiding superfluous phrases and unnecessary parentheses in my letters, both unmistakable proofs of a decline in mental activity. And it is noteworthy that the simpler the letter the more painful the effort to write it. At a scientific article I feel far more intelligent and at ease than at a letter of congratulation or a minute of proceedings. Another point: I find it easier to write German or English than to write Russian.

As regards my present way of life, I must give a foremost place to the insomnia from which I have suffered of late. If I were asked what constituted the chief and fundamental feature of my existence now, I should answer: insomnia. As in the past, from habit I undress and go to bed exactly at midnight. I fall asleep quickly, but before two o'clock I wake up and feel as though I had not slept at all. Sometimes I get out of bed and light a lamp. For an hour or two I walk up and down the room looking at the familiar photographs and pictures. When I am weary of walking about, I sit down at my desk. I sit motionless, thinking of nothing, conscious of no desires; if a book is lying before me, I mechanically move it closer and read it without any interest—in that way not long ago I mechanically read through in one night a whole novel, with the strange title *The Song the Lark was Singing*; or to occupy my attention I force myself to count to a thousand; or I imagine the face of one of my col-

leagues and begin trying to remember in what year and under what circumstances he entered the service. I like listening to sounds. Two rooms
away from me my daughter Liza says something rapidly in her sleep, or
my wife crosses the drawing-room with a candle and invariably drops the
matchbox; or a warped cupboard creaks; or the burner of the lamp suddenly begins to hum—and all these sounds, for some reason, excite me.

To lie awake at night means to be at every moment conscious of being
abnormal, and so I look forward with impatience to the morning and the
day, when I have a right to be awake. Many wearisome hours pass before
the cock crows in the yard. He is my first bringer of good tidings. As soon
as he crows I know that within an hour the porter will wake up below,
and, coughing angrily, will go upstairs to fetch something. And then a
pale light will begin gradually glimmering at the windows, voices will
sound in the street . . .

The day begins for me with the entrance of my wife. She comes in to
me in her petticoat, before she has done her hair, but after she has
washed, smelling of flower-scented eau-de-Cologne, looking as though
she had come in by chance. Every time she says exactly the same thing:

'Excuse me, I have just come for a minute . . . Have you had a bad
night again?'

Then she puts out the lamp, sits down near the table, and begins talking. I am no prophet, but I know what she will talk about. Every morning
it is exactly the same thing. Usually, after anxious enquiries concerning
my health, she suddenly mentions our son who is an officer serving in
Warsaw. After the twentieth of each month we send him fifty roubles, and
that serves as the chief topic of our conversation.

'Of course it is difficult for us,' my wife would sigh, 'but until he is
completely on his own feet it is our duty to help him. The boy is among
strangers, his pay is small . . . However, if you like, next month we won't
send him fifty, but forty. What do you think?'

Daily experience might have taught my wife that constantly talking
of our expenses does not reduce them, but my wife refuses to learn
from experience, and regularly every morning discusses our officer son,
and tells me that bread, thank God, is cheaper, while sugar is two
kopecks dearer—and all this in a tone as though she were telling me
something new.

I listen, mechanically assent, and, probably because I have had a bad
night, strange and inappropriate thoughts intrude themselves upon me. I
gaze at my wife and wonder like a child. I ask myself in perplexity, is it

possible that this old, very stout, ungainly woman, with her dull expression of petty anxiety and alarm about daily bread, with eyes dimmed by continual brooding over debts and money difficulties, who can talk of nothing but expenses and who smiles at nothing but things getting cheaper—is it possible that this woman is the same slender Varya with whom I fell in love so passionately for her fine, clear intelligence, for her pure soul, her beauty, and, as Othello his Desdemona, 'that she did pity' me for my studies? Could that woman be the same Varya who once bore me a son?

I look with strained attention into the face of this flabby, clumsy old woman, seeking in her my Varya, but of her past self nothing is left but her anxiety over my health and her manner of calling my salary 'our salary', and my cap 'our cap'. It is painful for me to look at her, and, to give her what little comfort I can, I let her say what she likes, and say nothing even when she passes unjust criticisms on other people or pitches into me for not having a private practice or not publishing textbooks.

Our conversation always ends in the same way. My wife suddenly remembers with dismay that I have not had my tea.

'What am I thinking about, sitting here?' she says, getting up. 'The samovar has been on the table ever so long, and here I stay gossiping. My goodness! how forgetful I am growing!'

She goes out quickly, and stops in the doorway to say:

'We owe Yegor five months' wages. Did you know that? You mustn't let the servants' wages pile up; how many times I have said it! It's much easier to pay ten roubles a month than fifty roubles every five months!'

As she goes out, she stops to say:

'The person I am sorriest for is our Liza. The girl studies at the Conservatoire, always mixes with people of good position, and goodness knows how she is dressed. Her fur coat is in such a state she is ashamed to show herself in the street. If she were somebody else's daughter it wouldn't matter, but of course everyone knows that her father is a distinguished professor, a Privy Counsellor.'

And having reproached me with my rank and reputation, she leaves at last. That is how my day begins. It does not improve as it goes on.

As I am drinking my tea, my Liza comes in wearing her fur coat and her cap, with her music in her hand, all ready to go to the Conservatoire. She is twenty-two. She looks younger, is pretty, and rather like my wife in her young days. She kisses me tenderly on my forehead and on my hand, and says:

'Good morning, Papa; are you quite well?'

As a child she was very fond of ice-cream, and I often used to take her to a confectioner's. Ice-cream was for her the measure of everything delightful. If she wanted to praise me she would say: 'You are as nice as cream, Papa.' We used to call one of her little fingers 'pistachio ice', the next, 'cream ice', the third 'raspberry', and so on. Usually when she came in to say good morning to me I used to sit her on my knee, kiss her little fingers, and say:

'Cream ice . . . pistachio . . . lemon . . .'

And now, from old habit, I kiss Liza's fingers and mutter: 'Pistachio . . . cream . . . lemon . . .' but the effect is utterly different. I am cold as ice and I am ashamed. When my daughter comes in to me and touches my forehead with her lips I start as though a bee had stung me on the head, give a forced smile, and turn my face away. Ever since I have been suffering from sleeplessness, one question sticks in my brain like a nail. My daughter often sees me, an old and distinguished man, blush painfully at being in debt to my footman; she sees how often anxiety over petty debts forces me to lay aside my work and to walk up and down the room for hours on end, thinking; but why is it she never comes to me in secret to whisper in my ear: 'Father, here is my watch, here are my bracelets, my ear-rings, my dresses . . . Pawn them all; you need the money . . .'? How is it that, seeing how her mother and I are placed in a false position and do our utmost to hide our poverty from people, she does not give up her expensive pleasure of music lessons? I would not accept her watch nor her bracelets, nor the sacrifice of her lessons—God forbid! That isn't what I need.

I think at the same time of my son, the officer in Warsaw. He is a clever, honest, and sober fellow. But that is not sufficient for me. I think if I had an old father, and if I knew there were moments when he was put to shame by his poverty, I should give up my officer's commission to somebody else, and should go out to earn my living as a workman. Such thoughts about my children poison me. What is the use of them? It is only a narrow-minded or embittered man who can harbour evil thoughts about ordinary people because they are not heroes. But enough of that!

At a quarter to ten I have to go and give a lecture to my dear boys. I dress and walk along the road which I have known for thirty years, and which has its history for me. Here is the big grey house with the chemist's shop; at this point there used to stand a little house, and in it was a beershop; in that beershop I thought out my thesis and wrote my first love-letter to Varya. I wrote it in pencil, on a page headed '*Historia morbi*'. Here there is a grocer's shop; at one time it was kept by a little Jew, who sold me cigarettes on credit; then by a fat peasant woman, who liked the students because 'every one of them has a mother'; now there is a red-haired shopkeeper sitting in it, a very stolid man who drinks tea from a copper teapot. And here are the gloomy gates of the University, which have long needed doing up; I see the bored porter in his sheepskin, the broom, the drifts of snow . . . On a boy coming fresh from the provinces and imagining that the temple of science must really be a temple, such gates cannot make a healthy impression. Altogether the dilapidated condition of the University buildings, the gloominess of the corridors, the griminess of the walls, the lack of light, the dejected aspect of the steps, the hatstands and the benches, take a prominent position among predisposing causes in the history of Russian pessimism . . . Here is our garden . . . I fancy it has grown neither better nor worse since I was a student. I don't like it. It would be far more sensible if there were tall pines and fine oaks growing here instead of sickly-looking lime-trees, yellow acacias, and skimpy pollard lilacs. The student, whose state of mind is in most cases created by his surroundings, ought in the place where he is studying to see facing him at every turn nothing but what is lofty, strong, and elegant . . . God preserve him from gaunt trees, broken windows, grey walls, and doors covered with torn oil-cloth!

When I go to my own entrance the door is flung wide open, and I am met by my old colleague, contemporary, and namesake, the porter Nikolay. As he lets me in he clears his throat and says:

'A frost, Your Excellency!'

Or, if my greatcoat is wet:

'Rain, Your Excellency!'

Then he runs on ahead of me and opens all the doors on my way. In my study he carefully takes off my fur coat, and while doing so manages to tell me some bit of University news. Thanks to the close intimacy existing between all the University porters and beadles, he knows everything that goes on in the four faculties, in the office, in the Rector's private room, in the library. What does he not know? When, for instance, the topic of the day is the retirement of a rector or dean, I hear him in conversation with the young porters mention the candidates for the post, explain that such a one would not be confirmed by the minister, that another would himself refuse to accept it, then drop into fantastic details concerning mysterious papers received in the office, secret conversations alleged to have taken place between the minister and the trustee, and so on. With the exception of these details, he almost always turns out to be right. His estimates of the candidates, though original, are very correct, too. If one wants to know in what year someone read his thesis, entered the service, retired, or died, then summon to your assistance the vast memory of that soldier, and he will not only tell you the year, the month and the day, but will furnish you also with the details that accompanied this or that event. Only one who loves can remember like that.

He is the guardian of the University traditions. From the porters who were his predecessors he has inherited many legends of University life, has added to that wealth much of his own gained during his time of service, and if you care to hear he will tell you many stories, short and long. He can tell one about extraordinary sages who knew *everything*, about remarkable Trojans who did not sleep for weeks, about numerous martyrs and victims of science; with him Good triumphs over Evil, the weak always vanquishes the strong, the wise man the fool, the humble the proud, the young the old. There is no need to take all these fables and legends for sterling coin; but filter them, and you will have left what is wanted: our fine traditions and the names of real heroes, recognised as such by all.

Our society's knowledge of the learned world consists of anecdotes about the extraordinary absent-mindedness of certain old professors, and two or three witticisms variously ascribed to Gruber, to me, and to Babukhin. For an educated public that is not much. If it loved science, learned men, and students, as Nikolay does, its literature would long ago have contained whole epics, records of sayings and doings—but, unfortunately, no such epics exist.

After telling me a piece of news, Nikolay assumes a severe expression, and conversation about business begins. If any outsider could at such times overhear Nikolay's free use of our terminology, he might perhaps imagine that he was a learned man disguised as a soldier. And, by the way, the rumours of the erudition of University porters are greatly exaggerated. It is true that Nikolay knows more than a hundred Latin words, knows how to put a skeleton together, sometimes prepares the apparatus and amuses the students by some long, learned quotation, but the by no means complicated theory of the circulation of the blood, for instance, is as much a mystery to him now as it was twenty years ago.

At the table in my study, bending low over some book or preparation, sits Pyotr Ignatyevich, my demonstrator, a modest and industrious but untalented man of thirty-five, already bald and corpulent. He works from morning to night, reads a lot, remembers well everything he has read—and in that way he is not a man, but pure gold; in all else he is a cart-horse or, in other words, a learned dullard. The cart-horse characteristics that show his lack of talent are these: his outlook is narrow and sharply limited by his speciality; outside his speciality he is as simple as a child. I remember, one morning I entered my study and said:

'Fancy! what a misfortune! They say Skobelev is dead.'

Nikolay crosses himself, but Pyotr Ignatyevich turns to me and asks:

'What Skobelev is that?'

Another time—somewhat earlier—I told him that Professor Perov was dead. Good Pyotr Ignatyevich asked:

'What did he lecture on?'

I believe if Patti had sung in his very ear, if a horde of Chinese had invaded Russia, if there had been an earthquake, he would not have moved a muscle, but screwing up his eye, would have gone on calmly looking through his microscope. What is he to Hecuba or Hecuba to him, in fact? I would give a good deal to see how this dry stick sleeps with his wife at night.

Another characteristic is his fanatical faith in the infallibility of science, and, above all, of everything written by the Germans. He believes in himself, in his preparations; knows the purpose of life, and knows nothing of the doubts and disappointments that turn the hair of talent grey. He has a slavish reverence for authorities and a complete lack of any desire for independent thought. To change his convictions is difficult, to argue with him impossible. How is one to argue with a man who is firmly persuaded that medicine is the finest of sciences, that doctors are the best of men, and that the traditions of the medical profession are superior to those of any other? Of the evil past of medicine only one tradition has been preserved—the white tie still worn by doctors; for a scholar, in fact, for any educated man, the only traditions that can exist are those of the University as a whole, with no distinction between medicine, law, etc. But it would be hard for Pyotr Ignatyevich to accept these facts, and he is ready to argue with you till the Day of Judgement.

I have a clear picture in my mind of his future. In the course of his life he will prepare many hundreds of chemicals of exceptional purity; he will write a number of dry and very accurate memoranda, will make some dozen conscientious translations, but he won't do anything striking. To do that one must have imagination, inventiveness, the gift of insight, and Pyotr Ignatyevich has nothing of the kind. In short, he is not a master in science, but a journeyman.

Pyotr Ignatyevich, Nikolay, and I talk in subdued tones. We are not quite ourselves. There is always a peculiar feeling when one hears through the doors a murmur as of the sea from the lecture-theatre. In the course of thirty years I have not grown accustomed to this feeling, and I experience it every morning. I nervously button up my coat, ask Nikolay superfluous questions, lose my temper . . . It is just as though I were frightened; it is not timidity, though, but something different which I can neither describe nor name.

Quite needlessly, I look at my watch and say:

'Well, it's time to go in.'

And we march into the room in the following order: foremost goes Nikolay, with the chemicals and apparatus or with a chart; after him I come; and then the cart-horse follows humbly, with hanging head; or, when necessary, a dead body is carried in first on a stretcher, followed by Nikolay, and so on. On my entrance the students all stand up, then they sit down, and the roar of the sea is suddenly hushed. Stillness reigns.

I know what I am going to lecture about, but I don't know how I am going to lecture, where I am going to begin or with what I am going to end. I haven't a single sentence ready in my head. But I have only to look round the lecture-hall (it is built in the form of an amphitheatre) and utter the stereotyped phrase, 'Last lecture we stopped at . . .' when sentences spring up from my soul in a long string, and I am carried away by my own eloquence. I speak with irresistible rapidity and passion, and it seems as though there were no force which could check the flow of my words. To lecture well—that is, with profit to the listeners and without boring them—one must have, besides talent, experience and a special knack; one must possess a clear conception of one's own powers, of the audience to whom one is lecturing, and of the subject of one's lecture. Moreover, one must be a man who knows what he is doing; one must keep a sharp look-out, and not for one second lose sight of what lies before one.

A good conductor, interpreting the composer's thought, does twenty things at once: reads the score, waves his baton, watches the singer, makes a motion sideways, first to the drum then to the wind instruments, and so on. I do just the same when I lecture. Before me a hundred and fifty faces, all unlike one another; three hundred eyes all looking straight into my face. My object is to dominate this many-headed hydra.

If every moment as I lecture I have a clear vision of the degree of its attention and its power of comprehension, then I am in control. The other foe I have to overcome is in myself. It is the infinite variety of forms, phenomena, laws, and the multitude of ideas of my own and other people's conditioned by them. Every moment I must have the skill to snatch out of that vast mass of material what is most important and necessary, and, as rapidly as my words flow, clothe my thought in a form in which it can be grasped by the hydra's intelligence, and may arouse its attention, and at the same time one must keep a sharp look-out that one's thoughts are conveyed, not just as they come, but in a certain order, essential for the correct composition of the picture I wish to sketch. Further, I endeavour to make my diction literary, my definitions brief and precise, my wording, as far as possible, simple and eloquent. Every minute I have to pull myself up and remember that I have only an hour and forty minutes at my disposal. In short, one has one's work cut out. At one and the same minute one has to play the part of scholar and teacher and orator, and it's a bad thing if the orator gets the upper hand of the scholar or of the teacher, or vice versa.

You lecture for a quarter of an hour, for half an hour, when you notice that the students are beginning to look at the ceiling, at Pyotr Ignatyevich; one is feeling for his handkerchief, another shifts in his seat, another smiles at his thoughts . . . That means their attention is flagging. Something must be done. Taking advantage of the first opportunity, I make some pun. A broad grin comes on to a hundred and fifty faces, their eyes shine brightly, the sound of the sea is audible for a brief moment . . . I laugh too. Their attention is refreshed, and I can go on.

No kind of sport, no kind of game or diversion, has ever given me such enjoyment as lecturing. Only at lectures have I been able to abandon myself entirely to passion, and have understood that inspiration is not an invention of the poets, but exists in real life, and I imagine Hercules after the most piquant of his exploits never felt such voluptuous exhaustion as I experienced after every lecture.

That was in the old times. Now at lectures I feel nothing but torture. Before half an hour is over I am conscious of an overwhelming weakness in my legs and my shoulders. I sit down in my chair, but I am not accustomed to lecture sitting down; a minute later I get up and go on standing, then sit down again. There is a dryness in my mouth, my voice grows husky, my head begins to go round . . . To conceal my condition from my audience I continually drink water, cough, often blow my nose as though

96

I were hindered by a cold, make puns inappropriately, and in the end break off earlier than I ought to. But above all I am ashamed.

My conscience and my intelligence tell me that the very best thing I could do now would be to deliver a farewell lecture to the boys, to say my last word to them, to bless them, and give up my post to a man younger and stronger than me. But, God be my judge, I have not courage enough to act according to my conscience.

Unfortunately, I am not a philosopher and not a theologian. I know perfectly well that I cannot live more than another six months; it might be supposed that I ought now to be chiefly concerned with the question of the shadowy life beyond the grave, and the visions that will visit my slumbers in the tomb. But for some reason my soul refuses to recognise these questions, though my mind is fully alive to their importance. Just as twenty, thirty years ago, so now, on the threshold of death, I am interested in nothing but science. As I yield up my last breath I shall still believe that science is the most important, the most splendid, the most essential thing in the life of man; that it always has been and will be the highest manifestation of love, and that only by means of science will man conquer himself and nature. This faith is perhaps naïve and may rest on false assumptions, but it is not my fault that I believe that and nothing else; I cannot overcome in myself this belief.

But that is not the point. I only ask people to be indulgent to my weakness, and to realise that to tear from the lecture-theatre and his pupils a man who is more interested in the history of the development of bone marrow than in the final purpose of creation would be equivalent to taking him and nailing him up in his coffin without waiting for him to be dead.

Sleeplessness and the consequent strain of combating increasing weakness leads to something strange in me. In the middle of my lecture tears suddenly rise in my throat, my eyes begin to smart, and I feel a passionate, hysterical desire to stretch out my hands before me and break into loud lamentation. I want to cry out in a loud voice that I, a famous man, have been sentenced by fate to the death penalty, that within some six months another man will be in control here in the lecture-theatre. I want to shriek that I am poisoned; new ideas such as I have not known before have poisoned the last days of my life, and are still stinging my brain like mosquitoes. And at that moment my position seems to me so awful that I want all my listeners to be horrified, to leap up from their seats and to rush in panic terror, with desperate screams, to the exit.

It is not easy to get through such moments.

After my lecture I sit at home and work. I read journals and monographs, or prepare my next lecture; sometimes I write something. I work with interruptions, as I have from time to time to see visitors.

There is a ring at the bell. It is a colleague come to discuss some business matter with me. He comes in to me with his hat and his stick, and, holding out both these objects to me, says:

'Only for a minute! Only for a minute! Sit down, *collega*! Only a couple of words.'

To begin with, we both try to show each other that we are extraordinarily polite and highly delighted to see each other. I make him sit down in an easy-chair, and he makes me sit down; as we do so, we cautiously pat each other on the back, touch each other's buttons, and it looks as though we were feeling each other and afraid of scorching our fingers. Both of us laugh, though we say nothing amusing. When we are seated we bow our heads towards each other and begin talking in subdued voices. However affectionately disposed we may be to one another, we cannot help adorning our conversation with all sorts of Chinese mannerisms, such as 'As you so justly observed', or 'I have already had the honour to inform you'; we cannot help laughing if one of us makes a joke, however unsuccessfully. When we have finished with business my colleague gets up impulsively and, waving his hat in the direction of my work, begins to say goodbye. Again we paw one another and laugh. I see him into the hall; then I assist my colleague to put on his coat, while he does all he can to decline this high honour. Then when Yegor opens the door my colleague declares that I shall catch cold, while I make a show of being ready to go even into the street with him. And when at last I go back into my study my face still goes on smiling, I suppose from inertia.

A little later another ring at the bell. Somebody comes into the hall, and is a long time coughing and taking off his things. Yegor announces a student. I tell him to ask him in. A minute later a young man of agreeable appearance comes in. For the last year our relationship has been strained; his examination answers are abominable, and I fail him. Every year I have some seven such hopefuls whom, to express it in the students' slang, I 'chivvy' or 'floor'. Those of them who fail in their examination through incapacity or illness usually bear their cross patiently and do not haggle with me; those who come to the house and haggle with me are always youths of sanguine temperament, broad natures, whose failure at examinations spoils their appetites and hinders them from visiting the opera with their usual regularity. I let the first class off easily, but the second I chivvy through a whole year.

'Sit down,' I say to my visitor; 'what have you to tell me?'

'Excuse me, Professor, for troubling you,' he begins, hesitating, and not looking me in the face. 'I would not have ventured to trouble you if it had not been . . . I have been up for your examination five times, and have been ploughed . . . I beg you, be so good as to mark me for a pass, because . . .'

The argument which all the sluggards bring forward on their own behalf is always the same; they have passed well in all their subjects and have only come to grief in mine, and that is the more surprising because they have always been particularly interested in my subject and knew it so well; their failure has always been entirely owing to some incomprehensible misunderstanding.

'Excuse me, my friend,' I say to the visitor; 'I cannot mark you for a pass. Go and read up the lectures and come to me again. Then we shall see.'

A pause. I feel an impulse to torment the student a little for liking beer and the opera better than science, and I say, with a sigh:

'To my mind, the best thing you can do now is to give up medicine altogether. If, with your abilities, you cannot succeed in passing the examination, it's evident that you have neither the desire nor the vocation for a doctor's calling.'

The sanguine youth's face lengthens.

'Excuse me, Professor,' he laughs, 'but that would be odd of me, to say the least. After studying for five years, all at once to give it up.'

'Oh, well! Better to have wasted five years than have to spend the rest of your life in doing work you don't care for.'

But at once I feel sorry for him, and I hasten to add:

'However, as you think best. And so read a little more and come again.'

'When?' the idle youth asks in a hollow voice.

'When you like. Tomorrow if you wish.'

And in his good-natured eyes I read:

'I can come all right, but of course you will plough me again, you beast!'

'Of course,' I say, 'you won't know more science through going in for my examination another fifteen times, but it is training your character, and you must be thankful for that.'

Silence follows. I get up and wait for my visitor to go, but he stands and looks towards the window, fingers his beard, and thinks. It grows boring.

The sanguine youth's voice is pleasant and mellow, his eyes are clever and ironical, his face is genial, though a little bloated from frequent indulgence in beer and excessive lying on the sofa; he looks as though he could tell me a lot of interesting things about the opera, about his affairs of the heart, and about comrades whom he likes. Unfortunately, it is not the thing to discuss these subjects; I should have been glad to listen to him.

'Professor, I give you my word of honour that if you mark me for a pass I . . . I'll . . .'

As soon as we reach the 'word of honour' I wave my hands and sit down at my desk. The student ponders a minute longer, and says dejectedly:

'In that case, goodbye . . . I beg your pardon.'

'Goodbye, my friend. Good luck to you.'

He goes irresolutely into the hall, slowly puts on his outdoor clothes, and, going out into the street, probably ponders for some time longer; unable to think of anything, except 'old devil,' inwardly addressed to me, he goes into a wretched restaurant to dine and drink beer, and then home to bed. Peace be to thy ashes, honest toiler!

A third ring at the bell. A young doctor, in a new black suit, gold spectacles, and of course a white tie, walks in. He introduces himself. I beg him to be seated, and ask what I can do for him. Not without emotion, the young devotee of science begins telling me that he has passed his examination as a doctor of medicine, and that he has now only to write his dissertation. He would like to work with me under my guidance, and he would be greatly obliged to me if I would give him a subject for his dissertation.

'Very glad to be of use to you, colleague,' I say, 'but just let us come to an understanding as to the meaning of a dissertation. That word is taken to mean a composition which is a product of independent creative effort. Is that not so? A work written on another man's subject and under another man's guidance is called something different . . .'

The doctor says nothing. I fly into a rage and jump up from my seat.

'Why is it you all come to me?' I cry angrily. 'Do I keep a shop? I don't deal in subjects. For the thousand-and-first time I ask you all to leave me in peace! Excuse my plain speaking, but I am quite sick of it!'

The doctor remains silent, but a faint flush is apparent on his cheek-bones. His face expresses a profound reverence for my fame and my learning, but from his eyes I can see he feels a contempt for my voice, my pitiful figure, and my nervous gesticulation. I impress him in my anger as an eccentric.

'I don't keep a shop,' I go on angrily. 'And it is a strange thing! Why don't you want to be independent? Why have you such a distaste for freedom?'

I say a great deal, but he still remains silent. By degrees I calm down, and of course give in. The doctor gets a subject from me for his thesis not worth a brass farthing, writes under my supervision a dissertation of no use to anyone, with dignity defends it in a dreary discussion, and receives a degree of no use to him.

The rings at the bell may follow one another endlessly, but I will confine my description here to four of them. The bell rings for the fourth time, and I hear familiar footsteps, the rustle of a dress, a dear voice . . .

Eighteen years ago a colleague of mine, an oculist, died leaving a little daughter Katya, a child of seven, and sixty thousand roubles. In his will he made me the child's guardian. Till she was ten years old Katya lived with us as one of the family, then she was sent to a boarding-school, and only spent the summer holidays with us. I never had time to look after her education. I kept an eye on it only at odd moments, and so I can say very little about her childhood.

The first thing I remember, and like so much in remembrance, is the extraordinary trustfulness with which she came into our house and let herself be treated by the doctors, a trustfulness which was always shining in her little face. She would sit somewhere out of the way, with her face bandaged, invariably watching something with attention; whether she saw me writing or turning over the pages of a book, or my wife bustling about, or the cook scrubbing a potato in the kitchen, or the dog playing, her eyes invariably expressed the same thought—that is, 'Everything that is done in this world is nice and sensible.' She was curious, and very fond of talking to me. Sometimes she would sit at the table opposite me, watching my movements and asking questions. It interested her to know what I was reading, what I did at the University, whether I was not afraid of the dead bodies, what I did with my salary.

'Do the students fight at the University?' she would ask.

'They do, dear.'

'And do you make them go down on their knees?'

'Yes, I do.'

And she thought it funny that the students fought and I made them go down on their knees, and she laughed. She was a gentle, patient, good child. It happened not infrequently that I saw something taken away from her, saw her punished without reason, or her curiosity left unsatisfied; at such times a look of sadness was mixed with the invariable expression of trustfulness on her face—that was all. I did not know how to take her part; only when I saw her sad I had an inclination to draw her to me and to commiserate with her like some old nurse: 'My poor little orphan one!'

I remember, too, that she was fond of fine clothes and of sprinkling herself with scent. In that respect she was like me. I, too, am fond of pretty clothes and nice scent.

I regret that I had not time nor inclination to watch over the rise and development of the passion which took complete possession of Katya when she was fourteen or fifteen. I mean her passionate love for the theatre. When she used to come from boarding-school and stay with us for the summer holidays, she talked of nothing with such pleasure and such warmth as of plays and actors. She bored us with her continual talk of the theatre. My wife and children would not listen to her. I was the only one who had not the courage to refuse to pay attention to her. When she had a longing to share her transports, she used to come into my study and say in an imploring tone:

'Nikolay Stepanych, do let me talk to you about the theatre!'

I pointed to the clock, and said:

'I'll give you half an hour—begin.'

Later on she used to bring with her dozens of portraits of actors and actresses which she worshipped; then she attempted several times to take part in private theatricals, and the upshot of it all was that when she left school she came to me and announced that she was born to be an actress.

I had never shared Katya's inclinations for the theatre. To my mind, if a play is good there is no need to trouble the actors in order that it may make the right impression; it is enough to read it. If the play is poor, no acting will make it good.

In my youth I often visited the theatre, and now my family takes a box twice a year and carries me off for a little distraction. Of course, that is not enough to give me the right to judge the theatre. In my opinion the theatre has become no better than it was thirty or forty years ago. Just as in the past, I can never find a glass of clean water in the corridors or foyers of the theatre. Just as in the past, the attendants fine me twenty kopecks for my fur coat, though there is nothing reprehensible in wearing a warm coat in winter. As in the past, for no sort of reason, music is played in the intervals, which adds something new and uncalled-for to the impression made by the play. As in the past, men go in the intervals and drink spirits in the buffet. If no progress can be seen in trifles, then it's pointless to seek it in what is more important. When an actor snared from head to foot by stage traditions and conventions tries to recite a simple ordinary speech, 'To be, or not to be,' not simply, but invariably with the accompaniment of hissing and convulsive movements all over his body, or when he tries to convince me at all costs that Chatsky, who talks so much with fools and loves a foolish woman, is a very clever man, and that *Woe From Wit* is not a dull play, the stage gives me the same feeling of conventionality which bored me so much forty years ago when I was regaled with the classical howling and beating on the breast. And every time I come out of the theatre more conservative than I go in.

The sentimental and confiding public may be persuaded that the stage, even in its present form, is a school; but anyone who is familiar with a school in its true sense will not be caught with that bait. I cannot say what will happen in fifty or a hundred years, but in its present condition the theatre can serve only as an entertainment. But this entertainment is too costly to deserve perpetuation. It robs the State of thousands of healthy and talented young men and women, who, if they had not devoted themselves to the theatre, might have been good doctors, farmers, schoolmistresses, officers; it robs the public of the evening hours—the best time for intellectual work and social intercourse. I say nothing of the waste of money and the moral damage to the spectator when he sees murder, fornication, or false witness unsuitably treated on the stage.

Katya was of an entirely different opinion. She assured me that the theatre, even in its present condition, was superior to the lecture-hall, to books, or to anything in the world. The stage was a power that united in itself all the arts, and actors were missionaries. No art nor science was capable of producing so strong and so certain an effect on the soul of man as the stage, and it was with good reason that an actor of medium quality enjoys greater popularity than the greatest scholar or artist. And no sort of public service could provide such enjoyment and gratification as the theatre.

103

And one fine day Katya joined a troupe of actors, and went off, I believe, to Ufa, taking away with her a good supply of money, a store of rainbow hopes, and the most aristocratic views of her work.

Her first letters on the journey were marvellous. I read them, and was simply amazed that those small sheets of paper could contain so much youth, purity of spirit, holy innocence, and at the same time subtle and apt judgements which would have done credit to a fine masculine intellect. It was more like a rapturous paean of praise she sent me than a mere description of the Volga, the countryside, the towns she visited, her companions, her failures and successes; every sentence was fragrant with that confiding trustfulness I was accustomed to read in her face—and at the same time there were a great many grammatical mistakes, and there was scarcely any punctuation at all.

Before six months had passed I received a highly poetical and enthusiastic letter beginning with the words, 'I have come to love . . .' This letter was accompanied by a photograph representing a young man with a shaven face, a wide-brimmed hat, and a plaid flung over his shoulder. The letters that followed were as splendid as before, but now commas and stops made their appearance in them, the grammatical mistakes disappeared, and there was a distinctly masculine flavour about them. Katya began writing to me how splendid it would be to build a great theatre somewhere on the Volga, on a co-operative basis, and to attract to this enterprise the rich merchants and the steamer owners; there would be a great deal of money in it; there would be vast audiences; the actors would play on co-operative terms . . . Possibly all this was really excellent, but it seemed to me that such schemes could only originate from a man's mind.

However that may have been, for a year and a half everything seemed to go well: Katya was in love, believed in her work, and was happy; but then I began to notice in her letters unmistakable signs of falling off. It began with Katya's complaining of her companions—this was the first and most ominous symptom; if a young scientific or literary man begins his career with bitter complaints about scientific and literary men, it is a sure sign that he is worn out and not fit for his work. Katya wrote to me that her companions did not attend the rehearsals and never knew their parts; that one could see in every one of them an utter disrespect for the public in the production of absurd plays, and in their behaviour on the stage; that for the sake of quick profit, which was all they talked about, actresses of the serious drama demeaned themselves by singing chansonnettes, while tragic actors sang comic songs making fun of deceived husbands and the pregnant condition of unfaithful wives, and so on. In fact, it was amazing that all this had not yet ruined the provincial stage, and that it could still maintain itself on such a rotten and unsubstantial footing.

In answer I wrote Katya a long and, I must confess, a very boring letter. Among other things, I wrote to her:

'I have more than once happened to converse with old actors, very worthy men, who showed a friendly disposition towards me; from my conversations with them I could understand that their work was controlled not so much by their own intelligence and free choice as by fashion and the mood of the public. The best of them had had to play in their day in tragedy, in operetta, in Parisian farces, and in extravaganzas, and they always seemed equally sure that they were on the right path and that they were of use. So, as you see, the cause of the evil must be sought, not in the actors, but, more deeply, in the art itself and in the attitude of the whole of society to it.'

This letter of mine only irritated Katya. She answered me:

'You and I are singing parts out of different operas. I wrote to you, not of the worthy men who showed a friendly disposition to you, but of a band of knaves who have nothing worthy about them. They are a horde of savages who have got on the stage simply because no one would have accepted them elsewhere, and who call themselves artists simply because they are impudent. There are numbers of dull-witted creatures, drunkards, intriguing schemers and slanderers, but there is not one person of talent among them. I cannot tell you how bitter it is to me that the art I love has fallen into the hands of people I detest; how bitter it is that the best men look on at evil from afar, not caring to come closer, and, instead of intervening, write ponderous commonplaces and utterly useless sermons . . .' And so on, all in the same style.

A little time passed, and I got this letter: 'I have been brutally deceived. I cannot go on living. Dispose of my money as you think best. I loved you as my father and my only friend. Goodbye.'

It turned out that *he*, too, belonged to the 'horde of savages'. Later on, from certain hints, I gathered that there had been an attempt at suicide. I believe Katya tried to poison herself. I imagine that she must have been seriously ill afterwards, as the next letter I got was from Yalta, where she had most probably been sent by the doctors. Her last letter contained a request to send her a thousand roubles to Yalta as quickly as possible, and ended with these words:

'Excuse the gloominess of this letter; yesterday I buried my child.'
After spending about a year in the Crimea, she returned home.

She had been about four years on her travels, and during those four years, I must confess, I had played a rather strange and unenviable part in regard to her. When in earlier days she had told me she was going on the stage, and then wrote to me of her love; when she was periodically overcome by extravagance, and I continually had to send her first one and then two thousand roubles; when she wrote to me of her intention to die, and then of the death of her baby, every time I was at a loss, and all my sympathy for her sufferings found no expression except that, after prolonged reflection, I wrote long, boring letters which I might just as well not have written. And yet I was like a father to her and loved her as a daughter!

Now Katya is living less than half a mile off. She has taken a flat of five rooms, and has installed herself fairly comfortably and in accordance with her taste. If anyone were to undertake to describe her surroundings, the most characteristic note in the picture would be indolence. For the indolent body there are soft couches, soft stools; for indolent feet soft rugs; for indolent eyes faded, dingy, or flat colours; for the indolent soul the walls are hung with a number of cheap fans and trivial pictures, in which the originality of the execution is more conspicuous than the subject; and the room contains a multitude of little tables and shelves filled with utterly useless articles of no value, and shapeless rags in place of curtains . . . All this, together with the dread of bright colours, of symmetry, and of empty space, bears witness not only to spiritual indolence, but also to a corruption of natural taste. For days on end Katya lies on a couch reading, principally novels and stories. She only goes out of the house once a day, in the afternoon, to see me.

I go on working while Katya sits silent not far from me on the sofa, wrapping herself in her shawl, as though she were cold. Either because I find her sympathetic or because I was used to her frequent visits when she was a little girl, her presence does not prevent me from concentrating. From time to time I mechanically ask her some question; she gives very brief replies; or, to rest for a minute, I turn round and watch her as she looks dreamily at some medical journal or the newspaper. And at such moments I notice that her face has lost the old look of confiding trustfulness. Her expression now is cold, apathetic, and absent-minded, like that of passengers who have had to wait too long for a train. She is dressed, as in the old days, simply and beautifully, but carelessly; her dress and her hair show visible traces of the sofas and rocking-chairs in which she spends whole days at a stretch. And she has lost the curiosity she used to have. She has ceased to ask me questions now, as though she had experienced everything in life and was expecting nothing new.

Towards four o'clock there are sounds of movement in the hall and in the drawing-room. Liza has come back from the Conservatoire, and has brought some girlfriends with her. We hear them playing on the piano, trying their voices and laughing; in the dining-room Yegor is laying the table, with the clatter of crockery.

'Goodbye,' says Katya. 'I won't go in and see your people today. They must excuse me. I haven't time. Come and visit me.'

While I am seeing her to the door, she looks me up and down grimly, and says with vexation:

'You are getting thinner and thinner! Why don't you consult a doctor? I'll call at Sergey Fyodorovich's and ask him to have a look at you.'

'There's no need, Katya.'

'I can't think where your people's eyes are! They are a nice lot, I must say!'

She puts on her fur coat abruptly, and as she does so two or three hairpins drop on to the floor from her carelessly arranged hair. She is too lazy and in too great a hurry to do her hair up; she awkwardly stuffs the falling curls under her hat, and goes away.

When I enter the dining-room my wife asks me:

'Was Katya with you just now? Why didn't she come in to see us? It's really strange . . .'

'Mamma,' Liza says to her reproachfully, 'let her alone, if she doesn't want to. We are not going down on our knees to her.'

'It's very neglectful, anyway. To sit for three hours in the study without remembering our existence! But of course she must do as she likes.'

Varya and Liza both hate Katya. This hatred is beyond my comprehension, and probably one would have to be a woman in order to understand it. I am ready to stake my life that of the hundred and fifty young men I see nearly every day in the lecture-theatre, and of the hundred elderly ones I meet every week, hardly one could be found capable of understanding their hatred and aversion for Katya's past—that is, for her having been a mother without being a wife, and for her having had an illegitimate child; and at the same time I cannot recall one woman or girl of my acquaintance who would not consciously or unconsciously harbour such feelings. And this is not because woman is purer or more virtuous than man: why, virtue and purity are not very different from vice if they are not free from evil feeling. I attribute this simply to the backwardness of woman. The mournful feeling of compassion and the pang of conscience experienced by a modern man at the sight of suffering is, to my mind, far greater proof of culture and moral elevation than hatred and aversion. Woman is as tearful and as coarse in her feelings now as she was in the Middle Ages, and to my thinking those who advise that she should be educated like a man are quite right.

My wife also dislikes Katya for having been an actress, for ingratitude, for pride, for eccentricity, and for the numerous vices which one woman can always find in another.

Besides my wife and daughter and me, there are dining with us two or three of my daughter's friends and Aleksandr Adolfovich Gnekker, her admirer and suitor. He is a fair-haired young man under thirty, of medium height, very stout and broad-shouldered, with red whiskers near his ears, and little waxed moustaches which make his plump smooth face look like a toy. He is dressed in a very short jacket, a coloured waistcoat, breeches very full at the top and very narrow at the ankle, with a large check pattern on them, and yellow boots without heels. He has prominent eyes like a crab's, his cravat is like a crab's neck, and I even fancy there is a smell of crab soup about the young man's whole person. He visits us every day, but no one in my family knows anything of his origin nor of the place of his education, nor of his means of livelihood. He neither plays nor sings, but has some connection with music and singing, sells somebody's pianos somewhere, is frequently at the Conservatoire, is acquainted with all the celebrities, and is a steward at the concerts; he criticises music with great authority, and I have noticed that people are eager to agree with him.

Rich people always have dependants hanging about them; the arts and sciences have the same. I believe there is not an art nor a science in the world free from 'foreign bodies' after the style of this Mr Gnekker. I am not a musician, and possibly I am mistaken in regard to Mr Gnekker, of whom, indeed, I know very little. But his air of authority and the dignity with which he takes his stand beside the piano when anyone is playing or singing strike me as very suspicious.

You may be ever so much of a gentleman and a Privy Counsellor, but if you have a daughter you cannot be immune from that petty-bourgeois atmosphere which is so often brought into your house and into your mood by the attentions of suitors, by matchmaking and marriage. I can never reconcile myself, for instance, to the expression of triumph on my wife's face every time Gnekker is in our company, nor can I reconcile myself to the bottles of Lafite, port, and sherry which are only brought out on his account, that he may see with his own eyes the liberal and luxurious way in which we live. I cannot tolerate the habit of spasmodic laughter Liza has picked up at the Conservatoire, and her way of screwing up her eyes whenever there are men in the room. Above all, I cannot understand why a creature utterly alien to my habits, my studies, my whole manner of life, completely different from the people I like, should come and see me every day, and every day should dine with me. My wife and my servants mysteriously whisper that he is a suitor, but still I don't understand his presence; it rouses in me the same wonder and perplexity as if they were to set a Zulu beside me at the table. And it seems strange to me, too, that my daughter, whom I am used to thinking of as a child, should love that cravat, those eyes, those soft cheeks . . .

In the old days I used to like my dinner, or at least was indifferent about it; now it excites in me no feeling but weariness and irritation. Ever since I became an 'Excellency' and one of the Deans of the Faculty my family has for some reason found it necessary to make a complete change in our menu and dining habits. Instead of the simple dishes to which I was accustomed when I was a student and when I was in practice, now they feed me with a purée with little white things like icicles floating about in it, and kidneys stewed in Madeira. My rank as a general and my fame have robbed me for ever of cabbage soup and savoury pies, and goose with apple sauce, and bream with boiled grain. They have robbed me of our maidservant Agasha, a chatty and laughter-loving old woman, instead of whom Yegor, a dull-witted and conceited fellow with a white glove on his right hand, waits at dinner. The intervals between the courses are short, but they seem immensely long because there is nothing to occupy them. There is none of the gaiety of the old days, the spontaneous talk, the jokes, the laughter; there is nothing of mutual affection and the joy which used to animate the children, my wife, and me when we met together at meals. For me, a busy man, dinner was a time of rest and reunion, and for my wife and children a fête—brief indeed, but bright and joyous—in which they knew that for half an hour I belonged, not to science, not to students, but to them alone. Our real exhilaration from one glass of wine is gone for ever, gone is Agasha, gone the bream with boiled grain, gone the uproar that greeted every little startling incident at dinner, such as the cat and dog fighting under the table, or Katya's bandage falling off her face into her soup-plate.

To describe our dinner nowadays is as unpalatable as to eat it. My wife's face wears a look of triumph and affected dignity, and her habitual expression of anxiety. She peers at our plates and says, 'I see you don't care for the joint. Tell me; you don't like it, do you?' and I am obliged to answer: 'There is no need for you to worry, my dear; the meat is very nice.' And she will say: 'You always stand up for me, Nikolay Stepanych, and you never tell the truth. Why is Aleksandr Adolfovich eating so little?' And so on in the same style all through dinner. Liza laughs spasmodically and screws up her eyes. I watch them both, and it is only now at dinner that it becomes absolutely clear to me that the inner life of these two has slipped away out of my ken. I have a feeling as though I had once lived at home with a real wife and children and that now I am dining as a guest in the house of a sham wife, and looking at a sham Liza. A startling change has taken place in both of them; I have missed the long process by which that change was effected, and it is no wonder that I can make nothing of it. Why did that change take place? I don't know. Perhaps the whole trouble is that God has not given my wife and daughter the same strength of character as me. From childhood I have been accustomed to resisting external influences, and have steeled myself pretty thoroughly. Such catastrophes in life as fame, the rank of a general, the transition from comfort to living beyond our means, acquaintance with celebrities, etc., have scarcely affected me, and I have remained safe and sound; but on my wife and Liza, who have not been through the same hardening process and are weak, all this has fallen like an avalanche of snow, overwhelming them.

Gnekker and the young ladies talk of fugues, of counterpoint, of singers and pianists, of Bach and Brahms, while my wife, afraid of their suspecting her of ignorance of music, smiles to them sympathetically and mutters: 'That's exquisite . . . really! You don't say so! . . .' Gnekker eats with solid dignity, jests with solid dignity, and condescendingly listens to the remarks of the young ladies. From time to time he is moved to speak in bad French, and then, for some reason or other, he thinks it necessary to address me as '*Votre Excellence*'.

And I am glum. Evidently I am a constraint to them and they are a constraint to me. I have never in my earlier days had a close knowledge of class antagonism, but now I am tormented by something of that sort. I am on the look-out for nothing but bad qualities in Gnekker; I quickly find them, and fret at the thought that a man not of my circle is sitting here as my daughter's suitor. His presence has a bad influence on me in other ways, too. As a rule, when I am alone or in the society of people I like, I never think of my own achievements, or, if I do recall them, they seem to me as trivial as though I had only completed my studies yesterday; but in the presence of people like Gnekker my achievements in science seem to be a lofty mountain the top of which vanishes into the clouds, while at its foot Gnekkers are running about scarcely visible to the naked eye.

After dinner I go into my study and there smoke my pipe, the only one in the whole day, the sole relic of my old bad habit of puffing from morning till night. While I am smoking my wife comes in and sits down to talk to me. Just as in the morning, I know beforehand what our conversation is going to be about.

'I must talk to you seriously, Nikolay Stepanych,' she begins. 'I mean about Liza . . . Why don't you pay attention?'

'To what?'

'You pretend to notice nothing. But that is not right. We can't shirk responsibility . . . Gnekker has intentions in regard to Liza . . . What will you say?'

'That he is a bad man I can't say, because I don't know him, but that I don't like him I have told you a thousand times already.'

'But you can't . . . you can't!'

She gets up and walks about in excitement.

'You can't take that attitude to a serious step,' she says. 'When it is a question of our daughter's happiness we must lay aside all personal feeling. I know you do not like him . . . Very good . . . if we refuse him now, if we break it all off, how can you be sure that Liza will not have a grievance against us all her life? Suitors are not plentiful nowadays, goodness knows, and it may happen that no other match will turn up . . . He is very much in love with Liza, and she seems to like him . . . Of course, he has no settled position, but that can't be helped. Please God, in time he will get one. He is of good family and well off.'

'Where did you learn that?'

'He told us so. His father has a large house in Kharkov and an estate in the neighbourhood. In short, Nikolay Stepanych, you absolutely must go to Kharkov.'

'What for?'

'You will find out all about him there . . . You know the professors there; they will help you. I would go myself, but I am a woman. I cannot . . .'

'I am not going to Kharkov,' I say morosely.

My wife is frightened, and a look of intense suffering comes into her face.

'For God's sake, Nikolay Stepanych,' she implores me, with tears in her voice—'for God's sake, take this burden off me! I am so worried!'

It is painful to look at her.

'Very well, Varya,' I say affectionately, 'if you wish it, then certainly I will go to Kharkov and do all you want.'

She presses her handkerchief to her eyes and goes off to her room to cry, and I am left alone.

A little later lights are brought in. The armchair and the lampshade cast familiar shadows that have long grown wearisome on the walls and on the floor, and when I look at them I feel as though the night had come and with it my accursed sleeplessness. I lie on my bed, then get up and walk about the room, then lie down again. As a rule it is after dinner, at the approach of evening, that my nervous excitement reaches its highest pitch. For no reason I begin crying and burying my head in the pillow. At such times I am afraid that someone may come in; I am afraid of suddenly dying; I am ashamed of my tears, and altogether there is something unbearable in my soul. I feel that I can no longer stand the sight of my lamp, or my books, or the shadows on the floor. I cannot bear the sound of the voices coming from the drawing-room. Some invisible and incomprehensible force is roughly thrusting me out of my flat. I leap up, dress hurriedly, and cautiously, that my family may not notice, slip out into the street. Where am I to go?

The answer to that question has long been ready in my brain. To Katya.

III

As a rule she is lying on the sofa or in a lounge-chair, reading. Seeing me, she raises her head languidly, sits up, and offers me her hand.

'You are always lying down,' I say, after pausing and taking breath. 'That's not good for you. You ought to occupy yourself with something.'

'What?'

'I say you ought to occupy yourself in some way.'

'With what? A woman can be nothing but a simple worker or an actress.'

'Well, if you can't be a worker, be an actress.'

She says nothing.

'You ought to get married,' I say, half in jest.

'There is no one to marry. There's no reason to, either.'

'You can't live like this.'

'Without a husband? Much that matters; I could have as many men as I like if I wanted to.'

'That's nasty, Katya.'

'What is nasty?'

'Why, what you have just said.'

Noticing that I am hurt and wishing to efface the disagreeable impression, Katya says:

'Let's go; come this way.'

She takes me into a very snug little room, and says, pointing to the writing-table:

'Look . . . I have got that ready for you. You shall work here. Come here every day and bring your work with you. They only hinder you there at home. Will you work here? Would you like to?'

Not to wound her by refusing, I answer that I will work here, and that I like the room very much. Then we both sit down in the snug little room and begin talking.

The warm, snug surroundings and the presence of a sympathetic person do not, as in the old days, arouse in me a feeling of pleasure, but an intense impulse to complain and grumble. I feel for some reason that if I lament and complain I shall feel better.

'Things are in a bad way with me, my dear—very bad . . .' I begin with a sigh.

'What is it?'

'You see how it is, my dear; the best and holiest right of kings is the right of mercy. And I have always felt myself a king, since I have made unlimited use of that right. I have never judged, I have been indulgent, I have readily forgiven everyone, right and left. Where others have protested and expressed indignation, I have only advised and persuaded. All my life it has been my endeavour that my company should not be a burden to my family, to my students, to my colleagues, to my servants. And I know that this attitude to people has had a good influence on all who have chanced to come into contact with me. But now I am not a king. Something is happening to me that is only excusable in a slave; day and night my brain is haunted by evil thoughts, and feelings such as I never knew before are brooding in my soul. I am full of hatred, and contempt, and indignation, and loathing, and dread. I have become excessively severe, exacting, irritable, ungracious, suspicious. Even things that in the old days would have provoked me only to an unnecessary jest and a good-natured laugh now arouse an oppressive feeling in me. My reasoning, too, has undergone a change: in the old days I despised money; now I harbour an evil feeling, not towards money, but towards the rich, as though they were to blame: in the old days I hated violence and tyranny, but now I hate the men who make use of violence, as though they alone were to blame, and not all of us who do not know how to educate each other. What does this mean? If these new ideas and new feelings have come from a change of convictions, what is that change due to? Can the world have grown worse and I better, or was I blind before and indifferent? If this change is the result of a general decline of physical and intellectual powers—I am ill, you know, and every day I am losing weight—my posi-tion is pitiable; it means that my new ideas are morbid and abnormal; I ought to be ashamed of them and think them of no consequence . . .'

'Illness has nothing to do with it,' Katya interrupts me; 'it's simply that your eyes are opened, that's all. You have seen what in the old days, for some reason, you refused to see. To my mind, what you ought to do, first of all, is to break with your family for good, and go away.'

'You are talking nonsense.'

'You don't love them; why be hypocritical? Can you call them a fam-ily? Nonentities! If they died today, no one would notice their absence tomorrow.'

Katya despises my wife and Liza as much as they hate her. One can hardly talk nowadays of people's having a right to despise one another. But if one looks at it from Katya's standpoint and recognises such a right,

114

one can see she has as much right to despise my wife and Liza as they have to hate her.

'Nonentities,' she goes on. 'Have you had dinner today? How was it they did not forget to tell you it was ready? How is it they still remember your existence?'

'Katya,' I say sternly, 'I beg you to be silent.'

'You think I enjoy talking about them? I should be glad not to know them at all. Heed my advice, my dear: give it all up and go away. Go abroad. The sooner the better.'

'What nonsense! What about the University?'

'The University, too. What is it to you? There's no sense in it, anyway. You have been lecturing for thirty years, and where are your pupils? Are many of them celebrated men of science? Count them up! And to multiply the doctors who exploit ignorance and pile up hundreds of thousands for themselves, there is no need to be a good and talented man. You are not wanted.'

'Good heavens! how harsh you are!' I cry in horror. 'How harsh you are! Be quiet or I will go away! I don't know how to answer the harsh things you say!'

The maid comes in and summons us to tea. At the samovar our conversation, thank God, changes. After voicing my grumble, I have a longing to give way to another weakness of old age, reminiscences. I tell Katya about my past, and to my great astonishment tell her incidents which, till then, I did not suspect of being still preserved in my memory, and she listens to me with tenderness, with pride, holding her breath. I am particularly fond of telling her how I was educated in a seminary and dreamed of going to the University.

'At times I used to walk about our seminary garden . . .' I tell her. 'If from some faraway tavern the wind floated sounds of a song and the squeaking of an accordion, or a sledge with bells dashed by the garden fence, it was quite enough to send a rush of happiness, filling not only my heart, but even my stomach, my legs, my arms . . . I would listen to the accordion or the bells dying away in the distance and imagine myself a doctor, and paint pictures, one better than another. And here, as you see, my dreams have come true. I have had more than I dared to dream of. For thirty years I have been a much-loved professor, I have had splendid comrades, I have enjoyed fame and honour. I have loved, married from passionate love, have had children. In fact, looking back upon it, I see my whole life as a fine composition arranged with talent. Now all that is left to me is not to spoil the end. For that I must die like a man. If death is really a thing to dread, I must meet it as a teacher, a man of science, and a citizen of a Christian country ought to meet it, with courage and untroubled soul. But I am spoiling the end. I am sinking, I fly to you, I beg for help, and you tell me "Sink; that is what you ought to do." '

But here there comes a ring at the front door. Katya and I recognise it, and say:

'It must be Mikhail Fyodorovich.'

And a minute later my colleague, the philologist Mikhail Fyodorovich, a tall, well-built man of fifty, clean-shaven, with thick grey hair and black eyebrows, walks in. He is a good-natured man and an excellent comrade. He comes of a fortunate and talented old noble family which has played a prominent part in the history of our literature and enlightenment. He is himself intelligent, talented, and very highly educated, but has his oddities. To a certain extent we are all odd and eccentric, but in his oddities there is something exceptional, apt to cause anxiety among his acquaintances. I know a good many people for whom his oddities completely obscure his good qualities.

Coming in to us, he slowly takes off his gloves and says in his velvety bass:

'Good evening. Are you having tea? That's just what I need. It's diabolically cold.'

Then he sits down at the table, takes a glass, and at once begins talking. What is most characteristic in his manner of talking is the continually jesting tone, a sort of mixture of philosophy and drollery as in Shakespeare's gravediggers. He is always talking about serious things, but he never speaks seriously. His judgements are always harsh and railing, but, thanks to his soft, even, jesting tone, the harshness and abuse do not jar upon the ear, and one soon grows used to them. Every evening he brings with him some five or six anecdotes from university life, and he usually begins with them when he sits down at the table.

'Oh, Lord!' he sighs, twitching his black eyebrows ironically. 'What comic people there are in the world!'

'Well?' asks Katya.

'As I was coming from my lecture this morning I met that old idiot N. N—— on the stairs . . . He was going along as usual, sticking out his chin like a horse, looking for someone to listen to his grumblings at his migraine, at his wife, and his students who won't attend his lectures. "Oh," I thought, "he has seen me—I am done for now; it is all up . . ." '

And so on in the same style. Or he will begin like this:

'I was yesterday at our friend Z. Z——'s public lecture. I wonder how it is our Alma Mater—don't speak of it after dark—dare display in public such noodles and patent dullards as that Z. Z——. Why, he is a European fool! Upon my word, you could not find another like him all over Europe! He lectures—can you imagine?—as though he were sucking a sugar-stick—sue, sue, sue . . . He is in a nervous funk; he can hardly decipher his own manuscript; his poor little thoughts crawl along like a bishop on a bicycle, and, what's worse, you can never make out what he is trying to say. The deadly dullness is awful, the very flies expire. It can only be compared with the boredom in the assembly-hall at the yearly meeting when the traditional address is read—damn it!'

And at once an abrupt transition:

'Three years ago—Nikolay Stepanovich here will remember it—I had to deliver that address. It was hot, stifling, my uniform cut me under the arms—it was deadly! I read for half an hour, for an hour, for an hour and a half, for two hours . . . "Come," I thought; "thank God, there are only ten pages left!" And at the end there were four pages that there was no need to read, and I reckoned to leave them out. "So there are only six really," I thought; "that is, only six pages left to read." But, only fancy, I chanced to glance before me, and, sitting in the front row, side by side, were a general with a ribbon on his breast and a bishop. The poor beggars were numb with boredom; they were staring with their eyes wide open to keep awake, and yet they were trying to put on an expression of attention and to pretend that they understood what I was saying and liked it. "Well," I thought, "since you like it you shall have it! I'll pay you out;" so I just gave them those four pages too.'

As is usual with ironical people, when he talks, nothing in his face smiles but his eyes and eyebrows. At such times there is no trace of hatred or spite in his eyes, but a great deal of humour, and that peculiar fox-like slyness which is only to be noticed in very observant people. Since I am speaking about his eyes, I've noticed another peculiarity in them. When he takes a glass from Katya, or listens to her speaking, or gazes after her as she goes out of the room for a moment, I notice in his eyes something gentle, beseeching, pure . . .

The maidservant takes away the samovar and puts on the table a large piece of cheese, some fruit, and a bottle of Crimean champagne—a rather poor wine of which Katya had grown fond in the Crimea. Mikhail Fyodorovich takes two packs of cards off the whatnot and begins to play patience. According to him, some varieties of patience require great concentration and attention, yet while he lays out the cards he continues to divert himself with talk. Katya watches his cards attentively, and more by gesture than by words helps him in his play. She drinks no more than a couple of glasses of wine the whole evening; I drink a quarter of a glass, and the rest of the bottle falls to the share of Mikhail Fyodorovich, who can drink a great deal and never get drunk.

Over our patience we settle various questions, principally of the higher order, and what we care for most of all—that is, science and learning—comes in for the roughest treatment.

'Science, thank God, has outlived its day,' says Mikhail Fyodorovich emphatically. 'Its song is sung. Yes, indeed. Mankind begins to feel the need to replace it by something else. It has grown on the soil of superstition, been nourished by superstition, and is now just as much the quintessence of superstition as its defunct grandams, alchemy, metaphysics, and philosophy. And, after all, what has it given to mankind? Why, the difference between the learned Europeans and the Chinese who have no science at all is trifling, purely external. The Chinese know nothing of science, but what have they lost thereby?'

'Flies know nothing of science, either,' I observe, 'but what of that?'

'There is no need to be angry, Nikolay Stepanych. I only say this here between ourselves . . . I am more careful than you think, and I am not going to say this in public—God forbid! The superstition exists in the multitude that the arts and sciences are superior to agriculture, commerce, superior to handicrafts. Our sect is maintained by that superstition, and it is not for you and me to destroy it. God forbid!'

After patience the younger generation comes in for a dressing too.

'Our audiences have degenerated,' sighs Mikhail Fyodorovich. 'Not to speak of ideals and all the rest of it, if only they were capable of work and rational thought! In fact, it's a case of "I look with mournful eyes on the young men of today." '

'Yes; they have degenerated horribly,' Katya agrees. 'Tell me, have you had one man of distinction among them for the last five or ten years?'

'I don't know how it is with the other professors, but I can't remember any among mine.'

'I have seen in my day many of your students and young scientists and many actors—well, I have never once been so fortunate as to meet—I won't say a hero or a man of talent, but even an interesting man. It's all the same grey mediocrity, puffed up with self-conceit.'

All this talk of degeneration always affects me as though I had accidentally overheard offensive talk about my own daughter. It offends me that these charges are wholesale, and rest on such worn-out commonplaces, on such wordy vapourings as degeneration and absence of ideals, or on references to the splendours of the past. Every accusation, even if it is uttered in ladies' society, ought to be formulated with all possible precision, or it is not an accusation, but idle disparagement, unworthy of decent people.

I am an old man, I have been lecturing for thirty years, but I notice neither degeneration nor lack of ideals, and I don't find that the present is worse than the past. My porter Nikolay, whose experience of this subject has its value, says that the students of today are neither better nor worse than those of the past.

If I were asked what I don't like in my pupils of today, I should answer the question, not straight off and not at length, but with a certain precision. I know their failings, and so have no need to resort to vague generalities. I don't like their smoking, drinking hard liquor, marrying late, and often being so irresponsible and careless that they will let one of their number be starving in their midst while they neglect to pay their subscriptions to the Students' Aid Society. They don't know modern languages, and they don't express themselves correctly in Russian; as recently as yesterday my colleague, the professor of hygiene, complained to me that he had to give twice as many lectures, because the students had a very poor knowledge of physics and were utterly ignorant of meteorology. They readily submit to the influence of the latest new writers, even when they are not first-rate, but they take absolutely no interest in classics such as Shakespeare, Marcus Aurelius, Epictetus, or Pascal, and this inability to distinguish the great from the small betrays their ignorance of practical life more than anything. All difficult questions that have more or less a social character (for instance the migration question) they settle by studying monographs on the subject, but not by way of scientific investigation or experiment, though that method is at their disposal and is more in keeping with their calling. They gladly become ward-surgeons, assistants, demonstrators, external teachers, and are ready to fill such posts till they are forty, though independence, a sense of freedom and personal initiative are no less necessary in science than, for instance, in art or commerce. I have pupils and listeners, but no successors and helpers, and so I love them and am touched by them, but am not proud of them. And so on, and so forth . . .

Such shortcomings, however numerous they may be, can give rise to a pessimistic or quarrelsome mood only in a faint-hearted and timid man. All these failings have a casual, transitory character, and are completely dependent on conditions of life; in some ten years they will have disappeared or given way to other fresh defects, which are all inevitable and will in their turn alarm the faint-hearted. The students' sins often vex me, but that vexation is nothing in comparison with the joy I have been experiencing now for the last thirty years when I talk to my pupils, lecture to them, observe their relationships, and compare them with people from other circles.

Mikhail Fyodorovich speaks evil of everything. Katya listens, and neither of them notices into what depths the apparently innocent diversion of finding fault with their neighbours is gradually drawing them. They are not conscious how by degrees simple talk passes into malicious mockery and jeering, and how they are both beginning to adopt the habits and methods of slander.

'Such killing types one meets with,' says Mikhail Fyodorovich. 'I went yesterday to our friend Yegor Petrovich's, and there I found a studious gentleman, one of your medicals in his third year, I believe. Such a face! . . . in the Dobrolyubov style, the imprint of profound thought on his brow; we got into talk. "Such doings, young man," said I. "I've read", said I, "that some German—I've forgotten his name—has created from the human brain a new kind of alkaloid, idiotine." What do you think? He believed it, and there was positively an expression of respect on his face, as though to say, "See what we fellows can do!" And the other day I went to the theatre. I took my seat. In the next row directly in front of me were sitting two men: one of "us fellows" and apparently a law student, the other a shaggy-looking figure, a medical student. The latter was as drunk as a cobbler. He did not look at the stage at all. He was dozing with his nose on his shirt-front. But as soon as an actor begins loudly reciting a monologue, or simply raises his voice, our friend starts, pokes his neighbour in the ribs, and asks, "What is he saying? Is it elevating?" "Yes," answers one of our fellows. "B-r-r-bravo!" roars the medical student. "Elevating! Bravo!" He had gone to the theatre, you see, the drunken blockhead, not for the sake of art, but for elevation! He wanted noble sentiments.'

Katya listens and laughs. She has a strange laugh; she catches her breath in rhythmically regular gasps, very much as though she were playing the accordion, and nothing in her face is laughing but her nostrils. I grow depressed and don't know what to say. Beside myself, I flare up, leap from my seat, and cry:

'Do leave off! Why are you sitting there like two toads, poisoning the air with your breath? Give over!'

And without waiting for them to finish their gossip I prepare to go home. And, indeed, it is high time: it is past ten.

'I will stay a little longer,' says Mikhail Fyodorovich. 'Will you allow me, Yekaterina Vladimirovna?'

'I will,' answers Katya.

'*Bene!* In that case send for another little bottle.'

They both accompany me with candles to the hall, and while I put on my fur coat, Mikhail Fyodorovich says:

'You have grown dreadfully thin and older looking, Nikolay Stepanovich. What's the matter with you? Are you ill?'

'Yes; I am not very well.'

'And you are not doing anything for it . . .' Katya puts in grimly.

'Why don't you? You can't go on like that! God helps those who help themselves, my dear fellow. Remember me to your wife and daughter, and make my apologies for not having been to see them. In a day or two, before I go abroad, I shall come to say goodbye. I shall be sure to. I am going away next week.'

I come away from Katya, irritated and alarmed by what has been said about my being ill, and dissatisfied with myself. I ask myself whether I really ought not to consult one of my colleagues. And at once I imagine how my colleague, after listening to me, would walk away to the window without speaking, would think a moment, then turn round to me and, trying to prevent my reading the truth in his face, would say in a careless tone: 'So far I see nothing serious, but at the same time, *collega*, I advise you to lay aside your work . . .' And that would deprive me of my last hope.

Who is without hope? Now that I am diagnosing my illness and prescribing for myself, from time to time I hope that I am deceived by my own ignorance, that I am mistaken about the albumen and the sugar I find, and about my heart and the swellings I have twice noticed in the mornings; when with the fervour of the hypochondriac I look through the textbooks of therapeutics and take a different medicine every day, I keep fancying that I shall hit upon something comforting. All that is petty.

Whether the sky is covered with clouds or the moon and the stars are shining, I turn my eyes towards it every evening and think that death will take me soon. One would expect that my thoughts at such times ought to be deep as the sky, brilliant, striking . . . But no! I think about myself, about my wife, about Liza, Gnekker, the students, people in general; my thoughts are evil, petty, I am insincere with myself, and at such times my theory of life may be expressed in the words the celebrated Arakcheyev said in one of his private letters: 'Nothing good can exist in the world without evil, and there is always more evil than good.' That is, everything is disgusting; there is nothing to live for, and the sixty-two years I have already lived must be reckoned as wasted. I catch myself in these thoughts, and try to persuade myself that they are accidental, temporary, and not deeply rooted in me, but at once I think:

'If so, what drives you every evening to those two toads?'

And I vow to myself that I will never go to Katya's again, though I know I shall go next evening.

Ringing the bell at the door and going upstairs, I feel that I have no family now and no desire to bring it back again. It is clear that the new Arakcheyev thoughts are not casual, temporary visitors, but have possession of my whole being. With my conscience ill at ease, dejected, languid, hardly able to move my limbs, feeling as though tons were added to my weight, I get into bed and soon fall asleep.

And then—insomnia . . .

IV

Summer begins and life is changed.

One fine morning Liza comes in to me and says in a jesting tone:

'Come, Your Excellency! We are ready.'

My Excellency is conducted into the street, and seated in a cab. As I go along, having nothing to do, I read the signboards from right to left. The word for 'inn', 'Traktir', reads 'Ritkart'; that could provide a baronial surname: Baroness Ritkart. Further on I drive through fields, by the graveyard, which makes absolutely no impression on me, though I shall soon lie in it; then I drive by forests and again by fields. There is nothing of interest. After two hours of driving, My Excellency is conducted into the lower storey of a summer villa and installed in a small, very cheerful little room with light blue wallpaper.

At night there is sleeplessness as before, but in the morning I do not put a good face upon it nor listen to my wife, but lie in bed. I do not sleep, but lie in the drowsy, half-conscious condition in which you know you are not asleep, but dreaming. At midday I get up and from habit sit down at my desk, but I do not work now; I amuse myself with French books in yellow covers, sent to me by Katya. Of course, it would be more patriotic to read Russian authors, but I must confess I cherish no particular liking for them. With the exception of two or three of the older writers, all our literature of today strikes me as not being literature, but a special sort of cottage industry, which exists simply in order to be encouraged, though people do not readily make use of its products. The very best of these cottage products cannot be called remarkable and cannot be sincerely praised without qualification. I must say the same of all the literary novelties I have read during the last ten or fifteen years; not one of them is remarkable, and not one of them can be praised without a 'but'. Cleverness, a good tone, but no talent; talent, a good tone, but no cleverness; or talent, cleverness, but not a good tone.

I don't say the French books have talent, cleverness, and a good tone. They don't satisfy me, either. But they are not so tedious as the Russian, and it is not unusual to find in them the chief element of artistic creation—the feeling of personal freedom which is lacking in the Russian authors. I don't remember one new book in which the author does not try from the first page to entangle himself in all sorts of conditions and contracts with his conscience. One is afraid to speak of the naked body; another ties himself up hand and foot in psychological analysis; a third must have a 'warm attitude to man'; a fourth purposely scrawls whole pages full of nature descriptions, so that he may not be suspected of writing tendentiously . . . One is bent upon being middle-class in his work, another must be a nobleman, and so on. There is intentionality, circumspection, and self-will, but they have neither the independence nor the courage to write freely, and therefore there is no creativeness.

All this applies to what are called *belles-lettres*.

As for serious treatises in Russian on sociology, for instance, on art, and so on, I do not read them simply from timidity. In my childhood and early youth I had for some reason a terror of doorkeepers and attendants at the theatre, and that terror has remained with me to this day. I am afraid of them even now. It is said that we are only afraid of what we do not understand. And, indeed, it is very difficult to understand why doorkeepers and theatre attendants are so self-important, haughty, and majestically impolite. I feel exactly the same vague terror when I read serious articles. Their extraordinary self-importance, their bantering lordly tone, their familiar manner towards foreign authors, their ability to spin idle words with dignity—all that is beyond my understanding; it is intimidating and utterly unlike the modesty and the quiet, gentlemanly tone to which I am accustomed when I read the works of our medical and scientific writers. It oppresses me to read not only the articles written by serious Russians, but even works translated or edited by them. The pretentious, edifying tone of the prefaces; the redundancy of remarks made by the translator, which prevent me from concentrating my attention; the question marks and '*sic*' in parenthesis scattered all over the book or article by the liberal translator, are to my mind an outrage on the author and on my independence as a reader.

Once I was summoned as an expert to a circuit court; in an interval one of my fellow-experts drew my attention to the rudeness of the public prosecutor towards the defendants, among whom there were two ladies of good education. I believe I did not exaggerate at all when I told him that the prosecutor's manner was no ruder than that of the authors of serious articles to one another. Their manners are, indeed, so rude that I cannot speak of them without distaste. They treat one another and the writers they criticise either with superfluous respect, at the sacrifice of their own dignity, or, on the contrary, with far more ruthlessness than I have shown in my notes and my thoughts in regard to my future son-in-law Gnekker. Accusations of insanity, of impure intentions, and, indeed, of every sort of crime, form an habitual ornament of serious articles. And that, as young medical men are fond of saying in their monographs, is the *ultima ratio*! Such ways must inevitably have an effect on the morals of the younger generation of writers, and so I am not at all surprised that in the new works with which our literature has been enriched during the last ten or fifteen years the heroes drink too much vodka and the heroines are not over-chaste.

I read French books, and I look out of the open window; I can see the spikes of my garden fence, two or three scraggy trees, and beyond the fence the road, the fields, and then a broad stretch of pine-wood. Often I admire a boy and girl, both flaxen-headed and ragged, who clamber on the fence and laugh at my baldness. In their shining little eyes I read, just as Elisha heard, 'Go up, thou bald head!' They are almost the only people who care nothing for my celebrity or my rank.

Visitors do not come to me every day now. I will only mention the visits of Nikolay and Pyotr Ignatyevich. Nikolay usually comes to me on holidays, with some pretext of business, though really to see me. He arrives very tipsy, a thing which never befalls him in the winter.

'What have you to tell me?' I ask, going out to him in the hall.

'Your Excellency!' he says, pressing his hand to his heart and looking at me with the ecstasy of a lover—'Your Excellency! God be my witness! Strike me dead on the spot! *Gaudeamus igitur juvenestus!*'

And he greedily kisses me on the shoulder, on the sleeve, and on the buttons.

'Is everything going well?' I ask him.

'Your Excellency! So help me God! . . .'

He persists in swearing by God's name for no sort of reason, and soon bores me, so I send him away to the kitchen, where they give him dinner.

Pyotr Ignatyevich visits me on holidays, too, with the special object of seeing me and sharing his thoughts with me. He usually sits down near my desk, modest, neat, and reasonable, and does not venture to cross his legs or put his elbows on the desk. All the time, in a soft, even, little voice, in rounded bookish phrases, he tells me various, to his mind, very interesting and piquant items of news which he has read in the magazines and journals. They are all alike and may be reduced to this type: 'A Frenchman has made a discovery; someone else, a German, has denounced him, proving that the discovery was made in 1870 by some American; while a third person, also a German, trumps them both by proving they both had made fools of themselves, mistaking bubbles of air for dark pigment under the microscope.' Even when he wants to amuse me, Pyotr Ignatyevich tells me things in the same lengthy, circumstantial manner as though he were defending a thesis, enumerating in detail the literary sources from which he is deriving his narrative, doing his utmost to be accurate as to the date and number of the journals and the name of everyone concerned, invariably mentioning it in full—Jean-Jacques Petit, never simply Petit. Sometimes he stays to dinner with us, and then during the whole of dinner-time he goes on telling me the same sort of piquant anecdotes, reducing everyone at table to a state of dejected boredom. If Gnekker and Liza begin talking before him of fugues and counterpoint, Brahms and Bach, he drops his eyes modestly, and is overcome with embarrassment; he is ashamed that such trivial subjects should be discussed in the presence of such serious people as him and me.

In my current state of mind five minutes of him is enough to sicken me as though I had been seeing and hearing him for an eternity. I hate the poor fellow. His soft, smooth voice and bookish language exhaust me, and his stories stupefy me . . . He cherishes the best of feelings for me, and talks to me simply in order to give me pleasure, and I repay him by peering at him as though I wanted to hypnotise him, and think, 'Go, go, go! . . .' But he is not amenable to thought-suggestion, and sits on and on and on . . .

While he is with me I can never shake off the thought, 'It's possible when I die he will be appointed to succeed me,' and my poor lecture-hall presents itself to me as an oasis in which the spring is dried up; and I am ungracious, silent, and surly with Pyotr Ignatyevich, as though he were to blame for such thoughts, and not I myself. When he begins, as usual, to extol German scientists, instead of making fun of him good-humouredly, as I used to do, I mutter sullenly:

'Asses, your Germans! . . .'

That is like the late Professor Nikita Krylov, who once, when he was bathing with Pirogov at Revel and vexed at the water being very cold, burst out with, 'Scoundrels, these Germans!' I behave badly with Pyotr Ignatyevich, and only when he is going away, and from the window I catch a glimpse of his grey hat behind the garden fence, I want to call out and say, 'Forgive me, my dear fellow!'

Dinner is even drearier than in the winter. Gnekker, whom I now hate and despise, dines with us almost every day. I used to endure his presence in silence, now I aim cutting remarks at him which make my wife and daughter blush. Carried away by evil feeling, I often say things that are simply stupid, and I don't know why I say them. So on one occasion it happened that I stared a long time at Gnekker, and, apropos of nothing, I fired off:

'An eagle may perchance swoop lower than a hen,
But never will the fowl soar upwards to the clouds . . .'

And the most vexatious thing is that the fowl Gnekker shows himself much cleverer than the eagle professor. Knowing that my wife and daughter are on his side, he adopts a course of meeting my gibes with condescending silence, as though to say:

'The old chap is in his dotage; what's the use of talking to him?'

Or he makes fun of me good-naturedly. It is remarkable how petty a man may become! I am capable of dreaming all dinner-time of how Gnekker will turn out to be an adventurer, how my wife and Liza will come to see their mistake, and how I will taunt them—and such absurd thoughts at a time when I am standing with one foot in the grave!

126

There are now, too, misunderstandings of which in the old days I had no idea except from hearsay. Though I am ashamed of it, I will describe one that occurred the other day after dinner.

I was sitting in my room smoking a pipe; my wife came in as usual, sat down, and began saying what a good thing it would be for me to go to Kharkov now while it is warm and I have free time, and there find out what sort of person our Gnekker is.

'Very good; I will go,' I assented.

My wife, pleased with me, got up and was going to the door, but turned back and said:

'By the way, I have another favour to ask of you. I know you will be angry, but it is my duty to warn you . . . Forgive my saying it, Nikolay Stepanych, but all our neighbours and acquaintances have begun talking about your being so often at Katya's. She is clever and well-educated; I don't deny that her company may be agreeable; but at your age and with your social position it seems strange that you should find pleasure in her society . . . Besides, she has such a reputation that . . .'

All the blood suddenly drained from my brain, my eyes flashed fire, I leaped up and, clutching at my head and stamping my feet, shouted in a voice unlike my own:

'Let me alone! let me alone! let me alone!'

Probably my face was terrible, my voice was strange, for my wife suddenly turned pale and began shrieking aloud in a despairing voice that was also unlike her own. Liza, Gnekker, then Yegor, came running in at our shouts . . .

'Let me alone!' I cried; 'let me alone! Go away!'

My legs turned numb as though they had ceased to exist; I felt myself falling into someone's arms; for a little while I still heard weeping, then sank into a swoon which lasted two or three hours.

Now about Katya; she comes to see me every day towards evening, and of course neither the neighbours nor our acquaintances can avoid noticing it. She comes in for a minute and carries me off for a drive with her. She has her own horse and a new chaise bought this summer. Altogether she lives in a grand manner; she has taken an expensive detached villa with a large garden, and has brought all her town furniture with her; she has two maids and a coachman . . . I often ask her:

'Katya, what will you live on when you have squandered your father's money?'

'Then we shall see,' she answers.

127

'That money, my dear, deserves to be treated more seriously. It was earned by a good man, by honest labour.'

'You have told me that already. I know it.'

At first we drive through the open country, then through the pine-wood which is visible from my window. Nature seems to me as beautiful as it always has been, though some evil spirit whispers to me that these pines and fir-trees, birds and white clouds in the sky will not notice my absence when in three or four months I am dead. Katya loves driving, and it is pleasant that the weather is fine and that I am sitting beside her. She is in good spirits and does not say harsh things.

'You are a very good man, Nikolay Stepanych,' she says. 'You are a rare specimen, and there isn't an actor who would understand how to play you. Me or Mikhail Fyodorych, for instance, any poor actor could do, but not you. And I envy you, I envy you horribly! Do you know what I am? What?'

She ponders for a minute, and then asks me:

'Nikolay Stepanych, I am a negative phenomenon! Yes?'

'Yes,' I answer.

'Hm! what am I to do?'

What answer was I to make her? It is easy to say 'work', or 'give your possessions to the poor', or 'know thyself', and because it is so easy to say that, I don't know what to answer.

My colleagues when they teach therapeutics advise 'the individual study of each separate case'. One has but to obey this advice to realise that the methods recommended in textbooks as the best and as providing a safe basis for treatment turn out to be quite unsuitable in individual cases. It is just the same in moral ailments.

But I must make some answer, and I say:

'You have too much free time, my dear; you absolutely must take up some occupation. After all, why shouldn't you be an actress again if it is your vocation?'

'I cannot!'

'Your tone and manner suggest that you are a victim. I don't like that, my dear; it is your own fault. Remember, you began by falling out with people and methods, but you have done nothing to make either better. You did not struggle against evil, but were cast down by it, and you are not the victim of the struggle, but of your own impotence. Well, of course you were young and inexperienced then; now it may all be different. Yes, really, go on the stage. You will work, you will serve a sacred art.'

'Don't pretend, Nikolay Stepanych,' Katya interrupts me. 'Let us make a compact once and for all; we will talk about actors, actresses, and authors, but we will let art alone. You are a splendid and rare person, but you don't know enough about art to regard it as really sacred. You have no instinct or feeling for art. You have been hard at work all your life, and have not had time to acquire that feeling. Anyway ... I don't like talk about art,' she goes on nervously. 'I don't like it! And, my goodness, how they have vulgarised it!'

'Who has vulgarised it?'

'Actors have vulgarised it by drunkenness, the newspapers by their familiar attitude, clever people by philosophy.'

'Philosophy has nothing to do with it.'

'Yes, it has. If anyone starts philosophising, that shows he lacks understanding.'

To avoid bitterness I hasten to change the subject, and then sit a long time silent. Only when we are driving out of the wood and turning towards Katya's villa I go back to my former question, and say:

'You still have not answered me, why you don't want to go on the stage.'

'Nikolay Stepanych, this is cruel!' she cries, and suddenly flushes all over. 'You want me to tell you the truth out loud? Very well, if ... if you want it! I have no talent! No talent and ... and a great deal of vanity! So there!'

After making this confession she turns her face away from me, and to hide the trembling of her hands tugs violently at the reins.

As we are driving towards her villa we see Mikhail Fyodorovich walking near the gate, impatiently awaiting us.

'That Mikhail Fyodorych again!' says Katya with vexation. 'Do rid me of him, please! I am sick and tired of him ... bother him!'

Mikhail Fyodorovich ought to have gone abroad long ago, but he puts off going from week to week. Of late there have been certain changes in him. He looks, as it were, sunken, has taken to drinking until he is tipsy, a thing which never used to happen to him before, and his black eyebrows are beginning to turn grey. When our chaise stops at the gate he does not conceal his joy and his impatience. He fussily helps me and Katya out, hurriedly asks questions, laughs, rubs his hands, and that gentle, imploring, pure expression, which I used to notice only in his eyes, is now suffused all over his face. He is glad and at the same time he is ashamed of his gladness, ashamed of his habit of spending every evening with Katya. And he thinks it necessary to explain his visit by some obvious absurdity such as: 'I was driving by on business, and I thought I would just look in for a minute.'

We all three go indoors; first we drink tea, then the familiar packs of cards, the big piece of cheese, the fruit, and the bottle of Crimean champagne are put upon the table. The subjects of our conversation are not new; they are just the same as in winter. We find fault with the University, the students, and literature and the theatre; the air grows thick and stifling with backbiting, and poisoned by the breath, not of two toads as in the winter, but of three. Besides the velvety baritone laugh and the giggle like the gasp of a concertina, the maid who waits upon us hears an unpleasant cracked 'Hee-hee!' like the chuckle of a general in a vaudeville.

V

There are terrible nights with thunder, lightning, rain, and wind, such as are called among the people 'sparrow nights'. There has been one such sparrow night in my personal life . . .

I woke up after midnight and leaped suddenly out of bed. It seemed to me for some reason that I was just about to die. Why did it seem so? I had no sensation in my body that suggested my immediate death, but my soul was oppressed with terror, as though I had suddenly seen a vast menacing glow of fire.

I rapidly struck a light, drank some water straight out of the decanter, then hurried to the open window. The weather outside was magnificent. There was a smell of hay and some other very sweet scent. I could see the spikes of the fence, the gaunt, drowsy trees by the window, the road, the dark streak of woodland; there was a serene, very bright moon in the sky and not a single cloud. Perfect stillness, not a leaf stirring. I felt that everything was looking at me and listening, waiting for me to die . . .

It was uncanny. I closed the window and ran to my bed. I felt for my pulse, and not finding it in my wrist, tried to find it in my temple, then in my chin, and again in my wrist, and everything I touched was cold and clammy with sweat. My breathing came more and more rapidly, my body was shivering, all my inside was in commotion; I had a sensation on my face and on my bald head as though they were covered with spiders' webs.

What should I do? Call my family? No; it would be no use. I could not imagine what my wife and Liza would do when they came in to me.

I hid my head under the pillow, closed my eyes, and waited and waited . . . My spine was cold; it seemed to be drawn inwards, and I felt as though death were coming upon me stealthily from behind . . .

'Kee-vee! kee-vee!' I heard a sudden shriek in the night's stillness, and did not know where it was—in my chest or outdoors. 'Kee-vee! kee-vee!'

My God, how terrible! I would have drunk some more water, but by then I was too frightened to open my eyes and I was afraid to raise my head. I was possessed by unaccountable animal terror, and I couldn't understand why I was so frightened: was it that I wanted to live, or that some new unknown pain was in store for me?

Upstairs, overhead, someone moaned or laughed . . . I listened. Soon afterwards there was a sound of footsteps on the stairs. Someone came hurriedly down, then went up again. A minute later there was a sound of steps downstairs again; someone stopped near my door and listened.

'Who is there?' I cried.

The door opened. I boldly opened my eyes, and saw my wife. Her face was pale and her eyes were tear-stained.

'You are not asleep, Nikolay Stepanych?' she asked.

'What is it?'

'For God's sake, go up and have a look at Liza; there is something the matter with her . . .'

'Very good, with pleasure,' I muttered, greatly relieved at not being alone. 'Very good, this minute . . .'

I followed my wife, heard what she said to me, and was too agitated to understand a word. Patches of light from her candle danced about the stairs, our long shadows trembled. My feet caught in the skirts of my dressing-gown; I gasped for breath, and felt as though something were pursuing me and trying to catch me from behind.

'I shall die on the spot, here on the staircase,' I thought. 'On the spot . . .' But we passed the staircase, the dark corridor with the Italian windows, and went into Liza's room. She was sitting on the bed in her night-dress, with her bare feet hanging down, and she was moaning.

'Oh, my God! Oh, my God!' she was muttering, screwing up her eyes at our candle. 'I can't bear it.'

'Liza, my child,' I said, 'what is it?'

Seeing me, she began crying out, and flung herself on my neck.

'My kind Papa! . . .' she sobbed—'my dear, good Papa . . . my darling, my pet, I don't know what is the matter with me . . . I am so miserable!'

She hugged me, kissed me, and babbled fond words I used to hear from her when she was a child.

'Calm yourself, my child. God be with you,' I said. 'There is no need to cry. I am miserable, too.'

I tried to tuck her in; my wife gave her water, and we awkwardly stumbled by her bedside; my shoulder jostled against her shoulder, and meanwhile I was thinking how the two of us used to give our children their bath.

'Help her! help her!' my wife implored me. 'Do something!'

What could I do? I could do nothing. There was some load on the girl's heart; but I did not understand, I knew nothing about it, and could only mutter:

'It's nothing, it's nothing; it will pass. Sleep, sleep!'

To make things worse, there was a sudden sound of dogs howling, at first subdued and uncertain, then loud, two dogs howling together. I had never attached significance to such omens as the howling of dogs or the shrieking of owls, but on that occasion it sent a pang to my heart, and I hastened to explain the howl to myself.

'It's nonsense,' I thought, 'the influence of one organism on another. The intensely strained condition of my nerves has been transmitted to my wife, Liza, the dog—that is all . . . Such transmission explains presentiments, forebodings . . .'

When a little later I went back to my room to write a prescription for Liza, I no longer thought I should die at once, but only had such a weight, such a feeling of oppression in my soul that I felt actually sorry that I had not died on the spot. For a long time I stood motionless in the middle of the room, pondering what to prescribe for Liza. But the moans overhead ceased, and I decided to prescribe nothing, and yet I went on standing there . . .

There was a deathly stillness, such a stillness, as some author has expressed it, that 'it rang in one's ears'. Time passed slowly; the streaks of moonlight on the windowsill did not shift their position, but seemed as though frozen . . . It was still some time before dawn.

But the gate in the fence creaked, someone stole in and, breaking a twig from one of those scraggy trees, cautiously tapped on the window with it.

'Nikolay Stepanych,' I heard a whisper. 'Nikolay Stepanych.'

I opened the window, and fancied I was dreaming: under the window, huddled against the wall, stood a woman in a black dress, with the moonlight bright upon her, looking at me with great eyes. Her face was pale, stern, and weird-looking in the moonlight, like marble, her chin was quivering.

'It is I,' she said—'I . . . Katya.'

In the moonlight all women's eyes look big and black, all people look taller and paler, and that was probably why I did not recognise her at first.

'What is it?'

'Forgive me!' she said. 'I suddenly felt unbearably miserable . . . I couldn't stand it, so came here. There was a light in your window and . . . and I decided to knock . . . I beg your pardon . . . Ah! if you knew how miserable I am! What are you doing just now?'

'Nothing . . . I can't sleep.'

'I had a feeling that there was something wrong, but that is nonsense.'

Her brows were raised, her eyes shone with tears, and her whole face was lit up with that familiar look of trustfulness which I had not seen for so long.

'Nikolay Stepanych,' she said imploringly, stretching out both hands to me, 'my precious friend, I beg you, I implore you . . . If you don't despise my affection and respect for you, consent to what I ask of you.'

'What is it?'

'Take my money from me!'

'Come! what an idea! What do I want with your money?'

'You'll go away somewhere for your health . . . You ought to go for your health. Will you take it? Yes? My dearest, yes?'

She looked greedily into my face and repeated: 'Yes, you will take it?'

'No, my dear, I won't take it . . .' I said. 'Thank you.'

She turned her back upon me and bowed her head. Probably I refused her in a tone which made further conversation about money impossible.

'Go home to bed,' I said. 'We will see each other tomorrow.'

'So you don't consider me your friend?' she asked dejectedly.

'I don't say that. But your money would be no use to me now.'

'I beg your pardon . . .' she said, dropping her voice a whole octave. 'I understand you . . . to be indebted to a person like me . . . a retired actress . . . But, goodbye . . .'

And she went away so quickly that I had not time even to say goodbye.

VI

I am in Kharkov.

As it would be useless to contend against my present mood and, indeed, beyond my power, I have made up my mind that the last days of my life shall at least be irreproachable externally. If I am unjust in regard to my wife and daughter, which I fully recognise, I will try and do as she wishes; since she wants me to go to Kharkov, I go to Kharkov. Besides, I have become of late so indifferent to everything that it is really all the same to me where I go, to Kharkov, or to Paris, or to Berdichev.

I arrived here at midday, and have put up at the hotel not far from the cathedral. The train was jolting, there were draughts, and now I am sitting on my bed, holding my head and expecting tic douloureux. I ought to have gone today to see some professors of my acquaintance, but I have neither the strength nor inclination.

The old corridor attendant comes in and asks whether I have my bed-linen. I detain him for five minutes, and put several questions to him about Gnekker, on whose account I have come here. The attendant turns out to be a native of Kharkov; he knows the town like the back of his hand, but does not remember any household bearing the surname of Gnekker. I question him about the estates—the same answer.

The clock in the corridor strikes one, then two, then three . . . These last months in which I am waiting for death seem much longer than the whole of my life. And I have never before been so ready to resign myself to the slowness of time as now. In the old days, when one sat in the station and waited for a train, or presided in an examination-room, a quarter of an hour would seem an eternity. Now I can sit all night on my bed without moving, and quite unconcernedly reflect that tomorrow will be followed by another night as long and colourless, and the day after tomorrow.

In the corridor it strikes five, six, seven . . . It grows dark.

There is a dull pain in my cheek, the tic beginning. To occupy myself with thoughts, I go back to my old point of view, when I was not so indifferent, and ask myself why I, a distinguished man, a Privy Counsellor, am sitting in this little hotel room, on this bed with the unfamiliar grey quilt. Why am I looking at that cheap tin washstand and listening to the whirr of the wretched clock in the corridor? Is all this in keeping with my fame and my lofty position? And I answer these questions with a jeer. I am amused by the *naïveté* with which I used in my youth to exaggerate the value of renown and of the exceptional position which celebrities are supposed to enjoy. I am famous, my name is pronounced with reverence, my portrait has been both in the *Cornfield* and in the *Universal Illustrated*; I have read my biography even in a German magazine. And what of all that? Here I am sitting utterly alone in a strange town, on a strange bed, rubbing my aching cheek with my hand . . . Domestic worries, the hard-heartedness of creditors, the rudeness of the railway servants, the inconveniences of the passport system, the expensive and unwholesome food in the refreshment-rooms, the general rudeness and coarseness in personal relationships—all this, and a great deal more which would take too long to enumerate, affects me as much as any tradesman who is famous only in his alley. In what way does my exceptional position find expression? Let's suppose that I am celebrated a thousand times over, that I am a hero of whom my country is proud. They publish bulletins of my illness in every paper, letters of sympathy come to me by post from my colleagues, my pupils, the general public; but all that does not prevent me from dying in a strange bed, in misery, in utter loneliness . . . Of course, no one is to blame for that; but I can't help disliking my popularity. I feel as though it has cheated me.

At ten o'clock I fall asleep, and in spite of the tic I sleep soundly, and should have gone on sleeping if I had not been awakened. Soon after one came a sudden knock at the door.

'Who is there?'

'A telegram.'

'You might have waited till tomorrow,' I say angrily, taking the telegram from the attendant. 'Now I shall not get to sleep again.'

'I am sorry. Your light was burning, so I thought you were not asleep.'

I tear open the telegram and look first at the signature. From my wife. What does she want?

'Gnekker was secretly married to Liza yesterday. Return.'

I read the telegram, and my dismay does not last long. I am dismayed, not by what Liza and Gnekker have done, but by the indifference with which I hear of their marriage. They say philosophers and the truly wise are indifferent. That is false: indifference is paralysis of the soul; it is premature death.

I go to bed again, and begin trying to think of something to occupy my mind. What am I to think about? I feel as though everything had been thought over already and there is nothing which could hold my attention now.

When daylight comes I sit up in bed with my arms round my knees, and to pass the time I try to know myself. 'Know thyself' is excellent and useful advice; it is only a pity that the ancients never thought to indicate the way to make use of this advice.

When I have wanted to understand somebody or myself, I have considered, not the actions, in which everything is relative, but the desires.

135

'Tell me what you want, and I will tell you what manner of man you are.'
And now I examine myself: what do I want?

I want our wives, children, friends and pupils to love in us, not our fame, not the brand and not the label, but to love us as ordinary men. Anything else? I should like to have had helpers and successors. Anything else? I should like to wake up in a hundred years' time and to have just a peep out of one eye at what is happening in science. I should like to have lived another ten years . . . What further?

Why, nothing further. I think and think for a long time, and can think of nothing more. And however much I might think, and however far my thoughts might travel, it is clear to me that my desires lack something vital, something very important. In my passion for science, in my desire to live, in this sitting on a strange bed, and in this striving to know myself— in all the thoughts, feelings, and ideas I form about everything, there is no common bond to connect it all into one whole. Every feeling and every thought exists apart in me; and in all my criticisms of science, the theatre, literature, my pupils, and in all the pictures my imagination draws, even the most skilful analyst could not find what is called a general idea, or the god of a living man.

And if there is not that, then there is nothing.

In such an impoverished state a serious ailment, the fear of death, the influence of circumstances and men were enough to turn upside-down and scatter in fragments all that I had once looked upon as my theory of life, and in which I had seen the meaning and joy of my existence. So there is nothing surprising in the fact that I have overshadowed the last months of my life with thoughts and feelings only worthy of a slave and barbarian, and that now I am indifferent and take no heed of the dawn. When a man lacks what is loftier and mightier than all external impressions, a bad cold is really enough to upset his equilibrium and make him begin to see an owl in every bird, to hear a dog howling in every sound. And all his pessimism or optimism with his thoughts great and small have at such times significance as symptoms and nothing more.

I am vanquished. If that is so, it is useless to go on thinking, it is useless to talk. I will sit and wait in silence for what is to come.

In the morning the corridor attendant brings me tea and a copy of the local newspaper. Mechanically I read the advertisements on the front page, the leading article, the extracts from the newspapers and journals, the chronicle of events . . . In the latter I find, among other things, the following paragraph: 'Our distinguished scholar, Professor Nikolay

Stepanovich So-and-so, arrived yesterday in Kharkov by express train, and is staying at the So-and-so Hotel.'

Apparently, illustrious names are created to live on their own account, apart from those that bear them. Now my name is promenading tranquilly about Kharkov; in another three months, engraved in gold letters on my monument, it will shine bright as the sun itself, while I shall be already under the moss.

A light tap at the door. Somebody wants me.

'Who is there? Come in.'

The door opens, and I step back surprised and hurriedly wrap my dressing-gown round me. Before me stands Katya.

'How do you do?' she says, breathless with running upstairs. 'You didn't expect me? I have come here, too . . . I have come, too!'

She sits down and goes on, hesitating and not looking at me.

'Why don't you speak to me? I have come, too . . . today . . . I found out that you were in this hotel, and have come to you.'

'Very glad to see you,' I say, shrugging my shoulders, 'but I am surprised. You seem to have dropped from the skies. Why have you come here?'

'Oh . . . I've simply come.'

Silence. Suddenly she jumps up impulsively and walks towards me.

'Nikolay Stepanych,' she says, turning pale and pressing her hands on her breast—'Nikolay Stepanych, I cannot go on living like this! I cannot! For God's sake, tell me quickly, this minute: what am I to do? Tell me, what am I to do?'

'What can I tell you?' I ask in perplexity. 'I can do nothing.'

'Tell me, I beseech you,' she goes on, breathing hard and trembling all over. 'I swear that I cannot go on living like this. It's too much for me!'

She sinks on a chair and begins sobbing. She flings her head back, wrings her hands, stamps her feet; her hat falls off and hangs bobbing on its elastic; her hair is dishevelled.

'Help me! help me!' she implores me. 'I cannot go on!'

She takes her handkerchief out of her travelling-bag, and with it pulls out several letters, which fall from her lap to the floor. I pick them up, and on one of them I recognise the handwriting of Mikhail Fyodorovich and accidentally read a bit of a word 'passionat . . .'

'There is nothing I can tell you, Katya,' I say.

'Help me!' she sobs, clutching at my hand and kissing it. 'You are my father, you know, my only friend! You are clever, educated; you have lived a long while; you have been a teacher! Tell me, what am I to do?'

'Upon my word, Katya, I don't know . . .'

I am utterly at a loss and confused, touched by her sobs, and hardly able to stand.

'Let us have lunch, Katya,' I say, with a forced smile. 'Give over crying.'

And at once I add in a sinking voice:

'I shall soon be gone, Katya . . .'

'Only one word, only one word!' she weeps, stretching out her hands to me. 'What am I to do?'

'You're an odd girl, really . . .' I mutter. 'I don't understand it! So sensible, and all at once . . . crying your eyes out . . .'

A silence follows. Katya straightens her hair, puts on her hat, then crumples up the letters and stuffs them in her bag—and all this deliberately, in silence. Her face, her bosom, and her gloves are wet with tears, but her expression now is cold and forbidding . . . I look at her, and feel ashamed that I am happier than she. The absence of what my philosophic colleagues call a general idea I have detected in myself only just before death, in the decline of my days, while the soul of this poor girl has known and will know no refuge all her life, all her life!

'Let us have lunch, Katya,' I say.

'No, thank you,' she answers coldly.

Another minute passes in silence.

'I don't like Kharkov,' I say; 'it's so grey here—such a grey town.'

'Yes, perhaps . . . It's ugly. I am here not for long, passing through. I am going on today.'

'Where?'

'To the Crimea . . . that is, to the Caucasus.'

'Oh! For long?'

'I don't know.'

Katya gets up, and, with a cold smile, holds out her hand without looking at me.

I want to ask her, 'Then, you won't be at my funeral?' but she does not look at me; her hand is cold and, as it were, strange. I escort her to the door in silence. She goes out, walks down the long corridor without looking back; she knows that I am looking after her, and most likely she will look back at the turn.

No, she did not look back. I've seen her black dress for the last time: her steps have died away . . . Farewell, my treasure!

138

Gusev

I

It was getting dark; it would soon be night.

Gusev, a discharged soldier, sat up in his hammock and said in an undertone:

'I say, Pavel Ivanych. A soldier at Suchan told me: while they were sailing a big fish came into collision with their ship and stove a hole in it.'

The nondescript individual whom he was addressing, and whom everyone in the ship's sickbay called Pavel Ivanych, was silent, as though he had not heard.

And again a stillness followed . . . The wind frolicked with the rigging, the screw throbbed, the waves lashed, the hammocks creaked, but the ear had long ago become accustomed to these sounds, and it seemed that everything around was asleep and silent. It was dreary. The three invalids—two soldiers and a sailor—who had been playing cards all day were asleep and talking in their dreams.

It seemed as though the ship were beginning to rock. The hammock slowly rose and fell under Gusev, as if it were heaving a sigh, and this was repeated once, twice, three times . . . Something crashed on to the floor with a clang: it must have been a jug falling down.

'The wind has broken loose from its chain . . .' said Gusev, listening.

This time Pavel Ivanych cleared his throat and answered irritably:

'One minute a vessel's running into a fish, the next, the wind's breaking loose from its chain . . . Is the wind a beast that it can break loose from its chain?'

'That's how christened folk talk.'

'They are as ignorant as you are then . . . They say all sorts of things. One must keep a head on one's shoulders and use one's reason. You are a senseless creature.'

Pavel Ivanych was subject to seasickness. When the sea was rough he was usually ill-humoured, and the merest trifle would make him irritable. Yet in Gusev's opinion there was absolutely nothing to be vexed about. What was there strange or wonderful, for instance, in the fish or in the wind's breaking loose from its chain? Suppose the fish were as big as a mountain and its back were as hard as a sturgeon's: and in the same way, supposing that away yonder at the end of the world there stood great stone walls and the fierce winds were chained up to the walls . . . If they had not broken loose, why did they tear about all over the sea like maniacs, and struggle to escape like dogs? If they were not chained up, what did become of them when it was calm?

Gusev pondered for a long time about fishes as big as a mountain and stout, rusty chains, then he began to feel bored and thought of his native region to which he was now returning after five years' service in the Far East. He pictured an immense pond covered with snow . . . On one side of the pond the red-brick building of the potteries with a tall chimney and clouds of black smoke; on the other side—a village . . . His brother Aleksey comes out in a sledge from the fifth yard from the end; behind him sits his little son Vanka in big felt boots, and his little girl Akulka, also wearing felt boots. Aleksey has been drinking, Vanka is laughing, Akulka's face he could not see, she had muffled herself up.

'You never know, he'll get the children frozen . . .' thought Gusev. 'Lord send them sense and judgement that they may honour their father and mother and not be wiser than their parents.'

'They want resoling,' a delirious sailor says in a bass voice. 'Yes, yes!'

Gusev's thoughts break off, and instead of a pond there suddenly appears apropos of nothing a huge bull's head without eyes, and the horse and sledge are not driving along, but are whirling round in a cloud of black smoke. But still he was glad he had seen his own folks. He held his breath from delight, shudders ran all over him, and his fingers twitched.

'The Lord let us meet again,' he muttered feverishly, but he at once opened his eyes and sought in the darkness for water.

He drank and lay back, and again the sledge was moving, then again the bull's head without eyes, smoke, clouds . . . And so on till daybreak.

II

The first outline visible in the darkness was a blue circle—the little round window; then little by little Gusev could distinguish his neighbour in the next hammock, Pavel Ivanych. The man slept sitting up, as he could not breathe lying down. His face was grey, his nose was long and sharp, his eyes looked huge from the terrible thinness of his face, his temples were sunken, his beard was skimpy, his hair was long . . . Looking at him you could not make out of what class he was, whether he were a gentleman, a merchant, or a peasant. Judging from his expression and his long hair he might have been a hermit or a lay brother in a monastery—but if one listened to what he said it seemed that he could not be a monk. He was worn out by his cough and his illness and by the stifling heat, and breathed with difficulty, moving his parched lips. Noticing that Gusev was looking at him he turned his face towards him and said:

'I begin to guess . . . Yes . . . I understand it all perfectly now.'

'What do you understand, Pavel Ivanych?'

'I'll tell you . . . It has always seemed strange to me that, terribly ill as you are, you should be placed here in a steamer where it is so hot and stifling and we are always being tossed up and down, where, in fact, everything threatens you with death; now it is all clear to me . . . Yes . . . Your doctors put you on the steamer to get rid of you. They get sick of looking after poor brutes like you . . . You don't pay them anything, you're a nuisance to them, and you spoil their records with your deaths—so, of course, you are just brutes! It's not difficult to get rid of you . . . All that is necessary is, in the first place, to have no conscience or humanity; and, secondly, to deceive the steamer authorities. The first condition need hardly be considered, in that respect we are artists; and one can always succeed in the second with a little practice. In a crowd of four hundred healthy soldiers and sailors half a dozen sick ones do not stand out; so they drove you all on to the steamer, mixed you with the healthy ones, hurriedly counted you over, and in the confusion nothing amiss was noticed, and when the steamer had started they saw that there were paralytics and consumptives in the last stage lying about on the deck . . .'

Gusev did not understand Pavel Ivanych; but supposing he was being blamed, he said in self-defence:

'I lay on the deck because I had not the strength to stand; when we were unloaded from the barge on to the ship I caught a fearful chill.'

'It's revolting,' Pavel Ivanych went on. 'The worst of it is they know perfectly well that you can't last out the long journey, and yet they put you here. Supposing you get as far as the Indian Ocean, what then? It's horrible to think of it . . . And that's their gratitude for your faithful, irreproachable service!'

Pavel Ivanych's eyes looked angry; he frowned contemptuously and said, gasping:

'Those are the people who ought to be plucked in the newspapers till their feathers fly in all directions.'

The two sick soldiers and the sailor were awake and already playing cards. The sailor was half reclining in his hammock, the soldiers were sitting near him on the floor in the most uncomfortable attitudes. One of the soldiers had his right arm in a sling, and the hand was swathed up in a regular bundle so that he held his cards under his right arm or in the crook of his elbow while he played with the left. The ship was rolling heavily. They could not stand up, nor drink tea, nor take their medicines.

'Were you an officer's servant?' Pavel Ivanych asked Gusev.

'Yes, an officer's servant.'

'My God, my God!' said Pavel Ivanych, and he shook his head mournfully. 'To tear a man out of his home, drag him twelve thousand miles away, then to drive him into consumption and . . . and what is it all for, one wonders? To turn him into a servant for some Captain Kopeykin or Midshipman Dyrka! How logical!'

'It's not hard work, Pavel Ivanych. You get up in the morning and clean the boots, put the samovar on, sweep the rooms, and then you have nothing more to do. The lieutenant spends all day drawing plans, but if you like you can say your prayers, if you like you can read a book or go out into the street. God grant everyone such a life.'

'Yes, very nice, the lieutenant draws plans, while you sit all day in the kitchen and pine for home . . . Plans indeed! . . . It is not plans that matter, but a human life. Life is not given twice, it must be treated mercifully.'

'Of course, Pavel Ivanych, a bad man gets no mercy anywhere, neither at home nor in the army, but if you live as you ought and obey orders, who has any need to insult you? The officers are educated gentlemen, they understand . . . In five years I was never once in prison, and I was never struck a blow, so help me God, but once.'

'What for?'

'For fighting. I have a heavy hand, Pavel Ivanych. Four Chinamen came into our yard; they were bringing firewood or something, I don't remember. Well, I was bored and I knocked them about a bit, one's nose began bleeding, damn the fellow . . . The lieutenant saw it through the little window, he was angry and gave me a box on the ear.'

'Foolish, pitiful man . . .' whispered Pavel Ivanych. 'You don't understand anything.'

He was utterly exhausted by the tossing of the ship and closed his eyes; his head alternately fell back and dropped forward on his chest. Several times he tried to lie down but nothing came of it; his difficulty in breathing prevented it.

'And what did you hit the four Chinamen for?' he asked a little while afterwards.

'Oh, nothing. They came into the yard, so I hit them.'

And a stillness followed . . . The card-players had been playing for two hours with enthusiasm and loud abuse of one another, but the motion of the ship overcame them, too; they threw aside their cards and lay down. Again Gusev saw the big pond, the brick building, the village . . . Again the sledge was coming along, again Vanka was laughing and Akulka, silly little thing, threw open her fur coat and stuck her feet out, as much as to say: 'Look, good people, my snowboots are not like Vanka's, they are new ones.'

'Five years old, and she has no sense yet,' Gusev muttered in delirium. 'Instead of kicking your legs you had better come and get your soldier uncle a drink. I will give you something nice.'

Then Andron with a flintlock gun on his shoulder was carrying a hare he had killed, and he was followed by the decrepit old Jew Isaychik, who offers to barter the hare for a piece of soap; then the black calf in the shed, then Domna sewing at a shirt and crying about something, and then again the bull's head without eyes, black smoke . . .

Overhead someone gave a loud shout, several sailors ran by, they seemed to be dragging something bulky over the deck, or something fell with a crash. Again they ran by . . . Had something gone wrong? Gusev raised his head, listened, and saw that the two soldiers and the sailor were playing cards again; Pavel Ivanych was sitting up moving his lips. It was stifling, one hadn't strength to breathe, one was thirsty, the water was warm, disgusting. The ship heaved as much as ever.

Suddenly something strange happened to one of the soldiers playing cards . . . He called hearts diamonds, got muddled in his score, and dropped his cards, then with a frightened, foolish smile looked round at all of them.

'I shan't be a minute, mates, I'll . . .' he said, and lay down on the floor.

Everybody was amazed. They called to him, he did not answer.

'Stepan, maybe you are feeling bad, eh?' the soldier with his arm in a sling asked him. 'Perhaps we had better bring the priest, eh?'

'Have a drink of water, Stepan . . .' said the sailor. 'Here, lad, drink.'

'Why are you knocking the jug against his teeth?' said Gusev angrily. 'Don't you see, turnip-head?'

'What?'

'What?' Gusev repeated, mimicking him. 'There is no breath in him, he is dead! That's what! What nonsensical people, Lord, have mercy on us . . .!'

143

III

The ship was not rocking and Pavel Ivanych was more cheerful. He was no longer ill-humoured. His face had a boastful, defiant, mocking expression. He looked as though he wanted to say: 'Yes, in a minute I will tell you something that will make you split your sides with laughing.' The little round window was open and a soft breeze was blowing on Pavel Ivanych. There was a sound of voices, of the plash of oars in the water . . . Just under the little window someone began droning in a high, unpleasant voice: no doubt it was a Chinaman singing.

'Here we are in the harbour,' said Pavel Ivanych, smiling ironically. 'Only another month and we shall be in Russia. Well, my worthy warriors! I shall arrive at Odessa and from there go straight to Kharkov. In Kharkov I have a friend, a literary man. I shall go to him and say, "Come, old man, put aside your horrid subjects, ladies' amours and the beauties of nature, and show up human depravity . . . Here are some real themes for you . . ." '

For a minute he pondered, then said:

'Gusev, do you know how I fooled them?'

'Fooled whom, Pavel Ivanych?'

'Why, these fellows . . . You know that on this steamer there is only a first-class and a third-class, and they allow only peasants—that is the riff-raff—to go in the third. If you're wearing a jacket and have the faintest resemblance to a gentleman or a bourgeois you must go first-class, if you please. You must fork out five hundred roubles if you die for it. Why, I ask, have you made such a rule? Do you want to raise the prestige of educated Russians thereby? "Not a bit of it. We don't let you go third-class simply because a decent person can't go third-class: it's horrible there and disgusting." Yes, indeed. I am very grateful for such solicitude for decent people's welfare. But in any case, whether it is nasty there or nice, five hundred roubles I haven't got. I haven't pilfered government money, I haven't exploited the natives, I haven't trafficked in contraband, I have flogged no one to death, so judge for yourself whether I have the right to travel first-class and even less to reckon myself of the educated class? But you won't get through to them with logic . . . One has to resort to deception. I put on a workman's coat and high boots, I assumed a drunken, servile mug and went to the agents: "Give us a little ticket, Your Honour," said I . . .'

'Why, what class do you belong to?' asked a sailor.

'The clergy. My father was an honest priest, he always told the great ones of this world the truth to their faces; and he suffered a lot in consequence.'

Pavel Ivanych was exhausted with talking and gasped for breath, but still went on:

'Yes, I always tell people the truth to their faces. I am not afraid of anyone or anything. There is a vast difference between me and all of you in that respect. You live in darkness, you are blind, crushed; you see nothing and what you do see you don't understand . . . You are told the wind breaks loose from its chain, that you are beasts, savages, and you believe it; they punch you in the neck, you kiss their hands; some animal in a sable-lined coat robs you and then tips you fifteen kopecks and you say: "Let me kiss your hand, sir." You are pariahs, pitiful people . . . I am a different sort. My eyes are open, I see it all as clearly as a hawk or an eagle when it soars above the earth, and I understand everything. I am a living protest. I see irresponsible tyranny—I protest. I see cant and hypocrisy—I protest. I see swine triumphant—I protest. And I cannot be suppressed, no Spanish Inquisition can make me hold my tongue. No . . . Cut out my tongue and I would protest in dumb show; shut me up in a cellar—I will shout from it to be heard half a mile away, or I will starve myself to death that they may have another weight on their black consciences. Kill me and I will haunt them with my ghost. All my acquaintances say to me: "You are a most insufferable person, Pavel Ivanych." I am proud of such a reputation. I have served three years in the Far East, and I shall be remembered there for a hundred years: I quarrelled with everyone. My friends write to me from Russia, "Don't come back," but here I am going back to spite them . . . yes . . . That is life as I understand it. That is what one can call life.'

Gusev was looking at the little window and was not listening. A boat was swaying on the transparent, softly turquoise water all bathed in hot, dazzling sunshine. In it there were naked Chinamen holding up cages with canaries and calling out:

'It sings, it sings!'

Another boat knocked against the first; the steam cutter darted by. And then there came another boat with a fat Chinaman sitting in it, eating rice with chopsticks. Languidly the water heaved, languidly the white seagulls hovered over it.

'I should like to give that fat fellow one in the neck,' thought Gusev, gazing at the stout Chinaman, with a yawn.

He dozed off, and it seemed to him that all nature was dozing, too.

145

Time flew swiftly by; imperceptibly the day passed, imperceptibly the darkness came on . . . The steamer was no longer standing still, but moving on further.

IV

Two days passed. Pavel Ivanych lay down instead of sitting up; his eyes were closed, his nose seemed to have grown sharper.

'Pavel Ivanych,' Gusev called to him. 'Hey, Pavel Ivanych.'

Pavel Ivanych opened his eyes and moved his lips.

'Are you feeling bad?'

'No . . . it's nothing . . .' answered Pavel Ivanych, gasping. 'Nothing; on the contrary . . . I am rather better . . . You see I can lie down . . . I am a little easier . . .'

'Well, thank God for that, Pavel Ivanych.'

'When I compare myself with you I am sorry for you . . . poor fellows. My lungs are all right, it is only a stomach cough . . . I can stand hell, let alone the Red Sea. Besides I take a critical attitude to my illness and to the medicines they give me. While you . . . you live in darkness . . . It's a wretched life for you, very, very wretched!'

The ship was not rolling, it was calm, but as hot and stifling as a bath-house; it was not only hard to speak but even hard to listen. Gusev hugged his knees, laid his head on them and thought of his home. Good heavens, what a relief it was to think of snow and cold in that stifling heat! You drive in a sledge, all at once the horses take fright at something and bolt . . . Regardless of the road, the ditches, the ravines, they dash like mad things, right through the village, over the pond by the pottery-works, out across the open fields. 'Hold on,' the pottery-hands and the peasants shout, meeting them. 'Hold on.' But why? Let the keen, cold wind beat in one's face and bite one's hands; let the lumps of snow, kicked up by the horses' hoofs, fall on one's cap, on one's back, down one's collar, on one's chest; let the runners ring on the snow, and the traces and the sledge be smashed, the devil take them one and all! And how delightful when the sledge upsets and you go flying full tilt into a drift, face downwards in the snow, and then you get up white all over with icicles on your moustaches; no cap, no gloves, your belt undone . . . People laugh, the dogs bark . . .

Pavel Ivanych half opened one eye, looked at Gusev with it, and asked softly:

146

'Gusev, did your commanding officer steal?'

'Who can tell, Pavel Ivanych! We can't say, it didn't reach us.'

And after that a long time passed in silence. Gusev brooded, muttered something in delirium, and kept drinking water; it was hard for him to talk and hard to listen, and he was afraid of being talked to. An hour passed, a second, a third; evening came on, then night, but he did not notice it. He still sat dreaming of the frost.

There was a sound as though someone came into the sickbay, and voices were audible, but a few minutes passed and all was still again.

'The kingdom of heaven and eternal rest,' said the soldier with his arm in a sling. 'He was a restless man.'

'What?' asked Gusev. 'Who?'

'He is dead, they have just carried him up.'

'Oh well,' muttered Gusev, yawning, 'the kingdom of heaven be his.'

'What do you think?' the soldier with his arm in a sling asked Gusev. 'Will he be in the kingdom of heaven or not?'

'Who is it you are talking about?'

'Pavel Ivanych.'

'He will be . . . he suffered so long. And there is another thing, he belonged to the clergy, and the priests always have a lot of relations. Their prayers will save him.'

The soldier with the sling sat down on a hammock near Gusev and said in an undertone:

'And you, Gusev, are not long for this world. You will never get to Russia.'

'Did the doctor or his assistant say so?' asked Gusev.

'It isn't that they said so, but one can see it . . . One can see at once when a man's going to die. You don't eat, you don't drink; it's dreadful to see how thin you've got. It's consumption, in fact. I say it, not to upset you, but because maybe you would like to receive communion and extreme unction. And if you have any money you had better give it to the senior officer.'

'I haven't written home . . .' Gusev sighed. 'I shall die and they won't know.'

'They'll hear of it,' the sick sailor said in a bass voice. 'When you die they will put it down in the *Gazette*, at Odessa they will send in a report to the commanding officer there and he will send it to the parish or somewhere . . .'

Gusev began to be uneasy after such a conversation and to feel a vague

147

yearning. He drank water—that didn't help; he dragged himself to the window and breathed the hot, moist air—that didn't help; he tried to think of home, of the frost—and nor did that help . . . At last it seemed to him one minute longer in the sickbay and he would certainly expire.

'It's stifling, mates . . .' he said. 'I'll go on deck. Help me up, for Christ's sake.'

'All right,' agreed the soldier with the sling. 'I'll carry you, you can't walk, hold on to my neck.'

Gusev put his arm round the soldier's neck, the latter put his unhurt arm round him and carried him up. On the deck sailors and discharged soldiers were lying asleep side by side; there were so many of them it was difficult to pass.

'Put your feet on the ground,' the soldier with the sling said softly. 'Follow me quietly, hold on to my shirt . . .'

It was dark. There was no light on deck, nor on the masts, nor anywhere on the sea around. At the furthest end of the ship the man on watch was standing perfectly still like a statue, and it looked as though he too were asleep. It seemed as though the steamer were abandoned to itself and were moving according to its own will.

'Now they will throw Pavel Ivanych into the sea,' said the soldier with the sling. 'In a sack and then into the water.'

'Yes, that's the rule.'

'But it's better to lie at home in the earth. At least, your mother comes to the grave and weeps.'

'Of course.'

There was a smell of hay and of dung. There were oxen standing with drooping heads by the ship's rail. One, two, three . . . eight of them! And there was a little horse. Gusev put out his hand to stroke it, but it shook its head, bared its teeth, and tried to bite his sleeve.

'Damned beast . . .' said Gusev angrily.

The two of them, he and the soldier, threaded their way to the bow of the ship, then stood at the rail and looked silently up and down. Overhead deep sky, bright stars, peace and stillness, exactly as at home in the village, below—darkness and disorder. The tall waves were resounding, no one could tell why. Whichever wave you looked at, each one was trying to rise higher than all the rest and was chasing and crushing the next one; after it a third as fierce and hideous flew noisily, with a glint of light on its white crest.

The sea has no sense and no pity. If the steamer had been smaller and not made of thick iron, the waves would have crushed it to pieces without the slightest compunction, and would have devoured all the people in it with no distinction of saints or sinners. The steamer also had a senseless and cruel expression. This monster with its huge beak was dashing onwards, cutting millions of waves in its path; it had no fear of the darkness nor the wind, nor of space, nor of solitude, caring for nothing, and if the ocean had its people this monster would have crushed them, too, without distinction of saints or sinners.

'Where are we now?' asked Gusev.

'I don't know. We must be in the ocean.'

'There is no sight of land . . .'

'No indeed! They say we shan't see it for seven days.'

The two soldiers watched the white foam with the phosphorus light on it and were silent, thinking. Gusev was the first to break the silence.

'There is nothing to be afraid of,' he said, 'only one is full of dread as though one were sitting in a dark forest; but if, for instance, they let a boat down on to the water this minute and an officer ordered me to go a hundred miles over the sea to catch fish, I'd go. Or, let's say, if a Christian were to fall into the water this minute, I'd go in after him. A German or a Chinaman I wouldn't save, but I'd go in after a Christian.'

'And are you afraid to die?'

'Yes. I am sorry for the folks at home. My brother at home, you know, isn't steady; he drinks, he beats his wife for nothing, he does not honour his parents. Everything will go to ruin without me, and Father and my old mother will be begging for their bread, I shouldn't wonder. But my legs won't bear me, brother, and it's hot here. Let's go to sleep.'

V

Gusev went back to the sickbay and got into his hammock. He was again tormented by a vague craving, and he could not make out what he wanted. There was a tight feeling in his chest, a throbbing in his head, his mouth was so dry that it was difficult for him to move his tongue. He dozed, and murmured in his sleep, and, worn out with nightmares, his cough, and the stifling heat, towards morning he fell into a sound sleep. He dreamed that they were just taking the bread out of the oven in the barracks and he climbed into the stove and had a steam bath in it, lashing himself with a bunch of birch-twigs. He slept for two days, and at midday on the third two sailors came down and carried him out of the sickbay.

He was sewn up in sailcloth and to make him heavier they put with him two iron weights. Sewn up in the sailcloth he looked like a carrot or a radish: broad at the head and narrow at the feet . . . Before sunset they brought him up to the deck and put him on a plank; one end of the plank lay on the side of the ship, the other on a box, placed on a stool. Round him stood the soldiers and the officers with their caps off.

'Blessed be the name of the Lord . . .' the priest began. 'As it was in the beginning, is now, and ever shall be.'

'Amen,' chanted three sailors.

The soldiers and the officers crossed themselves and looked away at the waves. It was strange that a man should be sewn up in sailcloth and should soon be flying into the sea. Was it possible that such a thing might happen to all of them?

The priest sprinkled earth upon Gusev and bowed down. They sang 'Eternal Memory'.

The man on watch duty tilted up the end of the plank, Gusev slid off and flew head foremost, turned a somersault in the air and splashed into the sea. He was covered with foam and for a moment looked as though he were wrapped in lace, but that moment passed and he disappeared in the waves.

He went rapidly towards the bottom. Would he reach it? It was said to be three miles to the bottom. After sinking sixty or seventy feet, he began moving more and more slowly, swaying rhythmically, as though he were hesitating and, carried along by the current, moved more rapidly sideways than downwards.

Then he was met by a shoal of the fish known as pilot-fish. Seeing the dark body the fish stopped as though petrified, and suddenly turned round and disappeared. In less than a minute they flew back swift as an arrow to Gusev, and began zigzagging round him in the water.

After that another dark body appeared. It was a shark. It swam under Gusev with dignity and no show of interest, as though it had not noticed him, and he sank upon its back, then it turned belly upwards, basking in the warm, transparent water and languidly opened its jaws with two rows of teeth. The pilot-fish are delighted, they stop to see what will happen next. After playing a little with the body the shark nonchalantly puts its jaws under it, cautiously touches it with its teeth, and the sailcloth is rent its full length from head to foot; one of the weights falls out and frightens the pilot-fish, and striking the shark on the ribs goes rapidly to the bottom.

Overhead at this time the clouds are massed together on the side

150

where the sun is setting; one cloud is like a triumphal arch, another like a lion, a third like a pair of scissors . . . From behind the clouds a broad, green shaft of light pierces through and stretches to the middle of the sky; a little later another, violet-coloured, lies beside it; next to that, one of gold, then one rose-coloured . . . The sky turns a soft lilac. Looking at this gorgeous, enchanting sky, at first the ocean scowls, but soon it, too, acquires tender, joyous, passionate colours which human speech would find hard to name.

The Grasshopper

I

All Olga Ivanovna's friends and acquaintances were at her wedding.

'Look at him; isn't it true that there is something about him?' she said to her friends, with a nod towards her husband, as though she wanted to explain why she was marrying a simple, very ordinary, and in no way remarkable man.

Her husband, Osip Stepanych Dymov, was a doctor, and only of the rank of titular counsellor. He was on the staff of two hospitals: in one a ward-surgeon and in the other a dissecting demonstrator. Every day from nine to twelve he saw patients and was busy in his ward, and after twelve o'clock he went by tram to the other hospital, where he dissected. His private practice was a small one, not worth more than five hundred roubles a year. That was all. What more could one say about him? Meanwhile, Olga Ivanovna and her friends and acquaintances were not quite ordinary people. Every one of them was remarkable in some way, and more or less famous; already had made a reputation and was looked upon as a celebrity; or if not yet a celebrity, gave brilliant promise of becoming one. There was an actor from the Dramatic Theatre, who was a great talent of established reputation, as well as an elegant, intelligent, and modest man, and an excellent reciter who was teaching Olga Ivanovna to recite; there was a singer from the opera, a good-natured, fat man who assured Olga Ivanovna, with a sigh, that she was ruining herself, that if she would take herself in hand and not be lazy she might make a remarkable singer; then there were several artists, and chief among them Ryabovsky, a very handsome, fair-haired young man of twenty-five who painted genre pieces, animal studies, and landscapes, was successful at exhibitions, and had sold his last picture for five hundred roubles. He put the finishing touches to Olga Ivanovna's sketches, and used to say she might achieve something. Then a cellist, whose instrument used to sob, and who openly declared that of all the ladies of his acquaintance the only one who could accompany him was Olga Ivanovna; then there was a literary man, young but already well known, who had written stories, novels, and plays. Who else? Why, Vasily Vasilyich, a gentleman landowner, amateur illustrator and vignettist, with a great feeling for the old Russian style, the old ballad and epic. On paper, on china, and on smoked plates, he produced literally marvels. In the midst

of this free artistic company, spoiled by fortune, though refined and modest, who recalled the existence of doctors only in times of illness, and to whom the name of Dymov sounded in no way different from peasant names such as Sidorov or Tarasov—in the midst of this company Dymov seemed strange, superfluous, and small, though he was tall and broadshouldered. He looked as though he were wearing somebody else's coat, and his beard was like a shopman's. Though if he had been a writer or an artist, they would have said that his beard reminded them of Zola.

The actor said to Olga Ivanovna that with her flaxen hair and in her wedding-dress she was very much like a graceful cherry-tree when it is covered all over with delicate white blossoms in spring.

'Oh, let me tell you', said Olga Ivanovna, taking his arm, 'how it all happened so suddenly. Listen, listen! . . . I must tell you that my father was on the same staff at the hospital as Dymov. When my poor father was taken ill, Dymov watched for days and nights on end at his bedside. Such self-sacrifice! Listen, Ryabovsky! You, my writer, listen; it is very interesting! Come nearer. Such self-sacrifice, such genuine sympathy! I sat up with my father, and did not sleep for nights, either. And all at once—the princess had won the hero's heart—my Dymov fell head over ears in love. Really, fate is so strange at times! Well, after my father's death he came to see me sometimes, met me in the street, and one fine evening, all of a sudden he proposed . . . like a bolt out of the blue . . . I lay awake all night, crying, and fell hellishly in love myself. And here, as you see, I am his wife. There really is something strong, powerful, bearlike about him, isn't there? Now his face is turned three-quarters towards us in a bad light, but when he turns round look at his forehead. Ryabovsky, what do you say to that forehead? Dymov, we are talking about you!' she called to her husband. 'Come here; hold out your honest hand to Ryabovsky . . . That's right, be friends.'

Dymov, with a naïve and good-natured smile, held out his hand to Ryabovsky, and said:

'Very glad to meet you. There was a Ryabovsky in my year at the medical school. Was he a relation of yours?'

II

Olga Ivanovna was twenty-two, Dymov was thirty-one. They got on splendidly together when they were married. Olga Ivanovna hung all her drawing-room walls with her own and other people's sketches, in frames

153

and without frames, and near the piano and furniture arranged picturesque corners with Chinese parasols, easels, daggers, busts, photographs, and rags of many colours . . . In the dining-room she papered the walls with peasant woodcuts, hung up bast shoes and sickles, stood a scythe and rake in one corner, and so achieved a dining-room in the Russian style. In her bedroom she draped the ceiling and the walls with dark cloths to make it like a cavern, hung a Venetian lantern over the beds, and at the door set a figure with a halberd. And everyone thought that the young couple had a very charming little home.

When she got up at eleven o'clock every morning, Olga Ivanovna played the piano or, if it were sunny, painted something in oils. Then between twelve and one she drove to her dressmaker's. As Dymov and she had very little money, barely enough to make ends meet, she and her dressmaker had to use great guile to enable her to appear constantly in new dresses and cause a sensation with them. Very often out of an old dyed dress, out of bits of tulle, lace, plush, and silk, costing nothing, perfect marvels were created, something bewitching—not a dress, but a dream. From the dressmaker's Olga Ivanovna usually drove to some actress of her acquaintance to hear the latest theatrical gossip, and incidentally to try and get hold of tickets for the first night of some new play or for a benefit performance. From the actress's she had to go to some artist's studio or to some exhibition or to see some celebrity—either to pay a visit or to issue an invitation or simply to have a chat. And everywhere she met with a cheerful and friendly welcome, and was assured that she was good, sweet, and special . . . Those whom she called great and famous received her as one of themselves, as an equal, and predicted with one voice that, with her talents, taste, and intelligence, she would do great things if she concentrated herself. She sang, she played the piano, she painted in oils, she sculpted, she took part in amateur theatricals; and all this not just anyhow, but always with talent, whether she made lanterns for an illumination or dressed up or tied somebody's cravat—everything she did was exceptionally graceful, artistic, and charming. But her talents showed themselves in nothing so clearly as in her faculty for quickly becoming acquainted and on intimate terms with celebrated people. No sooner did anyone become ever so little celebrated, and set people talking about him, than she made his acquaintance, got on friendly terms the same day, and invited him to her house. Every new acquaintance she made was a veritable feast-day for her. She adored celebrated people, was proud of them, dreamed of them every night. She craved for them, and could never satisfy her craving. The old ones departed and were forgotten, new ones came to replace them, but to these, too, she soon grew accustomed or was disappointed in them, and began eagerly seeking for fresh great men, finding them and seeking for them again. What for?

Between four and five she dined at home with her husband. His simplicity, good sense, and kind-heartedness moved and delighted her. She was constantly jumping up, impulsively hugging his head and showering kisses upon it.

'You are a clever, noble person, Dymov,' she used to say, 'but you have one very serious defect. You take absolutely no interest in art. You don't believe in music or painting.'

'I don't understand them,' he would say meekly. 'I have spent all my life working at natural science and medicine, and I have never had time to take an interest in the arts.'

'But, you know, that's awful, Dymov!'

'Why so? Your friends don't know anything of science or medicine, but you don't reproach them for that. Everyone has his own line. I don't understand landscapes and operas, but the way I look at it is that if one set of sensible people devote their whole lives to them, and other sensible people pay immense sums for them, they must be of use. I don't understand them, but not understanding is not the same as disbelief.'

'Let me shake your honest hand!'

After dinner Olga Ivanovna would drive off to see her friends, then to a theatre or to a concert, and she returned home after midnight. So it was every day.

On Wednesdays she had 'At Homes'. At these 'At Homes' the hostess and her guests did not play cards and did not dance, but entertained themselves with various arts. The actor from the Dramatic Theatre recited, a singer sang, artists sketched in the albums of which Olga Ivanovna had a great number, the cellist played, and the hostess herself sketched, sculpted, sang, and played accompaniments. In the intervals between the recitations, music, and singing, they talked and argued about literature, the theatre, and painting. There were no ladies present, for Olga Ivanovna considered all ladies wearisome and vulgar except for actresses and her own dressmaker. Not one of these entertainments passed without the hostess shuddering at every ring at the bell, and saying, with a triumphant expression, 'It is he,' meaning by 'he', of course, some new celebrity she had invited. Dymov was not in the drawing-room, and no one remembered his existence. But exactly at half-past eleven the door leading into the dining-room opened, and Dymov would appear with his good-natured, gentle smile and say, rubbing his hands:

'Come to supper, my friends.'

They all went into the dining-room, and every time found on the table exactly the same things: a dish of oysters, a piece of ham or veal, sardines, cheese, caviare, mushrooms, vodka, and two decanters of wine.

'My dear *maître d'hôtel*!' Olga Ivanovna would say, clasping her hands in delight, 'you are simply enchanting! My friends, look at his forehead! Dymov, turn your profile. Look! he has the face of a Bengal tiger and an expression as kind and sweet as a gazelle. Such a darling man!'

The visitors ate, and, looking at Dymov, thought, 'He really is a nice fellow,' but they soon forgot about him, and went on talking about the theatre, music, and painting.

The young couple were happy, and their life flowed on smoothly. The third week of their honeymoon was spent, however, not quite so happily—sadly, indeed. Dymov caught erysipelas in the hospital, was in bed for six days, and had to have his beautiful black hair cropped. Olga Ivanovna sat beside him and wept bitterly, but when he was better she put a white handkerchief on his shaven head and began to paint him as a Bedouin. And they were both in good spirits. Three days after he had begun to go back to the hospital he had another piece of misfortune.

'I have no luck, Mums,' he said one day at dinner. 'I had four dissections to do today, and I cut two of my fingers at one. And I did not notice it till I got home.'

Olga Ivanovna was alarmed. He smiled, and told her that it did not matter, and that he often cut his hands when he was dissecting.

'I get absorbed, Mums, and grow careless.'

Olga Ivanovna dreaded symptoms of blood-poisoning, and prayed about it every night, but all went well. And again life flowed on peaceful and happy, free from grief and anxiety. The present was splendid, and spring was approaching, already smiling in the distance, and promising a thousand delights. Of her happiness there shall be no end! In April, May and June a summer villa a long way from town; walks, sketching, fishing, nightingales; and then from July right until autumn an artists' tour on the Volga, and in this tour Olga Ivanovna would take part as an indispensable member of the society. She had already had made for her two travelling-dresses of linen, had bought paints, brushes, canvases, and a new palette for the journey. Almost every day Ryabovsky visited her to

156

see what progress she was making in her painting; when she showed him her painting, he used to thrust his hands deep into his pockets, compress his lips, sniff, and say:

'Ye—es! . . . That cloud of yours is screaming: it's not in the evening light. The foreground is somehow chewed up, and there is something, you know, not quite right . . . And your cottage is weighed down and whines pitifully. That corner ought to have been shown more in shadow, but on the whole it is not bad; I like it.'

And the more incomprehensibly he talked, the more readily Olga Ivanovna understood him.

III

After dinner on the second day of Trinity Week, Dymov bought some sweets and some savouries and went off to the villa to see his wife. He had not seen her for a fortnight, and missed her terribly. As he sat in the train and afterwards as he looked for his villa in a big wood, he felt all the while hungry and weary, and dreamed of how he would have supper in freedom with his wife, then tumble into bed and go to sleep. And he was delighted as he looked at his parcel, in which there was caviare, cheese, and white salmon.

The sun was setting by the time he found his villa and recognised it. The old servant told him that her mistress was not at home, but that most likely she would soon be back. The villa, very uninviting in appearance, with low ceilings papered with writing-paper and with uneven floors full of crevices, consisted of only three rooms. In one there was a bed, in the second there were canvases, brushes, greasy papers, and men's overcoats and hats lying about on the chairs and in the windows, while in the third Dymov found three unknown men; two were dark-haired and had beards, the other was clean-shaven and fat, apparently an actor. There was a samovar boiling on the table.

'What do you want?' asked the actor in a bass voice, looking at Dymov ungraciously. 'Do you want Olga Ivanovna? Wait a minute; she will be here soon.'

Dymov sat down and waited. One of the dark-haired men, looking sleepily and listlessly at him, poured himself a glass of tea, and asked:

'Perhaps you would like some tea?'

Dymov was both hungry and thirsty, but he refused tea for fear of spoiling his supper. Soon he heard footsteps and a familiar laugh; a door slammed, and Olga Ivanovna ran into the room, wearing a wide-brimmed hat and carrying a box in her hand; she was followed by Ryabovsky, red-cheeked and cheerful, carrying a big umbrella and a folding stool.

'Dymov!' cried Olga Ivanovna, and she flushed crimson with joy. 'Dymov!' she repeated, laying her head and both hands on his chest. 'Is it you? Why haven't you come for so long? Why? Why?'

'When could I, Mums? I am always busy, and whenever I am free it always happens somehow that the train does not fit.'

'But how glad I am to see you! I have been dreaming about you the whole night through, and I was afraid you must be ill. Ah! if you only knew how sweet you are! You have come in the nick of time! You will be my salvation! You are the only person who can save me! There is to be a most original wedding here tomorrow,' she went on, laughing, and tying her husband's cravat. 'A young telegraph clerk at the station, called Chikeldeyev, is getting married. He is a handsome young man and—well, not stupid, and you know there is something strong, bearlike in his face . . . One could paint him as a young Varangian. We summer visitors take a great interest in him, and have promised to be at his wedding . . . He is a lonely, timid man, not well off, and of course it would be a shame not to be sympathetic to him. Fancy! the wedding will be after the service; then we shall all walk from the church to the bride's lodgings . . . you can imagine: the wood, the birds singing, patches of sunlight on the grass, and all of us spots of different colours against the bright green background—very original, in the style of the French Impressionists. But, Dymov, what am I to wear in church?' said Olga Ivanovna, and she looked as though she were about to cry. 'I have nothing here, literally nothing! no dress, no flowers, no gloves . . . You must save me. Since you have come, fate itself decrees that you save me. Take the keys, my precious, go home and get my pink dress from the wardrobe. You remember it; it hangs in front . . . Then, in the storeroom, on the floor, on the right side, you will see two cardboard boxes. When you open the top one you will see tulle, heaps of tulle and rags of all sorts, and beneath them flowers. Take out all the flowers carefully, try not to crush them, darling; I will choose among them later . . . And buy me some gloves.'

'Very well,' said Dymov; 'I will go tomorrow and send them on to you.'

'Tomorrow?' asked Olga Ivanovna, and she looked at him in surprise. 'You won't have time tomorrow. The first train leaves tomorrow at nine, and the wedding's at eleven. No, darling, it must be today; it absolutely must be today. If you won't be able to come tomorrow, send them by a special messenger. Now, you must run along . . . The passenger train is due in a moment; don't miss it, darling.'

'Very well.'

'Oh, how sorry I am to let you go!' said Olga Ivanovna, and tears came into her eyes. 'And why did I promise that telegraph clerk, like a silly?'

Dymov hurriedly drank a glass of tea, picked up a roll and, smiling meekly, went to the station. And the caviare, the cheese, and the white salmon were eaten by the two dark-haired gentlemen and the fat actor.

IV

On a still moonlit night in July Olga Ivanovna was standing on the deck of a Volga steamer and looking alternately at the water and at the picturesque banks. Beside her stood Ryabovsky, telling her that the black shadows on the water were not shadows, but a dream, that it would be sweet to sink into forgetfulness, to die, to become a memory in the sight of that enchanted water with the fantastic glimmer, in sight of the fathomless sky and the mournful, dreamy shores that spoke of the vanity of our life and of the existence of something higher, blessed, and eternal. The past was vulgar and uninteresting, the future was trivial, and this marvellous night, which came but once in a lifetime, would soon be over, would blend with eternity; so why go on living?

And Olga Ivanovna listened to Ryabovsky's voice and to the silence of the night, thinking that she was immortal and would never die. The turquoise colour of the water, such as she had never seen before, the sky, the riverbanks, the black shadows, and the unaccountable joy that flooded her soul, all told her that she would become a great artist, and that somewhere in the distance, in the infinite space beyond the moonlight, success, glory, the love of the people, lay awaiting her . . . When she gazed steadily without blinking into the distance, she seemed to see crowds of people, lights, triumphant strains of music, shouts of delight, she herself in a white dress, and flowers showered upon her from all sides. She thought, too, that beside her, leaning with his elbows on the rail of the steamer, stood a really great man, a genius, one of God's elect . . . All that he had created until now was fine, new, and extraordinary, but what he would create in time, when with maturity his rare talent reached its full development, would be astounding, immeasurably sublime; and that could be seen in his face, in his manner of expressing himself and his attitude to nature. He talked of shadows, of the tones of evening, of the moonlight, in a special way, in a language of his own, so that one could not help feeling the fascination of his power over nature. He was very handsome, original, and his life, free, independent, aloof from all common cares, was like the life of a bird.

'It's growing cooler,' said Olga Ivanovna, and she gave a shudder.

Ryabovsky wrapped her in his cloak, and said mournfully:

'I feel that I am in your power; I am a slave. Why are you so enchanting today?'

He kept staring intently at her, and his eyes were terrible. And she felt afraid to look at him.

'I love you madly,' he whispered, breathing on her cheek. 'Say one word to me and I will not go on living; I will abandon art . . .' he muttered in violent emotion. 'Love me, love . . .'

'Don't talk like that,' said Olga Ivanovna, covering her eyes. 'It's frightening! What about Dymov?'

'What of Dymov? Who is Dymov? What is Dymov to me? The Volga, the moon, beauty, my love, my ecstasy, and Dymov does not exist . . . Ah! I know nothing . . . I don't care about the past; give me one moment, one instant!'

Olga Ivanovna's heart began to throb. She tried to think about her husband, but all her past, with her wedding, with Dymov, and with her 'At Homes', seemed to her petty, trivial, dingy, unnecessary, and far, far away . . . Yes, indeed, what of Dymov? Who is Dymov? What was Dymov to her? Had he any existence in nature, or was he only a dream?

'For him, a simple and ordinary man, the happiness he has had already is enough,' she thought, covering her face with her hands. 'Let others condemn me, let them curse me, but in spite of them all I will go to my ruin; I will go to my ruin! . . . One must experience everything in life. My God! how terrible and how glorious!'

'Well? Well?' muttered the artist, embracing her, and greedily kissing the hands with which she feebly tried to thrust him from her. 'You love me? Yes? Yes? Oh, what a night! A marvellous night!'

'Yes, what a night!' she whispered, looking into his eyes, which were glistening with tears.

Then she looked round quickly, embraced him, and kissed him on the lips.

'We are nearing Kineshma!' said someone on the other side of the deck.

They heard heavy footsteps; it was a waiter from the refreshment-bar.

'Waiter,' said Olga Ivanovna, laughing and crying with happiness, 'bring us some wine.'

The artist, pale with emotion, sat on the seat, looking at Olga Ivanovna with adoring, grateful eyes; then he closed his eyes, and said, smiling languidly:

'I am tired.'

And he leaned his head against the rail.

V

On the second of September the day was warm and still, but overcast. In the early morning a light mist had hung over the Volga, and after nine o'clock it had begun to spot with rain. And there seemed no hope of the sky clearing. Over their morning tea Ryabovsky told Olga Ivanovna that painting was the most ungrateful and boring art, that he was not an artist, that only fools thought he had any talent, and all at once, for no rhyme or reason, he snatched up a knife and with it scraped over his very best sketch. After his tea he sat plunged in gloom at the window and gazed at the Volga. And now the Volga was dingy, all of one even colour without a gleam of light, cold-looking. Everything, everything suggested the approach of dreary, gloomy autumn. And it seemed as though nature had removed now from the Volga the sumptuous green covers on its banks, the diamond reflections of the sunbeams, the transparent blue distance, and all its smart gala array, and had packed it away in boxes till the coming spring, and the crows were flying above the Volga and crying tauntingly, 'Bare, bare!'

Ryabovsky heard their cawing, and thought he had already faded and lost his talent, that everything in this world was relative, conditional, and stupid, and that he ought not to have got involved with this woman . . . In short, he was out of humour and depressed.

Olga Ivanovna sat behind the screen on the bed, and, passing her fingers through her lovely flaxen hair, pictured herself first in her drawing-room, then in the bedroom, then in her husband's study; her imagination carried her to the theatre, to the dressmaker, to her distinguished friends. What were they doing now? Did they think of her? The season had already begun, and it would be time to think about her 'At Homes'. And Dymov? Dear Dymov! With what gentleness and childlike pathos he kept begging her in his letters to make haste and come home!

Every month he sent her seventy-five roubles, and when she wrote to him that she had lent the artists a hundred roubles, he sent that hundred too. What a kind, generous-hearted man! The travelling wearied Olga Ivanovna; she was bored; and she longed to get away from the peasants, from the damp smell of the river, and to cast off the feeling of physical uncleanliness of which she was conscious all the time, living in the peasants' huts and wandering from village to village. If Ryabovsky had not given his word to the artists that he would stay with them till the twentieth of September, they might have gone away that very day. And how nice that would have been!

'My God!' moaned Ryabovsky. 'Will the sun never come out? I can't go on with a sunny landscape without the sun . . .'

'But you have a sketch with a cloudy sky,' said Olga Ivanovna, emerging from behind the screen. 'Do you remember, in the right foreground forest trees, on the left a herd of cows and geese? You might finish it now.'

'Oh!' the artist scowled. 'Finish it! Do you think I am such a fool that I don't know what I should do?'

'How you have changed towards me!' sighed Olga Ivanovna.

'And a good thing too!'

Olga Ivanovna's face quivered; she moved away to the stove and began to cry.

'Well, that's the last straw—crying! Do stop! I have a thousand reasons for tears, but I am not crying.'

'A thousand reasons!' wept Olga Ivanovna. 'The chief one is that you are weary of me. Yes!' she said, and broke into sobs. 'If one is to tell the truth, you are ashamed of our love. You keep trying to prevent the artists from noticing it, though it is impossible to conceal it, and they have known all about it for ever so long.'

'Olga, one thing I beg you,' said the artist in an imploring voice, laying his hand on his heart—'one thing; don't pester me! I want nothing else from you!'

'But swear that you love me still!'

'This is agony!' the artist hissed through his teeth, and he jumped up. 'It will end by my throwing myself into the Volga or going out of my mind! Leave me alone!'

'Come, kill me, kill me!' cried Olga Ivanovna. 'Kill me!'

She sobbed again, and went behind the screen. There was a swish of rain on the straw thatch of the hut. Ryabovsky clutched his head and strode up and down; then with a resolute face, as though bent on proving something to somebody, put on his cap, slung his gun over his shoulder, and went out of the hut.

After he had gone, Olga Ivanovna lay a long time on the bed, crying. At first she thought it would be a good thing to poison herself, so that when Ryabovsky came back he would find her dead; then her imagination carried her to her drawing-room, to her husband's study, and she pictured herself sitting motionless beside Dymov and enjoying the physical peace and cleanliness, and in the evening sitting in the theatre, listening to Masini. And a yearning for civilisation, for the noise and bustle of the town, for celebrated people, sent a pang to her heart. A peasant woman came into the hut and began in a leisurely way lighting the stove to prepare the dinner. There was a smell of charcoal fumes, and the air was filled with bluish smoke. The artists came in, in muddy high boots, their faces wet with rain, examined their sketches, and comforted themselves by saying that the Volga had its charms even in bad weather. On the wall the cheap clock went 'tic–tic–tic' . . . The flies, feeling chilled, crowded round the icons in the corner, buzzing, and one could hear the cockroaches scurrying about among the thick portfolios under the seats . . .

Ryabovsky came home as the sun was setting. He flung his cap on the table, and, without removing his muddy boots, sank pale and exhausted on the bench and closed his eyes.

'I am tired . . .' he said, and twitched his eyebrows, trying to raise his eyelids.

To be nice to him and to show she was not cross, Olga Ivanovna went up to him, gave him a silent kiss, and passed the comb through his fair hair. She meant to comb it for him.

'What's that?' he said, starting as though something cold had touched him, and he opened his eyes. 'What is it? Please leave me alone.'

He thrust her off, and moved away. And it seemed to her that there was a look of aversion and annoyance on his face.

At that moment the peasant woman cautiously carried him, in both hands, a plate of cabbage soup. And Olga Ivanovna could see both her thumbs in the soup. And the dirty peasant woman, standing with her stomach pulled in tight, and the cabbage soup which Ryabovsky began eating greedily, and the hut, and their whole way of life, which she at first had so loved for its simplicity and artistic disorder, seemed horrible to her now. She suddenly felt insulted, and said coldly:

'We must part for a time, or else from boredom we shall quarrel in earnest. I am sick of this; I am going today.'

'Going how? Astride on a broomstick?'

'Today is Thursday, so the steamer will be here at half-past nine.'

'Eh? Yes, yes . . . Well, go, then . . .' Ryabovsky said softly, wiping his mouth with a towel instead of a dinner napkin. 'You are bored and have nothing to do here, and one would have to be a great egoist to try and keep you. Go home, and we shall meet again after the twentieth.'

Olga Ivanovna packed in good spirits. Her cheeks positively glowed with pleasure. Could it really be true, she asked herself, that she would soon be writing in her drawing-room and sleeping in her bedroom, and dining with a cloth on the table? A weight was lifted from her heart, and she no longer felt angry with the artist.

'My paints and brushes I will leave with you, Ryabusha,' she said. 'You can bring what's left . . . Mind, now, don't be lazy here when I am gone; don't mope, but work. You are such a splendid fellow, Ryabusha!'

At nine o'clock Ryabovsky gave her a farewell kiss, in order, as she thought, to avoid kissing her on the steamer in front of the artists, and went with her to the landing-stage. The steamer soon came up and carried her away.

She arrived home two and a half days later. Breathless with excitement, she went, without taking off her hat or waterproof, into the drawing-room and thence into the dining-room. Dymov, with his waistcoat unbuttoned and no coat, was sitting at the table, sharpening a knife on a fork; before him lay a grouse on a plate. As Olga Ivanovna went into the flat she was convinced that it was essential to hide everything from her husband, and that she would have the strength and skill to do so; but now, when she saw his broad, meek, happy smile, and shining, joyful eyes, she felt that to deceive this man was as vile, revolting, impossible and out of her power as to bear false witness, to steal, or to kill, and in a flash she resolved to tell him all that had happened. Letting him kiss and embrace her, she sank down on her knees before him and hid her face.

'What is it, what is it, Mums?' he asked tenderly. 'Were you homesick?'

She raised her face, red with shame, and gazed at him with a guilty and imploring look, but fear and shame prevented her from telling him the truth.

'Nothing,' she said; 'it's just nothing . . .'

'Let us sit down,' he said, raising her and seating her at the table.

'That's right, eat the grouse. You are starving, poor darling.'

She eagerly breathed in the atmosphere of home and ate the grouse, while he watched her with tenderness and laughed with delight.

VI

Apparently, by the middle of the winter Dymov began to suspect that he was being deceived. As though his conscience was not clear, he could not look his wife straight in the eyes, did not smile with delight when he met her, and to avoid being left alone with her, he often brought in to dinner his colleague, Korostelyov, a little close-cropped man with a crumpled face, who kept buttoning and unbuttoning his jacket with embarrassment when he talked to Olga Ivanovna, and then with his right hand tweaked his left moustache. At dinner the two doctors remarked that a displacement of the diaphragm was sometimes accompanied by irregularities of the heart, or that multiple neuritis was more common of late, or that Dymov had the day before found a cancer of the lower abdomen while dissecting a corpse with the diagnosis of pernicious anaemia. And it seemed as though they were talking of medicine only to give Olga Ivanovna a chance of being silent—that is, of not lying. After dinner Korostelyov sat down to the piano, while Dymov sighed and said to him:

'Ah, brother—never mind! Play something sad.'

Raising his shoulders and stretching his fingers wide apart, Korostelyov played some chords and began singing in a tenor voice, 'Show me the abode where the Russian peasant does not groan,' while Dymov sighed once more, propped his head on his fist, and sank into thought.

Olga Ivanovna had been extremely imprudent in her conduct of late. Every morning she woke up in a very bad humour and with the thought that she no longer cared for Ryabovsky, and that, thank God, it was all over now. But as she drank her coffee she reflected that Ryabovsky had robbed her of her husband, and that now she was left with neither her husband nor Ryabovsky; then she remembered talk she had heard among her acquaintances of a picture Ryabovsky was preparing for the exhibition, something striking, a mixture of genre and landscape, in the style of Polenov, about which everyone who had been to his studio went into raptures; and this, of course, she mused, he had created under her influence, and altogether, thanks to her influence, he had greatly changed for the

165

better. Her influence was so beneficial and essential that if she were to leave him he might perhaps go to ruin. And she remembered, too, that the last time he had come to see her in a greatcoat with flecks on it and a new tie, he had asked her languidly:

'Am I handsome?'

And with his elegance, his long curls, and his blue eyes, he really was very handsome (or perhaps it only seemed so), and he had been affectionate to her.

Considering and remembering many things, Olga Ivanovna dressed and in great agitation drove to Ryabovsky's studio. She found him in high spirits, and enchanted with his really magnificent picture. He was dancing about and playing the fool and answering serious questions with jokes. Olga Ivanovna was jealous of the picture and hated it, but from politeness she stood before the picture for five minutes in silence, and, heaving a sigh, as though before a holy shrine, said softly:

'Yes, you have never painted anything like it before. Do you know, it is positively awe-inspiring?'

And then she began beseeching him to love her and not to cast her off, to have pity on her in her misery and her wretchedness. She shed tears, kissed his hands, insisted on his swearing that he loved her, told him that without her good influence he would go astray and be ruined. And, when she had spoilt his good-humour, feeling herself humiliated, she would drive off to her dressmaker or to an actress of her acquaintance to try and get theatre tickets.

If she did not find him at his studio she left a letter in which she swore that if he did not come to see her that day she would poison herself. He was scared, came to see her, and stayed to dinner. Regardless of her husband's presence, he would say rude things to her, and she would answer him in the same way. Both felt they were a burden to each other, that they were tyrants and enemies, and felt angry, and in their wrath did not notice that their behaviour was unseemly, and that even Korostelyov, with his close-cropped head, saw it all. After dinner Ryabovsky made haste to say goodbye and get away.

'Where are you off to?' Olga Ivanovna would ask him in the hall, looking at him with hatred.

Scowling and screwing up his eyes, he mentioned some lady of their acquaintance, and it was evident that he was laughing at her jealousy and wanted to annoy her. She went to her bedroom and lay down on her bed; from jealousy, anger, a sense of humiliation and shame, she bit the pillow and began sobbing aloud. Dymov left Korostelyov in the drawing-room, went into the bedroom, and with a bewildered and embarrassed face said softly:

'Don't cry so loud, Mums; there's no need. You must be quiet about it. You must not let people see . . . You know what's done is done, and can't be mended.'

Not knowing how to ease the burden of her jealousy, which actually set her temples throbbing with pain, and thinking still that things might be set right, she would wash, powder her tear-stained face, and fly off to the lady mentioned.

Not finding Ryabovsky with her, she would drive off to a second, then to a third. At first she was ashamed to rush about like this, but afterwards she got used to it, and it sometimes happened that in one evening she would make the round of all her female acquaintances in search of Ryabovsky, and everyone was aware of this.

One day she said to Ryabovsky of her husband:

'That man crushes me with his magnanimity.'

This phrase pleased her so much that when she met the artists who knew of her affair with Ryabovsky she said every time of her husband, with a vigorous movement of her arm:

'That man crushes me with his magnanimity.'

Their manner of life was the same as it had been the year before. On Wednesdays they were 'At Home'; an actor recited, the artists sketched. The cellist played, a singer sang, and invariably at half-past eleven the door leading to the dining-room opened and Dymov, smiling, said:

'Come to supper, gentlemen.'

As before, Olga Ivanovna hunted celebrities, found them, was not satisfied, and went in pursuit of fresh ones. As before, she came back late every night; but now Dymov was not, as last year, asleep, but sitting in his study at work of some sort. He went to bed at three o'clock and got up at eight.

One evening when she was getting ready to go to the theatre and standing before a tall mirror, Dymov came into her bedroom, wearing his dress-coat and a white tie. He was smiling gently and looked into his wife's face joyfully, as in the old days; his face was radiant.

'I have just been defending my thesis,' he said, sitting down and stroking his knees.

'Defending?' asked Olga Ivanovna.

'Aha!' he laughed, and he craned his neck to see his wife's face in the mirror, for she was still standing with her back to him, doing up her hair. 'Aha,' he repeated, 'do you know it's very possible they may offer me the Readership in General Pathology? It seems like it.'

It was evident from his beaming, blissful face that if Olga Ivanovna had shared his joy and triumph he would have forgiven her everything, both the present and the future, and would have forgotten everything, but she did not understand what was meant by a 'readership' or by 'general pathology'; besides, she was afraid of being late for the theatre, and she said nothing.

He sat there for another two minutes, and with a guilty smile went away.

VII

It had been a most troubled day.

Dymov had a very bad headache; he did not drink his tea in the morning, and did not go to the hospital, but spent the whole time lying on his sofa in the study. Olga Ivanovna went as usual at midday to see Ryabovsky, to show him her still-life sketch, and to ask him why he had not been to see her the evening before. The sketch seemed worthless to her, and she had painted it only in order to have an additional reason for visiting the artist.

She went in to him without ringing, and as she was taking off her galoshes in the entry she heard a sound as of something running softly in the studio, with a feminine rustle of skirts; and as she hastened to peep in she caught a momentary glimpse of a piece of brown petticoat, which vanished behind a big picture draped, together with the easel, with black calico down to the floor. There could be no doubt that a woman was hiding there. How often Olga Ivanovna herself had taken refuge behind that picture!

Ryabovsky, evidently much embarrassed, held out both hands to her, as though surprised at her arrival, and said with a forced smile:

'Ah—ah! Very glad to see you! Anything nice to tell me?'

Olga Ivanovna's eyes filled with tears. She felt ashamed and bitter, and would not for a million roubles have consented to speak in the presence of an outsider, her rival, that deceitful woman who was standing now behind the picture, and probably giggling malignantly.

'I have brought you a sketch,' she said timidly in a thin voice, and her lips quivered. '*Nature morte*.'

'Ah—ah! . . . A sketch?'

The artist took the sketch in his hands, and as he examined it walked, as it were mechanically, into the other room.

Olga Ivanovna followed him obediently.

'*Nature morte* . . . first sort,' he muttered, falling into rhyme. 'Kurort . . . sport . . . port . . .'

From the studio came the sound of hurried footsteps and the rustle of a skirt.

So *she* had gone. Olga Ivanovna wanted to scream aloud, to hit the artist on the head with something heavy and then leave, but she could see nothing through her tears, was crushed by her shame, and felt herself, not Olga Ivanovna, not an artist, but a little insect.

'I am tired . . .' said the artist languidly, looking at the sketch and tossing his head as though struggling with drowsiness. 'It's very nice, of course, but a sketch today, a sketch last year, another sketch in a month . . . I wonder you are not bored with them. If I were you I should give up painting and work seriously at music or something. You're not an artist, you know, but a musician. But you can't imagine how tired I am! I'll tell them to bring us some tea, shall I?'

He went out of the room, and Olga Ivanovna heard him give some order to his footman. To avoid farewells and explanations, and above all to avoid bursting into sobs, she ran as fast as she could, before Ryabovsky came back, to the entry, put on her galoshes, and went out into the street; then she breathed easily, and felt she was free for ever from Ryabovsky and from painting and from the burden of shame which had so crushed her in the studio. It was all over!

She drove to her dressmaker's; then to see Barnay, who had arrived only the day before; from Barnay to a music-shop, and all the time she was thinking how she would write Ryabovsky a cold, harsh letter full of personal dignity, and how in the spring or the summer she would go with Dymov to the Crimea, free herself finally there from the past, and begin a new life.

On getting home late in the evening she sat down in the drawing-room, without taking off her things, to begin the letter. Ryabovsky had told her she was not an artist, and to pay him back she would write to him now that he painted the same thing every year, and said exactly the same thing every day; that he was at a standstill, and that nothing more would come of him than had come already. She wanted to write, too, that he owed a great deal to her good influence, and that if he was going wrong it was only because her influence was paralysed by various dubious persons like the one who had been hiding behind the picture that day.

'Mums!' Dymov called from the study, without opening the door. 'Mums!'

'What is it?'

'Don't come in to me, but only come to the door—that's right . . . The day before yesterday I must have caught diphtheria at the hospital, and now . . . I am ill. Make haste and send for Korostelyov.'

Olga Ivanovna always called her husband by his surname, as she did all the men of her acquaintance; she disliked his Christian name, Osip, because it reminded her of the servant Osip in Gogol's play and because it rhymed with 'gossip'. But now she cried:

'Osip, it cannot be!'

'Send for him; I feel ill,' Dymov said behind the door, and she could hear him go back to the sofa and lie down. 'Send!' she heard his voice faintly.

'Good heavens!' thought Olga Ivanovna, turning chill with horror. 'It must be dangerous!'

For no reason she took the candle and went into her bedroom, and there, pondering what she must do, glanced casually at herself in the mirror. With her pale, frightened face, in a jacket with sleeves high on the shoulders, with yellow flounces at the front, and with stripes running in unusual directions on her skirt, she seemed to herself horrible and disgusting. She suddenly felt acutely sorry for Dymov, for his boundless love for her, for his young life, and even for the desolate little bed in which he had not slept for so long; and she remembered his habitual, gentle, resigned smile. She wept bitterly, and wrote an imploring letter to Korostelyov. It was two o'clock in the night.

VIII

When towards eight o'clock in the morning Olga Ivanovna, her head heavy from want of sleep and her hair unbrushed, came out of her bedroom, looking unattractive and with a guilty expression on her face, a gentleman with a black beard, apparently the doctor, passed by her into the hall. There was a smell of medicines. Korostelyov was standing near the study door, twisting his left moustache with his right hand.

'Excuse me, I can't let you go in,' he said surlily to Olga Ivanovna; 'it's catching. Besides, it's no use, really; he is delirious, anyway.'

'Has he really got diphtheria?' Olga Ivanovna asked in a whisper.

'People who wantonly risk infection ought to be hauled up and punished for it,' muttered Korostelyov, not answering Olga Ivanovna's question. 'Do you know how he caught it? On Tuesday he was sucking up the mucus through a pipette from a boy with diphtheria. And what for? It was stupid . . . Sheer folly . . .'

'Is it very dangerous?' asked Olga Ivanovna.

'Yes; they say it is the malignant form. We ought to send for Shrek, really.'

A little red-haired man with a long nose and a Jewish accent arrived; then a tall, stooping, shaggy individual, who looked like a head deacon; then a stout young man with a red face and spectacles. These were doctors who came to watch by turns beside their colleague. Korostelyov did not go home when his turn was over, but remained and wandered about the rooms like a shadow. The maid kept getting tea for the various doctors, and was constantly running to the chemist, and there was no one to tidy the rooms. There was a dismal stillness in the flat.

Olga Ivanovna sat in her bedroom and thought that God was punishing her for having deceived her husband. That silent, uncomplaining, incomprehensible creature, robbed by his meekness of all personality and will, weak from excessive kindness, was suffering in obscurity over there on his sofa, and had not complained. Yet if he were to complain even in delirium, the doctors watching by his bedside would learn that diphtheria was not the only cause of his sufferings. They would ask Korostelyov. He knew all about it, and it was not for nothing that he looked at his friend's wife with eyes that seemed to say that she was the real chief villain and diphtheria was only her accomplice. She did not think now of the moonlit evening on the Volga, nor the words of love, nor that poetical life in the hut. She thought only that from an idle whim, from self-indulgence, she had sullied herself all over from head to foot in something filthy, sticky, which one could never wash off . . .

'Oh, how dreadfully false I've been!' she thought, recalling the troubled love she had known with Ryabovsky. 'Curse it all! . . .'

At four o'clock she dined with Korostelyov. He did nothing but scowl and drink red wine, and did not eat a morsel. She ate nothing, either. One moment she was praying inwardly and vowing to God that if Dymov recovered she would love him again and be a faithful wife to him. Then, forgetting herself for a minute, she would look at Korostelyov, and think: 'Surely it must be dull to be a humble, obscure person, not remarkable in any way, especially with such a crumpled face and bad manners!' Then it seemed to her that God would strike her dead that very minute for not having once been in her husband's study, through fear of infection. But mainly she had a dull, despondent feeling and a conviction that her life was spoilt, and that it could never be set right . . .

After dinner darkness came on. When Olga Ivanovna went into the drawing-room Korostelyov was asleep on the sofa, with a gold-embroidered silk cushion under his head.

'Khee-poo-ah,' he snored—'khee-poo-ah.'

And the doctors as they came to sit up and went away again did not notice this disorder. The fact that a strange man was asleep and snoring in the drawing-room, and the sketches on the walls and the quaint decoration of the room, and the fact that the lady of the house was dishevelled and untidy—all that aroused not the slightest interest now. One of the doctors chanced to laugh at something, and the laugh had a strange and timid sound that made one's heart ache.

When Olga Ivanovna went into the drawing-room a second time, Korostelyov was not asleep, but sitting up and smoking.

'He has diphtheria of the nasal cavity,' he said in a low voice, 'and his heart is not working properly now. Things are in a bad way, really.'

'But you will send for Shrek?' said Olga Ivanovna.

'He has been already. It was he noticed that the diphtheria had passed into the nose. What's the use of Shrek! Shrek's no use at all, really. He is Shrek, I am Korostelyov, that's all there is to it.'

Time dragged on fearfully slowly. Olga Ivanovna lay down in her clothes on her bed, that had not been made all day, and sank into a doze. She dreamed that the whole flat was filled up from floor to ceiling with a huge piece of iron, and that if they could only get the iron out they would all be light-hearted and happy. Waking, she realised that it was not the iron but Dymov's illness that was weighing on her.

'*Nature morte*, port . . .' she thought, sinking into forgetfulness again. 'Sport . . . Kurort . . . and what of Shrek? Shrek . . . trek . . . wreck . . . And where are my friends now? Do they know that we are in trouble? Lord, save . . . spare! Shrek . . . trek . . .'

And again the iron was there . . . Time dragged on slowly, though the clock downstairs struck frequently. And bells were continually ringing as the doctors arrived . . . The housemaid came in with an empty glass on a tray, and asked, 'Shall I make the bed, madam?' and getting no answer, went away.

The clock below struck the hour. She dreamed of the rain on the Volga; and again someone came into her bedroom—a stranger, she thought. Olga Ivanovna jumped up, and recognised Korostelyov.

'What time is it?' she asked.

'About three.'

'Well, what is it?'

'What, indeed! . . . I've come to tell you he is dying . . .'

He gave a sob, sat down on the bed beside her, and wiped away the tears with his sleeve. She could not grasp it at once, but turned cold all over and began slowly crossing herself.

'He is dying,' he repeated in a shrill voice, and again he gave a sob. 'He is dying because he sacrificed himself. What a loss for science!' he said bitterly. 'Compare him with all of us. He was a great man, an extraordinary man! What gifts! What hopes we all had of him!' Korostelyov went on, wringing his hands: 'Merciful God, he would have been a scientist in a million. Osip Dymov, what have you done—oh, my God!'

Korostelyov covered his face with both hands in despair, and shook his head.

'And what moral strength,' he went on, seeming to grow more and more exasperated with someone. 'Not a man, but a pure, good, loving soul, and clean as crystal. He served science and died for science. And he worked like an ox night and day—no one spared him—and this young scientist, a future professor, had to take a private practice and work at translations at night to pay for these . . . vile rags!'

Korostelyov looked with hatred at Olga Ivanovna, snatched at the sheet with both hands and angrily tore it, as though it were to blame.

'He did not spare himself, and others did not spare him. Oh, what's the use of talking!'

'Yes, he was a very special man,' said a bass voice in the drawing-room.

Olga Ivanovna remembered her whole life with him from beginning to end, with all its details, and suddenly she understood that he really was an extraordinary, special, and, compared with everyone else she knew, a great man. And remembering how her late father and all the other doctors had regarded him, she realised that they all had seen in him a future celebrity. The walls, the ceiling, the lamp, and the carpet on the floor, winked at her sarcastically, as if trying to say, 'You were blind! you were blind!' With a wail she flung herself out of the bedroom, dashed by some unknown man in the drawing-room, and ran into her husband's study. He was lying motionless on the sofa, covered to the waist with a quilt. His face was fearfully thin and sunken, and was of a greyish-yellow colour such as is never seen in the living; only from his forehead, black eyebrows and his familiar smile, could he be recognised as Dymov. Olga Ivanovna hurriedly felt his chest, forehead, and hands. His chest was still warm, but his forehead and hands were unpleasantly cold, and his half-open eyes looked, not at Olga Ivanovna, but at the quilt.

'Dymov!' she called loudly, 'Dymov!' She wanted to explain to him that it had been a mistake, that all was not lost, that life might still be beautiful and happy, that he was an extraordinary, special, great man, and that she would worship him all her life and bow down in homage and holy awe before him . . .

'Dymov!' she called him, patting him on the shoulder, unable to believe that he would never wake again. 'Dymov! Dymov!'

In the drawing-room Korostelyov was saying to the housemaid:

'Why keep asking? Go to the churchwarden's lodge and enquire where the alms-women live. They'll wash the body and lay it out, and do everything that is necessary.'

In Exile

Old Semyon, nicknamed Canny, and a young Tartar, whom no one knew by name, were sitting on the river-bank by the camp-fire; the other three ferrymen were in the hut. Semyon, an old man of sixty, lean and toothless, but broad-shouldered and still healthy-looking, was drunk; he would have gone in to sleep long before, but he had a bottle in his pocket and he was afraid that the fellows in the hut would ask him for vodka. The Tartar was ill and weary, and wrapping himself up in his rags was describing how nice it was in the Simbirsk province, and what a beautiful and clever wife he had left behind at home. He was not more than twenty-five, and now by the light of the camp-fire, with his pale and sick, mournful face, he looked like a boy.

'To be sure, it is not paradise here,' said Canny. 'You can see for yourself, the water, the bare banks, clay, and nothing else . . . Easter has long passed and yet there is ice on the river, and this morning there was snow . . .'

'It's bad! it's bad!' said the Tartar, and looked round him in terror.

The dark, cold river was flowing ten paces away; it grumbled, lapped against the hollow clay banks and raced on swiftly towards the faraway sea. Close to the bank there was the dark blur of a big barge, which the ferrymen called a 'karbas'. Far away on the other bank, lights, dying down and flickering up again, zigzagged like little snakes; they were burning last year's grass. And beyond the little snakes there was darkness again. Little icicles could be heard knocking against the barge. It was damp and cold . . .

The Tartar glanced at the sky. There were as many stars as at home, and the same blackness all round, but something was lacking. At home in Simbirsk province the stars were quite different, and so was the sky.

'It's bad! it's bad!' he repeated.

'You will get used to it,' said Canny, and he laughed. 'Now you are young and foolish, the milk is hardly dry on your lips, and it seems to you in your foolishness that you are more wretched than anyone; but the time will come when you will say to yourself: "I wish no one a better life than mine." Just look at me. Within a week the floods will be over and we shall set up the ferry; you will all go wandering off about Siberia while I shall stay and shall begin crossing from bank to bank. I've been going like that for twenty-two years, day and night. The pike and the salmon are under the water while I am on the water. And thank God for it, I want nothing; God grant everyone such a life.'

The Tartar threw some dry twigs on the camp-fire, lay down closer to the blaze, and said:

'My father is a sick man. When he dies my mother and wife will come here. They have promised.'

'And what do you want your wife and mother for?' asked Canny. 'That's mere foolishness, my lad. It's the devil confounding you, damn his soul! Don't you listen to him, the cursed one. Don't let him have his way. He is on at you about the women, but you spite him; say, "I don't want them!" He is on at you about freedom, but you stand up to him and say: "I don't want it!" I want nothing, neither father nor mother, nor wife, nor freedom, nor post, nor paddock; I want nothing, damn their souls!'

Canny took a swig at the bottle and went on:

'I am not a simple peasant, not of the working class, but the son of a deacon, and when I was free I lived in Kursk; I used to wear a frock-coat, and now I have brought myself to such a pass that I can sleep naked on the ground and eat grass. And I wish no one a better life. I want nothing and I am afraid of nobody, and the way I look at it is that there is nobody richer and freer than I am. When they sent me here from Russia from the first day I dug my heels in: I want nothing! The devil was at me about my wife and about my home and about freedom, but I told him: "I want nothing." I stuck to it, and here you see I live well, and I don't complain, but if any-one gives way to the devil and listens to him, if only once, he is lost, there is no salvation for him: he is sunk in the bog to the crown of his head and will never get out.

'It is not only a foolish peasant like you, but even gentlemen, well-educated people, are lost. Fifteen years ago they sent a gentleman here from Russia. He hadn't shared something with his brothers and had forged something in a will. They did say he was a prince or a baron, but maybe he was simply an official—who knows? Well, the gentleman arrived here, and first thing he bought himself a house and land in Mukhortinskoye. "I want to live by my own work," says he, "in the sweat of my brow, for I am not a gentleman now," says he, "but a settler." "Well," says I, "God help you, that's the right thing." He was a young man then, busy and careful; he used to mow and catch fish and ride forty miles on horseback. Only this is what happened: from the very first year

176

he took to riding to Gyrino for the post; he used to stand on my ferry and sigh: "Ah, Semyon, how long it is since they sent me any money from home!" "You don't want money, Vasily Sergeich," says I. "What use is it to you? You cast away the past, and forget it as though it had never been at all, as though it had been a dream, and begin to live anew. Don't listen to the devil," says I; "he will bring you to no good, he'll draw you into a snare. Now you want money," says I, "but in a very little while you'll be wanting something else, and then more and more. If you want to be happy," says I, "the chief thing is not to want anything. Yes . . . If," says I, "if fate has wronged you and me cruelly, it's no good asking for her favour and bowing down to her, you should despise her and laugh at her, or else she will laugh at you." That's what I said to him . . .

'Two years later I ferried him across to this side, and he was rubbing his hands and laughing. "I am going to Gyrino to meet my wife," says he. "She was sorry for me," says he; "she has come. She is good and kind." And he was breathless with joy. So a day later he came with his wife. A beautiful young lady in a hat; in her arms was a baby girl. And lots of luggage of all sorts. And my Vasily Sergeich was fussing round her; he couldn't take his eyes off her and couldn't say enough in praise of her. "Yes, brother Semyon, even in Siberia people can live!" "Oh, all right," thinks I, "it will be a different tale presently." And from that time forward he went almost every week to enquire whether money had not come from Russia. He needed a lot of money. "She is ruining her youth and beauty here in Siberia for my sake," says he, "and sharing my bitter lot with me, and so I ought", says he, "to provide her with every comfort . . ."

'To make it livelier for the lady he made acquaintance with the officials and all sorts of riff-raff. And of course he had to give food and drink to all that crew, and there had to be a piano and a shaggy lap-dog on the sofa—plague take it! . . . Luxury, in fact, self-indulgence. The lady did not stay with him long. How could she? The clay, the water, the cold, no vegetables for you, no fruit. All around you, ignorant and drunken people and no sort of manners, and she was a spoilt lady from Petersburg or Moscow . . . To be sure she moped. Besides, her husband, say what you like, was not a gentleman now, but a settler—not the same rank.

'Three years later, I remember, on the eve of the Assumption, there was shouting from the further bank. I went over with the ferry, and what do I see but the lady, all wrapped up, and with her a young gentleman, an official. A sledge with three horses . . . I ferried them across here, they got in and away like the wind. They were soon lost to sight. And towards morning Vasily Sergeich galloped up with a pair of horses. "Did my wife come this way with a gentleman in spectacles, Semyon?" "She did," said I; "you may look for the wind in the fields!" He galloped in pursuit of them. For five days and nights he was riding after them. When I ferried him over to the other side afterwards, he flung himself on the ferry and beat his head on the boards and howled. "So that's how it is," says I. I laughed, and reminded him "people can live even in Siberia!" And he beat his head harder than ever . . .

'Then he began longing for freedom. His wife had slipped off to Russia, and of course he was drawn there to see her and to get her away from her lover. And he took, my lad, to galloping almost every day, either to the post or to the town to see the commanding officer; he kept sending in petitions for them to have mercy on him and let him go back home; and he used to say that he had spent some two hundred roubles on telegrams alone. He sold his land and mortgaged his house to the Jews. He grew grey and bent, and yellow in the face, as though he was consumptive. If he talked to you he would go, khee—khee—khee, . . . and there were tears in his eyes. He kept rushing about like this with petitions for eight years, but now he has grown brighter and more cheerful again: he has found another whim to give way to. You see, his daughter has grown up. He looks at her, and she is the apple of his eye. And to tell the truth she is all right, good-looking, with black eyebrows and a lively disposition. Every Sunday he used to ride with her to church in Gyrino. They used to stand on the ferry, side by side, she would laugh and he could not take his eyes off her. "Yes, Semyon," says he, "people can live even in Siberia. Even in Siberia there is happiness. Look," says he, "what a daughter I have ! I warrant you wouldn't find another like her for a thousand miles around." "Your daughter is all right," says I, "that's true, certainly." But to myself I thought: "Wait a bit, the wench is young, her blood is dancing, she wants to live, and there is no life here." And she did begin to pine, my lad . . . She faded and faded, fell ill, and now she can hardly crawl about. Consumption.

'So you see what Siberian happiness is, damn its soul! You see how people can live in Siberia . . . He has taken to going from one doctor to another and bringing them home with him. As soon as he hears that one or two hundred miles away there is a doctor or a quack, he will drive to fetch him. A terrible lot of money he has spent on doctors, and to my thinking he had better have spent the money on drink . . . She'll die just the same. She is certain to die, and then it will be all over with him. He'll hang himself from grief or run away to Russia—that's a sure thing. He'll run away and they'll catch him, then he will be tried, sent to prison, he will have a taste of the lash . . .'

'Good! good!' muttered the Tartar, shivering with cold.

'What is good?' asked Canny.

'His wife, his daughter . . . What of prison and what of sorrow!—anyway, he did see his wife and his daughter . . . You say, want nothing. But "nothing" is bad! His wife lived with him three years—that was a gift from God. "Nothing" is bad, but three years is good. How not understand?'

Shivering and hesitating, with effort picking out the Russian words of which he knew but few, the Tartar said that God forbid one should fall sick and die in a strange land, and be buried in the cold, dark earth; that if his wife came to him for one day, even for one hour, then for such happiness he would be ready to bear any suffering and to thank God. Better one day of happiness than nothing.

Then he described again what a beautiful and clever wife he had left at home. Then, clutching his head in both hands, he began crying and assuring Semyon that he was not guilty, and was suffering for nothing. His two brothers and an uncle had carried off a peasant's horses, and had beaten the old man till he was half dead, and the commune had not judged fairly, but had contrived a sentence by which all the three brothers were sent to Siberia, while the uncle, a rich man, was left at home.

'You will get u-used to it!' said Semyon.

The Tartar was silent, and stared with tear-stained eyes at the fire; his face expressed bewilderment and fear, as though he still did not understand why he was here in the darkness and the damp, beside strangers, and not in Simbirsk province.

Canny lay near the fire, chuckled at something, and began humming a song in an undertone.

'What joy has she with her father?' he said a little later. 'He loves her and he rejoices in her, that's true; but, mate, you must mind your p's and q's with him, he is a strict old man, a harsh old man. And young wenches don't want strictness. They want affection and ha-ha-ha! and ho-ho-ho! and scent and pomade. Yes . . . Ah! life, life,' sighed Semyon, and he got up heavily. 'The vodka is all gone, so it's time to sleep. Eh? I am going, my lad . . .'

Left alone, the Tartar put on more twigs, lay down and stared at the fire; he began thinking of his own village and of his wife. If his wife could only come for a month, for a day; and then if she wished she could go back again. Better a month or even a day than nothing. But if his wife kept her promise and came, what would he have to feed her on? Where could she live here?

'If there were not something to eat, how could she live?' the Tartar asked aloud.

He was paid only ten kopecks for working all day and all night at the oar; it is true that travellers gave him tips for tea and for vodka, but the men shared all they received among themselves, and gave nothing to the Tartar, but only laughed at him. And from poverty he was hungry, cold, and frightened . . . Now, when his whole body was aching and shivering, he ought to go into the hut and lie down to sleep; but he had nothing to cover him there, and it was colder than on the river-bank; here he had nothing to cover him either, but at least he could make up the fire . . .

In another week, when the floods were quite over and they set the ferry going, none of the ferrymen but Semyon would be wanted, and the Tartar would begin walking from village to village begging for alms and for work. His wife was only seventeen; she was beautiful, spoilt, and shy; could she possibly walk from village to village begging alms with her face unveiled? No, it was terrible even to think of that . . .

It was already getting light; the barge, the bushes of willow on the water, and the waves could be clearly discerned, and if one looked round there was the steep clay slope; at the bottom a hut thatched with dingy brown straw, and the huts of the village lay clustered higher up. The cocks were already crowing in the village.

The rusty-red clay slope, the barge, the river, the strange, unkind people, hunger, cold, illness, perhaps all that was not real. Most likely it was all a dream, thought the Tartar. He felt that he was asleep and heard his own snoring . . . Of course he was at home in the Simbirsk province, and he had only to call his wife by name for her to answer; and in the next room was his mother . . . What terrible dreams there are, though! What are they for? The Tartar smiled and opened his eyes. What river was this, the Volga?

Snow was falling.

'Boat!' was shouted on the further side. 'Boat!'

The Tartar woke up, and went to wake his mates and row over to the other side. The ferrymen came on to the river-bank, putting on their torn sheepskins as they walked, swearing with voices husky from sleepiness and shivering from the cold. On waking from their sleep, the river, from which came a breath of piercing cold, struck them as revolting and horrible. They jumped into the barge without hurrying themselves . . . The Tartar and the three ferrymen took the long, broad-bladed oars, which in the darkness looked like the claws of crabs; Semyon leaned his stomach against the tiller. The shout on the other side still continued, and two shots were fired from a revolver, probably with the idea that the ferrymen were asleep or had gone to the tavern in the village.

'All right, you have plenty of time,' said Canny in the tone of a man convinced that there was no necessity in this world to hurry—that it would lead to nothing, anyway.

The heavy, clumsy barge moved away from the bank and floated between the willow-bushes, and only the willows slowly receding showed that the barge was not standing still but moving. The ferrymen swung the oars evenly in time; Canny lay with his stomach on the tiller, and, describing a semicircle in the air, flew from one side to the other. In the darkness it looked as though the men were sitting on some antediluvian animal with long paws, and were sailing on it towards a cold, desolate land, the land of which one sometimes dreams in nightmares.

They passed beyond the willows and floated out into the open. The creak and regular splash of the oars was heard on the further shore, and a shout came: 'Make haste! make haste!'

Another ten minutes passed, and the barge banged heavily against the landing-stage.

'And it keeps sprinkling and sprinkling,' muttered Semyon, wiping the snow from his face; 'and where it all comes from God only knows.'

On the bank stood a thin man of medium height, in a jacket lined with fox-fur and in a white lambskin cap. He was standing at a little distance from his horses and not moving; he had a gloomy, concentrated expression, as though he were trying to remember something and angry with his untrustworthy memory. When Semyon went up to him and took off his cap, smiling, he said:

'I am hastening to Anastasyevka. My daughter's worse again, and they say that there is a new doctor at Anastasyevka.'

They dragged the carriage on to the barge and floated back. The man whom Semyon addressed as Vasily Sergeich stood all the time motionless, tightly compressing his thick lips and staring out into space; when his coachman asked permission to smoke in his presence he made no answer, as though he had not heard. Semyon, lying with his stomach on the tiller, looked mockingly at him and said:

'Even in Siberia people can live—can li–ive!'

There was a triumphant expression on Canny's face, as though he had proved something and was delighted that things had happened as he had foretold. The unhappy helpless look of the man in the foxskin coat evidently afforded him great pleasure.

'It's muddy driving now, Vasily Sergeich,' he said when the horses were harnessed again on the bank. 'You should have put off going for another fortnight, when it will be drier. Or else not have gone at all . . . If any good would come of your going—but as you know yourself, people have been driving about for years and years, day and night, and it's always been no use. That's the truth.'

Vasily Sergeich tipped him without a word, got into his carriage and drove off.

'There, he has galloped off for a doctor!' said Semyon, shivering from the cold. 'But looking for a good doctor is like chasing the wind in the fields or catching the devil by the tail, plague take your soul! What an odd chap, Lord forgive me a sinner!'

The Tartar went up to Canny, and, looking at him with hatred and repulsion, quivering, and mixing Tartar words with his broken Russian, said:

'He is good . . . good; but you are bad! You are bad! The gentleman is a good soul, excellent, and you are a beast, bad! The gentleman is alive, but you are a dead carcass . . . God created man to be alive, and to have joy and grief and sorrow; but you want nothing, so you are not alive, you are stone, clay! A stone wants nothing and you want nothing. You are a stone, and God does not love you, but He loves the gentleman!'

Everyone laughed; the Tartar frowned contemptuously, and with a wave of his hand wrapped himself in his rags and went to the camp-fire. The ferrymen and Semyon sauntered to the hut.

'It's cold,' said one ferryman huskily as he stretched himself on the straw with which the damp clay floor was covered.

'Yes, it's not warm,' another agreed. 'It's a hard life . . .'

They all lay down. The door was thrown open by the wind and the snow drifted into the hut; nobody felt inclined to get up and shut the door: they were cold, and it was too much trouble.

'I am all right,' said Semyon as he began to doze. 'I wouldn't wish anyone a better life.'

'You are a tough one, we all know. Even the devils won't take you!'

Sounds like a dog's howling came from outside.

'What's that? Who's there?'

'It's the Tartar crying.'

'I say . . . He's an odd one!'

'He'll get u–used to it!' said Semyon, and at once fell asleep.

The others were soon asleep too. And the door remained unclosed.

Ward No. 6

In the hospital yard there stands a small lodge surrounded by a perfect forest of burdocks, nettles, and wild hemp. Its roof is rusty, the chimney is tumbling down, the steps at the front door are rotting away and overgrown with grass, and there are only traces left of the stucco. The front of the lodge faces the hospital; at the back it looks out into the open country, from which it is separated by the grey hospital fence with nails on it. These nails, with their points upwards, and the fence, and the lodge itself, have that peculiar, desolate, God-forsaken look which is only found in our hospital and prison buildings.

If you are not afraid of being stung by the nettles, come by the narrow footpath that leads to the lodge, and let us see what is going on inside. Opening the first door, we walk into the porch. Here along the walls and by the stove every sort of hospital rubbish lies littered about. Mattresses, old tattered dressing-gowns, trousers, blue striped shirts, boots and shoes no good for anything—all these remnants are piled up in heaps, mixed up and crumpled, mouldering and giving out a sickly smell.

The porter, Nikita, an old soldier wearing rusty good-conduct stripes, is always lying on the litter with a pipe between his teeth. He has a grim, surly, battered-looking face, overhanging eyebrows which give him the expression of a sheep-dog of the steppes, and a red nose; he is short and looks thin and scraggy, but he is of imposing deportment and his fists are huge. He belongs to the class of simple-hearted, practical, and dull-witted people, prompt in carrying out orders, who like discipline better than anything in the world, and so are convinced that it is their duty to beat people. He showers blows on the face, on the chest, on the back, on whatever comes first, and is convinced that there would be no order in the place if he did not.

Next you come into a big, spacious room which fills up the whole lodge except for the porch. Here the walls are painted a dirty blue, the ceiling is as sooty as in a hut without a chimney—it is evident that in the winter the stove smokes and the room is full of fumes. The windows are disfigured by iron gratings on the inside. The wooden floor is grey and full of splinters. There is a stench of sour cabbage, of smouldering wicks, of bugs, and of ammonia, and at first this stench gives you the impression of having walked into a menagerie . . .

There are bedsteads screwed to the floor. Men in blue hospital dressing-gowns, and wearing nightcaps in the old style, are sitting and lying on them. These are the lunatics.

In all, there are five of them here. Only one is of the upper class, the rest are all artisans. The one nearest the door—a tall, lean workman with shining red whiskers and tear-stained eyes—sits with his head propped on his hand, staring at the same point. Day and night he grieves, shaking his head, sighing and smiling bitterly. He rarely takes a part in conversation and usually makes no answer to questions; he eats and drinks mechanically when food is offered him. From his agonising, throbbing cough, his thinness, and the flush on his cheeks, one may judge that he is in the first stage of consumption. Next to him is a little, alert, very lively old man, with a pointed beard and curly black hair like a negro's. By day he walks up and down the ward from window to window, or sits on his bed, cross-legged like a Turk, and ceaselessly, as a bullfinch, whistles, softly sings and titters. He shows his childish gaiety and lively character at night also when he gets up to say his prayers—that is, to beat himself on the chest with his fists, and to scratch with his fingers at the door. This is the Jew Moyseyka, an imbecile, who went crazy twenty years ago when his hat factory was burnt down.

And of all the inhabitants of Ward No. 6, he is the only one who is allowed to go out of the lodge, and even out of the yard into the street. He has enjoyed this privilege for years, probably because he is an old inhabitant of the hospital—a quiet, harmless imbecile, the buffoon of the town, where people are used to seeing him surrounded by boys and dogs. In his wretched gown, in his absurd nightcap, and in slippers, sometimes with bare legs and even without trousers, he walks about the streets, stopping at the gates and little shops, and begging for a kopeck. In one place they will give him some kvass, in another some bread, in another a kopeck, so that he generally goes back to the ward feeling rich and well-fed. Everything that he brings back Nikita takes from him for his own benefit. The soldier does this roughly, angrily turning the Jew's pockets inside out, and calling God to witness that he will not let him go into the street again, and that a breach of the regulations is worse to him than anything in the world.

Moyseyka likes to make himself useful. He gives his companions water, and covers them up when they are asleep; he promises each of them to bring him back a kopeck, and to make him a new cap; he feeds

185

with a spoon his neighbour on the left, who is paralysed. He acts in this way, not from compassion nor from any considerations of a humane kind, but through imitation, involuntarily submitting to Gromov, his neighbour on the right.

Ivan Dmitrich Gromov, a man of thirty-three, who is a gentleman by birth, and has been a bailiff and provincial secretary, suffers from persecution mania. He either lies curled up in bed or walks from corner to corner as though for exercise; he very rarely sits down. He is always excited, agitated, and overwrought by a sort of vague, undefined expectation. The faintest rustle in the porch or shout in the yard is enough to make him raise his head and begin listening: are they coming for him? Are they looking for him? And at such times his face expresses the utmost uneasiness and repulsion.

I like his broad face with its high cheekbones, always pale and unhappy, and reflecting, as though in a mirror, a soul tormented by conflict and long-continued terror. His grimaces are strange and abnormal, but the delicate lines traced on his face by profound, genuine suffering show intelligence and sense, and there is a warm and healthy light in his eyes. I like the man himself, courteous, anxious to be of use, and extraordinarily gentle to everyone except Nikita. When anyone drops a button or a spoon, he jumps up from his bed quickly and picks it up; every day he says good morning to his companions, and when he goes to bed he wishes them good night.

Besides his continually overwrought condition and his grimaces, his madness shows itself in the following way also. Sometimes in the evenings he wraps himself in his dressing-gown, and, trembling all over, with his teeth chattering, begins walking rapidly from corner to corner and between the bedsteads. It seems as though he is in a violent fever. From the way he suddenly stops and glances at his companions, it can be seen that he is longing to say something very important, but, apparently reflecting that they would not listen or would not understand him, he shakes his head impatiently and goes on pacing up and down. But soon the desire to speak gets the upper hand of every consideration, and he will let himself go and speak fervently and passionately. His talk is disordered and feverish like delirium, disconnected, and not always intelligible, but, on the other hand, something extremely fine may be felt in it, both in the words and the voice. When he talks you recognise in him the lunatic and the human being. It is difficult to reproduce on paper his insane talk. He speaks of the baseness of mankind, of violence trampling on justice, of the glorious life which will one day be upon earth, of the window-gratings, which remind him every minute of the stupidity and cruelty of oppressors. It makes a disorderly, incoherent pot-pourri of themes old but not yet out of date.

II

Some twelve or fifteen years ago an official called Gromov, a highly respectable and prosperous person, was living in his own house in the principal street of the town. He had two sons, Sergey and Ivan. When Sergey was a student in his fourth year he was taken ill with galloping consumption and died, and his death was, as it were, the first of a whole series of calamities which suddenly descended on the Gromov family. Within a week of Sergey's funeral the old father was put on trial for fraud and misappropriation, and he died of typhoid in the prison hospital soon afterwards. The house, with all their belongings, was sold by auction, and Ivan Dmitrich and his mother were left entirely without means.

Hitherto, in his father's lifetime, Ivan Dmitrich, who was studying at the University of Petersburg, had received an allowance of sixty or seventy roubles a month, and had had no conception of poverty; now he had to make an abrupt change in his life. He had to spend his time from morning to night giving lessons for next to nothing, to work at copying, and with all that to go hungry, as all his earnings were sent to keep his mother. Ivan Dmitrich could not stand such a life; he lost heart and strength, and, giving up the University, went home.

Here, in the little town, through connections he obtained the post of teacher in the district school, but could not get on with his colleagues, was not liked by the boys, and soon gave up the post. His mother died. He was for six months without work, living on nothing but bread and water; then he became a bailiff. He kept this post until he was dismissed because of illness.

He had never even in his young student days given the impression of being perfectly healthy. He had always been pale, thin, and prone to catch cold; he ate little and slept badly. A single glass of wine went to his head and made him hysterical. He always had a craving for society, but, owing to his irritable temperament and suspiciousness, he never became very intimate with anyone, and had no friends. He always spoke with contempt of his fellow-townsmen, saying that their coarse ignorance and sleepy animal existence seemed to him loathsome and horrible. He spoke in a loud tenor, ardently, and invariably either with scorn and indignation, or with wonder and enthusiasm, and always with perfect sincerity. Whatever one talked to him about he always brought it round to the same subject: that life was dull and stifling in the town; that the townspeople had no lofty interests, but lived a dingy, meaningless life, diversified by violence, coarse profligacy, and hypocrisy; that scoundrels were well fed and clothed, while honest men lived from hand to mouth; that they needed schools, a progressive local paper, a theatre, public lectures, solidarity among the intelligentsia; that society must recognise its failings and be horrified. In his criticisms of people he laid on the colours thick, using only black and white, and no fine shades; mankind was divided for him into honest men and scoundrels: there was nothing in between. He always spoke with passion and delight of women and of love, but he had never been in love.

In town, despite the severity of his judgements and his nervousness, he was liked, and behind his back was spoken of affectionately as Vanya. His innate refinement and readiness to be of service, his decency, his moral purity, and his shabby coat, his frail appearance and family misfortunes, aroused a kind, warm, sorrowful feeling. Moreover, he was well educated and well read; according to the townspeople's notions, he knew everything, and was in their eyes something like a walking encyclopaedia.

He had read a great deal. He would sit at the club, nervously pulling at his beard and looking through the magazines and books; and from his face one could see that he was not reading, but devouring the pages, scarcely giving himself time to digest what he read. It must be supposed that reading was one of his morbid habits, as he fell upon anything that came into his hands with equal avidity, even last year's newspapers and calendars. At home he always read lying down.

III

One autumn morning Ivan Dmitrich, turning up the collar of his greatcoat and splashing through the mud, made his way by side-streets and back lanes to see some artisan, and to collect some payment that was owing. He was in a gloomy mood, as he always was in the morning. In one of the side-streets he was met by two convicts in fetters and an escort of four soldiers with rifles. Ivan Dmitrich had very often met convicts before, and they had always excited feelings of compassion and discomfort in him; but now this meeting made a peculiar, strange impression on him. It suddenly seemed to him for some reason that he, too, might be put into fetters and led through the mud to prison like that. After visiting the artisan, on the way home he met near the post office a police superintendent of his acquaintance, who greeted him and walked a few paces along the street with him, and for some reason this seemed to him suspicious. At home he could not get the convicts or the soldiers with their rifles out of his head all day, and an unaccountable inward agitation prevented him from reading or concentrating his mind. In the evening he did not light his lamp, and at night he could not sleep, but kept thinking that he might be arrested, put into fetters, and thrown into prison. He did not know of any harm he had done, and could be certain that he would never be guilty of murder, arson, or theft in the future either; but was it not easy to commit a crime by accident, unconsciously, and was not false witness always possible, and, indeed, miscarriage of justice? It was not without good reason that the age-long experience of the simple people teaches that beggary and prison are ills none can be safe from. A miscarriage of justice is very possible the way legal proceedings are conducted nowadays, and it would come as no surprise. People who have an official, professional relation to other men's sufferings—for instance, judges, police officers, doctors—in the course of time, through habit, grow so callous that they cannot, even if they wish it, take anything but a formal attitude to their clients; in this respect they are no different from the peasant who slaughters sheep and calves in the backyard, and does not notice the blood. With this formal, soulless attitude to human personality the judge needs but one thing—time—in order to deprive an innocent man of all rights of property, and to condemn him to penal servitude. Only the time spent on performing certain formalities for which the judge is paid his salary, and then—it is all over. Then you may look in vain for justice and defence in this dirty, wretched little town a hundred and fifty miles from a railway station! And, indeed, is it not absurd even to think of justice when every kind of violence is accepted by society as a rational and consistent necessity, and every act of mercy—for instance, a verdict of acquittal—calls forth a whole outburst of dissatisfied and revengeful feeling?

In the morning Ivan Dmitrich got up from his bed in a state of horror, with cold perspiration on his forehead, completely convinced that he might be arrested any minute. Since his gloomy thoughts of yesterday had haunted him so long, he thought, it must be that there was some truth in them. They could not, indeed, have come into his mind without any grounds whatever.

189

A policeman walking slowly passed by the windows: that was not for nothing. Here were two men standing still and silent near the house. Why were they silent? And agonising days and nights followed for Ivan Dmitrich. Everyone who passed by the windows or came into the yard seemed to him a spy or a detective. At midday the chief of the police usually drove down the street with a pair of horses; he was going from his estate near the town to the police department; but Ivan Dmitrich fancied every time that he was driving especially quickly, and that he had a peculiar expression: it was evident that he was in haste to announce that there was a very important criminal in the town. Ivan Dmitrich started at every ring of the bell and knock on the gate, and was agitated whenever he came upon anyone new at his landlady's; when he met police officers and gendarmes he smiled and began whistling so as to seem unconcerned. He could not sleep for whole nights in succession expecting to be arrested, but he snored loudly and sighed as though in deep sleep, so that his landlady might think he was asleep; for if he could not sleep it meant that he was tormented by pangs of conscience—what a piece of evidence! Facts and common sense persuaded him that all these terrors were nonsense and morbidity, that if one looked at the matter more broadly there was nothing really terrible in arrest and imprisonment—so long as one's conscience is at ease; but the more sensibly and logically he reasoned, the more acute and agonising his mental distress became. It might be compared with the story of a hermit who tried to cut a dwelling-place for himself in a virgin forest: the more zealously he worked with his axe, the thicker the forest grew. In the end Ivan Dmitrich, seeing it was useless, gave up reasoning altogether, and abandoned himself entirely to despair and dread.

He began to avoid people and to seek solitude. His official work had been distasteful to him before: now it became unbearable to him. He was afraid they would somehow get him into trouble, would put a bribe in his pocket unnoticed and then denounce him, or that he would accidentally make a mistake in official papers that would seem tantamount to fraud, or would lose other people's money. It is strange that his imagination had never at other times been so agile and inventive as now, when every day he thought of thousands of different reasons for being seriously anxious over his freedom and honour; but, on the other hand, his interest in the outer world, in books in particular, grew noticeably fainter, and his memory began to fail him.

In the spring when the snow melted there were found in the ravine near the cemetery two half-decomposed corpses—the bodies of an old woman and a boy bearing the traces of death by violence. Nothing was talked of in town but these bodies and their unknown murderers. That people might not think he had been guilty of the crime, Ivan Dmitrich walked about the streets, smiling, and when he met acquaintances he turned pale, flushed, and began declaring that there was no greater crime than the murder of the weak and defenceless. But this duplicity soon exhausted him, and after some reflection he decided that in his position the best thing to do was to hide in his landlady's cellar. He sat in the cellar all day and then all night, then another day, was fearfully cold, and, waiting till dusk, stole secretly like a thief back to his room. He stood in the middle of the room till day-break, listening without stirring. Very early in the morning, before sun-rise, some workmen came into the house. Ivan Dmitrich knew perfectly well that they had come to mend the stove in the kitchen, but his fear told him that they were police officers disguised as workmen. He slipped stealthily out of the flat, and, overcome by terror, ran along the street without his cap and coat. Dogs raced after him barking, a peasant shouted somewhere behind him, the wind whistled in his ears, and it seemed to Ivan Dmitrich that the violence of the whole world was massed together behind his back and was chasing after him.

He was stopped and brought home, and his landlady sent for a doctor. Doctor Andrey Yefimych, of whom we shall have more to say hereafter, prescribed cold compresses on his head and laurel drops, shook his head sadly, and went away, telling the landlady he would not come again, as one should not interfere with people who are going out of their minds. As he had not the means to live at home and be nursed, Ivan Dmitrich was soon sent to the hospital, and was there put into the ward for venereal patients. He could not sleep at night, was full of whims and fancies, and disturbed the patients, and was soon afterwards, by Andrey Yefimych's orders, transferred to Ward No. 6.

Within a year Ivan Dmitrich was completely forgotten in the town, and his books, heaped up by his landlady in a sledge in the shed, were pil-fered by boys.

IV

Ivan Dmitrich's neighbour on the left is, as I have said already, the Jew Moyseyka; his neighbour to the right is a peasant so rolling in fat that he is almost spherical, with a blankly stupid face, utterly devoid of thought.

This is a motionless, gluttonous, unclean animal who has long ago lost all powers of thought or feeling. An acrid, stifling stench always comes from him.

Nikita, who has to clean up after him, beats him terribly with all his might, not sparing his fists; and what is dreadful is not his being beaten— that one can get used to—but the fact that this stupefied creature does not respond to the blows with a sound or a movement, nor by a look in the eyes, but only sways a little like a heavy barrel.

The fifth and last inhabitant of Ward No. 6 is a man of the artisan class who had once been a sorter in the post office, a thinnish, fair little man with a good-natured but rather sly face. To judge from the bright, cheerful look in his calm and intelligent eyes, he is rather a deep one, and has some very important and pleasant secret. He keeps under his pillow and under his mattress something that he never shows anyone, not from fear of its being taken from him and stolen, but from modesty. Sometimes he goes to the window, and turning his back to his companions, puts something on his breast, and bending his head, looks at it; if you go up to him at such a moment, he is overcome with confusion and snatches something off his breast. But it is not difficult to guess his secret.

'Congratulate me,' he often says to Ivan Dmitrich; 'I have been presented with the Stanislav order of the second degree with the star. The second degree with the star is only given to foreigners, but for some reason they want to make an exception for me,' he says with a smile, shrugging his shoulders in perplexity. 'That I must confess I did not expect.'

'I don't understand anything about that,' Ivan Dmitrich replies morosely.

'But do you know what I shall attain to sooner or later?' the former sorter persists, screwing up his eyes slyly. 'I shall certainly get the Swedish "Polar Star". That's an order it is worth working for, a white cross with a black ribbon. It's very beautiful.'

Probably in no other place is life so monotonous as in this ward. In the morning the patients, except the paralytic and the fat peasant, wash in the porch at a big tub and wipe themselves with the skirts of their dressing-gowns; after that they drink tea out of tin mugs which Nikita brings them from the main building. Everyone is allowed one mugful. At midday they have soup made from sour cabbage and boiled grain, in the evening their supper consists of grain left from dinner. In the intervals they lie down, sleep, look out of the window, and walk from one corner to the other. And so every day. Even the former sorter always talks of the same orders.

Fresh faces are rarely seen in Ward No. 6. The doctor has not taken in any new mental cases for a long time, and the people who are fond of visiting lunatic asylums are few in this world. Once every two months Semyon Lazarich, the barber, appears in the ward. How he cuts the patients' hair, and how Nikita helps him to do it, and what a trepidation the lunatics are always thrown into by the arrival of the drunken, smiling barber, we will not describe.

No one even looks into the ward except the barber. The patients are condemned to see day after day no one but Nikita.

A rather strange rumour has, however, been circulating in the hospital of late.

It is rumoured that the doctor has begun to visit Ward No. 6.

V

A strange rumour!

Doctor Andrey Yefimych Ragin is a remarkable man in his own way. They say that when he was young he was very religious, and prepared himself for a clerical career, and that when he had finished his studies at the high school in 1863 he intended to enter a theological academy, but that his father, a surgeon and doctor of medicine, jeered at him and declared point-blank that he would disown him if he became a priest. How far this is true I don't know, but Andrey Yefimych himself has more than once confessed that he has never had a natural bent for medicine or science in general.

However that may have been, when he finished his studies in the medical faculty he did not enter the priesthood. He showed no special devoutness, and was no more like a priest at the beginning of his medical career than he is now.

His exterior is heavy, coarse like a peasant's; his face, beard, flat hair, and tough, clumsy figure suggest an overfed, intemperate, and harsh innkeeper on the high road. His face is surly-looking and covered with blue veins, his eyes are little and his nose is red. With his height and broad shoulders he has huge hands and feet; one would think that a blow from his fist would knock the life out of anyone, but his step is soft, and his walk is cautious and insinuating; when he meets anyone in a narrow passage he is always the first to stop and make way, and to say, not in a bass, as one would expect, but in a high, soft tenor: 'I beg your pardon!' He has a little swelling on his neck which prevents him from wearing stiff starched collars, and so he always goes about in soft linen or cotton shirts. Altogether he does not dress like a doctor. He wears the same suit for ten years, and the new clothes, which he usually buys at a Jewish shop, look as shabby and crumpled on him as his old ones; he sees patients and dines and pays visits all in the same coat; but this is not due to niggardliness, but to complete carelessness about his appearance.

When Andrey Yefimych came to the town to take up his duties the 'charitable institution' was in a terrible condition. One could hardly breathe for the stench in the wards, in the passages, and in the courtyards of the hospital. The hospital servants, the nurses, and their children slept in the wards together with the patients. They complained that cockroaches, bedbugs, and mice made life impossible. The surgical wards were never free from erysipelas. There were only two scalpels and not one thermometer in the whole hospital; potatoes were kept in the baths. The superintendent, the housekeeper, and the medical assistant robbed the patients, and of the old doctor, Andrey Yefimych's predecessor, people declared that he secretly sold the hospital alcohol, and that he kept a regular harem consisting of nurses and female patients. These disorderly proceedings were perfectly well known in the town, and were even exaggerated, but people took them calmly; some justified them on the ground that there were only peasants and working-men in the hospital, who could not be dissatisfied, since they were much worse off at home than in the hospital—they couldn't be fed on woodcocks! Others said in excuse that the town alone, without help from the local district council, the zemstvo, was not equal to maintaining a good hospital; thank God for having one at all, even a poor one. And the newly formed zemstvo did not open infirmaries either in the town or the neighbourhood, relying on the fact that the town already had its hospital.

After looking over the hospital Andrey Yefimych came to the conclusion that it was an immoral institution and extremely prejudicial to the health of the townspeople. In his opinion the most sensible thing that could be done was to let out the patients and close the hospital. But he reflected that his will alone was not enough to do this, and that it would be useless; if physical and moral impurity were driven out of one place, they would only move to another; one must wait for it to wither away of itself. Besides, if people open a hospital and put up with having it, it must be because they need it; superstition and all the nastiness and abominations of daily life were necessary, since in process of time they worked out to something sensible, just as manure turns into black earth. There was nothing on earth so good that it had not something nasty about its first origin.

When Andrey Yefimych undertook his duties he was apparently not greatly concerned about the irregularities at the hospital. He only asked the attendants and nurses not to sleep in the wards, and had two cupboards of instruments put up; the superintendent, the housekeeper, the medical assistant, and the erysipelas remained unchanged.

Andrey Yefimych loved intelligence and honesty intensely, but he had no strength of will nor belief in his right to organise an intelligent and honest life about him. He was absolutely unable to give orders, to forbid things, and to insist. It seemed as though he had taken a vow never to raise his voice and never to make use of the imperative. It was difficult for him to say 'Give' or 'Bring'; when he wanted his meals he would cough hesitatingly and say to the cook: 'How about tea? . . .' or 'How about dinner? . . .' To dismiss the superintendent or to tell him to stop stealing, or to abolish that unnecessary parasitic post altogether, was absolutely beyond his powers. When Andrey Yefimych was deceived or flattered, or accounts he knew to be crooked were brought him to sign, he would turn as red as a crab and feel guilty, and yet he would still sign the accounts. When the patients complained to him of being hungry or of the roughness of the nurses, he would be embarrassed and mutter guiltily: 'Very well, very well, I will go into it later . . . Most likely there is some misunderstanding . . .'

At first Andrey Yefimych worked very zealously. He saw patients every day from morning till dinner-time, performed operations, and even attended confinements. The ladies said of him that he was attentive and clever at diagnosing diseases, especially those of women and children. But in process of time the work unmistakably wearied him by its monotony and obvious uselessness. Today one sees thirty patients, and tomorrow they have increased to thirty-five, the next day forty, and so on from day to day, from year to year, while the mortality in the town did not decrease and the patients kept on coming. To be any real help to forty patients between morning and dinner was not physically possible, so it could lead only to deception. If twelve thousand patients were seen in a year it meant, if one looked at it simply, that twelve thousand people were deceived. To put those who were seriously ill into wards, and to treat them according to the principles of science, was impossible, too, because

195

though there were principles there was no science; if he were to put aside philosophy and pedantically follow the rules as other doctors did, the most necessary things were cleanliness and ventilation instead of dirt, wholesome nourishment instead of broth made of stinking, sour cabbage, and good assistants instead of thieves.

And, indeed, why hinder people dying if death is the normal and legitimate end of everyone? What is gained if some shopkeeper or clerk lives an extra five or ten years? If the aim of medicine is by drugs to alleviate suffering, the question inevitably arises: why alleviate it? In the first place, they say that suffering leads man to perfection; and in the second, if mankind really learns to alleviate its sufferings with pills and drops, it will completely abandon religion and philosophy, in which it has hitherto found not merely protection from all sorts of trouble, but even happiness. Pushkin suffered terrible agonies before his death, poor Heine lay paralysed for several years; why, then, should not some Andrey Yefimych or Matryona Savishna be ill, since their lives had nothing of importance in them, and would have been entirely empty and like the life of an amoeba except for suffering?

Oppressed by such reflections, Andrey Yefimych relaxed his efforts and gave up visiting the hospital every day.

VI

This is how his life passed. As a rule he got up at eight o'clock in the morning, dressed, and drank his tea. Then he sat down in his study to read, or went to the hospital. At the hospital the out-patients were sitting in the dark, narrow little corridor waiting to be seen by the doctor. The nurses and the attendants, tramping with their boots over the brick floors, ran by them; gaunt-looking patients in dressing-gowns passed; dead bodies and vessels full of filth were carried by; the children were crying, and there was a cold draught. Andrey Yefimych knew that such surroundings were torture to feverish, consumptive, and impressionable patients; but what could be done? In the consulting-room he was met by his assistant, Sergey Sergeich—a fat little man with a plump, well-washed, shaven face, with soft, smooth manners, wearing a new loosely cut suit, and looking more like a senator than a medical assistant. He had an immense practice in the town, wore a white tie, and considered himself more proficient than the doctor, who had no practice. In the corner of the consulting-room there stood a huge icon in a shrine with a heavy lamp in front of it, and near it a candle-stand with a white cover on it. On the walls hung portraits of bishops, a view of the Svyatogorsky Monastery, and wreaths of dried cornflowers. Sergey Sergeich was religious, and liked solemnity and decorum. The icon had been put up at his expense; at his instructions one of the patients read the hymns of praise in the consulting-room on Sundays, and after the reading Sergey Sergeich himself went through the ward with a censer and burned incense.

There were a great many patients, but time was short, and so the work was confined to the asking of a few brief questions and the administration of some drugs, such as castor oil or volatile ointment. Andrey Yefimych would sit with his cheek resting in his hand, lost in thought and asking questions mechanically. Sergey Sergeich sat down too, rubbing his hands, and from time to time putting in his word.

'We suffer pain and poverty', he would say, 'because we do not pray to merciful God as we should. Yes!'

Andrey Yefimych never performed any operations when he was seeing patients; he had long ago given up doing so, and the sight of blood upset him. When he had to open a child's mouth in order to look at its throat, and the child cried and tried to defend itself with its little hands, the noise in his ears made his head go round and brought tears into his eyes. He would make haste to prescribe a drug, and motion to the woman to take the child away.

He was soon wearied by the timidity of the patients and their incoherence, by the proximity of the pious Sergey Sergeich, by the portraits on the walls, and by his own questions which he had asked over and over again for twenty years. And he would go away after seeing five or six patients. The rest would be seen by his assistant in his absence.

With the agreeable thought that, thank God, he had no private practice now, and that no one would interrupt him, Andrey Yefimych sat down at his desk immediately on reaching home and began reading. He read a great deal and always with great enjoyment. Half his salary went on buying books, and of the six rooms that made up his abode three were heaped up with books and old magazines. He liked best of all works on history and philosophy; the only medical publication to which he subscribed was *The Doctor*, of which he always read the last pages first. He would always go on reading for several hours without a break and without being weary. He did not read as rapidly and impulsively as Ivan Dmitrich had done in the past, but slowly and with concentration, often pausing over a passage which he liked or did not find intelligible. Near the book there always stood a decanter of vodka, and a salted cucumber or a pickled apple lay beside it, not on a plate, but on the baize table-cloth. Every half-hour he would pour himself a glass of vodka and drink it without taking his eyes off the book. Then without looking at it he would feel for the cucumber and bite off a bit.

At three o'clock he would go cautiously to the kitchen door, cough, and say: 'Daryushka, what about dinner? . . .'

After his dinner—a rather poor and untidily served one—Andrey Yefimych would walk up and down his rooms with his arms folded, thinking. The clock would strike four, then five, and still he would be walking up and down thinking. Occasionally the kitchen door would creak, and the red, sleepy face of Daryushka would appear.

'Andrey Yefimych, isn't it time for you to have your beer?' she would ask anxiously.

'No, it is not time yet . . .' he would answer. 'I'll wait a little . . . I'll wait a little . . .'

Towards evening the postmaster, Mikhail Averyanych, the only man in the town whose society did not bore Andrey Yefimych, would come in. Mikhail Averyanych had once been a very rich landowner, and had served in the cavalry, but had come to ruin, and was forced by poverty to take a job in the post office late in life. He had a hale and hearty appearance, lux-uriant grey whiskers, the manners of a well-bred man, and a loud, pleasant voice. He was good-natured and emotional, but hot-tempered. When anyone in the post office made a protest, expressed disagreement, or merely began to argue, Mikhail Averyanych would turn crimson, shake all over, and shout in a voice of thunder, 'Hold your tongue!' so that the post office had long enjoyed the reputation of an institution which it was terrifying to visit. Mikhail Averyanych liked and respected Andrey Yefimych for his culture and the loftiness of his soul; he treated the other inhabitants of the town superciliously, as though they were his subordinates.

'Here I am,' he would say, going in to Andrey Yefimych. 'Good evening, my dear fellow! I'll be bound, you are getting sick of me, aren't you?'

'On the contrary, I am delighted,' said the doctor. 'I am always glad to see you.'

The friends would sit down on the sofa in the study and for some time would smoke in silence.

'Daryushka, what about some beer?' Andrey Yefimych would say.

They would drink their first bottle still in silence, the doctor brooding and Mikhail Averyanych with a gay and animated face, like a man who has something very interesting to tell. The doctor was always the one to begin the conversation.

'What a pity,' he would say quietly and slowly, shaking his head and not looking his friend in the face (he never looked anyone in the face)—'what a great pity it is that there are no people in our town who are capable of carrying on intelligent and interesting conversation, or care to do so. It is an immense privation for us. Even the educated class do not rise above vulgarity; the level of their development, I assure you, is not a bit higher than that of the lower orders.'

'Perfectly true. I agree.'

'You know, of course,' the doctor went on quietly and deliberately, 'that everything in this world is insignificant and uninteresting except the higher spiritual manifestations of the human mind. Intellect draws a sharp line between the animals and man, suggests the divinity of the latter, and to some extent even takes the place of immortality, which does not exist. Consequently the intellect is the only possible source of enjoyment. We see and hear of no trace of intellect about us, so we are deprived of enjoyment. We have books, it is true, but that is not at all the same as living talk and conversation. If you will allow me to make a not quite apt comparison: books are the printed score, while talk is the singing.'

'Perfectly true.'

A silence would follow. Daryushka would come out of the kitchen and with an expression of blank dejection stand in the doorway to listen, with her face propped on her fist.

'Ah!' Mikhail Averyanych would sigh. 'To expect intelligence of this generation!'

And he would describe how wholesome, entertaining, and interesting life had been in the past. How intelligent the educated class in Russia used to be, and what lofty ideas it had of honour and friendship; how they used to lend money without an IOU, and it was thought a disgrace not to give a helping hand to a comrade in need; and what campaigns, what adventures, what skirmishes, what comrades, what women! And the Caucasus, what a marvellous country! The wife of a battalion commander, a strange woman, used to put on an officer's uniform and drive off into the mountains in the evening, alone, without a guide. It was said that she had a love-affair with some princeling in a native village.

'Queen of heaven, Holy Mother . . .' Daryushka would sigh.

'And how we drank! And how we ate! And what desperate liberals we were!'

Andrey Yefimych would listen without hearing; he was musing as he sipped his beer.

'I often dream of intellectual people and conversation with them,' he said suddenly, interrupting Mikhail Averyanych. 'My father gave me an excellent education, but under the influence of the ideas of the sixties made me become a doctor. I believe if I had not obeyed him then, by now I should have been in the very centre of the intellectual movement. Most likely I should have become a member of some university. Of course, intellect, too, is transient and not eternal, but you know why I cherish a partiality for it. Life is a vexatious trap; when a thinking man reaches maturity and attains to full consciousness he cannot help feeling that he is in a trap from which there is no escape. Indeed, he is summoned without his choice by fortuitous circumstances from non-existence into life . . . What for? He tries to find out the meaning and purpose of his existence; he is told nothing, or he is told absurdities; he knocks and it is not opened to him; death comes to him—also without his choice. And so, just as in prison men held together by common misfortune feel more at ease when they are together, so one does not notice the trap in life when people with a bent for analysis and generalisation meet together and pass their time in the interchange of proud and free ideas. In that sense the intellect is the source of an enjoyment nothing can replace.'

'Perfectly true.'

Not looking his friend in the face, Andrey Yefimych would go on, quietly and with pauses, talking about intellectual people and conversation with them, and Mikhail Averyanych would listen attentively and agree: 'Perfectly true.'

'And you do not believe in the immortality of the soul?' the postmaster would ask suddenly.

'No, my dear Mikhail Averyanych; I do not believe in it, and have no grounds for believing in it.'

'I must own I doubt it too. And yet I have a feeling as though I shall never die. Oh, I think to myself: "Old fogey, it is time you were dead!" But there is a little voice in my soul says: "Don't believe it; you won't die." '

Soon after nine o'clock Mikhail Averyanych would go away. As he put on his fur coat in the entry he would say with a sigh:

'What a wilderness fate has carried us to, though, really! What's most vexatious of all is to have to die here. Ah! . . .'

VII

After seeing his friend out Andrey Yefimych would sit down at the table and begin reading again. The stillness of the evening, and afterwards of the night, was not broken by a single sound, and it seemed as though time were standing still and brooding with the doctor over the book, and as though there were nothing in existence but this book and the lamp with the green shade. The doctor's coarse peasant-like face was gradually lit up by a smile of delight and warm tenderness over the progress of the human intellect. Oh, why is not man immortal? he thought. What is the good of the brain centres and convolutions, what is the good of sight, speech, self-consciousness, genius, if it is all destined to depart into the soil, and in the end to grow cold together with the earth's crust, and then for millions of years to fly with the earth round the sun with no meaning and no purpose? To do that there was no need at all to draw man with his lofty, almost godlike intellect out of non-existence, and then, as though in mockery, to turn him into clay. The transmutation of matter! But what cowardice to comfort oneself with that cheap substitute for immortality! The unconscious processes that take place in nature are lower even than the stupidity of man, since in stupidity there is, at least, consciousness and will, while in those processes there is absolutely nothing. Only the coward who has more fear of death than dignity can comfort himself with the notion that his body will in time live again in the grass, in stones, in a toad . . . To find one's immortality in the transmutation of matter is as strange as to prophesy a brilliant future for the case after a precious violin has been broken and become useless.

When the clock struck, Andrey Yefimych would sink back into his chair and close his eyes to think a little. And under the influence of the fine ideas of which he had been reading he would, unawares, recall his past and his present. The past was hateful—better not to think of it. And it was the same in the present as in the past. He knew that at the very time when his thoughts were floating together with the cooling earth round the sun, in the main building beside his abode people were suffering in sickness and physical filth; someone perhaps could not sleep and was making war upon the insects, someone was being infected by erysipelas, or moaning over too tight a bandage; perhaps the patients were playing cards with the nurses and drinking vodka. According to the yearly return, twelve thousand people had been deceived; the whole hospital rested as it had done twenty years ago on thieving, squabbles, gossip, nepotism, on gross quackery, and, as before, it was an immoral institution extremely injurious to the health of its inhabitants. He knew that Nikita knocked the patients about behind the barred windows of Ward No. 6, and that Moyseyka went about the town every day begging for alms.

On the other hand, he knew very well that a fabulous change had taken place in medicine during the last twenty-five years. When he was studying at the University he had fancied that medicine would soon be overtaken by the fate of alchemy and metaphysics; but now when he was reading at night the science of medicine touched him and excited his wonder, and even delight. What unexpected brilliance, what a revolution! Thanks to the antiseptics, operations were performed such as the great Pirogov had considered impossible even *in spe*. Ordinary zemstvo doctors were venturing to perform the resection of the kneecap; of abdominal operations only one per cent was fatal; while gravel was considered such a trifle that they did not even write about it. A radical cure for syphilis had been discovered. And the theory of heredity, hypnotism, the discoveries of Pasteur and of Koch, hygiene based on statistics, and the work of our zemstvo doctors!

Psychiatry with its modern classification of mental diseases, methods of diagnosis, and treatment, was a kind of Mount Everest in comparison with what had been in the past. They no longer poured cold water on the heads of lunatics nor put strait-jackets upon them; they treated them with humanity, and even, so it was stated in the papers, devised balls and entertainments for them. Andrey Yefimych knew that with modern tastes and views such an abomination as Ward No. 6 was possible only a hundred and fifty miles from a railway in a little town where the mayor and all the town council were half-illiterate tradesmen who looked upon the doctor as an oracle who must be believed without any criticism even if he had poured molten lead into their mouths; in any other place the public and the newspapers would long ago have torn this little Bastille to pieces.

'But, after all, what of it?' Andrey Yefimych would ask himself, opening his eyes. 'There are antiseptics, there is Koch, there is Pasteur, but the essential reality has not altered a bit; ill-health and mortality are still the same. They devise balls and entertainments for the mad, but still they don't let them go free; so it's all nonsense and vanity, and there is no difference in reality between the best Vienna clinic and my hospital.' But depression and a feeling akin to envy prevented him from feeling indifferent; it must have been from exhaustion. His heavy head sank on to the book, he put his hands under his face to make it softer, and thought: 'I serve a pernicious institution and receive a salary from people whom I am deceiving. I am not honest, but then, I of myself am nothing, I am only part of an inevitable social evil: all local officials are pernicious and receive their salary for doing nothing . . . And so for my dishonesty it is not I who am to blame, but the times . . . If I had been born two hundred years later I should have been different . . .'

When it struck three he would put out his lamp and go into his bedroom; he was not sleepy.

VIII

Two years before, the zemstvo in a generous mood had decided to allow three hundred roubles a year to pay for additional medical service in the town till the zemstvo hospital should be opened, and the district doctor, Yevgeny Fyodorych Khobotov, was invited to the town to assist Andrey Yefimych. He was a very young man—not yet thirty—tall and dark, with broad cheekbones and little eyes; his forefathers had probably come from one of the many alien races of Russia. He arrived in the town without a farthing, with a small portmanteau, and a plain young woman whom he called his cook. This woman had a baby at the breast. Yevgeny Fyodorych used to go about in a peaked cap and high boots, and in the winter wore a sheepskin coat. He made great friends with Sergey Sergeich, the medical assistant, and with the treasurer, but kept aloof from the other officials, and for some reason called them aristocrats. He had only one book in his lodgings, *The Latest Prescriptions of the Vienna Clinic for 1881*. When he went to a patient he always took this book with him. He played billiards in the evening at the club: he did not like cards. He was very fond of using in conversation such expressions as 'red tape', 'canting soft soap', 'shut up with your finicking . . .'

He visited the hospital twice a week, made the round of the wards, and saw out-patients. The complete absence of antiseptics and the cupping roused his indignation, but he did not introduce any new system, being afraid of offending Andrey Yefimych. He regarded his colleague as a sly old rascal, suspected him of being a man of large means, and secretly envied him. He would have been very glad to have his post.

IX

On a spring evening towards the end of March, when there was no snow left on the ground and the starlings were singing in the hospital garden, the doctor went out to see his friend the postmaster as far as the gate. At that very moment the Jew Moyseyka, returning with his booty, came into the yard. He had no cap on, and his bare feet were thrust into galoshes; in his hand he had a little bag of alms.

'Give me a kopeck!' he said to the doctor, smiling, and shivering with cold. Andrey Yefimych, who could never refuse anyone anything, gave him a ten-kopeck piece.

'How bad that is!' he thought, looking at the Jew's bare feet with their thin red ankles. 'Why, it's wet.'

And stirred by a feeling akin both to pity and disgust, he followed the Jew into the lodge, looking now at his bald head, now at his ankles. As the doctor went in, Nikita jumped up from his heap of litter and stood to attention.

'Good day, Nikita,' Andrey Yefimych said mildly. 'That Jew should be provided with boots or something, he will catch cold.'

'Certainly, Your Honour. I'll inform the superintendent.'

'Please do; ask him in my name. Tell him that I asked.'

The door into the ward was open. Ivan Dmitrich, lying propped on his elbow on the bed, listened in alarm to the unfamiliar voice, and suddenly recognised the doctor. He trembled all over with anger, jumped up, and with a red and wrathful face, with his eyes starting out of his head, ran out into the middle of the ward.

'The doctor has come!' he shouted, and broke into a laugh. 'At last! Gentlemen, I congratulate you. The doctor is honouring us with a visit! Cursed reptile!' he shrieked, and stamped in a frenzy such as had never been seen in the ward before. 'Kill the reptile! No, killing's too good. Drown him in the latrine!'

Andrey Yefimych, hearing this, looked into the ward from the entry and asked mildly:

'What for?'

'What for?' shouted Ivan Dmitrich, going up to him with a menacing air and convulsively wrapping himself in his dressing-gown. 'What for? Thief!' he said with revulsion, moving his lips as though he would spit at him. 'Quack! hangman!'

'Calm yourself,' said Andrey Yefimych, smiling guiltily. 'I assure you I have never stolen anything; and as to the rest, most likely you greatly exaggerate. I see you are angry with me. Calm yourself, I beg, if you can, and tell me coolly: what are you angry for?'

'Well, why are you keeping me here?'

'Because you are ill.'

'Yes, I am ill. But you know dozens, hundreds of madmen are walking about in freedom because your ignorance is incapable of distinguishing them from the sane. Why am I and these poor wretches to be shut up here like scapegoats for all the rest? You, your assistant, the superintendent, and all your hospital rabble, are immeasurably inferior to every one of us morally; why then are we shut up and you are not? Where's the logic of that?'

'Morality and logic don't come into it, it all depends on chance. If anyone is shut up he has to stay, and if anyone is not shut up he can walk about, that's all. There is neither morality nor logic in my being a doctor and your being a mental patient, there is nothing but idle chance.'

'That twaddle I don't understand . . .' Ivan Dmitrich uttered in a hollow voice, and he sat down on his bed.

Moyseyka, whom Nikita did not venture to search in the presence of the doctor, laid out on his bed pieces of bread, bits of paper, and little bones, and, still shivering with cold, began rapidly in a singsong voice saying something in Yiddish. He probably imagined that he had opened a shop.

'Let me out,' said Ivan Dmitrich, and his voice quivered.

'I cannot.'

'But why, why?'

'Because it is not in my power. Think, what use will it be to you if I do let you out? Go. The townspeople or the police will detain you and bring you back.'

'Yes, yes, that's true,' said Ivan Dmitrich, and he rubbed his forehead. 'It's awful! But what am I to do, what?'

Andrey Yefimych liked Ivan Dmitrich's voice and his intelligent young face with its grimaces. He longed to be kind to the young man and soothe him; he sat down on the bed beside him, thought, and said:

'You ask me what to do. The very best thing in your position would be to run away. But, unfortunately, that is useless. You would be detained. When society protects itself from the criminal, mentally deranged, or otherwise inconvenient people, it is invincible. There is only one thing left for you: to resign yourself to the thought that your presence here is inevitable.'

'It is no use to anyone.'

'So long as prisons and madhouses exist someone must be shut up in them. If not you, I. If not I, some third person. Wait till in the distant future prisons and madhouses no longer exist, and there will be neither bars on the windows nor hospital gowns. Of course, that time will come sooner or later.'

Ivan Dmitrich smiled ironically.

'You are jesting,' he said, screwing up his eyes. 'Such gentlemen as you and your assistant Nikita have nothing to do with the future, but you may be sure, sir, better days will come! I may express myself tritely, you may laugh, but the dawn of a new life is at hand; truth and justice will triumph, and—our turn will come! I shall not live to see it, I shall perish, but some people's great-grandsons will see it. I greet them with all my heart and rejoice, rejoice with them! Onward! God be your help, friends!'

With shining eyes Ivan Dmitrich got up, and stretching his hands towards the window, went on with emotion in his voice:

'From behind these bars I bless you! Hurrah for truth and justice! I rejoice!'

'I see no particular reason to rejoice,' said Andrey Yefimych, who thought Ivan Dmitrich's emotion theatrical, though he was delighted by it. 'Prisons and madhouses there will not be, and truth, as you have just expressed it, will triumph; but the essence of things, you know, will not change, the laws of nature will still remain the same. People will suffer pain, grow old, and die just as they do now. However magnificent a dawn lit up your life, you would still in the end be nailed up in a coffin and thrown into a pit.'

'And immortality?'

'Oh, come, now!'

'You don't believe in it, but I do. Somebody in Dostoyevsky or Voltaire says that if there had not been a God men would have invented him. And I firmly believe that if there is no immortality the great intellect of man will sooner or later invent it.'

'Well said,' observed Andrey Yefimych, smiling with pleasure; 'it's a good thing you have faith. With such a belief one may live happily even enclosed within walls. You have studied somewhere, I presume?'

'Yes, I have been to university, but did not complete my studies.'

'You are a reflective and a thoughtful man. In any surroundings you can find tranquillity in yourself. Free and deep thinking which aspires to comprehend life, and complete contempt for the foolish bustle of the world—those are two blessings beyond any that man has ever known. And you can possess them even though you lived behind threefold bars. Diogenes lived in a tub, yet he was happier than all the kings of the earth.'

'Your Diogenes was a blockhead,' said Ivan Dmitrich morosely. 'Why do you talk to me about Diogenes and some foolish comprehension of life?' he cried, growing suddenly angry and leaping up. 'I love life; I love it passionately. I have a persecution mania, a continual agonising terror; but there are moments when I am overwhelmed by the thirst for life, and then I am afraid of going mad. I have a tremendous desire to live, tremendous!'

He walked up and down the ward in agitation, and said, dropping his voice:

'When I dream, I am haunted by phantoms. People come to me, I hear voices and music, and I fancy I am walking through woods or by the sea-shore, and I long so passionately for bustle, for interests . . . Come, tell me, what news is there?' asked Ivan Dmitrich; 'what's happening?'

'Do you wish to know about the town or in general?'

'Well, tell me first about the town, and then in general.'

'Well, in the town it is appallingly dull . . . There's no one to say a word to, no one to listen to. There are no new people. A young doctor called Khobotov has come here recently.'

'He came in my time. Well, he is a lout, isn't he?'

'Yes, he is a man of no culture. It's strange, you know . . . Judging by every sign, there is no intellectual stagnation in our capital cities; there is movement—so there must be real people there too; but for some reason they always send us such men as I would rather not see. It's an unlucky town!'

'Yes, it is an unlucky town,' sighed Ivan Dmitrich, and he laughed. 'And how are things in general? What are they writing in the papers and reviews?'

It was by now dark in the ward. The doctor got up, and, standing, began to describe what was being written abroad and in Russia, and the trends in thought that could now be discerned. Ivan Dmitrich listened attentively and put questions, but suddenly, as though recalling something terrible, clutched at his head and lay down on the bed with his back to the doctor.

'What's the matter?' asked Andrey Yefimych.

'You will not hear another word from me,' said Ivan Dmitrich rudely. 'Leave me alone.'

'But why?'

'I tell you, leave me alone. Why the devil do you persist?'

Andrey Yefimych shrugged his shoulders, heaved a sigh, and went out. As he crossed the entry he said: 'You might clear up here, Nikita . . . there's an awfully stuffy smell.'

'Certainly, Your Honour.'

'What an agreeable young man!' thought Andrey Yefimych, going back to his flat. 'In all the years I have been living here I do believe he is the first person I have met with whom one can talk. He is capable of reasoning and is interested in just the right things.'

While he was reading, and afterwards, while he was going to bed, he kept thinking about Ivan Dmitrich, and when he woke next morning he remembered that he had the day before made the acquaintance of an intelligent and interesting man, and determined to visit him again as soon as possible.

X

Ivan Dmitrich was lying in the same position as on the previous day, with his head clutched in both hands and his legs drawn up. His face was not visible.

'Good day, my friend,' said Andrey Yefimych. 'You are not asleep, are you?'

'In the first place, I am not your friend,' Ivan Dmitrich articulated into the pillow; 'and in the second, your efforts are useless; you will not get one word out of me.'

'Strange,' muttered Andrey Yefimych in confusion. 'Yesterday we talked peacefully, but suddenly for some reason you took offence and broke off all at once . . . Probably I expressed myself awkwardly, or perhaps gave utterance to some idea which did not fit in with your convictions . . .'

'Yes, expect me to trust you!' said Ivan Dmitrich, sitting up and looking at the doctor with irony and unease. His eyes were red. 'You can go and spy and probe somewhere else, it's no use your doing it here. I knew yesterday what you had come for.'

'A strange fancy,' laughed the doctor. 'So you suppose me to be a spy?'

'Yes, I do . . . A spy or a doctor who has been charged to test me—it's all the same—'

'Oh, excuse me, what an odd fellow you really are!'

The doctor sat down on a stool near the bed and shook his head reproachfully.

'But let us suppose you are right,' he said, 'let us suppose that I am treacherously trying to trap you into saying something so as to betray you to the police. You would be arrested and then tried. But would you be any worse off being tried and in prison than you are here? If you are banished to a settlement, or even sent to penal servitude, would it be worse than being shut up in this ward? I imagine it would be no worse . . . What, then, are you afraid of?'

These words evidently had an effect on Ivan Dmitrich. He sat down quietly.

It was between four and five in the afternoon—the time when Andrey Yefimych usually walked up and down his rooms, and Daryushka asked whether it was not time for his beer. It was a still, bright day.

'I came out for a walk after dinner, and here I have come, as you see,' said the doctor. 'It really is spring.'

'What month is it? March?' asked Ivan Dmitrich.

'Yes, the end of March.'

'Is it very muddy?'

'No, not very. There are already paths in the garden.'

'It would be nice now to drive in an open carriage somewhere into the country,' said Ivan Dmitrich, rubbing his red eyes as though he were just awake, 'then to come home to a warm, snug study, and . . . and to have a decent doctor to cure one's headache . . . It's so long since I have lived like a human being. It's disgusting here! Insufferably disgusting!'

After his excitement of the previous day he was exhausted and listless, and spoke unwillingly. His fingers twitched, and from his face it could be seen that he had a splitting headache.

'There is no real difference between a warm, snug study and this ward,' said Andrey Yefimych. 'A man's peace and contentment do not lie outside him, but within himself.'

'What do you mean?'

'The ordinary man looks for good and evil in external things—that is, in a carriage or a study—but a thinking man looks for it within himself.'

'You should go and preach that philosophy in Greece, where it's warm and fragrant with the scent of pomegranates, but it doesn't suit our climate. With whom was it I was talking of Diogenes? Was it with you?'

'Yes, with me yesterday.'

'Diogenes did not need a study or warm accommodation; it's hot there without those things. You can lie in your tub and eat oranges and olives. But were he to live in Russia, he'd be begging to be let indoors in May, let alone December. He'd be doubled up with the cold.'

'No. One can be insensible to cold as to every other pain. Marcus Aurelius says: "A pain is a vivid idea of pain; make an effort of will to change that idea, dismiss it, cease to complain, and the pain will disappear." That is true. A wise man, or simply a reflective, thoughtful man, is distinguished precisely by his contempt for suffering; he is always contented and surprised at nothing.'

'Then I am an idiot, since I suffer and am discontented and surprised at the baseness of mankind.'

'You are wrong in that; if you reflect more on the subject you will understand how insignificant is all that external world that agitates us. One must strive to comprehend life, and in this lies true happiness.'

'Comprehend . . .' repeated Ivan Dmitrich, frowning. 'External, internal . . . Excuse me, but I don't understand it. I only know,' he said, getting up and looking angrily at the doctor—'I only know that God has created me of warm blood and nerves, yes, indeed! If organic tissue is capable of life it must react to every stimulus. And I do! To pain I respond with tears and outcries, to baseness with indignation, to filth with loathing. To my mind, that constitutes life. The lower the organism, the less sensitive it is, and the more feebly it reacts to stimulus; and the higher it is, the more responsively and vigorously it reacts to reality. How is it you don't know that? A doctor, and not know such trifles! To despise suffering, to be always contented, and to be surprised at nothing, one must reach this condition'—and Ivan Dmitrich pointed to the peasant who was a mass of fat—'or to harden oneself by suffering to such a point that one loses all sensibility to it—that is, in other words, to cease to live. You must excuse me, I am not a sage or a philosopher,' Ivan Dmitrich continued with irritation, 'and I don't understand anything about it. I am not capable of reasoning.'

'On the contrary, your reasoning is excellent.'

'The Stoics, whom you are parodying, were remarkable people, but their doctrine crystallised two thousand years ago and has not advanced, and will not advance, an inch forward, since it is not practical or living. It had a success only with the minority which spends its life in savouring all sorts of theories and ruminating over them; the majority did not understand it. A doctrine which advocates indifference to wealth and to the comforts of life, and a contempt for suffering and death, is quite unintelligible to the vast majority of men, since that majority has never known wealth or the comforts of life; and to despise suffering would mean despising life itself, since man's entire essence is made up of the sensations of hunger, cold, injury, loss, and a Hamlet-like dread of death. The whole of life lies in these sensations; one may be oppressed by it, one may hate it, but one cannot despise it. And so I repeat, the doctrine of the Stoics can never have a future; from the beginning of time up to today you see continually increasing the struggle, the sensibility to pain, the capacity of responding to stimulus.'

Ivan Dmitrich suddenly lost the thread of his thoughts, stopped, and rubbed his forehead with vexation.

'I meant to say something important, but I have lost it,' he said. 'What was I saying? Oh yes! This is what I mean: one of the Stoics sold himself into slavery to redeem his neighbour, so, you see, even a Stoic reacted to stimulus, since, for such a generous act as the destruction of oneself for the sake of one's neighbour, he must have had a soul capable of pity and indignation. Here in prison I have forgotten everything I learned, or else I could have recalled something else. Take Christ, for instance: Christ responded to reality by weeping, smiling, being sorrowful and moved to wrath, even overcome by misery. He did not go to meet His sufferings with a smile, He did not despise death, but prayed in the Garden of Gethsemane that this cup might pass Him by.'

Ivan Dmitrich laughed and sat down.

'Granted that a man's peace and contentment lie not outside but within himself,' he said, 'granted that one must despise suffering and not be surprised at anything, yet on what ground do you preach this theory? Are you a sage? A philosopher?'

'No, I am not a philosopher, but everyone ought to preach it because it is reasonable.'

'No, I want to know how it is that you consider yourself competent to judge of "comprehension", contempt for suffering, and so on. Have you ever suffered? Have you any idea of suffering? Allow me to ask you, were you ever thrashed in your childhood?'

'No, my parents had an aversion for corporal punishment.'

'My father used to flog me cruelly; my father was a harsh, sickly Government clerk with a long nose and a yellow neck. But let us talk of you. No one has laid a finger on you all your life, no one has scared you or beaten you; you are as strong as a horse. You grew up under your father's wing and studied at his expense, and then you dropped at once into a sinecure. For more than twenty years you have lived rent-free with heating, lighting, and service all provided, and had the right to work how you pleased and as much as you pleased, even to do nothing. You were naturally a flabby, lazy man, and so you have tried to arrange your life so that nothing should disturb you or make you move. You have handed over your work to your assistant and the rest of the rabble while you sit in peace and warmth, accumulate money, read, amuse yourself with reflections about all sorts of lofty nonsense, and' (Ivan Dmitrich looked at the doctor's red nose) 'with boozing; in fact, you have seen nothing of life, you know absolutely nothing of it, and are only theoretically acquainted with reality; you despise suffering and are surprised at nothing for a very simple reason: vanity of vanities, the external and the internal, contempt for life, for suffering and for death, comprehension, true happiness— that's the philosophy that suits the Russian sluggard best. You see a peasant beating his wife, for instance. Why interfere? Let him beat her, they will both die sooner or later, anyway; and, besides, he who beats injures by his blows, not the person he is beating, but himself. To get drunk is stupid and unseemly, but if you drink you die, and if you don't drink you die. A peasant woman comes with toothache . . . well, what of it? Pain is the idea of pain, and besides "you can't live in this world without illness; we shall all die, and so, go away, woman, don't hinder me from thinking and drinking vodka". A young man asks advice, what he is to do, how he is to live; anyone else would think before answering, but you have got the answer ready: strive for "comprehension" or for true happiness. And what is that fantastic "true happiness"? There's no answer, of course. We are kept here behind barred windows, tortured, left to rot; but that is very good and reasonable, because there is no difference at all between this ward and a warm, snug study. A convenient philosophy. You can do nothing, and your conscience is clear, and you feel you are wise . . . No, sir, it is not philosophy, it's not thinking, it's not breadth of vision, but laziness, fakirism, drowsy stupefaction. Yes,' cried Ivan Dmitrich, getting angry again, 'you despise suffering, but I'll be bound if you pinch your finger in the door you will howl at the top of your voice.'

'And perhaps I shouldn't howl,' said Andrey Yefimych, with a gentle smile.

'Oh, I dare say! Well, if you were stricken by paralysis, or supposing some fool or bully took advantage of his position and rank to insult you in public, and if you knew he could do it with impunity, then you would understand what it means to fob people off with comprehension and true happiness.'

'That's original,' said Andrey Yefimych, laughing with pleasure and rubbing his hands. 'I am agreeably struck by your inclination to generalise, and the sketch of my character you have just drawn is simply brilliant. I must confess that talking to you gives me great pleasure. Well, I've listened to you, and now you must graciously listen to me.'

XI

This conversation went on for about an hour longer, and apparently made a deep impression on Andrey Yefimych. He began going to the ward every day. He went there in the mornings and after dinner, and often the dusk of evening found him in conversation with Ivan Dmitrich. At first Ivan Dmitrich kept aloof from him, suspected him of evil designs, and openly expressed his hostility. But afterwards he got used to him, and his abrupt manner changed to one of condescending irony.

Soon it was all over the hospital that the doctor, Andrey Yefimych, had taken to visiting Ward No. 6. No one—neither his assistant, nor Nikita, nor the nurses—could conceive why he went there, why he stayed there for hours on end, what he was talking about, and why he did not write prescriptions. His actions seemed strange. Often Mikhail Averyanych did not find him at home, which had never happened in the past, and Daryushka was greatly perturbed, for the doctor drank his beer now at no definite time, and sometimes was even late for dinner.

One day—it was at the end of June—Dr Khobotov went to see Andrey Yefimych about something. Not finding him at home, he proceeded to look for him in the yard; there he was told that the old doctor had gone to see the mental patients. Entering the lodge and stopping in the porch, Khobotov heard the following conversation:

'We shall never agree, and you will not succeed in converting me to your faith,' Ivan Dmitrich was saying irritably; 'you are utterly ignorant of reality, and you have never known suffering, but have only like a leech fed on the sufferings of others, while I have been in continual suffering from the day of my birth till today. For that reason, I tell you frankly,

I consider myself superior to you and more competent in every respect. It's not for you to teach me.'

'I have absolutely no ambition to convert you to my faith,' said Andrey Yefimych gently, and with regret that the other refused to understand him. 'And that's not the point, my friend; what matters is not that you have suffered and I have not. Joy and suffering are passing; let us leave them, never mind them. What matters is that you and I think; we see in each other people who are capable of thinking and reasoning, and that is a common bond between us however different our views. If you knew, my friend, how sick I am of universal folly, ineptitude, stupidity, and with what delight I always talk with you! You are an intelligent man, and I enjoy your company.'

Khobotov opened the door an inch and glanced into the ward; Ivan Dmitrich in his nightcap and the doctor Andrey Yefimych were sitting side by side on the bed. The madman was grimacing, twitching, and convulsively wrapping himself in his gown, while the doctor sat motionless with bowed head, and his face was red and looked helpless and sorrowful. Khobotov shrugged his shoulders, grinned, and exchanged glances with Nikita. Nikita shrugged his shoulders too.

Next day Khobotov went to the lodge, accompanied by the assistant. Both stood in the porch and listened.

'I fancy our old man has gone clean off his chump!' said Khobotov as he came out of the lodge.

'Lord have mercy upon us sinners!' sighed the decorous Sergey Sergeich, scrupulously avoiding the puddles that he might not muddy his polished boots. 'I must own, honoured Yevgeny Fyodorych, I have been expecting it for a long time.'

XII

After this Andrey Yefimych began to notice a mysterious air all around him. The attendants, the nurses, and the patients looked at him inquisitively when they met him, and then whispered together. The superintendent's little daughter Masha, whom he liked to meet in the hospital garden, for some reason ran away from him now when he went up with a smile to stroke her on the head. The postmaster no longer said, 'Perfectly true,' as he listened to him, but in unaccountable confusion muttered, 'Yes, yes, yes . . .' and looked at him with a grieved and thoughtful expression; for some reason he took to advising his friend to give up vodka and beer, but as a man of delicate feeling he did not say this directly, but hinted at it, telling him first about the commanding officer of his battalion, an excellent man, and then about the regimental chaplain, a capital fellow, both of whom drank and fell ill, but on giving up drinking completely regained their health. On two or three occasions Andrey Yefimych was visited by his colleague Khobotov, who also advised him to give up hard liquor, and for no apparent reason recommended him to take potassium bromide.

In August Andrey Yefimych got a letter from the mayor of the town asking him to come on very important business. On arriving at the town hall at the appointed hour, Andrey Yefimych found there the military commander, the superintendent of the district school, a member of the town council, Khobotov, and a plump, fair-haired gentleman who was introduced to him as a doctor. This doctor, with a Polish surname difficult to pronounce, lived at a pedigree stud-farm twenty miles away, and was now passing through the town.

'There's something that concerns you,' said the member of the town council, addressing Andrey Yefimych after they had all greeted one another and sat down at the table. 'Here Yevgeny Fyodorych says that there is not room for the dispensary in the main building, and that it ought to be transferred to one of the lodges. That's of no consequence—of course it can be transferred, but the point is that the lodge needs major repairs.'

'Yes, it would need repair,' said Andrey Yefimych after a moment's thought. 'If the corner lodge, for instance, were fitted up as a dispensary, I imagine it would cost at least five hundred roubles. An unproductive expenditure!'

Everyone was silent for a while.

'I had the honour of submitting to you ten years ago', Andrey Yefimych went on in a low voice, 'that the hospital in its present form is a luxury for the town beyond its means. It was built in the forties, but things were different then. The town spends too much on unnecessary buildings and superfluous staff. I believe with a different system two model hospitals might be maintained for the same money.'

'Well, let us have a different system, then!' the member of the town council said briskly.

'I have already had the honour of submitting to you that the medical department should be transferred to the supervision of the zemstvo.'

'Yes, transfer the money to the zemstvo and they will steal it,' laughed the fair-haired doctor.

'That's what it always comes to,' the member of the council agreed, and he also laughed.

Andrey Yefimych looked with apathetic, lustreless eyes at the fair-haired doctor and said: 'One must have justice.'

Again there was silence. Tea was brought in. The military commander, for some reason much embarrassed, touched Andrey Yefimych's hand across the table and said:

'You have quite forgotten us, doctor. But of course you are a hermit: you don't play cards and don't like women. You would be bored with fellows like us.'

They all began saying how boring it was for a decent person to live in such a town. No theatre, no music, and at the last dance at the club there had been about twenty ladies and only two gentlemen. The young men did not dance, but spent all their time crowding round the refreshment-bar or playing cards.

Not looking at anyone and speaking slowly in a low voice, Andrey Yefimych began saying what a pity, what a terrible pity it was that the townspeople should waste their vital energy, their hearts and their minds on cards and gossip, and should have neither the power nor the inclination to spend their time in interesting conversation and reading, and should refuse to take advantage of the enjoyments of the mind. The mind alone was interesting and worthy of attention, all the rest was base and petty. Khobotov listened to his colleague attentively and suddenly asked:

'Andrey Yefimych, what day of the month is it?'

Having received an answer, the fair-haired doctor and he, in the tone of examiners conscious of their lack of skill, began asking Andrey Yefimych what day of the week it was, how many days there were in the year, and whether it was true that there was a remarkable prophet living in Ward No. 6.

In response to the last question Andrey Yefimych turned rather red and said: 'Yes, he is mentally ill, but he is an interesting young man.'

They asked him no other questions.

When he was putting on his overcoat in the porch, the military commander laid a hand on his shoulder and said with a sigh:

'It's time for us old fellows to rest!'

As he came out of the hall, Andrey Yefimych understood that it had been a committee appointed to enquire into his mental condition. He recalled the questions that had been asked him, flushed crimson, and for some reason, for the first time in his life, felt bitterly grieved for medical science.

'My God . . .' he thought, remembering how these doctors had just examined him, 'why, they have only lately been hearing lectures on psychiatry, they have taken an examination—so why this crass ignorance? They have no conception of psychiatry!'

And for the first time in his life he felt insulted and moved to anger.

In the evening of the same day Mikhail Averyanych came to see him. The postmaster went up to him without waiting to greet him, took him by both hands, and said in an agitated voice:

'My dear fellow, my dear friend, show me that you believe in my genuine affection and look on me as your friend!' And preventing Andrey Yefimych from speaking, he went on, growing excited: 'I love you for your culture and nobility of soul. Listen to me, my dear fellow. The rules of their profession compel the doctors to conceal the truth from you, but I blurt out the plain truth like a soldier. You are not well! Excuse me, my dear fellow, but it is the truth; everyone around you has been noticing it for a long time. Doctor Yevgeny Fyodorych has just told me that it is essential for you to rest and distract your mind for the sake of your health. Perfectly true! Excellent! In a day or two I am taking a holiday and am going away for a sniff of a different atmosphere. Show that you are a friend to me, let us go together! Let us go for a jaunt as in the good old days.'

'I feel perfectly well,' said Andrey Yefimych after a moment's thought. 'I can't go away. Allow me to show you my friendship in some other way.'

To go away for no reason, without his books, without Daryushka, without his beer, to break abruptly with his routine of twenty years—the idea at first struck him as wild and fantastic, but he remembered the conversation with the committee and the depressed mood in which he had returned home, and the thought of a brief absence from the town in which stupid people looked on him as a madman seemed pleasant to him.

'And where precisely do you intend to go?' he asked.

'To Moscow, to Petersburg, to Warsaw . . . I spent the five happiest years of my life in Warsaw. What a marvellous city! Let us go, my dear fellow!'

XIII

A week later it was suggested to Andrey Yefimych that he should have a rest—that is, send in his resignation—a suggestion he received with indifference, and a week later still, Mikhail Averyanych and he were sitting in a springless carriage driving to the nearest railway station. The days were cool and bright, with a blue sky and a clear horizon. They spent two days driving the hundred and fifty miles to the railway station, and stayed two nights on the way. When at the posting station the glasses given them for their tea had not been properly washed, or the drivers were slow in harnessing the horses, Mikhail Averyanych would turn crimson, and quivering all over would shout:

'Hold your tongue! Don't argue!'

And in the carriage he talked without ceasing for a moment, describing his campaigns in the Caucasus and in Poland. What adventures he had had, what meetings! He talked loudly and opened his eyes so wide with wonder that he might well be thought to be lying. Moreover, as he talked he breathed in Andrey Yefimych's face and laughed into his ear. This bothered the doctor and prevented him from thinking and concentrating.

In the train they travelled, for economy, third-class in a non-smoking compartment. Half the passengers were decent people. Mikhail Averyanych soon made friends with everyone and, moving from one seat to another, kept saying loudly that they ought not to travel by these appalling lines. It was a regular swindle! A very different thing riding on a good horse: one could do seventy miles a day and still feel fresh and well after it. And our bad harvests were due to the draining of the Pinsk marshes; altogether, the way things were done was dreadful. He got excited, talked loudly, and would not let others speak. This endless chatter to the accompaniment of loud laughter and expressive gestures wearied Andrey Yefimych.

'Which of us is the madman?' he thought with vexation. 'I, who try not to disturb my fellow-passengers in any way, or this egoist who thinks that he is cleverer and more interesting than anyone here, and so will leave no one in peace?'

In Moscow Mikhail Averyanych put on a military coat without epaulettes and trousers with red braid. He wore a military cap and overcoat in the street, and soldiers saluted him. It seemed now to Andrey

Yefimych that his companion was a man who had squandered all that was good and kept only what was bad of those characteristics of a country gentleman that he had once possessed. He liked to be waited on even when it was quite unnecessary. The matches would be lying before him on the table, and he could see them, yet he would shout to the waiter to give him the matches; he did not hesitate to appear before a maidservant in nothing but his underclothes; he used the familiar mode of address to all footmen indiscriminately, even old men, and when he was angry called them fools and blockheads. This, Andrey Yefimych thought, was lordly, but disgusting.

First of all Mikhail Averyanych led his friend to the Iverskaya Madonna. He prayed fervently, shedding tears and bowing down to the ground, and when he had finished, heaved a deep sigh and said:

'Even though one does not believe, it makes one somehow feel easier when one prays a little. Kiss the icon, my dear fellow.'

Andrey Yefimych was embarrassed and he kissed the image, while Mikhail Averyanych pursed his lips and, shaking his head, prayed in a whisper, and again tears came into his eyes. Then they went to the Kremlin and looked there at the Tsar-cannon and the Tsar-bell, and even touched them with their fingers, admired the view over the river, visited St Saviour's and the Rumyantsev Museum.

They dined at Testov's. Mikhail Averyanych perused the menu, stroking his whiskers, and said in the tone of a gourmet accustomed to dine in restaurants:

'We shall see what you give us to eat today, my angel!'

XIV

The doctor walked about, looked at things, ate and drank, but he had all the while one feeling: annoyance with Mikhail Averyanych. He longed to have a rest from his friend, to get away from him, to hide himself, while the friend thought it his duty not to let the doctor move a step away from him, and to provide him with as many distractions as possible. When there was nothing to look at he entertained him with conversation. For two days Andrey Yefimych endured it, but on the third he announced to his friend that he was ill and wanted to stay at home for the whole day; his friend replied that in that case he would stay too—that really he needed rest, for he was run off his legs already. Andrey Yefimych lay on the sofa, with his face to the back and, clenching his teeth, listened to his friend, who ardently assured him that sooner or later France would certainly thrash Germany, that there were a great many scoundrels in Moscow, and that it was impossible to judge a horse's quality by its outward appearance. The doctor began to have a buzzing in his ears and palpitations of the heart, but out of delicacy could not bring himself to beg his friend to go away or hold his tongue. Fortunately Mikhail Averyanych grew weary of sitting in the hotel room, and after dinner he went out for a walk.

As soon as he was alone Andrey Yefimych abandoned himself to a feeling of relief. How pleasant to lie motionless on the sofa and to know that one is alone in the room! Real happiness is impossible without solitude. The fallen angel betrayed God probably because he longed for solitude, of which the angels know nothing. Andrey Yefimych wanted to think about what he had seen and heard during the last few days, but he could not get Mikhail Averyanych out of his head.

'Why, he has taken a holiday and come with me out of friendship, out of generosity,' thought the doctor with vexation. 'Nothing could be worse than this friendly supervision. I suppose he is good-natured and generous and a lively fellow, but he is a bore. An insufferable bore. In the same way there are people who never say anything but what is clever and good, yet one feels that they are dull-witted people.'

On the following days Andrey Yefimych declared himself ill and would not leave the hotel room; he lay with his face to the back of the sofa, and suffered agonies of weariness when his friend entertained him with conversation, or rested when his friend was absent. He was vexed with himself for having come, and with his friend, who grew every day more talkative and more free and easy; he could not succeed in attuning his thoughts to a serious and lofty level.

'This is what I get from the real life Ivan Dmitrich talked about,' he thought, angry at his own pettiness. 'It's of no consequence, though . . . I shall return home, and everything will go on as before . . .'

It was the same thing in Petersburg too; for whole days on end he did not leave the hotel room, but lay on the sofa and only got up to drink beer.

Mikhail Averyanych was all haste to travel to Warsaw.

'My dear man, what should I go there for?' said Andrey Yefimych in an imploring voice. 'You go alone and let me go home! I beg you!'

'On no account,' protested Mikhail Averyanych. 'It's a marvellous city. I spent there the five happiest years of my life!'

Andrey Yefimych had not the strength of will to insist on his own way, and much against his inclination went to Warsaw. There he did not leave the hotel room, but lay on the sofa, furious with himself, with his friend, and with the waiters, who obstinately refused to understand Russian; while Mikhail Averyanych, healthy, hearty, and full of spirits as usual, went about the town from morning to night, looking up his old acquaintances. Several times he did not return home at night. After one night spent in some unknown haunt he came home early in the morning, in a violently excited condition, with a red face and tousled hair. For a long time he walked up and down the rooms muttering something to himself, then stopped and said:

'Honour before everything.'

After walking up and down a little longer he clutched his head in both hands and pronounced in a tragic voice:

'Yes, honour before everything! Accursed be the moment when the idea first entered my head to visit this Babylon! My dear friend,' he added, addressing the doctor, 'you may despise me, I have gambled and lost; lend me five hundred roubles!'

Andrey Yefimych counted out five hundred roubles and gave them to his friend without a word. The latter, still crimson with shame and anger, incoherently articulated some pointless vow, put on his cap, and went out. Returning two hours later he flopped into an easy-chair, heaved a loud sigh, and said:

'My honour is saved. Let us go, my friend; I do not care to remain another hour in this accursed city. Scoundrels! Austrian spies!'

By the time the friends were back in their own town it was November, and deep snow was lying in the streets. Dr Khobotov had Andrey Yefimych's post; he was still living in his old lodgings, waiting for Andrey Yefimych to arrive and clear out of the hospital apartments. The plain woman whom he called his cook was already established in one of the lodges.

Fresh scandals about the hospital were going the round of the town. It was said that the plain woman had quarrelled with the superintendent, and that the latter had crawled on his knees before her begging forgiveness. On the very first day he arrived Andrey Yefimych had to seek new lodgings.

'My friend,' the postmaster said to him timidly, 'excuse an indiscreet question: what means have you at your disposal?'

Andrey Yefimych, without a word, counted out his money and said: 'Eighty-six roubles.'

'I don't mean that,' Mikhail Averyanych blurted out in confusion, misunderstanding him; 'I mean, what have you to live on?'

'I tell you, eighty-six roubles . . . I have nothing else.'

Mikhail Averyanych looked upon the doctor as an honest and honourable man, yet he suspected that he had accumulated a fortune of at least twenty thousand. Now, learning that Andrey Yefimych was a beggar, that he had nothing to live on, he was for some reason suddenly moved to tears and embraced his friend.

XV

Andrey Yefimych now lodged in a little house with three windows owned by a tradeswoman, Belova. There were only three rooms besides the kitchen in this little house. The doctor lived in two of them which looked on to the street, while Daryushka and the landlady with her three children lived in the third room and the kitchen. Sometimes the landlady's lover, a drunken peasant who was rowdy and reduced the children and Daryushka to terror, would come for the night. When he arrived and established himself in the kitchen and demanded vodka, they all felt very uncomfortable, and the doctor would be moved by pity to take the crying children into his room and let them sleep on his floor, and this gave him great satisfaction.

He got up as before at eight o'clock, and after his morning tea sat down to read his old books and magazines: he had no money for new ones. Either because the books were old, or perhaps because of the change in his surroundings, reading exhausted him, and did not grip his attention as before. That he might not spend his time in idleness he made a detailed catalogue of his books and gummed little labels on their backs, and this mechanical, painstaking work seemed to him more interesting than reading. The monotonous, painstaking work lulled his thoughts to sleep in some unaccountable way, and time passed quickly while he thought of nothing. Even sitting in the kitchen, peeling potatoes with Daryushka or picking over the buckwheat grain, seemed interesting to him. On Saturdays and Sundays he went to church. Standing near the wall and half closing his eyes, he listened to the singing and thought of his father, of his mother, of the University, of the religions of the world; he felt calm and melancholy, and when he came out of the church he regretted that the service was so soon over. He went twice to the hospital to talk to Ivan Dmitrich. But on both occasions Ivan Dmitrich was unusually excited and ill-humoured; he bade the doctor leave him in peace, as he had long been sick of empty chatter, and declared that, in return for all his sufferings, he asked from the damned scoundrels only one favour—solitary confinement. Surely they would not refuse him even that? On both occasions when Andrey Yefimych was taking leave of him and wishing him good night, he snarled:

'Go to hell!'

And Andrey Yefimych did not know now whether to go to him for a third time or not. He longed to go.

In the old days Andrey Yefimych used to walk about his rooms and think in the interval after dinner, but now from dinner-time till evening tea he lay on the sofa with his face to the back and gave himself up to trivial thoughts which he could not struggle against. He was mortified that after more than twenty years of service he had been given neither a pension nor any assistance. It is true that he had not done his work honestly, but, then, all who are in the Service get a pension without distinction whether they are honest or not. Contemporary justice lies precisely in the bestowal of grades, orders, and pensions, not for moral qualities or capacities, but for service whatever it may have been like. Why should he be the sole exception? He had no money at all. He was ashamed to pass by the shop and look at the woman who owned it. He owed thirty-two roubles for beer already. There was money owing to the landlady also. Daryushka sold old clothes and books on the sly, and told lies to the landlady, saying that the doctor was about to receive a large sum of money.

He was angry with himself for having wasted on travelling the thousand roubles he had saved up. How useful that thousand would have been now! He was vexed that people would not leave him in peace. Khobotov thought it his duty to look in on his sick colleague from time to time. Everything about him was revolting to Andrey Yefimych—his well-fed face and vulgar, condescending tone, and his use of the word 'colleague', and his high top-boots; the most revolting thing was that he thought it was his duty to treat Andrey Yefimych, and thought that he really was treating him. On every visit he brought a bottle of potassium bromide and rhubarb pills.

Mikhail Averyanych, too, thought it his duty to visit his friend and entertain him. Every time he went in to Andrey Yefimych with an affectation of ease and forced laughter, and began assuring him that he was looking very well today, and that, thank God, he was on the high road to recovery, and from this it could be concluded that he regarded his friend's condition as hopeless. He had not yet repaid his Warsaw debt, and was overwhelmed by shame; he was tense, and so tried to laugh louder and talk more amusingly. His anecdotes and descriptions seemed endless now, and were an agony both to Andrey Yefimych and himself.

In his presence Andrey Yefimych usually lay on the sofa with his face to the wall, and listened with his teeth clenched; his soul was oppressed with rankling disgust, and after every visit from his friend he felt as though this disgust had risen higher, and was mounting into his throat.

To stifle petty thoughts he made haste to reflect that he himself, and Khobotov, and Mikhail Averyanych, would all sooner or later perish without leaving any trace on the world. If one imagined some spirit flying by the earthly globe in space in a million years he would see nothing but clay and bare rocks. Everything—culture and the moral law—would pass away and not even a burdock would grow out of them. Of what consequence was shame because of a shopkeeper, of what consequence was the insignificant Khobotov or the wearisome friendship of Mikhail Averyanych? It was all trivial and nonsensical.

But such reflections did not help him now. Scarcely had he imagined the earthly globe in a million years, when Khobotov in his high top-boots or Mikhail Averyanych with his forced laugh would appear from behind a bare rock, and he even heard the shamefaced whisper: 'That Warsaw debt . . . I will repay it in a day or two, my dear fellow . . . Without fail.'

XVI

One day Mikhail Averyanych came after dinner when Andrey Yefimych was lying on the sofa. It so happened that Khobotov arrived at the same time with his potassium bromide. Andrey Yefimych got up heavily and sat down, leaning both arms on the sofa.

'You have a much better colour today than you had yesterday, my dear man,' began Mikhail Averyanych. 'Yes, you look splendid. Upon my soul, you do!'

'It's high time you were well, colleague,' said Khobotov, yawning. 'I'll be bound, you are sick of this red tape.'

'And we shall recover,' said Mikhail Averyanych cheerfully. 'We shall live another hundred years! To be sure!'

'If not a hundred, then at least twenty,' Khobotov said reassuringly. 'It's all right, all right, colleague; don't lose heart . . . So shut up with your finicking.'

'We'll show what we can do,' laughed Mikhail Averyanych, and he slapped his friend on the knee. 'We'll show them yet! Next summer, please God, we shall be off to the Caucasus, and we will ride all over it on horseback—trot, trot, trot! And when we are back from the Caucasus I shouldn't wonder if we will all dance at the wedding.' Mikhail Averyanych gave a sly wink. 'We'll marry you off, my dear boy, we'll marry you . . .'

Andrey Yefimych felt suddenly that the rising disgust had mounted to his throat; his heart began beating violently.

'That's vulgar,' he said, getting up quickly and walking away to the window. 'Don't you understand that you are talking vulgar nonsense?'

He meant to go on softly and politely, but against his will he suddenly clenched his fists and raised them above his head.

'Leave me alone,' he shouted in a voice unlike his own, flushing crimson and shaking all over. 'Get out, both of you!'

Mikhail Averyanych and Khobotov stood up and stared at him, first with amazement and then with alarm.

'Get out, both of you!' Andrey Yefimych went on shouting. 'Stupid people! Foolish people! I don't want either your friendship or your medicines, stupid man! It's vulgar! Horrible!'

Khobotov and Mikhail Averyanych, looking at each other in bewilderment, staggered to the door and went out. Andrey Yefimych snatched up the bottle of potassium bromide and flung it after them; the bottle broke with a crash on the threshold.

'Go to the devil!' he shouted in a tearful voice, running out into the passage. 'To the devil!'

When his guests were gone Andrey Yefimych lay down on the sofa, trembling as though in a fever, and went on for a long while repeating: 'Stupid people! Foolish people!'

When he was calmer, what occurred to him first of all was the thought that poor Mikhail Averyanych must be feeling fearfully ashamed and depressed now, and that it was all quite dreadful. Nothing like this had ever happened before. Where was his intelligence and his tact? Where was his comprehension of things and his philosophical indifference?

The doctor could not sleep all night for shame and vexation with himself, and at ten o'clock next morning he went to the post office and apologised to the postmaster.

'We won't think again of what has happened,' Mikhail Averyanych, greatly touched, said with a sigh, warmly pressing his hand. 'Let bygones be bygones. Lyubavkin,' he suddenly shouted so loud that all the postmen and customers started, 'give me a chair; and you wait,' he shouted to a peasant woman who was stretching out a registered letter to him through the grating. 'Can't you see that I am busy? We will not remember the past,' he went on, affectionately addressing Andrey Yefimych; 'sit down, I beg you, my dear fellow.'

For a minute he stroked his knees in silence, and then said:

'I have never had a thought of taking offence. Illness is no joke, I understand. Your attack frightened the doctor and me yesterday, and we had a long talk about you afterwards. My dear friend, why won't you treat your illness seriously? You can't go on like this . . . Excuse me for speaking openly as a friend,' whispered Mikhail Averyanych. 'You live in the most unfavourable surroundings, in a crowd, in uncleanliness, no one to look after you, no money for proper treatment . . . My dear friend, the doctor and I implore you with all our hearts, listen to our advice: go into hospital! There you will have wholesome food and attendance and treatment. Though, between ourselves, Yevgeny Fyodorych is *mauvais ton*, yet he does understand his work, you can fully rely upon him. He has promised me he will look after you.'

Andrey Yefimych was touched by the postmaster's genuine sympathy and the tears which suddenly glittered on his cheeks.

'My honoured friend, don't believe it!' he whispered, laying his hand on his heart; 'don't believe them. It's all a sham. My illness is only that in twenty years I have only found one intelligent man in the whole town, and he is mad. I am not ill at all, it's simply that I have got into a vicious circle, and there is no way out. I don't care; I am ready for anything.'

'Go into hospital, my dear fellow.'

'I don't care if it were into the pit.'

'Give me your word, my dear man, that you will obey Yevgeny Fyodorych in everything.'

'If you wish, I give you my word. But I repeat, my honoured friend, I have got into a vicious circle. Now everything, even the genuine sympathy of my friends, leads to the same thing—to my ruin. I am going to my ruin, and I have the courage to admit it.'

'My dear fellow, you will recover.'

'What's the use of saying that?' said Andrey Yefimych, with irritation. 'There are few men who at the end of their lives do not experience what I am experiencing now. When you are told that you have something such as bad kidneys or an enlarged heart, and you begin being treated for it, or are told you are mad or a criminal—that is, in short, when people suddenly turn their attention to you—you may be sure you have got into a vicious circle from which you will not escape. You will try to escape and only make things worse. You had better give in, for no human efforts can save you. So it seems to me.'

Meanwhile the public was crowding at the grating. That he might not be in their way, Andrey Yefimych got up and began to take his leave. Mikhail Averyanych made him promise on his honour once more, and escorted him to the outer door.

Towards evening on the same day Khobotov, in his sheepskin and his high top-boots, suddenly made his appearance, and said to Andrey Yefimych in a tone as though nothing had happened the day before:

'I have come on business, colleague. I have come to ask you whether you would not join me in a consultation. Eh?'

Thinking that Khobotov wanted to distract his mind with an outing, or perhaps really to enable him to earn something, Andrey Yefimych put on his coat and hat, and went out with him into the street. He was glad of the opportunity to smooth over his fault of the previous day and to be reconciled, and in his heart thanked Khobotov, who did not even allude to yesterday's scene and was evidently sparing him. One would never have expected such delicacy from this uncultured man.

'Where is your invalid?' asked Andrey Yefimych.

'In the hospital . . . I have long wanted to show him to you. A very interesting case.'

They went into the hospital yard and, going round the main building, turned towards the lodge where the mental cases were kept, and all this, for some reason, in silence. When they went into the lodge Nikita as usual jumped up and stood to attention.

'One of the patients here has a lung complication,' Khobotov said in an undertone, going into the ward with Andrey Yefimych. 'You wait here, I'll be back directly. I am going for a stethoscope.'

And he went away.

XVII

Dusk was falling. Ivan Dmitrich was lying on his bed with his face thrust into his pillow; the paralytic was sitting motionless, crying quietly and moving his lips. The fat peasant and the former sorter were asleep. It was quiet.

Andrey Yefimych sat on Ivan Dmitrich's bed and waited. But half an hour passed, and instead of Khobotov, Nikita came into the ward clutching a dressing-gown, someone's linen, and a pair of slippers.

'Please change your things, Your Honour,' he said softly. 'Here is your bed; come this way,' he added, pointing to an empty bedstead which had obviously just been brought into the ward. 'It's all right; please God, you will recover.'

Andrey Yefimych understood it all. Without saying a word he crossed to the bed to which Nikita pointed and sat down; seeing that Nikita was standing waiting, he undressed entirely and he felt ashamed. Then he put on the hospital clothes; the drawers were very short, the shirt was too long, and the dressing-gown smelt of smoked fish.

'Please God, you will recover,' repeated Nikita, and he gathered up Andrey Yefimych's clothes, went out, and shut the door after him.

'No matter . . .' thought Andrey Yefimych, wrapping himself in his dressing-gown in a shamefaced way and feeling that he looked like a convict in his new costume. 'It's no matter . . . It does not matter whether it's a dress-coat or a uniform or this dressing-gown . . .'

But how about his watch? And the notebook that was in the side-pocket? And his cigarettes? Where had Nikita taken his clothes? Now perhaps to the day of his death he would never again put on trousers, a waistcoat, and high boots. It was all somehow strange and even incomprehensible at first. Andrey Yefimych was even now convinced that there was no difference between his landlady's house and Ward No. 6, that everything in this world was nonsense and vanity of vanities. And yet his hands were trembling, his feet were cold, and he was filled with dread at the thought that soon Ivan Dmitrich would get up and see that he was in a dressing-gown. He got up and walked across the room and sat down again.

Here he had been sitting already half an hour, an hour, and he was miserably sick of it: was it really possible to live here a day, a week, and even years like these people? Why, he had been sitting here, had walked about and sat down again; he could get up and look out of the window and walk from corner to corner again, and then what? Sit thus all the time, like a statue, thinking? No, that was scarcely possible.

Andrey Yefimych lay down, but at once got up, wiped the cold sweat from his brow with his sleeve, and felt that his whole face smelt of smoked fish. He walked about again.

'It's some misunderstanding . . .' he said, spreading his hands in perplexity. 'It must be sorted out. There is a misunderstanding . . .'

Meanwhile Ivan Dmitrich woke up; he sat up and propped his cheeks on his fists. He spat. Then he glanced lazily at the doctor, and apparently at first did not understand; but soon his sleepy face grew malicious and mocking.

'Aha! so they have put you in here, too, old fellow?' he said in a voice husky from sleepiness, screwing up one eye. 'Very glad to see you. You sucked the blood of others, and now they will suck yours. Excellent!'

'It's a misunderstanding . . .' Andrey Yefimych blurted out, frightened by Ivan Dmitrich's words; he shrugged his shoulders and repeated: 'It's some misunderstanding . . .'

Ivan Dmitrich spat again and lay down.

'Cursed life,' he grumbled, 'and what's so bitter and insulting, this life will not end with a reward for our sufferings, it will not end with apotheosis as it would in an opera, but with death; peasants will come and drag one's dead body by the arms and legs into a cellar. Ugh! Well, it does not matter . . . We shall have our good time in the next world . . . I shall come here as a ghost from the next world and frighten these reptiles. I'll turn their hair grey.'

Moyseyka returned, and, seeing the doctor, held out his hand.

'Give me one little kopeck,' he said.

XVIII

Andrey Yefimych walked away to the window and looked out into the open country. It was getting dark, and on the horizon to the right a cold crimson moon was rising. Not far from the hospital fence, not much more than two hundred yards away, stood a tall white house enclosed by a stone wall. That was the prison.

'So this is real life,' thought Andrey Yefimych, and he felt frightened.

The moon and the prison, and the nails on the fence, and the faraway flames at the bone-charring factory were all frightening. Behind him there was the sound of a sigh. Andrey Yefimych looked round and saw a man with glittering stars and orders on his breast, who was smiling and slyly winking. And this, too, seemed frightening.

Andrey Yefimych assured himself that there was nothing special about the moon or the prison, that even sane persons wear orders, and that everything in time will decay and turn to earth, but he was suddenly overcome with despair; he clutched at the grating with both hands and shook it with all his might. The strong grating did not yield.

Then that it might not be so frightening he went to Ivan Dmitrich's bed and sat down.

'I have lost heart, my dear fellow,' he muttered, trembling and wiping away the cold sweat, 'I have lost heart.'

'You should be philosophical,' said Ivan Dmitrich ironically.

'My God, my God . . . Yes, yes . . . You were pleased to say once that there was no philosophy in Russia, but that all people, even the paltriest, talk philosophy. But, you know, the philosophising of the paltriest does not harm anyone,' said Andrey Yefimych in a tone as if he wanted to cry and complain. 'Why, then, that malignant laugh, my friend, and how can these paltry creatures help philosophising if they are not satisfied? For an intelligent, educated man, made in God's image, proud and freedom-loving, to have no alternative but to be a doctor in a filthy, stupid, wretched little town, and to spend his whole life among bottles, leeches, mustard plasters! Quackery, narrowness, vulgarity! Oh, my God!'

'You are talking nonsense. If you don't like being a doctor you should have gone in for being a statesman.'

'I could not, I could not do anything. We are weak, my dear friend . . . I used to be indifferent. I reasoned boldly and soundly, but at the first coarse touch of life upon me I have lost heart . . . Prostration . . . We are weak, we are poor creatures . . . and you, too, my dear friend, you are intelligent, generous, you imbibed good impulses with your mother's milk, but you had hardly entered upon life when you were exhausted and fell ill . . . Weak, weak!'

As evening approached, Andrey Yefimych was continually tormented by another persistent sensation besides terror and the feeling of resentment. At last he realised that he was longing for a smoke and for beer.

'I am going out, my friend,' he said. 'I will tell them to bring a light; I can't put up with this . . . I can't stand it . . .'

Andrey Yefimych went to the door and opened it, but at once Nikita jumped up and barred his way.

'Where are you going? You can't, you can't!' he said. 'It's bedtime.'

'But I'm only going out for a minute to walk about the yard,' said Andrey Yefimych timidly.

'You can't, you can't; it's forbidden. You know that yourself.'

Nikita slammed the door and barred it with his back.

'But what difference will it make to anyone if I go out?' asked Andrey Yefimych, shrugging his shoulders. 'I don't understand. Nikita, I must go out!' he said in a trembling voice. 'I must.'

'Don't cause trouble, that's bad,' Nikita admonished him.

'This is abominable,' Ivan Dmitrich cried suddenly, and he jumped up. 'What right has he not to let you out? How dare they keep us here? I believe it is clearly laid down in the law that no one can be deprived of freedom without trial! This is violence! Tyranny!'

'Of course it's tyranny,' said Andrey Yefimych, encouraged by Ivan Dmitrich's outburst. 'I must go out, I need to. He has no right! Open, I tell you.'

'Do you hear, you dull-witted brute?' cried Ivan Dmitrich, and he banged on the door with his fist. 'Open the door, or I will break it down! Torturer!'

'Open the door,' cried Andrey Yefimych, trembling all over; 'I insist!'

'Talk away!' Nikita answered through the door, 'talk away . . .'

'At least, go and call Yevgeny Fyodorych! Say that I beg him to come for a minute!'

'His Honour will come of himself tomorrow.'

'They will never let us out,' Ivan Dmitrich was going on meanwhile. 'They will leave us to rot here! Oh, Lord, can there really be no hell in the next world, and will these wretches be forgiven? Where is justice? Open the door, you wretch! I am choking!' he cried in a hoarse voice, and flung himself at the door. 'I'll dash out my brains, you murderers!'

Nikita opened the door quickly, and roughly with both his hands and his knee shoved Andrey Yefimych back, then swung his arm and punched him in the face with his fist. It seemed to Andrey Yefimych as though a huge salt wave enveloped him from his head downwards and dragged him to the bed; there really was a salt taste in his mouth: most likely the blood was running from his teeth. He waved his arms as though he were trying to swim out and clutched at a bedstead, and at the same moment felt Nikita hit him twice on the back.

Ivan Dmitrich gave a loud scream. He must have been beaten too.

Then all was still, the faint moonlight came through the grating, and a shadow like a net lay on the floor. It was frightening. Andrey Yefimych lay and held his breath: he was expecting with horror to be struck again. He felt as though someone had taken a sickle, thrust it into him, and turned it round several times in his breast and bowels. He bit the pillow from pain and clenched his teeth, and all at once through the chaos in his brain there flashed the frightening, unbearable thought that these people, who seemed now like black shadows in the moonlight, had to endure such pain day by day for years. How could it have happened that for more than

231

twenty years he had not known this and had refused to know it? He knew nothing of pain, had no conception of it, so he was not to blame, but his conscience, as inexorable and as rough as Nikita, made him turn cold from the back of his neck to his heels. He leaped up, tried to cry out with all his might, and to run in haste to kill Nikita, and then Khobotov, the superintendent and the assistant, and then himself; but no sound came from his chest, and his legs would not obey him. Gasping for breath, he tore at the dressing-gown and the shirt on his breast, rent them, and fell senseless on the bed.

XIX

Next morning his head ached, there was a droning in his ears and a feeling of infirmity all over. He was not ashamed at recalling his weakness the day before. He had been cowardly, had even been afraid of the moon, had openly expressed thoughts and feelings such as he had not suspected in himself before; for instance, the thought that the paltry people who philosophised were really dissatisfied. But now nothing mattered to him.

He ate nothing, he drank nothing. He lay motionless and silent.

'It is all the same to me,' he thought when they asked him questions. 'I shan't answer . . . It's all the same to me.'

After dinner Mikhail Averyanych brought him a quarter of a pound of tea and a pound of fruit pastilles. Daryushka came too and stood for a whole hour by the bed with an expression of dull grief on her face. Dr Khobotov visited him. He brought a bottle of potassium bromide and told Nikita to fumigate the ward with something.

Towards evening Andrey Yefimych died of an apoplectic stroke. At first he had a violent shivering fit and a feeling of sickness; something revolting, as it seemed, penetrating through his whole body, even to his finger-tips, stretched from his stomach to his head and flooded his eyes and ears. There was a greenness before his eyes. Andrey Yefimych understood that his end had come, and remembered that Ivan Dmitrich, Mikhail Averyanych, and millions of people believed in immortality. And what if it really existed? But he did not want immortality, and he thought of it only for one instant. A herd of deer, extraordinarily beautiful and graceful, of which he had been reading the day before, ran by him; then a peasant woman stretched out her hand to him with a registered letter . . . Mikhail Averyanych said something, then it all vanished, and Andrey Yefimych sank into oblivion for ever.

The hospital porters came, took him by his arms and his legs, and carried him away to the chapel.

There he lay on the table, with open eyes, and the moon shed its light upon him at night. In the morning Sergey Sergeich came, prayed piously before the crucifix, and closed his former chief's eyes.

Next day Andrey Yefimych was buried. Mikhail Averyanych and Daryushka were the only people at the funeral.

The Black Monk

I

Andrey Vasilyich Kovrin, who held a master's degree at the University, had exhausted himself, and had upset his nerves. He did not send for a doctor, but casually, over a bottle of wine, he spoke to a friend who was a doctor, and the latter advised him to spend the spring and summer in the country. Very opportunely a long letter came from Tanya Pesotskaya, who asked him to come and stay with them at Borisovka. And he made up his mind that he really must go.

To begin with—that was in April—he went to his own home, Kovrinka, and there spent three weeks in solitude; then, as soon as the roads were passable, he set off in a carriage to visit Pesotsky, his former guardian, who had brought him up, and was a horticulturist well known all over Russia. The distance from Kovrinka to Borisovka was less than fifty miles. To drive along a soft road in May in a comfortable carriage with springs was a real pleasure.

Pesotsky had an immense house with columns and carved lions, off which the stucco was peeling, and with a footman in swallow-tails at the entrance. The old park, laid out in the English style, gloomy and severe, stretched for almost three-quarters of a mile to the river, and there ended in a steep, precipitous clay bank, where pines grew with bare roots that looked like shaggy paws; the water shone below with an unfriendly gleam, and the sandpipers flew up with a plaintive cry— mood enough to make one want to sit down and write a ballad. But near the house itself, in the courtyard and orchard, which together with the nurseries covered eighty acres, it was all life and gaiety even in bad weather. Such marvellous roses, lilies, camellias; such tulips of all pos- sible shades, from glistening white to sooty black—such a wealth of flowers, in fact, Kovrin had never seen anywhere as at Pesotsky's. It was only the beginning of spring, and the real glory of the flower-beds was still hidden away in the hot-houses. But even the flowers along the avenues, and here and there in the flower-beds, were enough to make one feel, as one walked about the garden, as though one were in a realm of tender colours, especially in the early morning when the dew was glis- tening on every petal.

The decorative part of the garden, which Pesotsky contemptuously described as rubbish, had at one time in his childhood given Kovrin an impression of fairyland.

Every sort of caprice, of elaborate monstrosity and mockery of nature was here. There were espaliers of fruit-trees, a pear-tree in the shape of a pyramidal poplar, spherical oaks and lime-trees, an apple-tree in the shape of an umbrella, plum-trees trained into arches, crests, candelabra, and even into the number 1862—the year when Pesotsky first took up horticulture. One came across, too, lovely, graceful trees with strong, straight stems like palms, and it was only by looking intently that one could recognise these trees as gooseberries or currants. But what made the garden most cheerful and gave it a lively air, was the continual coming and going in it, from early morning till evening; people with wheelbarrows, shovels, and watering-cans swarmed round the trees and bushes, in the avenues and the flower-beds, like ants . . .

Kovrin arrived at Pesotsky's at ten o'clock in the evening. He found Tanya and her father, Yegor Semyonych, in great anxiety. The clear star-lit sky and the thermometer foretold a frost towards morning, and meanwhile Ivan Karlych, the gardener, had gone into the town, and they had no one to rely upon. At supper they talked of nothing but the morning frost, and it was decided that Tanya should not go to bed, and between twelve and one should walk through the garden, and see that everything was done properly, and Yegor Semyonych should get up at three o'clock or even earlier.

Kovrin sat with Tanya all evening, and after midnight went out with her into the garden. It was cold. There was a strong smell of burning already in the garden. In the big orchard, which was called the commercial garden, and which brought Yegor Semyonych several thousand clear profit every year, a thick, black, acrid smoke was creeping over the ground and, curling round the trees, was saving those thousands from the frost. Here the trees were arranged as on a chessboard, in straight and regular rows like ranks of soldiers, and this severe pedantic regularity, and the fact that all the trees were of the same size, and had tops and trunks all exactly alike, made them look monotonous and even dreary. Kovrin and Tanya walked along the rows where fires of dung, straw, and all sorts of refuse were smouldering, and from time to time they were met by labourers who wandered in the smoke like shadows. The only trees in flower were the cherries, plums, and certain sorts of apples, but the whole garden was plunged in smoke, and it was only near the nurseries that Kovrin could breathe freely.

'Even as a child I used to sneeze from the smoke here,' he said, shrugging his shoulders, 'but to this day I don't understand how smoke can keep off frost.'

'Smoke takes the place of clouds when there are none . . .' answered Tanya.

'And what do you want clouds for?'

'In overcast and cloudy weather there is no frost.'

'You don't say so.'

He laughed and took her arm. Her broad, very earnest face, chilled with the frost, with her delicate black eyebrows, the turned-up collar of her coat, which prevented her moving her head freely, and the whole of her thin, graceful figure, with her skirts tucked up on account of the dew, touched him.

'Good heavens! she is grown-up,' he said. 'When I went away from here last, five years ago, you were still a child. You were such a thin, long-legged creature, with your hair hanging on your shoulders; you used to wear short frocks, and I used to tease you, calling you a heron . . . What time does!'

'Yes, five years!' sighed Tanya. 'Much water has flowed since then. Tell me, Andryusha, honestly,' she began eagerly, looking him in the face, 'do you feel strange with us now? But why do I ask you? You are a man, you live your own interesting life, you are somebody . . . To grow apart is so natural! But however that may be, Andryusha, I want you to think of us as your people. We have a right to that.'

'I do, Tanya.'

'On your word of honour?'

'Yes, on my word of honour.'

'You were surprised this evening that we have so many of your photographs. You know my father adores you. Sometimes it seems to me that he loves you more than he loves me. He is proud of you. You are a clever, extraordinary man, you have made a brilliant career for yourself, and he is convinced that you have turned out like this because he brought you up. I don't try to prevent him from thinking so. Let him.'

Dawn was already breaking, and that was especially perceptible from the distinctness with which the coils of smoke and the tops of the trees began to stand out in the air. Nightingales were singing, and the call of quails drifted from the fields.

'It's time we were asleep, though,' said Tanya, 'and it's cold, too.' She took his arm. 'Thank you for coming, Andryusha. We have only

236

uninteresting acquaintances, and not many of them. We have only the garden, the garden, the garden, and nothing else. Standards, half-standards,' she laughed. 'Oporto apples, rennets, borovinkas, budded stocks, grafted stocks . . . All, all our life has gone into the garden. I never even dream of anything but apples and pears. Of course, it is very nice and useful, but sometimes one longs for something else for variety. I remember that when you used to come to us for the summer holidays, or simply a visit, it always seemed to be fresher and brighter in the house, as though the covers had been taken off the chandelier and the furniture. I was only a little girl then, but yet I understood it.'

She spoke with great feeling. For some reason the idea came into his head that in the course of the summer he might grow fond of this little, weak, talkative creature, might be carried away and fall in love; in their position it was so possible and natural! This thought touched and amused him; he bent down to her sweet, preoccupied face and hummed softly:

> 'Onegin, I shall not conceal it,
> I love, I love Tatyana madly . . .'

By the time they reached the house, Yegor Semyonych had got up. Kovrin did not feel sleepy; he talked to the old man and went to the garden with him. Yegor Semyonych was a tall, broad-shouldered, corpulent man, and he suffered from asthma, yet he always walked so fast that it was difficult to keep up with him. He had an extremely preoccupied air; he was always hurrying somewhere, with an expression that suggested that if he were one minute late all would be ruined!

'Here is a business, brother . . .' he began, standing still to take breath. 'On the surface of the ground, as you see, is frost; but if you raise the thermometer on a stick fourteen feet above the ground, there it is warm . . . Why is that?'

'I really don't know,' said Kovrin, and he laughed.

'Hm! . . . One can't know everything, of course . . . However large the intellect may be, you can't find room for everything in it. I suppose you still go in chiefly for philosophy?'

'Yes, I lecture in psychology; but I am working on philosophy.'

'And it does not bore you?'

'On the contrary, it's all I live for.'

'Well, God bless you! . . .' said Yegor Semyonych, meditatively

237

stroking his grey whiskers. 'God bless you! . . . I am delighted for you . . . delighted, my boy . . .'

But suddenly he listened, and, with a terrible face, ran off and quickly disappeared behind the trees in a cloud of smoke.

'Who tied this horse to an apple-tree?' Kovrin heard his despairing, heart-rending cry. 'Who is the base scoundrel who has dared to tie this horse to an apple-tree? My God, my God! They have ruined everything; they have spoilt everything; they have done everything filthy, horrible, and abominable. The orchard's done for, the orchard's ruined. My God!'

When he came back to Kovrin, his face looked exhausted and mortified.

'What is one to do with these accursed people?' he said in a tearful voice, flinging up his hands. 'Styopka was carting dung at night, and tied the horse to an apple-tree! He twisted the reins round it, the rascal, as tightly as he could, so that the bark is rubbed off in three places. What do you think of that! I spoke to him and he stands like a post and only blinks his eyes. Hanging is too good for him.'

Growing calmer, he embraced Kovrin and kissed him on the cheek.

'Well, God bless you! . . . God bless you! . . .' he muttered. 'I am very glad you have come. Unutterably glad . . . Thank you.'

Then, with the same rapid step and preoccupied face, he made the round of the whole garden, and showed his former ward all his greenhouses and hothouses, his covered-in garden, and two apiaries which he called the marvel of our century.

While they were walking the sun rose, flooding the garden with brilliant light. It grew warm. Foreseeing a long, bright, cheerful day, Kovrin recollected that it was only the beginning of May, and that he had before him a whole summer as bright, cheerful, and long; and suddenly there stirred in his chest a joyous, youthful feeling, such as he used to experience in his childhood, running about in that garden. And he hugged the old man and kissed him affectionately. Both of them, deeply moved, went indoors and drank tea out of old-fashioned china cups, with cream and satisfying krendels made with milk and eggs; and these trifles reminded Kovrin again of his childhood and boyhood. The delightful present was blended with the impressions of the past that stirred within him; he felt constrained, but happy.

He waited till Tanya was awake and had coffee with her, went for a walk, then retired to his room and sat down to work. He read attentively, making notes, and from time to time raised his eyes to glance at the open windows or at the fresh, still-dewy flowers in the vases on the table; and again he lowered his eyes to his book, and it seemed to him as though every vein in his body was quivering and fluttering with pleasure.

II

In the country he led just as nervous and restless a life as in town. He read and wrote a great deal, he studied Italian, and when he was out for a walk, thought with pleasure that he would soon sit down to work again. He slept so little that everyone wondered at him; if he accidentally dozed for half an hour in the daytime, he would lie awake all night, and, after a sleepless night, would feel cheerful and vigorous as though nothing had happened.

He talked a great deal, drank wine, and smoked expensive cigars. Very often, almost every day, young ladies of neighbouring families would come to the Pesotskys', and would sing and play the piano with Tanya; sometimes a young neighbour who was a good violinist would come, too. Kovrin listened with eagerness to the music and singing, and was exhausted by it, and this showed itself by his eyes closing and his head falling to one side.

One day he was sitting on the balcony after evening tea, reading. At the same time, in the drawing-room, Tanya taking soprano, one of the young ladies a contralto, and the young man with his violin, were practising a well-known serenade of Braga's. Kovrin listened to the words—they were Russian—and could not understand their meaning. At last, leaving his book and listening attentively, he understood: a maiden, full of sick fancies, heard one night in her garden mysterious sounds, so strange and lovely that she was obliged to recognise them as a holy harmony which is unintelligible to us mortals, and so flies back to heaven. Kovrin's eyes began to close. He got up, and in exhaustion walked up and down the drawing-room, and then the dining-room. When the singing was over he took Tanya's arm, and with her went out on to the balcony.

'I have been thinking all day of a legend,' he said. 'I don't remember whether I have read it somewhere or heard it, but it is a strange and almost grotesque legend. To begin with, it is not very lucid. A thousand years ago a monk, dressed in black, wandered about the desert, some-where in Syria or Arabia . . . Some miles from where he was, some fishermen saw another black monk, who was moving slowly over the surface of a lake. This second monk was a mirage. Now forget all the laws of optics, which the legend seems not to recognise, and listen to the rest. From that mirage there was cast another mirage, then from that other a third, so that the image of the black monk began to be repeated endlessly from one layer of the atmosphere to another. So that he was seen at one time in Africa, at another in Spain, then in Italy, then in the Far North . . . Then he passed beyond the earth's atmosphere, and now he is wandering throughout the universe, yet never finding conditions in which he might disappear. Possibly he may be seen now on Mars or in some star of the Southern Cross. But, my dear, the real point on which the whole legend hangs is that, exactly a thousand years from the day when the monk walked in the desert, the mirage will return to the earth's atmosphere again and will appear to men. And it seems that the thousand years is almost up . . . According to the legend, we may look out for the black monk today or tomorrow.'

'A strange mirage,' said Tanya, who did not like the legend.

'But the most wonderful part of it all,' laughed Kovrin, 'is that I simply cannot recall where I got this legend from. Have I read it somewhere? Have I heard it? Or perhaps I dreamed of the black monk. I swear I don't remember. But the legend interests me. I have been thinking about it all day.'

Letting Tanya go back to her visitors, he went out of the house, and, lost in meditation, walked by the flower-beds. The sun was already setting. The flowers, having just been watered, gave forth a damp, irritating fragrance. Indoors they began singing again, and from afar the violin had the effect of a human voice. Kovrin, racking his brains to remember where he had read or heard the legend, turned slowly towards the park, and did not notice that he had reached the river. By a little path that ran along the steep bank, between the bare roots, he went down to the water, disturbed the sandpipers there and frightened two ducks. The last rays of the setting sun still threw light here and there on the gloomy pines, but it was quite dark on the surface of the river. Kovrin crossed to the other side by the narrow bridge. Before him lay a wide field covered with young rye not yet in blossom. There was no living habitation, no living soul in the distance, and it seemed as though the little path, if one went along it, would take one to the unknown, mysterious place where the sun had just gone down, and where the evening glow was flaming in immensity and splendour.

'How open, how free, how still it is here!' thought Kovrin, walking along the path. 'And it feels as though all the world were watching me, hiding and waiting for me to understand it . . .'

But then waves began running across the rye, and a light evening breeze softly touched his uncovered head. A minute later there was another gust of wind, but stronger—the rye began rustling, and he heard behind him the hollow murmur of the pines. Kovrin stood still in amazement. On the horizon there rose up from the earth to the sky, like a whirlwind or a waterspout, a tall black column. Its outline was indistinct, but from the first instant it could be seen that it was not standing still, but moving with fearful rapidity, moving straight towards Kovrin, and the nearer it came the smaller and the more distinct it was. Kovrin leapt aside into the rye to make way for it, and was only just in time.

A monk, dressed in black, with grey hair and black eyebrows, his arms crossed over his breast, floated by him . . . His bare feet did not touch the earth. After he had floated about seven yards beyond him, he looked round at Kovrin, and nodded to him with a friendly but sly smile. But what a pale, fearfully pale, thin face! Beginning to grow larger again, he flew across the river, collided noiselessly with the clay bank and pines, and passing through them, vanished like smoke.

'So, you see,' muttered Kovrin, 'there must be truth in the legend.'

Without trying to explain to himself the strange apparition, glad that he had succeeded in seeing so near and so distinctly, not only the monk's black garments, but even his face and eyes, agreeably excited, he went back to the house.

In the park and in the garden people were moving about quietly, in the house they were playing—so he alone had seen the monk. He had an intense desire to tell Tanya and Yegor Semyonych all about it, but he reflected that they would certainly think his words sheer delirium, and that would frighten them; he had better say nothing.

He laughed aloud, sang, and danced the mazurka; he was in high spirits, and all of them, the visitors and Tanya, thought he had a peculiar look, radiant and inspired, and that he was very interesting.

III

After supper, when the visitors had gone, he went to his room and lay down on the sofa: he wanted to think about the monk. But a minute later Tanya came in.

'Here, Andryusha, read Father's articles,' she said, giving him a bundle of pamphlets and offprints. 'They are splendid articles. He writes wonderfully.'

'Wonderfully, indeed!' said Yegor Semyonych, following her and giving a forced smile; he was ashamed. 'Don't listen to her, please; don't read them! Though, if you want to go to sleep, read them by all means; they are a fine soporific.'

'I think they are excellent articles,' said Tanya, with deep conviction. 'You read them, Andryusha, and persuade Father to write more often. He could write a complete manual of horticulture.'

Yegor Semyonych gave an awkward laugh, blushed, and began uttering the phrases usually employed by embarrassed authors. Finally, he began to give way.

'In that case, begin with Gaucher's article and these Russian articles,' he muttered, turning over the pamphlets with a trembling hand, 'or else you won't understand. Before you read my objections, you must know what I am objecting to. But it's all nonsense . . . tiresome stuff. Besides, I believe it's bedtime.'

Tanya went away. Yegor Semyonych sat down on the sofa by Kovrin and heaved a deep sigh.

'Yes, my boy . . .' he began after a pause. 'That's how it is, my dear Master. Here I write articles, and take part in exhibitions, and receive medals . . . Pesotsky, they say, has apples the size of a human head, and Pesotsky, they say, has made his fortune with his garden. In short, "Kochubey is rich and glorious." But one asks oneself: what is it all for? The garden is certainly fine, a model. It's not so much a garden as a regular institution, which is of the greatest public importance because it marks, so to say, a new era in Russian agriculture and Russian industry. But, what's it for? What's the point of it?'

'The fact speaks for itself.'

'I do not mean in that sense. I meant to ask: what will happen to the garden when I die? In the condition in which you see it now, it would not last for one month without me. The whole secret of success lies not in its being a big garden or a great number of labourers being employed in it, but in the fact that I love the work. Do you understand? I love it perhaps more than myself. Look at me; I do everything myself. I work from morning to night: I do all the grafting myself, the pruning myself, the planting myself. I do it all myself: when anyone helps me I am jealous and irritable, even rude. The whole secret lies in loving it—that is, in the sharp eye of the owner, and in the owner's hands, and in the feeling that makes one, when one goes anywhere for an hour's visit, sit, ill at ease, with one's heart far away, afraid that something may have happened in the garden. But when I die, who will look after it? Who will work? The gardener? The labourers? Yes? But I tell you, my dear fellow, the worst enemy in the garden is not a hare, not a cockchafer, and not the frost, but any out-side person.'

'And Tanya?' asked Kovrin, laughing. 'She can't be more harmful than a hare? She loves the work and understands it.'

'Yes, she loves it and understands it. If after my death the garden goes to her and she is the mistress, of course nothing better could be wished. But if, which God forbid, she should marry,' Yegor Semyonych whis-pered, and looked with frightened eyes at Kovrin, 'that's just it. If she marries and children come, she will have no time to think about the gar-den. What I fear most is: she will marry some fine gentleman, and he will be greedy, and he will lease the garden to market-women, and everything will go to the devil the very first year! In our work females are the scourge of God!'

Yegor Semyonych sighed and paused for a while.

'Perhaps it is egoism, but I tell you frankly: I don't want Tanya to get married. I am afraid of it! There is one young dandy comes to see us, bringing his violin and scraping on it; I know Tanya will not marry him, I know it quite well; but I can't bear to see him! Altogether, my boy, I am very odd. I admit it.'

Yegor Semyonych got up and walked about the room in excitement, and it was evident that he wanted to say something very important, but could not bring himself to it.

'I am very fond of you, and so I am going to speak to you openly,' he decided at last, thrusting his hands into his pockets. 'I deal plainly with certain delicate questions, and say exactly what I think, and I cannot endure so-called hidden thoughts. I will speak plainly: you are the only man to whom I should not be afraid to marry my daughter. You are a clever man with a good heart, and would not let my beloved work go to ruin; and the chief reason is that I love you as a son, and I am proud of you. If Tanya and you were to fall in love, then—well! I should be very glad and even happy. I tell you this plainly, without mincing matters, as an honest man.'

Kovrin laughed. Yegor Semyonych opened the door to go out, and stood in the doorway.

'If Tanya and you had a son, I would make a horticulturist of him,' he said, after a moment's thought. 'However, this is idle dreaming. Good night.'

Left alone, Kovrin settled himself more comfortably and started on the articles. The title of one was 'On Intercropping'; of another, 'A Few Words on the Remarks of Monsieur Z. concerning the Trenching of the Soil for a New Garden'; a third, 'Additional Matter concerning Grafting with a Dormant Bud'; and they were all of the same sort. But what a restless, jerky tone! What nervous, almost hysterical passion! Here was an article, one would have thought, with a most peaceable title and uncontroversial contents: it dealt with the Russian Antonovka apple. But Yegor Semyonych began it with '*Audiatur altera pars*,' and finished it with '*Sapienti sat*'; and between these two quotations a perfect torrent of venomous phrases directed at 'the learned ignorance of our recognised horticultural authorities, who observe nature from the height of their university chairs', or at Monsieur Gaucher, 'whose success has been the work of the vulgar and the dilettanti'. And then followed an inappropriate, affected, and insincere regret that peasants who stole fruit and broke the branches could not nowadays be flogged.

'It is beautiful, charming, healthy work, but even here there is strife and passion,' thought Kovrin. 'I suppose that everywhere and in all careers men of ideas are nervous, and marked by exaggerated sensitivity. Most likely it must be so.'

He thought of Tanya, who was so pleased with Yegor Semyonych's articles. Small, pale, and so thin that her collar-bones stuck out, her eyes, wide-open, dark and intelligent, had an intent gaze, as though looking for something. She walked like her father with little, hurried steps. She talked a great deal and was fond of arguing, accompanying every phrase, however insignificant, with expressive mimicry and gesticulation. No doubt she was nervous in the extreme.

Kovrin went on reading the articles, but he understood nothing, and stopped. The same pleasant excitement with which he had earlier in the evening danced the mazurka and listened to the music was now mastering him again and rousing a multitude of thoughts. He got up and began walking about the room, thinking of the black monk. It occurred to him that if this strange, supernatural monk had appeared to him only, that meant that he was ill and was already having hallucinations. This reflection frightened him, but not for long.

'But I feel happy, and I am doing no harm to anyone; so there is nothing bad in my hallucinations,' he thought; and he felt happy again.

He sat down on the sofa and clasped his hands round his head. Restraining the unaccountable joy which filled his whole being, he then paced up and down again, and sat down to his work. But the thoughts that he read in the book did not satisfy him. He wanted something gigantic, unfathomable, stupendous. Towards morning he undressed and reluctantly went to bed: he really ought to sleep.

When he heard the footsteps of Yegor Semyonych going out into the garden, Kovrin rang the bell and asked the footman to bring him some wine. He drank with relish several glasses of Lafite, then wrapped himself up, head and all; his consciousness grew clouded and he fell asleep.

IV

Yegor Semyonych and Tanya often quarrelled and said nasty things to each other.

They squabbled about something one morning. Tanya burst out crying and went to her room. She would not come down to dinner nor to tea. At first Yegor Semyonych went about looking sulky and dignified, as if to show that for him the claims of justice and good order were more important than anything else in the world; but he could not keep it up for long, and soon sank into depression. He walked about the park dejectedly, continually sighing: 'Oh, my God! My God!' and at dinner did not eat a morsel. At last, guilty and conscience-stricken, he knocked at the locked door and called timidly:

'Tanya! Tanya!'

And from behind the door came a faint voice, weak with crying but still determined:

'Leave me alone, if you please.'

The depression of the master and mistress was reflected in the whole household, even in the labourers working in the garden. Kovrin was absorbed in his interesting work, but at last he, too, felt miserable and uncomfortable. To dissipate the general ill-humour in some way, he made up his mind to intervene, and towards evening he knocked at Tanya's door. He was admitted.

'Fie, fie, for shame!' he began playfully, looking with surprise at Tanya's tear-stained, woebegone face, flushed in patches with crying. 'Is it really so serious? Fie, fie!'

'But if you knew how he tortures me!' she said, and floods of scalding tears streamed from her large eyes. 'He torments me to death,' she went on, wringing her hands. 'I said nothing to him . . . nothing . . . I only said that there was no need to keep . . . too many labourers . . . if we could hire them by the day when we wanted them. You know . . . you know the labourers have been doing nothing for a whole week . . . I . . . I . . . only said that, and he shouted and . . . said . . . a lot of horrible insulting things to me. What for?'

'There, there,' said Kovrin, smoothing her hair. 'You've quarrelled with each other, you've cried, and that's enough. You must not be angry for long—that's wrong . . . all the more as he loves you beyond everything.'

'He has . . . has spoiled my whole life,' Tanya went on, sobbing. 'I hear nothing but abuse and . . . insults. He thinks I am of no use in the house. Well! He is right. I shall go away tomorrow; I shall become a telegraph clerk . . . I don't care . . .'

'Come, come, come . . . You mustn't cry, Tanya. You mustn't, dear . . . Both of you are hot-tempered and irritable, and you are both to blame. Come along; I will reconcile you.'

Kovrin talked affectionately and persuasively, while she went on crying, twitching her shoulders and wringing her hands, as though some terrible misfortune had really befallen her. He felt all the sorrier for her because her grief was not a serious one, yet she suffered deeply. What trivialities were enough to make this little creature miserable for a whole day, perhaps for her whole life! Comforting Tanya, Kovrin thought that, apart from this girl and her father, he might hunt the world over and would not find people who would love him as one of themselves, as one of their kindred. If it had not been for these two he might very likely, having lost his father and mother in early childhood, never to the day of his death have known what was meant by genuine affection and that naïve, uncritical love which is only lavished on very close blood relations; and he felt that the nerves of this weeping, shaking girl responded to his half-sick, overstrained nerves like iron to a magnet. He never could have loved a healthy, strong, rosy-cheeked woman, but pale, weak, unhappy Tanya attracted him.

And he enjoyed stroking her hair and her shoulders, pressing her hand and wiping away her tears . . . At last she stopped crying. She went on for a long time complaining of her father and her hard, insufferable life in that house, entreating Kovrin to put himself in her place; then she began, little by little, smiling, and sighing that God had given her such a bad temper. At last, laughing aloud, she called herself a fool, and ran out of the room.

When a little later Kovrin went into the garden, Yegor Semyonych and Tanya were walking side by side along an avenue as though nothing had happened, and both were eating rye bread with salt on it, as both were hungry.

V

Glad that he had been so successful in the role of peacemaker, Kovrin went into the park. Sitting on a garden seat, thinking, he heard the rattle of carriages and women's laughter—visitors were arriving. When the shades of evening began falling on the garden, the sounds of the violin and singing voices reached him indistinctly, and that reminded him of the black monk. Where, in what land or on what planet, was that optical absurdity now moving?

Hardly had he recalled the legend and pictured in his imagination the dark apparition he had seen in the rye-field, when, from behind a pine-tree exactly opposite, there came out noiselessly, without the slightest rustle, a man of medium height with uncovered grey head, all in black, and barefooted like a beggar, and his black eyebrows stood out conspicuously on his pale, death-like face. Nodding his head graciously, this beggar or pilgrim came noiselessly to the seat and sat down, and Kovrin recognised him as the black monk.

For a minute they looked at one another, Kovrin with amazement, and the monk with tenderness, and, just as before, with a little slyness, and a somewhat crafty expression.

'But you are a mirage,' said Kovrin. 'Why are you here and sitting still? That does not fit in with the legend.'

'That does not matter,' the monk answered after a pause and in a low voice, turning his face towards him. 'The legend, the mirage and I are all the products of your excited imagination. I am a phantom.'

'Then you don't exist?' asked Kovrin.

'You can think as you like,' said the monk, with a faint smile. 'I exist in your imagination, and your imagination is part of nature, so I exist in nature.'

'You have a very old, wise, and extremely expressive face, as though you really had lived more than a thousand years,' said Kovrin. 'I did not know that my imagination was capable of creating such phenomena. But

247

why do you look at me with such delight? Do you like me?'

'Yes, you are one of those few who are justly called God's chosen. You serve eternal truth. Your thoughts, your intentions, the marvellous studies you are engaged in, and all your life, bear a divine, heavenly stamp, since they are consecrated to the rational and the beautiful—that is, to what is eternal.'

'You said "eternal truth" . . . But is eternal truth of use to man and within his reach, if there is no eternal life?'

'There is eternal life,' said the monk.

'Do you believe in the immortality of man?'

'Yes, of course. A grand, brilliant future is in store for you, for mankind. And the more there are like you on earth, the sooner will this future be realised. Without you who serve the higher principle and live in full understanding and freedom, mankind would be of little account; developing in a natural way, it would have to wait a long time for the end of its earthly history. You will lead it some thousands of years earlier into the kingdom of eternal truth—and therein lies your supreme service. You are the incarnation of the blessing of God, which rests upon men.'

'And what is the object of eternal life?' asked Kovrin.

'As of all life—enjoyment. True enjoyment lies in knowledge, and eternal life will provide innumerable and inexhaustible sources of knowledge, and in that sense it has been said: "In my Father's house are many mansions." '

'If only you knew how pleasant it is to hear you!' said Kovrin, rubbing his hands with satisfaction.

'I am very glad.'

'But I know that when you go away I shall be worried by the question of your reality. You are a phantom, an hallucination. So I am mentally ill, not normal?'

'What if you are? Why trouble yourself? You are ill because you have overworked and exhausted yourself, and that means that you have sacrificed your health to the idea, and the time is near at hand when you will give up life itself to it. What could be better? That is the goal towards which all divinely endowed, noble natures strive.'

'If I know I am mentally ill, can I trust myself?'

'And are you sure that the men of genius, whom all men trust, did not see phantoms, too? The learned nowadays say that genius is allied to madness. My friend, only the common herd are healthy and normal people. Reflections upon the neurasthenia of the age, nervous exhaustion

248

and degeneracy, etcetera, can only seriously disturb those who place the purpose of life in the present—that is, the common herd.'

'The Romans used to say: *Mens sana in corpore sano.*'

'Not everything the Greeks and the Romans said is true. Exaltation, enthusiasm, ecstasy—all that distinguishes prophets, poets, martyrs for the idea, from the common folk—are repellent to the animal side of man—that is, his physical health. I repeat, if you want to be healthy and normal, join the herd.'

'Strange that you repeat what often comes into my mind,' said Kovrin. 'It is as though you had seen and overheard my secret thoughts. But don't let us talk about me. What do you mean by "eternal truth"?'

The monk did not answer. Kovrin looked at him and could not distinguish his face. His features grew blurred and misty. Then the monk's head and arms began to disappear; his body seemed merged into the seat and the evening twilight, and he vanished altogether.

'The hallucination is over,' said Kovrin; and he laughed. 'It's a pity.'

He went back to the house, light-hearted and happy. What little the monk had said to him had flattered, not his vanity, but his whole soul, his whole being. To be one of the chosen, to serve eternal truth, to stand in the ranks of those who would make mankind worthy of the kingdom of God some thousands of years sooner—that is, to free men from some thousands of years of unnecessary struggle, sin, and suffering; to sacrifice to the idea everything—youth, strength, health; to be ready to die for the common good—what an exalted, what a happy destiny! He recalled his past—pure, chaste, industrious; he remembered what he had learned himself and what he had taught to others, and decided that there was no exaggeration in the monk's words.

Tanya came to meet him in the park: she was by now wearing a different dress.

'Are you here?' she said. 'And we have been looking and looking for you . . . But what is the matter with you?' she asked in wonder, glancing at his radiant, ecstatic face and his eyes full of tears. 'How strange you are, Andryusha!'

'I am pleased, Tanya,' said Kovrin, laying his hands on her shoulders. 'I am more than pleased: I am happy. Tanya, darling Tanya, you are an extremely attractive person. Dear Tanya, I am so glad, so glad!'

He kissed both her hands ardently, and went on:

'I have just experienced some exalted, wonderful, unearthly moments. But I can't tell you all about it or you would call me mad and not believe me. Let us talk of you. Dear, delightful Tanya! I love you, and am used to loving you. To have you near me, to meet you a dozen times a day, has become a necessary part of my existence; I don't know how I shall do without you when I go back home.'

'Oh,' laughed Tanya, 'you will forget about us in two days. We are humble people and you are a great man.'

'No; let us talk in earnest!' he said. 'I shall take you with me, Tanya. Yes? Will you come with me? Will you be mine?'

'Oh,' said Tanya, and tried to laugh again, but the laugh would not come, and red patches appeared on her face.

She began breathing quickly and walked very fast, but not to the house, but further into the park.

'I'd not expected this . . . not expected,' she said, wringing her hands as if in despair.

And Kovrin followed her and went on talking, with the same radiant, rapturous face:

'I want a love that will captivate me completely; and that love only you, Tanya, can give me. I am happy! So happy!'

She was overwhelmed, she stooped and shrank, and seemed ten years older all at once, while he thought her beautiful and expressed his rapture aloud:

'How lovely she is!'

VI

Learning from Kovrin that not only had they fallen in love, but that there would even be a wedding, Yegor Semyonych spent a long time in pacing from one corner of the room to the other, trying to conceal his agitation. His hands began trembling, his neck swelled and turned purple, he ordered his racing carriage and drove off somewhere. Tanya, seeing how he lashed the horse, and how he pulled his cap over his ears, understood what he was feeling, shut herself up in her room, and cried the whole day.

In the hothouses the peaches and plums were already ripe; the packing and despatching of these tender and fragile goods to Moscow took a great deal of care, work, and trouble. Owing to the fact that the summer was very hot and dry, it was necessary to water every tree, and a great deal of time and labour was spent on this. Numbers of caterpillars made their appearance, which, to Kovrin's disgust, the labourers and even Yegor

Semyonych and Tanya squashed with their fingers. In addition, they had already to book autumn orders for fruit and trees, and to conduct a great deal of correspondence. And at the very busiest time, when no one seemed to have a free moment, work in the fields took more than half their labourers from the garden. Yegor Semyonych, sunburnt, exhausted, ill-humoured, galloped from the fields to the garden and back again; he cried that he was being torn to pieces, and that he would put a bullet through his brains.

Then came the fuss and worry of the trousseau, to which the Pesot-skys attached a good deal of importance. Everyone's head was in a whirl from the snipping of the scissors, the rattle of sewing-machines, the smell of hot irons, and the caprices of the dressmaker, a huffy and nervous lady. And, as ill-luck would have it, visitors came every day, who had to be entertained, fed, and even put up for the night. But all this hard labour passed unnoticed as though in a fog. Tanya felt that love and happiness had taken her unawares, though she had, since she was fourteen, for some reason been convinced that Kovrin would marry her and no one else. She was bewildered, could not grasp it, could not believe herself . . . At one moment such joy would swoop down upon her that she longed to fly away to the clouds and there pray to God, at another moment she would remember that in August she would have to part from her home and leave her father; or, goodness knows why, the idea would occur to her that she was worthless, insignificant and unworthy of a great man like Kovrin—and she would go to her room, lock herself in, and cry bitterly for several hours. When there were visitors, she would suddenly fancy that Kovrin looked extraordinarily handsome, and that all the women were in love with him and envying her, and her soul was filled with pride and rapture, as though she had conquered the whole world; but he had only to smile politely at any young lady for her to be trembling with jealousy, to retreat to her room—and tears again. These new sensations possessed her completely; she helped her father mechanically, without noticing peaches, caterpillars or labourers, or how rapidly the time was passing.

It was almost the same with Yegor Semyonych. He worked from morning till night, was always in a hurry, was irritable, and flew into rages, but all of this was in a sort of spellbound dream. It seemed as though there were two men in him: one was the real Yegor Semyonych, who was moved to indignation, and clutched his head in despair when he heard of some irregularity from Ivan Karlovich the gardener; and another—not the real one—who seemed as though he were half drunk, would interrupt a business conversation at half a word, touch the gardener on the shoulder, and begin muttering:

'Say what you like, but blood really counts. His mother was a wonderful woman, most high-minded and intelligent. It was a pleasure to look at her good, bright, pure face; it was like the face of an angel. She drew splendidly, wrote verses, spoke five foreign languages, sang . . . Poor thing! she died of consumption. The kingdom of heaven be hers.'

The unreal Yegor Semyonych sighed, and after a pause went on:

'When he was a boy and growing up in my house, he had the same angelic face, good and bright. The way he looks and talks and moves is as soft and elegant as his mother's. And his intellect! We were always struck by his intellect. To be sure, it's not for nothing he's a Master of Arts! Not for nothing! And wait a bit, Ivan Karlych, what will he be in ten years' time? He will be far above us!'

But at this point the real Yegor Semyonych, suddenly coming to himself, would make a terrible face, clutch his head and cry:

'The devils! They have spoilt everything! They have ruined everything! It's abominable! The orchard's done for, the orchard's ruined!'

Kovrin, meanwhile, worked with the same ardour as before, and did not notice the general commotion. Love only added fuel to the flames. After every talk with Tanya he went to his room, happy and triumphant, took up his book or his manuscript with the same passion with which he had just kissed Tanya and told her of his love. What the black monk had told him of God's chosen, of eternal truth, of the brilliant future of mankind and so on, gave peculiar and extraordinary significance to his work, and filled his soul with pride and a consciousness of his own eminence. Once or twice a week, in the park or in the house, he met the black monk and had long conversations with him, yet this did not alarm him, but, on the contrary, delighted him, as he was now firmly convinced that such apparitions only visited outstanding, chosen people who devote themselves to the service of the idea.

One day the monk appeared at dinner-time and sat in the dining-room by the window. Kovrin was delighted, and very adroitly began a conversation with Yegor Semyonych and Tanya which might be of interest to the monk; the black-robed visitor listened and nodded his head graciously, and Yegor Semyonych and Tanya listened, too, and smiled gaily without suspecting that Kovrin was not talking to them but to his hallucination.

Imperceptibly the Fast of the Assumption was approaching, and soon after came the wedding, which, at Yegor Semyonych's express desire, was celebrated with 'a flourish'—that is, with senseless festivities that lasted for two whole days and nights. Three thousand roubles' worth of food and drink was consumed, but the music of the wretched hired band, the noisy toasts, the scurrying to and fro of the footmen, the uproar and crowding, prevented people from appreciating the taste of the expensive wines and the wonderful delicacies ordered from Moscow.

VII

One long winter night Kovrin was lying in bed, reading a French novel. Poor Tanya, who had headaches in the evenings from living in town, to which she was not accustomed, had been asleep a long while, and, from time to time, uttered incoherent phrases in her restless dreams.

It struck three o'clock. Kovrin put out the light and lay down to sleep, lay for a long time with his eyes closed, but could not get to sleep because, as he fancied, the room was very hot and Tanya was talking in her sleep. At half-past four he lit the candle again, and this time he saw the black monk sitting in an armchair near the bed.

'Good morning,' said the monk, and after a brief pause he asked: 'What are you thinking of now?'

'Of fame,' answered Kovrin. 'In the French novel I have just been reading, there is a description of a young scholar, who does silly things and pines away through longing for fame. I can't understand such longing.'

'Because you are wise. Your attitude towards fame is one of indifference, as towards a toy which does not interest you.'

'Yes, that is true.'

'Renown does not allure you. What is there flattering, amusing, or edifying in their carving your name on a tombstone, only for time to rub off the inscription together with the gilding? Moreover, happily there are too many of you for the weak memory of mankind to be able to retain your names.'

'Of course,' agreed Kovrin. 'Besides, why should they be remembered? But let us talk of something else. Of happiness, for instance. What is happiness?'

When the clock struck five, he was sitting on the bed, dangling his feet on the carpet, talking to the monk:

'In ancient times a happy man eventually grew frightened of his happiness—it was so great!—and to propitiate the gods he brought as a sacrifice his favourite ring. Do you know, I, too, like Polykrates, begin to be uneasy about my happiness. It seems strange to me that from morning to night I feel nothing but joy; it fills my whole being and stifles all my other feelings. I don't know what sadness, grief, or boredom are. I have difficulty in sleeping, I suffer from insomnia, but I am not bored. I say it in earnest; I begin to feel perplexed.'

'But why?' the monk asked in wonder. 'Is joy a supernatural feeling? Ought it not to be the normal state of man? The more highly a man is developed on the intellectual and moral side, the freer he is, the more pleasure life gives him. Socrates, Diogenes, and Marcus Aurelius were joyful, not sorrowful. And the Apostle tells us: "Rejoice always"; "Rejoice and be happy." '

'But what if the gods grow wrathful?' Kovrin jested, and he laughed. 'If they take from me comfort and make me go cold and hungry, that will scarcely be to my liking.'

Meanwhile Tanya woke up, and looked with amazement and horror at her husband. He was talking, addressing the armchair, laughing and gesticulating; his eyes were gleaming, and there was something strange in his laugh.

'Andryusha, whom are you talking to?' she asked, clutching the hand he stretched out to the monk. 'Andryusha! Whom?'

'Oh! Whom?' said Kovrin in confusion. 'Why, to him . . . He is sitting here,' he said, pointing to the black monk.

'There is no one here . . . no one! Andryusha, you are ill!'

Tanya embraced her husband and held him tight, as though protecting him from apparitions, and put her hand over his eyes.

'You are ill!' she sobbed, trembling all over. 'Forgive me, my precious, my dear one, but I have noticed for a long time that your mind is clouded in some way . . . You are mentally ill, Andryusha . . .'

Her trembling infected him, too. He glanced once more at the armchair, which was now empty, felt a sudden weakness in his arms and legs, took fright, and began dressing.

'It's nothing, Tanya, nothing,' he muttered, shivering. 'I really am not quite well . . . it's time I admitted that.'

'I noticed long ago . . . and Father has noticed too,' she said, trying to suppress her sobs. 'You talk to yourself, smile somehow strangely . . . and you can't sleep. Oh, my God, my God, save us!' she said in terror. 'But don't be frightened, Andryusha, for God's sake don't be frightened . . .'

She began dressing, too. Only now, looking at her, Kovrin realised the danger of his position—realised the meaning of the black monk and his conversations with him. It was clear to him now that he was mad.

Neither of them knew why they dressed and went into the dining-room: she in front and he following her. There they found Yegor Semyonych standing in his dressing-gown and with a candle in his hand. He was staying with them, and had been awakened by Tanya's sobs.

'Don't be frightened, Andryusha,' Tanya was saying, shivering as though in a fever; 'don't be frightened . . . Father, it will all pass . . . it will all pass . . .'

Kovrin was too much agitated to speak. He wanted to say to his father-in-law in a playful tone: 'Congratulate me; it appears I have gone out of my mind;' but he could only move his lips and smile bitterly.

At nine o'clock in the morning they put on his jacket and fur coat, wrapped him up in a shawl, and took him in a carriage to a doctor. He began to receive treatment.

VIII

Summer had come again, and the doctor advised their going into the country. Kovrin had recovered; he had stopped seeing the black monk, and he needed only to build up his strength. Staying at his father-in-law's in the country, he drank a great deal of milk, worked for only two hours out of the twenty-four, and neither smoked nor drank wine.

On the evening before Elijah's Day they had an evening service in the house. When the sexton was handing the priest the censer the immense old room smelt like a graveyard, and Kovrin felt bored. He went out into the garden. Without noticing the gorgeous flowers, he walked about the garden, sat for a while on a bench, then strolled about the park; reaching the river, he went down and then stood lost in thought, looking at the water. The sullen pines with their shaggy roots, which had seen him a year before so young, so joyful and confident, were not whispering now, but standing mute and motionless, as though they did not recognise him. And, indeed, his head was closely cropped, his beautiful long hair was gone, his step was sluggish, his face was fuller and paler than last summer.

He crossed by the footbridge to the other side. Where the year before there had been rye there were oats, reaped, and lying in rows. The sun had set and there was a broad stretch of glowing red on the horizon, a sign of windy weather next day. It was still. Looking in the direction from which the year before the black monk had first appeared, Kovrin stood for twenty minutes, till the evening glow had begun to fade . . .

When, listless and dissatisfied, he returned home the service was over. Yegor Semyonych and Tanya were sitting on the steps of the veranda, drinking tea. They were talking of something, but, seeing Kovrin, ceased at once, and he concluded from their faces that their talk had been about him.

'I believe it is time for you to have your milk,' Tanya said to her husband.

'No, it's not time yet . . .' he replied, sitting down on the bottom step. 'Drink it yourself; I don't want it.'

Tanya exchanged a troubled glance with her father, and said in a guilty voice:

'You know yourself that milk does you good.'

'Yes, a great deal of good!' Kovrin laughed. 'I congratulate you: I have gained another pound in weight since Friday.' He pressed his head tightly in his hands and said miserably: 'Why, oh why have you cured me? Preparations of bromide, idleness, hot baths, supervision, cowardly fear of every mouthful, of every step—all this will finally reduce me to idiocy. I was going out of my mind, I had megalomania; but then I was cheerful, confident, and even happy; I was interesting and original. Now I have become more sensible and stolid, but I am just like everyone else: I am a mediocrity; I am weary of life . . . Oh, how cruelly you have treated me! . . . I saw hallucinations, but what harm did that do to anyone? I ask, what harm did that do anyone?'

'Goodness knows what you are saying!' sighed Yegor Semyonych. 'It's wearisome to listen to.'

'Then don't listen.'

The presence of other people, especially Yegor Semyonych, irritated Kovrin now; he answered him drily, coldly, and even rudely, and invariably looked at him with irony and hatred, while Yegor Semyonych was overcome with confusion and cleared his throat guiltily, though he was not conscious of any fault in himself. At a loss to understand why their charming and affectionate relationship had changed so abruptly, Tanya huddled up to her father and looked anxiously in his face; she wanted to understand but could not, and all that was clear to her was that their relationship was growing worse and worse every day, that of late her father had begun to look much older, and her husband had grown irritable, capricious, quarrelsome and uninteresting. She could no longer laugh or sing; at dinner she ate nothing; she did not sleep for nights on end, expecting something awful, and was so worn out that on one occasion she lay in a dead faint from dinner-time till evening. During the service she thought her father was crying, and now while the three of them were sitting together on the terrace she made an effort not to think of it.

'How fortunate Buddha, Muhammad, and Shakespeare were that their kind relations and doctors did not cure them of their ecstasy and their inspiration,' said Kovrin. 'If Muhammad had taken bromide for his nerves, had worked only two hours out of the twenty-four, and had drunk milk, that remarkable man would have left no more trace after him than his dog. Doctors and kind relations will end by stupefying mankind, making mediocrity pass for genius and bringing civilisation to ruin. If only you knew,' Kovrin said with annoyance, 'how grateful I am to you.'

He felt intense irritation, and to avoid saying too much, he got up quickly and went into the house. It was still, and the fragrance of the tobacco-plant and the marvel of Peru floated in at the open window. The moonlight lay in green patches on the floor and on the piano in the big dark dining-room. Kovrin remembered the raptures of the previous summer when there had been the same scent of the marvel of Peru and the moon had shone in at the window. To recapture the mood of last year he went quickly to his study, lit a strong cigar, and told the footman to bring him some wine. But the cigar left a bitter and disgusting taste in his mouth, and the wine had not the same flavour as it had the year before. And so great is the effect of giving up a habit, the cigar and the two gulps of wine made him giddy, and brought on palpitations of the heart, so that he was obliged to take potassium bromide.

Before going to bed, Tanya said to him:

'Father adores you. You are cross with him about something, and it is killing him. Look at him; he is ageing, not from day to day, but by the hour. I entreat you, Andryusha, for God's sake, for the sake of your own dead father, for the sake of my peace of mind, be kind to him.'

'I can't, I don't want to.'

'But why?' asked Tanya, beginning to tremble all over. 'Explain why.'

'Because I don't like him, that's all,' said Kovrin casually; and he shrugged his shoulders. 'But we won't talk about him: he is your father.'

'I can't understand, I can't,' said Tanya, pressing her hands to her

257

temples and staring at a fixed point. 'Something incomprehensible, awful, is going on in our house. You have changed, grown unlike yourself . . . You, a clever, extraordinary man, are irritated over trifles, you meddle in petty squabbles . . . Such trivial things excite you, that sometimes one is simply amazed and can't believe that it is you. Come, come, don't be angry, don't be angry,' she went on, kissing his hands, frightened of her own words. 'You are clever, kind, noble. You will be fair to Father. He is so good.'

'He is not good; he is just good-natured. Burlesque old uncles like your father, with well-fed, good-natured faces, extraordinarily hospitable and eccentric, at one time used to touch me and amuse me in novels and in farces and in life; now I dislike them. They are egoists to the marrow of their bones. What disgusts me most of all is their being so well-fed, and that purely bovine or hoggish optimism of a full stomach.'

Tanya sat down on the bed and laid her head on the pillow.

'This is torture,' she said, and from her voice it was evident that she was utterly exhausted, and that it was hard for her to speak. 'Not one moment of peace since the winter . . . Why, it's awful! My God! I am so wretched.'

'Oh, of course, I am Herod, and you and your father are the innocents. Of course.'

His face seemed to Tanya ugly and unpleasant. Hatred and an ironical expression did not suit him. And, indeed, she had noticed before that there was something lacking in his face, as though ever since his hair had been cut his face had changed, too. She wanted to say something wounding to him, but immediately she caught herself in this antagonistic feeling, grew frightened and walked out of the bedroom.

IX

Kovrin received a professorship at the University. His inaugural lecture was fixed for the second of December, and a notice to that effect was hung up in the corridor at the University. But on the day appointed he informed the authorities, by telegram, that he was prevented by illness from giving the lecture.

He had a haemorrhage from the throat. He often spat blood, but it happened twice or so each month that there was a considerable loss of blood, and then he grew extremely weak and sank into a drowsy condition. This illness did not particularly frighten him, as he knew that his mother had lived for ten years or longer suffering from the same disease, and the doctors assured him that there was no danger, and had only advised him to avoid excitement, to lead a regular life, and to speak as little as possible.

In January again his lecture did not take place for the same reason, and in February it was too late to begin the course. It had to be postponed to the following year.

By now he was living not with Tanya, but with another woman, who was two years older than he was, and who looked after him as though he were a baby. He was in a calm and tranquil state of mind; he readily gave in to her, and when Varvara Nikolayevna—that was the name of his friend—decided to take him to the Crimea, he agreed, though he had a presentiment that no good would come of this trip.

They reached Sevastopol in the evening and stopped at an hotel to rest and go on the next day to Yalta. They were both exhausted by the journey. Varvara Nikolayevna had some tea, went to bed and was soon asleep. But Kovrin did not go to bed. An hour before starting for the station, he had received a letter from Tanya, and had not brought himself to open it, and now it was lying in his coat pocket, and the thought of it disturbed him disagreeably. At the bottom of his heart he genuinely considered now that his marriage to Tanya had been a mistake. He was glad that their separation was final, and the thought of that woman who in the end had turned into a living relic personified, in whom everything seemed dead except her big, staring, intelligent eyes—the thought of her roused in him nothing but pity and annoyance with himself. The handwriting on the envelope reminded him how cruel and unjust he had been two years before, how he had worked off his anger at his spiritual emptiness, his boredom, his loneliness, and his dissatisfaction with life by revenging himself on people in no way to blame. He remembered, also, how he had torn up his dissertation and all the articles he had written during his illness, and how he had thrown them out of the window, and the bits of paper had fluttered in the wind and caught on the trees and flowers. In every line of them he saw strange, utterly groundless pretension, shallow defiance, arrogance, megalomania; and they made him feel as though he were reading a description of his vices. But when the last manuscript had been torn up and sent flying out of the window, he felt, for some reason, suddenly bitter and angry; he had gone to his wife and said a great many unpleasant things to her. My God, how he had tormented her! One day, wanting to cause her pain, he told her that her father had played a very unattractive part in their romance, that he had asked him to marry her. Yegor Semyonych accidentally overheard this, ran into the room, and, in his despair, could not utter a word, could only stamp and make a strange, bellowing sound as though he had lost the power of speech, and Tanya, looking at her father, had uttered a heart-rending shriek and fallen into a swoon. It was hideous.

All this came back into his memory as he looked at the familiar writing. Kovrin went out on to the balcony; it was still warm weather and there was a smell of the sea. The wonderful bay reflected the moon and the lights, and was of a colour for which it is difficult to find a name. It was a soft and tender blending of dark blue and green; in places the water was like blue vitriol, and in places it seemed as though the moonlight were liquefied and filling the bay instead of water. And what harmony of colours, what an atmosphere of peace, calm, and sublimity!

In the lower storey under the balcony the windows were probably open, for women's voices and laughter could be heard distinctly. Apparently there was a party.

Kovrin made an effort, tore open the envelope, and, returning to his room, read:

My father has just died. I owe that to you, for you have killed him. Our garden is being ruined; strangers are managing it already—that is, the very thing is happening that poor Father dreaded. That, too, I owe to you. I hate you with my whole soul, and I hope you may soon perish. Oh, how wretched I am! Insufferable anguish is burning my soul . . . My curses on you. I took you for an extraordinary man, a genius; I loved you, but you turned out to be a madman . . .

Kovrin could read no more, he tore up the letter and threw it away. He was overcome by an uneasiness that was akin to terror. Varvara Niko-layevna was asleep behind the screen, and he could hear her breathing. From the lower storey came the sounds of laughter and women's voices, but he felt as though in the whole hotel there were no living soul but him. Because Tanya, unhappy, broken by sorrow, had cursed him in her letter and hoped for his perdition, he felt horrified and kept glancing hurriedly at the door, as though he were afraid that the mysterious force which two years before had wrought such havoc in his life and in the life of those closest to him might come into the room and master him once more.

He knew by experience that when his nerves were out of hand the best thing for him to do was work. He must sit down at the table and force himself, at all costs, to concentrate his mind on some one thought. He took from his red portfolio a notebook containing a sketch of a short compilatory piece, which he had planned in case he should find it dull in the Crimea with nothing to do. He sat down at the table and began working on this plan, and it seemed to him that his calm, peaceful, indifferent mood was coming back. The notebook with the sketch even led him to meditation on the vanity of the world. He thought how much life exacts for the worthless or very commonplace blessings it can give a man. For instance, to gain, before forty, a university chair, to be an ordinary professor, to expound ordinary and second-hand thoughts in dull, heavy, insipid language—in fact, to reach the position of a mediocre scholar, he, Kovrin, had had to study for fifteen years, to work day and night, to endure a terrible mental illness, to experience an unhappy marriage, and to do a great number of stupid and unjust things which it would have been pleasant not to remember. Kovrin recognised clearly, now, that he was a mediocrity, and readily resigned himself to it, as he considered that every man ought to be satisfied with what he is.

The sketch would have soothed him completely, but the torn letter showed white on the floor and prevented him from concentrating. He got up from the table, picked up the pieces of the letter and threw them out of the window, but there was a light wind blowing from the sea, and the bits of paper were scattered on the windowsill. Again he was overcome by uneasiness akin to terror, and he felt as though in the whole hotel there were no living soul but himself . . . He went out on the balcony. The bay, like a living thing, looked at him with its multitude of light-blue, dark-blue, turquoise and fiery eyes, and beckoned to him. It really was hot and oppressive—the kind of weather to go for a bathe.

Suddenly in the lower storey under the balcony a violin began playing, and two soft feminine voices began singing. It was something familiar. The song was about a maiden, full of sick fancies, who heard one night in her garden mysterious sounds, and decided that this was a holy harmony which is unintelligible to us mortals . . . Kovrin caught his breath and there was a pang of sadness in his heart, and a thrill of the sweet, exquisite delight he had so long forgotten began to stir in his breast.

A tall black column, like a whirlwind or a waterspout, appeared on the further side of the bay. It moved with fearful rapidity across the bay, towards the hotel, growing smaller and darker as it came, and Kovrin only just had time to get out of the way to let it pass . . . The monk with bare grey head, black eyebrows, barefoot, his arms crossed over his breast, floated by him, and stood still in the middle of the room.

'Why did you not believe me?' he asked reproachfully, looking affectionately at Kovrin. 'If you had believed me then, that you were a genius, you would not have spent these two years so gloomily and so wretchedly.'

Kovrin now believed that he was one of God's chosen and a genius; he vividly recalled all his past conversations with the black monk and tried to speak, but the blood flowed from his throat on to his breast, and not knowing what he was doing, he passed his hands over his breast, and his cuffs were soaked with blood. He tried to call Varvara Nikolayevna, who was asleep behind the screen, he made an effort and said:

'Tanya!'

He fell on the floor and, propping himself on his arms, called again:

'Tanya!'

He called Tanya, called to the great garden with the gorgeous flowers sprinkled with dew, called to the park, the pines with their shaggy roots, the rye-field, his marvellous learning, his youth, courage, joy—called to life, which was so lovely. He saw on the floor near his face a great pool of blood, and was too weak to utter a word, but an unspeakable, infinite happiness flooded his whole being. Below, under the balcony, they were playing the serenade, and the black monk whispered to him that he was a genius, and that he was dying only because his frail human body had lost its balance and could no longer serve as the mortal garb of genius.

When Varvara Nikolayevna woke up and came out from behind the screen, Kovrin was dead, and a blissful smile was frozen on his face.

Rothschild's Fiddle

The town was a little one, worse than a village, and it was inhabited almost exclusively by old people who died with an infrequency that was really annoying. For the hospital and the prison very few coffins were needed. In short, business was bad. If Yakov Ivanov had been an undertaker in the chief town of the province he would certainly have had a house of his own, and people would have addressed him as Yakov Matveich; here in this wretched little town people called him simply Yakov; his nickname in the street was for some reason Bronze, and he lived in a poor way like a humble peasant, in a little old hut in which there was only one room, and in this room he and Marfa, the stove, a double bed, the coffins, his bench, and all their belongings were crowded together.

Yakov made good, solid coffins. For peasants and working people he made them to fit himself, and never got it wrong, for there were none taller and stronger than he, even in the prison, though he was already seventy. For gentry and for women he made them to measure, and used an iron foot-rule for the purpose. He was very unwilling to take orders for children's coffins, and made them straight off without measurements, contemptuously, and when he was paid for the work he always said:

'I must confess I don't like rubbishy jobs.'

Apart from his trade, playing the fiddle brought him in a small income.

The Jews' orchestra conducted by Moisey Ilyich Shakhkes, the tinsmith, who took more than half their receipts for himself, played as a rule at weddings in the town. As Yakov played very well on the fiddle, especially Russian songs, Shakhkes sometimes invited him to join the orchestra at a fee of half a rouble a day, in addition to tips from the visitors. When Bronze sat in the orchestra, first of all his face became crimson and perspiring; it was hot, there was a suffocating smell of garlic, the fiddle squeaked, the double-bass wheezed close to his right ear, while the flute wailed at his left, played by a gaunt, red-haired Jew who had a perfect network of red and blue veins all over his face, and who bore the name of the famous millionaire Rothschild. And this accursed Jew contrived to play even the liveliest things plaintively. For no apparent reason Yakov little by little became possessed by hatred and contempt for the Jews, and especially for Rothschild; he began to pick quarrels with him, rail at him in unseemly language and once even tried to strike him, and Rothschild was offended and said, looking at him ferociously:

'If it were not that I respect you for your talent, I would have sent you flying out of the window.'

Then he began to weep. And because of this Bronze was not often asked to play in the orchestra; he was only sent for in case of extreme necessity in the absence of one of the Jews.

Yakov was never in a good temper, as he was continually having to put up with terrible losses. For instance, it was a sin to work on Sundays or Saints' days, and Monday was an unlucky day, so that in the course of the year there were some two hundred days on which, whether he liked it or not, he had to sit with his hands folded. And only think, what a loss that meant! If anyone in the town had a wedding without music, or if Shakhkes did not send for Yakov, that was a loss, too. The superintendent of the prison was ill for two years and was wasting away, and Yakov was impatiently waiting for him to die, but the superintendent went off to the chief town of the province to be treated, and chose to die there. There's a loss for you, ten roubles at least, as there would have been an expensive coffin to make, lined with brocade. The thought of his losses haunted Yakov, especially at night; he laid his fiddle on the bed beside him, and when all sorts of rubbish came into his mind he touched a string; the fiddle gave out a sound in the darkness, and he felt better.

On the sixth of May of the previous year Marfa had suddenly been taken ill. The old woman's breathing was laboured, she drank a great deal of water, and she staggered as she walked, yet she lit the stove in the morning and even went herself to get water. Towards evening she lay down. Yakov played his fiddle all day; when it was quite dark he took the book in which he used every day to put down his losses, and, feeling bored, he began adding up the total for the year. It came to more than a thousand roubles. This so agitated him that he flung the reckoning beads down, and trampled them under his feet. Then he picked up the reckoning beads, and again spent a long time clicking them and heaving deep, strained sighs. His face was crimson and wet with perspiration. He thought that if he had put that lost thousand roubles in the bank, the interest for a year would have been at least forty roubles, so that forty roubles was a loss too. In fact, wherever one turned there were losses and nothing else.

'Yakov!' Marfa called unexpectedly. 'I am dying.'

He looked round at his wife. Her face was rosy with fever, unusually bright and joyful. Bronze, accustomed to seeing her face always pale, timid, and unhappy, was bewildered. It seemed as if she really were dying and were glad that she was going away for ever from that hut, from the coffins, and from Yakov . . . And she gazed at the ceiling and moved her lips, and her expression was one of happiness, as though she saw death as her deliverer and were whispering to him.

It was daybreak; from the window one could see the flush of dawn. Looking at the old woman, Yakov for some reason remembered that not once in his life had he been affectionate to her, he had not pitied her, had never once thought to buy her a kerchief, or to bring her home some dainty from a wedding, but had done nothing but shout at her, scold her for his losses, shake his fists at her; it is true he had never actually beaten her, but he had frightened her, and at such times she had always been numb with terror. Why, he had forbidden her to drink tea because they spent too much without that, and she drank only hot water. And he understood why she had such a strange, joyful face now, and he was overcome with dread.

As soon as it was morning he borrowed a horse from a neighbour and took Marfa to the hospital. There were not many patients there, and so he had not long to wait, only three hours. To his great satisfaction the patients were not being received by the doctor, who was himself ill, but by the assistant, Maksim Nikolaich, an old man of whom everyone in the town used to say that, though he drank and was quarrelsome, he knew more than the doctor.

'I wish you good day,' said Yakov, leading his old woman into the consulting-room. 'You must excuse us, Maksim Nikolaich, we are always troubling you with our trivial affairs. Here you see my better half is ailing, the partner of my life, as they say, if you will excuse the expression . . .'

Knitting his grizzled brows and stroking his whiskers the assistant began to examine the old woman, and she sat on a stool, a wasted, bent figure with a sharp nose and open mouth, looking like a bird that wants to drink.

'Hm . . . Ah! . . .' the assistant said slowly, and he heaved a sigh. 'Influenza and possibly fever. There's typhus in the town now. Well, the old woman has lived her life, thank God . . . How old is she?'

'She'll be seventy in another year, Maksim Nikolaich.'

'Well, the old woman has lived her life, it's time to say goodbye.'

'You are quite right in what you say, of course, Maksim Nikolaich,' said Yakov, smiling from politeness, 'and we thank you feelingly for your kindness, but allow me to say that every insect wants to live.'

'To be sure,' said the assistant, in a tone which suggested that it depended upon him whether the woman lived or died. 'Well, then, my good fellow, put a cold compress on her head, and give her these powders twice a day, and so goodbye. *Bonjour.*'

From the expression on his face Yakov saw that things were bad, and that no powders would be any help; it was clear to him that Marfa would die very soon, if not today, tomorrow. He nudged the assistant's elbow, winked at him, and said in a low voice:

'If you would just cup her, Maksim Nikolaich.'

'I have no time, I have no time, my good fellow. Take your old woman and go in God's name. Goodbye.'

'Be so gracious,' Yakov besought him. 'You know yourself that if, let us say, it were her stomach or her inside that were bad, then powders or drops would do, but you see she has got a chill! In a chill the first thing is to let blood, Maksim Nikolaich.'

But the assistant had already sent for the next patient, and a peasant woman came into the consulting-room with a boy.

'Go along, go along,' he said to Yakov, frowning. 'It's no use to—'

'In that case put on leeches, anyway! We shall pray for you for ever.'

The assistant flew into a rage and shouted:

'You speak to me again! You blockhead . . .'

Yakov flew into a rage too, and he turned crimson all over, but he did not utter a word. He took Marfa on his arm and led her out of the room. Only when they were sitting in the cart he looked morosely and ironically at the hospital, and said:

'A nice set of artists they've planted there! I bet he would have cupped a rich man, but even a leech he grudges to the poor. The Herods!'

When they got home and went into the hut, Marfa stood for ten minutes holding on to the stove. It seemed to her that if she were to lie down Yakov would talk to her about his losses, and scold her for lying down and not wanting to work. Yakov looked at her drearily and thought that tomorrow was St John the Divine's, and next day St Nicholas the Miracle-Worker's, and the day after that was Sunday, and then Monday, an unlucky day. For four days he would not be able to work, and most likely Marfa would die on one of those days; so he would have to make the coffin today. He picked up his iron rule, went up to the old woman and measured her. Then she lay down, and he crossed himself and began to make her coffin.

When the work was finished Bronze put on his spectacles and wrote in his book: 'Marfa Ivanova's coffin, two roubles, forty kopecks.'

And he heaved a sigh. The old woman lay all the time silent with her eyes closed. But in the evening, when it got dark, she suddenly called the old man.

'Do you remember, Yakov,' she asked, looking at him joyfully. 'Do you remember fifty years ago God gave us a little baby with flaxen hair? We used always to be sitting by the river then, singing songs . . . under the willow-tree,' and, laughing bitterly, she added: 'The baby girl died.'

Yakov racked his memory, but could not remember the baby or the willow-tree.

'You're imagining it,' he said.

The priest arrived; he administered the sacrament and extreme unction. Then Marfa began muttering something unintelligible, and towards morning she died. Old women, neighbours, washed her, dressed her, and laid her in the coffin. To avoid paying the sacristan, Yakov read the psalms over the body himself, and they got nothing out of him for the grave, as the gravedigger was a crony of his. Four peasants carried the coffin to the graveyard, not for money, but from respect. The coffin was followed by old women, beggars, and a couple of holy simpletons, and the people who met it crossed themselves piously . . . And Yakov was very pleased that it was so creditable, decorous, and cheap, and had caused no offence to anyone. As he took his last leave of Marfa he touched the coffin and thought: 'A good piece of work!'

But as he was going back from the cemetery he was overcome by acute depression. He didn't feel very well: his breathing was laboured and feverish, his legs went weak, and he had an enormous thirst. And thoughts of all sorts crowded into his mind. He remembered again that all his life he had never pitied Marfa, had never been affectionate to her. The fifty-two years they had lived in the same hut had dragged on a long, long time, but it had somehow happened that in all that time he had never once thought of her, had paid no attention to her, as though she had been a cat or a dog. And yet, every day, she had lit the stove, had cooked and baked, had fetched the water, chopped the wood, slept with him in the same bed, and when he came home drunk from the weddings always reverently hung his fiddle on the wall and put him to bed, and all this in silence, with a timid, anxious expression.

267

Rothschild, smiling and bowing, came to meet Yakov.

'I was looking for you, Uncle,' he said. 'Moysey Ilyich sends you his greetings and bids you come to him at once.'

Yakov felt in no mood for this. He wanted to weep.

'Leave me alone,' he said, and walked on.

'How can you?' Rothschild said, flustered, running on in front. 'Moysey Ilyich will be offended! He bade you come at once!'

Yakov was revolted at the Jew's gasping for breath and blinking, and having so many red freckles on his face. And it was disgusting to look at his green coat with black patches on it, and all his fragile, refined figure.

'Why are you pestering me, you garlic?' shouted Yakov. 'Don't persist!'

The Jew got angry and shouted too:

'Not so noisy, please, or I'll send you flying over the fence!'

'Get out of my sight!' roared Yakov, and rushed at him with his fists. 'You wretches make life impossible!'

Rothschild, half dead with terror, crouched down and waved his hands above his head, as though parrying some blows; then he leapt up and ran away as fast as his legs could carry him: as he ran he gave little skips and kept clasping his hands, and Yakov could see how his long, thin spine quivered. Some boys, delighted at the incident, ran after him shouting 'Jew! Jew!' Some dogs joined in the chase, barking. Someone burst into a roar of laughter, then gave a whistle; the dogs barked with even more noise and unanimity. Then a dog must have bitten Rothschild, as a desperate, painful scream was heard.

Yakov went for a walk on the grazing ground, then wandered on at random in the outskirts of the town, while the street-boys shouted:

'Bronze is coming! Bronze is coming!'

He reached the river, where the sandpipers hovered in the air uttering shrill cries and the ducks quacked. The sun was burning hot, and there was a glitter from the water, so that it hurt the eyes to look at it. Yakov walked by a path along the bank and saw a plump, rosy-cheeked lady come out of a bathing-place, and thought about her: 'Ugh! You otter!'

Not far from the bathing-place boys were catching crayfish with bits of meat; seeing him, they began shouting spitefully, 'Bronze! Bronze!' And then he saw an old spreading willow-tree with a big hollow in it, and crow's nests on top . . . And suddenly there rose up vividly in Yakov's memory a baby with flaxen hair, and the willow-tree Marfa had spoken of. Why, that is it, the same willow-tree—green, still, and sorrowful . . . How old it has grown, poor thing!

He sat down under it and began to recall the past. On the other bank, where now there was the water-meadow, in those days there stood a big birch-wood, and yonder on the bare hillside that could be seen on the horizon an old, old pine-forest used to be a bluish patch. Big boats used to sail on the river. But now it was all smooth and unruffled, and on the other bank there stood now only one birch-tree, youthful and slender like a young lady, and there was nothing on the river but ducks and geese, and one could hardly believe there had ever been boats on it. It seemed as though even the geese were fewer than of old. Yakov shut his eyes, and in his imagination huge flocks of white geese soared, meeting one another.

He wondered how it had happened that for the last forty or fifty years of his life he had never once been to the river, or if he had been there he had paid it no attention. Why, it was a decent-sized river, not a trivial one; he might have gone in for fishing and sold the fish to merchants, officials, and the barkeeper at the station, and then have put money in the bank; he might have sailed in a boat from one estate to another, playing the fiddle, and people of all classes would have paid to hear him; he might have tried getting big boats afloat again—that would be better than making coffins; he might have bred geese, killed them, and sent them in the winter to Moscow. Why, the feathers alone would mount up to ten roubles a year. But he had missed his chance: he had done nothing of this. What losses! Ah! What losses! And if he had gone in for all those things at once—catching fish and playing the fiddle, and sailing the boats and killing geese—what a fortune he would have made! But nothing of this had happened, even in his dreams; life had passed uselessly without any pleasure, had been wasted for nothing, not even a pinch of snuff; nothing lay ahead, and if one looked back—there was nothing but losses, and such terrible ones, it made one cold all over. And why was it a man could not live so as to avoid these losses and misfortunes? He wondered why they had cut down the birch-copse and the pine-forest. Why was the grazing ground unused? Why do people always do what they shouldn't? Why had Yakov all his life scolded, bellowed, shaken his fists, ill-treated his wife, and, one might ask, what necessity was there for him to frighten and insult the Jew just now? Why did people in general hinder each other from living? What losses come as a result! What terrible losses! If it were not for hatred and malice people would get immense benefit from one another.

In the evening and the night he had visions of the baby, of the willow, of fish, of slaughtered geese, and Marfa looking in profile like a bird that wants to drink, and the pale, pitiful face of Rothschild, and ugly faces crowded in from all directions, muttering of losses. He tossed from side to side, and got out of bed half a dozen times to play the fiddle.

In the morning he rose with an effort and went to the hospital. The same Maksim Nikolaich told him to put a cold compress on his head, and gave him some powders, and from his tone and facial expression Yakov realised that things were bad and that no powders would be any help. As he went home afterwards, he reflected that death would be nothing but a benefit; he would not have to eat or drink, or pay taxes or offend people, and, as a man lies in his grave not for one year but for hundreds and thousands, if one reckoned it up the gain would be enormous. A man's life meant loss: death meant gain. This reflection was, of course, a just one, and yet it was bitter and offensive; why was the way of the world so strange, that life, which is given to man only once, passes away without any benefit?

He was not sorry to die, but at home, as soon as he saw his fiddle, it sent a pang to his heart and he felt sorry. He could not take the fiddle with him to the grave, and now it would be left forlorn, and the same thing would happen to it as to the birch-copse and the pine-forest. Everything in this world was wasted and would be wasted! Yakov went out of the hut and sat on the doorstep, pressing the fiddle to his chest. Thinking of his wasted, profitless life, he began to play, he did not know what, but it was plaintive and touching, and tears trickled down his cheeks. And the harder he thought, the more mournfully the fiddle sang.

The latch clicked a couple of times, and Rothschild appeared at the gate. He walked across half the yard boldly, but seeing Yakov he stopped short, and seemed to shrink together, and, probably from terror, began making signs with his hands as though he wanted to show on his fingers what o'clock it was.

'Come along, it's all right,' said Yakov in a friendly tone, and he beckoned him to approach. 'Come along!'

Looking at him mistrustfully and apprehensively, Rothschild began to advance, and stopped seven feet off.

'Be so good as not to beat me,' he said, ducking. 'Moysey Ilyich has sent me again. "Don't be afraid," he said; "go to Yakov again and tell him," he said, "we can't get on without him." There is a wedding on Wednesday . . . Ye—es! Mr Shapovalov is marrying his daughter to a good man . . . And it will be a grand wedding, oo-oo!' added the Jew, screwing up one eye.

'I can't come,' said Yakov, breathing hard. 'I'm ill, brother.'

And he began playing again, and the tears gushed from his eyes on to the fiddle. Rothschild listened attentively, standing sideways to him and folding his arms on his chest. The scared and perplexed expression on his face, little by little, changed to a look of woe and suffering; he rolled his eyes as though he were experiencing an agonising ecstasy, and said, 'Vakhhh!' And tears slowly ran down his cheeks and trickled on to his greenish coat.

And Yakov lay in bed all the rest of the day grieving. In the evening, when the priest confessing him asked whether he remembered any special sin he had committed, then, straining his failing memory, he thought again of Marfa's unhappy face, and the despairing shriek of the Jew when the dog bit him, and said, hardly audibly, 'Give the fiddle to Rothschild.'

'Very well,' answered the priest.

And now everyone in the town asks where Rothschild got such a fine fiddle. Did he buy it or steal it? Or perhaps it came to him as a pledge. He gave up the flute long ago, and now plays nothing but the fiddle. The same plaintive sounds flow from his bow, as came once from his flute, but when he tries to repeat what Yakov played, sitting on the doorstep, the effect is so sad and sorrowful that his audience weep, and he himself rolls his eyes and says 'Vakhhh! . . .' And this new melody is so much liked in the town that the merchants and officials continually send for Rothschild and make him play it again and again.

The Student

The weather at first was fine and still. Thrushes sang, and nearby in the marshes something living plaintively moaned, as if blowing into an empty bottle. A lone woodcock flew over, and a shot rang out in the spring air, rumbling cheerfully. But when it grew dark in the wood, a cold piercing wind blew unseasonably from the east; everything fell silent. Needles of ice stretched across the pools, and the wood became comfortless, dull and desolate. Winter was in the air.

Ivan Velikopolsky, a student at the ecclesiastical academy and son of a lowly sexton, was keeping to the path through the water-meadow as he made his way home from the shoot. His fingers were numb, and his face burned in the wind. It seemed to him that this sudden cold had destroyed the order and harmony in everything, that nature herself had taken fright, and that was why the evening darkness had descended more rapidly than normal. All around was deserted and somehow unusually gloomy. A light shone only in the widows' allotments by the river; far around, and in the village three miles away, everything was submerged in the cold evening mist. The student remembered that, when he left the house, his mother was sitting barefoot on the porch floor, cleaning the samovar, while his father lay on the stove, coughing. As it was Good Friday they had cooked nothing at home, and he had felt tormented by hunger. And now, huddling from the cold, the student reflected that just such a wind had blown in the days of Ryurik, and of Ivan the Terrible, and of Peter the Great, and that in those days, too, there had been just such desperate poverty, and famine, the same hole-ridden thatched roofs, ignorance, misery, the same desert all around, gloom, a feeling of oppression—all these horrors had been, were now, and always would be, and, even a thousand years from now, life would be no better. And he did not feel like going home.

The allotments were called the widows' because they were kept by two widows, a mother and her daughter. A fire was burning brightly, crackling and lighting up the ploughed land far around. Widow Vasilisa, a tall, plump old woman in a man's sheepskin coat, stood by, pensively eyeing the flames; her daughter Lukerya, small, pock-marked, with a rather stupid face, was sitting on the ground, washing a pot and spoons. They had evidently just had supper. Men's voices could be heard; the local workmen were watering their horses at the river.

'So winter's come back,' said the student, as he drew near the fire. 'Good evening to you!'

Vasilisa shuddered, but immediately recognised him and gave a welcoming smile.

'I didn't recognise you at first, God be with you,' she said. 'That's a good sign—it means you'll be rich.'

They began to talk. Vasilisa, a woman of much experience, who had once been a wet-nurse, then a nanny, for her masters, expressed herself delicately, and a soft, sedate smile never left her face; her daughter Lukerya, a peasant woman often beaten by her husband, merely screwed up her eyes at the student and remained silent, and she wore a strange expression, like that of a deaf-mute.

'On a cold night just like this the Apostle Peter warmed himself by a fire,' said the student, stretching out his hands to the flames. 'So it was cold then, too. Ah, what a dreadful night that was, Granny! An extraordinarily long and dismal night!'

He looked around at the darkness, shook his head abruptly, and asked:

'I suppose you were in church yesterday for the Twelve Gospel Readings?'

'I was,' Vasilisa replied.

'If you recall, at the Last Supper Peter said to Jesus: "I am ready to go with thee, both into prison, and to death." And the Lord answered: "I tell thee, Peter, the cock shall not crow this day, before that thou shalt thrice deny that thou knowest me." After supper Jesus in the garden was exceeding sorrowful, even unto death, and He prayed, but poor Peter grew weary in spirit, he felt weak, his eyelids were heavy, and he simply could not fight off sleep. He slept. Then, as you heard, Judas that same night kissed Jesus and betrayed Him to His tormentors. They led Him bound to the high priest and smote Him, and Peter, exhausted, tortured by anguish and alarm—you know, not having slept enough—foreseeing that very soon something horrible was going to happen on earth, went after Him . . . He loved Jesus passionately, forgetting all else, and now he saw afar off that they smote Him . . .'

Lukerya put down the spoons and gazed fixedly at the student.

'They came to the high priest,' he continued; 'they began to question Jesus, and meanwhile the workmen kindled a fire in the midst of the hall, for it was cold, and they warmed themselves. Peter stood with them by the fire, and also warmed himself, as I am doing now. One woman saw him and said: "This fellow was also with Jesus", meaning that he, too, should be taken for questioning. And all the workmen near the fire must have looked at him suspiciously and sternly, for he was troubled and said: "I know Him not." A little later someone else recognised him as one of Jesus's disciples and said: "Thou art also of them." But he denied again. And for the third time someone addressed him: "Did not I see thee in the garden with Him today?" He denied a third time. And after this time immediately the cock crew, and Peter, looking afar off upon Jesus, remembered the words that He had said to him at supper . . . He remembered, came to his senses, left the hall, and started weeping bitterly, bitterly. It says in the Gospel: "And he went out, and wept bitterly." I can imagine: a still, still, dark, dark garden, and in the stillness dull sobbing can scarcely be heard . . .'

The student sighed and sank into thought. Continuing to smile, Vasilisa suddenly broke into sobs; large, copious tears flowed down her cheeks, and with her sleeve she shielded her face from the fire, as if ashamed of her tears, while Lukerya, looking fixedly at the student, blushed, and her expression became mournful and strained, like that of someone who is suppressing intense pain.

The workmen were returning from the river, and one of them on horseback was quite close, and the light from the fire quivered upon him. The student wished the widows good night, and went on his way. And again darkness set in, and his hands began to freeze. A cruel wind was blowing, winter was indeed returning, and it did not feel as if Easter Sunday was only two days away.

Now the student thought of Vasilisa: if she had started weeping, then everything that happened to Peter on that dreadful night had some connection with her . . .

He glanced back. The solitary light flickered calmly in the dark, and near it no people could be seen. The student again thought that if Vasilisa had started weeping, and her daughter had been troubled, then evidently the story he had just been telling, which had happened nineteen centuries ago, had some connection with the present—with these two women and, probably, with this deserted village, with himself, and with all people. If the old woman had started weeping, it was not because he could tell a story movingly, but because Peter was close to her, and because her whole being was interested in what happened in Peter's soul.

And joy suddenly stirred in his soul, and he even stopped for a moment to draw breath. The past, he thought, is linked to the present by

274

an unbroken chain of events, flowing one from the other. And it seemed to him that he had just seen both ends of this chain: he had touched one end, whereupon the other had trembled.

And when he was crossing the river by ferry, and then, climbing the hill, looked towards his native village and the west, where the cold crimson sunset shone in a narrow streak, he reflected that truth and beauty, which had governed human life there, in the garden and in the hall of the high priest, had continued unbroken to this day and had, apparently, always been the main element in human life and on earth as a whole; and a feeling of youth, health, strength—he was only twenty-two years old—and an inexpressibly sweet expectation of happiness, unknown, mysterious happiness, gradually took hold of him, and life seemed to him enchanting, wonderful, and full of noble meaning.

The House with the Mezzanine

AN ARTIST'S STORY

I

It was six or seven years ago when I was living in one of the districts of the province of T——, on the estate of a young landowner called Belokurov, who used to get up very early, wear a peasant tunic, drink beer in the evenings, and continually complain to me that he never met with sympathy from anyone. He lived in the lodge in the garden, and I in the old manor-house, in a huge room with columns, where there was no furniture except a wide sofa on which I used to sleep, and a table on which I used to lay out patience. There was always, even in still weather, a droning noise in the old Amosov stoves, and during thunderstorms the whole house shook and seemed to be cracking into pieces; and it was rather terrifying, especially at night, when all the ten big windows were suddenly lit by lightning.

Condemned by destiny to perpetual idleness, I did absolutely nothing. For hours on end I gazed out of the window at the sky, at the birds, at the avenues, read everything that the post brought me, slept. Sometimes I went out of the house and wandered about till late in the evening.

One day as I was returning home, I accidentally strayed into a place I did not know. The sun was already sinking, and the shades of evening lay across the flowering rye. Two rows of old, closely planted, very tall fir-trees stood like two dense walls forming a beautiful, gloomy avenue. I easily climbed over the fence and walked along this avenue, slipping on the fir-needles which lay two inches deep on the ground. It was still and dark, and only here and there on the high treetops the vivid golden light quivered and made rainbows in the spiders' webs. There was a strong, almost stifling smell of resin. Then I turned into a long avenue of limes. Here, too, all was desolation and age; last year's leaves rustled mournfully under my feet and in the twilight shadows lurked between the trees. From the old orchard on the right came the faint, reluctant note of the golden oriole, who must have been old too. But at last the limes ended. I walked by a white house with a terrace and a mezzanine, and there suddenly opened before me a view of a courtyard, a large pond with a bathing-place, a group of green willows, and a village on the further bank, with a high, narrow belfry on which there glittered a cross reflecting the setting sun.

For a moment I sensed the enchantment of something near and very familiar, as though I had seen that landscape at some time in my childhood.

By the white stone gates which led from the yard to the fields, old-fashioned solid gates with lions on them, were standing two girls. One of them, the elder, a slim, pale, very beautiful girl with a heap of chestnut hair and a little obstinate mouth, had a severe expression and scarcely took notice of me, while the other, who was still very young, not more than seventeen or eighteen, and was also slim and pale, with a large mouth and large eyes, looked at me with astonishment as I passed by, said something in English, and was overcome with embarrassment. And it seemed to me that these two charming faces, too, had long been familiar to me. And I returned home feeling as though I had had a pleasant dream.

One morning soon afterwards, as Belokurov and I were walking near the house, a carriage drove unexpectedly into the yard, rustling over the grass, and in it was sitting one of those girls. It was the elder one. She had come to ask for subscriptions for some villagers whose cottages had been burnt down. Speaking with great earnestness and precision, and not looking at us, she told us how many houses in the village of Siyanovo had been burnt, how many men, women, and children were left homeless, and what steps were proposed, to begin with, by the Relief Committee, of which she was now a member. After handing us the subscription list for our signatures, she put it away and immediately began to take her leave.

'You have quite forgotten us, Pyotr Petrovich,' she said to Belokurov as she shook hands with him. 'Do come, and if Monsieur N. (she mentioned my name) cares to make the acquaintance of admirers of his work, and will come and see us, Mother and I will be delighted.'

I bowed.

When she had gone Pyotr Petrovich began to tell me about her. The girl was, he said, of good family, and her name was Lidiya Volchaninova, and the estate on which she lived with her mother and sister, like the village on the other side of the pond, was called Shelkovka. Her father had once held an important position in Moscow, and had died with the rank of Privy Counsellor. Although they had ample means, the Volchaninovs lived on their estate summer and winter without going away. Lidiya was a teacher in the zemstvo school in her own village, and received a salary of twenty-five roubles a month. She spent nothing on herself but her salary, and was proud of earning her own living.

'An interesting family,' said Belokurov. 'Let's go over one day. They will be delighted to see you.'

One afternoon on a holiday we thought of the Volchaninovs, and went to Shelkovka to see them. They—the mother and two daughters—were at home. The mother, Yekaterina Pavlovna, who at one time had apparently been beautiful, but was now asthmatic, sad, vague, and prematurely plump, tried to entertain me with conversation about painting. Having heard from her daughter that I might come to Shelkovka, she had hurriedly recalled two or three of my landscapes which she had seen in exhibitions in Moscow, and now asked what I meant to express by them. Lidiya, or as they all called her, Lida, talked more to Belokurov than to me. Earnest and unsmiling, she asked him why he was not on the local district council, the zemstvo, and why he had not attended any of its meetings.

'It's not right, Pyotr Petrovich,' she said reproachfully. 'It's not right. It's too bad.'

'That's true, Lida—that's true,' her mother agreed. 'It isn't right.'

'Our whole district is in the hands of Balagin,' Lida went on, addressing me. 'He is the chairman of the Zemstvo Board, and he has distributed all the posts in the district among his nephews and sons-in-law; and he does as he likes. He ought to be opposed. The young men ought to make a strong party, but you can see what our young men are like. It's too bad, Pyotr Petrovich!'

The younger sister, Zhenya, was silent while they were talking of the zemstvo. She took no part in serious conversations. She was not regarded as quite grown-up by her family, and, like a baby, was always addressed as Misyus, her childhood name for *Miss*, her English governess. She kept on looking at me with curiosity, and when I glanced at the photographs in the album, she explained to me: 'That's Uncle . . . that's Godfather,' moving her finger across the photographs. As she did so she touched me with her shoulder like a child, and I had a close view of her delicate, undeveloped chest, her slender shoulders, her plait, and her thin little body tightly drawn in by her sash.

We played croquet and lawn tennis, we walked about the garden, drank tea, and then sat a long time over supper. After my huge empty room with columns, I felt, as it were, at home in this small snug house where there were no oleographs on the walls and where the servants were spoken to with civility. And everything seemed to me young and pure, thanks to the presence of Lida and Misyus, and there was an atmosphere of refinement over everything. At supper Lida talked to Belokurov again of the zemstvo, of Balagin, and of school libraries. She was an energetic, sincere girl, with convictions, and it was interesting to listen to her, though she talked a great deal and in a loud voice—perhaps because she was accustomed to talking at school. On the other hand, Pyotr Petrovich, who had retained from his student days the habit of turning every conversation into an argument, was tedious, flat, long-winded, and unmistakably anxious to appear clever and progressive. Gesticulating, he upset a sauce-boat with his sleeve, making a huge pool on the table-cloth, but no one except me appeared to notice it.

It was dark and still as we went home.

'Good breeding is shown, not by not upsetting the sauce, but by not noticing it when somebody else does,' said Belokurov, with a sigh. 'Yes, a splendid, intellectual family! I've lost touch with decent people; it's dreadful how I've lost touch! It's all work, work, work!'

He talked of how hard one had to work if one wanted to be a model farmer. And I thought what a heavy, sluggish fellow he was! Whenever he talked of anything serious he articulated 'Er-er' with intense effort, and worked just as he talked—slowly, always late and missing deadlines. I had little faith in his business capacity if only from the fact that when I gave him letters to post he carried them in his pocket for weeks on end.

'The hardest thing of all,' he muttered as he walked beside me—'the hardest thing of all is that, work as one may, one meets with no sympathy from anyone. No sympathy!'

II

I began visiting the Volchaninovs. As a rule I sat on the lower step of the terrace; I was plagued by self-dissatisfaction; I regretted my life passing so rapidly and uninterestingly, and felt as though I would like to tear out of my breast the heart which had grown so heavy. And meanwhile I heard talk on the terrace, the rustling of dresses, the pages of a book being turned. I soon grew accustomed to the idea that during the day Lida received patients, handed out books, and often went into the village with a parasol and no hat, and in the evening talked loudly of the zemstvo and schools. This slim, beautiful, invariably austere girl, with her

279

small well-defined mouth, always said drily when the conversation turned to serious subjects:

'This is of no interest to you.'

She did not like me. She disliked me because I was a landscape painter and did not in my pictures portray the privations of the peasants, and because, as she fancied, I was indifferent to what she put such faith in. I remember when I was travelling on the banks of Lake Baykal, I met a Buryat girl on horseback, wearing a shirt and trousers of blue Chinese canvas; I asked her if she would sell me her pipe. While we talked she looked contemptuously at my European face and hat, and in a moment she was bored with talking to me; she shouted to her horse and galloped off. And in just the same way Lida despised me as a foreigner. She never outwardly expressed her disinclination, but I sensed it, and sitting on the lower step of the terrace, I felt irritated, and said that treating peasants when one was not a doctor was deceiving them, and that it was easy to be a philanthropist when one had six thousand acres.

Meanwhile her sister Misyus had no cares, and spent her life in complete idleness just as I did. When she got up in the morning she immediately took up a book and sat down to read on the terrace in a deep armchair, with her feet hardly touching the ground, or hid herself with her book in the lime-avenue, or walked out into the fields. She spent the whole day reading, poring greedily over her book, and only from the tired, dazed look in her eyes and the extreme pallor of her face could one divine how this continual reading exhausted her brain. When I arrived she would flush a little, leave her book, and looking into my face with her big eyes, would tell me eagerly of anything that had happened—for instance, that the chimney had been on fire in the servants' hall, or that one of the men had caught a huge fish in the pond. On ordinary days she usually wore a light blouse and a dark-blue skirt. We went for walks together, picked cherries for making jam, went out in the boat. When she jumped up to reach a cherry or worked at the oars, her thin, weak arms showed through her transparent sleeves. Or I painted a sketch, and she stood beside me watching rapturously.

One Sunday at the end of July I came to the Volchaninovs towards nine o'clock in the morning. I walked about the park, keeping a good distance from the house, looking for white mushrooms, of which there were a great number that summer, and noting their position so as to come and pick them afterwards with Zhenya. There was a warm breeze. I saw Zhenya and her mother, both in light holiday dresses, coming home from church, with Zhenya holding on to her hat in the wind. Afterwards I heard them having tea on the terrace.

For a carefree person like me, trying to find justification for my perpetual idleness, those holiday mornings in our country houses in summer have always had a particular charm. When the green garden, still wet with dew, is all sparkling in the sun and looks radiant with happiness, when there is a scent of mignonette and oleander near the house, when the young people have just come back from church and are drinking tea in the garden, all so charmingly dressed and cheerful, and one knows that all these healthy, well-fed, beautiful people are going to do nothing the whole day long, one wishes that all life were like that. Now, too, I had the same thought, and walked about the garden prepared to walk thus, aimless and unoccupied, the whole day, the whole summer.

Zhenya came out with a basket; she had a look on her face as though she knew she would find me in the garden, or had a presentiment of it. We gathered mushrooms and talked, and when she asked a question she walked a little ahead so as to see my face.

'A miracle happened in the village yesterday,' she said. 'The lame woman Pelageya has been ill for a year. No doctors or medicines helped; but yesterday an old woman came and whispered something over her, and her illness disappeared.'

'That's nothing much,' I said. 'You mustn't look for miracles only among sick people and old women. Isn't health a miracle? And life itself? Whatever is beyond understanding is a miracle.'

'But aren't you afraid of what is beyond understanding?'

'No. Phenomena I don't understand I face boldly, and am not overwhelmed by them. I am above them. Man ought to recognise himself as superior to lions, tigers, stars, superior to everything in nature, even what seems miraculous and is beyond his understanding, or else he is not a man, but a mouse afraid of everything.'

Zhenya believed that as an artist I knew a very great deal, and that I could guess correctly what I did not know. She longed for me to initiate her into the domain of the Eternal and the Beautiful—into that higher world in which, as she imagined, I was quite at home. And she talked to me of God, of eternal life, of the miraculous. And I, who could never admit that my self and my imagination would be lost for ever after death, answered: 'Yes, people are immortal'; 'Yes, eternal life awaits us.' And she listened, believed, and did not ask for proof.

As we were going home she stopped suddenly and said:

281

'Our Lida is a remarkable person—isn't she? I love her very dearly, and would give my life for her any minute. But tell me'—Zhenya touched my sleeve with her finger—'tell me, why do you always argue with her? Why are you irritated?'

'Because she is wrong.'

Zhenya shook her head and tears came into her eyes.

'How incomprehensible that is!' she said.

At that moment Lida had just returned from somewhere, and standing by the steps with a whip in her hand, a slim, beautiful figure in the sunlight, she was giving some orders to a workman. Talking loudly, she hurriedly received two or three sick villagers; then with a busy and anxious face she walked about the rooms, opening one cupboard after another, and went upstairs to the mezzanine. It was a long time before they could find her and call her to dinner, and she came in when we had finished our soup. All these tiny details I remember with tenderness, and that whole day I remember vividly, though nothing special happened. After dinner Zhenya lay in a deep armchair reading, while I sat upon the bottom step of the terrace. We were silent. The whole sky was overcast with clouds, and it began to spot with fine rain. It was hot; the wind had dropped, and it seemed as though the day would never end. Yekaterina Pavlovna came out on the terrace, looking drowsy and carrying a fan.

'Oh, Mother,' said Zhenya, kissing her hand, 'it's not good for you to sleep in the day.'

They adored each other. When one went into the garden, the other would stand on the terrace, and, looking towards the trees, call 'Aa—oo, Zhenya!' or 'Mother, where are you?' They always said their prayers together, and had the same faith; and they understood each other perfectly even when they did not speak. And their attitude to people was the same. Yekaterina Pavlovna, too, grew quickly used to me and fond of me, and when I did not come for two or three days, sent to ask if I were well. She, too, gazed at my sketches with enthusiasm, and with the same openness and readiness to chatter as Misyus, she told me what had happened, and confided to me her domestic secrets.

She went in awe of her elder daughter. Lida did not care for endearments, she talked only of serious matters; she lived her life apart, and to her mother and sister was as sacred and enigmatic a person as an admiral, always sitting in his cabin, is to his sailors.

'Our Lida is a remarkable person,' the mother would often say. 'Isn't she?'

Now, too, while it was drizzling with rain, we talked of Lida.

'She is a remarkable person,' said her mother, and added in an undertone, like a conspirator, looking about her timidly: 'You wouldn't easily find another like her; only, do you know, I am beginning to feel a little uneasy. The school, the dispensary, books—all that's very good, but why go to extremes? She is twenty-three, you know; it's time for her to think seriously of herself. With her books and her dispensary life will slip by, unnoticed . . . She must get married.'

Zhenya, pale from reading, with her hair disarranged, raised her head and said as if to herself, looking at her mother:

'Mother, everything is in God's hands.'

And again she buried herself in her book.

Belokurov came in his tunic and embroidered shirt. We played croquet and tennis, then when it was dark, sat a long time over supper, and Lida again talked about schools and about Balagin, who had the whole district under his thumb. As I went away from the Volchaninovs that evening, I carried away the impression of a long, long idle day, with a melancholy awareness that everything ends in this world, however long it may be.

Zhenya saw us out to the gate, and perhaps because she had been with me all day, from morning till night, I felt somewhat bored without her, and that all this charming family was near and dear to me, and for the first time that summer I had a yearning to paint.

'Tell me, why do you lead such a boring, colourless life?' I asked Belokurov as I went home. 'My life is boring, difficult, and monotonous because I am an artist, a strange person. From my earliest days I've been wrung by envy, self-dissatisfaction, doubts about my work. I'm always poor, I'm a wanderer, but you—you're a healthy, normal man, a landowner, and a gentleman. Why do you live in such an uninteresting way? Why do you get so little out of life? Why haven't you, for instance, fallen in love with Lida or Zhenya?'

'You forget that I love another woman,' answered Belokurov.

He was referring to his friend, Lyubov Ivanovna, who shared the lodge with him. Every day I saw this lady, very plump, rotund, and dignified, not unlike a fattened goose, walking about the garden, in the Russian national dress and beads, always carrying a parasol; and the servant was continually calling her in to dinner or to tea. Three years before she had taken one of the lodges for a summer holiday, and had settled down at Belokurov's, apparently for ever. She was ten years older than he was, and kept a firm grip on him, so much so that he had to ask her permission when he went out of the house. She often sobbed in a deep masculine voice, and then I used to send word to her that if she did not stop, I would move out; and she stopped.

When we got home Belokurov sat down on the sofa and frowned thoughtfully, and I began walking up and down the room, conscious of a soft emotion as though I were in love. I wanted to talk about the Volchaninovs.

'Lida could only fall in love with a member of the zemstvo, as devoted to schools and hospitals as she is,' I said. 'Oh, for the sake of a girl like that one might not only join the zemstvo, but even wear out iron shoes, like the girl in the fairy-tale. And Misyus? What a sweet creature she is, that Misyus!'

Belokurov, drawling out 'Er—er,' began a long-winded disquisition on the malady of the age—pessimism. He talked confidently, in a tone that suggested that I was opposing him. Hundreds of miles of desolate, monotonous, burnt-up steppe cannot induce such melancholia as one man when he sits and talks, and one does not know when he will go away.

'It's not a question of pessimism or optimism,' I said irritably; 'it's simply that ninety-nine per cent of people have no sense.'

Belokurov saw this as aimed at himself, took offence, and went away.

III

'The Prince is staying at Malozyomovo, and he asks to be remembered to you,' said Lida to her mother. She had just come in, and was taking off her gloves. 'He gave me a great deal of interesting news . . . He promised to raise the question of a medical relief centre at Malozyomovo again at the provincial assembly, but he says the chances are slight.' And turning to me, she said: 'Excuse me, I always forget that this cannot be interesting to you.'

I felt irritated.

'Why not interesting to me?' I asked, shrugging my shoulders. 'You do not care to know my opinion, but I assure you the question interests me keenly.'

'Indeed?'

'Yes. In my opinion a medical relief centre at Malozyomovo is quite unnecessary.'

My irritation infected her; she looked at me, screwing up her eyes, and asked:

284

'What is necessary? Landscapes?'

'Landscapes are not, either. Nothing is.'

She finished taking off her gloves, and opened the newspaper, which had just been brought from the post. A minute later she said quietly, evidently restraining herself:

'Last week Anna died in childbirth, and if there had been a medical relief centre near, she would have lived. And I think even landscape painters ought to have some convictions on that subject.'

'I have a very definite conviction on that subject, I assure you,' I answered; but she hid behind the newspaper, as though unwilling to listen to me. 'To my mind, all these schools, dispensaries, libraries, medical relief centres, under present conditions, only serve to aggravate the enslavement of the people. The peasants are fettered by a great chain, and you do not break this chain, but only add fresh links to it—there's my conviction for you.'

She raised her eyes to me and smiled ironically, while I went on trying to formulate my main idea.

'What matters is not that Anna died in childbirth, but that all these Annas, Mavras, Pelageyas, toil from early morning till dark, fall ill from working beyond their strength, all their lives tremble for their sick and hungry children, all their lives fear death and disease, all their lives receive treatment, they fade and age early, and die in filth and stench. Their children begin the same story over again as soon as they grow up, and so it goes on for hundreds of years and billions of men live worse than beasts—in continual terror, for a mere crust of bread. The whole horror of their position lies in their never having time to think of their souls, of their image and likeness. Cold, hunger, animal terror, the burden of toil, like avalanches of snow, block for them every way to spiritual activity—that is, to what distinguishes man from a beast and what is the only thing which makes life worth living. You go to their aid with hospitals and schools, but you don't free them from their fetters; on the contrary, you enslave them further, since, by introducing new prejudices, you increase the number of their needs, to say nothing of the fact that they've got to pay the zemstvo for plasters and books, and so toil harder than ever.'

'I am not going to argue with you,' said Lida, putting down the paper. 'I've heard all that before. I will only say one thing: one cannot sit with one's hands in one's lap. It's true that we are not saving humanity, and perhaps we make a great many mistakes; but we do what we can, and we are right. The highest and holiest task for a civilised being is to serve his neighbours, and we try to serve them as best we can. You don't like it, but one can't please everyone.'

'That's true, Lida,' said her mother—'that's true.'

In Lida's presence she was always a little timid, and looked at her nervously as she talked, afraid of saying something superfluous or out of place. And she never contradicted her, but always agreed: 'That's true, Lida—that's true.'

'Teaching the peasants to read and write, books with wretched precepts and rhymes, and medical relief centres, cannot diminish either ignorance or the death-rate, just as the light from your windows cannot light up this huge garden,' said I. 'You give nothing. By meddling in these people's lives you only create new needs in them, and new demands on their labour.'

'But, good heavens! One must do something!' said Lida with vexation, and from her tone one could see that she thought my arguments worthless and despised them.

'The people must be freed from hard physical labour,' said I. 'We must lighten their yoke, let them have time to breathe, that they may not spend all their lives at the stove, at the wash-tub, and in the fields, but may also have time to think of their souls, of God—to develop their spiritual capacities. The vocation of every man is spiritual activity—the perpetual search for truth and the meaning of life. Make coarse animal labour unnecessary for them, let them feel themselves free, and then you will see what a mockery these dispensaries and books really are. Once a man recognises his true vocation, he can only be satisfied by religion, science, and art, and not by these trifles.'

'Free them from labour?' laughed Lida. 'But is that possible?'

'Yes. Take upon yourself a share of their labour. If all of us, townspeople and country people, all without exception, would agree to divide between us the labour which mankind spends on the satisfaction of its physical needs, each of us would perhaps need to work only for two or three hours a day. Imagine that we all, rich and poor, work only for three hours a day, and the rest of our time is free. Imagine further that in order to depend even less upon our bodies and to labour less, we invent machines to replace our work, we try to cut down our needs to a minimum. We would train ourselves and our children so that they should not be afraid of hunger and cold, and then we wouldn't be continually trembling for their health like Anna, Mavra, and Pelageya. Imagine that we

286

don't seek treatment, don't keep dispensaries, tobacco factories, distil-
leries—how much free time we would all have! All of us together would
devote our leisure to science and to art. Just as the peasants sometimes
work as a community when mending the roads, so all of us together, as a
community, would search for truth and the meaning of life, and I am convinced that the truth would be discovered very quickly; man would
escape from this continual, agonising, oppressive dread of death, and
even from death itself.'

'You contradict yourself, though,' said Lida. 'You talk about science,
and are yourself opposed to elementary education.'

'Elementary education when a man has nothing to read but the signs
on public-houses and sometimes books which he cannot understand—
such education has existed among us since the times of Ryurik; Gogol's
Petrushka has been reading for ever so long, yet the village has remained
the same as in the days of Ryurik. What is needed is not elementary education, but freedom for a wide development of our spiritual capacities.
What is needed is not schools, but universities.'

'You are opposed to medicine, too.'

'Yes. It would be necessary only for the study of diseases as natural
phenomena, but not for curing them. If one must cure, it should not be
diseases, but their causes. Remove the principal cause—physical labour,
and then there will be no diseases. I don't believe in a science that cures
disease,' I went on excitedly. 'When science and art are real, they aspire
not to temporary, individual goals, but to the eternal and universal—they
seek for truth and the meaning of life, they seek for God, for the soul, but
when they are tied down to the needs and requirements of the day, to dispensaries and libraries, they only complicate and burden life. We have
plenty of doctors, chemists, lawyers, plenty of people can read and write,
but we are totally without biologists, mathematicians, philosophers,
poets. The whole of our intelligence, the whole of our spiritual energy, is
spent on satisfying temporary, passing needs. Scientists, writers, artists,
are hard at work; thanks to them, the conveniences of life are multiplied
from day to day. Our physical demands increase, yet truth is still a long
way off, and man still remains the most rapacious and dirty animal;
everything is tending to the degeneration of the majority of mankind, and
the loss for ever of all fitness for life. In such conditions an artist's work
has no meaning, and the more talented he is, the stranger and the more
unintelligible is his position, since when one looks into it, it is evident
that he is working for the amusement of a rapacious and unclean animal,

and is supporting the existing order. And I don't care to work and I won't work . . . Nothing is needed; let the earth sink to perdition!'

'Misyus, leave the room!' said Lida to her sister, apparently thinking my words harmful to such a young girl.

Zhenya looked mournfully at her mother and sister, and left the room.

'These are the charming things people say when they want to justify their indifference,' said Lida. 'It is easier to disapprove of schools and hospitals, than to teach or heal.'

'That's true, Lida—that's true,' her mother agreed.

'You threaten to give up working,' continued Lida. 'You evidently set a high value on your work. Let us stop arguing; we shall never see eye to eye, since I put the most imperfect dispensary or library of which you have just spoken so contemptuously on a higher level than any land-scape.' And turning at once to her mother, she began speaking in quite a different tone: 'The Prince is very much changed, and much thinner than when he was with us last. He is being sent to Vichy.'

She told her mother about the Prince in order to avoid talking to me. Her face glowed, and to hide her emotion she bent low over the table as though she were short-sighted, and made a show of reading the news-paper. My presence was disagreeable to her. I said goodbye and went home.

IV

It was quite still out of doors; the village on the further side of the pond was already asleep; there was not a light to be seen, and only the stars were faintly reflected in the pond. At the gate with the lions on it Zhenya was standing motionless, waiting to see me off.

'Everyone is asleep in the village,' I said to her, trying to make out her face in the darkness, and I saw her mournful dark eyes fixed upon me. 'The publican and the horse-stealers are sound asleep, while we, respectable people, argue and annoy each other.'

It was a melancholy August night—melancholy because there was already a feeling of autumn; the moon was rising behind a purple cloud, and it shed a faint light upon the road and on the dark fields of winter corn by the sides. From time to time a star fell. Zhenya walked beside me along the road, and tried not to look at the sky, that she might not see the falling stars, which for some reason frightened her.

'I believe you are right,' she said, shivering in the damp night air. 'If people, all together, could devote themselves to spiritual activity, they would soon know everything.'

'Of course. We are higher beings, and if we were really to recognise the whole force of human genius and lived only for higher aims, we should in the end become like gods. But that will never be—mankind will degenerate and no traces of genius remain.'

When the gates were out of sight, Zhenya stopped and hurriedly shook hands with me.

'Goodnight,' she said, shivering; she had nothing but her blouse over her shoulders and was huddling from the cold. 'Come tomorrow.'

I felt wretched at the thought of being left alone, annoyed and dissatisfied with myself and other people; and I, too, tried not to look at the falling stars.

'Stay another minute,' I said to her, 'I beg you.'

I loved Zhenya. I must have loved her because she met me when I came and saw me off when I went away; because she looked at me tenderly and with admiration. How touchingly fine were her pale face, slender neck, slender arms, her weakness, her idleness, her reading. And intelligence? I suspected that she had exceptional intelligence. I admired the breadth of her views, perhaps because they were different from those of the stern, beautiful Lida, who disliked me. Zhenya liked me because I was an artist. I had conquered her heart by my talent, and had a passionate desire to paint for her sake alone; and I dreamed of her as of my little queen who with me would possess those trees, those fields, the mists, the dawn, the exquisite and wondrous scenery in the midst of which I still felt hopelessly solitary and useless.

'Stay another minute,' I begged her. 'I beseech you.'

I took off my overcoat and put it over her frozen shoulders; afraid of looking ugly and absurd in a man's overcoat, she laughed, threw it off, and at that instant I put my arms round her and covered her face, shoulders, and hands with kisses.

'Till tomorrow,' she whispered, and softly, as though afraid of breaking the silence of the night, she embraced me. 'We have no secrets from one another. I must tell my mother and my sister at once . . . It's so dreadful! Mother is all right; Mother likes you—but Lida!'

She ran to the gates.

'Goodbye!' she called.

And then for two minutes I heard her running. I did not want to go home, and I had nothing to go for. I stood for a little time hesitating, and made my way slowly back, to look once more at the house in which she lived, the sweet, simple old house, which seemed to be watching me from the windows of its mezzanine, and understanding everything. I walked by the terrace, sat on the seat by the tennis-court, in the dark under the old elm-tree, and looked from there at the house. In the windows of the mezzanine where Misyus lived there appeared a bright light, which changed to a soft green—they had covered the lamp with the shade. Shadows began to move . . . I was full of tenderness, peace, and satisfaction with myself—satisfaction at having been able to be carried away by my feelings and fall in love, and at the same time I was uncomfortable at the thought that only a few steps away from me, in one of the rooms of that house there was Lida, who disliked and perhaps hated me. I went on sitting there wondering whether Zhenya would come out; I listened and fancied I heard voices talking in the mezzanine.

About an hour passed. The green light went out, and the shadows were no longer visible. The moon was standing high above the house, and lighting up the sleeping garden and the paths; the dahlias and the roses in front of the house could be seen distinctly, and seemed all the same colour. It began to grow very cold. I went out of the garden, picked up my coat on the road, and slowly wandered home.

When next day after dinner I came to the Volchaninovs, the glass door into the garden was wide open. I sat for a while on the terrace, expecting Zhenya every minute to appear from behind the flower-beds on the lawn, or from one of the avenues, or that I should hear her voice from the house. Then I walked into the drawing-room, the dining-room. There was not a soul to be seen. From the dining-room I walked down the long corridor to the hall, and back. In this corridor there were several doors, and through one of them I heard the voice of Lida:

' "God . . . sent . . . a crow," ' she said in a loud, emphatic voice, probably dictating—' "God sent a crow a piece of cheese . . . A crow . . . A piece of cheese . . ." Who's there?' she called suddenly, hearing my steps.

'It's I.'

'Ah! Excuse me, I cannot come out to you this minute; I'm giving Dasha her lesson.'

'Is Yekaterina Pavlovna in the garden?'

'No, she went away with my sister this morning to our aunt in the province of Penza. And in the winter they will probably go abroad,' she added after a pause. ' "Go-od sent . . . the cro-ow . . . a piece . . . of cheese . . ." Have you written it?'

I went into the hall, and stared vacantly at the pond and the village, and the sound reached me of 'A piece of cheese . . . God sent the crow a piece of cheese.'

And I left the place by the same way I had first arrived, but in reverse order—from the yard into the garden past the house, then down the avenue of lime-trees . . . At this point I was overtaken by a small boy who gave me a note: 'I told my sister everything and she insists on my parting from you,' I read. 'I could not grieve her by disobeying. God will give you happiness. Forgive me. If only you knew how bitterly my mother and I are crying!'

Then there was the dark fir-avenue, the broken-down fence . . . In the field where once the rye was in flower and the quails were calling, now there were cows and hobbled horses. On the slopes there were bright green patches of winter corn. A sober workaday mood came over me and I felt ashamed of all I had said at the Volchaninovs', and, as before, I felt bored by life. When I got home, I packed and set off that evening for Petersburg.

I never saw the Volchaninovs again. Not long ago, on my way to the Crimea, I met Belokurov in the train. As before, he was wearing a peasant tunic and an embroidered shirt, and when I asked how he was, he replied that, God be praised, he was well. We began talking. He had sold his old estate and bought another smaller one, in the name of Lyubov Ivanovna. He could tell me little about the Volchaninovs. Lida, he said, was still living in Shelkovka and teaching in the school; she had by degrees succeeded in gathering round her a circle of like-minded people who made a strong party, and at the last election had turned out Balagin, who till then held the whole district under his thumb. About Zhenya he could merely tell me that she did not live at home, and that he did not know where she was.

I am already beginning to forget the house with the mezzanine, and only sometimes when I am painting or reading I suddenly, apropos of nothing, remember the green light in the window, and the sound of my footsteps as I walked home through the fields at night, with my heart full of love, rubbing my hands in the cold. And still more rarely, at moments when I am sad and depressed by loneliness, I have dim memories, and little by little I begin to feel that I am remembered, too—that someone is waiting for me, and that we shall meet again . . .

Misyus, where are you?

Peasants

I

Nikolay Chikildeyev, a waiter in the Moscow hotel, the Slavyansky Bazaar, had fallen ill. His legs went numb and his gait was affected, so that on one occasion, as he was going along the corridor, he tumbled and fell down with a tray full of ham and peas. He had to leave his job. All his own savings and his wife's were spent on doctors and medicines; they had nothing left to live upon. He felt bored without work, and he decided he must go home to his village. It is better to be ill at home, and living there is cheaper; and it is a true saying that the walls of home are a help.

He reached his Zhukovo towards evening. In memories of childhood he had pictured his home as bright, snug, comfortable. Now, going into the hut, he felt frightened; it was so dark, crowded, and unclean. His wife Olga and his daughter Sasha, who had come with him, kept looking in bewilderment at the big untidy stove, which took up almost half the hut and was black with soot and flies. What a horde of flies! The stove leaned on one side, the beams lay slanting on the walls, and it looked as though the hut were about to fall to pieces. In the corner facing the door, next to the icons, bottle labels and newspaper cuttings were stuck on the walls instead of pictures. The poverty, such poverty! None of the grown-ups was at home; they were all out harvesting. On the stove sat a white-headed girl of about eight, unwashed and apathetic; she did not even glance at them as they came in. On the floor a white cat was rubbing herself against the oven fork.

'Puss, puss!' Sasha called to her. 'Puss!'

'She can't hear,' said the little girl; 'she has gone deaf.'

'Why?'

'Oh, she was beaten.'

Nikolay and Olga realised from the first glance what life was like here, but said nothing to one another; in silence they put down their bundles, and they went out into the street in silence. Their hut was the third from the end, and seemed the very poorest and oldest-looking; the second was no better; but the last one had an iron roof, and curtains in the windows. That hut stood apart, not enclosed; it was a tavern. The huts were in a single row, and the whole of the little village—quiet and dreamy, with willows, elders, and rowan trees peeping out from the yards—had an attractive look.

Beyond the peasants' homesteads there was a slope down to the river, so steep and precipitous that huge stones jutted out bare here and there through the clay. Along the slope, near these stones and holes dug by the potters, ran winding paths; bits of broken pottery, some brown, some red, lay piled up in heaps, and below there stretched a broad, level, bright green meadow, which had already been mowed, and in which the peasants' cattle were now wandering. The river, half a mile from the village, ran twisting and turning, with beautiful leafy banks; beyond it another broad meadow, a herd of cattle, long strings of white geese; then, as on this side, a steep ascent uphill, and on top of the hill a hamlet, and a church with five domes, and at a little distance the manor-house.

'It's lovely here in your parts!' said Olga, crossing herself at the sight of the church. 'What spaciousness, oh Lord!'

Just at that moment the bell began ringing for service (it was Saturday evening). Two little girls, down below, who were dragging a pail of water, looked round at the church to listen to the bell.

'At about this time they'll be serving dinner at the Slavyansky Bazaar,' said Nikolay dreamily.

Sitting on the edge of the slope, Nikolay and Olga watched the sun setting, watched the gold and crimson sky reflected in the river, in the church windows, and in the entire air—which was soft and still and unutterably pure as it never was in Moscow. And when the sun had set the flocks and herds passed, bleating and lowing; geese flew across from the far side of the river, and all sank into silence; the soft light died away in the air, and the dusk of evening swiftly closed in.

Meanwhile Nikolay's father and mother, two gaunt, bent, toothless old people, identical in height, came back. The women—the sisters-in-law Marya and Fyokla—who had been working on the landowner's estate beyond the river, arrived home, too. Marya, the wife of Nikolay's brother Kiryak, had six children, and Fyokla, the wife of Nikolay's brother Denis—who had been taken into the army—had two; and when Nikolay, going into the hut, saw all the family, all those bodies big and little moving about on the plank beds, in the hanging cradles and in all the corners, and when he saw the greed with which the old father and the women ate the black bread, dipping it in water, he realised he had made a mistake in coming here, sick, penniless, and with a family, too—a great mistake!

'And where is Kiryak?' he asked after they had exchanged greetings.

'He is in service at the merchant's,' answered his father; 'a keeper in the woods. He is not a bad peasant, but too fond of his glass.'

'He is no great help!' said the old woman tearfully. 'Our men are a wretched lot; they bring nothing into the house, but take plenty out. Kiryak drinks, and so does the old man; it is no use hiding a sin; he knows his way to the tavern. The Heavenly Mother is wroth.'

In honour of the visitors they brought out the samovar. The tea smelt of fish; the sugar was grey and had been nibbled at; cockroaches scurried over the bread and crockery. The tea tasted disgusting, and the conversation was disgusting, too—about nothing but poverty and illnesses. But before they had time to empty their first cups there came a loud, prolonged, drunken shout from the yard:

'Ma-arya!'

'It sounds like Kiryak coming,' said the old man. 'Talk of the devil.'

Everyone fell silent. And again, soon afterwards, the same shout, coarse and drawn-out as though it came out of the earth:

'Ma-arya!'

Marya, the elder sister-in-law, turned pale and huddled against the stove, and it was strange to see the look of terror on the face of this strong, broad-shouldered, ugly woman. Her daughter, the child who had been sitting on the stove and looked so apathetic, suddenly broke into loud weeping.

'What are you howling for, you plague?' Fyokla, a handsome woman, also strong and broad-shouldered, shouted to her. 'He won't kill you, you know!'

From his old father Nikolay had learned that Marya was afraid to live in the forest with Kiryak, and that when he was drunk he always came for her, made a row, and beat her mercilessly.

'Ma-arya!' the shout sounded just outside the door.

'Protect me, for the love of Christ, good people!' babbled Marya, breathing as though she had been plunged into very cold water. 'Protect me, kind people . . .'

All the children in the hut began crying, and looking at them, Sasha, too, began to cry. They heard a drunken cough, and a tall, black-bearded peasant wearing a winter cap came into the hut, and was the more terrible because his face could not be seen in the dim light of the little lamp. It was Kiryak. Going up to his wife, he swung his arm and punched her in the face with his fist. Stunned by the blow, she did not utter a sound but sat down, and her nose instantly began bleeding.

'What a disgrace! What a disgrace!' muttered the old man, clambering up on to the stove. 'Before visitors, too! It's a sin!'

The old mother sat silent, bowed, lost in thought; Fyokla rocked the cradle.

Evidently conscious of inspiring fear, and pleased at doing so, Kiryak seized Marya by the arm, dragged her towards the door, and bellowed like an animal in order to seem still more terrible; but at that moment he suddenly caught sight of the visitors and stopped.

'Oh, they've come . . .' he said, letting his wife go; 'my own brother and his family . . .'

Staggering and opening wide his red, drunken eyes, he prayed to the icon and went on:

'My brother and his family have come to the parental home . . . from Moscow, I suppose. The great capital Moscow, to be sure, the mother of cities . . . Excuse me.'

He sank down on the bench near the samovar and began drinking tea, sipping it loudly from the saucer in the midst of general silence . . . He drank a dozen cups, then reclined on the bench and began snoring.

They started getting ready for bed. Nikolay, as an invalid, was put on the stove with his old father; Sasha lay down on the floor, while Olga went with the other women into the barn.

'Aye, aye, dearie,' she said, lying down on the hay beside Marya; 'you won't mend your trouble with tears. Bear it in patience, that is all. It is written in the Scriptures: "Whosoever shall smite thee on the right cheek, offer him the left one also . . ." Aye, aye, dearie.'

Then in a low singsong murmur she told them about Moscow, about her own life, how she had been a chambermaid in furnished lodgings.

'And in Moscow the houses are big, built of brick,' she said; 'and there are ever so many churches, forty times forty, dearie; and they are all gentry in the houses, so handsome and so proper!'

Marya told her that she had never been to Moscow, nor even to their own district town; she could not read or write, and knew no prayers, not even the 'Our Father'. Both she and Fyokla, the other sister-in-law, who was sitting a little way off listening, were extremely ignorant and could understand nothing. They both disliked their husbands; Marya was afraid of Kiryak, and whenever he stayed with her she was shaking with fear, and always got a headache from the fumes of vodka and tobacco of which he reeked. And in answer to the question whether she did not miss her husband, Fyokla answered with vexation:

'Miss him! Huh!'

They talked a little and sank into silence.

It was cool, and a cock crowed at the top of his voice near the barn, preventing them from sleeping. When the bluish morning light was already peeping through all the crevices, Fyokla got up stealthily and went out, and then they heard the sound of her bare feet running off somewhere.

II

Olga went to church, and took Marya with her. As they went down the path towards the meadow both were in good spirits. Olga liked the spaciousness, and Marya felt that in her sister-in-law she had someone near and akin to her. The sun was rising. Low over the meadow floated a drowsy hawk. The river looked gloomy; there was a haze hovering over it here and there, but on the further bank a streak of light already stretched across the hill. The church was gleaming, and in the manor garden the rooks were cawing furiously.

'The old man is all right,' Marya told her, 'but Granny is strict; she is continually nagging. Our own grain lasted till Lent. We buy flour now at the tavern. She is angry about it; she says we eat too much.'

'Aye, aye, dearie! Bear it in patience, that is all. It is written: "Come unto Me, all ye that labour and are heavy laden." '

Olga spoke sedately, rhythmically, and she walked like a pilgrim woman, with a rapid, fussy step. Every day she read the gospel, read it aloud like a deacon; a great deal of it she did not understand, but the words of the gospel moved her to tears, and words like 'forasmuch as' and 'verily' she pronounced with a sweet flutter at her heart. She believed in God, in the Holy Mother, in the Saints; she believed one must not offend anyone in the world—not simple folks, nor Germans, nor gypsies, nor Jews—and woe even to those who have no compassion for the beasts. She believed this was written in the Holy Scriptures; and so, when she pronounced phrases from Holy Writ, even though she did not understand them, her face grew softer, compassionate, and radiant.

'What parts do you come from?' Marya asked her.

'I am from Vladimir. Only I was taken to Moscow long ago, when I was eight years old.'

They reached the river. On the far side a woman was standing at the water's edge, undressing.

'It's our Fyokla,' said Marya, recognising her. 'She has been over the river to the manor yard. To the stewards. She is a shameless hussy and foul-mouthed—dreadfully!'

Fyokla, young and vigorous as a girl, with her black eyebrows and her loose hair, jumped off the bank and began splashing the water with her feet, and waves ran in all directions from her.

'Shameless—dreadfully!' repeated Marya.

The river was crossed by a rickety little log bridge, and directly below it in the clear, limpid water was a shoal of broad-headed chub. The dew was glistening on the green bushes that looked into the water. There was a feeling of warmth; it was comforting! What a beautiful morning! And how beautiful life would be in this world, in all likelihood, if it were not for poverty, horrible, hopeless poverty, from which one can find no refuge! One had only to look round at the village to remember vividly all that had happened the day before, and the illusion of happiness which seemed to surround them vanished instantly.

They reached the church. Marya stood at the entrance, and did not dare to go further. She did not dare to sit down either. Though they only began ringing for Mass between eight and nine, she remained standing the whole time.

While the gospel was being read the crowd suddenly parted to make way for the family from the great house. Two young girls in white frocks and wide-brimmed hats walked in; with them a chubby, rosy boy in a sailor-suit. Their appearance touched Olga; she made up her mind from the first glance that they were refined, well-educated, handsome people. Marya looked at them from under her brows, sullenly, dejectedly, as though they were not human beings coming in, but monsters who might crush her if she did not step aside.

And every time the deacon boomed out something in his bass voice she fancied she heard the shout 'Ma-arya!'—and she shuddered.

III

The arrival of the visitors was already known in the village, and directly after Mass a number of people gathered together in the hut. The Leony-chevs and Matveichevs and the Ilyichovs came to enquire about their relations who were in service in Moscow. All the lads of Zhukovo who could read and write were packed off to Moscow and hired out as butlers or waiters (while from the village on the other side of the river the boys all became bakers), and that had been the custom since the days of serfdom long ago when a certain Luka Ivanych, a peasant from Zhukovo, now a legendary figure, who had been a waiter in one of the Moscow clubs, would take none but his fellow-villagers into his service, and the latter, upon establishing themselves, sent for their relatives and found jobs for them in taverns and restaurants; and from that time the village of Zhukovo was always called among the inhabitants of the surrounding districts Lackeytown. Nikolay had been taken to Moscow when he was eleven, and Ivan Makarych, one of the Matveichevs, at that time a head waiter in the 'Hermitage' garden, had found him a job. And now, addressing the Matveichevs, Nikolay said emphatically:

'Ivan Makarych was my benefactor, and I am bound to pray for him day and night, as it is owing to him that I became someone.'

'Goodness me!' a tall old woman, the sister of Ivan Makarych, said tearfully, 'and not a word have we heard about him, poor dear.'

'In the winter he was in service at Aumont's, and this season there was a rumour he was somewhere out of town, in the gardens . . . He has aged! In the old days he would bring home as much as ten roubles a day in the summer-time, but now things are very quiet everywhere. The old man's suffering.'

The women looked at Nikolay's feet, shod in felt boots, and at his pale face, and said mournfully:

'You're not making much, Nikolay Osipych; you're not making much! No, indeed!'

And they all fussed over Sasha. She was ten years old, but she was little and very thin, and might have been taken for no more than seven. Among the other little girls, with their sunburnt faces and roughly cropped hair, dressed in long faded smocks, she, so white, with her big dark eyes, with a red ribbon in her hair, looked funny, as though she were some little wild creature that had been caught and brought into the hut.

'She can read, too,' Olga boasted, looking tenderly at her daughter. 'Read a little, child!' she said, taking the gospel from her bundle. 'You read, and the good Christian people will listen.'

The gospel was an old and heavy one in a leather binding, with dog-eared edges, and it exuded a smell as though monks had come into the hut. Sasha raised her eyebrows and began in a loud rhythmic chant:

' "And the angel of the Lord . . . appeareth to Joseph in a dream, saying unto him: Arise, and take the Babe and His Mother." '

'The Babe and His Mother,' Olga repeated, and flushed all over with emotion.

' "And flee into Egypt . . . and tarry there until such time as . . ." '

At the word 'tarry' Olga could not refrain from tears. Looking at her, Marya began to whimper, and after her Ivan Makarych's sister. The old father cleared his throat, and bustled about to find a present for his granddaughter, but, finding nothing, gave up with a wave of his hand. And when the reading was over the neighbours dispersed to their homes, feeling touched and very much pleased with Olga and Sasha.

As it was a holiday, the family spent the whole day at home. The old woman, whom her husband, her daughters-in-law, and her grandchildren all alike called Granny, tried to do everything herself; she heated the stove and set the samovar with her own hands, even waited at the midday meal, and then complained that she was worn out with work. And all the time she was anxious lest anyone should eat a piece too much, or lest her husband and daughters-in-law should sit idle. At one moment she would hear the tavern-keeper's geese going round the back of the huts to her kitchen-garden, and she would run out of the hut with a long stick and spend half an hour screaming shrilly by her cabbages, which were as gaunt and scraggy as herself; on another occasion she fancied that a crow was after her chickens, and she rushed to attack it, shrieking abuse. She was cross and grumbling from morning till night. And often she raised such an outcry that passers-by stopped in the street.

She showed no affection towards her old man, reviling him as a lazy-bones and a plague. He was not a responsible, reliable peasant, and perhaps if she had not been continually nagging at him he would not have worked at all, but would have simply sat on the stove and talked. He talked to his son at great length about certain enemies of his, complained of the insults he said he had to put up with every day from the neighbours, and it was tedious to listen to him.

'Yes,' he would say, standing with his arms akimbo, 'yes . . . A week after the Exaltation of the Cross I sold my hay willingly at ninety kopecks a hundredweight . . . Well and good . . . So you see I was taking the hay in the morning with a good will; I was interfering with no one. As ill luck would have it, I see the village elder, Antip Sedelnikov, coming out of the tavern. "Where are you taking it, you ruffian?" says he, and bashes me on the ear.'

Kiryak had a fearful headache after his drinking bout, and was ashamed to face his brother.

'What vodka does! Ah, my God!' he muttered, shaking his aching head. 'For the love of Christ, forgive me, brother and sister; I'm really very sorry.'

As it was a holiday, they bought a herring at the tavern and made a soup of the herring's head. At midday they all sat down to drink tea, and went on drinking it for a long time, till they were bathed in sweat; they looked swollen from the tea-drinking, and only then began sipping the soup, all helping themselves out of one bowl. But Granny hid the herring.

In the evening a potter began firing pots by the ravine. In the meadow below the girls got up a choral dance and sang songs. They played the concertina. And on the other side of the river a kiln for baking pots was lit, too, and the girls sang songs, and from afar that singing sounded soft and musical. The peasants were noisy in and outside the tavern. They were singing with drunken voices, all out of tune, and swearing at one another, so that Olga could only shudder and say:

'Oh, Holy Saints!'

She was amazed that the abuse was incessant, and those who were loudest and most persistent in swearing were the old men with one foot in the grave. And the girls and children heard this abuse, and were not in the least embarrassed, and clearly they were used to it from the cradle.

It was past midnight, the kilns on both sides of the river had gone out, but in the meadow below and in the tavern the merrymaking continued. The old father and Kiryak, both drunk, walking arm-in-arm and jostling each other, went to the barn where Olga and Marya were lying.

'Let her alone,' the old man urged him; 'let her alone . . . She is a harmless woman . . . It's a sin . . .'

'Ma-arya!' shouted Kiryak.

'Let her be . . . It's a sin . . . She is not a bad woman.'

Both stopped by the barn for a minute and went on.

'I lo-ove the flowers of the fi-ield,' the old man began singing suddenly in a high, piercing tenor. 'I lo-ove to gather them in the meadows!'

Then he spat, and with a filthy oath went into the hut.

IV

Granny put Sasha by her kitchen-garden and told her to keep watch so that the geese didn't get in. It was a hot August day. The tavern-keeper's geese could make their way into the kitchen-garden by the backs of the huts, but now they were busily engaged picking up oats by the tavern, peacefully conversing, and only the gander craned his head high as though trying to see whether the old woman were coming with her stick. The other geese might come up from below, but they were now grazing far away on the other side of the river, stretched out in a long white garland across the meadow. Sasha stood about a little, became bored, and, seeing that the geese were not coming, went off to the ravine.

There she saw Marya's eldest daughter Motka, who was standing motionless on a huge stone, staring at the church. Marya had given birth to thirteen children, but only six survived, all girls, not one boy, and the eldest was eight. Motka in a long smock was standing barefoot in the full glare of the sun; the sun was blazing down on her head, but she did not notice, and seemed as if turned to stone. Sasha stood beside her and said, looking at the church:

'God lives in the church. Men have lamps and candles, but God has little green and red and blue lamps like little eyes. At night God walks about the church, and with Him the Holy Mother of God and Saint Nicholas, thud, thud, thud! . . . And the watchman is terrified, terrified! Aye, aye, dearie,' she added, imitating her mother. 'And when the end of the world comes all the churches will be carried up to heaven.'

'With the-ir be-ells?' Motka asked in her deep voice, drawling every syllable.

'With their bells. And when the end of the world comes, the good will go to paradise, but the angry will burn in fire eternal and unquenchable, dearie. To my mother as well as to Marya God will say: "You never offended anyone, and for that go to the right to paradise"; but to Kiryak and to Granny He will say: "You go to the left into the fire." And anyone who has eaten meat in Lent will go into the fire, too.'

She looked upwards at the sky, opening wide her eyes, and said:

'Look at the sky without blinking, and you will see the angels.'

Motka began looking at the sky, too, and a minute passed in silence.

'Do you see them?' asked Sasha.

'No,' said Motka in her deep voice.

'But I can. Little angels are flying about the sky and flap, flap their little wings, just like mosquitoes.'

Motka thought for a little, gazing at the ground, and asked:

'Will Granny burn?'

'She will, dearie.'

From the stone an even gentle slope ran down to the bottom, covered with soft green grass, which one longed to lie on or touch with one's hands . . . Sasha lay down and rolled to the bottom. Motka with a grave, severe face, puffing out her cheeks, lay down, too, and rolled to the bottom, and as she did so, her smock rode right up to her shoulders.

'What fun it is!' said Sasha, delighted.

They walked up to the top to roll down again, but at that moment they heard a shrill, familiar voice. Oh, how awful it was! Granny, a toothless, bony, hunchbacked figure, with short grey hair which was fluttering in the wind, was driving the geese out of the kitchen-garden with a long stick, shouting:

'They have trampled all the cabbages, the damned brutes! I'd cut your throats, thrice-accursed plagues! Blast you!'

She saw the little girls, flung down the stick and picked up a switch, and, seizing Sasha by the neck with her fingers, thin and hard as gnarled branches, began whipping her. Sasha cried with pain and terror, while the gander, waddling and craning his neck, went up to the old woman and hissed at her, and when he went back to his flock all the geese greeted him approvingly 'Ga-ga-ga!' Then Granny proceeded to whip Motka, and Motka's smock rode up again. In despair, crying loudly, Sasha went to the hut to complain. Motka followed her; she, too, was crying on a deeper note, without wiping her tears, and her face was as wet as if it had been dipped in water.

'Holy Saints!' cried Olga, aghast, as the two came into the hut. 'Queen of heaven!'

Sasha began her tale, just when Granny walked in with a storm of shrieks and abuse; then Fyokla flew into a rage, and there was uproar in the hut.

'Never mind, never mind!' Olga, pale and upset, tried to comfort them, stroking Sasha's head. 'She is your grandmother; it is a sin to be angry with her. Never mind, my child.'

Nikolay, who was worn out already by the everlasting din, hunger, stifling fumes, and stench, who hated and despised this poverty, and who felt ashamed that his wife and daughter should see his father and mother, swung his legs off the stove and said in an irritable, tearful voice, addressing his mother:

'You must not beat her! You have no right to beat her!'

'You lie rotting on the stove, you wretched creature!' Fyokla shouted at him spitefully. 'The devil inflicted you all on us, eating us out of house and home.'

Sasha and Motka and all the little girls in the hut huddled on the stove in the corner behind Nikolay's back, and listened in silent terror, and their little hearts could be heard beating. Whenever there is someone in a family who has long been hopelessly ill, there come painful moments when all his relatives timidly, secretly, deep down, long for his death; and only children fear the death of someone near them, and always feel horrified at the thought of it. And now the little girls, with bated breath, with a mournful look on their faces, gazed at Nikolay and thought that he was soon to die; and they wanted to cry and say something friendly and compassionate to him.

He pressed close to Olga, as though seeking protection, and said to her softly in a quavering voice:

'Olya darling, I can't stay here any longer. It's more than I can bear. For God's sake, for the love of Christ, write to your sister Klavdiya Abramovna. Let her sell and pawn everything she has; let her send us the money. We will go away from here. Oh, Lord,' he went on miserably, 'to have one more look at Moscow! If I could see it in my dreams, the dear place!'

And when the evening came on, and it grew dark in the hut, it was so dismal that it was hard to utter a word. Granny, ill-tempered, soaked some crusts of rye bread in a cup, and spent a long time, a whole hour, sucking at them. Marya, after milking the cow, brought in a pail of milk and set it on a bench; then Granny poured it from the pail into jugs just as slowly and deliberately, evidently pleased that it was now the Fast of the Assumption, so that no one would drink milk and it would be left untouched. And she only poured out a very little in a saucer for Fyokla's baby. When Marya and she carried the jugs down to the cellar Motka suddenly stirred, clambered down from the stove and, going to the bench where stood the wooden cup full of crusts, splashed into it some milk from the saucer.

Granny, coming back into the hut, sat down to her soaked crusts again, while Sasha and Motka, sitting on the stove, gazed at her, and they were glad that she had broken her fast and now would go to hell. They were comforted and lay down to sleep, and Sasha as she dozed off imagined the Day of Judgement: a huge stove was burning, like a potter's kiln, and the Evil One, with horns like a cow's, and black all over, was driving Granny into the fire with a long stick, just as Granny herself had lately driven the geese.

V

On the day of the Feast of the Assumption, between ten and eleven in the evening, the girls and lads who were merrymaking in the meadow suddenly raised a hue and cry, and ran in the direction of the village; and those who were sitting on the edge of the ravine could not at first make out what was the matter.

'Fire! Fire!' they heard desperate shouts from below. 'The village is on fire!'

Those who were sitting above looked round, and a terrible and extraordinary spectacle met their eyes. On the thatched roof of one of the end huts stood a column of flame, seven feet high, which curled and scattered sparks in all directions like a fountain. And all at once the whole roof burst into bright flame, and the crackling of fire was heard.

The light of the moon dimmed, and the whole village was now bathed in a red quivering glow: black shadows moved over the ground, there was a smell of burning, and those who ran up from below were all gasping and could not speak for trembling; they jostled against each other, fell down and, in the unaccustomed brightness, they could hardly see or recognise one another. It was terrifying. What seemed especially terrifying was that doves were flying over the fire in the smoke; and in the tavern, where they did not yet know of the fire, people were still singing and playing the concertina as if nothing had happened.

'Uncle Semyon's on fire,' shouted a loud, coarse voice.

Marya was rushing around outside her hut, weeping and wringing her hands, while her teeth chattered, though the fire was a long way off at the other end of the village. Nikolay came out in high felt boots, the children ran out in their little smocks. Near the village constable's hut an iron sheet was struck. Boom, boom, boom! . . . floated through the air, and this repeated, relentless sound sent a pang to the heart and turned one cold. The old women stood with the holy icons. Sheep, calves, cows were driven out of the backyards into the street; boxes, sheepskins, tubs were carried out. A black stallion, who was kept apart from the drove of horses because he kicked and injured them, on being set free ran once or twice up and down the village, neighing and pawing the ground; then suddenly stopped short near a cart and began kicking it with his hind legs.

They began ringing the bells too, in the church on the other side of the river.

Near the burning hut it was hot and so light that one could distinctly see every blade of grass. Semyon, a red-haired peasant with a long nose, wearing a jacket and a cap pulled down right over his ears, sat on one of the boxes which they had managed to drag out; his wife was lying on her face, moaning and distracted. A little old man of eighty, with a big beard, who looked like a gnome—not one of the villagers, though obviously connected in some way with the fire—walked about bareheaded, with a white bundle in his arms. The glare was reflected on his bald head. The village elder, Antip Sedelnikov, as swarthy and black-haired as a gypsy, went up to the hut with an axe, and hacked out the windows one after another—no one knew why—then began chopping up the front steps.

'Women, water!' he shouted. 'Bring the engine! Look sharp!'

The peasants, who had been carousing in the tavern just before, dragged the engine up. They were all drunk; they kept stumbling and falling down, and all had a helpless expression and tears in their eyes.

'Wenches, water!' shouted the elder, who was drunk, too. 'Look sharp, wenches!'

The women and wenches ran downhill to where there was a spring, and kept hauling pails and buckets of water up the hill, and, pouring it into the engine, ran off again. Olga and Marya and Sasha and Motka all hauled water. The women and the boys pumped the water; the pipe hissed, and the elder, directing it now at the door, now at the windows, held back the stream with his finger, which made it hiss more sharply still.

'Bravo, Antip!' voices shouted approvingly. 'That's the way!'

Antip went inside the hut into the fire and shouted from within:

'Pump! Bestir yourselves, good Christian folk, in such a terrible mischance!'

The peasants stood round in a crowd, doing nothing but stare at the fire. No one knew what to do, no one had the sense to do anything, though all about there were stacks of wheat, hay, barns, and piles of fag-gots. Kiryak and old Osip, his father, both tipsy, were standing there, too. And as though to justify his idleness, old Osip said, addressing the woman who lay on the ground:

'Why thrash about, old girl? The hut's insured—why worry?'

Semyon, addressing himself first to one person and then to another, kept describing how the fire had started.

'That old man, the one with the bundle, is a house-serf of General Zhukov's . . . He was cook at our general's, God rest his soul! He came over this evening: "Let me stay the night," says he . . . Well, we had a glass, to be sure . . . The wife got the samovar—she was going to give the old fellow tea, but, as ill luck would have it, she put the samovar in the porch. The sparks from the pipe must have blown straight up to the thatch; that's how it was. We were almost burnt ourselves. And the old fellow's cap has been burnt: what a shame!'

And the sheet of iron was struck tirelessly, and the bells kept ring-ing in the church the other side of the river. In the glow of the fire Olga, breathless, looking with horror at the red sheep and the pink doves flying in the smoke, kept running down the hill and up again. It seemed to her that this ringing went to her heart with a sharp stab, that the fire would never end, that Sasha was lost . . . And when the ceiling of the hut fell in with a crash, the thought that now the whole village would be burnt made her weak and faint, and she could not go on fetching water, but sat down by the ravine, placing the buckets near her; beside her and below, the peasant women sat wailing as though at a wake.

Then the stewards and workmen from the manorial estate the other side of the river arrived in two carts, bringing with them a fire-engine. A very young student in an unbuttoned white tunic rode up on horseback. There was a thud of axes. They put a ladder to the burning framework of the house, and five men ran up it at once. Ahead of them all was the stu-dent, who was red in the face and shouting in a harsh, hoarse voice, and in a tone as though extinguishing fires was his normal occupation. They pulled the house to pieces, a beam at a time; they dismantled the cattle-shed, the fences, and the nearest haystack.

'Don't let them break it all up!' cried stern voices in the crowd. 'Don't let them.'

Kiryak made his way to the hut with a resolute air, as though he meant to prevent the newcomers from breaking up the hut, but one of the workmen turned him back with a blow in his neck. There was the sound of laughter, the workman dealt him another blow, Kiryak fell down, and crawled back into the crowd on his hands and knees.

Two handsome girls in hats, probably the student's sisters, came from the other side of the river. They stood a little way off, looking at the fire. The beams that had been dragged apart were no longer burning, but were smoking vigorously; the student, who was working the hose, turned the water, first on the beams, then on the peasants, then on the women who were bringing the water.

'George!' the girls called to him reproachfully in anxiety, 'George!'

The fire was over. And only when they began to disperse did they notice that the day was breaking, that everyone was pale and rather dark in the face, as it always seems in the early morning when the last stars are going out. As they parted, the peasants laughed and made jokes about General Zhukov's cook and his cap which had been burnt; they were already willing to turn the fire into a joke, and even seemed sorry that it had ended so soon.

'How well you put out the fire, sir!' said Olga to the student. 'You ought to visit us in Moscow: there we have a fire every day.'

'Why, do you come from Moscow?' asked one of the young ladies.

'Yes, miss. My husband was a waiter at the Slavyansky Bazaar. And this is my daughter,' she said, indicating Sasha, who was cold and huddling up to her. 'She is a Moscow girl, too.'

The two young ladies said something in French to the student, and he gave Sasha a twenty-kopeck piece.

Old Osip saw this, and there was a gleam of hope in his face.

'We must thank God, Your Honour, there was no wind,' he said, addressing the student, 'or else we should have been all burnt up in a jiffy. Your Honour, kind gentlefolks,' he added in embarrassment in a lower tone, 'the morning's chilly . . . something to warm me up . . . half a bottle to Your Honour's health.'

Nothing was given him, and coughing and spitting he slouched home. Olga stood afterwards at the end of the street and watched the two carts crossing the river by the ford and the gentlefolk walking across the meadow; a carriage was waiting for them on the far side. Going into the hut, she told her husband with delight:

'Such good people! And so handsome! The young ladies were like cherubim.'

'Plague take them!' Fyokla, half-asleep, said spitefully.

307

VI

Marya considered herself unhappy, and said that she very much wanted to die; Fyokla, on the other hand, found all this life to her taste: the poverty, the uncleanliness, and the incessant abuse. She ate what was given her without discrimination; slept anywhere, on whatever came to hand. She would empty the slops right by the porch, would splash them out from the doorway, and then walk barefoot through the puddle. And from the very first day she hated Olga and Nikolay precisely because they disliked this life.

'We shall see what you'll find to eat here, you Moscow gentry!' she said malignantly. 'We shall see!'

One morning—it was at the beginning of September—Fyokla, vigorous, good-looking, and rosy from the cold, brought up two pails of water; Marya and Olga were sitting at the table drinking tea.

'Tea and sugar,' said Fyokla sarcastically. 'What fine ladies!' she added, setting down the pails. 'You have taken to the fashion of tea every day. You better look out that you don't burst with your tea-drinking,' she went on, looking with hatred at Olga. 'That's how you got your fat mug in Moscow, you lump of flesh!' She swung the yoke and hit Olga such a blow on the shoulder that the two sisters-in-law could only clasp their hands and say:

'Oh, Holy Saints!'

Then Fyokla went down to the river to wash the clothes, swearing all the time so loudly that she could be heard in the hut.

The day passed and was followed by the long autumn evening. They wound silk in the hut; everyone except Fyokla: she had gone over the river. They got the silk from a factory close by, and the whole family working together earned next to nothing, twenty kopecks a week.

'Things were better in the old days under the gentry,' said the old father as he wound silk. 'You worked and ate and slept, everything in its turn. At dinner you had cabbage soup and boiled grain, and at supper the same again. Cucumbers and cabbage in plenty: you could eat to your heart's content, as much as you wanted. And there was more strictness. Everyone knew his place.'

The hut was lit by a single little lamp, which burned dimly and smoked. When someone screened the lamp and a big shadow fell across the window, the bright moonlight could be seen. Old Osip, speaking slowly, told them how people used to live before the Emancipation of 1861; how in these very parts, where life was now so poor and dreary, they used to hunt with harriers, greyhounds, special trios of huntsmen, and when they went out as beaters the peasants were given vodka; how whole wagonloads of game used to be sent to Moscow for the young masters; how the bad were beaten with rods or sent away to the Tver estate, while the good were rewarded. And Granny also had a tale to tell. She remembered everything, absolutely everything. She talked about her mistress, a kind, God-fearing woman, whose husband was a profligate and a rake, and all of whose daughters made unlucky marriages: one married a drunkard, another a workman, a third eloped secretly (Granny herself, at that time a young girl, helped in the elopement), and all three, like their mother, died early from grief. And remembering all this, Granny even shed a few tears.

Suddenly someone knocked at the door, and they all started.

'Uncle Osip, give me a night's lodging.'

The little bald old man, General Zhukov's cook, the one whose cap had been burnt, walked in. He sat down and listened, then he, too, began telling stories of all sorts. Nikolay, sitting on the stove with his legs dangling, listened and asked questions about the dishes that were prepared in the old days for the gentry. They talked of rissoles, cutlets, various soups and sauces, and the cook, who also remembered everything very clearly, mentioned dishes that are no longer served. There was one, for instance—a dish made of bulls' eyes, which was called 'on waking up in the morning'.

'And used you to do cutlets *maréchal*?' asked Nikolay.

'No.'

Nikolay shook his head reproachfully and said:

'Tut, tut! Call yourself a cook!'

The little girls sitting and lying on the stove stared down without blinking; it seemed as though there were a great many of them, like cherubim in the clouds. They liked the stories: they sighed, shuddered and turned pale with alternate rapture and terror, and they listened breathlessly, afraid to stir, to Granny, whose stories were the most interesting of all.

They lay down to sleep in silence; and the old people, troubled and excited by their stories, thought how precious was youth, of which, no matter what it was really like, nothing remains in the memory but what was vivid, joyful, touching, and how dreadful and cold was death, which was not far off—better not think of that! The lamp went out. And the dusk, and the two little windows sharply illuminated in the moonlight, and the stillness and the creak of the cradle, reminded them for some reason that life was over, that nothing one could do would bring it back . . . You doze off, you forget yourself, and suddenly someone touches your shoulder or breathes on your cheek—and sleep is gone; your body feels numb, and thoughts of death keep invading your mind. You turn on the other side: death is forgotten, but old dreary, sickening thoughts of poverty, of food, of how dear flour is getting, stray through the mind, and a little later you remember again that life is over and you cannot bring it back . . .

'Oh Lord!' sighed the cook.

Someone gave a soft, soft tap at the window. It must be Fyokla come back. Olga got up and, yawning and whispering a prayer, opened the door, then drew the bolt in the porch, but no one came in; only from the street came a cold draught and a sudden brightness from the moonlight. The street, still and deserted, and the moon itself floating across the sky, could be seen through the open door.

'Who is there?' called Olga.

'Me,' she heard the answer—'it's me.'

Near the door, crouching against the wall, stood Fyokla, stark naked. She was shivering with cold, her teeth were chattering, and in the bright moonlight she looked very pale, strange, and beautiful. The shadows on her, and the bright moonlight on her skin, stood out vividly, and her dark eyebrows and firm, youthful bosom were defined with particular clarity.

'The ruffians over there undressed me and turned me out like this,' she said. 'I walked home without my clothes . . . naked as a baby. Bring me something to put on.'

'But go inside!' Olga said softly, beginning to shiver, too.

'I don't want the old folks to see.' Granny was, in fact, already stirring and muttering, and the old father asked: 'Who is there?' Olga brought her own smock and skirt, dressed Fyokla, and then both went softly into the hut, trying not to bang the doors.

'Is that you, you sleek one?' Granny grumbled angrily, guessing who it was. 'Fie upon you, night-walker! . . . Blast you!'

'It's all right, it's all right,' whispered Olga, wrapping Fyokla up; 'it's all right, dearie.'

All was stillness again. They always slept badly in the hut; everyone was kept awake by something worrying and persistent: the old man by the pain in his back, Granny by anxiety and anger, Marya by terror, the children by itching and hunger. Now, too, their sleep was troubled; they kept turning from side to side, talking in their sleep, getting up for a drink.

Fyokla suddenly broke into a loud, coarse howl, but immediately checked herself, and only uttered sobs from time to time, growing softer and on a lower note, until she lapsed into silence. From time to time from the other side of the river there floated the sound of the striking of the hours; but time seemed out of joint—five was struck and then three.

'Oh Lord!' sighed the cook.

Looking at the windows, it was difficult to tell whether it was still moonlight or already dawn. Marya got up and went out, and she could be heard milking the cow and saying, 'Stea-dy!' Granny went out, too. It was still dark in the hut, but all the objects were now visible.

Nikolay, who had not slept all night, got down from the stove. He took his dress-coat out of a green box, put it on, and going to the window, stroked the sleeves and took hold of the coat-tails—and smiled. Then he carefully took off the coat, put it away in his box, and lay down again.

Marya came back and began stoking the stove. She was evidently hardly awake, and was gradually waking up as she walked. Probably she had had some dream, or the stories of the night before came into her mind as, stretching luxuriously before the stove, she said:

'No, freedom is better.'

VII

The master arrived—that was what the villagers called the police inspector. When he would come and what he was coming for had been known for the past week. There were only forty households in Zhukovo, but more than two thousand roubles of arrears of rates and taxes had accumulated.

The police inspector stopped at the tavern. He drank there two glasses of tea, and then went on foot to the village elder's hut, near which a crowd of those in arrears stood waiting. The elder, Antip Sedelnikov, was, in spite of his youth—he was only a little over thirty—strict and always on the side of the authorities, though he himself was poor and did not pay his taxes regularly. Evidently he enjoyed being elder, and liked the sense of authority, which he could only display by strictness. In the village council the peasants were afraid of him and obeyed him. It would sometimes happen that he would pounce on a drunken man in the street or near the tavern, tie his hands behind him, and put him in the lock-up. On one occasion he even put Granny in the lock-up because she went to the village council instead of Osip, and began swearing, and he kept her there for a whole day and night. He had never lived in a town or read a book, but somewhere or other had picked up various learned expressions, and loved to deploy them in conversation, and he was respected for this, though he was not always understood.

When Osip came into the village elder's hut with his tax book, the police inspector, a lean old man with long, grey side-whiskers, in a grey double-breasted jacket, was sitting at a table in the icon corner, writing something. It was clean in the hut; all the walls were dotted with pictures cut out of the illustrated papers, and in the most conspicuous place near the icons there was a portrait of Battenberg, ex-prince of Bulgaria. By the table stood Antip Sedelnikov with his arms folded.

'There is one hundred and nineteen roubles standing against him,' he said when it came to Osip's turn. 'Before Easter he paid a rouble, and he has not paid a kopeck since.'

The police inspector raised his eyes to Osip and asked:

'Why is this, brother?'

'Show Divine mercy, Your Honour,' Osip began, growing agitated. 'Allow me to say, last year the gentleman at Lyutoretsk said to me, "Osip," he said, "sell your hay . . . you sell it," he said. Why? I had thirty hundredweight for sale; the women mowed it on the water-meadow. Well, we struck a bargain . . . All was fine, willingly . . .'

He complained of the elder, and kept turning round to the peasants as though inviting them to bear witness; his face flushed red and perspired, and his eyes grew sharp and angry.

'I don't know why you are saying all this,' said the police inspector. 'I am asking you . . . I am asking you why you don't pay your arrears. You don't pay, any of you, and am I to be held responsible for you?'

'I can't do it.'

'His words are of no consequence, Your Honour,' said the elder. 'The Chikildeyevs certainly are an impoverished lot, but if you just ask the others, the root of it all is vodka, and they're always making mischief. They have no sort of understanding.'

The police inspector wrote something down, and said to Osip quietly, in an even tone, as though he were asking him for water:

'Clear off.'

Soon he went away; and when he got into his cheap chaise and coughed, it could be seen from the very expression of his long thin back that he was no longer thinking of Osip or of the village elder, nor of the Zhukovo arrears, but was pondering on his own affairs. Before he had gone three-quarters of a mile Antip Sedelnikov was already confiscating the samovar from the Chikildeyevs' hut, followed by Granny, screaming shrilly and straining her chest:

'I won't let you have it, I won't let you have it, damn you!'

He walked rapidly with long steps, and she pursued him panting, almost falling over, a bent, ferocious figure; her kerchief slipped on to her shoulders, her grey hair with greenish lights on it was blown about in the wind. She suddenly stopped short, and like a real folk rebel, began to beat her breast with her fists and shout louder than ever in a singsong voice, as though she were sobbing:

'Good Christians and believers in God! Neighbours, they have ill-treated me! Kind friends, they have oppressed me! Oh, oh! dear people, take my part.'

'Granny, Granny!' said the village elder sternly, 'have some sense in your head!'

It was hopelessly dreary in the Chikildeyevs' hut without the samovar; there was something humiliating in this loss, something insulting, as though the honour of the hut had been violated. Better if the elder had carried off the table, all the benches, all the pots—it would not have seemed so empty. Granny screamed, Marya cried, and the little girls, looking at her, cried, too. The old father, feeling guilty, sat in the corner with bowed head and said nothing. And Nikolay, too, was silent. Granny loved him and was sorry for him, but now, forgetting her pity, she fell upon him with abuse, with reproaches, shaking her fists right in his face. She shouted that it was all his fault; why had he sent them so little when he boasted in his letters that he was getting fifty roubles a month at the Slavyansky Bazaar? Why had he come here, and with his family, too? If he died, who would provide the money for his funeral . . .? And it was pitiful to look at Nikolay, Olga, and Sasha.

The old father cleared his throat, took his cap, and went off to the village elder. It was already getting dark. Antip Sedelnikov was soldering something by the stove, puffing out his cheeks; there was a smell of burning. His children, emaciated and unwashed, no better than the Chikildeyevs, were scrambling about the floor; his wife, an ugly, freckled woman with a large stomach, was winding silk. They were a poor, unlucky family, and Antip was the only one who looked vigorous and handsome. On a bench there were five samovars standing in a row. The old man said his prayer to Battenberg and said:

'Antip, show Divine mercy. Give me back the samovar, for the love of Christ!'

'Bring three roubles, then you shall have it.'

'I can't do it!'

Antip puffed out his cheeks, the fire roared and hissed, and the glow was reflected in the samovars. The old man crumpled up his cap and said after a moment's thought:

'Give it back!'

The swarthy elder looked quite black, and was like a magician; he turned round to Osip and said sternly and rapidly:

'It all depends on the rural captain. On the twenty-sixth instant you can state the grounds for your dissatisfaction before the administrative session, verbally or in writing.'

Osip did not understand a word, but he was satisfied with that and went home.

Ten days later the police inspector came again, stayed an hour and went away. During those days the weather had turned cold and windy; the river had been frozen for some time past, but still there was no snow, and people found it difficult to get about. One holiday evening some of the neighbours came into Osip's to sit and have a talk. They did not light the lamp, as it would have been a sin to work, but talked in the darkness. There were some items of news, all rather unpleasant. In two or three households hens had been taken for the arrears, and had been sent to the district police station, and there they had died because no one had fed them; they had taken sheep, and while they were being driven away tied to one another, shifted into another cart at each village, one of them had died. And now they were discussing the question: who was to blame?

'The local district council, the zemstvo,' said Osip. 'Who else?'

'Of course it is the zemstvo.'

The zemstvo was blamed for everything—for the arrears, and for the oppressions, and for the failure of the crops, though not one of them knew what was meant by the zemstvo. And all this dated from the time when well-to-do peasants who had factories, shops, and inns of their own became members of the zemstvo, grew dissatisfied, and took to swearing at the zemstvo in their factories and taverns.

They talked of God's not sending any snow; they had to bring in wood for fuel, and there was no driving nor walking in the frozen ruts. In the old days fifteen to twenty years ago conversation was much more interesting in Zhukovo. In those days every old man looked as though he were treasuring some secret; as though he knew something and was expecting something. They used to talk about a certificate with a gold seal, about the division of lands, about new land, about treasures; they hinted at something. Now the people of Zhukovo had no secrets at all; their whole life was open in the sight of all, and they could talk of nothing but poverty, food, and the absence of snow . . .

There was a pause. Then they thought again of the hens, of the sheep, and began discussing whose fault it was.

'The zemstvo,' said Osip wearily. 'Who else?'

VIII

The parish church was four miles away at Kosogorovo, and the peasants only attended it when they had to, for baptisms, weddings, or funerals; they went for prayers to the church across the river. On holidays in fine weather the girls dressed up in their best and went in a crowd together to Mass, and it was a cheering sight to see them in their red, yellow, and green dresses crossing the meadow; in bad weather they all stayed at home. They took communion in the parish church. From each of those who did not manage in Lent to go to confession in readiness for the sacrament the parish priest, going the round of the huts with the cross at Easter, took fifteen kopecks.

The old father did not believe in God, for he hardly ever thought about Him; he recognised the supernatural, but considered it only affected women, and when religion or miracles were discussed before him, or a question were put to him, he would say reluctantly, scratching himself:

'Who can tell!'

Granny believed, but her faith was somewhat hazy; everything was mixed up in her memory, and she could scarcely begin to think of sins, of death, of the salvation of the soul, before poverty and her daily cares took possession of her mind, and she instantly forgot what she was thinking about. She did not remember the prayers, and usually in the evenings, before lying down to sleep, she would stand before the icons and whisper:

'Holy Mother of Kazan, Holy Mother of Smolensk, Holy Mother of Troyeruchitsa . . .'

Marya and Fyokla crossed themselves, fasted, and took the sacrament every year, but understood nothing. The children were not taught to pray, nothing was told them about God, and no moral principles were instilled into them; they were only forbidden to eat meat or milk in Lent. In the other families it was much the same: there were few who believed, few who understood. At the same time everyone loved the Holy Scripture, loved it with a tender, reverent love; but they had no Bible, there was no one to read it and explain it, and because Olga sometimes read them the gospel, they respected her, and they all addressed her and Sasha with particular politeness.

For church holidays and services Olga often went to neighbouring villages, and to the district town, in which there were two monasteries and twenty-seven churches. She was sunk in thought, and when she was on these pilgrimages she quite forgot her family, and only when she got home again suddenly made the joyful discovery that she had a husband and daughter, and then she would say, smiling and radiant:

'God has sent me such blessings!'

What went on in the village revolted and tormented her. On Elijah's Day they drank, at the Assumption they drank, at the Exaltation of the Cross they drank. The Feast of the Intercession was the parish holiday for Zhukovo, and the peasants used to drink then for three days; they squandered on drink fifty roubles belonging to the commune, and then collected more for vodka from all the households. On the first day of the feast the Chikildeyevs killed a sheep and ate of it in the morning, at dinner-time, and in the evening; they ate it ravenously, and the children got up at night to eat more. Kiryak was fearfully drunk for three whole days; he drank up everything, even his boots and cap, and beat Marya so terribly that they had to pour water over her. And then they all felt ashamed and sickened.

However, even in Zhukovo, in this Lackeytown, there was one occasion of genuine religious fervour. This was in August, when throughout the district they carried from village to village the Holy Mother, Giver of Life. It was still and overcast on the day when they expected Her at Zhukovo. The girls set off in the morning to meet the icon, in their bright holiday dresses, and brought Her towards evening, in procession with the cross and with singing, while the bells pealed in the church across the river. An immense crowd of villagers and strangers flooded the street; there was noise, dust, a great crush . . . And the old father and Granny and Kiryak—all stretched out their hands to the icon, looked eagerly at it and said, weeping:

'Our protector! Mother! Protector!'

All seemed suddenly to realise that there was not a void between earth and heaven, that the rich and the powerful had not taken possession of everything, that there was still a refuge from injury, from slavish bondage, from crushing, unendurable poverty, from the terrible vodka.

'Protector! Mother!' sobbed Marya. 'Mother!'

But the thanksgiving service ended and the icon was carried away, and everything went on as before; and again the sound of coarse drunken voices rose from the tavern.

Only the well-to-do peasants were afraid of death; the richer they were the less they believed in God and in the redemption of souls, and only through fear of their mortal end did they light candles and have services said for them, to be on the safe side. The peasants who were poorer did not fear death. The old father and Granny were told to their faces that they had lived too long, that it was time they were dead, and they did not mind. They bluntly told Fyokla in Nikolay's presence that when Nikolay died her husband Denis would get exemption—to return home from the army. And Marya, far from fearing death, regretted that it was so slow in coming, and was glad when her children died.

Death they did not fear, but of every disease they had an exaggerated terror. The merest trifle was enough—a stomach upset, a slight chill, and Granny would be wrapped up on the stove, and would begin moaning loudly and incessantly:

'I am dy-ing!'

The old father hurried off for the priest, and Granny received the sacrament and extreme unction. They often talked of colds, of worms, of tumours which move in the stomach and coil round to the heart. Above all, they were afraid of catching cold, and so put on thick clothes even in the summer and warmed themselves at the stove. Granny was fond of being doctored, and often went to the hospital, where she used to say she was not seventy, but fifty-eight; she supposed that if the doctor knew her real age he would not treat her, but would say it was time she died instead of receiving treatment. She usually left for the hospital early in the morning, taking with her two or three of the little girls, and came back in the evening, hungry and ill-tempered—with drops for herself and ointments for the little girls. Once she took Nikolay, who swallowed drops for a fortnight afterwards, and said he felt better.

Granny knew all the doctors and their assistants and the quacks for twenty miles around, and not one of them she liked. At the Intercession, when the priest went round the huts carrying the cross, the sexton told her that in the town near the prison lived an old man who had been a medical orderly in the army and was very good, and advised her to try him. Granny took his advice. When the first snow fell she drove to the town and fetched an old man with a big beard, a converted Jew, in a long gown, whose face was covered with blue veins. There were labourers at work in the hut at the time: an old tailor, in terrible spectacles, was cutting a waistcoat out of some rags, and two young men were making felt boots out of wool; Kiryak, who had been dismissed from his job for drunkenness, and now lived at home, was sitting beside the tailor and mending a bridle. And it was crowded, stifling, and foul-smelling in the hut. The converted Jew examined Nikolay and said that it was necessary to try cupping.

He put on the cups, and the old tailor, Kiryak, and the little girls stood and looked on, and it seemed to them that they saw the disease being drawn out of Nikolay; and Nikolay, too, watched how the cups suckling at his breast gradually filled with dark blood, and felt as though there really were something coming out of him, and smiled with pleasure.

'It's a fine thing,' said the tailor. 'Please God, it will do you good.'

The Jew put on twelve cups and then another twelve, drank some tea, and went away. Nikolay began shivering; his face grew thin, and, as the women expressed it, shrank into a fist; his fingers turned blue. He wrapped himself up in a quilt and in a sheepskin, but got colder and colder. Towards evening he became greatly distressed; asked to be laid on the ground, asked the tailor not to smoke; then he fell silent beneath the sheepskin and towards morning he died.

IX

Oh, what a grim, what a long winter!

Their own grain did not last beyond Christmas, and they had to buy flour. Kiryak, who lived at home now, was rowdy in the evenings, terrifying everyone, and in the mornings he was tormented by headaches and shame; and he was a pitiful sight. In the stall the starving cow bellowed day and night—a heart-rending sound to Granny and Marya. And as ill luck would have it, there were continuous sharp frosts, the snow drifted in high heaps, and the winter dragged on. At Annunciation there was a real winter blizzard, and snow fell in Holy Week.

But in spite of it all the winter did end. At the beginning of April there came warm days and frosty nights. Winter would not give way, but one warm day overpowered it at last, and the streams began to flow and the birds began to sing. The whole meadow and the bushes near the river were drowned in the spring floods, and all the space between Zhukovo and the far side was filled by a vast sheet of water, from which wild ducks rose up in numerous flocks. Every evening the spring sunset, flaming among gorgeous clouds, offered something new, extraordinary, amazing—a spectacle one later finds incredible, when one sees those same colours and those same clouds in a painting.

The cranes flew swiftly, swiftly, with mournful cries, as if inviting others to accompany them. Standing on the edge of the ravine, Olga gazed at the flooded meadow, at the sunshine, at the bright church, that seemed to have grown younger; and her tears flowed and her breath came in gasps from her passionate longing to go away somewhere, far away to the edge of the world. It was already settled that she should go back to Moscow to be a chambermaid, and that Kiryak should set off with her to get a job as a porter or something. Oh, to go away as soon as possible!

When it grew dry and warm they got ready to set off. Olga and Sasha, with satchels on their backs and shoes of plaited bark on their feet, came out before daybreak; Marya came out, too, to see them on their way. Kiryak was not well, and was kept at home for another week. For the last time Olga prayed looking at the church and thought of her husband, and though she did not shed tears, her face puckered up and seemed ugly like an old woman's. During the winter she had grown thinner and plainer, and her hair had turned a little grey, and instead of the old look of sweetness and the pleasant smile on her face, she had the resigned, mournful expression left by the sorrows she had been through, and there was something fixed and vacant in her eyes, as though she did not hear what was said. She was sorry to part from the village and the peasants. She remembered how they had carried out Nikolay, and how a requiem had been ordered for him at every hut, and all had shed tears in sympathy with her grief. In the course of the summer and winter there had been hours and days when it seemed as though these people lived worse than the beasts, and to live with them was terrible; they were coarse, dishonest, filthy, and drunken; they did not live in harmony, but quarrelled continually, because they distrusted and feared and did not respect one another. Who keeps the tavern and makes the people drunken? The peasant. Who wastes and spends on drink the funds of the commune, of the schools, of the church? The peasant. Who stole from his neighbours, set fire to their property, gave false witness at the court for a bottle of vodka? At meetings of the zemstvo and other local bodies, who was the first to rail against the peasants? The peasant. Yes, to live with them was terrible; and yet, they were human beings, they suffered and wept like human beings, and there was nothing in their lives for which one could not find excuse. Hard labour that made the whole body ache at night, the cruel winters, the scanty harvests, the overcrowding; and no help, nor any hope of help. Those who were richer and stronger than they were could be no help, as they themselves were coarse, dishonest, drunken, and abused one another just as revoltingly; the paltriest little clerk or official treated the peasants as though they were tramps, and addressed even the village elders and churchwardens as inferiors, and considered they had a right to do so. And, indeed, can any sort of help or good example be given by mercenary, greedy, depraved, and idle persons who only visit the village in order to insult, to cheat, and to terrorise? Olga remembered the pitiful, humiliated look of the old people when in the winter Kiryak had been taken to be flogged . . . And now she felt sorry for all these people, painfully so, and as she walked on she kept looking back at the huts.

After walking two miles with them Marya said goodbye, then kneeling, and falling forward with her face on the earth, she began wailing:

'Again I am left alone. Alas, for poor me! poor and unhappy! . . .'

And she wailed like this for a long time, and for a long time Olga and Sasha could still see her on her knees, bowing down to someone at the side and clutching her head in her hands, while the rooks flew above her.

The sun rose high; it became hot. Zhukovo was left far behind. Walking was pleasant. Olga and Sasha soon forgot both the village and Marya; they felt cheerful and everything entertained them. Now they came upon an ancient burial mound, now upon a row of telegraph posts running one after another into the distance and disappearing on the horizon, and the wires hummed mysteriously. Then they saw a homestead, all wreathed in green foliage; from it there came a scent of dampness, of hemp, and it seemed for some reason that happy people lived there. Then they came upon a horse's skeleton whitening in solitude in the open fields. And the larks trilled unceasingly, the quails called to one another, and the landrail cried as though someone were really scraping at an old iron rail.

At midday Olga and Sasha reached a big village. There in the broad street they met the little old man who was General Zhukov's cook. He was hot, and his red, perspiring bald head gleamed in the sunlight. Olga and he did not recognise each other, then looked round at the same moment, recognised each other, and went their separate ways without saying a word. Stopping near the hut which looked newest and most prosperous, Olga bowed down before the open windows, and said in a loud, thin, chanting voice:

'Good Christian folk, give alms, for the love of Christ, that God's blessing may be upon you, and that your parents may be in the kingdom of heaven in peace eternal.'

'Good Christian folk,' Sasha began chanting, 'give, for the love of Christ, that God's blessing, the kingdom of heaven . . .'

Ionych

I

When visitors to the provincial capital S—— complained of the dreariness and monotony of life, the inhabitants of the town, as though defending themselves, declared that it was very nice in S——, that there was a library, a theatre, a club, and dances; and, finally, that there were clever, agreeable, and interesting families with whom one could make acquaintance. And they used to point to the Turkin family as the most educated and talented.

This family lived in their own house in the principal street, near the Governor's. Ivan Petrovich Turkin himself—a stout, handsome, dark man with whiskers—used to arrange amateur performances for charity, and himself used to play elderly generals and cough very amusingly. He knew a number of anecdotes, charades, proverbs, and was fond of joking and making witticisms, and he always wore an expression from which it was impossible to tell whether he were joking or in earnest. His wife, Vera Iosifovna—a thin, nice-looking lady with a pince-nez—used to write novels and stories, and willingly read them aloud to her visitors. The daughter, Yekaterina Ivanovna, a young girl, used to play on the piano. In short, every member of the family had a special talent. The Turkins welcomed visitors, and good-humouredly displayed their talents with heartfelt simplicity. Their stone house was roomy and cool in summer; half of the windows looked into a shady old garden, where nightingales sang in the springtime. When there were visitors in the house, there was a clatter of knives in the kitchen and a smell of fried onions in the yard—and that was always a sure sign of a plentiful and tasty supper to follow.

And as soon as Dmitry Ionych Startsev was appointed as district doctor, and took up his abode at Dyalizh, six miles from S——, he, too, was told that as a cultivated man he must make the acquaintance of the Turkins. In the winter he was introduced to Ivan Petrovich in the street; they talked about the weather, about the theatre, about the cholera; an invitation followed. On a holiday in spring—it was Ascension Day—after seeing his patients, Startsev set off for town in search of a little recreation and to make some purchases. He walked in a leisurely way (he did not yet own any horses), humming all the time:

In town he dined, went for a walk in the gardens, then Ivan Petrovich's invitation came into his mind, as it were by itself, and he decided to call on the Turkins and see what sort of people they were.

'How do you do, please?' said Ivan Petrovich, meeting him on the steps. 'Delighted, delighted to see such an agreeable visitor. Come along; I will introduce you to my better half. I tell him, Verochka,' he went on, as he presented the doctor to his wife—'I tell him that he has no human right to stay at home in a hospital; he ought to devote his leisure to society. Oughtn't he, darling?'

'Sit here,' said Vera Iosifovna, making her visitor sit down beside her. 'You can dance attendance on me. My husband is jealous—he is an Othello; but we will try and behave so well that he will notice nothing.'

'Ah, you naughty chicken!' Ivan Petrovich muttered tenderly, and he kissed her on the forehead. 'You have come just in the nick of time,' he said, addressing the doctor again. 'My better half has written a ginormous novel, and she is going to read it aloud today.'

'Dear *Jean*,' said Vera Iosifovna to her husband, '*dites que l'on nous donne du thé.*'

Startsev was introduced to Yekaterina Ivanovna, a girl of eighteen, very much like her mother, thin and nice-looking. Her expression was still childish and her waist was soft and slim; and her virginal, well-developed bosom, healthy and beautiful, spoke of spring, real spring.

Then they drank tea with jam, honey, and sweetmeats, and with very tasty cakes, which melted in the mouth. As the evening came on, other visitors gradually arrived, and Ivan Petrovich fixed his laughing eyes on each of them and said:

'How do you do, please?'

Then they all sat down in the drawing-room with very serious faces, and Vera Iosifovna read her novel. She began like this: 'The frost was intensifying . . .' The windows were wide open; from the kitchen came the clatter of knives and the smell of fried onions . . . It was comfortable in the soft deep armchair; the lights had such a friendly twinkle in the twilight of the drawing-room, and at this moment on a summer evening when sounds of voices and laughter floated in from the street with the scent of lilac from the yard, it was difficult to grasp that the frost could be intensifying, and that the setting sun was lighting with its chilly rays a solitary wayfarer upon a snowy plain. Vera Iosifovna read how a beautiful young countess founded schools, hospitals, libraries, in her village, and fell in love with a wandering artist; she read of things that never happen in real life, and yet it was pleasant and cosy to listen to, and such agreeable, serene thoughts kept coming into one's mind,—one had no desire to get up.

'Not badsome . . .' Ivan Petrovich said softly.

And one of the visitors, listening with his thoughts far, far away, said hardly audibly:

'Yes . . . indeed . . .'

One hour passed, another. In the town gardens close by, a band was playing and a choir was singing. When Vera Iosifovna shut her manuscript book, the company was silent for five minutes, listening to a folk-song sung by the choir, and this song conveyed what was not in the novel but happens in real life.

'Do you publish your work in magazines?' Startsev asked Vera Iosifovna.

'No,' she answered. 'I never publish. I write and put it away in my cupboard. Why publish?' she explained. 'We have enough to live on.'

And for some reason everyone sighed.

'And now, Kitten, you play something,' Ivan Petrovich said to his daughter.

The lid of the piano was raised and the music lying ready was opened. Yekaterina Ivanovna sat down and banged on the keys with both hands, and then banged again with all her might, and then again and again; her shoulders and bosom shook. She obstinately banged on the same notes, and it sounded as if she would not stop until she had hammered the keys into the piano. The drawing-room was filled with the din; everything was resounding; the floor, the ceiling, the furniture . . . Yekaterina Ivanovna was playing a difficult passage, interesting simply on account of its difficulty, long and monotonous, and Startsev, listening, pictured stones dropping down a steep hill and going on dropping, and he wished they would stop dropping; and at the same time Yekaterina Ivanovna, pink from her exertions, strong and vigorous, with a lock of hair falling over her forehead, attracted him very much. After the winter spent at Dyalizh among patients and peasants, to sit in a drawing-room, to watch this young, elegant, and, probably, pure creature, and to listen to these noisy, tedious but still cultured sounds, was so pleasant, so new . . .

'Well, Kitten, you have played as never before,' said Ivan Petrovich, with tears in his eyes, when his daughter had finished and stood up. 'Die, Denis; you won't write anything better.'

All flocked round her, congratulated her, expressed astonishment, declared that it was ages since they had heard such music, and she listened in silence with a faint smile, and triumph was written all over her.

'Splendid, superb!'

'Splendid,' said Startsev, too, carried away by the general enthusiasm. 'Where have you studied?' he asked Yekaterina Ivanovna. 'At the Conservatoire?'

'No, I am only preparing for the Conservatoire, and till now have been working with Madame Zavlovskaya.'

'Did you go to the high school here?'

'Oh no,' Vera Iosifovna interposed. 'We have teachers for her at home; there might be bad influences at the high school or a boarding-school, you know. While a young girl is growing up, she ought to be under no influence but her mother's.'

'All the same, I'm going to the Conservatoire,' said Yekaterina Ivanovna.

'No. Kitten loves her mamma. Kitten won't grieve Papa and Mamma.'

'No, I am going, I am going,' said Yekaterina Ivanovna, with playful caprice, stamping her foot.

And at supper it was Ivan Petrovich who displayed his talents. Laughing only with his eyes, he told anecdotes, made witticisms, asked ridiculous riddles and answered them himself, talking the whole time in his extraordinary language, evolved in the course of prolonged practice in wit and evidently now ingrained as a habit: 'Not badsome', 'Ginormous', 'Thank you most dumbly', and so on.

But that was not all. When the guests, replete and satisfied, trooped into the hall, looking for their coats and sticks, there bustled about them the footman Pavlusha, or, as he was called in the family, Pava—a lad of fourteen with shaven head and chubby cheeks.

'Come, Pava, perform!' Ivan Petrovich said to him.

Pava struck an attitude, flung up his arm, and said in a tragic tone: 'Unhappy woman, die!'

And everyone roared with laughter.

'It's entertaining,' thought Startsev, as he went out into the street.

He called in at a restaurant and drank some beer, then set off to walk home to Dyalizh; he walked all the way singing:

'Thy voice to me so languid and caressing . . .'

On going to bed, he felt not the slightest fatigue after the six-mile walk. On the contrary, he felt as though he could with pleasure have walked another dozen miles.

'Not badsome,' he thought, and laughed as he fell asleep.

II

Startsev kept meaning to go to the Turkins' again, but there was a great deal of work in the hospital, and he was unable to find free time. In this way more than a year passed in toil and solitude. But one day a letter in a light-blue envelope was brought to him from town . . .

Vera Iosifovna had been suffering for some time from migraine, but now since Kitten frightened her every day by saying that she was going away to the Conservatoire, the attacks had become more frequent. All the doctors of the town had been at the Turkins'; now it was the district doctor's turn. Vera Iosifovna wrote him a touching letter in which she begged him to come and relieve her sufferings. Startsev went, and after that he began to come often, very often to the Turkins' . . . He really was of some help to Vera Iosifovna, and she was already telling all her visitors that he was a wonderful and extraordinary doctor. But it was not for the sake of her migraine that he visited the Turkins now . . .

It was a holiday. Yekaterina Ivanovna finished her long, wearisome exercises on the piano. Then they sat a long time in the dining-room, drinking tea, and Ivan Petrovich told some amusing story. Then the bell rang and he had to go into the hall to welcome a guest; Startsev took advantage of the momentary confusion, and whispered to Yekaterina Ivanovna in great agitation:

'For God's sake, I entreat you, don't torment me; let us go into the garden!'

She shrugged her shoulders, as though perplexed and not knowing what he wanted of her, but she got up and went.

'You play the piano for three or four hours,' he said, following her; 'then you sit with your mother, and there is no chance to speak to you. Give me a quarter of an hour at least, I beg you.'

Autumn was approaching, and it was quiet and melancholy in the old garden; brown leaves lay thick in the walks. It was already beginning to get dark early.

'I haven't seen you for a whole week,' Startsev continued, 'and if you only knew what suffering it is! Let us sit down. Listen to me.'

They had a favourite place in the garden: a bench beneath an old spreading maple. And now they sat down on this bench.

'What do you want?' asked Yekaterina Ivanovna drily, in a matter-of-fact tone.

'I haven't seen you for a whole week; I haven't heard you for so long. I yearn passionately, I thirst for your voice. Speak.'

She enchanted him by her freshness, the naïve expression of her eyes and cheeks. Even in the way her dress hung on her, he saw something extraordinarily charming, touching in its simplicity and naïve grace; and at the same time, in spite of this *naïveté*, she seemed to him very clever and developed beyond her years. He could talk with her about literature, about art, about anything; could complain to her of life, of people, though it sometimes happened in the middle of a serious conversation that she would laugh inappropriately or run away into the house. Like almost all the girls in S——, she had read a great deal (as a rule, people read very little in S——, and at the lending library they said if it were not for the girls and the young Jews, they might as well shut up the library). This afforded Startsev infinite delight; he used to ask her eagerly every time what she had been reading the past few days, and listened enthralled while she told him.

'What have you been reading this week since I saw you last?' he asked now. 'Do please tell me.'

'I have been reading Pisemsky.'

'What exactly?'

'His novel, *A Thousand Souls*,' answered Kitten. 'And what a funny name Pisemsky had—Aleksey Feofilaktych!'

'Where are you going?' cried Startsev in horror, as she suddenly got up and walked towards the house. 'I must talk to you; I want to explain myself . . . Stay with me just five minutes, I implore you!'

She stopped as though she wanted to say something, then awkwardly thrust a note into his hand, ran into the house and sat down to the piano again.

'Be in the cemetery,' Startsev read, 'at eleven o'clock tonight, near the tomb of Demetti.'

'Well, that's not at all clever,' he thought, coming to his senses. 'Why the cemetery? What for?'

It was clear: Kitten was playing a prank. Who would seriously dream of making an assignation at night in the cemetery far out of the town, when it might easily have been arranged in the street or the town gardens? And was it proper for him—a district doctor, a clever, staid man—to be sighing, receiving notes, to hang about cemeteries, to do silly things that even schoolboys think ridiculous nowadays? What would this romance lead to? What would his colleagues say when they found out? Such were Startsev's reflections as he wandered round the tables at the club, yet at half-past ten he suddenly set off for the cemetery.

By now he had his own pair of horses, and a coachman called Pante-leymon, in a velvet waistcoat. The moon was shining. It was still and warm, but warm as it is in autumn. Dogs were howling in the suburb near the slaughter-house. Startsev left his horses in one of the side-streets at the edge of the town, and walked on foot to the cemetery.

'We all have our oddities,' he thought. 'Kitten is odd, too; and—who knows?—perhaps she is not joking, perhaps she will come'; and he aban-doned himself to this faint, vain hope, and it intoxicated him.

He walked for a third of a mile through a field; the cemetery showed as a dark streak in the distance, like a forest or big garden. The wall of white stone came into sight, the gate . . . In the moonlight he could read on the gate: 'For the hour is coming, in the which . . .' Startsev went in at the wicket-gate, and before anything else he saw the white crosses and tombs on both sides of a broad avenue, and the black shadows from them and the poplars; and for a long way round it was all white and black, and the slumbering trees bowed their branches over the white stones. It seemed lighter here than in the field; the maple-leaves stood out sharply like paws on the yellow sand of the avenues and on the stones, and the inscriptions on the tombs could be clearly read. At first Startsev was struck by what he was now seeing for the first time in his life, and what he would probably never see again; a world unlike anything else, a world in which the moonlight was so soft and tender, as if here were its cradle, where there was no life, none whatever; but in every dark poplar, in every grave, one felt the presence of a mystery, promising a life which was gentle, beautiful, eternal. The stones and faded flowers, together with the autumn scent of the leaves, all told of forgiveness, melancholy, and peace.

All was silence around; the stars looked down from the sky with pro-found meekness, and Startsev's footsteps sounded loud and out of place, and only when the church clock began striking and he imagined himself dead, buried here for ever, he felt as though someone were looking at

him, and for a moment he thought that it was not peace and tranquillity, but stifled despair, the blank misery of non-existence . . .

Demetti's tomb was in the form of a shrine with an angel at the top. The Italian opera had once visited S—— and one of the singers had died; she was buried here, and this monument put up to her. No one in the town remembered her now, but the icon-lamp at the entrance reflected the moonlight, and seemed to be alight.

There was no one, and, indeed, who would come here at midnight? But Startsev waited, and as though the moonlight aroused his passion, he waited passionately, and, in his imagination, pictured kisses and embraces. He sat near the monument for half an hour, then paced up and down the side-avenues, with his hat in his hand, waiting and thinking how many women and girls were buried in these tombs who once had been beautiful and enchanting, who had loved, at night burned with passion, surrendering to caresses. How wickedly Mother Nature jests at man's expense, and how painful is this knowledge!

Such were Startsev's thoughts, and at the same time he wanted to cry out that he wanted love, that he was eager for it at all costs. To his eyes they were no longer slabs of marble, but beautiful white bodies in the moonlight; he saw shapes hiding bashfully in the shadows of the trees, felt their warmth, and his yearning was oppressive . . .

And as though a curtain were lowered, the moon went behind some clouds, and suddenly all was darkness. Startsev could scarcely find the gate—by now it was as dark as on an autumn night. Then he wandered about for an hour and a half, looking for the side-street in which he had left his horses.

'I am tired; I can scarcely stand,' he said to Panteleymon.

And settling blissfully in his carriage, he thought: 'Ah! I mustn't put on weight!'

III

The following evening he went to the Turkins' to propose. But the timing was not right, since Yekaterina Ivanovna was in her own room having her hair done by a hairdresser. She was getting ready to go to a dance at the club.

He had to sit for a long while again in the dining-room drinking tea. Ivan Petrovich, seeing that his visitor was bored and preoccupied, drew some notes out of his waistcoat pocket, and read a comic letter from a

329

German steward, saying that he was making a cattlelog of all the break-ages on the estate, and that there was a whole in one of the sealings.

'I expect they will give a decent dowry,' thought Startsev, listening absent-mindedly.

After a sleepless night, he was in a state of stupefaction, as though he had been given something sweet and soporific to drink; his mood was hazy, yet joyful and warm, and at the same time a cold, heavy part of his brain was reflecting:

'Stop before it's too late! Is she a match for you? She is spoilt, whimsi-cal, sleeps till two o'clock in the afternoon, while you are a sexton's son, a district doctor . . .'

'What of it?' he thought. 'I don't care.'

'Besides, if you marry her,' the part of his brain went on, 'then her relations will make you give up your district work and live in the town.'

'What of it?' he thought, 'if it must be the town, so be it. They will give a dowry; we'll set up house properly.'

At last Yekaterina Ivanovna came in, wearing a ball-dress, with a low neck, looking fresh and pretty; and Startsev admired her so much, and went into such rapture, that he could say nothing, but simply stared at her and laughed.

She began to say goodbye, and he—he had no reason for staying now—got up, saying that it was time for him to go home; his patients were waiting for him.

'Well, that can't be helped,' said Ivan Petrovich. 'Go, and you might take Kitten to the club on the way.'

It was spotting with rain; it was very dark, and they could only tell where the horses were by Panteleymon's husky cough. The hood of the carriage was put up.

'I have five buttons on my coat, but I can only fasten four; you have nine buttons on your coat, but you can only fascinate,' said Ivan Petro-vich as he put his daughter into the carriage. 'Off! Goodbye, please!'

They drove off.

'I went to the cemetery yesterday,' Startsev began. 'How ungenerous and merciless it was of you . . .'

'You went to the cemetery?'

'Yes, I went there and waited till almost two o'clock. I suffered . . .'

'Well, suffer, if you cannot understand a joke.'

Yekaterina Ivanovna, pleased at having played such a clever trick on a man who was in love with her, and at being the object of such intense love, burst out laughing and suddenly uttered a shriek of terror, for, at that very moment, the horses turned sharply in at the gate of the club, and the carriage tilted to one side. Startsev put his arm round Yekaterina Ivanovna's waist; in her fright she clung on to him, and he could not restrain himself, and passionately kissed her on the lips and on the chin, and embraced her more tightly.

'That's enough,' she said drily.

And a minute later she was not in the carriage, and a policeman near the lighted entrance of the club shouted in a repulsive voice to Panteleymon:

'What are you stopping for, you crow? Drive on.'

Startsev drove home, but soon afterwards returned. Attired in a borrowed dress-suit and a stiff white tie which kept chafing at his neck and trying to slip off his collar, he was sitting at midnight in the club drawing-room, and was saying animatedly to Yekaterina Ivanovna:

'Ah, how little those people know who have never loved! It seems to me that no one has ever described love truthfully, and I doubt whether this tender, joyful, agonising feeling can be described, and anyone who has once experienced it would not attempt to put it into words. What's the use of humming and hawing? What's the use of unnecessary fine words? My love is boundless . . . I beg, I beseech you,' Startsev brought out at last, 'be my wife!'

'Dmitry Ionych, said Yekaterina Ivanovna, with a very serious face, after a moment's thought—'Dmitry Ionych, I am very grateful to you for the honour. I respect you, but . . .' she got up and continued standing, 'but, forgive me, I cannot be your wife. Let us talk seriously. Dmitry Ionych, you know I love art more than anything in life. I adore music, I love it frantically; I have dedicated my whole life to it. I want to be an artist; I want fame, success, freedom, and you want me to go on living in this town, to go on living this empty, useless life, which has become unbearable to me. To become a wife—oh no, forgive me! One must strive towards a lofty, glorious goal, and married life would bind me for ever. Dmitry Ionych' (she smiled faintly as she pronounced his name; she thought of 'Aleksey Feofilaktych')—'Dmitry Ionych, you are a good, clever, honourable man; you are better than anyone . . .' Tears came into her eyes. 'I feel for you with my whole heart, but . . . but you will understand . . .'

And she turned away and left the drawing-room in order not to cry.

Startsev's heart stopped beating anxiously. Going out of the club into the street, he first of all tore off the stiff tie and drew a deep breath. He was a little ashamed and his vanity was wounded—he had not expected a refusal—and could not believe that all his dreams, his hopes and yearnings, had led him to such a stupid end, as in some little play at an amateur performance. And he was sorry for his feeling, for that love of his, so sorry that he felt like bursting into tears or belabouring with his umbrella Panteleymon's broad back.

For three days he could not concentrate on anything, he could not eat or sleep; but when the news reached him that Yekaterina Ivanovna had gone away to Moscow to enter the Conservatoire, he grew calmer and began to live as before.

Afterwards, remembering sometimes how he had wandered about the cemetery or how he had driven all over town in search of a dress-suit, he stretched lazily and said:

'What a lot of trouble, though!'

IV

Four years had passed. Startsev already had a large practice in the town. Every morning he hurriedly saw his patients at Dyalizh, then he drove in to see his town patients. By now he drove, not a pair, but a team of three with bells on them, and he returned home late at night. He had put on weight and was quite corpulent, and was not very fond of walking, as he suffered from breathlessness. Panteleymon also had put on weight, and the broader he grew, the more mournfully he sighed and complained of his bitter fate: driving had got him down!

Startsev used to visit various households and met many people, but did not draw close to anyone. The inhabitants irritated him by their conversation, their outlook on life, and even their appearance. Experience taught him by degrees that while he played cards or lunched with one of these people, the man was a peaceable, friendly, and even intelligent human being; but as soon as one talked of anything not edible, for instance, of politics or science, he would be completely at a loss, or would expound a philosophy so stupid and malicious that there was nothing else to do but wave one's hand in despair and go away. Even when Startsev tried to talk to liberal citizens, saying, for instance, that humanity, thank God, was progressing, and that one day it would be possible to dispense with passports and capital punishment, these citizens would look at him askance and suspiciously and ask: 'Then anyone can murder anybody he chooses in the street?' And when, in company, at tea or supper, Startsev observed that one should work, and that one ought not to live without working, everyone took this as a reproach, and began to get angry and argue aggressively. For all that, the inhabitants did nothing, absolutely nothing, and took no interest in anything, and it was quite impossible to think of what to talk to them about. So Startsev avoided conversation, and confined himself to eating and playing whist; and when there was a family celebration in some household and he was invited to a meal, then he sat and ate in silence, looking at his plate. And everything that was said at the time was uninteresting, unjust, and stupid; he felt irritated and disturbed, but held his tongue, and, because he sat glumly silent and looked at his plate, he was nicknamed in the town 'the haughty Pole', though he never had been a Pole.

All such diversions as the theatre and concerts he declined, but he played whist every evening for about three hours with enjoyment. He had one other diversion to which he took imperceptibly, little by little: in the evening he would extract from his pockets the banknotes he had gained by his practice, and sometimes there were stuffed in his pockets notes— yellow and green, and smelling of scent and vinegar and incense and fish oil—up to the value of seventy roubles; and when they amounted to several hundred he carted them to the Mutual Credit Bank and deposited them in his current account.

He was only twice at the Turkins' in the course of the four years after Yekaterina Ivanovna had gone away, on each occasion at the invitation of Vera Iosifovna, who was still undergoing treatment for migraine. Every summer Yekaterina Ivanovna came to stay with her parents, but he did not once see her; it somehow never happened.

But now four years had passed. One still, warm morning a letter was brought to the hospital. Vera Iosifovna wrote to Dmitry Ionych that she was missing him very much, and begged him to come and seen her, and to relieve her sufferings; and, by the way, it was her birthday today. Below was a postscript: 'I join in Mother's request.—K[itten].'

Startsev considered, and in the evening he went to the Turkins'.

'How do you do, please?' Ivan Petrovich met him, smiling with his eyes only. 'Bongjour.'

Vera Iosifovna, white-haired and looking much older, shook Startsev's hand, sighed affectedly, and said:

'You don't care to dance attendance on me, doctor. You never come and see us; I am too old for you. But now someone young has come; perhaps she will be more fortunate.'

And Kitten? She had grown thinner, paler, had become more handsome and more graceful; but now she was Yekaterina Ivanovna, not Kitten; she had lost her freshness and look of childish *naïveté*. And in her expression and manners there was something new—guilty and diffident, as though she did not feel at home here in the Turkins' house.

'It's so long since we met!' she said, giving Startsev her hand, and he could see that her heart was beating with excitement; and gazing at him intently and curiously, she went on: 'You've put on weight! You look sunburnt and more manly, but on the whole you have changed very little.'

Now, too, he found her attractive, very attractive, but there was something lacking in her, or else something superfluous—he could not himself have said exactly what it was, but something prevented him from feeling as before. He did not like her pallor, her new expression, her faint smile, her voice, and soon afterwards he disliked her clothes, too, the armchair in which she was sitting; he disliked something in the past when he had almost married her. He remembered his love, the dreams and hopes which had stirred him four years before—and he felt awkward.

They had tea with cakes. Then Vera Iosifovna read her novel aloud; she read of things that never happen in real life, and Startsev listened, looked at her handsome grey head, and waited for her to finish.

'It's not writing badly that makes one third-rate,' he thought, 'but writing badly and failing to conceal it.'

'Not badsome,' said Ivan Petrovich.

Then Yekaterina Ivanovna played long and noisily on the piano, and when she finished she was profusely thanked and warmly praised.

'It's a good thing I didn't marry her,' thought Startsev.

She looked at him, and evidently expected him to invite her into the garden, but he remained silent.

'Let's have a talk,' she said, going up to him. 'How are you getting on? What are you doing? How are things? I have been thinking about you all these days,' she went on nervously. 'I wanted to write to you, wanted to come to Dyalizh to see you. I made up my mind to go, but then I thought better of it. God knows how you regard me now; I have been looking forward to seeing you today with such emotion. For goodness' sake let's go into the garden.'

They went into the garden and sat down on the bench beneath the old maple, just as they had done four years before. It was dark.

'How are you getting on?' asked Yekaterina Ivanovna.

'Oh, all right; not too badly,' answered Startsev.

And he could think of nothing more. They were silent.

'I feel so stirred up!' said Yekaterina Ivanovna, and she hid her face in her hands. 'But take no notice. I am so happy to be at home; I am so glad to see everyone. I can't get used to it. So many memories! I thought we should talk without stopping till morning.'

Now he saw her face near, her shining eyes, and in the darkness she looked younger than in the room, and even her former childish expression seemed to have returned. And indeed she was looking at him with naïve curiosity, as though she wanted to get a closer view and understanding of the man who had loved her so ardently, with such tenderness, and so unhappily; her eyes thanked him for that love. And he remembered all that had been, every minute detail; how he had wandered about the cemetery, how he had returned home in the morning exhausted, and he suddenly felt sad and regretted the past. A small light began to gleam in his heart.

'Do you remember how I took you to the dance at the club?' he asked. 'It was dark and rainy then . . .'

The light was now glowing in his heart, and he longed to talk, to complain about life . . .

'Ah!' he said with a sigh. 'You ask how I am living. How do we live here? We don't. We put on weight, we grow old and slack. Day after day passes; life slips by without colour, without impressions, without thought . . . In the daytime working for gain, and in the evening the club, the company of card-players, alcoholics, raucous-voiced gentlemen whom I can't endure. What's good about that?'

'But you have your work—a noble aim in life. You used to be so fond of talking of your hospital. I was such a strange girl then; I imagined I was a great pianist. Nowadays all young ladies play the piano, and I played, too, like everybody else, and there was nothing special about me. I am just as much a pianist as my mother is a writer. And of course I didn't understand you then, but afterwards in Moscow I often thought of you. I thought of no one but you. What happiness to be a district doctor; to help the suffering; to serve the people! What happiness!' Yekaterina Ivanovna repeated with enthusiasm. 'When I thought of you in Moscow, you seemed to me so ideal, so lofty . . .'

335

Startsev remembered the banknotes he would extract with such pleasure from his pockets in the evening, and the light in his heart went out.

He got up to go into the house. She took his arm.

'You are the best man I've known in my life,' she continued. 'We will see each other and talk, won't we? Promise me. I am not a pianist; I have no illusions about myself now, and I will not play in your presence or talk of music.'

When they had gone into the house, and when Startsev saw in the lamplight her face, and her sad, grateful, searching eyes fixed upon him, he felt uneasy and thought again:

'It's a good thing I didn't marry her then.'

He began to take his leave.

'You have no human right to go before supper,' said Ivan Petrovich as he saw him off. 'It's extremely perpendicular on your part. Come, perform!' he added, addressing Pava in the hall.

Pava, no longer a boy, but a young man with moustaches, struck an attitude, flung up his arm, and spoke in a tragic voice:

'Unhappy woman, die!'

All this irritated Startsev. Getting into his carriage, and looking at the dark house and garden which had once been so precious and dear to him, he remembered everything at once—Vera Iosifovna's novels and Kitten's noisy playing, and Ivan Petrovich's jokes and Pava's tragic attitude, and thought that if the most talented people in the town were so third-rate, what must the town be like?

Three days later Pava brought a letter from Yekaterina Ivanovna.

'You don't come and see us—why?' she wrote to him. 'I am afraid that you have changed towards us. I am afraid, and I am terrified at the very thought of it. Reassure me; come and tell me that all is well. I must talk to you.—Your Y. T.'

He read this letter, thought a while, and said to Pava:

'Tell them, my good fellow, that I can't come today; I am very busy. Say I will come in three days or so.'

But three days passed, a week passed, and still he did not go. Happening once to drive past the Turkins' house, he remembered that he ought to call in, if only for a moment, but he thought a while . . . and drove on.

And he never went to the Turkins' again.

V

Several more years have passed. Startsev has put on even more weight, he has grown fat, breathes heavily, and already walks with his head thrown back. When, plump and red in the face, he drives with his bells and team of three horses, and Panteleymon, also plump and red in the face with his thick beefy neck, sits on the box, holding his arms stiffly out as if they were made of wood, and shouts to oncoming drivers: 'Keep to the ri-i-ight!'—it is an impressive sight; one might think it was not a mortal, but some heathen deity in his chariot. He has an immense practice in town, no time to breathe, and already has an estate and two houses in the town, and he is looking out for a third, more profitable one; and when at the Mutual Credit Bank he is told of a house that is up for auction, he goes to that house without ceremony, and, marching through all the rooms, regardless of half-dressed women and children who gaze at him in amazement and alarm, he prods at the doors with his stick, and says:

'Is that the study? Is that a bedroom? And what's here?'

And as he does so he breathes heavily and wipes the sweat from his brow.

He has a lot of trouble, but still he does not give up his work as district doctor; he is greedy for gain, and he tries to be in all places at once. At Dyalizh and in the town he is called simply 'Ionych': 'Where is Ionych off to?' or 'Shouldn't we call Ionych to a consultation?'

Probably because his throat is covered with rolls of fat, his voice has changed; it has become thin and sharp. His temper has changed, too: he has grown ill-humoured and irritable. When he sees his patients he is usually in a bad mood; he taps the floor brusquely with his stick, and shouts in his disagreeable voice:

'Kindly confine yourself to answering my questions! Don't talk so much!'

He is solitary. He leads a dreary life; nothing interests him.

During all the time he has lived at Dyalizh his love for Kitten was his only joy, and probably his last. In the evenings he plays whist at the club, and then sits alone at a big table and has supper. Ivan, the oldest and most respectable of the waiters, serves him, hands him Lafite No. 17, and everyone at the club—the members of the committee, the cook and waiters—knows what he likes and what he doesn't like; they do their very utmost to satisfy him, or else he might fly into a rage and bang the floor with his stick.

As he eats his supper, he turns round from time to time and interrupts some conversation:

'What are you on about? Eh? Who?'

And when at a neighbouring table there is talk of the Turkins, he asks:

'What Turkins do you mean? The ones whose daughter plays on the piano?'

That is all that can be said about him.

And the Turkins? Ivan Petrovich has grown no older; he is not changed in the least, and still makes jokes and tells anecdotes. Vera Iosifovna still reads her novels to her visitors willingly and with heartfelt simplicity. And Kitten plays the piano for about four hours every day. She has grown visibly older, is constantly ailing, and every autumn goes to the Crimea with her mother. When Ivan Petrovich sees them off at the station, he wipes his tears as the train starts, and shouts:

'Goodbye, please!'

And waves his handkerchief.

Encased

After returning late, the hunters had decided to bed down for the night in a barn belonging to village elder Prokofy on the very edge of Mironosit-skoye village. There were only two of them: Ivan Ivanych, a veterinary surgeon, and Burkin, a schoolmaster. Ivan Ivanych had a rather strange, double-barrelled surname, Chimsha-Himalaisky, which did not suit him at all, and everyone in the province knew him simply as Ivan Ivanych. He lived on a stud-farm close to the town and had come on this expedition to enjoy some fresh air, whereas Burkin, the schoolmaster, spent every summer as a guest of Count P.'s family and was very much at home in these parts.

They were not asleep. Ivan Ivanych, a tall thin old man with a big moustache, was sitting outside the barn smoking a pipe in the moonlight, while Burkin lay inside on the hay, invisible in the darkness.

They were telling various stories. The conversation turned to Mavra, the village elder's wife, a healthy woman of normal intelligence, who had never once been outside her own village, had never seen a town or rail-way, and for the past ten years had sat behind her stove and only ever gone out at night.

'Nothing so remarkable in that,' Burkin said. 'There are plenty of people in the world who are solitary by nature and try to retire into their shells, like hermit-crabs or snails. Maybe it's some kind of atavistic throwback to the time when our ancestors were not social animals but lived in their own solitary lairs, or maybe it's just one of the variants of human nature—who knows? I'm not a natural scientist and such questions aren't in my line. All I'm saying is that people like Mavra aren't uncommon. I can think of one straight away. Name of Belikov. He was the Greek master at our school and died in the town two months ago. You'll have heard of him, no doubt. The remarkable thing about him was that even in the hottest weather he would go out in galoshes and with an umbrella and always wearing a warm padded coat. He had a cover for his umbrella, a grey shammy-leather case for his pocket-watch, and when he took out his penknife to sharpen a pencil, even that had a little case of its own. His face, too, seemed encased, as he always hid it in his upturned collar. He wore dark glasses and a pullover, stuffed his ears with cotton-wool, and whenever he took a cab, gave orders for the hood to be raised.

In brief, the man displayed a persistent, insuperable urge to surround himself with a membrane, to make a kind of casing that would isolate and protect him from external influences. Reality irritated and scared him, kept him in a state of permanent anxiety, and perhaps it was to justify his timidity and revulsion from the present that he always praised the past and a world that had never existed. The ancient languages, which he taught, were essentially just like the galoshes and umbrella in which he took refuge from the real world.

' "Oh, how sonorous and beautiful the Greek language is!" he would say with a sugary expression; and as if to prove his point, he would half-close his eyes, raise his finger and say the word *anthropos*.

'His thoughts, too, Belikov endeavoured to encase. The only things clear to him were official regulations and newspaper articles in which something was forbidden. If there was an official regulation banning pupils from being out after nine at night, or some article appeared banning sexual intercourse, that was clear and definite: it's banned, the matter's settled. But in anything that was authorised or permitted he always detected a dubious element, something not fully spelled out and unclear. Whenever an amateur dramatic society or a reading-room or a tea-shop was authorised in the town, he would shake his head and say quietly:

' "Well, yes, it's a good idea, of course—but what if it leads to something?"

'Any infringement of the rules, any deviation or departure from them, would make him despondent, however little it might have to do with him. If a colleague was late for church service, or the boys were rumoured to have been up to some prank, or a member of staff from the girls' school was seen out late with an officer, he became very worried and kept saying that it might lead to something. At staff meetings he simply wore us down with his cautious, suspicious attitude, with those encased ideas of his about bad behaviour in the boys' and girls' schools, and the awful din in the classrooms—oh dear, suppose the authorities hear about this, suppose it leads to something—and wouldn't it be a good idea to expel Petrov from the second year and Yegorov from the fourth? And what happened? With his sighs and his whining, his dark glasses on that pale little face—it was a small kind of face like a ferret's—he put such pressure on us that we caved in, gave Petrov and Yegorov bad marks for conduct, put them in detention and eventually expelled them both. He had a strange habit of going round our lodgings. He'd call on a teacher, sit down and say nothing, and appear to be making an inspection. He'd sit like that in silence for an hour or two and go away. He called this "maintaining good relations with his colleagues", but it was obvious he found it a strain visiting us and sitting like that, and did so only because he considered it his duty as a colleague. We teachers were scared of him. Even the Headmaster was scared of him. Just imagine, our teachers are thoroughly decent, thinking people, brought up on Turgenev and Shchedrin, and yet this little man with his galoshes and umbrella held the whole school under his thumb for all of fifteen years! And not only the school, the whole town! Our ladies never arranged any home theatricals on a Saturday in case he found out, and the clergy took care not to eat meat on fast days or play cards when he was around. Because of Belikov and his like, during the past ten or fifteen years people in our town have become scared of everything. Scared of talking in a loud voice, of sending letters, making new acquaintances, reading books, afraid of helping the poor, of teaching people to read and write . . .'

Ivan Ivanych wanted to say something and cleared his throat, but first lit his pipe, glanced at the moon and only then said in measured tones:

'Yes. Decent, thinking people, they read their Shchedrin and Turgenev, their Henry Buckle and the rest of them, and yet they submitted, they put up with it . . . Yes, that's the way things are.'

'Belikov and I lived in the same house,' Burkin continued, 'on the same floor. Our doors were facing, so we often met, and I knew his domestic life. It was the same story there: dressing-gown and nightcap, shutters and bolts, a whole series of bans and restrictions of every kind, and worrying about what things might lead to. Fasting is bad for you, but you mustn't eat meat on fast days or people will say Belikov doesn't observe the fasts, so he ate perch fried in butter, which wasn't Lenten food, but wasn't exactly prohibited either. For fear of gossip he did not keep any female servants, only a cook, Afanasy, a drunken old half-wit of about sixty, who had once served as a batman and could knock up a meal of sorts. This Afanasy usually stood outside the door with his arms folded, forever mumbling the same words and sighing deeply:

' "Far too many of *them* around these days!"

'Belikov's bedroom was small and box-like, and his bed was a four-poster. When he lay down, he pulled the bedding over his head. It was hot and stuffy, the wind was knocking on the closed doors and droning in the stove. Sighs came from the kitchen, ominous sighs . . . He felt scared beneath his blanket. He was afraid something might happen, that

Afanasy might cut his throat or thieves break in, and all night long he had nightmares, so that in the morning, when we walked to school together, he was pale and lifeless, he was obviously terrified of the school he was going to with its masses of people, all this was deeply repellent to him, and even having to walk alongside me was a strain for a solitary nature like his.

' "What an awful din from the classrooms," he would say, as if trying to find an explanation for his depressed mood. "Indescribable."

'And believe it or not, this teacher of Greek, this man in a case, nearly got married.'

Ivan Ivanych glanced quickly into the barn and said:

'You're joking!'

'No, he nearly got married, strange as it may seem. A new master was appointed to teach history and geography, name of Kovalenko, Mikhail Savvich, a Ukrainian. When he arrived, he had his sister Varenka with him. He was a tall, swarthy young man with huge hands, his face alone told you he had a bass voice and so he had, boom-boom-boom, like something from a barrel . . . She wasn't young, about thirty, but tall and well built like him, with dark eyebrows and red cheeks. In brief, not a maiden but a ripe peach, full of noise and energy, singing Ukrainian songs all the time and laughing . . . The least thing and she'd go off into peals of loud laughter: ha-ha-ha! The first time, I remember, that we really got to know the Kovalenkos was at the Head's name-day party. Amid those grim, bottled-up old teachers, for whom parties were more like an official duty, suddenly we see a new Aphrodite rising from the foam: arms on hips, laughing, singing and dancing . . . She gave a heartfelt rendering of "Winds A-blowing", then another song, and a third, and bowled us all over, Belikov included. He sat down next to her and said with a sugary smile:

' "The delicacy and pleasing sonority of Ukrainian remind me of ancient Greek."

'She was flattered, and began telling him with great intensity of feeling about the farm she owned in the Gadyach district, it was where her dear mother lived, and you should just see the pears they have down there, and the melons, and the pumpkins! And did he know the Ukrainians have a word for "pumpkin" which is the same as the Russian word for "pub", and the borsch they make using tomatoes and egg-plants is "so tasty, so tasty, it's simply terrific!"

'We listened and listened and suddenly we all had the same thought.

' "Why don't we get them married?" the Head's wife said to me quietly.

'For some reason we all called to mind that our Belikov was a bachelor and were puzzled we'd never noticed this before, had somehow quite overlooked this important detail in his life. What was his attitude to women, how did he resolve this vital question? Previously it hadn't been of the slightest interest to us; maybe we couldn't even conceive that a man who wore galoshes in all weathers and slept in a four-poster could love anyone.

' "He's well over forty, she's thirty," the Head's wife elaborated. "I think she'd have him."

'What a lot of stupid, unnecessary things we get up to in the provinces out of sheer boredom! And all because we fail to do what *is* necessary. Why this sudden need to marry off Belikov when you couldn't even imagine him as a married man? The Head's wife, the inspector's wife and all the school ladies perked up and even looked prettier, as if they'd discovered a purpose in life. The Head's wife takes a box at the theatre, and whom do we see sitting there but Varenka, holding this fan if you please, beaming and happy, with the small, hunched-up Belikov beside her, looking as if he'd been prised from home with a pair of pincers. I throw a party and the ladies insist that I invite Belikov and Varenka. In brief, the wheels began to turn. Varenka, it emerged, was quite keen to get married. Living with her brother was no great fun, they did nothing but argue and swear at each other for days on end. Here's a typical scene. Kovalenko's walking down the street, healthy, tall and gangling, wearing an embroidered shirt, with a quiff of hair pushing out from under his cap. He's carrying a parcel of books in one hand and a thick knobbly stick in the other. His sister is walking behind him, also carrying books.

' "But you haven't read it, Mikhailik!" she's arguing loudly. "I tell you, I swear to you, you simply haven't read it!"

' "And I say I have!" Kovalenko shouts, banging his stick on the pavement.

' "Oh, for Heaven's sake, Minchik! Why get so worked up when we're talking about a matter of principle?"

' "And I tell you I have read it!" Kovalenko shouts even louder.

'At home, as soon as anyone turned up, they immediately began squabbling. She was probably tired of living like that and wanted a place of her own, and there was also her age to consider: she was in no position to pick and choose, but must take anyone going, even a teacher of Greek. For most of our young ladies getting married, after all, is what matters, and never mind to whom. Be that as it may, Varenka began to show our Belikov a marked partiality.

'And Belikov? He used to call on Kovalenko, as he did the rest of us. He'd arrive, sit down and say nothing. And while he sat there in silence, Varenka would sing him "Winds A-blowing", or gaze at him thoughtfully with her dark eyes, or suddenly burst out laughing:

' "Ha-ha-ha!"

'Where love is concerned and especially marriage, people are easily influenced. All his colleagues and all the ladies began to assure Belikov that he ought to marry, that he had no other alternative in life; we all congratulated him, and uttered various po-faced banalities about marriage being a serious step and so on; and Varenka *was* quite good-looking, an interesting person, the daughter of a state counsellor with her own farm, and most important of all, she was the first woman who had shown him genuine affection—his head was turned and he decided he really must marry.'

'That was the time to get his galoshes and umbrella off him,' said Ivan Ivanych.

'Couldn't be done, would you believe it? He put a portrait of Varenka on his desk, kept coming in to talk to me about Varenka and family life and marriage being a serious step, visited the Kovalenkos frequently, but didn't change his way of life in the slightest. On the contrary, his decision to marry seemed to affect his health, he became thin and pale and appeared to retreat even further into his shell.

' "I like Varvara Savvishna," he said to me, twisting his face into a weak little smile, "and I know everyone must marry, but . . . but all this, you know, has been rather sudden . . . I must think it over."

' "What's there to think over?" I reply. "Just get married."

' "No, marriage is a serious step, one must first weigh up one's future duties and responsibilities . . . in case it should lead to anything later. I'm so worried, I can't sleep at all now. To be honest, I'm apprehensive. She and her brother have such strange views, they look at things in such a strange kind of way somehow, they've got lively characters. Get married, and before you know what's happening, you'll be caught up in some incident."

'And he didn't propose but kept delaying, much to the annoyance of the Head's wife and all our ladies; kept weighing up his future duties and responsibilities, while at the same time he went out with Varenka almost every day, perhaps because he felt he had to in his position, and came in

to talk to me about family life. In all probability he would eventually have proposed, and one of those stupid, unnecessary marriages would have taken place that occur by the thousand because we're bored and have nothing better to do, had not the most *kolossalische Skandal* suddenly erupted. I should mention that Varenka's brother, Kovalenko, had hated Belikov from the first day of their acquaintance and couldn't stand him.

' "I don't know how you put up with that loathsome little sneak," he would say to us, shrugging his shoulders. "Gentlemen, gentlemen, how can you go on living in such a foul, stifling atmosphere? You're not educators or teachers, you're time-servers. This isn't a temple of learning, it's a police station, it smells as sour as a sentry-box. No, my friends, I'll spend a while longer with you, then I'm off to the farm to catch crayfish and teach the local boys. And you can stay on here with that Judas of yours, blast him."

'Or else he'd laugh, laugh until he cried, first in a deep bass, then in a squeaky little treble.

' "Why does he just sit there?" he would ask me, reverting to his native Ukrainian accent and gesturing helplessly. "What does he want? He just sits and stares."

'He even nicknamed Belikov "The Bloodsucker". Needless to say, we refrained from mentioning that his sister Varenka was intending to marry this same "Bloodsucker". And when the Head's wife said to him once what a good idea it would be to fix up his sister with such a reliable, universally respected man as Belikov, he scowled and muttered:

' "No concern of mine. Let her marry a viper if she wants to. I don't stick my nose into other people's business."

'Now on with the story. Some joker drew a caricature. It showed Belikov in galoshes with his trousers rolled up, carrying his umbrella and walking arm in arm with Varenka. Underneath was the caption "The Lovesick Anthropos". It had caught his expression to a T. The artist must have been hard at it for several nights, because we all received a copy—all the teachers at the boys' and girls' schools and the theological college, plus the town officials. Belikov received one, too. The caricature had a profoundly depressing effect on him.

'So, it's the first of May, a Sunday, and he and I are leaving the house together. Masters and boys have arranged to meet at the school and then all go walking to a small wood beyond the town. Belikov's face is green and gloomier than a thundercloud.

345

' "What bad, wicked people there are in the world!" he said, and his lips trembled.

'I even felt sorry for him. Then as we were walking along, who should suddenly appear but Kovalenko, riding a bicycle, and behind him, also on a bicycle, Varenka, red in the face and exhausted, but cheerful and happy.

' "We're going on ahead!" she shouts. "Isn't it a *wonderful* day? Simply terrific!"

'And they disappeared from view. My Belikov's face turns from green to white. He stops dead in his tracks, looks at me and asks:

' "What *is* going on? Or do my eyes deceive me? Can bicycling be regarded as a proper activity for schoolmasters and for women?"

' "What's improper about it?" I said. "Let them ride as much as they like."

' "But how can you say that?" he shouted, astonished by my calmness. "What on earth do you mean?"

'And he was so overcome that he refused to go on and returned home.

'Next day he was rubbing his hands nervously all the time and shaking, and looked obviously unwell. For the first time in his life he cancelled his classes and went home. He did not have a meal, but towards evening wrapped himself up well, even though it was a perfect summer's day, and took himself off to the Kovalenkos. He found only the brother at home, Varenka was out.

' "Please take a seat," Kovalenko said coldly and frowned. He looked half-asleep, having only just finished resting after his meal, and was in a very bad temper.

'Belikov sat there in silence for about ten minutes and then began:

' "I have come here to relieve my mind of a very, very heavy burden. Some lampoonist has made a comic representation of myself and another individual, who is close to both of us. It is my duty to assure you that I am in no way to blame. I never gave the least grounds for such ridicule. On the contrary, I behaved throughout with perfect propriety."

'Kovalenko sat there fuming and said nothing. Belikov waited a while, then went on quietly in a sorrowful voice:

' "There is something else I have to say to you. I have been teaching a long time, whereas you are only just starting in the profession, and it is my duty as a senior colleague to give you a warning. You go bicycling, and such an amusement is most improper in one who bears responsibility for educating the young."

' "Why so?" Kovalenko said in a deep voice.

346

' "Do I really need to go into explanations, Mikhail Savvich, isn't it obvious? If a teacher goes bicycling, then what can be expected from the pupils? Next thing we know, they'll be walking on their heads! And if it's not been officially sanctioned, it's not allowed. I was appalled yesterday! When I caught sight of your sister, I nearly fainted. A woman or a girl on a bicycle is quite shocking."

' "What exactly is it you want?"

' "One thing only, Mikhail Savvich, to warn you. You are a young man with your future ahead of you, you must behave with very, very great caution, but you—you don't bother, oh dear me no, you don't bother at all! You wear an embroidered shirt, you're always carrying books around in the street, and now on top of everything there's this bicycle. The Headmaster will find out that you and your sister ride bicycles, then it'll reach the school governor . . . That won't be so pleasant."

' "The fact that my sister and I ride bicycles is no one's concern but ours!" Kovalenko said, turning crimson. "If anyone starts interfering in my domestic and family life, I'll see him in hell."

'Belikov turned pale and stood up.

' "If you adopt that tone with me, I cannot continue," he said. "I must ask you never to express yourself like that in my presence about our superiors. You must show proper respect for the authorities."

' "When did I say anything critical of the authorities?" Kovalenko asked, glaring at him. "Please leave me in peace. I'm an honest man and have no wish to talk to a gentleman of your sort. I don't like informers."

'Belikov fussed about nervously and began hastily putting on his coat, an expression of horror on his face. No one had ever used such strong language to him before.

' "You may say what you wish, but I must warn you of one thing," he said, going out on to the landing from the hall. "Someone may have been listening to us, and in case they misinterpret our conversation and it might lead to something, I shall have to report its substance to the Headmaster . . . in general terms. It is my bounden duty."

' "Go on then, report away!"

'Seizing him from behind by the collar, Kovalenko gave him a push and Belikov tumbled downstairs, his galoshes thumping. It was a long steep staircase, but he reached the bottom safely, stood up and felt his nose to see if his glasses were broken. But at the very moment when he was tumbling down, Varenka came in with two ladies. They were standing at the bottom watching. For Belikov this was the worst thing that

347

could have happened. Better to break his neck or both legs than become a laughing-stock: now the whole town's going to find out, it'll reach the Headmaster and the Governor—oh dear, what will that lead to—they'll draw a new caricature, and it'll end up with him being forced to resign . . .

'When he had got to his feet, Varenka saw who it was and looking at his comic face, his rumpled coat and his galoshes, and not realising what had happened but assuming he had fallen downstairs by accident, she could not contain herself. Her laughter echoed all over the house:

' "Ha–ha–ha!"

'And that peal of loud laughter brought everything to an end: the courtship and Belikov's earthly existence. He did not hear what Varenka was saying to him, he did not see anything. Returning home, he first removed her portrait from the desk, then lay down and was never to rise again.

'Three days later Afanasy came in to ask me if he should send for the doctor, as something was wrong with the master. I went in to Belikov. He was lying in the four-poster, covered with a blanket, and not speaking; in answer to my questions he said yes or no—and nothing more. Meanwhile Afanasy was prowling round, gloomy, scowling, sighing deeply and stinking to high heaven of vodka.

'A month later Belikov died. We all attended his funeral: both schools, that is, and the theological college. Now that he was lying in his coffin, his expression was mild, pleasant, and even cheerful, as if he were glad to have been put at last in a case from which he would never emerge. Yes, he had attained his ideal! As if in his honour, the weather during the funeral was dull and rainy, and we were all wearing galoshes and carrying umbrellas. Varenka was at the funeral, too, and when the coffin was lowered into the grave, she burst into tears. I've noticed that Ukrainian women either laugh or cry, they don't have a mood in between.

'Burying people like Belikov is a great pleasure, I have to admit. On the way back from the cemetery, our faces wore expressions of modest sobriety; no one wanted to reveal this feeling of pleasure, the kind of pleasure we had experienced long long ago as children, when the grown-ups went out and we ran round the garden for an hour or two enjoying absolute freedom. Freedom, freedom! Even a hint, even a faint hope of its possibility, makes the spirit soar, doesn't it?

'We got back from the cemetery in an excellent mood. But not a week had gone by before life was as grim, tiring and fatuous as ever, a life that

348

was not banned officially, but was not fully authorised either; there was no improvement. We might have buried one Belikov, but how many other encased men had been left behind, and how many more are still to come!'

'Yes, that's the way things are,' said Ivan Ivanych and lit his pipe.

'How many more are still to come!' Burkin repeated.

The schoolmaster came out of the barn. He was a short fat man, completely bald, with a black beard almost down to his waist. Two dogs came out with him.

'That's quite a moon!' he said, looking upwards.

It was already midnight. To the right the whole village was visible, the long road stretching three miles into the distance. A deep quiet sleep pervaded everything; there was no sound or movement; how could everything in nature be so quiet? The sight of a wide village road in the moonlight with its huts, its hayricks and its sleeping willows has a quieting effect on the soul; that sense of repose, of being sheltered by the darkness of night from toil, worry and grief, give it a sad gentle beauty, the stars seem to look down on it with tender kindness, evil is no more and all's well with the world. Beyond the edge of the village to the left, open fields began, stretching far away to the horizon, and there, too, no sound or movement came from the whole of that wide moonlit expanse.

'Yes, that's the way things are,' Ivan Ivanych repeated. 'And what of our own lives, crowded together in towns without fresh air, compiling useless reports and playing cards—isn't that a kind of case? Spending all our time among idlers and pettifoggers, and stupid empty-headed women, talking and hearing all kinds of rubbish—isn't that a kind of case? If you like, I'll tell you a very instructive story.'

'No, it's time to go to sleep,' Burkin said. 'Tell me tomorrow.'

They both went into the barn and lay down on the hay. Both had covered themselves and dozed off when suddenly they caught the tip-tap of light footsteps . . . Someone was walking near the barn, taking a few steps, stopping, then a minute later, tip-tap . . . The dogs began growling.

'That's Mavra,' Burkin said.

The footsteps died away.

'To see and hear people lying,' Ivan Ivanych said, turning over, 'and to be called a fool because you put up with such lies; to bear insults and humiliations, not to dare to proclaim that you are on the side of free, honest people, but to lie and smile yourself, and all for the sake of a crust of bread, a roof over your head, some worthless rank—no, it's impossible to go on living like that!'

349

'Now you're on to a different theme, Ivan Ivanych,' the schoolmaster said. 'Let's get some sleep.'

Ten minutes later Burkin was already sleeping. But Ivan Ivanych kept turning over and sighing, then he got up, went outside again and sat down in the doorway to light his pipe.

Gooseberries

The whole sky had been overcast with rainclouds from early morning; it was a still day, not hot, but dreary, as it is in grey dull weather when the clouds have been hanging over the fields for a long while, when one expects rain and it does not come. Ivan Ivanych, the veterinary surgeon, and Burkin, the schoolmaster, were already tired from walking, and the fields seemed to them endless. Far ahead they could just see the windmills of the village of Mironositskoye; on the right stretched a row of hillocks which disappeared in the distance beyond the village, and they both knew that this was the bank of the river, where there were meadows, green willows, homesteads, and that if you stood on one of the hillocks you could see the same vast plain, telegraph wires, and a train which from afar looked like a crawling caterpillar, and that in clear weather you could even see the town. Now, in still weather, when all nature seemed mild and dreamy, Ivan Ivanych and Burkin were filled with love of these fields, and both thought how great, how beautiful a land it was.

'Last time we were in the village elder Prokofy's barn,' said Burkin, 'you were about to tell me a story.'

'Yes; I meant to tell you about my brother.'

Ivan Ivanych heaved a deep sigh and lit a pipe in readiness to tell his story, but just at that moment the rain began. And five minutes later heavy rain came down, covering the sky, and it was hard to guess when it would be over. Ivan Ivanych and Burkin stopped in hesitation; the dogs, already drenched, stood with their tails between their legs gazing at them fondly.

'We must take shelter somewhere,' said Burkin. 'Let's go to Alyokhin's; it's close by.'

'Come along.'

They turned aside and walked through mown fields, sometimes going straight forward, sometimes turning to the right, till they came out on the road. Soon they saw poplars, a garden, then the red roofs of barns; the river shone, and a view opened on to a broad expanse of water with a windmill and a white bathing-pool: this was Sofyino, where Alyokhin lived.

The watermill was at work, drowning the sound of the rain; the dam was shaking. Here wet horses with drooping heads were standing near their carts, and men were walking about covered with sacks. It was damp, muddy, and desolate; the water looked cold and malignant. Ivan Ivanych and Burkin were already conscious of a feeling of wetness, dirtiness, and discomfort all over; their feet were heavy with mud, and when, crossing the dam, they went up to Alyokhin's barns, they were silent, as if they were angry with one another.

In one of the barns there was the sound of a winnowing machine, the door was open, and clouds of dust were coming from it. In the doorway stood Alyokhin himself, a man of forty, tall and stout, with long hair, more like a professor or an artist than a landowner. He wore a white shirt that badly needed washing, a rope for a belt, drawers instead of trousers, and his boots, too, were plastered with mud and straw. His eyes and nose were black with dust. He recognised Ivan Ivanych and Burkin, and was apparently delighted to see them.

'Go into the house, gentlemen,' he said, smiling; 'I'll come directly, this minute.'

It was a big two-storeyed house. Alyokhin lived in the lower storey, in two rooms with arched ceilings and little windows, where the bailiffs had once lived; here everything was plain, and there was a smell of rye bread, cheap vodka, and harness. He went upstairs into the best rooms only on rare occasions, when visitors came. Ivan Ivanych and Burkin were met in the house by a maidservant, a young woman so beautiful that they both stood still and looked at one another.

'You can't imagine how delighted I am to see you, my friends,' said Alyokhin, following them into the hall. 'What a surprise! Pelageya,' he said, addressing the girl, 'give our visitors something to change into. And, by the way, I will change too. Only I must first go and wash, for I do believe I haven't washed since spring. Wouldn't you like to come into the bathing-pool while they get things ready here?'

Beautiful Pelageya, so polite and soft-looking, brought them towels and soap, and Alyokhin went to the bathing-pool with his guests.

'Yes, it's ages since I had a wash,' he said, undressing. 'I have got a nice bathing-pool, as you see—my father built it—but I somehow never have time to wash.'

He sat down on a step and soaped his long hair and his neck, and the water round him turned brown.

'Yes, I must say,' said Ivan Ivanych meaningfully, looking at his head.

'It's ages since I had a wash . . .' Alyokhin repeated with embarrassment, giving himself a second soaping, and the water near him turned dark blue, like ink.

Ivan Ivanych went outside, plunged into the water with a loud splash, and swam in the rain, flinging his arms out wide. He stirred the water into waves which set the white lilies bobbing up and down; he swam to the very middle of the millpond and dived, and came up a minute later in another place, and swam on, and kept on diving, trying to touch the bottom.

'Oh, my goodness!' he repeated continually, enjoying himself thoroughly. 'Oh, my goodness!' He swam to the mill, talked to the peasants there about something, then returned and lay on his back in the middle of the pond, turning his face to the rain. Burkin and Alyokhin were dressed and ready to go, but he still went on swimming and diving. 'Oh, my goodness! . . .' he said. 'Oh, Lord, have mercy!'

'That's enough!' Burkin shouted to him.

They went back to the house. And only when the lamp was lit in the big drawing-room upstairs, and Burkin and Ivan Ivanych, attired in silk dressing-gowns and warm slippers, were sitting in armchairs; and Alyokhin, washed and combed, in a new coat, was walking about the drawing-room, evidently enjoying the feeling of warmth, cleanliness, dry clothes, and light shoes; and when the beautiful Pelageya, stepping noiselessly on the carpet and smiling softly, served tea and jam on a tray—only then did Ivan Ivanych begin his story, and it seemed as though not only Burkin and Alyokhin were listening, but also the ladies, young and old, and the officers who gazed down sternly and calmly from their gilt picture-frames.

'There are two of us brothers,' he began, 'I, Ivan Ivanych, and my brother, Nikolay Ivanych, two years younger. I went in for a learned profession and became a veterinary surgeon, while Nikolay sat in a Government office from the time he was nineteen. Our father, Chimsha-Himalaisky, was a soldier's son, but he rose to be an officer and left us a little estate and the rank of nobility. After his death the little estate went in debts and legal expenses; but, anyway, we had spent our childhood roaming free in the countryside. Like peasant children, we passed our days and nights in the fields and the woods, looked after horses, stripped the bark off the trees, fished, and so on . . . And, you know, anyone who has once in his life fished for ruff or has seen the migrating of the thrushes in autumn, as they drift in flocks over the village on bright, cool days, that person will never be a townsman, and will have a yearning for freedom to the day of his death. My brother was miserable in the Government office. Years passed by, and he went on sitting in the same place, went on writing the same papers and thinking of one and the same thing—how to get into the country. And this yearning by degrees turned into a definite desire, a dream of purchasing a little farm somewhere on the banks of a river or lake.

'He was a gentle, good-natured fellow, and I was fond of him, but I never sympathised with this desire to shut himself up for the rest of his life in a little farm of his own. People often say that a man needs no more than six feet of earth. But six feet is what a corpse needs, not a man. And they say, too, nowadays, that if our intellectual classes are attracted to the land and aspire to own a farm, then that's a good thing. But these farms are just the same as six feet of earth. To retreat from town, from the struggle, from the bustle of life, to retreat and bury oneself in one's farm—that's not life, it's egoism, laziness, it's a kind of monasticism, but monasticism without heroic deeds. A man does not need six feet of earth or a farm, but the entire globe, the whole of nature, where he can have room to display all the qualities and facets of his free spirit.

'My brother Nikolay, sitting in his office, dreamed of how he would eat his own cabbage-soup, which would fill the whole yard with such a savoury smell, eat his meals on the green grass, sleep in the sunshine, sit for hours on end on a bench by the gate gazing at the fields and the forest. Gardening books and all those agricultural tips in calendars were his delight, his favourite spiritual sustenance; he enjoyed reading newspapers, too, but the only things he read in them were the advertisements of so many acres of arable land and meadows with farm, river, garden, mill and millponds, all for sale. And his imagination pictured the garden-paths, flowers and fruit, starling cotes, the carp in the pond, and all that sort of thing, you know. These imaginary pictures varied according to the advertisements which he came across, but for some reason every one of them always featured gooseberries. He could not imagine a homestead, or any idyllic nook, without gooseberries.

' "Country life has its conveniences," he would sometimes say. "You sit on the veranda and drink tea, while your ducks swim on the pond, there is a delicious smell everywhere, and . . . and the gooseberries are growing."

'He used to draw a map of his property, and in every map there were the same things: (a) manor-house, (b) servants' quarters, (c) kitchen-garden, (d) gooseberry-bushes. He lived frugally: he cut down on food

354

and drink, dressed any old how, like a beggar, and kept on saving and putting money in the bank. He grew terribly mean. It was painful to look at him, and I used to give him hand-outs and send him presents for Christmas and Easter, but he used to save those too. Once a man is obsessed by some idea, there's nothing one can do.

'Years passed: he was transferred to another province. He was over forty, and still reading the advertisements in the papers and saving up. Then I heard he had married. Still with the same object of buying a farm and having gooseberries, he married an elderly and ugly widow without a trace of feeling for her, but simply because she had filthy lucre. He went on living frugally with her, and kept her short of food, while he put her money in the bank in his name.

'Her first husband had been a postmaster, and with him she was accustomed to pies and liqueurs, while with her second husband she did not even get enough black bread; she began to pine away with that sort of life, and three years later she gave up the ghost. And I need hardly say that my brother never for one moment imagined that he was responsible for her death. Money, like vodka, does strange things to a man. In our town there was a merchant who, before he died, ordered a plateful of honey and ate up all his money and lottery tickets with the honey, so that no one might reap the benefit. While I was inspecting cattle at a railway station, a cattle-dealer fell under an engine and had his leg cut off. We carried him into the waiting-room, the blood was flowing—it was a horrible sight—and he kept asking them to look for his leg and was dreadfully anxious; there were twenty roubles in the boot on the leg that had been cut off, and he was afraid they would be lost.'

'Now you're on to a different theme,' said Burkin.

'Following his wife's death', Ivan Ivanych went on, after thinking for half a minute, 'my brother began seeking an estate for himself. Of course, you may search for five years and still end by making a mistake, and buying something quite different from what you have dreamed of. My brother Nikolay bought through an agent a mortgaged estate of three hundred and thirty acres, with a manor-house, with servants' quarters, with a park, but with no orchard, no gooseberry-bushes, and no duck-pond; there was a river, but the water in it was the colour of coffee, because on one side of the estate there was a brickyard and on the other a factory for burning bones. But my Nikolay Ivanych was not disheartened; he ordered twenty gooseberry-bushes, planted them, and began living as a country gentleman.

'Last year I went to pay him a visit. I thought I would go and see what his property was like. In his letters my brother called his estate "Chumbaroklova Waste, alias Himalaiskoye". I reached "alias Himalaiskoye" in the afternoon. It was hot. Everywhere there were ditches, fences, hedges, fir-trees planted in rows, and there was no knowing how to get to the yard, where to put one's horse. I went up to the house, and was met by a fat red dog that looked like a pig. It wanted to bark, but it was too lazy. The cook, a fat, barefooted woman, came out of the kitchen, and she, too, looked like a pig, and said that her master was resting after dinner. I went in to see my brother. He was sitting up in bed with a quilt over his legs; he had grown older, fatter, flabby; his cheeks, nose, and lips all stuck out—he looked as though he might grunt into the quilt at any moment.

'We embraced each other, and shed tears of joy and of sadness at the thought that we had once been young and now were both grey-headed and not long for this world. He dressed, and led me out to show me his estate.

' "Well, how are you getting on here?" I asked.

' "Oh, all right, thank God; I am getting on very well."

'He was no longer a poor timid clerk, but a real landowner, a gentleman. He was already accustomed to this role, and had developed a taste for it. He ate a great deal, washed in the bath-house, was growing stout, and he was already at law with the village commune and both factories, and took umbrage when the peasants did not call him "Your Honour". And he concerned himself with the salvation of his soul in a substantial, gentlemanly manner, and performed deeds of charity, not simply, but with an air of consequence. And what deeds of charity? He treated the peasants for every sort of disease with soda and castor oil, and on his name-day held a thanksgiving service in the middle of the village, and then treated the peasants to a gallon of vodka—he thought that was the thing to do. Oh, those horrible gallons of vodka! One day the fat landowner hauls the peasants up before the district captain for trespass, and next day, in honour of a holiday, treats them to a gallon of vodka, and they drink and shout "Hurrah!" and when they are drunk bow down to his feet. A change of life for the better, and being well-fed and idle, develop in a Russian the most insolent self-conceit. Nikolay Ivanych, who at one time in the Government office was afraid to have any views of his own, now uttered words of wisdom, in a ministerial tone: "Education is essential, but for the peasants it is premature." "Corporal punishment is harmful as a rule, but in some cases it is necessary and indispensable."

' "I know the peasants and understand how to deal with them," he would say. "The peasants like me. I need only to hold up my little finger and the peasants will do anything I want."

'And all this, observe, was uttered with a wise, benevolent smile. He repeated twenty times over "We noblemen", "I as a noble"; obviously he did not remember that our grandfather was a peasant, and our father a soldier. Even our surname Chimsha-Himalaisky, in reality so absurd, now seemed to him melodious, distinguished, and very refined.

'But the point just now is not he, but myself. I want to tell you about the change that took place in me during the brief hours I spent at his country place. In the evening, when we were drinking tea, the cook put on the table a plateful of gooseberries. They were not bought, but his own gooseberries, gathered for the first time since the bushes were planted. Nikolay Ivanych laughed and looked for a minute in silence at the gooseberries, with tears in his eyes; he could not speak for excitement. Then he placed one gooseberry in his mouth, looked at me with the triumph of a child who has at last received his favourite toy, and said:

' "How delicious!"

'And he ate them greedily, continually repeating, "Ah, how delicious! Do taste them!"

'They were sour and unripe, but, as Pushkin says:

> "Dearer to us is the falsehood that exalts us
> Than hosts of baser truths."

'I beheld a happy man whose cherished dream was so evidently fulfilled, who had attained his aim in life, gained what he wanted, who was satisfied with his fate and himself. There is always, for some reason, an element of sadness mingled with my thoughts of human happiness, and, on this occasion, at the sight of a happy man I was overcome by an oppressive feeling that was close to despair. I felt particularly oppressed at night. A bed had been made up for me in the room next to my brother's bedroom, and I could hear that he was awake, and that he kept getting up and going to the plate of gooseberries and taking one. I reflected how many satisfied, happy people there really are! What a crushing force they are! Just look at our life: the insolence and idleness of the strong, the ignorance and brutishness of the weak, incredible poverty all around, overcrowding, degeneration, drunkenness, hypocrisy, lying . . . Yet all is calm and stillness in the houses and in the

357

streets; of the fifty thousand living in the town, there is not one who would cry out, who would give voice to his indignation. We see people going to market for provisions, eating by day, sleeping by night, talking their silly nonsense, getting married, growing old, serenely lugging their dead to the cemetery; but we do not see and we do not hear those who suffer, and what is terrible in life takes place somewhere off-stage. Everything is calm and still, and nothing protests but mute statistics: so many people gone mad, so many gallons of vodka drunk, so many children dead from malnutrition . . . And this order of things is evidently necessary; evidently the happy man only feels at ease because the unhappy bear their burden in silence, and without that silence happiness would be impossible. It's a case of mass hypnosis. There ought to be behind the door of every happy, contented man someone tapping with a little hammer, as a continual reminder that there are unhappy people; that however happy he may be, life will show him her claws sooner or later, misfortune will strike—disease, poverty, losses, and no one will see or hear him, just as now he neither sees nor hears others. But there is no man with a little hammer; the happy man lives at ease, and petty daily cares faintly stir him, like the wind in the aspen-tree—and all is well with the world.

'That night I realised that I, too, had been happy and contented,' Ivan Ivanych continued, getting up. 'I, too, at dinner and at the hunt liked to pontificate on life and religion, and on how to manage the peasantry. I, too, used to say that science was enlightenment, that education was essential, but for the simple people reading and writing sufficed for now. Freedom is good, I used to say, as necessary as air, but we must wait a little. Yes, I used to talk like that, but now I ask, "Why are we to wait?" ' asked Ivan Ivanych, looking angrily at Burkin. 'Why wait, I ask you? What grounds have we for waiting? I shall be told, it can't be done all at once; every idea takes shape in life gradually, in its due time. But who says that? Where is the proof that it's right? You will cite the natural order of things, the legitimate sequence of phenomena; but is there order and legitimacy in the notion that I, a living, thinking being, should stand over a chasm and wait for it to close by itself, or to fill up with mud, when perhaps I might leap over it or build a bridge across it? And again, I ask, why wait? Wait, when we're too weak to live, and yet we must live and we long to live!

'I went away from my brother's early in the morning, and ever since then it has been unbearable for me to visit the town. I am oppressed by its

358

calm and stillness; I am afraid to look at the windows, for there is no spectacle more painful to me now than the sight of a happy family sitting round the table drinking tea. I am old and unfit for the struggle; I am not even capable of hatred; I can only grieve inwardly, feel irritated and vexed; but at night my head seethes with thoughts, and I cannot sleep . . . Ah, if only I were young!'

Ivan Ivanych walked to and fro in excitement, and repeated: 'If only I were young!'

He suddenly went up to Alyokhin and began pressing first one of his hands and then the other.

'Pavel Konstantinych,' he said in an imploring voice, 'don't be calm and contented, don't let yourself be lulled! While you are young, strong, confident, do not tire of doing good! There is no happiness, and nor should there be; but if there is a meaning and aim in life, that meaning and aim is not our happiness, but something greater and more rational. Do good!'

And all this Ivan Ivanych said with a pitiful, suppliant smile, as if he were asking a personal favour.

Then all three sat in armchairs in separate corners of the drawing-room and were silent. Ivan Ivanych's story had not satisfied either Burkin or Alyokhin. When the generals and ladies gazed down from their gilt frames, looking in the dusk as though they were alive, it was dreary to listen to the story of a poor clerk who ate gooseberries. They felt inclined, for some reason, to listen and talk about elegant people, about women. And sitting in a drawing-room where everything—the chandelier in its covers, the armchairs, and the carpet under their feet—reminded them that those very people who were now gazing down from their frames had once moved about, sat, drunk tea in this room, and the beautiful Pelageya moving noiselessly about—all this was better than any story.

Alyokhin felt terribly sleepy; he had got up early, before three o'clock in the morning, to work on his farm, and now his eyes kept closing; but he was afraid his visitors might tell some interesting story in his absence, and so he lingered on. He did not try to fathom whether what Ivan Ivanych had just said was right and true. His visitors did not talk of groats, nor of hay, nor of tar, but of something that had no direct bearing on his life, and he was glad and wanted them to continue . . .

'It's bedtime, though,' said Burkin, getting up. 'Allow me to wish you good night.'

Alyokhin said good night and went downstairs to his own domain, while the visitors remained upstairs. They had been given a large room containing two old, elaborately carved beds, and in the corner was an ivory crucifix. The wide cool beds, which had been prepared by the beautiful Pelageya, smelt agreeably of clean linen.

Ivan Ivanych undressed in silence and climbed into bed.

'Lord forgive us sinners!' he said, and drew the blanket over his head.

His pipe lying on the table smelt strongly of stale tobacco, and Burkin could not sleep for a long while, and kept wondering where the oppressive smell came from.

Rain pattered on the window-panes all night.

About Love

At lunch next day they were served very tasty pies, crayfish, and mutton cutlets; and while they were eating, Nikanor, the cook, came up to ask what the visitors would like for dinner. He was a man of medium height, with a puffy face and little eyes; he was close-shaven, and it looked as though his moustaches had not been shaved, but plucked.

Alyokhin told his guests that the beautiful Pelageya was in love with this cook. As he drank and was of a violent character, she did not want to marry him, but was willing to live in sin. Yet he was very devout, and his religious convictions would not allow him to live in sin; he insisted on her marrying him, and would consent to nothing else, and when he was drunk he used to curse her and even beat her. Whenever he got drunk she used to hide upstairs and sob, and then Alyokhin and the servants stayed in the house, to defend her should the need arise.

They began talking about love.

'How love is born,' said Alyokhin, 'why Pelageya didn't fall for somebody more closely matching her spiritual and external qualities, and why she fell for Nikanor, that ugly snout—we all call him "The Snout"—since questions of personal happiness are so important in love—all that is unknown; one can take what view one likes. So far only one incontestable truth has been uttered about love: "This is a great mystery." Everything else that has been written or said about love is not a solution, but only a formulation of questions which have remained unanswered. The explanation which would seem to fit one case does not apply in a dozen others, and the very best thing, to my mind, would be to explain every case individually without attempting to generalise. We ought, as the doctors say, to individualise each case.'

'Perfectly true,' Burkin assented.

'We Russians, decent people, have a partiality for these questions that remain unanswered. Love is usually poeticised, adorned with roses and nightingales; we Russians adorn our love with these momentous questions, and select the most uninteresting of them, too. In Moscow, when I was a student, I had a friend who shared my life, a charming lady, and every time I held her in my arms she was wondering about her monthly allowance and the price of a pound of beef. In the same way, when we are in love we never tire of asking ourselves questions: whether it is honourable or dishonourable, sensible or stupid, what this love is leading to, and so on. Whether this is a good thing or not I don't know, but that it is obstructive, unsatisfactory, and irritating, I do know.'

It looked as though he wanted to tell some story. People who lead a solitary existence always have something in their hearts which they are eager to talk about. In town bachelors visit the baths and the restaurants on purpose to talk, and sometimes tell the most interesting things to bath attendants and waiters; in the country, as a rule, they unburden themselves to their guests. One could see now through the windows a grey sky and trees drenched in the rain; one couldn't go out in such weather, so nothing remained but to tell stories and listen.

'I have lived at Sofyino and been farming for a long time,' Alyokhin began, 'ever since I left the University. I am an idle gentleman by upbringing, a studious person by disposition; but there was a big debt owing on the estate when I came here, and as my father was in debt partly because he had spent so much on my education, I decided not to go away, but to work till I had paid off the debt. That was my decision and I set to work, not, I must confess, without some repugnance. The land here doesn't yield much, and if one is not to farm at a loss one must employ serfs or hired labourers, which is almost the same thing, or put it on a peasant footing—that is, work the fields oneself, with one's family. There is no middle way. But in those days I did not go into such subtleties. I didn't leave a clod of earth unturned; I gathered together all the peasants, men and women, from the neighbouring villages; the work went on at a tremendous pace. I myself ploughed and sowed and reaped, and was bored doing it, and frowned with disgust, like a village cat driven by hunger to eat cucumbers in the kitchen-garden. My body ached, and I slept as I walked. At first it seemed to me that I could easily reconcile this life of toil with my cultured habits; to do so, I thought, all that is necessary is to maintain a certain external order in life. I established myself upstairs here in the best rooms, and ordered them to bring me coffee and liqueur after lunch and dinner, and my bedtime reading every night was the *European Herald*. But one day our priest, Father Ivan, came and drank up all my liqueur at one sitting; and the *European Herald* also went to the priest's daughters; as in the summer, especially at haymaking, I did not manage to get to my bed at all, and slept in the sledge in the barn, or somewhere in the forester's lodge—what chance was there of reading? Little by little I moved downstairs, began dining in the servants' kitchen, and of my former luxury nothing remains but the servants who were in my father's service, and whom it would be painful to dismiss.

'In the first years I was elected here as an honorary justice of the peace. I used to have to go to the town and take part in the assizes and the circuit court, and this was a pleasant change for me. When you live here for two or three months without a break, especially in the winter, you begin at last to pine for a black coat. And in the circuit court there were frock-coats, and uniforms, and dress-coats, too, all lawyers, men who have received a sound education; I had someone to talk to. After sleeping in the sledge and dining in the kitchen, to sit in an armchair, in clean linen and smart shoes, with a chain on one's waistcoat, is such luxury!

'I received a warm welcome in the town. I made friends eagerly. And of all my acquaintanceships the most meaningful and, to tell the truth, the most agreeable to me was my acquaintance with Luganovich, the vice-chairman of the circuit court. You both know him: a most charming man. It all happened just after a celebrated case of arson; the preliminary investigation lasted two days; we were exhausted. Luganovich looked at me and said:

' "Well, now, come round to dinner with me."

'This was unexpected, as I knew Luganovich hardly at all, only officially, and I had never been to his house. I just went back to my hotel room to change and then set off to dinner. And here I had occasion to meet Anna Alekseyevna, Luganovich's wife. At that time she was still very young, no more than twenty-two, and her first baby had been born some six months before. It is all a thing of the past; and now I should find it difficult to define what was so extraordinary about her, what it was in her attracted me so much; at the time, at dinner, it was all irresistibly clear to me. I saw a young, beautiful, good, cultured, fascinating woman, such as I had never met before; and I felt at once that she was close and already familiar, as though that face, those cordial, intelligent eyes, I had seen somewhere in my child-hood, in the album which lay upon my mother's chest of drawers.

'Four Jews had been charged with arson, as part of a gang, and, to my mind, quite groundlessly. At dinner I was very excited, I was distressed, and I don't recall what I said, but Anna Alekseyevna kept shaking her head and saying to her husband:

' "Dmitry, how can that be?"

'Luganovich is a good-natured fellow, one of those simple-hearted people who firmly believe that, if a man is put on trial, then he must be guilty, and to express doubt about the correctness of a sentence cannot be done except in legal form on paper, but never at dinner or in private conversation.

' "You and I did not set fire to the place," he said softly, "so we're not put on trial, or thrown into prison."

'And both husband and wife tried to make me eat and drink as much as possible. From some trifling details, from the way they made the coffee together, for instance, and from the way they understood each other at half a word, I could gather that they lived in peace and harmony, and that they were glad of a visitor. After dinner they played a duet on the piano; then it got dark, and I went home. This was at the beginning of spring.

'After that I spent the whole summer at Sofyino without a break, and I had no time to think of the town, either, but the memory of that graceful fair-haired woman remained with me all those days; I did not think of her, but it was as though her light shadow lay upon my heart.

'In the late autumn there was a theatrical performance in town for some charity. I went into the Governor's box (I was invited to go there in the interval); I looked, and there was Anna Alekseyevna sitting beside the Governor's wife; and again the same irresistible, thrilling impression of beauty and sweet, caressing eyes, and again the same feeling of closeness. We sat side by side, then went to the foyer.

' "You've grown thinner," she said; "have you been ill?"

' "Yes, I've had rheumatism in my shoulder, and in rainy weather I can't sleep."

' "You look dispirited. In the spring, when you came to dinner, you were younger, more confident. You were animated then, and talked a great deal; you were very interesting, and I confess I was a little carried away by you. For some reason I often remembered you during the summer, and when I was getting ready for the theatre today I thought I should see you."

'And she laughed.

' "But you look dispirited today," she repeated; "it makes you seem older."

'The next day I lunched at the Luganovichs'. After lunch they drove out to their summer villa, in order to make arrangements there for the winter, and I went with them. I returned with them to the town, and at midnight drank tea with them in quiet domestic surroundings, while the fire glowed, and the young mother kept going to see if her baby girl was asleep. And after that, every time I went to town I never failed to visit the

Luganovichs. They grew used to me, and I grew used to them. As a rule I went in unannounced, like one of the family.

' "Who is there?" I would hear from a faraway room in the drawling voice that seemed to me so lovely.

' "It is Pavel Konstantinych," answered the maid or the nurse.

'Anna Alekseyevna would come out to me with an anxious face, and would ask every time:

' "Why is it so long since you've been? Has anything happened?"

'Her eyes, the noble, elegant hand she gave me, her indoor dress, the way she did her hair, her voice, her step, always produced the same impression on me of something new and extraordinary in my life, and very important. We talked together for hours, and were silent for hours, immersed in our own thoughts, or she played for me on the piano. If there were no one at home I stayed and waited, talked to the nurse, played with the child, or lay on the sofa in the study and read the newspaper; and when Anna Alekseyevna came back I met her in the hall, took all her parcels from her, and for some reason I carried those parcels every time with as much love, with as much delight, as a little boy.

'There is a proverb that if a peasant woman has no troubles she will buy a pig. The Luganovichs had no troubles, so they made friends with me. If I was absent from town for long, then I must be ill or something must have happened to me, and both of them grew extremely worried. They were worried that I, an educated man with a knowledge of languages, should, instead of devoting myself to science or literary work, live in the country, rush round like a squirrel in a cage, work hard with never a kopeck to show for it. They fancied that I was miserable, and that I only talked, laughed, and ate to conceal my sufferings, and even at cheerful moments when I felt fine I was aware of their searching eyes fixed upon me. They were particularly touching when I really was depressed, when I was being harassed by a creditor or lacked ready money to pay some bill. The two of them, husband and wife, would whisper together at the window; then he would come to me and say with a solemn face:

' "If you are short of money at the present time, Pavel Konstantinych, my wife and I beg you not to hesitate to borrow from us."

'And he would blush to his ears with emotion. And it would happen that, after whispering in the same way at the window, he would come up to me, with red ears, and say:

' "My wife and I earnestly beg you to accept this gift."

'And he would give me cuff-links, a cigar-case, or a lamp, and I would send them game, butter, and flowers from the country. They both, by the way, had considerable means of their own. In early days I often borrowed money, and was not very particular about it—borrowed wherever I could—but nothing in the world would have induced me to borrow from the Luganovichs. That goes without saying!

'I was unhappy. At home, in the fields, and in the barn, I thought of her; I tried to understand the mystery of a beautiful, intelligent young woman who had married an uninteresting, almost an old man (her husband was over forty), and had children by him; to understand the mystery of this uninteresting, good-natured, simple-hearted man, who reasoned with such boring common sense, at balls and evening parties hovered near the solid citizens, looking listless and superfluous, with a submissive, detached expression, as if he had been brought there for sale, who yet believed in his right to be happy, to have children by her; and I kept trying to understand why she had met him first and not me, and why such a terrible mistake had to happen in our lives.

'And when I went to the town I saw every time from her eyes that she was expecting me, and she would confess to me herself that she had had a peculiar feeling all that day and had guessed that I should come. We talked for hours, and were silent, yet we did not confess our love to each other, but timidly and jealously concealed it. We were afraid of everything that might reveal our secret to ourselves. I loved her tenderly, deeply, but I reasoned and kept asking myself what our love could lead to if we had not the strength to fight it. It seemed incredible that my gentle, melancholy love might crudely disrupt the happy life of her husband, her children, and all the household in which I was so loved and trusted. Would that be honourable? She would go away with me, but where? Where could I take her? It would have been a different matter if I had led a beautiful, interesting life—if, for instance, I had been struggling for the liberation of my country, or had been a celebrated scholar, actor or painter; but as it was it would mean taking her from one everyday humdrum existence to another as humdrum or perhaps more so. And how long would our happiness last? What would happen to her if I fell ill or died, or if we simply stopped loving one another?

'And she apparently reasoned in the same way. She thought of her husband, her children, and of her mother, who loved Luganovich like a son. If she abandoned herself to her feelings she would have to lie, or else to tell the truth, and in her position either course would have been equally terrible and awkward. And she was tormented by the question whether her love would bring me happiness—would it not complicate my life, which, as it was, was hard enough and full of all sorts of misfortune? She fancied she was not young enough for me, not industrious or energetic enough to begin a new life, and she often talked to her husband of the importance of my marrying a girl of intelligence and merit who would be a capable housewife and helpmate—and she would immediately add that it would be difficult to find such a girl in the entire town.

'Meanwhile the years were passing. Anna Alekseyevna now had two children. When I arrived at the Luganovichs' the servants smiled cordially, the children shouted that Uncle Pavel Konstantinych had come, and flung their arms round my neck; everyone was overjoyed. They did not understand what was happening in my soul, and thought that I, too, was overjoyed. Everyone looked upon me as a noble being. Grown-ups and children alike felt that a noble being was walking about their rooms, and that gave a peculiar charm to their manner towards me, as though in my presence their life, too, was purer and more beautiful. Anna Alekseyevna and I used to go to the theatre together, always walking there; we used to sit side by side in the stalls, our shoulders touching. I would take the opera-glass from her hands without a word, and feel at that moment that she was close to me, that she was mine, that we could not live without each other; but by some strange misunderstanding, when we came out of the theatre we always said goodbye and parted as though we were strangers. Goodness knows what people were already saying about us in town, but in all they said there was not a single word of truth.

'In the latter years Anna Alekseyevna took to going away for frequent visits to her mother or to her sister; she began to suffer from low spirits, she began to recognise that her life was spoilt and unsatisfied, and at times she did not want to see her husband or her children. She was now being treated for neurasthenia.

'We were silent, we kept on being silent, and in the presence of outsiders she displayed a strange irritation towards me; whatever I talked about, she disagreed with me, and if I had an argument she sided with my opponent. If I dropped anything, she would say coldly:

' "My congratulations."

'If I forgot to take the opera-glass when we were going to the theatre, she would say afterwards:

' "I knew you would forget it."

'Happily or unhappily, there is nothing in our lives that does not end

367

sooner or later. The time of parting came, as Luganovich was appointed court chairman in one of the western provinces. They had to sell their furniture, their horses, their summer villa. When they drove out to the villa and, returning, glanced back, to look for the last time at the garden, at the green roof, everyone was sad, and I realised that I had to say good-bye not only to the villa. It was arranged that at the end of August we should see Anna Alekseyevna off to the Crimea, where the doctors were sending her, and that a little later Luganovich and the children would leave for their western province.

'There was a great crowd of us to see Anna Alekseyevna off. When she had said goodbye to her husband and her children and there was only a moment left before the third bell, I ran into her compartment to put a basket, which she had almost forgotten, on the rack, and I had to say goodbye. When our eyes met in the compartment our strength of mind deserted us both; I took her in my arms, she pressed her face to my chest, and tears flowed from her eyes. Kissing her face, her shoulders, her hands wet with tears—oh, how unhappy we were!—I confessed my love for her, and with a burning pain in my heart I realised how unnecessary, petty, and how deceptive all that had hindered us from loving was. I realised that, when you love, in your reasoning about that love you must start from what is highest, from what is more important than happiness or unhappiness, sin or virtue in their accepted meaning, or you must not reason at all.

'I kissed her for the last time, pressed her hand, and we parted for ever. The train had already started. I went into the next compartment—it was empty—and until I reached the first station I sat there crying. Then I walked home to Sofyino . . .'

While Alyokhin was telling his story, the rain stopped and the sun came out. Burkin and Ivan Ivanych went out on the balcony, from which there was a fine view over the garden and the millpond, which was shining now in the sunlight like a mirror. They admired it, and at the same time they were sorry that this man with the kind, clever eyes, who had told them his story with such genuine feeling, should indeed be rushing round this huge estate like a squirrel in a cage instead of devoting himself to science or something else which would have made his life more pleasant; and they thought what a sorrowful face Anna Alekseyevna must have had when he said goodbye to her in the railway carriage and kissed her face and shoulders. Both of them had seen her in the town, and Burkin was acquainted with her and found her beautiful.

A Doctor's Visit

The Professor received a telegram from the Lyalikovs' factory; he was asked to come as soon as possible. The daughter of some Madame Lyalikova, apparently the owner of the factory, was ill, and that was all that one could understand from this long, incoherent telegram. And the Professor did not go himself, but sent instead his house-surgeon, Korolyov.

It was two stops by train from Moscow, and then a drive of three miles from the station. A carriage with three horses had been sent to the station to meet Korolyov; the coachman wore a hat with a peacock's feather in it, and answered every question in a loud voice like a soldier:

'No, sir!' 'Certainly, sir!'

It was Saturday evening; the sun was setting. Workers were coming in crowds from the factory to the station, and they bowed to the carriage in which Korolyov was driving. And he was enchanted by the evening, the farmhouses, and the villas to either side, and the birch-trees, and the quiet atmosphere all around, when it seemed that, together with the workers on the eve of their holiday, the fields and the woods and the sun were preparing to rest—to rest and, perhaps, to pray . . .

He was born and had grown up in Moscow; he did not know country life, and had never taken any interest in factories, or been inside one. But he had occasionally read about factories, and had been in the houses of factory owners and had talked to them; and whenever he saw a factory far or near, he always thought how quiet and peaceable it was outside, but inside there was surely the crass ignorance and dull-witted egoism of the owners, the wearisome, unhealthy toil of the workers, squabbling, vermin, vodka. And now when the workers timidly and deferentially made way for the carriage, in their faces, their caps, their walk, he perceived physical impurity, drunkenness, nervous exhaustion, bewilderment.

They drove in at the factory gates. On each side he caught glimpses of the workers' little houses, the faces of women, quilts and linen on the front steps. 'Look out!' shouted the coachman, giving full rein to the horses. They came to a wide grassless courtyard, with five immense blocks of buildings with tall chimneys a little distance from one another, warehouses and barracks, and over everything a sort of grey powder as though from dust. Here and there, like oases in the desert, there were pitiful gardens, and the green and red roofs of the houses in which the managers and clerks lived. The coachman suddenly pulled up the horses, and the carriage stopped at the house, which had been newly painted grey; here was a flower-garden, with a lilac bush covered with dust, and on the yellow steps at the front door there was a strong smell of paint.

'Please come in, doctor,' said women's voices in the porch and the entry, and at the same time he heard sighs and whisperings. 'Please walk in . . . We've been expecting you so long . . . we're so worried. Here, this way.'

Madame Lyalikova—a stout elderly lady wearing a black silk dress with fashionable sleeves, but, judging from her face, a simple uneducated woman—looked anxiously at the doctor, and could not bring herself to offer him her hand; she did not dare. Beside her stood a person with short hair and a pince-nez; she was wearing a blouse of many colours, and was very thin and no longer young. The servants called her Khristina Dmitriyevna, and Korolyov guessed that this was the governess. Probably, as the person of most education in the house, she had been charged to meet and receive the doctor, for she began immediately, in great haste, stating the causes of the illness, giving trivial and tiresome details, but without saying who was ill or what was the matter.

The doctor and the governess were sitting talking while the lady of the house stood motionless at the door, waiting. From the conversation Korolyov learned that the patient was Madame Lyalikova's only daughter and heiress, a girl of twenty, called Liza; she had been ill for a long time, and had consulted various doctors, and the previous night she had suffered till morning from such violent palpitations of the heart, that no one in the house had slept, and they had been afraid she might die.

'She has been, one might say, ailing since infancy,' said Khristina Dmitriyevna in a singsong voice, continually wiping her lips with her hand. 'The doctors say it is nerves; but when she was a little girl she had scrofula, and the doctors drove it back inside her, so I think it may be that.'

They went to see the invalid. Fully grown-up, big and tall, but ugly like her mother, with the same little eyes and disproportionately wide lower part of the face, lying with her hair uncombed, muffled up to the chin, she at once appeared to Korolyov as an unfortunate and destitute creature, sheltered and cared for here out of charity, and he could hardly believe that she was the heiress of those five immense factory blocks.

'I am the doctor come to see you,' said Korolyov. 'Good evening.'

He introduced himself and shook her hand, a large, cold, ugly hand;

370

she sat up, and, evidently accustomed to doctors, let herself be sounded, without showing the least concern that her shoulders and chest were uncovered.

'I have palpitations of the heart,' she said. 'It was so awful all night . . . I almost died of fright! Do give me something.'

'I will, I will! Calm down.'

Korolyov examined her and shrugged his shoulders.

'The heart is all right,' he said; 'all's well, and as it should be. Your nerves must have been playing up a little, but that's very common. The attack's over now, it seems; lie down and get some sleep.'

At that moment a lamp was brought into the bedroom. The patient screwed up her eyes at the light, then suddenly put her hands to her head and burst into sobs. And the appearance of a destitute, ugly creature vanished, and Korolyov no longer noticed her little eyes or the crudely disproportionate lower part of her face. He saw a soft, suffering expression which was so intelligent and touching; she seemed to him altogether graceful, feminine, and simple; and he longed to calm her, not with medicine, nor advice, but with simple, kindly words. Her mother cradled her head and hugged her. What despair, what grief was in the old woman's face! She, her mother, had reared her and brought her up, spared nothing, and devoted her whole life to having her daughter taught French, dancing, music; had engaged a dozen teachers for her; had consulted the best doctors, kept a governess. And now she could not understand the reason for these tears, why there was so much misery, she could not understand, and was bewildered; and she had a guilty, agitated, despairing expression, as if she had omitted something very important, had left something undone, had let someone remain uninvited—but whom, she did not know.

'Lizanka, you are crying again . . . again,' she said, hugging her daughter to her. 'My own, my darling, my child, tell me, what's the matter? Have pity on me! Tell me.'

Both wept bitterly. Korolyov sat down on the edge of the bed and took Liza's hand.

'That's enough, there's no need to cry,' he said kindly. 'Why, there is nothing in the world that is worth all these tears. Come, we won't cry; there's no need . . .'

But to himself he thought:

'It's high time she was married . . .'

'Our doctor at the factory gave her some bromide,' said the governess, 'but I notice it only makes her worse. I should have thought that if she is given anything for the heart it ought to be drops . . . I forget the name . . . Lily of the valley, isn't it?'

And there followed all sorts of details. She interrupted the doctor, preventing him from speaking, and there was a look of effort on her face, as if she supposed that, as the woman of most education in the house, she was obliged to conduct a continuous conversation with the doctor, and on no other subject but medicine.

Korolyov became bored.

'I can find no special symptoms,' he said, addressing the mother as he went out of the bedroom. 'If your daughter is being treated by the factory doctor, let him go on treating her. The treatment so far has been correct, and I see no reason for changing your doctor. Why change? It's such an ordinary illness; there's nothing seriously wrong.'

He spoke deliberately as he put on his gloves, while Madame Lyalikova stood without moving, and looked at him with her tearful eyes.

'I have half an hour to catch the ten-o'clock train,' he said. 'I hope I am not too late.'

'But can't you stay?' she asked, and tears trickled down her cheeks again. 'I am ashamed to trouble you, but if you would be so good . . . For the love of God,' she went on in an undertone, glancing towards the door, 'do stay tonight with us! She is all I have . . . my only daughter . . . She frightened me last night; I can't get over it . . . Don't go away, for goodness' sake! . . .'

He wanted to tell her that he had a great deal of work in Moscow, that his family were expecting him home; it was disagreeable to him to spend all evening and all night in a strange house quite needlessly; but he looked at her face, heaved a sigh, and began taking off his gloves without a word.

All the lamps and candles were lit in his honour in the drawing-room and the dining-room. He sat down at the piano and began turning over the music. Then he looked at the pictures on the walls, at the portraits. The pictures, oil-paintings in gold frames, showed views of the Crimea—a stormy sea with a ship, a Catholic monk with a wine-glass; and all this was soulless, prettified, third-rate . . . There was not a single beautiful, interesting face among the portraits, nothing but broad cheekbones and goggling eyes. Lyalikov, Liza's father, had a low forehead and a self-satisfied expression; his uniform sat like a sack on his bulky plebeian figure; on his breast was a medal and a Red Cross badge. There was little sign of culture, and the luxury was senseless and haphazard, and as awkward as that uniform. The floors irritated him with their glittering polish, and the chandelier irritated him, and he was reminded for some reason of the story of the merchant who used to go to the baths with a medal round his neck . . .

He heard a whispering in the entry; someone was softly snoring. And suddenly from outside came harsh, abrupt, metallic sounds, such as Korolyov had never heard before, and which he did not understand now; they roused strange, unpleasant echoes in his soul.

'I believe nothing would induce me to live here . . .' he thought, and went back to the music-books again.

'Doctor, please come to supper!' the governess called him in a low voice.

He went in to supper. The table was large and laid with a vast number of dishes and wines, but there were only two to supper: himself and Khristina Dmitriyevna. She drank Madeira, ate rapidly, and talked, looking at him through her pince-nez:

'Our workers are very contented. We have performances at the factory every winter; the workers themselves act. They have lectures with a magic lantern, a splendid tea-room, and everything they want. They are extremely devoted to us, and when they heard that Lizanka was worse they had a service sung for her. Though they have no education, they have their feelings, too.'

'It seems you have no man in the house,' said Korolyov.

'Not one. Pyotr Nikanorych died a year and a half ago, and left us alone. There are just the three of us. In the summer we live here, and in winter we live in Moscow, in Polyanka Street. I have been living with them for eleven years—as one of the family.'

At supper they served sturgeon, chicken rissoles, and stewed fruit; the wines were French, and very expensive.

'Please don't stand on ceremony, doctor,' said Khristina Dmitriyevna, eating and wiping her mouth with her fist, and it was evident she found her life here exceedingly pleasant. 'Please have some more.'

After supper the doctor was shown to his room, where a bed had been made up for him, but he did not feel sleepy. The room was stuffy and it smelt of paint; he put on his coat and went out.

It was cool in the open air; there was already a glimmer of dawn, and all the five blocks of buildings, with their tall chimneys, barracks, and warehouses, stood out clearly in the damp air. As it was a holiday, no one was working, and the windows were dark, and in only one of the buildings a furnace was still burning; two windows showed crimson, and now and then fire mixed with smoke came from the chimney. Far away beyond the yard frogs were croaking and a nightingale sang.

Looking at the factory buildings and the barracks, where the workers slept, he thought again what he always thought when he saw a factory. They may have performances for the workers, magic lanterns, factory doctors, and improvements of all sorts, but, none the less, the workers he had met that day on his way from the station did not look any different from those he had seen long ago in his childhood, before there were factory performances and improvements. As a doctor proficient at diagnosing chronic diseases, whose fundamental cause was incomprehensible and incurable, he regarded factories as something baffling, whose cause was also unclear and insurmountable, and all the improvements in the life of the factory hands he looked upon not as superfluous, but as comparable with the treatment of incurable illnesses.

'There is something baffling here, of course . . .' he thought, looking at the crimson windows. 'Fifteen hundred or two thousand factory hands work without rest in unhealthy conditions, making cheap cotton goods, living on the verge of starvation, and only waking from this nightmare at rare intervals in the tavern; a hundred people act as overseers, and the entire life of that hundred is spent in imposing fines, in swearing and acting unjustly, and only two or three so-called owners enjoy the profits, though they don't work at all, and despise their cheap cotton. But what are these profits, and how are they enjoyed? Madame Lyalikova and her daughter are unhappy, they're a pitiful sight; the only one who gets any pleasure out of life is Khristina Dmitriyevna, a stupid old maid wearing a pince-nez. And so it appears that all these five blocks of buildings are at work, and cheap cotton is sold in the Eastern markets, simply in order that Khristina Dmitriyevna may eat her sturgeon and drink Madeira.'

Suddenly strange sounds rang out, the same sounds Korolyov had heard before supper. Someone was striking on a sheet of metal near one of the buildings; he struck a note, and then at once checked the vibrations, so that short, harsh, discordant sounds were produced, rather like 'Dair . . . dair . . . dair . . .' Then there was half a minute of stillness, and from another building came sounds equally abrupt and unpleasant, lower bass notes: 'Drin . . . drin . . . drin . . .' Eleven times. Evidently it was the watchmen striking the hour.

Near the third building he heard: 'Zhak . . . zhak . . . zhak . . .' And so it was near all the buildings, and then behind the barracks and beyond the gates. And in the stillness of the night it seemed as though these sounds were uttered by a monster with crimson eyes—the devil himself, who controlled the owners and the workers alike, and was deceiving both.

Korolyov went out of the yard into the open country.

'Who goes there?' someone called to him at the gates in a coarse voice.

'It's just like a prison,' he thought, and made no answer.

Here the nightingales and the frogs could be heard more distinctly, and one could sense it was a May night. From the station came the noise of a train; somewhere in the distance drowsy cocks were crowing; but, all the same, the night was still, the world was sleeping peacefully. In a field not far from the factory there was the framework of a house and heaps of building material. Korolyov sat down on some planks and went on thinking.

'The only person who feels happy here is the governess, and the factory works for her pleasure. But that's mere appearance: she is only a figurehead. The main person, for whom everything is being done, is the devil.'

And he thought about the devil, in whom he did not believe, and he glanced round at the two windows where the fire was gleaming. It seemed to him that out of those crimson eyes the devil himself was looking at him—that unknown force that had created the relations between the strong and the weak, that coarse blunder which could never be corrected. The strong must shackle the weak—such was the law of nature; but only in a newspaper article or in a school-book was that intelligible and easily grasped. In the hotchpotch of everyday life, in the tangle of trivialities from which human relations were woven, it was no longer a law, but a logical absurdity, when the strong and the weak were both equally victims of their mutual relations, involuntarily submitting to some directing force, unknown, standing outside life, apart from man.

Thus thought Korolyov, sitting on those planks, and little by little he was possessed by a feeling that this unknown and mysterious force really was close by and looking at him. Meanwhile the East was growing paler, time passed rapidly. When there was not a soul anywhere near, as if everything were dead, the five buildings and their chimneys against the grey background of the dawn had a peculiar look—not the same as by day; one forgot altogether that inside were steam engines, electricity,

375

telephones, and kept thinking of pile-dwellings, of the Stone Age, feeling the presence of a crude, unconscious force . . .

And again came the sound: 'Dair . . . dair . . . dair . . . dair . . .' twelve times. Then there was stillness, stillness for half a minute, and at the other end of the yard there rang out:

'Drin . . . drin . . . drin . . .'

'Terribly unpleasant!' thought Korolyov.

'Zhak . . . zhak . . .' resounded from a third place, abruptly, harshly, as though with annoyance—'zhak . . . zhak . . .'

And it took four minutes to strike twelve. Then there was a hush; and again it seemed as if everything were dead.

Korolyov sat a little longer, then went to the house, but sat up for a good while longer. In the adjoining rooms there was whispering, a sound of shuffling slippers and bare feet.

'Can she be having another attack?' thought Korolyov.

He went out to have a look at the patient. By now it was quite light in the rooms, and a faint glimmer of sunlight, piercing through the morning mist, quivered on the floor and on the wall of the drawing-room. The door of Liza's room was open, and she was sitting in an armchair beside her bed, with her hair uncombed, wearing a dressing-gown and wrapped in a shawl. The blinds were down on the windows.

'How do you feel?' asked Korolyov.

'Thank you for asking.'

He touched her pulse, then straightened her hair, that had fallen over her forehead.

'You're not sleeping,' he said. 'It's beautiful weather outside. It's spring. The nightingales are singing, yet you sit in the dark and keep thinking of something.'

She listened and looked into his face; her eyes were sorrowful and intelligent, and it was apparent that she wanted to say something to him.

'Does this happen to you often?' he asked.

She moved her lips, and answered:

'Often, I feel wretched almost every night.'

At that moment the watchmen in the yard began striking two o'clock. They heard 'dair . . . dair . . .', and she shuddered.

'Does this tapping worry you?' he asked.

'I don't know. Everything here worries me,' she answered, and pondered. 'Everything worries me. I hear sympathy in your voice; I felt as soon as I saw you that I could speak to you about anything.'

'Do speak, I beg you.'

'I want to tell you my opinion. It seems to me that I have no illness, but that I am worried and frightened, because it has to be so and cannot be otherwise. Even the healthiest person can't help worrying if, for instance, a robber is lurking beneath his window. I am constantly receiving treatment,' she went on, looking at her knees, and she gave a shy smile. 'I am very grateful, of course, and I don't deny that treatment is useful; but I should like to talk, not with a doctor, but with some close friend who would understand me and convince me whether I was right or wrong.'

'Have you no friends?' asked Korolyov.

'I am lonely. I have a mother; I love her, but, all the same, I am lonely. That's the way it is . . . Lonely people read a great deal, but say little and hear little. Life for them is mysterious; they are mystics and often see the devil when he isn't there. Lermontov's Tamara was lonely and she saw the devil.'

'Do you read a great deal?'

'Yes. You see, my whole time is free from morning till night. I read by day, and by night my head is empty; instead of thoughts there are kinds of shadows.'

'Do you see anything at night?' asked Korolyov.

'No, but I sense . . .'

She smiled again, raised her eyes to the doctor, and looked at him so sorrowfully, so intelligently; and it seemed to him that she trusted him, and that she wanted to speak frankly to him, and that she had the same thoughts as he did. But she was silent, perhaps waiting for him to speak.

And he knew what to say to her. It was clear to him that she needed as soon as possible to abandon the five buildings and the million if she had it—to abandon this devil that looked out at night; it was clear to him, too, that she thought so herself, and was only waiting for someone she trusted to confirm her opinion.

But he did not know how to say it. How? One is wary of asking men under sentence what they have been sentenced for; and in the same way it is awkward to ask very rich people why they need so much money, why they make such poor use of their wealth, why they don't give it up, even when they see it as the source of their unhappiness; and if one begins to speak of this, one usually becomes bashful, awkward and long-winded.

'How is one to say it?' Korolyov wondered. 'And is it necessary to speak?'

377

And he said what he meant in a roundabout way:

'In your capacity as a factory owner and a wealthy heiress you are dissatisfied; you don't believe in your own rights; and now you can't sleep. That, of course, is better than if you were satisfied, slept soundly, and thought all was well with the world. Your sleeplessness does you credit; at all events, it's a good sign. Indeed, such a conversation as ours would have been unthinkable for our parents. At night they did not talk, but slept soundly; we, our generation, sleep badly, are restless, talk a great deal, and are always trying to decide whether we are right or not. For our children or grandchildren that question— whether they are right or not—will already have been decided. They will see things more clearly than we do. Life will be good in fifty years' time; it's just a pity we won't be around. It would be interesting to have a little look.'

'What will our children and grandchildren do?' asked Liza.

'I don't know . . . I suppose they will give it all up and go away.'

'Go where?'

'Where? . . . Why, wherever they like,' said Korolyov; and he laughed. 'There are many places a decent, intelligent person can go to.'

He glanced at his watch.

'The sun has risen, though,' he said. 'It's time you were asleep. Get into your nightclothes and have a good sleep. I'm very glad to have made your acquaintance,' he went on, pressing her hand. 'You're a splendid, interesting person. Good night!'

He went to his room and climbed into bed.

In the morning when the carriage was brought round they all came out on to the steps to see him off. Liza, pale and exhausted, was in a white dress as though for a holiday, with a flower in her hair; she looked at him, as yesterday, sorrowfully and intelligently, smiled and talked, and with such an expression as if she wanted to tell him something special, important—him alone. They could hear the larks trilling and the church bells pealing. The windows in the factory buildings were sparkling gaily, and, driving across the yard and afterwards along the road to the station, Korolyov no longer called to mind the workers, or the pile-dwellings, or the devil, but thought of the time, perhaps close at hand, when life would be as bright and joyous as that still Sunday morning; and he thought how pleasant it was on such a spring morning to drive with three horses in a fine carriage, and to bask in the sunshine.

On Official Duty

The acting examining magistrate and the district doctor were going to an inquest in the village of Syrnya. On the road they were overtaken by a snowstorm; they spent a long time going round in circles, and arrived, not at midday, as they had intended, but in the evening when it was dark. They put up for the night in a hut belonging to the local council, the zemstvo. It so happened that in this hut the dead body was lying—the corpse of the zemstvo insurance agent, Lesnitsky, who had arrived in Syrnya three days before and, upon settling in this hut and ordering a samovar, had shot himself, to the great surprise of everyone; and the fact that he had ended his life so strangely, with the samovar in front of him and his food spread out on the table, led many people to suspect that it was a case of murder; an inquest was necessary.

In the outer room the doctor and the examining magistrate shook the snow off themselves, stamping their feet. And meanwhile the old village constable, Ilya Loshadin, stood by, holding a little tin lamp. There was a strong smell of paraffin.

'Who are you?' asked the doctor.

'Conshtable . . .' answered the constable.

He used to spell it 'conshtable' when he signed the receipts at the post office.

'And where are the witnesses?'

'They must have gone to tea, Your Honour.'

On the right was the parlour, the travellers' or gentry's room; on the left a room for the common people, with a big stove and sleeping-benches. The doctor and the examining magistrate, followed by the constable, holding the lamp above his head, went into the parlour. Here a still, long body covered with white linen was lying on the floor close to the table-legs. In the dim light of the lamp they could clearly see, besides the white covering, new rubber galoshes, and everything was uncanny and sinister: the dark walls, and the silence, and those galoshes, and the stillness of the dead body. On the table stood a samovar, cold long ago; and round it parcels, probably the dead man's food.

'To shoot oneself in the zemstvo hut, how tactless!' said the doctor. 'If one does want to put a bullet through one's brains, one ought to do it at home in some outhouse.'

379

He sank on to a bench, just as he was, in his cap, his fur coat, and his felt overboots; his fellow-traveller, the examining magistrate, sat down opposite.

'These hysterical neurotics are great egoists,' the doctor went on grimly. 'If a neurotic sleeps in the same room as you, he rustles his newspaper; when he dines with you, he starts a scene with his wife, completely ignoring your presence; and when he feels inclined to shoot himself, he shoots himself in a village in a zemstvo hut, so as to give the maximum of bother to everybody. These gentlemen in every circumstance of life think only of themselves. Only of themselves! That's why old folk so dislike our "nervous age". '

'Old folk dislike so many things,' said the examining magistrate, yawning. 'You should point out to the old folk what the difference is between the suicides of the past and the suicides of today. In the past the so-called gentleman shot himself because he had embezzled Government money, but nowadays it is because he is sick of life, depressed . . . Which is better?'

'Sick of life, depressed; but you must admit that he might have shot himself somewhere else.'

'Such trouble!' said the constable, 'such trouble! It's a real affliction. The people are very upset, Your Honour; they haven't slept these three nights. The children are crying. The cows ought to be milked, but the women won't go to the stall—they are afraid . . . for fear the gentleman should appear to them in the darkness. Of course they are silly women, but some of the men are frightened too. As soon as it is dark they won't go by the hut on their own, but only in a flock together. And the witnesses too . . .'

Dr Starchenko, a middle-aged man in spectacles with a dark beard, and the examining magistrate Lyzhin, a fair-haired man, still young, who had taken his degree only two years before and looked more like a student than an official, sat in silence, musing. They were vexed that they were late. Now they had to wait till morning, and to stay here for the night, though it was not yet six o'clock; and they had before them a long evening, a dark night, boredom, uncomfortable beds, cockroaches, and cold in the morning; and, listening to the blizzard that howled in the chimney and in the loft, they both thought how all this was unlike the life which they would have chosen for themselves and of which they had once dreamed, and how far away they both were from their contemporaries, who were at that moment walking about the lighted streets in town, not noticing the weather, or were getting ready for the theatre, or sitting in their studies over a book. Oh, what they would have given now, just to stroll along the Nevsky Prospect, or along Petrovka in Moscow, to listen to decent singing, to sit for an hour or so in a restaurant!

'Oo-oo-oo-oo!' sang the storm in the loft, and something outside slammed viciously, probably the signboard on the hut. 'Oo-oo-oo-oo!'

'You can do as you please, but I have no desire to stay here,' said Starchenko, getting up. 'It's not six yet, it's too early to go to bed; I am off. Von Taunitz lives not far from here, only a couple of miles from Syrnya. I shall go to see him and spend the evening there. Constable, run and tell my coachman not to take the horses out. And what are you going to do?' he asked Lyzhin.

'I don't know; I expect I shall go to sleep.'

The doctor wrapped himself in his fur coat and went out. Lyzhin could hear him talking to the coachman and the bells beginning to quiver on the frozen horses. He drove off.

'It is not nice for you, sir, to spend the night in here,' said the constable; 'come into the other room. It's dirty, but for one night it won't matter. I'll get a samovar from a peasant and put it on. Then I'll pile up some hay for you, and you can go to sleep, and God bless you, Your Honour.'

A little later the examining magistrate was sitting in the room for common people, drinking tea, while Loshadin, the constable, was standing at the door talking. He was an old man of over sixty, short and very thin, bent and white, with a naïve smile on his face and watery eyes; and he kept smacking his lips as though he were sucking a sweet. He was wearing a short sheepskin coat and felt boots, and held a stick in his hands all the time. The youth of the examining magistrate evidently aroused his compassion, and that was probably why he addressed him in this familiar way.

'The elder Fyodor Makarych gave orders that he was to be informed when the police superintendent or the examining magistrate came,' he said, 'so I suppose I must go now . . . It's nearly three miles to the district office, and the storm, the snowdrifts, are something terrible—I probably won't get there before midnight. Ugh! how the wind roars!'

'I don't need the elder,' said Lyzhin. 'There is nothing for him to do here.'

He looked at the old man with curiosity, and asked:

'Tell me, Grandfather, how many years have you been constable?'

'How many? Why, thirty years. Five years after the Freedom I began as constable, that's how I reckon it. And from that time I've been going every day since. Other people have holidays, but I am always on the go. When it's Easter and the church bells are ringing and Christ is Risen, I still go about with my bag—to the treasury, to the post, to the police superintendent's lodgings, to the rural captain, to the tax inspector, to the municipal office, to the gentry, to the peasants, to all orthodox Christians. I carry parcels, notices, tax papers, letters, forms of all sorts, circulars, and to be sure, kind sir, Your Honour, there are such forms nowadays, so as to note down the numbers—yellow, white, and red—and every gentleman or priest or well-to-do peasant must write down a dozen times in the year how much he has sown and harvested, how many quarters or hundredweight he has of rye, how many of oats, how many of hay, and what the weather's like, you know, and insects, too, of all sorts. To be sure, you can write what you like, it's only a regulation, but I have to go and hand out the notices and then go again and collect them. Here, for instance, there's no need to cut open the gentleman; you know yourself it's a silly thing, it's only dirtying your hands, and here you have been put to trouble, Your Honour; you have come because it's the regulation; you can't help it. For thirty years I have been going round according to regulation. In the summer it is all right, it's warm and dry; but in winter and autumn it's uncomfortable. At times I have been almost drowned and almost frozen; all sorts of things have happened—wicked people set on me in the forest and took away my bag; I've been beaten, and I've been before a court of law.'

'What were you accused of?'

'Of fraud.'

'How do you mean?'

'Why, you see, Khrisanf Grigoryev, the clerk, sold the contractor some boards belonging to someone else—cheated him, in fact. I was mixed up in it. They sent me to the tavern for vodka; well, the clerk did not share with me—did not even offer me a glass; but as through my poverty I was—in appearance, I mean—not a man to be relied upon, not a man of any worth, we were both brought to trial; he was sent to prison, but, praise God! I was acquitted on all counts. They read a notice, you know, in the court. And they were all in uniforms—in the court, I mean. I can tell you, Your Honour, my duties for anyone not used to them are terrible, absolutely killing; but to me it's nothing. In fact, my feet ache when I am not walking. And at home it is worse for me. At home you have to stoke the stove for the clerk in the district office, fetch water for him, and clean his boots.'

'And what wages do you get?' Lyzhin asked.

'Eighty-four roubles a year.'

'I'll bet you get other little sums coming in. You do, don't you?'

'Other little sums? No, indeed! Gentlemen nowadays don't often give tips. Gentlemen nowadays are strict, they take offence at anything. If you bring them a notice they are offended, if you take off your cap before them they are offended. "You have come to the wrong entrance," they say. "You are a drunkard," they say. "You smell of onion; you are a block-head; you are the son of a bitch." There are kind-hearted ones, of course; but what do you get from them? They only laugh and call you all sorts of names. Mr Altukhin, for instance, he is a good-natured gentleman; and if you look at him he seems sober and in his right mind, but as soon as he sees me he shouts and does not know what he means himself. He gave me such a name. "You," said he . . .' The constable uttered some word, but in such a low voice that it was impossible to make out what he said.

'What?' Lyzhin asked. 'Say it again.'

' "Administration",' the constable repeated aloud. 'He has been calling me that for a long while, for the last six years. "Hallo, Administration!" But I don't mind; let him, who cares? Sometimes a lady will send a glass of vodka and a bit of pie, and you drink to her health. But peasants give more; peasants are more kind-hearted, they have the fear of God in their hearts: one will give a morsel of bread, another a drop of cabbage soup, another will stand you a glass. The village elders treat you to tea in the tavern. Now the witnesses have gone to their tea. "Loshadin," they said, "you stay here and keep watch for us," and they gave me a kopeck each. You see, they are frightened, not being used to it, and yesterday they gave me fifteen kopecks and brought me a glass.'

'And you, aren't you frightened?'

'I am, sir; but of course it's my duty, there is no getting away from it. In the summer I was taking a convict to the town, and he set upon me and gave me such a drubbing! And all around were fields, forest—how could I get away from him? It's just the same here. I remember the gentleman, Mr Lesnitsky, when he was so high, and I knew his father and mother. I am from the village of Nedoshchotova, and they, the Lesnitsky family, were only three-quarters of a mile from us, even less, their land's next to ours. And old Mr Lesnitsky had an unmarried sister, a God-fearing and tender-hearted lady. Lord keep the soul of Thy servant Yuliya, eternal memory to her! She never married, and when she was dying she divided all her property; she left three hundred acres to the monastery, and six hundred to the commune of peasants of Nedoshchotova to pray for her soul; but her brother, the master, hid the will, they do say he burnt it in the stove, and took all the land for himself. He thought, to be sure, it was to his advantage; but—nay, wait a bit, you won't get on in the world through injustice, brother. The master did not go to confession for twenty years after. He kept away from the church, to be sure, and died unrepentant. He burst. He was a very fat man, so he burst lengthways. Then everything was taken from the young master, from Seryozha, to pay the debts—everything there was. Well, he had not gone very far in his studies, he couldn't do anything, and the chairman of the Rural Board, his uncle—"I'll take him"—Seryozha, I mean—thinks he, "for an agent; let him collect the insurance, that's not a difficult job." But the gentleman was young and proud, he wanted to be living on a grander scale and in better style and with more freedom. To be sure, it was a comedown for him to be jolting about the district in a wretched cart and talking to the peasants; he would walk and keep looking at the ground, looking and saying nothing; if you called his name right in his ear, "Sergey Sergeich!" he would look round like this, "Eh?" and look down at the ground again. And now you see he has laid hands on himself. There's no sense in it, Your Honour, it's not right, and there's no making out what's the meaning of it, merciful Lord! Say your father was rich and you are poor; that hurts, of course, but there, you have to put up with it. I used to live in good style, too; I had two horses, Your Honour, three cows, I used to keep twenty head of sheep; but the time has come, and I am left with nothing but a wretched bag, and even that is not mine but Government property. And now in our Nedoshchotova, if the truth be told, my house is the worst of the lot. From riches to rags—that's my path.'

'How was it you became so poor?' asked the examining magistrate.

'My sons knock back the vodka. I can't tell you how they drink, you wouldn't believe it.'

Lyzhin listened and thought how he, Lyzhin, would go back sooner or later to Moscow, while this old man would stay here for ever, and would always be walking and walking. And how many times in his life he would meet such battered, unkempt old men, men 'not of any worth', in whose souls were somehow blended fifteen kopecks, a glass of vodka, and a profound belief that you won't get on in this world through injustice.

Then he grew tired of listening, and told the old man to bring him some hay for his bed. There was an iron bedstead with a pillow and a quilt in the travellers' room, and it could be fetched in; but the dead man had been lying by it for nearly three days (and perhaps sitting on it just before his death), and it would be disagreeable to sleep upon it now . . .

'It's only half-past seven,' thought Lyzhin, glancing at his watch. 'How awful!'

He was not sleepy, but having nothing to do to pass away the time, he lay down and covered himself with a rug. Loshadin went in and out several times, clearing away the tea-things; smacking his lips and sighing, he kept tramping round the table; at last he took his little lamp and went out, and, looking at his long grey hair and his bent figure from behind, Lyzhin thought:

'Just like a wizard in an opera.'

It was dark. The moon must have been behind the clouds, as the windows and the snow on the window-frames could be seen distinctly.

'Oo-oo-oo-oo!' sang the storm. 'Oo-oo-oo-oo!'

'Ho-ho-ly Sa-aints!' wailed a woman in the loft, or it sounded like that. 'Ho-ho-ly Sa-aints!'

'B-bookh!' something outside banged against the wall. 'Trakh!'

The examining magistrate listened: there was no woman up there, it was the wind howling. He felt cold, and he put his fur coat over his rug. As he got warm he thought how far all this—the snowstorm, and the hut, and the old man, and the dead body lying in the next room—how far it all was from the life he would have chosen for himself, and how alien it all was to him, how petty, and uninteresting. If this man had killed himself in Moscow or somewhere near Moscow, and he had had to hold an inquest there, it would have been interesting, important, and perhaps he might even have been afraid to sleep in the next room to the corpse. Here, nearly a thousand miles from Moscow, everything appeared somehow in a different light; it was not life, they were not human beings, but something only existing 'according to regulation', as Loshadin would have said; all this would leave not the faintest trace in his memory, and would be forgotten as soon as he, Lyzhin, drove away from Syrnya. The motherland, the real Russia, was Moscow, Petersburg; but here he was in the provinces, the colonies. When one dreamed of playing a leading role, of becoming popular, of being, for instance, examining magistrate in particularly important cases or prosecutor in a circuit court, of being a society lion, one always thought of Moscow. To live, one must be in Moscow; here one cared for nothing, grew easily resigned to one's insignificant role, and expected only one thing of life—to get out and away as quickly as possible. And in his imagination Lyzhin moved about the Moscow streets, went into the familiar houses, met his relatives, his comrades, and there was a sweet pang in his heart at the thought that he was only twenty-six, and that if in five or ten years he could break away from here and get to Moscow, even then it would not be too late and he would still have a whole life before him. And as he sank into oblivion, as his thoughts became confused, he imagined the long corridors of the court in Moscow, himself delivering a speech, his sisters, the orchestra which for some reason kept droning: 'Oo-oo-oo! Oo-oo-oo!'

'B-bookh! Trakh!' sounded again. 'Bookh!'

And he suddenly recalled how one day, when he was talking to the bookkeeper in the little office of the Rural Board, a thin, pale gentleman with black hair and dark eyes walked in; he had a disagreeable look in his eyes such as one sees in people who have slept too long after dinner, and it spoilt his delicate, intelligent profile; and the high boots he was wearing did not suit him, but looked clumsy. The bookkeeper had introduced him: 'This is our zemstvo agent.'

'So that was Lesnitsky . . . this same man . . .' Lyzhin reflected now.

He recalled Lesnitsky's soft voice, imagined his gait, and it seemed to him that someone was walking beside him now with a step like Lesnitsky's.

All at once he felt frightened, his head turned cold.

'Who's there?' he asked in alarm.

'The conshtable!'

'What do you want here?'

'I have come to ask, Your Honour—you said this evening that you did not want the elder, but I am afraid he may be angry. He told me to go to him. Shouldn't I go?'

'That's enough, you bother me,' said Lyzhin with vexation, and he covered himself up again.

'He may be angry . . . I'll go, Your Honour. I hope you will be comfortable,' and Loshadin went out.

In the passage there was coughing and murmuring. The witnesses must have returned.

'We'll let those poor beggars get away early tomorrow . . .' thought the examining magistrate; 'we'll begin the inquest as soon as it is daylight.'

He began sinking into oblivion when suddenly there were steps again, not timid this time but rapid and noisy. There was the slam of a door, voices, the scratching of a match . . .

'Are you asleep? Are you asleep?' Dr Starchenko was asking him hurriedly and angrily as he struck one match after another; he was covered with snow, and brought a chill air in with him. 'Are you asleep? Get up! Let's go to von Taunitz's. He has sent his own horses for you. Come along. There, at any rate, you will have supper, and sleep like a human being. You see, I've come for you myself. The horses are splendid, we shall be there in twenty minutes.'

'And what time is it now?'

'A quarter past ten.'

Lyzhin, sleepy and discontented, put on his felt overboots, his fur-lined coat, his cap and hood, and went out with the doctor. The frost was not very severe, but a violent and piercing wind was blowing and driving along the street clouds of snow which seemed to be racing away in terror; high drifts were heaped up already under the fences and at the doorways. The doctor and the examining magistrate got into the sledge, and the white coachman bent over them to button up the cover. They were both hot.

'We're off!'

They drove through the village. 'Cutting a feathery furrow,' thought the examining magistrate listlessly, watching the action of the trace-horse's legs. There were lights in all the huts, as though it were the eve of a great holiday: the peasants had not gone to bed because they were afraid of the dead body. The coachman preserved a sullen silence, probably he had felt bored while waiting by the zemstvo hut, and now he, too, was thinking of the dead man.

'At the Taunitzs',' said Starchenko, 'they all set upon me when they heard that you were left to spend the night in the hut, and asked me why I did not bring you with me.'

As they drove out of the village, at the turning the coachman suddenly shouted at the top of his voice: 'Get out of the way!'

They caught a glimpse of a man: he was standing up to his knees in the snow, moving off the road and staring at the horses. The examining magistrate saw a stick with a crook, and a beard and a bag, and he fancied that it was Loshadin, and even fancied that he was smiling. He flashed by and disappeared.

The road ran at first along the edge of the forest, then along a broad

387

forest clearing; they caught glimpses of old pines and a young birch-copse, and tall, gnarled young oak-trees standing singly in the glades where the wood had lately been cut; but soon the air was blurred in clouds of snow. The coachman said he could see the forest; the examining magistrate could see nothing but the trace-horse. The wind blew on their backs.

All at once the horses stopped.

'Well, what is it now?' asked Starchenko crossly.

The coachman got down from the box without a word and began running round the sledge, treading on his heels; he made larger and larger circles, getting further and further away from the sledge, and it looked as though he were dancing; at last he came back and began to turn off to the right.

'You've lost the road, eh?' asked Starchenko.

'It's all ri-ight . . .'

Then there was a little village and not a single light in it. Again the forest and the fields. Again they lost the road, and the coachman got down from the box and danced. The sledge flew along a dark avenue, flew swiftly on. And the fiery trace-horse's hoofs knocked against the front of the sledge. Here there was a fearful roaring sound from the trees, and nothing could be seen, as though they were flying towards an abyss; and all at once the bright light of an entrance and windows flashed upon their eyes, and they heard the good-natured barking of dogs, and voices . . . They had arrived.

While they were taking off their fur coats and felt boots in the hall below, 'Un petit verre de Clicquot' was being played on the piano upstairs, and they could hear children beating time with their feet. Immediately on going in they were aware of the snug warmth and special smell of the old apartments of a mansion where, whatever the weather outside, life is so warm and clean and comfortable.

'That's capital!' said von Taunitz, a fat man with an incredibly thick neck and with whiskers, as he shook the examining magistrate's hand. 'That's capital! You are very welcome, delighted to make your acquaintance. We are colleagues to some extent, you know. At one time I was deputy prosecutor; but not for long, only two years. I came here to look after the estate, and here I have grown old—an old fogey, in fact. You are very welcome,' he went on, evidently restraining his voice so as not to speak too loud; he was going upstairs with his guests. 'I have no wife, she's dead. But here, I will introduce my daughters,' and, turning round, he shouted down the stairs in a voice of thunder: 'Tell Ignat to have the sledge ready at eight o'clock tomorrow morning.'

His four daughters, young and pretty girls, all wearing grey dresses and with their hair done up in the same style, and their cousin, also young and attractive, with her children, were in the drawing-room. Starchenko, who knew them already, began at once to beg them to sing something, and two of the young ladies spent a long time declaring they could not sing and that they had no music; then the cousin sat down to the piano, and with trembling voices, they sang a duet from *The Queen of Spades*. Again 'Un petit verre de Clicquot' was played, and the children skipped about, beating time with their feet. And Starchenko skipped about too. Everybody roared with laughter.

Then the children said good night and went off to bed. The examining magistrate laughed, danced a quadrille, flirted, and kept wondering whether it was not all a dream? The section for the common people in the zemstvo hut, the heap of hay in the corner, the rustling of cockroaches, the revolting poverty-stricken surroundings, the voices of the witnesses, the wind, the snowstorm, the danger of losing the road; and then all at once these magnificent, bright rooms, the sounds of the piano, lovely girls, curly-headed children, the gay, happy laughter—such a transformation seemed to him like a fairy-tale, and it seemed incredible that such transformations were possible within the space of some two miles, and in the course of one hour. And dreary thoughts prevented him from enjoying himself, and he kept thinking this was not life here, but bits of life, fragments, that everything here was accidental, that one could draw no conclusions from it; and he even felt sorry for these girls, who were living and would end their lives here in the wilds, in the provinces, far away from cultured surroundings, where nothing is accidental, but everything is in accordance with reason and law, and where, for instance, every suicide is intelligible, so that one can explain why it has happened and what its significance is in the general scheme of things. He supposed that if the life surrounding him here in the wilds were not intelligible to him, and if he could not see it, this meant that it did not exist at all.

At supper the conversation turned to Lesnitsky.

'He left a wife and child,' said Starchenko. 'I would forbid neurotics, and all people whose nervous system is out of order, to marry; I would deprive them of the right and possibility of multiplying their kind. To bring into the world children suffering from nervous disorder is a crime.'

'He was an unfortunate young man,' said von Taunitz, sighing gently and shaking his head. 'What a lot one must suffer and think about before one brings oneself to take one's own life . . . a young life! Such a misfortune may happen in any family, and that is awful. It is hard to bear such a thing, insufferable . . .'

And all the girls listened in silence with grave faces, looking at their father. Lyzhin felt that he, too, must say something, but he couldn't think of anything, and merely said:

'Yes, suicide is an undesirable phenomenon.'

He slept in a warm room, in a soft bed covered with a quilt under which there were fine clean sheets, but for some reason he did not feel comfortable; perhaps because the doctor and von Taunitz were, for a long time, talking in the adjoining room, and overhead he heard, above the ceiling and in the stove, the snowstorm roaring just as in the zemstvo hut, and as plaintively howling: 'Oo-oo-oo-oo!'

Taunitz's wife had died two years before, and he was still unable to resign himself to his loss and, whatever he was talking about, always mentioned his wife; and there was no trace of a prosecutor left about him now.

'Is it possible that I could ever reach such a state?' thought Lyzhin, as he fell asleep, still hearing through the wall his host's subdued, almost bereaved, voice.

The examining magistrate did not sleep soundly. He felt hot and uncomfortable, and it seemed to him in his sleep that he was not in Taunitz's house, and not in a soft clean bed, but still on the hay in the zemstvo hut, hearing the murmur of the witnesses; he fancied that Lesnitsky was close by, not fifteen paces away. In his dreams he remembered again how the zemstvo agent, black-haired and pale, wearing dusty high boots, had come into the bookkeeper's office. 'This is our zemstvo agent . . .'

Then he dreamed that Lesnitsky and Loshadin the constable were walking through the open country in the snow, side by side, supporting each other; the snowstorm was whirling above them, the wind was blowing on their backs, but they walked on, singing: 'We go on, and on, and on . . .'

The old man was like a wizard in an opera, and both of them were singing as though they were on the stage:

'We go on, and on, and on . . . You are in the warmth, in the light and snugness, but we are walking in the frost and the storm, through the deep snow . . . We know nothing of ease, we know nothing of joy . . . We bear all the burden of this life, yours and ours . . . Oo-oo-oo! We go on, and on, and on . . .'

Lyzhin woke and sat up in bed. What a confused, nasty dream! And why had he dreamed of the constable and the agent together? What nonsense! And now while Lyzhin's heart was throbbing violently and he was sitting on his bed, holding his head in his hands, it seemed to him that there really was something in common between the lives of this insurance agent and the constable. Had they not indeed gone side by side in life, holding on to one another? Some link, invisible, but significant and essential, existed between them, even between them and Taunitz and between all men, all men; in this life, even in the remotest wilds, nothing is accidental, everything is imbued by a single common idea, everything has one soul, one aim, and, to understand this, it is not enough to think, it is not enough to reason, one must have also, it seems, the gift of insight into life, a gift which is evidently not bestowed on all. And the unfortunate man who had broken down and killed himself—the 'neurotic', as the doctor called him—and the old peasant who spent every day of his life going from one man to another, were only accidental, were fragments of life for someone who thought of his own life as accidental, but were parts of one organism—marvellous and rational—for someone who thought of his own life as part of that universal whole and understood it. So thought Lyzhin, and it was a thought that had long lain hidden in his soul, and only now had it unfolded broadly and clearly in his conscious mind.

He lay down and began to fall asleep; and again they were going along together, singing: 'We go on, and on, and on . . . We take from life what is hardest and bitterest in it, and we leave you what is easy and joyful; and sitting at supper, you can coldly and sensibly discuss why we suffer and perish, and why we are not as healthy and contented as you.'

What they were singing had occurred to him before, but that thought had been somewhere in the background behind his other thoughts, and flickered timidly like a distant light in foggy weather. And he felt that this suicide and the peasant's sufferings lay upon his conscience, too; to resign oneself to the fact that these people, submissive to their fate, had taken up the burden of what was hardest and darkest in life—how awful! To resign oneself to that, while desiring for oneself a life full of light and vivacity among happy, contented people, and to be continually dreaming of such a life, means dreaming of further suicides of men crushed by toil and anxiety, or of the weak and the outcast of whom people only talk sometimes at supper with annoyance or mockery, without going to their help . . . And again:

'We go on, and on, and on . . .' as though someone were beating with a hammer on his temples.

He woke early in the morning with a headache, roused by a noise; in the next room von Taunitz was saying loudly to the doctor:

'It's impossible for you to go now. See what it's like outside! Don't argue, you had better ask the coachman; he won't take you in such weather for a million.'

'But it's only two miles,' said the doctor in an imploring voice.

'Even if it were only half a mile. If you can't, then you can't. Directly you drive out of the gates it is sheer hell, you would be off the road in a minute. Nothing will induce me to let you go, you can say what you like.'

'It's bound to be quieter towards evening,' said the peasant who was stoking the stove.

And in the next room the doctor began talking of the rigorous climate and its influence on the Russian character, of the long winters which, by preventing the freedom of movement, hinder the intellectual develop-ment of the people; and Lyzhin listened with annoyance to these observations and looked out of the window at the snowdrifts, piled up against the fence. He gazed at the white dust which covered the whole visible expanse, at the trees which bowed their heads despairingly to right and then to left, listened to the howling and the banging, and thought gloomily:

'Well, what moral can anyone draw? It's a blizzard and that's all . . .'

At midday they had lunch, then wandered aimlessly about the house; they went to the windows.

'And Lesnitsky is lying there,' thought Lyzhin, watching the whirling snow, which raced furiously round and round upon the drifts. 'Lesnitsky is lying there, the witnesses are waiting . . .'

They talked of the weather, saying that the snowstorm usually lasted two days and nights, rarely longer. At six o'clock they had dinner, then they played cards, sang, danced; finally, they had supper. The day was over, they went to bed.

In the night, towards morning, everything calmed down. When they got up and looked out of the windows, the bare willows with their feebly drooping branches were standing perfectly motionless; it was dull and still, as if nature now were ashamed of its orgy, of its mad nights, and the licence it had given to its passions. The horses, harnessed in tandem, had been waiting at the front door since five o'clock in the morning. When it was fully daylight the doctor and the examining magistrate put on their fur coats and felt boots, and, saying goodbye to their host, went out.

At the steps beside the coachman stood the familiar figure of the con-shtable, Ilya Loshadin, with an old leather bag across his shoulder and no cap on his head, all covered with snow, and his face was red and wet with perspiration. The footman who had come out to help the guests into the sledge and cover their legs looked at him sternly and said:

'What are you standing here for, you old devil? Clear off!'

'Your Honour, the people are anxious,' said Loshadin, smiling naïvely all over his face, and evidently pleased at seeing at last the people he had waited for so long. 'The people are very anxious, the children are crying . . . They thought, Your Honour, that you had gone back to the town again. Show us Divine mercy, be our benefactors . . .'

The doctor and the examining magistrate said nothing, got into the sledge, and drove to Syrnya.

The Darling

Olenka, the daughter of retired collegiate assessor Plemyannikov, sat on the porch in her yard, lost in thought. It was hot, the flies wouldn't leave her alone, and it was bliss to think it would soon be evening. Dark rain-clouds were moving up from the east, preceded by occasional wafts of humid air.

In the middle of the yard Snookin, manager-proprietor of the Tivoli Pleasure Gardens, who lodged across the yard in Olenka's *fliegel*, stood gazing at the sky.

'Not again!' he was saying in despair. 'Not rain again! Day after day, day after day, rain, rain, rain! Just my luck! What I have to put up with! I'm ruined! I'm losing huge sums every day!'

Throwing up his hands, he turned to Olenka and said:

'You see what our life's like, Olga Semyonovna. Enough to make you weep! You work hard and do your best, you worry and have sleepless nights, you're always thinking of improvements—and what's the result? Take audiences for a start. They're nothing but ignorant savages. I give them the best operetta and pantomime, top-quality burlesque, but is that what they want? Do they appreciate it? No, they want some vulgar little peepshow. Then take the weather. Rain almost every evening. The tenth of May it started, and it's been at it right through May and June. Appalling! The public stays away, but who has to pay the rent, I ask you? Who has to pay the performers?'

Clouds began gathering at the same time next day.

'Oh yes, let it all come!' Snookin said, laughing hysterically. 'Let it flood the whole Gardens and take me with it! I don't deserve any happiness in this world or the next! Let the performers take me to court! Why stop at that? Make it penal servitude in Siberia! The scaffold! Ha-ha-ha!'

It was the same next day . . .

Olenka said nothing but listened to Snookin gravely, and sometimes tears came to her eyes. In the end his misfortunes moved her and she fell in love with him. He was short and skinny, with a sallow complexion and hair combed back off the temples, he spoke in a high-pitched tenor, twisting his mouth as he did so, and his face wore an expression of permanent despair—yet he aroused in her deep and genuine emotion. She was constantly in love with someone and could not live otherwise. Previously she had loved her Papa, now an invalid sitting in his armchair in a darkened room and breathing with difficulty; then she had loved her aunt, who came to visit them every other year from Bryansk; and earlier still she had loved the French master at her school. She was a quiet, good-natured, tender-hearted girl, with soft gentle eyes, and in the best of health. Looking at her plump rosy cheeks and soft white neck with its dark birthmark, at the innocent, kindly smile on her face whenever she was listening to something pleasant, men said to themselves, 'yes, not a bad one, that,' and smiled, too, while her female visitors could not refrain from seizing her by the hand in the middle of a conversation and exclaiming with delight:

'You're such a darling!'

The house she had lived in all her life and was due to inherit stood on the edge of town in Gypsy Lane, not far from the Tivoli, so that in the evenings and at night, hearing the band playing and the rockets going off with a bang, she imagined this was Snookin challenging his fate and taking his chief enemy, the indifferent public, by storm; her heart would melt, she didn't feel a bit sleepy, and when he returned home in the early hours, she would knock softly on her bedroom window and letting him see through the curtains only her face and one shoulder, smile affectionately . . .

He proposed and they were married. Now that he could see her neck and both her plump healthy shoulders properly, he threw up his hands and said:

'You darling, you!'

He was happy, but since it rained on the wedding day *and* on the wedding night, the look of despair never left his face.

Life went well after the marriage. She sat in his box-office, supervised the Gardens, wrote down expenses and paid out salaries, and you'd catch a glimpse of her rosy cheeks and sweetly innocent, radiant smile at the box-office window one moment, behind stage the next, and now in the refreshment bar. Already she was telling her friends that nothing in the world was so remarkable, so important and necessary as the theatre, and only in the theatre could you experience real enjoyment and become an educated, civilised human being.

'But does the public appreciate that?' she would say. 'What they want is a peepshow. Yesterday we did *Faust Inside Out* and almost all the boxes were empty, but if we'd put on something vulgar, me and Vanya, we'd have been packed out, I can tell you. Tomorrow we're doing

Orpheus in the Underworld, me and Vanya, why don't you come?'

Whatever Snookin said about the theatre and the actors, she repeated. Like him, she despised the public for its indifference to art and its ignorance, interfered in rehearsals, corrected the actors and made sure the musicians behaved, and whenever there was a bad notice in the local press, she would cry and then go round to the editorial office to have it out with them.

The actors were fond of her and called her 'Me and Vanya' and 'The Darling'. She felt sorry for them and gave them small loans, and if they let her down, she just had a quiet cry and said nothing to her husband.

Life went well that winter, too. They hired the town theatre for the whole season and rented it out for short periods to a Ukrainian troupe, a conjuror, and the local amateur dramatic company. Olenka put on weight and positively radiated well-being, but Snookin looked thin and sallow, and complained of huge losses, even though business was quite good all winter. At night he coughed and she gave him raspberry or lime-blossom tea to drink, rubbed him with eau-de-Cologne and wrapped him in her soft shawls.

'My wonderful little man!' she would say with complete sincerity, as she stroked his hair. 'My handsome little man!'

During Lent he went off to Moscow to engage a new company, and in his absence she couldn't sleep, but sat by the window looking at the stars. She was like the hens, she thought, which stay awake all night and are restive when the cock isn't in the hen-house. Snookin was delayed in Moscow but said he'd be back by Easter, and his letters were already giving her instructions about the Tivoli. But on the Sunday before Easter, late at night, there was a sudden ominous knocking outside. Someone was banging on the gate until it started booming like a barrel. The sleepy cook ran to answer, her bare feet splashing in the puddles.

'Open up, please!' someone outside was saying in a deep bass. 'Telegram for you!'

Olenka had received telegrams from her husband before, but now for some reason she felt petrified. She opened it with trembling hands and read as follows:

Ivan Petrovich died suddenly today suchly await instructions funreal Tuesday.

That was what the telegram said, 'funreal' and the other meaningless word 'suchly'; it was signed by the producer of the operetta company.

'My precious!' Olenka sobbed. 'My sweet precious little Vanya! Why did I ever meet you? Why did I come to know you and love you? Who's going to look after your poor wretched Olenka now you've abandoned her?'

Snookin was buried on the Tuesday at the Vagankovo Cemetery in Moscow. Olenka returned home on Wednesday and as soon as she entered her room, flung herself down on the bed and sobbed so loudly she could be heard in the street and the neighbouring yards.

'Poor darling!' the women neighbours said, crossing themselves. 'She *is* taking it badly, poor darling Olga Semyonovna!'

Three months later Olenka, in full mourning, was returning home sadly one day from church. It so happened that a neighbour of hers, Vasily Andreich Pustovalov, manager of the merchant Babakayev's timber-yard, was also returning from church and walking alongside her. He was wearing a straw hat and a white waistcoat with a gold watch-chain, and looked more like a landowner than a tradesman.

'Everything has to take its proper course, Olga Semyonovna,' he was saying soberly, with a sympathetic note in his voice, 'and if someone dear to us dies, that means it is God's wish, so we must contain ourselves and bear it with resignation.'

After seeing Olenka to her gate, he said goodbye and walked on. For the rest of the day she kept hearing that sober voice, and she had only to close her eyes to picture his dark beard to herself. She liked him very much. Evidently she had made an impression on him, too, for not long afterwards an elderly lady, whom she scarcely knew, came to drink coffee with her, and had no sooner sat down at the table than she started talking about Pustovalov, what a good, reliable man he was and how any young lady would be delighted to have him for a husband. Three days later Pustovalov himself paid her a visit, stayed no more than about ten minutes and said little, but Olenka fell for him so completely that she lay awake all night feeling hot and feverish, and next morning sent for the elderly lady. The match was quickly arranged, then came the wedding.

Life went well for Pustovalov and Olenka after their marriage. He would usually stay at the timber-yard until lunch and then go out on business, whereupon Olenka would take his place and stay in the office until evening, doing the accounts and despatching orders.

'Timber's going up by twenty per cent a year now,' she would tell customers and friends. 'In the past we used to get our timber locally, but now, imagine, my Vasya has to fetch it every year from Mogilyov

Province. And the freight charges!' she would say, covering both cheeks with her hands in horror. 'The freight charges!'

She felt that she had been dealing in timber for ages and ages, and it was the most vitally important thing in life, and the words joist, batten, offcut, purlin, round beam, short beam, frame and slab, were like dear old friends to her. At night she dreamed of whole mountains of boards and battens, of never-ending convoys of carts carrying timber somewhere far beyond the town; she dreamed of a whole regiment of beams, thirty feet by nine inches, marching upright into battle against the timber-yard, and how beams, joists and slabs banged together with the resounding thud of dry wood, falling over and then righting themselves, piling up on top of each other. Olenka would cry out in her sleep and Pustovalov would say to her tenderly:

'What's the matter, Olenka dear? Better cross yourself!'

Whatever thoughts her husband had, she had also. If he thought the room was too hot or business had become quiet, she thought the same. Her husband did not like any entertainments and on holidays stayed at home; so did she.

'You're always at home or in the office,' friends said to her. 'You should go to the theatre, darling, or the circus.'

'Me and Vasya have no time for theatres,' she replied soberly. 'We're working folk, we can't be bothered with trifles. What do people see in those theatres, anyway?'

On Saturdays she and Pustovalov attended the all-night vigil, and on feast days early-morning service. Afterwards, walking home side by side, they both looked deeply moved, they smelt fragrant, and her silk dress rustled agreeably. At home they drank tea, with rich white bread and various jams, then they had pie. Every day at noon the yard and the street outside the gates were filled with the appetising smell of borsch and roast lamb or duck, or fish on fast days, and no one could walk past without beginning to feel hungry. In the office the samovar was always on the boil, and customers were treated to tea and buns. Once a week the couple went to the baths and walked home side by side, both red in the face.

'We're not complaining,' Olenka told her friends. 'Life's going well, praise be to God. May God grant everyone as good a life as me and Vasya.'

When Pustovalov went off to Mogilyov Province for timber, she missed him terribly and could not sleep at night for crying. Sometimes she had an evening visit from the young man renting her *fliegel*, a regimental vet called Smirnin. He would tell her about something or they'd play cards, and this cheered her up. She was particularly interested to hear about his own family life: he was married with a son, but had separated from his wife because she'd been unfaithful, and now he hated her and sent her forty roubles a month for the boy's maintenance. As she listened, Olenka sighed and shook her head, and felt sorry for him.

'The Lord be with you,' she would say, bidding him good night and lighting him to the top of the stairs with a candle. 'It was kind of you to while away your time with me, may God and the Holy Mother watch over you . . .'

She always expressed herself in the same sober, judicious tones, imitating her husband. The vet was already disappearing behind the downstairs door when she would call him back and say:

'Vladimir Platonych, don't you think you should make it up with your wife? Forgive her, if only for your son's sake! That little chap knows just what's going on, be sure of that.'

When Pustovalov returned, she would tell him in a hushed voice about the vet and his unhappy family situation, and both would sigh, shake their heads and talk of how the boy must be missing his father; then, by some strange association of ideas they would both kneel before the icons, prostrate themselves and pray that God might send them children.

Thus did the Pustovalovs live for six years, quietly and peacefully, in love and complete harmony. But one winter's day at the yard Vasily Andreich went out bareheaded to despatch some timber after drinking hot tea, caught cold and fell ill. He was treated by the best doctors, but the illness took its course and he died four months later.

Olenka had become a widow again.

'Who will look after me now, my precious?' she sobbed, after burying her husband. 'How can I possibly live without you? I'm so wretched and unhappy! Pity me, good people, I'm all alone now . . .'

She wore a black dress with weepers, having vowed never to wear a hat or gloves again, went out seldom and then only to church or to her husband's grave, and lived at home like a nun. Six months passed before she discarded the weepers and began opening her shutters. Some mornings she was to be seen shopping for food in the market with her cook, but people could only surmise how she was living now and what her domestic arrangements were. They surmised when they saw her, for example, sitting in her little garden drinking tea with the vet while he read the newspaper out to her, and also when she bumped into a female friend at the post office and was heard to say:

'Our town has no proper veterinary inspection and that gives rise to many illnesses. You're always hearing of people being infected by milk or catching diseases from horses and cows. We really ought to treat the health of domestic animals as seriously as we do that of human beings.'

She repeated the vet's thoughts and now shared his opinions on everything. It was clear that she could not survive even for a year without an attachment and had found her new happiness in the *fliegel* next door. Anyone else would have been condemned for this, but no one could think ill of Olenka, her whole life was so transparent. She and the vet did not tell anyone about the change that had taken place in their relationship and tried to conceal it, but without success, because Olenka could not keep a secret. When regimental colleagues came to visit him and she was pouring out their tea or serving supper, she would start talking about cattle plague, pearl disease, and the municipal slaughter-houses. This made him terribly embarrassed, and as the guests were leaving, he would seize her by the arm and hiss angrily:

'Haven't I told you before not to talk about things you don't understand? When we vets are talking shop, please don't butt in. It's extremely tedious.'

She would look at him in alarm and astonishment, and say:

'But Volodya dear, what *am* I to talk about?!'

With tears in her eyes she embraced him and begged him not to be angry, and they were both happy.

But this happiness did not last long. The vet departed with his regiment, and since they had been transferred somewhere very distant, practically to Siberia, his departure was permanent.

Olenka was left on her own.

This time she was completely on her own. Her father had long since died, and his armchair, with one leg missing, was gathering dust in the attic. She became plain and thin, and people meeting her in the street no longer looked at her and smiled as they used to; her best years were evidently gone for good, now a new, unknown life was beginning that did not bear thinking about. In the evenings Olenka sat on her porch and could hear the band playing and the rockets going off at the Tivoli, but this no longer made her think of anything. She gazed apathetically at her empty yard, had no thoughts or desires, and when night fell, went to bed and dreamed of her empty yard. She seemed reluctant even to eat or drink.

But the worst thing of all was no longer having any opinions. She saw objects round her and understood everything that was going on, but she could not form opinions about anything and did not know what to talk about. How awful it is not to have an opinion! You see a bottle, for example, standing there, or the rain falling, or a peasant going along in his cart, but what the bottle or rain or peasant are for, what sense they make, you can't say and couldn't say, even if they offered you a thousand roubles. In Snookin's and Pustovalov's time, and then with the vet, Olenka could explain everything and give her opinion on any subject you liked, whereas now her mind and heart were as empty as the yard outside. It was a horrible, bitter sensation, like a mouthful of wormwood.

The town has gradually expanded in all directions. Gypsy Lane is now called a street, and where the Tivoli and the timber-yards once stood, houses have sprung up and there are a number of side-streets. How time flies! Olenka's house looks dingy, the roof has rusted, the shed is leaning to one side, and the yard is completely overgrown with weeds and stinging nettles. Olenka herself has grown older and plainer. In summer she sits on her porch, with the same feeling of emptiness, boredom and bitterness in her soul as before, in winter she sits by her window gazing at the snow. If she feels the breath of spring, or hears the sound of cathedral bells carried on the wind, memories suddenly flood in, tugging at her heart-strings, and copious tears stream down her face; but this lasts only a minute, then the same emptiness and sense of futility returns. Her black cat Bryska snuggles up to her, purring softly, but Olenka is unmoved by these feline caresses. Is that what she needs? No, she needs the kind of love that will possess her completely, mind and soul, that will provide her with thoughts and a direction in life, and warm her ageing blood. She bundles black Bryska off her lap and says irritably:

'Go away . . . I don't want you here!'

It's the same day after day, year after year—she doesn't have a single joy in life or a single opinion. Whatever Mavra the cook says is good enough.

One hot July day, towards evening, when the town cattle were being driven past and clouds of dust had filled the yard, all of a sudden someone knocked at the gate. Olenka went to open it herself, took one look and was completely dumbfounded: Smirnin the vet was standing there, grey-haired and in civilian clothes. Suddenly everything came back to her, she broke down and burst into tears, laid her head on his chest without saying a word, and was so overcome that afterwards she had no recollection of how they went into the house together and sat down to drink tea.

'Vladimir Platonych,' she murmured, trembling with joy, 'dearest! Whatever brings you here?'

'I'd like to settle down here permanently,' he told her. 'I've resigned my commission and come to try my luck as a civilian, leading a settled life. Then there's my son, he's growing up and it's time he went to grammar school. I've made it up with my wife, you know.'

'And where is she now?' Olenka asked.

'At the hotel with the boy while I go round looking for lodgings.'

'But good heavens, have *my* house, dear! Far better than lodgings. Oh heavens above, I don't want any rent,' Olenka went on, becoming agitated and bursting into tears again. 'You live here and the *fliegel* will do for me. Wonderful!'

Next day they were already painting the roof and whitewashing the walls, and Olenka was walking about the yard, arms on hips, giving orders. Her face shone with its old smile, and everything about her was fresh and lively, as if she had just woken from a long sleep. The vet's wife arrived, a thin, unattractive woman with short hair and a peevish expression. With her came the boy, Sasha, who was small for his age (he was over nine) and chubby, with bright blue eyes and dimpled cheeks. He had no sooner set foot in the yard than he began chasing the cat, and his merry, joyful laughter rang out.

'Is that your cat, Auntie?' he asked Olenka. 'When it has babies, will you give us one, please? Mamma's scared stiff of mice.'

Olenka chatted to him and gave him tea, and suddenly felt a warm glow and pleasurable tightening in her heart, as if this boy were her own son. And when he was sitting in the dining-room repeating his lessons in the evenings, she would look at him with tenderness and pity, and whisper:

'My precious, my pretty little child . . . You're so clever and your skin is so fair.'

'An island,' he read out, 'is an area of dry land surrounded on all sides by water.'

'An island is an area of dry land . . .' she repeated, and this was the first opinion she had expressed with confidence after all those years of silence and emptiness of mind.

Now she had her own opinions and talked to Sasha's parents over supper about how hard children had to work at grammar school these days, but all the same a classical education was better than a modern one, because every career was open to you afterwards—doctor, engineer, whatever you wished.

Sasha had begun attending the grammar school. His mother went away to her sister's in Kharkov and did not come back, his father went off somewhere every day to inspect herds and might be away for three days at a time, and Olenka felt that Sasha was being completely neglected, his parents didn't want him and he must be starving to death; so she transferred him to her *fliegel* and fixed him up in a little room there.

Six months have now passed since Sasha began living in her *fliegel*. Every morning Olenka goes into his room: he is fast asleep with his hand under his cheek, breathing imperceptibly. She is sorry to have to wake him.

'Sashenka,' she says sadly, 'get up, dear! Time for school.'

He gets up, dresses, says his prayers, and then sits down to drink tea; he drinks three glasses and consumes two large rolls and half a French loaf with butter. Still not fully awake, he is in a bad mood.

'You didn't learn your fable properly, you know, Sashenka,' Olenka says, looking at him as if about to see him off on a long journey. 'What a worry you are to me. You *must* make an effort to learn, dear, and do as the teachers say.'

'Oh, stop nagging!' says Sasha.

Then he walks along the street to school, a small boy in a big cap, with a satchel on his back. Olenka follows silently behind.

'Sashenka-a!' she calls.

He looks round, and she pops a date or a caramel into his hand. When they turn into the school street, he feels ashamed at being followed by this tall, stout woman, looks round and says:

'You go home now, Auntie, I'll do the last bit on my own.'

She stops and keeps her eyes fixed on him until he disappears through the school entrance. Oh, how she loves him! Not one of her previous attachments has been so deep, never before has she surrendered herself so wholeheartedly, unselfishly and joyfully as now, when her maternal feelings are being kindled more and more. For this boy, who is not hers, for his cap and his dimpled cheeks, she would give away her whole life, and do so with gladness and tears of emotion. Why? Who can possibly say why?

After seeing Sasha off, she returns home quietly, feeling so calm and contented, and overflowing with love. In these last six months her face has become younger, she is smiling and radiant, and people meeting

403

her in the street feel pleasure as they look at her, and say:

'Olga Semyonovna darling, good morning! How are you, darling?'

'They have to work so hard at grammar school these days,' she tells them in the market. 'It's no laughing matter. Yesterday the first year had a fable to learn by heart *and* a Latin translation *and* a maths problem . . . How can a small boy cope?'

She goes on to talk about teachers and lessons and textbooks—repeating exactly what Sasha tells her.

Between two and three they have their meal together, and in the evening they do Sasha's homework together and cry. Putting him to bed, she spends a long time making the sign of the cross over him and whispering a prayer, then, on going to bed herself, she pictures that distant hazy future when Sasha has finished his degree and become a doctor or an engineer, has his own large house with horses and a carriage, marries and has children . . . She falls asleep still thinking about it all, and tears run down her cheeks from her closed eyes. The black cat lies purring by her side: mrr, mrr, mrr . . .

Suddenly there's a loud knock at the gate. Olenka wakes up, too terrified to breathe. Her heart is thumping. Half a minute passes, then there's another knock.

'It's a telegram from Kharkov,' she thinks, beginning to tremble all over. 'Sasha's mother wants him to live with her in Kharkov . . . Oh heavens!'

She is in despair. Her head, arms and legs turn cold, she feels the unhappiest person in the world. But another minute passes and she hears voices. It's the vet, he's come back from his club.

'Oh, thank God,' she thinks.

Gradually the pressure on her heart eases and she feels relaxed again. She lies down and thinks of Sasha, who is sleeping soundly in the room next door. From time to time he starts talking in his sleep:

'I'll show you! Get out! Stop fighting!'

The Lady with the Dog

I

It was said that a new person had appeared on the sea-front: a lady with a little dog. Dmitry Dmitrich Gurov had already been a fortnight in Yalta, and grown accustomed to its ways; now he, too, had begun to take an interest in new arrivals. Sitting in Vernet's outside café, he saw, walking on the sea-front, a fair-haired young lady of medium height, wearing a beret; a white Pomeranian dog was running behind her.

And afterwards he met her in the public gardens and in the square several times a day. She walked alone, always wearing the same beret, and accompanied by the white Pomeranian; no one knew who she was, and everyone called her simply 'the lady with the dog'.

'If she is here alone without a husband or friends, it might be worth making her acquaintance,' Gurov reflected.

He was under forty, but he had a daughter already twelve years old, and two sons at school. He had been married young, when he was a student in his second year, and by now his wife seemed half as old again as he. She was a tall, erect woman with dark eyebrows, staid and dignified, and she called herself an 'intellectual'. She read a great deal, favoured changes in spelling, called her husband, not Dmitry, but Dimitry, and he secretly considered her unintelligent, narrow, inelegant, was afraid of her, and did not like to be at home. He had begun being unfaithful to her long ago—had been unfaithful to her often, and, probably on that account, almost always spoke ill of women, and when they were talked about in his presence, used to call them 'the lower race'.

It seemed to him that he had been sufficiently schooled by bitter experience to call them what he liked, and yet he could not live for two days on end without this 'lower race'. In the society of men he was bored and uncomfortable, with them he was cold and uncommunicative; but when he was in the company of women he felt free, and knew what to say to them and how to behave; and he was at ease with them even when he was silent. In his appearance, in his character, in his whole nature, there was something attractive and elusive which allured women and disposed them in his favour; he knew that, and some force seemed to draw him, too, to them.

Experience often repeated, truly bitter experience, had taught him long ago that with decent people, especially Moscow people—always sluggish and irresolute—every intimacy, which at first so agreeably diversifies life and appears as a light and charming adventure, inevitably grows into a vast problem of extreme intricacy, and the situation eventually becomes unbearable. But at every fresh meeting with an interesting woman this experience seemed to slip from his memory, and he was eager for life, and everything seemed so simple and amusing.

One evening he was dining in the gardens, and the lady in the beret came up slowly to take the next table. Her expression, her gait, her dress, and the way she did her hair told him that she was from decent society, and married, that she was in Yalta for the first time and alone, and that she was bored here . . . Stories about the looseness of morals in places like Yalta are largely untrue; he despised them, and knew that such stories were for the most part made up by persons who would themselves have been glad to sin if they had been able; but when the lady sat down at the next table three paces from him, he remembered these tales of easy conquests, of trips to the mountains, and the tempting thought of a swift, fleeting love-affair, a romance with an unknown woman, whose name he did not know, suddenly took possession of him.

He beckoned coaxingly to the Pomeranian, and when the dog came up to him he shook his finger at it. The Pomeranian growled. Gurov shook his finger again.

The lady glanced at him and at once lowered her eyes.

'He doesn't bite,' she said, and blushed.

'May I give him a bone?' And when she nodded he asked courteously, 'Have you been long in Yalta?'

'Five days.'

'Well, I've nearly lasted a fortnight.'

There was a brief silence.

'Time goes fast, and yet it is so boring here!' she said, not looking at him.

'That's only the fashion to say it is boring here. A provincial will live in Belyov or Zhizdra and not be bored, but when he comes here it's "Oh, the boredom! Oh, the dust!" One would think he came from Granada.'

She laughed. Then both continued eating in silence, like strangers, but after dinner they walked side by side; and there sprang up between them the light jesting conversation of people who are free and contented, to whom it does not matter where they go or what they talk about. They walked and talked of the strange light on the sea; the water was of a soft warm lilac hue, and there was a golden streak from the moon upon it. They talked of how sultry it was after a hot day. Gurov told her that he came from Moscow, that he had taken his degree in the arts, but had a post in a bank; that he had trained as an opera-singer, but had given it up, that he owned two houses in Moscow . . . And from her he learnt that she had grown up in Petersburg, but had lived in S—— since her marriage two years ago, that she was staying another month in Yalta, and that her husband, who needed a holiday too, might perhaps come and fetch her. She was not sure whether her husband had a post with the Provincial Council or the Rural Board—and was amused by her own ignorance.

And Gurov learnt, too, that she was called Anna Sergeyevna.

Afterwards he thought about her in his room at the hotel—thought she would certainly meet him next day; that was bound to happen. As he got into bed he recalled that she had been a schoolgirl not long ago, doing lessons like his own daughter; he recalled the diffidence, the stiffness, that was still manifest in her laugh and her manner of talking with a stranger. This must have been the first time in her life she had been alone in surroundings in which she was followed, looked at, and spoken to merely from a secret motive which she could hardly fail to guess. He recalled her slender, delicate neck, her lovely grey eyes.

'There's something pitiful about her, anyway,' he thought, as he started to fall asleep.

II

A week had passed since their first meeting. It was a holiday. Indoors was sultry, while in the streets the wind whirled the dust round and round, and blew people's hats off. It was a thirsty day, and Gurov often went into the café, and pressed Anna Sergeyevna to have syrup and water or an ice. There was no escape from the heat.

In the evening when the wind had dropped a little, they went out on to the pier to see the steamer come in. There were a great many people strolling about on the landing-stage; they had gathered to welcome some-one, bringing bouquets. And two features of the festive Yalta crowd were very conspicuous: the elderly ladies were dressed like young ones, and there were great numbers of generals.

Owing to the roughness of the sea, the steamer arrived late, after the sun had set, and it manoeuvred for a long time before it reached the pier. Anna Sergeyevna gazed through her lorgnette at the steamer and the passengers as though looking for acquaintances, and when she turned to Gurov her eyes were shining. She talked a great deal and asked disconnected questions, forgetting next moment what she had asked; then she lost her lorgnette in the crush.

The festive crowd began to disperse; it was too dark to see people's faces. The wind had completely dropped, but Gurov and Anna Sergeyevna still stood as if waiting for someone else to disembark. Anna Sergeyevna was silent now, and sniffed her flowers without looking at Gurov.

'The weather is better now that it's evening,' he said. 'Where shall we go? Shall we drive somewhere?'

She made no answer.

Then he stared at her intently, and all at once put his arm round her and kissed her on the lips, and breathed in the moisture and the fragrance of her flowers; and he immediately glanced around anxiously, wondering whether anyone had seen them.

'Let's go to your room,' he said softly. And both walked quickly.

In her room it was sultry and smelt of the scent she had bought at the Japanese shop. Gurov looked at her and thought: 'What different people one meets in life!' From the past he preserved memories of light-hearted, good-natured women, who loved cheerfully and were grateful to him for their happiness, however brief it might be; and of women like his wife who loved without any genuine feeling, with superfluous phrases, affectedly, hysterically, with an expression that suggested that it was not love nor passion, but something more significant; and of two or three others, very beautiful, cold women, on whose faces he had glimpsed a rapacious expression—an obstinate desire to snatch from life more than it could give, and these were capricious, unreflecting, domineering, unintelligent women no longer in their first youth, and when Gurov cooled towards them their beauty aroused his hatred, and the lace on their underclothes seemed to him like a lizard's scales.

But in this case there was still the diffidence, the stiffness of inexperienced youth, an awkward feeling; and there was a sense of consternation as if someone had suddenly knocked at the door. The attitude of Anna Sergeyevna—this 'lady with the dog'—to what had happened was somehow peculiar, very grave, as though it were her fall—so it seemed, and it was strange and inappropriate. Her features had sunk and faded, and down each side of her face her long hair hung sadly; she mused in a dejected pose like 'the sinful woman' in an old-fashioned picture.

'It's wrong,' she said. 'You will be the first not to respect me now.'

There was a water-melon on the table. Gurov cut himself a slice and began eating it without haste. There followed at least half an hour of silence.

Anna Sergeyevna was touching; there was about her the purity of a decent, naïve woman who had seen little of life. The solitary candle burning on the table threw a faint light on her face, yet it was clear that she felt very unhappy.

'Why should I lose respect for you?' asked Gurov. 'You don't know what you are saying.'

'God forgive me,' she said, and her eyes filled with tears. 'It's awful.'

'You seem to be trying to justify yourself.'

'Justify? No. I am a bad, low woman; I despise myself and have no thought of justification. It's not my husband but myself I have deceived. And not only just now; I have been deceiving myself for a long time. My husband may be a good, honest man, but he is a lackey! I don't know what he does there, what his work is, but I know he is a lackey! I was twenty when I married him. I was tormented by curiosity; I wanted something better. "There must be a different sort of life," I said to myself. I wanted to live! To live, and live! . . . I was fired by curiosity . . . you don't understand, but, I swear to God, I could not control myself; something happened to me; I could not be restrained. I told my husband I was ill, and came here . . . And here I have been walking about as though I were dazed, like a mad creature; . . . and now I have become a vulgar, contemptible woman whom anyone may despise.'

Gurov felt bored already, listening to her. He was irritated by the naïve tone, by this remorse, so unexpected and inopportune; but for the tears in her eyes, he might have thought she was jesting or acting a role.

'I don't understand,' he said softly. 'What is it you want?'

She hid her face on his breast and pressed close to him.

'Believe me, believe me, I beseech you . . .' she said. 'I love a pure, honest life, and sin is loathsome to me. I don't know what I am doing. Simple people say: "The Evil One has beguiled me." And I may say of myself now that the Evil One has beguiled me.'

'Hush, that's enough! . . .' he muttered.

He looked into her staring, frightened eyes, kissed her, talked softly and affectionately, and gradually she calmed down, and her gaiety returned; they both began to laugh.

Afterwards when they went out there was not a soul on the sea-front. The town with its cypresses seemed quite dead, but the sea still broke noisily on the shore; a single barge was rocking on the waves, and a lantern was blinking sleepily on it.

They found a cab and drove to Oreanda.

'I learnt your surname in the hall just now: it was written on the board—von Diederitz,' said Gurov. 'Is your husband German?'

'No; I believe his grandfather was German, but he is Orthodox Russian himself.'

At Oreanda they sat on a bench not far from the church, looked down at the sea, and were silent. Yalta was barely visible through the morning mist; white clouds stood motionless on the mountain-tops. The leaves did not stir on the trees, cicadas chirred, and the monotonous hollow sound of the sea, rising up from below, spoke of peace, of the eternal sleep that awaits us. So it must have sounded when there was no Yalta, no Oreanda here; so it sounds now, and it will sound as indifferently and monotonously when we are no more. And in this constancy, in this complete indifference to the life and death of each one of us, there lies hidden, perhaps, a pledge of our eternal salvation, of the unceasing movement of life upon earth, of unceasing progress towards perfection. Sitting beside a young woman who in the dawn seemed so lovely, soothed and spellbound in these magical surroundings—the sea, mountains, clouds, the open sky—Gurov reflected that, in essence, if one considers it carefully, everything is beautiful in this world: everything except what we think or do ourselves when we forget the higher aims of existence and our human dignity.

A man walked up to them—probably a watchman—looked at them and walked away. And this detail seemed mysterious and lovely, too. They saw a steamer arrive from Feodosiya, with its lights out, illuminated by the dawn.

'There is dew on the grass,' said Anna Sergeyevna, after a silence.

'Yes. It's time to go home.'

They went back to the town.

Then they met every day at twelve o'clock on the sea-front, lunched and dined together, went for walks, admired the sea. She complained that she slept badly, that her heart throbbed violently; asked the same questions, troubled now by jealousy and now by the fear that he did not respect her sufficiently. And often in the square or gardens, when there was no one near them, he suddenly drew her to him and kissed her passionately. Complete idleness, these kisses in broad daylight, glancing round in fear lest someone see them, the heat, the smell of the sea, and the continual passing to and fro of idle, festive, well-fed people, seemed to transform him; he told Anna Sergeyevna how lovely she was, how fascinating. He was impetuously passionate, he would not move a step away from her, while she was often pensive and continually urged him to admit that he did not respect her, did not love her in the least, and regarded her as nothing but a common woman. Quite late almost every evening they drove somewhere out of town, to Oreanda or to the waterfall; and the expedition was always a success, the scenery invariably impressed them as grand and beautiful.

They were expecting her husband to arrive, but he sent a letter, saying that there was something wrong with his eyes, and begging his wife to come home as quickly as possible. Anna Sergeyevna made haste to leave.

'It's a good thing I am going away,' she said to Gurov. 'This is fate itself.'

She set off by carriage and he accompanied her. They drove for a whole day. When she took her seat in the express train, and when the second bell had rung, she said:

'Let me look at you once more . . . look at you once again. That's right.'

She did not shed tears, but was so sad that she seemed ill, and her face was quivering.

'I shall remember you . . . think of you,' she said. 'God be with you; be happy. Don't think badly of me. We are parting for ever—it must be so, for we ought never to have met. Well, God be with you.'

The train moved off rapidly, its lights soon vanished from sight, and a minute later there was no sound of it, as if everything had conspired to end as quickly as possible that sweet delirium, that madness. Left alone on the platform, and gazing into the dark distance, Gurov listened to the chirp of the grasshoppers and the hum of the telegraph wires, feeling as though he had only just awoken. And he reflected that this had been another episode or adventure in his life, and it, too, was at an end, and nothing was left but a memory . . . He was moved, sad, and felt a slight remorse. This young woman whom he would never meet again had not been happy with him; he had been cordial and affectionate with her, and yet in his manner, his tone, and his caresses there had been a shade of light irony, the coarse condescension of a successful male who was, moreover, almost twice her age. She had always called him kind, exceptional, lofty; obviously he had seemed to her different from what he really was, and so he had unintentionally deceived her . . .

Here at the station there was already a scent of autumn; the evening was cool.

'It's time for me to go north, too,' thought Gurov as he left the platform. 'High time!'

III

Back home in Moscow everything was in its winter routine; the stoves were heated, and in the morning it was still dark when the children were having breakfast and getting ready for school, and the nurse would light the lamp for a short while. The frosts had already begun. When the first snow has fallen, on the first day of sledge-driving it is pleasant to see the white earth, the white roofs, to draw soft, delicious breath, and the season brings back the days of one's youth. The old limes and birches, white with hoar-frost, have a good-natured expression; they are dearer to one's heart than cypresses and palms, and near them one does not yearn for mountains and the sea.

Gurov was Moscow born; he arrived in Moscow on a fine frosty day, and when he put on his fur coat and warm gloves, and walked along Petrovka, and when on Saturday evening he heard the ringing of the bells, his recent trip and the places he had seen lost all charm for him. Little by little he became absorbed in Moscow life, and avidly read three newspapers a day, while claiming that he read no Moscow newspapers on principle! He already felt a longing to go to restaurants, clubs, dinner-parties, anniversary celebrations, and he felt flattered at entertaining distinguished lawyers and actors, and at playing cards with a professor at the doctors' club. He could already eat a whole portion of 'hotpot' straight from the frying-pan . . .

In another month, he fancied, the image of Anna Sergeyevna would be shrouded in mist in his memory, and only from time to time would visit him in his dreams with a touching smile, as others did. But more than a month passed, real winter had come, and everything was still clear in his memory as if he had parted from Anna Sergeyevna only the day before. And his memories flared up more and more brightly. When in the evening stillness he heard from his study the voices of his children, preparing their lessons, or when he listened to a popular song or a barrel-organ in a restaurant, or a blizzard howled in the chimney, suddenly everything would rise up in his memory: what had happened on the pier, and that early morning with mist on the mountains, and the steamer coming from Feodosiya, and the kisses. He would pace a long time about his room, remembering and smiling; then his memories passed into dreams, and in his fancy the past was mingled with what was yet to come. Anna Sergeyevna did not come to him in his dreams, but followed him about everywhere like a shadow and haunted him. When he shut his eyes he saw her as if she were standing before him, and she seemed to him lovelier, younger, tenderer than she really was; and he imagined himself finer than he had been in Yalta. In the evenings she peeped out at him from the bookcase, from the fireplace, from the corner—he heard her breathing, the caressing rustle of her dress. In the street he watched the women, looking for someone like her.

He was tormented by an intense desire to share his memories with someone. But at home it was impossible to talk of his love, and he had no one outside; he could not talk to his tenants nor to anyone at the bank. And what was there to talk of? Had he been in love then? Had there been anything beautiful, poetical, or edifying or simply interesting in his relations with Anna Sergeyevna? And so he had to talk vaguely of love, and women, and no one guessed what he meant; only his wife twitched her dark eyebrows, and said: 'The role of lady-killer does not suit you at all, Dimitry.'

One evening, coming out of the doctors' club with an official with whom he had been playing cards, he could not resist saying:

'If only you knew what a fascinating woman I met in Yalta!'

The official climbed into his sledge and was driving away, but turned suddenly and shouted:

'Dmitry Dmitrich!'

'What?'

'You were right this evening: the sturgeon was a bit off!'

These words, so ordinary, for some reason infuriated Gurov, and struck him as degrading and unclean. What savage manners, what people! What senseless nights, what uninteresting, uneventful days! Frantic card-playing, gluttony, drunkenness, perpetual talk on a single topic. Useless pursuits and perpetual talk absorb the better part of one's time, the better part of one's strength, until all that remains is a tailless, wingless life, a mere trifle, and there is no refuge and no escape—it's like being in a madhouse or a prison!

Gurov did not sleep all night, and was filled with fury. And he had a headache all the next day. And on the following nights he slept badly; he sat up in bed, thinking, or paced up and down his room. He was sick of his children, sick of the bank; he had no desire to go anywhere or to talk of anything.

In the holidays in December he prepared for a journey, and told his wife he was going to Petersburg to do something in the interests of a young friend—and he set off for S——. What for? He himself did not really know. He wanted to see Anna Sergeyevna and to talk with her—to arrange a meeting, if possible.

He reached S—— in the morning, and took the best room at the hotel, in which the floor was covered with grey army cloth, and on the table was an inkstand, grey with dust and adorned with a figure on horseback, with his hat raised aloft in one hand, and his head broken off. The hotel porter gave him the necessary information; von Diederitz lived in a house of his own in Old Pottery Street—it was not far from the hotel; he was rich and lived in fine style, and had his own horses; everyone in the town knew him. The porter pronounced the name 'Dridirits'.

Gurov went without haste to Old Pottery Street and found the house. Just opposite the house stretched a long grey fence adorned with nails.

'That fence is enough to make one flee,' thought Gurov, looking from the fence to the windows of the house and back again.

He considered: today was a holiday, and the husband would probably be at home. And in any case it would be tactless to go into the house and upset her. If he were to send her a note it might fall into her husband's hands, and that might ruin everything. The best thing was to trust to chance. And he kept walking up and down the street and by the fence, waiting for this chance. He saw a beggar go in at the gate and dogs fly at him; then an hour later he heard a piano, and the sounds were faint and indistinct. It must be Anna Sergeyevna playing. The front door suddenly opened, and an old woman came out, followed by the familiar white Pomeranian. Gurov was on the point of calling to the dog, but his heart suddenly raced, and in his excitement he could not remember the dog's name.

He walked up and down, and loathed the grey fence more and more, and by now he thought irritably that Anna Sergeyevna had forgotten him, and was perhaps already amusing herself with someone else, and that was very natural in a young woman who had nothing to look at from morning till night but this confounded fence. He went back to his hotel room and sat for a long while on the sofa, not knowing what to do, then he had dinner and a long nap.

'How stupid and distressing it is!' he thought when he woke and looked at the dark windows; it was already evening. 'Now I've had a good sleep for some reason. What shall I do at night?'

He sat on the bed, which was covered by a cheap grey blanket, of the kind one sees in hospitals, and he taunted himself in his vexation:

'So much for your lady with the dog . . . So much for your adventure . . . Now you can grin and bear it . . .'

That morning at the station a poster in large letters had caught his eye. *The Geisha* was to be performed for the first time. He remembered this and went to the theatre.

'It's quite possible she attends first nights,' he thought.

The theatre was full. As in all provincial theatres, there was a haze above the chandelier, the gallery was noisy and restless; in the front row the local dandies were standing up before the beginning of the performance, with their hands behind them; in the Governor's box the Governor's daughter, wearing a feather boa, was sitting in the front seat, while the Governor himself lurked modestly behind the curtain with only his hands visible; the orchestra was a long time tuning up; the stage curtain swayed. While the audience were coming in and taking their seats, Gurov's eyes were searching eagerly.

Anna Sergeyevna, too, came in. She sat down in the third row, and when Gurov looked at her his heart contracted, and he understood clearly that for him there was in the whole world no creature so near, so precious, and so important to him; this little woman, in no way remarkable, lost in a provincial crowd, with a vulgar lorgnette in her hand, filled his whole life now, was his sorrow and his joy, the one happiness that he now desired for himself, and to the sounds of that atrocious orchestra, of those wretched screeching violins, he thought how lovely she was. He thought and dreamed.

A young man with small side-whiskers, tall and stooping, came in with Anna Sergeyevna and sat down beside her; he bent his head at every step and seemed to be continually bowing. Most likely this was the husband whom at Yalta, in a rush of bitter feeling, she had called a lackey. And there really was in his long figure, his side-whiskers, and the small bald patch on his head, something of the lackey's obsequiousness; his smile was sugary, and the badge of some learned society gleamed in his button-hole, like a waiter's number tag.

During the first interval the husband went out to smoke; she remained in her seat. Gurov, who was sitting in the stalls, too, went up to her and said in a trembling voice, with a forced smile:

'Good evening.'

She glanced at him and turned pale, then glanced again with horror, unable to believe her eyes, and tightly gripped the fan and the lorgnette in her hands, evidently struggling with herself not to faint. Both were silent. She was sitting, he was standing, frightened by her confusion and not venturing to sit down beside her. The violins and the flute began tuning up. Suddenly it became frightening; it felt as if they were being stared at from every box. She got up and went quickly to the door; he followed her, and both walked aimlessly along passages, and up and down stairs, and figures in legal, scholastic, and civil service uniforms, all wearing badges, flitted before their eyes. They caught glimpses of ladies, of fur coats hanging on pegs; a draught enveloped them with the smell of cigarette ends. And Gurov, whose heart was beating violently, thought:

'Oh, heavens! Why are these people here and this orchestra! . . .'

And at that instant he recalled how when he had seen Anna Sergeyevna off, that evening at the station, he had told himself that every-thing was over and they would never meet again. And yet the end was still so far!

On the narrow, gloomy staircase over which was written 'Entrance to Circle', she stopped.

'How you frightened me!' she said, breathing hard, still pale and over-whelmed. 'Oh, how you frightened me! I feel scarcely alive. Why have you come? Why?'

'But do understand, Anna, do understand . . .' he said hastily in a low voice. 'I beg you to understand . . .'

She looked at him with dread, with entreaty, with love; she looked at him intently, to hold his features more firmly in her memory.

'I am so unhappy,' she went on, not heeding him. 'I've thought only of you all this time; thinking of you kept me alive. And I wanted to forget, to forget you; but why, oh why, have you come?'

On the landing above them two schoolboys were smoking and looking

416

down, but that meant nothing to Gurov; he drew Anna Sergeyevna to him, and began kissing her face, her cheeks, and her hands.

'What are you doing, what are you doing!' she cried in horror, pushing him away. 'We are mad. Go away today; go away at once . . . I implore you by all that is sacred, I beg you . . . Somebody's coming!'

Someone was ascending the stairs.

'You must go away,' Anna Sergeyevna went on in a whisper. 'Do you hear, Dmitry Dmitrich? I will come and see you in Moscow. I have never been happy; I am miserable now, and I never, never shall be happy, never! Don't make me suffer even more! I swear I'll come to Moscow. But now let us part! My precious, good, dear one, we must part!'

She pressed his hand and began rapidly going downstairs, looking round at him, and from her eyes he could see that she really was unhappy. Gurov stood for a little while, listened, then, when everything was quiet, he found his coat and left the theatre.

IV

And Anna Sergeyevna began coming to see him in Moscow. Once every two or three months she left S——, telling her husband that she was going to consult a professor about a female complaint—and her husband believed her, and did not believe her. In Moscow she stayed at the Slavyansky Bazaar hotel, and at once sent a man in a red cap to Gurov. Gurov went to see her, and no one in Moscow knew of it.

He was going to see her in this manner one winter morning (the messenger had come the evening before when he was out). With him walked his daughter, whom he wanted to take to school: it was on the way. Snow was falling in big moist flakes.

'It's three degrees above freezing-point, and yet it is snowing,' said Gurov to his daughter. 'The thaw is only on the surface of the earth; there is quite a different temperature in the upper layers of the atmosphere.'

'Why doesn't it thunder in winter, Papa?'

He explained that, too. He talked, thinking all the while that he was going to see *her*, and no living soul knew of it, and probably never would know. He had two lives: one open, seen and known by all who cared to know, full of relative truth and of relative falsehood, exactly like the lives of his friends and acquaintances; and another life running its course in secret. And through some strange, perhaps accidental, conjunction of circumstances, everything that was important, interesting and essential to him, in which he was sincere and did not deceive himself, everything that made up the core of his life, was hidden from other people; and all that was false in him, the outer shell in which he hid himself to conceal the truth—such as, for instance, his work in the bank, his arguments at the club, his 'lower race', his presence with his wife at anniversary celebrations—all that was open. And he judged of others by himself, not believing in what he saw, and always supposing that every man kept his real, most interesting life under the cover of secrecy, as under the cover of night. Each individual existence is based on secrecy, and this, perhaps, is partly why civilised man is so anxious that personal privacy should be respected.

After leaving his daughter at school, Gurov went on to the Slavyansky Bazaar. He took off his fur coat below, went upstairs, and softly knocked at the door. Anna Sergeyevna, wearing his favourite grey dress, exhausted by the journey and the suspense, had been expecting him since the evening before. She was pale; she looked at him, and did not smile, and he had hardly come in when she fell on his breast. Their kiss was slow and prolonged, as if they had not met for two years.

'Well, how are you getting on there?' he asked. 'What news?'

'Wait; I'll tell you directly . . . I can't talk.'

She could not speak; she was crying. She turned away from him, and pressed her handkerchief to her eyes.

'Let her have her cry. I'll sit down and wait,' he thought, and he sat down in an armchair.

Then he rang and asked for tea to be brought to him, and while he drank his tea she remained standing with her back to him, facing the window. She was crying from emotion, from the sorrowful awareness that their life had taken such a sad course; they could meet only in secret, hiding away from people, like thieves! Was not their life ruined?

'Please stop!' he said.

It was evident to him that this love of theirs would not soon be over, one could not know when. Anna Sergeyevna grew more and more attached to him. She adored him, and it was unthinkable to say to her that all this must end one day; besides, she would not have believed it.

He went up to her and took her by the shoulders to say something affectionate and cheering, and at that moment he saw himself in the mirror.

His hair was already beginning to turn grey. And it seemed strange to him that he had grown so much older, so much plainer during the last few years. The shoulders on which his hands rested were warm and quivering. He felt compassion for this life, still so warm and lovely, but probably already not far from beginning to fade and wither like his own. Why did she love him so much? Women had never seen him as he really was, and they loved in him not himself, but the man created by their imagination, whom they had been eagerly seeking all their lives; and afterwards, when they noticed their mistake, they loved him all the same. And not one of them had been happy with him. Time passed, he met them, became intimate, parted, but he had never been in love; it was anything you like, but not love.

And only now when his head was grey had he fallen truly, really in love—for the first time in his life.

Anna Sergeyevna and he loved one another like people very close and akin, like husband and wife, like tender friends; it seemed to them that fate itself had meant them for one another, and they could not understand why he had a wife and she a husband; and it was as if they were two birds of passage, a male and a female, caught and forced to live in different cages. They forgave each other for what they were ashamed of in their past, they forgave everything in the present, and felt that this love of theirs had changed them both.

In moments of dejection in the past he had comforted himself with any reasoning that came into his mind, but now he had no use for reasoning; he felt profound compassion, he wanted to be sincere and tender . . .

'Don't cry, my darling,' he said. 'You've had your cry; that's enough . . . Let's talk now, let's think of some plan.'

Then they spent a long while taking counsel together, talked of how to avoid this necessity for furtiveness, deception, living in different towns and not seeing each other for long periods. How could they be free from these intolerable bonds?

'How? How?' he asked, clutching his head. 'How?'

And it seemed as if in a little while the solution would be found, and then a new, beautiful life would begin; and it was clear to both of them that the end was still far, far away, and that the most complicated and difficult part was only just beginning.

In the Ravine

I

The village of Ukleyevo lay in a ravine so that only the belfry and the chimneys of the calico-printing factories could be seen from the high road and the railway station. When visitors asked what village this was, they were told:

'That's the one where the sexton ate all the caviare at the funeral.'

Once, during a funeral banquet at factory-owner Kostyukov's house, an elderly sexton saw among the savouries some unpressed caviare and began eating it greedily; people nudged him, tugged his sleeve, but he was in a transport of delight: he felt nothing, and merely went on eating. He ate up all the caviare, though it was a four-pound jar. And years had passed since then, the sexton had long been dead, but the caviare was still remembered. Whether life was so poor here or people had not wit enough to notice anything but that unimportant incident of ten years before—at all events, they had nothing else to tell about the village of Ukleyevo.

The village was never free from fever, and there was boggy mud even in the summer, especially under the fences over which hung old willow-trees that provided broad shade. Here there was always a smell from the factory refuse and the acetic acid used in the processing of cotton print.

The three cotton factories and the tannery were not in the village itself but on the outskirts and a little way off. They were small factories, and no more than four hundred workmen were employed in all of them. The tannery often made the water in the little river stink; the refuse contaminated the meadows, the peasants' cattle suffered from anthrax, and orders were given that the factory should be closed. It was considered closed, but went on working in secret with the connivance of the local police inspector and the district doctor, who were paid ten roubles a month by the owner. In the whole village there were only two decent houses built of brick with iron roofs; one of them contained the council offices, in the other, a two-storeyed house just opposite the church, there lived a shopkeeper from Yepifan called Grigory Petrov Tsybukin.

Grigory kept a grocer's shop, but that was only for appearance's sake: in reality he sold vodka, cattle, hides, grain, and pigs; he traded in anything that came to hand, and when, for instance, magpies were wanted abroad for ladies' hats, he made some thirty kopecks on every pair of birds; he bought up timber, lent money at interest, and was altogether a resourceful old man.

He had two sons. The elder, Anisim, was in the police, in the criminal investigation department, and was rarely at home. The younger, Stepan, had gone in for trade and helped his father, but no great help was expected from him as he was weak in health and deaf; his wife Aksinya, a handsome woman with a good figure, who wore a hat and carried a parasol on holidays, got up early and went to bed late, and ran about all day long, picking up her skirts and jingling her keys, going from the granary to the cellar and from there to the shop, and old Tsybukin looked at her good-humouredly while his eyes glowed, and at such moments he regretted she had not been married to his elder son instead of to the younger one, who was deaf and evidently had little appreciation of female beauty.

The old man always had a fondness for family life, and he loved his family more than anything on earth, especially his elder son, the detective, and his daughter-in-law. Aksinya had no sooner married the deaf son than she began to display an extraordinary gift for business, and knew who could be allowed to run up a bill and who could not; she kept the keys and would not trust them even to her husband; she clicked away on the counting frame, looked at the horses' teeth like a peasant, and was always laughing or shouting; and whatever she did or said the old man was simply delighted and muttered:

'What a daughter-in-law! What a beauty!'

He was a widower, but a year after his son's marriage he could not resist getting married himself. A girl was found for him, living twenty miles from Ukleyevo, called Varvara Nikolayevna, no longer very young, but handsome, stately, and belonging to a decent family. As soon as she was installed in the upper-storey room everything in the house seemed to brighten up as if new glass had been put into all the windows. The lamps gleamed before the icons, the tables were covered with snow-white cloths, flowers with red buds made their appearance in the windows and in the front garden, and at dinner, instead of eating from a communal bowl, each person had a separate plate set before him. Varvara Nikolayevna had a pleasant, friendly smile, and it seemed as though the whole house were smiling, too. Beggars and pilgrims, male and female, began to come into the yard, a thing which had never happened in the past; the plaintive singsong voices of the Ukleyevo peasant women and the apologetic coughs of weak, haggard men, who had been dismissed from the factory for drunkenness, were heard under the windows. Varvara helped them with money, with bread, with old clothes, and afterwards, when she felt more at home, began taking things out of the shop. One day the deaf man saw her take four ounces of tea and that disturbed him.

'Here, Mother's taken four ounces of tea,' he informed his father afterwards; 'who's that to be charged to?'

The old man made no reply but stood still and thought a moment, moving his eyebrows, and then went upstairs to his wife.

'Varvarushka, if you want anything out of the shop,' he said affectionately, 'take it, my dear. Take it and welcome; don't hesitate.'

And next day the deaf man, running across the yard, called to her:

'If there is anything you want, Mother, take it.'

There was something new, something cheerful and light-hearted in her giving of alms, just as there was in the icon-lamps and the little red flowers. When just before fasts, or at the village church festival which lasted three days, they sold the peasants tainted salt meat, smelling so strong it was hard to stand near the barrel, and let drunken men pawn scythes, caps, and their wives' kerchiefs; when the factory hands, stupefied with bad vodka, lay rolling in the mud, and sin seemed to hover like dense fog in the air, then it was a relief to think that up there in the house there was a gentle, neatly dressed woman who had nothing to do with salt meat or vodka; her charity acted in those heavy, hazy days like a safety-valve in a machine.

The days in Tsybukin's house were spent in business cares. Before the sun had risen Aksinya was panting and puffing as she washed in the outer room, and the samovar was boiling in the kitchen with an ominous hum. Old Grigory Petrov, dressed in a long black coat, cotton breeches and shiny top-boots, such a dapper little figure, walked about the rooms, tapping with his little heels like the father-in-law in a popular song. The shop was opened. When it was daylight a racing droshky was brought up to the front door and the old man sprang jauntily on to it, pulling his big cap down to his ears; and, looking at him, no one would have said he was fifty-six. His wife and daughter-in-law saw him off, and at such times when he was wearing a nice, clean coat, and had in the droshky a huge black stallion that cost three hundred roubles, the old man did not like the peasants to come up to him with their complaints and petitions; he hated the peasants and disdained them, and if he saw some peasant waiting at the gate, he would shout angrily:

'Why are you standing there? Move on!'

Or if it were a beggar, he would say:

'God will provide!'

He used to drive off on business; his wife, in a dark dress and a black apron, tidied the rooms or helped in the kitchen. Aksinya attended to the shop, and from the yard could be heard the clink of bottles and money, her laughter and shouting, and the anger of customers whom she had offended; and at the same time it was evident that the secret sale of vodka was already going on in the shop. The deaf man sat in the shop, too, or walked about the street bareheaded, with his hands in his pockets looking absent-mindedly now at the huts, now at the sky overhead. Six times a day they drank tea; four times a day they sat down to meals; and in the evening they counted their takings, noted them down, and then slept soundly.

All three cotton factories in Ukleyevo and the houses of the factory owners—Khrymin Seniors, Khrymin Juniors, and Kostyukov—were connected by telephone. The telephone was laid on in the council offices, too, but it soon ceased to work there, as it became infested by bugs and cockroaches. The elder of the rural district was semi-literate and began every word in official documents with a capital letter. But when the telephone was spoiled he said:

'Yes, we'll find it hard now without a telephone.'

The Khrymin Seniors were continually at law with the Juniors, and sometimes the Juniors quarrelled among themselves and began going to law, and their factory did not work for a month or two until they were reconciled again, and this entertained the people of Ukleyevo, as there was a great deal of talk and gossip occasioned by every quarrel. On holidays Kostyukov and the Juniors would go out driving, and dashed about Ukleyevo, running over the calves. Aksinya, in her Sunday best, rustling her starched petticoats, would promenade up and down the street near her shop; the Juniors would snatch her up and carry her off as if by force. Then old Tsybukin would drive out to show off his new horse, taking Varvara with him.

In the evening, after the driving, when people were going to bed, an expensive concertina was played in the Juniors' yard and, if it were a moonlit night, those sounds sent a thrill of delight to the heart, and Ukleyevo no longer seemed a wretched hole.

II

The elder son Anisim came home very rarely, only on major holidays, but he often sent by a returning villager presents and letters written in very good writing by some other hand, always on a sheet of foolscap in the form of a petition. The letters were full of expressions that Anisim never made use of in conversation: 'Dear Papa and Mamma, I send you a pound of flower tea for the satisfaction of your physical needs.'

At the bottom of every letter was scratched, as though with a broken pen: 'Anisim Tsybukin,' and again in the same excellent hand: 'Agent.'

The letters were read aloud several times, and the old father, touched, red with emotion, would say:

'So, he did not care to stay at home, he has gone in for learning. Well, let him! Every man to his own job!'

Once, just before Shrovetide, there was heavy rain and sleet; the old man and Varvara went to the window to look at it, and lo and behold! Anisim drove up in a sledge from the station. He was completely unexpected. He came indoors, looking anxious and troubled about something, and he remained the same all the time; there was something offhand in his manner. He was in no haste to go away, and it seemed as if he might have been dismissed from the service. Varvara was pleased at his arrival; she looked at him with a sly expression, sighed, and shook her head.

'How is this, my friends?' she said. 'Tut, tut, the lad's in his twenty-eighth year, and he is still leading a merry bachelor life; tut, tut, tut . . .'

From the other room her soft, even speech sounded like tut, tut, tut. She began whispering with her husband and Aksinya, and their faces also assumed a sly and mysterious, conspiratorial expression.

They decided to marry Anisim off.

'Oh, tut, tut . . . the younger brother was married off long ago,' said Varvara, 'and you're still unwed, like a cockerel in a shed. What's the use of that? Tut, tut, you will be married, please God, then as you choose—you will go back to your work and your wife will remain here at home to help us. There is no order in your life, young man, and I see you've forgotten what order is. Tut, tut, it's nothing but trouble with all you townspeople.'

When the Tsybukins married, since they were rich, the most handsome girls were chosen to be their brides. For Anisim, too, they found a handsome one. He himself was unattractive and insignificant, with a feeble, sickly build, and short of stature; he had fat, bulging cheeks which looked as if he were puffing them out; his eyes were sharp, unblinking; his beard was red and scanty, and when he was thinking he always put it into his mouth and chewed upon it; moreover he often drank too much, and that was noticeable in his face and his walk. But when he was informed that they had found a very beautiful bride for him, he said:

'Oh well, I am no fright myself. All of us Tsybukins are handsome, I may say.'

The village of Torguyevo was near the town. Half of it had lately been incorporated into the town, the other half remained a village. In the first—the town half—there was a widow living in her own little house; she had a sister living with her who was quite poor and went out to work by the day, and this sister had a daughter called Lipa, a girl who went out to work, too. People in Torguyevo were already talking about Lipa's good looks, but her terrible poverty put everyone off; people reckoned that some widower or elderly man would marry her regardless of her poverty, or would perhaps take her to himself without marriage, and then her mother would be cared for, too. Varvara heard about Lipa from the matchmakers, and she drove over to Torguyevo.

Then a visit of inspection was arranged at the aunt's, with lunch and wine all as it should be, and Lipa wore a new pink dress made especially for this occasion, and a crimson ribbon like a flame gleamed in her hair. She was pale-faced, thin, and frail, with soft, delicate features sunburnt from working in the open air; a shy, mournful smile always hovered about her face, and there was a childlike look in her eyes, trustful and inquisitive.

She was young, still a little girl, her bosom was scarcely developed, but she could be married because she had reached the legal age. She really was beautiful, and the only thing that might be thought unappealing was her big masculine hands which hung idle now like two big claws.

'There is no dowry—and we don't mind,' said Tsybukin to the aunt. 'We took a wife from a poor family for our son Stepan, too, and now we can't praise her too highly. In house and in business alike she has hands of gold.'

Lipa stood in the doorway and looked as though she would say: 'Do with me as you will, I trust you,' while her mother Praskovya the work-woman hid herself in the kitchen, numb with shyness. Once, in her youth, a merchant whose floors she was scrubbing stamped at her in a rage; she went chill with terror and remained frightened for life. Because she was frightened her arms and legs always trembled and her cheeks twitched. Sitting in the kitchen she tried to hear what the visitors were saying, and she kept crossing herself, pressing her fingers to her forehead, and glancing at the icon. Anisim, slightly drunk, opened the door into the kitchen and said in an offhand way:

'Why are you sitting out here, precious Mamma? We miss you!'

And Praskovya, overcome with timidity, pressing her hands to her lean, emaciated bosom, replied:

'Oh, not at all . . . It's very kind of you.'

After the visit of inspection the wedding day was fixed. Then Anisim walked about the rooms at home whistling, or suddenly thinking of something, started brooding and stared piercingly at the floor, as if his eyes sought to probe to the very depths of the earth. He expressed neither pleasure that he was to be married, married so soon, on Low Sunday, nor a desire to see his bride, but simply went on whistling. And it was evident that he was only getting married because his father and stepmother wished him to, and because it was the custom in the village to marry the son in order to have a woman to help in the house. When he was leaving he seemed in no hurry, and his behaviour as a whole was different from on previous visits—he was strangely offhand and said all the wrong things.

III

In the village of Shikalova lived two dressmakers, sisters, belonging to the Flagellant sect. The new clothes for the wedding were ordered from them, and they often came over for fittings, and stayed a long while drinking tea. They made for Varvara a brown dress with black lace and bugles, and for Aksinya a light-green dress with a yellow front, with a train. When the dressmakers had finished their work Tsybukin paid them not in money but in goods from his shop, and they went away sadly, carrying parcels of tallow candles and sardines which they did not in the least need, and when they got out of the village into the open country they sat down on a hillock and wept.

Anisim arrived three days before the wedding, rigged out in new clothes from top to toe. He had shiny rubber galoshes, and instead of a tie wore a red cord with beads on it, and over his shoulders he had draped a coat, which was also new.

426

After praying solemnly before the icon, he greeted his father and gave him ten silver roubles and ten half-roubles; to Varvara he gave the same, and to Aksinya twenty quarter-roubles. The main charm of these presents lay in the fact that all the coins, as if specially chosen, were brand-new and glittered in the sun. Trying to appear grave and solemn, Anisim pursed up his face and puffed out his cheeks, and he smelt of spirits. Probably he had visited the refreshment bar at every station. And again there was an offhandness about the man—something superfluous. Then Anisim had lunch and drank tea with the old man, while Varvara turned the new coins over in her hands and enquired about villagers who had gone to live in the town.

'They are all right, thank God, they're doing well,' said Anisim. 'Only something has happened to Ivan Yegorov: his old wife Sofya Nikiforovna has died. From consumption. They ordered the memorial dinner for the repose of her soul at the confectioner's for two-and-a-half roubles a head. And there was real wine. Those who were peasants from our village— they paid two-and-a-half roubles, too. They ate nothing. What does a peasant know about sauce!'

'Two-and-a-half,' said his father, shaking his head.

'Well, it's not like the country there. You go into a restaurant to have a snack, you ask for one thing and another, others join in, you have a drink—and before you know, it's already daylight and you've three or four roubles each to pay. And when you're with Samorodov he likes to have coffee with brandy after everything, and brandy is sixty kopecks a glass.'

'He's making it all up,' said the old man with delight; 'he's making it all up!'

'I am always with Samorodov now. It is Samorodov who writes my letters to you. He writes splendidly. And if I were to tell you, Mamma,' Anisim went on cheerfully, addressing Varvara, 'the sort of fellow that Samorodov is, you wouldn't believe me. We call him Mukhtar because he's like an Armenian—black all over. I can see through him, I know all his affairs like the back of my hand, and he feels that, and he always follows me about, we are quite inseparable. He seems a bit scared, but he can't live without me. Where I go he goes. I have a reliable, true eye, Mamma. One sees a peasant selling a shirt in the market-place. "Stop, that shirt's stolen." And truly it turns out to be so: the shirt was a stolen one.'

'How can you tell?' asked Varvara.

'I just have an eye for it. I know nothing about the shirt, only for some reason I seem drawn to it: it's stolen, and that's all I can say. In our department they have a saying, "Anisim has gone to shoot snipe!" That means looking for stolen goods. Yes . . . Anybody can steal, but it is another thing to hang on to the booty! The earth is wide, but there is nowhere to hide stolen goods.'

'In our village a ram and two ewes were carried off last week from the Guntorevs,' said Varvara, and she heaved a sigh, 'and there is no one to try and find them . . . Oh, tut, tut . . .'

'Well, I might have a try. I don't mind.'

The day of the wedding arrived. It was a cool but bright, cheerful April day. People were driving about Ukleyevo from early morning with pairs or teams of three horses decked with many-coloured ribbons on their yokes and manes, with a jingle of bells. The rooks, disturbed by this activity, were cawing noisily in the willows, and the starlings sang their loudest unceasingly as if rejoicing that there was a wedding at the Tsybukins'.

Indoors the tables were already covered with long fish, smoked hams, stuffed fowls, boxes of sprats, salted and pickled savouries, and numerous bottles of vodka and wine; there was a smell of smoked sausage and of sour lobster. Old Tsybukin walked about near the tables, tapping with his little heels and sharpening the knives against each other. They kept calling Varvara and asking for things, and she was constantly running, breathlessly and looking distracted, into the kitchen, where the chef from Kostyukov's and the head cook, a woman, from Khrymin Juniors' had been at work since early morning. Aksinya, with her hair curled, in her stays without her dress on, in new squeaky boots, flew about the yard like a whirlwind showing glimpses of her bare knees and bosom.

It was noisy, there was a sound of scolding and oaths; passers-by stopped at the wide-open gates, and in everything there was a feeling that something extraordinary was happening.

'They have gone for the bride!'

The bells began jingling and died away far beyond the village . . . Between two and three o'clock people ran up: again there was a jingling of bells: they were bringing the bride! The church was full, the candelabra blazed, the choristers were singing from sheet music, as old Tsybukin had wished. The glare of the lights and the bright coloured dresses dazzled Lipa; she felt as though the choristers' loud voices were hitting her on the head with a hammer. Her shoes and the stays, which she had put on for the first time in her life, pinched her, and her face looked as if she had just come round after fainting; she gazed about without understanding. Anisim, in his black coat with a red cord instead of a tie, stared at the same spot lost in thought, and when the choristers shouted loudly he hurriedly crossed himself. He felt touched and disposed to weep. This church was familiar to him from earliest childhood; at one time his late mother used to bring him here to take the sacrament; at one time he used to sing in the choir with the other boys; every icon he remembered so well, every corner. And now he was being married, he had to take a wife for propriety, but he was not thinking of that, he had forgotten his wedding completely. Tears dimmed his eyes so that he could not see the icons, he felt heavy at heart; he prayed and besought God that the inevitable disasters, that were ready to burst upon him any day now, might somehow pass him by as stormclouds in time of drought pass over the village without yielding one drop of rain. And so many sins were heaped up in the past, so many sins, it was all so inescapable, so irretrievable that it seemed absurd even to ask forgiveness. But he did ask forgiveness, and even gave a loud sob, but no one took any notice of that, since they all supposed he had had a drop too much.

There was a sound of a fretful childish wail:

'Take me away, Mamma darling!'

'Quiet there!' cried the priest.

When they returned from the church people ran after them; there were crowds, too, round the shop, round the gates, and in the yard under the windows. The peasant women came to sing songs of congratulation. The young couple had scarcely crossed the threshold when the choristers, who were already standing in the entrance-hall with their sheet music, broke into a loud chant at the top of their voices; a band ordered expressly from the town began playing. Sparkling Don wine was brought in tall wine-glasses, and Yelizarov, a carpenter who did jobs by contract, a tall, gaunt old man with eyebrows so bushy that his eyes could scarcely be seen, said, addressing the newly-weds:

'Anisim and you, my child, love one another, live in God's way, little children, and the Heavenly Mother will not abandon you.'

He leaned his face on the old father's shoulder and gave a sob.

'Grigory Petrov, let us weep, let us weep with joy!' he said in a thin voice, and then at once burst out laughing in a loud bass guffaw. 'Ho-ho-ho! This is a fine daughter-in-law for you too! Everything is in its place in her; all runs smoothly, no creaking, the mechanism works well, lots of nuts and bolts.'

He was a native of the Yegoryevsky district, but had worked in the factories in Ukleyevo and the neighbourhood since youth, and had made Ukleyevo his home. He had been a familiar figure for years, as old and gaunt and lanky as now, and for years he had been nicknamed 'Crutch'. Perhaps because for over forty years he had been occupied in repairing the factory machinery he judged everybody and everything by its soundness or its need of repair. And before sitting down at table he tried several chairs to see whether they were sound, and he touched the salmon also.

After the sparkling wine, they all sat down at table. The guests talked, moving their chairs. The choristers sang in the entrance-hall. The band was playing, and at the same time the peasant women in the yard were singing their songs in unison—and there was an awful cacophony which made one's head spin.

Crutch fidgeted in his chair and prodded his neighbours with his elbows, prevented them from talking, and laughed and cried alternately.

'Little children, little children, little children,' he muttered rapidly. 'Aksinya my dear, Varvara darling, we will all live in peace and harmony, my dear little axes . . .'

He drank little and was now drunk from only one glass of English bitters. The revolting bitters, made from nobody knows what, intoxicated everyone who drank it as though it had stunned them. Their speech became slurred.

The local clergy, clerks from the factories with their wives, tradesmen and tavern-keepers from other villages were present. The clerk and the elder of the rural district who had served together for fourteen years, and who had during all that time never signed a single document nor let a single person out of the council offices without deceiving or insulting him, were sitting now side by side, both fat and well-fed, and it seemed as though they were so steeped in injustice and falsehood that even the skin of their faces was somehow peculiar, fraudulent. The clerk's wife, a scrawny woman with a squint, had brought all her children with her, and like a bird of prey looked aslant at the plates and snatched anything she could get hold of to put in her own or her children's pockets.

Lipa sat petrified, still with the same expression as in church. Anisim had not said a single word to her since he had made her acquaintance, so that he did not yet know the sound of her voice; and now, sitting beside her, he remained silent and went on drinking English bitters, and when he got drunk he began talking to an aunt who was sitting opposite:

'I have a friend called Samorodov. A very special man. He is by rank an honorary citizen, and he can talk. But I can see right through him, Auntie, and he feels it. Pray join me in drinking to the health of Samorodov, Auntie!'

Varvara, worn out and distracted, walked round the table pressing the guests to eat, and was evidently pleased that there were so many dishes and that everything was so lavish—no one could disparage them now. The sun set, but the dinner went on; the guests were beyond knowing what they were eating or drinking, it was impossible to distinguish what was said, and only from time to time when the band was quiet some peasant woman could be heard shouting from the yard:

'They have sucked the blood out of us, the Herods; a plague upon them!'

In the evening they danced to the band. The Khrymin Juniors came, bringing their wine, and one of them, when dancing a quadrille, held a bottle in each hand and a wine-glass in his mouth, and that made everyone laugh. In the middle of the quadrille they suddenly bent their knees and danced in a squatting position; Aksinya in green flew by like a flash, stirring up a wind with her train. Someone trod on her flounce and Crutch shouted:

'Hey, they have torn off her skirting-board! Children!'

Aksinya had naïve grey eyes which rarely blinked, and a naïve smile played continually on her face. And in those unblinking eyes, and in that little head on the long neck, and in her slenderness there was something snake-like; all in green but for her yellow front, she looked with a smile on her face as a viper looks out of the young rye in springtime at a passer-by, stretching itself and lifting its head. The Khrymins were free in their behaviour to her, and it was very noticeable that she was on intimate terms with the elder of them. But her deaf husband saw nothing, he did not look at her; he sat with his legs crossed and ate nuts, cracking them so loudly that it sounded like pistol shots.

But, behold, old Tsybukin himself walked into the middle of the room and waved his handkerchief as a sign that he, too, wanted to dance a Russian dance, and all over the house and from the crowd in the yard rose a roar of approbation:

431

'*He's* going to dance! *He* himself!'

Varvara danced, but the old man only waved his handkerchief and kicked up his heels, yet the people in the yard, propped against one another, peeping in at the windows, were in raptures, and for a moment forgave him everything—his wealth and his insults.

'Well done, Grigory Petrov!' was heard in the crowd. 'That's right, do your best! You can still play your part! Ha-ha!'

It all ended late, after one o'clock in the morning. Anisim, staggering, went to take his leave of the choristers and bandsmen, and gave each of them a new half-rouble. His father, who was not swaying but seemed to be leaning on one leg, saw his guests off, and said to each of them:

'The wedding cost two thousand.'

As the party was breaking up, someone took the Shikalova innkeeper's good coat instead of his own old one, and Anisim suddenly flew into a rage and began shouting:

'Stop, I'll find it at once! I know who stole it! Stop!'

He ran out into the street and pursued someone. Anisim was caught, brought back home and shoved, drunken, red with anger, and wet, into the room where the aunt was undressing Lipa, and he was locked in.

IV

Five days had passed. Anisim, who was ready to leave, went upstairs to say goodbye to Varvara. All the lamps were burning before her icons, there was a smell of incense, while she sat at the window knitting a stocking of red wool.

'You have not stayed with us long,' she said. 'You've been bored, I dare say. Oh, tut, tut . . . We live comfortably; we have plenty of everything. We celebrated your wedding properly, in good style; your father says it came to two thousand. In fact we live like merchants, only it's dreary. We treat the people very badly. My heart aches, my dear; how we treat them, my goodness! Whether we exchange a horse or buy something or hire a labourer—it's all cheating. Cheating and cheating. The Lenten oil in the shop is bitter, rancid, the people have tar that is better. But surely, pray tell me, couldn't we sell good oil?'

'Every man to his own job, Mamma.'

'But you know we all have to die? You really ought to talk to your father! . . .'

'You should talk to him yourself.'

'Well, if I do, he says exactly what you do: "Every man to his own job." In the next world they'll know what job we've been put to! God's judgement is just.'

'Of course no one will know,' said Anisim, and he heaved a sigh. 'There is no God, anyway, Mamma, so what knowing can there be?'

Varvara looked at him with surprise, burst out laughing, and clasped her hands. Because she was so genuinely surprised at his words and looked at him as though he were odd, he was embarrassed.

'Perhaps there is a God, only there is no faith,' he said. 'When I was being married I felt uneasy. Just as you may take an egg from under a hen and there is a chicken chirping in it, so my conscience began to chirp in me, and while I was being married I thought all the time: there is a God! But when I left the church it was the same as usual. And indeed, how can I tell whether there is a God or not? We are not taught the right things from childhood, and while the babe is still at his mother's breast he is only taught "every man to his own job". Father does not believe in God, either. You were saying that Guntorev had some sheep stolen . . . I discovered: it was a Shikalova peasant stole them; he stole them, but Father's got the fleeces . . . So much for faith!'

Anisim winked and shook his head.

'The elder does not believe in God, either,' he went on. 'And the clerk and the sexton, too. And as for their going to church and keeping the fasts, that is simply to prevent people talking ill of them, and in case there really may be a Day of Judgement. Nowadays people say that the end of the world has come because people have grown weaker, do not honour their parents, and so on. All that is nonsense. My idea, Mamma, is that all our trouble is because there is so little conscience in people. I see through things, Mamma, and I understand. If a man has a stolen shirt I see it. A man sits in a tavern and you fancy he is drinking tea and no more, but to me the tea is neither here nor there; I see further, that he has no conscience. You can go about all day and not meet one person with a conscience. And the whole reason is that they don't know whether there is a God or not . . . Well, goodbye, Mamma, keep alive and well, don't think badly of me.'

Anisim bowed down at Varvara's feet.

'I thank you for everything, Mamma,' he said. 'You are a great gain to our family. You are a very worthy woman, and I am very pleased with you.'

Much moved, Anisim went out, but returned again and said:

'Samorodov has got me mixed up in something: I shall be either rich

433

or ruined. If anything happens, then you must comfort my father, Mamma.'

'Oh nonsense, don't you worry, tut, tut, tut . . . God is merciful. And Anisim, you should be affectionate to your wife, instead of giving each other sulky looks as you do; you might smile at least.'

'Yes, she's a strange one,' said Anisim, and he gave a sigh. 'She doesn't understand anything, she never speaks. She is very young, let her grow up.'

A tall, sleek white stallion, harnessed to a cabriolet, was already standing at the front door.

Old Tsybukin jumped in jauntily at a run and took the reins. Anisim kissed Varvara, Aksinya, and his brother. On the steps Lipa, too, was standing; she was standing motionless, looking away, and it seemed as though she had not come to see him off but just by chance for some unknown reason. Anisim went up to her and lightly touched her cheek with his lips.

'Goodbye,' he said.

And without looking at him she gave a strange smile; her face began to quiver, and everyone for some reason felt sorry for her. Anisim, too, leaped aboard and set his arms akimbo, for he considered himself good-looking.

When they drove up out of the ravine Anisim kept looking back towards the village. It was a warm, bright day. The cattle were being driven out for the first time, and the peasant girls and women were walking by the herd in their holiday dresses. A brown bull bellowed, glad to be free, and pawed the ground with his forefeet. On all sides, above and below, the larks were singing. Anisim looked round at the elegant white church—it had only lately been whitewashed—and he thought how he had been praying in it five days before; he looked round at the school with its green roof, at the little river in which he once used to bathe and catch fish, and joy stirred in his heart, and he wished that a wall might rise up from the ground and prevent him from going further, and that he might be left with nothing but the past.

At the station they went to the refreshment room and drank a glass of sherry. His father felt in his pocket for his purse to pay.

'I'll treat you,' said Anisim. The old man, touched and delighted, slapped him on the shoulder, and winked to the waiter as much as to say, 'See what a fine son I have got.'

434

'You ought to stay at home in the business, Anisim,' he said; 'you would be worth any price to me! I would shower gold on you from head to foot, my son.'

'It can't be done, Papa.'

The sherry was sour and smelt of sealing-wax, but they had another glass.

When old Tsybukin returned home from the station, at first he did not recognise his younger daughter-in-law. As soon as her husband had driven out of the yard, Lipa was transformed and suddenly cheered up. Wearing a worn old skirt, with her feet bare and her sleeves rolled up to the shoulders, she was scrubbing the stairs in the porch and singing in a silvery little voice, and when she brought out a big tub of dirty water and looked up at the sun with her childlike smile it seemed as if she, too, were a lark.

An old labourer who was passing by the door shook his head and cleared his throat.

'Yes, indeed, your daughters-in-law, Grigory Petrov, are a blessing from God,' he said. 'Not women, but real treasures!'

V

On Friday, the eighth of July, Yelizarov, nicknamed Crutch, and Lipa were returning from the village of Kazanskoye, where they had been on a pilgrimage to mark the church holiday in honour of the Holy Mother of Kazan. A good distance after them walked Lipa's mother Praskovya, who always fell behind, as she was ill and short of breath. It was drawing towards evening.

'A-a-a . . .' said Crutch, wondering as he listened to Lipa. 'A-a! . . . We-ell!'

'I am very fond of jam, Ilya Makarych,' said Lipa. 'I sit down in my little corner and drink tea and eat jam. Or I drink it with Varvara Nikolavna, and she tells some story full of feeling. They have a lot of jam—four jars. They say, "Have some, Lipa; eat as much as you like." '

'A-a-a, four jars!'

'They live very well. They have white bread with their tea; and beef, too, as much as you want. They live very well, only I am frightened there, Ilya Makarych. Oh, oh, how frightened I am!'

'Why are you frightened, child?' asked Crutch, and he looked back to see if Praskovya was very far behind.

'To begin with, when the wedding had been celebrated I was afraid of Anisim Grigoryich. Anisim Grigoryich did nothing, he didn't ill-treat me, only when he comes near me a cold shiver runs all over me, through all my bones. And I did not sleep one night, I trembled all over and kept praying to God. And now I am afraid of Aksinya, Ilya Makarych. It's not that she does anything, she is always laughing, but sometimes she glances at the window, and her eyes are so fierce and there is a glint of green in them—like a sheep's eyes in the shed. The Khrymin Juniors are leading her astray: "Your old man", they tell her, "has a bit of land at Butyokino, over a hundred acres," they say, "and there is sand and water there, so you, Aksyusha," they say, "should build a brickyard there and we will go shares with you." Bricks now are twenty roubles a thousand, it's a profitable business. Yesterday at dinner Aksinya said to my father-in-law: "I want to build a brickyard at Butyokino; I'm going into business on my own account." She laughed as she said it. And Grigory Petrovich's face darkened, you could see he did not like it. "As long as I live," he said, "the family must not break up, we must all work together." She flashed her eyes and gritted her teeth . . . Fritters were served, but she wouldn't eat them.'

'A-a-a! . . .' Crutch was surprised. 'She wouldn't eat them!'

'And tell me, if you please, when does she sleep?' Lipa went on. 'She sleeps for half an hour, then jumps up and keeps walking and walking about to see whether the peasants have set fire to something, or stolen something . . . I am frightened of her, Ilya Makarych! And the Khrymin Juniors did not go to bed after the wedding, but drove to town to go to law with each other; and folks do say it's all on account of Aksinya. Two of the brothers have promised to build her a brickyard, but the third is offended, and the factory has been at a standstill for a month, and my uncle Prokhor is without work and goes from house to house begging for crusts. "Hadn't you better go working on the land or sawing up wood, meanwhile, Uncle?" I tell him; "why disgrace yourself?" "I've got out of the habit of peasant's work," he says; "I don't know how to do anything, Lipa dear! . . ." '

They stopped to rest and wait for Praskovya near a copse of young aspen-trees. Yelizarov had been doing contract work for a long time, but he had no horse, going on foot all over the district with nothing but a little bag of bread and onions, and walking along with big strides, swinging his arms. And it was difficult to keep up with him.

At the entrance to the copse stood a milestone. Yelizarov touched it, to see if it was sound. Praskovya reached them, out of breath. Her wrinkled face, with its perpetual look of fear, was beaming with happiness; she had been at church today like anyone else, then she had been to the fair and had drunk pear kvass there! For her this was unusual, and it even seemed to her now that she had lived for her own pleasure that day for the first time in her life. After resting, all three of them went on together. The sun was setting, and its beams filtered through the copse, casting a light on the trunks of the trees. There was a faint sound of voices ahead. The Ukleyevo girls had long before pushed on ahead but had lingered in the copse, probably gathering mushrooms.

'Hey, wenches!' cried Yelizarov. 'Hey, my beauties!'

There was a sound of laughter in response.

'Crutch is coming! Crutch! The old fogey!'

And the echo laughed, too. And then the copse was left behind. The tops of the factory chimneys came into view. The cross on the belfry glittered: this was the village, 'the one where the sexton ate all the caviare at the funeral'. Now they were almost home; they only had to go down into the big ravine. Lipa and Praskovya, who had been walking barefooted, sat down on the grass to put on their boots; Yelizarov sat down with them. From on high, Ukleyevo seemed beautiful and peaceful with its willow-trees, its white church, and its little river, and the only blots on the picture were the factory roofs, painted for reasons of economy a hideous gloomy colour. On the slope on the further side they could see the rye—some in stacks and sheaves here and there as though strewn about by the storm, and some freshly cut lying in swathes; the oats, too, were ripe and glistened now in the sun like mother-of-pearl. It was harvest-time. Today was a holiday, tomorrow they would harvest the rye and carry the hay, and then Sunday, a holiday again; every day there were mutterings of distant thunder. It was misty and looked like rain, and, gazing now at the fields, everyone thought, God grant we gather the harvest in time; and everyone felt cheerful and joyful and anxious at heart.

'Mowers ask a high price nowadays,' said Praskovya. 'One rouble forty kopecks a day.'

People kept coming and coming from the fair at Kazanskoye; peasant women, factory workers in new caps, beggars, children . . . Here a cart would drive by stirring up the dust and behind it would run an unsold horse, and it seemed glad it had not been sold; then a cow was led along by the horns, resisting stubbornly; then a cart again, and in it drunken peasants dangling their legs. An old woman led a little boy in a big cap and big boots; the boy was tired out with the heat and the heavy boots which prevented him from bending his legs at the knees, and yet he blew unceasingly with all his might on a tin trumpet. They had gone down the slope and turned into the street, but the trumpet could still be heard.

'Our factory owners don't seem quite themselves . . .' said Yelizarov. 'There's trouble. Kostyukov is angry with me. "Too many boards have gone on the cornices." "Too many? As many as were needed, Vasily Danilych; I don't eat them with my porridge." "How can you speak to me like that?" said he, "you good-for-nothing blockhead! Don't forget yourself! It was I made you a contractor." "That's nothing so wonderful," said I. "Even before I was a contractor I used to drink tea every day." "You're all rascals . . ." he said. I said nothing. "We are rascals in this world," thought I, "and you will be rascals in the next . . ." Ha-ha-ha! The following day he was softer. "Don't be cross with me for my words, Makarych," he said. "If I said too much," says he, "what of it? I am a merchant of the first guild, your superior—you ought to hold your tongue." "You", said I, "are a merchant of the first guild and I am a carpenter, that's correct. And Saint Joseph was a carpenter, too. Ours is a righteous calling and pleasing to God, and if you are pleased to be my superior you are very welcome to it, Vasily Danilych." And later on, after that conversation I mean, I thought: "Who is the superior? A merchant of the first guild or a carpenter?" The carpenter must be, children!'

Crutch thought a minute and added:

'Yes, that's how it is, children. He who labours, he who is long-suffering is the superior.'

By now the sun had set and a thick mist as white as milk was rising over the river, in the churchyard, and in the open spaces round the factories. Now when the darkness was coming on rapidly, when lights were twinkling below, and when it seemed as if the mist were hiding a fathomless abyss, Lipa and her mother who were born in poverty and prepared to live so till the end, giving up to others everything except their frightened, gentle souls, may have fancied for a minute perhaps that in this vast mysterious world, among the endless series of lives, they, too, counted for something, and they, too, were superior to someone; they liked sitting here on high, they smiled happily and forgot that they would still have to go back down.

At last they were home again. The mowers were sitting on the ground at the gates and near the shop. As a rule the Ukleyevo peasants would not work for Tsybukin, and they had to hire strangers, and now in the darkness the men sitting there all seemed to have long black beards. The shop was open, and through the doorway they could see the deaf man playing draughts with a boy. The mowers were singing softly, barely audibly, or loudly demanding their wages for the previous day, but they were not paid for fear they should go away before tomorrow. Old Tsybukin, with his coat off, was sitting in his waistcoat, drinking tea with Aksinya, under the birch-tree by the porch; a lamp was burning on the table.

'I say, Grandfather,' a mower called from outside the gates, as if taunting him, 'pay us half anyway! Hey, Grandfather!'

And at once there was the sound of laughter, and then again they sang barely audibly . . . Crutch, too, sat down to have some tea.

'We have been at the fair, you know,' he began telling them. 'We've had a good time, a very good time, my children, praise the Lord. But an unfortunate thing happened: Sashka the blacksmith bought some tobacco and gave the shopman half a rouble, you see. And the half-rouble was a false one'—Crutch went on, and he glanced round; he meant to speak in a whisper, but he spoke in a smothered, husky voice which was audible to everyone. 'The half-rouble turned out to be a bad one. He was asked where he got it. "Anisim Tsybukin gave it me," he said. "When I went to his wedding," he said. They called the constable, took the man away . . . Look out, Petrovich, that nothing comes of it, no talk . . .'

'Grandfather!' the same voice called tauntingly outside the gates. 'Gra-andfather!'

A silence followed.

'Ah, little children, little children, little children . . .' Crutch muttered rapidly, and he got up. He was overcome with drowsiness. 'Well, thank you for the tea, for the sugar, little children. It's time to sleep. I am like a bit of rotten timber nowadays, my beams are crumbling under me. Ho-ho-ho!'

And, as he left, he said:

'I suppose it's time I was dead.'

And he sobbed. Old Tsybukin did not finish his tea but sat for a while, pondering; and his face looked as if he were listening to the footsteps of Crutch, who was far away down the street.

'Sashka the blacksmith told a lie, I expect,' said Aksinya, guessing his thoughts.

He went into the house and came back a little later with a parcel; he opened it, and there was the gleam of roubles—perfectly new coins. He took one, tried it with his teeth, flung it on the tray; then flung down another.

'The roubles really are false . . .' he said, looking at Aksinya and seeming

439

perplexed. 'It's them . . . Anisim brought them that time, his present. Take them, daughter,' he whispered, and thrust the parcel into her hands. 'Take them and throw them down the well . . . Confound them! And mind there is no talk. Nothing must come of it . . . Take away the samovar, put out the light . . .'

Lipa and Praskovya sitting in the barn saw the lights go out one after the other; only upstairs in Varvara's room the blue and red icon-lamps gleamed, and a feeling of peace, content, and happy ignorance seemed to float down from there. Praskovya could never get used to her daughter's being married to a rich man, and when she came she huddled timidly in the entrance-hall with a pleading smile on her face, and tea and sugar were sent out to her. And Lipa, too, could not get used to it either, and after her husband had gone away she did not sleep in her bed, but lay down anywhere to sleep, in the kitchen or the barn, and every day she scrubbed the floors or washed the clothes, and felt as though she were hired by the day. And now, on returning from the pilgrimage, they drank tea in the kitchen with the cook, then they went into the barn and lay down on the ground between the sledge and the wall. It was dark there and smelt of horse-collars. The lights went out around the house, then they could hear the deaf man shutting up the shop, the mowers settling themselves about the yard to sleep. In the distance at the Khrymin Juniors' they were playing on the expensive concertina . . . Praskovya and Lipa began to go to sleep.

And when they were awakened by somebody's steps it was bright moonlight; at the entrance to the barn stood Aksinya with her bedding in her arms.

'Maybe it's a bit cooler here,' she said; then she came in and lay down almost on the threshold so that the moonlight fell full upon her.

She did not sleep, but breathed heavily, tossing from side to side with the heat, throwing off almost all the bedclothes. And in the magic moon-light what a beautiful, what a proud animal she was! A little time passed, and then steps were heard again: the old father, white all over, appeared in the doorway.

'Aksinya,' he called, 'are you there?'

'What is it?' she responded angrily.

'I told you just now to throw the money down the well, have you done so?'

'What next, throwing good money into the water! I gave it to the mowers . . .'

'Oh my God!' cried the old man, dumbfounded and alarmed. 'Oh my God! you mischievous woman . . .'

440

He clasped his hands and went away, and he kept muttering something as he left. And a little later Aksinya sat up and sighed heavily with annoyance, then got up and, gathering her bedclothes in her arms, went out.

'Why did you marry me into this family, Mother?' said Lipa.

'People have to marry, dear daughter. It was not us who ordained it.'

And a feeling of inconsolable grief was ready to take possession of them. But it seemed to them that someone was looking down from the height of the heavens, from out of that starry blue, and could see everything that happened in Ukleyevo, and was watching over them. And no matter how great the evil, yet the night was calm and beautiful, yet in God's world there is and will be truth, just as calm and beautiful, and everything on earth is only waiting to blend with truth, even as the moonlight blends with the night.

And, comforted, they huddled together, and fell asleep.

VI

News had come long ago that Anisim had been put in prison for coining and circulating false money. Months passed, more than half a year passed, the long winter was over, spring had begun, and everyone in the house and the village had grown used to the fact that Anisim was in prison. And when anyone walked by the house or the shop at night he would remember that Anisim was in prison; and, when they rang at the churchyard, for some reason that, too, reminded them that he was in prison awaiting trial.

It seemed as though a shadow lay over the homestead. The house looked darker, the roof was rustier, the heavy, iron-bound door into the shop, which was painted green, was covered with cracks, or, as the deaf man expressed it, 'blisters'; and old Tsybukin seemed to have grown dingy, too. He had long given up cutting his hair and beard, and looked shaggy. He no longer sprang jauntily into his chaise, nor shouted to beggars: 'God will provide!' His strength was on the wane, and that was evident in everything. People were less afraid of him now, and the constable drew up a formal charge against him in the shop though he received his regular bribe as before; and three times the old man was summoned to town to be tried for illicit dealing in spirits, and the case was continually adjourned owing to the non-appearance of witnesses, and old Tsybukin was worn out with worry.

441

He often went to see his son, hired somebody, addressed petitions to somebody else, donated a holy banner to some church. He presented the governor of the prison in which Anisim was confined with a silver glass-holder bearing the enamelled inscription: 'The soul knows its right measure'—together with a long spoon.

'There is no one to put in a word for us,' said Varvara. 'Tut, tut . . . You ought to ask one of the gentlefolk, they would write to the head officials . . . At least they might let him out on bail! Why wear the poor fellow out?'

She, too, was distressed, but had grown stouter and whiter; she lit the lamps before her icons as before, and saw that everything in the house was clean, and regaled the guests with jam and apple-cheese. The deaf man and Aksinya served in the shop. A new project was in progress—the brickyard in Butyokino—and Aksinya went there almost every day in the chaise. She drove herself, and when she met acquaintances she stretched out her neck like a snake in the young rye, and smiled naïvely and enigmatically. Lipa spent her time playing with the baby which had been born to her just before Lent. It was a tiny, thin, pitiful little baby, and it was strange that it should cry and gaze about and be considered a human being, and even be called Nikifor. He lay in his cradle, and Lipa would walk away towards the door and say, bowing to him:

'Good day, Nikifor Anisimych!'

And she would rush up to him and kiss him. Then she would walk away to the door, bow, and again say:

'Good day, Nikifor Anisimych!'

And he kicked up his little red legs, and his crying was mixed with laughter like the carpenter Yelizarov's.

At last the day of the trial was fixed. The old man set off five days before. Then they heard that the peasants called as witnesses had been fetched; their old workman who had received a summons went too.

The trial was on a Thursday. But Sunday had passed, and the old man was still not back, and there was no news. Towards the evening on Tuesday Varvara was sitting at the open window, listening for her husband to come. In the next room Lipa was playing with her baby. She was tossing him up in her arms and saying with delight:

'You will grow up ever so big, ever so big. You will be a peasant, we shall go out work together! We shall go out to work together!'

'Come, come,' said Varvara, offended. 'Go out to work, what an idea, you silly girl! He will be a merchant! . . .'

Lipa began singing softly, but a minute later she forgot herself and again:

'You will grow up ever so big, ever so big. You will be a peasant, we shall go out to work together!'

'There she is, at it again!'

Lipa, with Nikifor in her arms, stood still in the doorway and asked:

'Why do I love him so much, Mamma? Why do I feel so sorry for him?' she went on in a quivering voice, and her eyes glistened with tears. 'Who is he? What is he like? As light as a little feather, as a little crumb, but I love him; I love him like a real person. He can't do anything, he can't talk, and yet I know what he wants from his dear little eyes.'

Varvara listened keenly: the sound of the evening train coming into the station reached her. Had her husband come? She did not hear or understand what Lipa was saying, she had no idea how the time passed, but only trembled all over—not from dread, but intense curiosity. She saw a cart full of peasants rumble quickly by. It was the witnesses coming back from the station. When the cart passed the shop the old workman jumped out and walked into the yard. She could hear him being greeted in the yard and being asked some questions . . .

'Deprivation of rights and all his property,' he said loudly, 'and six years' penal servitude in Siberia.'

She could see Aksinya come out of the shop by the back way; she had just been selling kerosene, and in one hand held a bottle and in the other a funnel, and in her mouth she had some silver coins.

'Where is Father?' she asked, lisping.

'At the station,' answered the labourer. ' "When it gets a little darker," he said, "then I shall come." '

And when it became known in the yard that Anisim was sentenced to penal servitude, the cook in the kitchen suddenly broke into a wail as though at a funeral, imagining that this was what propriety demanded:

'There is no one to care for us now you have gone, Anisim Grigoryich, our bright falcon . . .'

The dogs began barking in alarm. Varvara ran to the window and, rushing about in distress, shouted to the cook, straining her voice with all her might:

'Sto-op, Stepanida, sto-op! Don't torment us, for the love of Christ!'

They forgot to set the samovar, they could think of nothing. Only Lipa could not make out what it was all about and went on playing with her baby.

When the old man arrived from the station they asked him no questions. He greeted them and walked through all the rooms in silence; he had no supper.

'There was no one to put in a word for us . . .' Varvara began when they were alone. 'I said you should have asked some of the gentlefolk, you would not heed me at the time . . . A petition would . . .'

'I tried to put in a word,' said the old man with a wave of his hand. 'When Anisim was condemned I went to the gentleman who was defending him. "It's no use now," he said, "it's too late"; and Anisim himself said that it's too late. But all the same as I came out of the court I made an agreement with a lawyer, I paid him something in advance. I'll wait a week and then I will go again. Surely God will provide.'

Again the old man walked through all the rooms, and when he went back to Varvara he said:

'I must be ill. My head's in a sort of . . . fog. My thoughts are in a haze.'

He closed the door so that Lipa might not hear, and went on softly:

'I am unhappy about my money. Do you remember, the week after Easter before his wedding, Anisim brought me some new roubles and half-roubles? One parcel I hid away at the time, but the others I mixed with my own money . . . When my uncle Dmitry Filatych—the kingdom of heaven be his—was alive, he used constantly to go on journeys to Moscow and to the Crimea to buy goods. He had a wife, and this same wife, when he was away buying goods, used to carry on with other men. She had half a dozen children. And when Uncle was in his cups he would laugh and say: "I never can make out," he used to say, "which are my children and which are other people's." An easy-going disposition, to be sure. And in the same way now I can't make out which are genuine coins and which are false ones. And it seems to me that they are all false.'

'Nonsense, God bless you.'

'I buy a ticket at the station, I give the man three roubles, and I keep fancying they are false. And I am frightened. I must be ill.'

'There's no denying it, we are all in God's hands . . . Oh, tut, tut . . .' said Varvara, and she shook her head. 'You ought to think about this, Petrovich . . . You never know, anything may happen, you are not a young man. See they don't wrong your grandchild when you are dead and gone. Oh, I am afraid they will wrong Nikifor! He has as good as no father, his mother's young and foolish . . . you ought to transfer something to his name, the poor little boy, at least the land, Butyokino, say, Petrovich, really! Think it over!' Varvara went on persuading him. 'He's such a

444

sweet little boy, I'm sorry for him! You go tomorrow and sign the papers; why put it off?'

'I'd forgotten about my grandson,' said Tsybukin. 'I must go and say hello to him. So you say the boy is all right? Well, let him grow, please God.'

He opened the door and, crooking his finger, beckoned to Lipa. She went up to him with the baby in her arms.

'If there is anything you want, Lipa dear, just ask for it,' he said. 'And eat anything you like, we don't grudge it, so long as you keep well . . .' He made the sign of the cross over the baby. 'And take care of my grandson. My son is gone, but my grandson is left.'

Tears rolled down his cheeks; he gave a sob and went away. Soon afterwards he went to bed and slept soundly after seven sleepless nights.

VII

The old man went to the town for a short while. Someone told Aksinya that he had gone to the notary to make his will and that he was leaving Butyokino, the very place where she had set up a brickyard, to Nikifor, his grandson. She was informed of this in the morning when the old man and Varvara were sitting near the steps under the birch-tree, drinking their tea. She closed the shop in the front and at the back, gathered together all the keys she had, and flung them at the old man's feet.

'I am not going on working for you!' she began in a loud voice, and suddenly broke into sobs. 'It seems I am not your daughter-in-law, but a servant! Everybody's jeering and saying, "See what a servant the Tsybukins have got hold of!" I did not come to you as a hired labourer! I'm not a beggar, I'm not a slave, I have a father and mother.'

She did not wipe away her tears, she glared at the old man with eyes full of tears, vindictive, squinting with wrath; her face and neck were red and tense, as she was shouting at the top of her voice.

'I don't intend to go on being a slave!' she continued. 'I am worn out! When it comes to work, sitting in the shop day in and day out, sneaking out at night for vodka—that is my share, but when it comes to giving away some land, then that's for the convict's wife and her imp. She's the mistress here, the fine lady, and I'm her servant! Give her everything, the convict's wife, and may it choke her; I am going home! Find yourselves some other fool, you damned Herods!'

445

The old man had never in his life scolded or punished his children, and had never dreamed that one of his family could speak to him rudely or behave disrespectfully; and now he was very frightened; he ran into the house and hid there behind the cupboard. And Varvara felt so flustered that she could not get up from her seat, and only waved her hands before her as if she were warding off a bee.

'Oh Holy Saints! what's this?' she muttered in horror. 'Why is she shouting so? Oh, tut, tut . . . People will hear! Hush. Oh, hush!'

'They've given Butyokino to the convict's wife,' Aksinya went on bawling. 'Give her everything now, I don't want anything from you! Go to hell! You're all a gang of thieves! I've seen my fill, I've had enough! You've robbed everyone who came your way; you've robbed old and young alike, you brigands! And who has been selling vodka without a licence? And those false coins? You've filled coffers with false coins, and now I'm of no more use!'

A crowd had gathered by now at the open gate and was staring into the yard.

'Let the people look!' bawled Aksinya. 'I'll shame you all! You shall burn with shame! You shall grovel at my feet! Hey, Stepan!' she called to the deaf man. 'Let's go home this minute! Let's go to my father and mother; I don't want to live with convicts. Get ready!'

Clothes were hanging on lines stretched across the yard; she snatched her still wet skirts and blouses and flung them into the deaf man's arms. Then in her fury she dashed about the yard, snatched down everything— including other people's clothes—threw it on the ground and trampled on it.

'Holy Saints, stop her!' moaned Varvara. 'What's she doing? Give her Butyokino! Give it her, for the Lord's sake!'

'Well! Wha-at a woman!' people were saying at the gate. 'Such a wo-oman! She's really letting fly!'

Aksinya ran into the kitchen where washing was going on. Lipa was washing alone, the cook had gone to the river to rinse the clothes. Steam was rising from the tub and from the cauldron near the stove, and the kitchen was dark and stifling from the mist. On the floor was a heap of unwashed clothes, and Nikifor, kicking up his little red legs, had been placed on a bench near them so that if he fell he should not hurt himself. Just as Aksinya came in Lipa took the former's chemise out of the heap and put it in the tub, and was stretching out her hand to a big ladle of boiling water which was standing on the table . . .

446

'Give it here,' said Aksinya, looking at her with hatred, and snatched the chemise from the tub. 'It's not your business to touch my clothes! You're a convict's wife, and ought to know your place and who you are.'

Lipa gazed at her, taken aback, and did not understand, but suddenly she caught the look Aksinya turned upon the child, and suddenly she understood and went numb all over . . .

'You've taken my land, so here you are!'

Saying this, Aksinya snatched up the ladle of boiling water and flung it over Nikifor.

After this there was heard a scream such as had never been heard in Ukleyevo, and no one would have believed that a little weak creature like Lipa could scream like that. And suddenly it was quiet outside. Aksinya walked silently into the house, with her habitual naïve smile . . . The deaf man kept moving about the yard with his arms full of clothes, then he began hanging them up again, silently, without haste. And until the cook came back from the river no one ventured to go into the kitchen and see what was there.

VIII

Nikifor was taken to the district hospital, and towards evening he died there. Lipa did not wait for them to come for her, but wrapped the dead baby in its little blanket and carried it home.

The hospital, a new one, recently built, with large windows, stood high up on a hill; it was glittering from the setting sun and looked as if it were on fire inside. There was a small village below. Lipa went down along the road, and before reaching the village sat down by a little pond. A woman brought a horse down to drink, and the horse would not drink.

'What more do you want?' said the woman softly, quite bewildered. 'What do you want?'

A boy in a red shirt, sitting at the water's edge, was washing his father's boots. And not another soul was in sight either in the village or on the hill.

'It's not drinking,' said Lipa, looking at the horse.

Then the woman and the boy with the boots went away, and there was no one to be seen. The sun went to bed wrapped in cloth of gold and purple, and long clouds, red and lilac, stretched across the sky, to guard its slumbers. Somewhere far away a bittern boomed, a hollow, melancholy

447

sound like a cow locked in a barn. The boom of that mysterious bird was heard every spring, but no one knew what it was like or where it lived. At the top of the hill by the hospital, in the bushes close to the pond, beyond the village and in the fields all around, nightingales were trilling. A cuckoo was counting someone's age, but kept losing count and beginning again. In the pond the frogs, straining themselves, called angrily to one another, and one could even make out their words: 'That's what you are! That's what you are!' What a noise there was! It seemed that all these creatures were singing and shouting so that no one might sleep on this spring night, so that all, even the angry frogs, might appreciate and relish every minute: for life is given only once!

A silver half-moon was shining in the sky; there were many stars. Lipa had no idea how long she sat by the pond, but when she got up and walked on, everybody was asleep in the little village, and there was not a single light. It must have been eight miles to her home, but she had not the strength, and knew not where to go: the moon gleamed now in front, now on the right, and the same cuckoo kept calling in a voice grown husky, with a chuckle as though taunting her: 'Heh, look out, you'll lose your way!' Lipa walked rapidly; the kerchief fell from her head . . . She gazed at the sky and wondered where her baby's soul was now: was it following her, or floating there on high among the stars, and thinking no longer of his mother? Oh, how lonely it was in the open country at night, amid this singing when one cannot sing oneself, amid the incessant cries of joy when one cannot oneself be joyful, when from the sky the moon looks down, also lonely, not caring whether it is spring or winter, whether people are alive or dead . . . When there is grief in one's heart it is hard to be without people. If only her mother, Praskovya, had been with her, or Crutch, or the cook, or some peasant!

'Boo-oo!' boomed the bittern. 'Boo-oo!'

And suddenly she heard clearly the sound of human speech:

'Harness the horses, Vavila!'

By the wayside a camp-fire was burning ahead of her; the flames had died down, there were only red embers. She could hear the horses munching. In the darkness she could see the outlines of two carts, one with a barrel, the other, a lower one, with sacks, and the figures of two men: one was leading a horse to put it into the shafts, the other was standing motionless by the fire with his hands behind his back. A dog growled near the cart. The one who was leading the horse stopped and said:

'It seems someone's coming down the road.'

448

'Sharik, be quiet!' the other called to the dog.

And from his voice one could tell that this other man was old. Lipa stopped and said:

'God be with you!'

The old man went up to her and answered not immediately:

'Good evening!'

'Your dog won't bite, will he, Grandfather?'

'No, come along, he won't touch you.'

'I have been at the hospital,' said Lipa after a pause. 'My little son died there. Now I am carrying him home.'

It must have been unpleasant for the old man to hear this, for he moved away and said hurriedly:

'Never mind, my dear. It's God's will. You are very slow, lad,' he added, turning to his companion. 'Get a move on!'

'Your yoke's not there,' said the lad; 'I can't see it.'

'You're a right charlie, Vavila.'

The old man picked up an ember, blew on it—only his eyes and nose were lit up—then, when they had found the yoke, he went with the light to Lipa and looked at her, and his look expressed compassion and tenderness.

'You are a mother,' he said; 'every mother grieves for her child.'

And he sighed and shook his head as he said this. Vavila threw something on the fire, stamped on it—and at once it grew very dark; the vision vanished, and as before there were only the fields, the sky with the stars, and the noise of the birds preventing each other from sleeping. And the landrail called, it seemed, in the very place where the fire had been.

But a minute passed, and again she could see the carts and the old man and lanky Vavila. The carts creaked as they went out on the road.

'Are you holy men?' Lipa asked the old man.

'No. We are from Firsanovo.'

'You looked at me just now and my heart was softened. And the lad is so gentle. So I thought you must be holy men.'

'Are you going far?'

'To Ukleyevo.'

'Get in, we will give you a lift as far as Kuzmyonki. Then you go straight on and we turn off to the left.'

Vavila got into the cart with the barrel and the old man and Lipa got into the other. They moved at a walking pace, Vavila in front.

'My baby was in torment all day,' said Lipa. 'He looked at me with his little eyes and said nothing; he wanted to speak and could not. Holy Father, Queen of Heaven! In my grief I kept falling down on the floor. I stood up and fell down by the bedside. And tell me, Grandfather, why a little one should be tormented before his death? When a grown-up person, a man or woman, is in torment their sins are forgiven, but why a little one, when he has no sins? Why?'

'Who knows?' answered the old man.

They drove on for half an hour in silence.

'We can't know everything, the whys and wherefores,' said the old man. 'It is ordained for a bird to have two wings, not four, because it is able to fly with two; and so it is ordained for man not to know everything but only a half or a quarter. What he needs to know in order to live, that much he knows.'

'It's easier for me to go on foot, Grandfather. Now my heart is all of a tremble.'

'Never mind, sit still.'

The old man yawned and made the sign of the cross over his mouth.

'Never mind,' he repeated. 'Yours is not the worst of sorrows. Life is long, there will be good and bad to come, there will be everything. Great is Mother Russia,' he said, and looked round to either side. 'I have been all over Russia, and I have seen everything in her, and you may believe my words, my dear. There will be good and there will be bad. I've often been to Siberia, and I have been to the Amur River and the Altay Mountains and I settled in Siberia; I worked the land there, then I felt homesick for Mother Russia and I returned to my native village. We came back to Russia on foot; and I remember we went on a ferry, and I was thin as thin, all in rags, barefoot, freezing with cold, and sucking a crust, and a gentleman who was on the ferry—the kingdom of heaven be his if he is dead—looked at me pitifully, and his tears started flowing. "Ah," he said, "your bread is black, your days are black ..." And when I got home, as the saying is, there was neither stick nor stall; I had a wife, but I left her behind in Siberia, she was buried there. So I worked as a farm-labourer. And yet I tell you: since then I have had good as well as bad. Now I do not want to die, my dear, I would be glad to live another twenty years; so there has been more good than bad. And great is our Mother Russia!' he said, and again he gazed to each side and glanced back.

'Grandfather,' Lipa asked, 'when a person dies, how many days does his soul walk the earth?'

'Who knows? Let's ask Vavila here, he has been to school. Now they teach them everything. Vavila!' the old man called.

'What?'

'Vavila, when a person dies, how many days does his soul walk the earth?'

Vavila stopped the horse and only then answered:

'Nine days. My uncle Kirilla died and his soul lived in our hut thirteen days after.'

'How do you know?'

'For thirteen days there was a knocking in the stove.'

'Well, that's all right. Go on,' said the old man, and it could be seen that he did not believe a word of it.

Near Kuzmyonki the carts turned on to the high road while Lipa went straight on. Already it was getting light. As she went down into the ravine the Ukleyevo huts and the church were hidden in fog. It was cold, and it seemed to her that the same cuckoo was calling still.

When Lipa reached home the cattle had not yet been driven out; everyone was asleep. She sat down on the steps and waited. The old man was the first to come out; at a glance he understood all that had happened, and for a long time he could not utter a word, but only made a smacking sound with his lips.

'Ah, Lipa,' he said, 'you did not take care of my grandchild . . .'

Varvara was woken. She clasped her hands and broke into sobs, and immediately began laying out the baby.

'And he was such a pretty child . . .' she said. 'Oh tut, tut . . . You only had the one child, and you did not take care of him, you silly girl . . .'

There was a requiem service in the morning and the evening. The funeral took place the next day, and after it the guests and the priests ate a great deal, and with such greed that one might have thought that they had not tasted food for ages. Lipa waited at table, and the priest, lifting his fork on which was speared a pickled mushroom, said to her:

'Do not grieve for the babe. For of such is the kingdom of heaven.'

And only when they had all left did Lipa realise fully that there was no Nikifor and never would be, she realised this and broke into sobs. And she did not know what room to go into to sob, for she felt that after her child's death there was no place for her in this house, that she had no reason to be here, she was superfluous; and the others felt it, too.

451

'What are you wailing for?' Aksinya suddenly shouted, appearing in the doorway; to mark the funeral she was dressed all in new clothes and had powdered her face. 'Shut up!'

Lipa tried to stop but could not, and sobbed louder than ever.

'Do you hear?' shouted Aksinya, and she stamped her foot in a violent rage. 'Who is it I am speaking to? Clear out of here and don't set foot in this house again, you convict's wife. Clear off!'

'There, there, there,' fussed the old man. 'Aksyusha, calm down, my girl . . . She is crying, it's only natural . . . her child is dead . . .'

' "It's only natural," ' Aksinya mimicked him. 'Let her stay the night here, but don't let me see a trace of her tomorrow! "It's only natural!" . . .' she mimicked him again, and, laughing, she went off to the shop.

Early next morning Lipa went home to her mother at Torguyevo.

IX

At the present time the roof and door of the shop have been repainted and shine like new, there are cheerful geraniums in the windows as before, and what happened in Tsybukin's house and yard three years ago is almost forgotten.

Old Grigory Petrovich is still considered the master, but in reality everything has passed into Aksinya's hands; she buys and sells, and nothing can be done without her consent. The brickyard is working well; and as bricks are wanted for the railway their price has gone up to twenty-four roubles a thousand; peasant women and girls cart the bricks to the station and load them up in trucks and earn a quarter-rouble a day for that work.

Aksinya has gone into partnership with the Khrymins, and their factory is now called 'Khrymin Juniors and Co.'. They have opened a tavern near the station, and now the expensive concertina is played not at the factory but in this tavern, and the postmaster often goes there, and he, too, is engaged in some sort of business, and the station-master, too. Khrymin Juniors have presented deaf Stepan with a gold watch, and he keeps taking it out of his pocket and holding it to his ear.

People in the village say of Aksinya that she has become a person of great power; and it is true that when she drives in the morning to her brickyard, handsome and happy, with a naïve smile on her face, and afterwards when she is giving orders there, she conveys an air of great power. Everyone is afraid of her at home and in the village and at the brickyard. When she goes to the post-office the postmaster jumps up and says to her:

'I humbly beg you to be seated, Kseniya Abramovna!'

A certain landowner, middle-aged but foppish, in a tunic of fine cloth and patent leather high boots, once sold her a horse, and was so carried away by talking to her that he knocked down his price to meet her wishes. He held her hand a long time and, looking into her merry, sly, naïve eyes, said:

'For a woman like you, Kseniya Abramovna, I would do anything in the world. Only say when we can meet where no one will interrupt us?'

'Why, whenever you wish!'

And since then the middle-aged fop drives up to the shop almost every day to drink beer. And the beer is horrid, bitter as wormwood. The landowner shakes his head, but he drinks it.

Old Tsybukin no longer takes part in the business. He keeps no money in his pockets, because he cannot distinguish between the good and the false, but he is silent, and tells no one about this weakness of his. He has become forgetful, and if they don't give him food he does not ask for it. They have grown used to having dinner without him, and Varvara often says:

'He went to bed again yesterday without any supper.'

And she says it casually because she is used to it. For some reason, summer and winter alike, he wears a fur coat, and only on very hot days he does not go out at all, but stays at home. As a rule, putting on his fur coat, wrapping it round him and turning up his collar, he walks about the village, along the road to the station, or sits from morning till night on the seat near the church gates. He sits there without stirring. Passers-by bow to him, but he does not respond, for as before he dislikes the peasants. If he is asked a question he answers quite rationally and politely, but briefly.

There is a rumour going about in the village that his daughter-in-law has turned him out of the house and gives him nothing to eat, and that he lives on charity; some are glad, others are sorry for him.

Varvara has grown even fatter and whiter, and as before she is active in good works, and Aksinya does not interfere with her. There is so much jam now that they have no time to eat it before the fresh fruit comes in; it crystallises, and Varvara almost weeps, not knowing what to do with it.

They have begun to forget about Anisim. A letter once arrived from him written in verse on a big sheet of paper in the form of a petition, still in the same splendid handwriting. Evidently his friend Samorodov was sharing his punishment. Under the verses in an ugly, scarcely legible handwriting there was a single line: 'I am ill here all the time; I feel wretched, for the love of Christ help me!'

Towards evening—it was a fine autumn day—old Tsybukin was sitting near the church gates, with the collar of his fur coat turned up, and nothing could be seen of him but his nose and the peak of his cap. At the other end of the long seat was Yelizarov the contractor, and beside him Yakov the school watchman, a toothless old man of seventy. Crutch and the watchman were talking.

'Children ought to give food and drink to the old . . . Honour thy father and thy mother . . .' Yakov was saying with irritation, 'while she, this daughter-in-law, has turned her father-in-law out of his own house; the old man has neither food nor drink, where is he to go? He hasn't had a morsel for these three days.'

'Three days!' said Crutch, amazed.

'Here he sits, and never a word. He has grown feeble. But why keep silent? He ought to prosecute her, she'd not get away with it in court.'

'Who got away with it in court?' asked Crutch, not hearing.

'What?'

'The woman's all right, she's a hard worker. In their line of business they can't get on without that . . . without sin, I mean . . .'

'Out of his own house,' Yakov went on with irritation. 'Build up your own house first, before you turn others out. She is a nice one, to be sure! A pla-ague!'

Tsybukin listened and did not stir.

'Whether it's your own house or others' it makes no difference so long as it is warm and the women don't scold . . .' said Crutch, and he laughed. 'When I was young I was very fond of my Nastasya. She was a quiet woman. And she used to be always at it: "Buy a house, Makarych! Buy a house, Makarych! Buy a horse, Makarych!" She was dying and yet she kept on saying, "Buy yourself a racing droshky, Makarych, so you won't have to walk." But I bought her nothing but gingerbread.'

'Her husband's deaf and stupid,' Yakov went on, not hearing Crutch; 'a real fool, a proper goose. He can't understand anything. Hit a goose on the head with a stick and even then it won't understand.'

Crutch got up to go home to the factory. Yakov also got up, and both of them went off together, still talking. When they had gone fifty paces old Tsybukin got up, too, and shuffled along after them, stepping uncertainly as though on slippery ice.

The village was already plunged in twilight and the sun gleamed only on the upper part of the road which wound like a snake up the slope. Old women were returning from the woods and children with them; they were bringing baskets of forest mushrooms. Peasant women and girls came in a crowd from the station where they had been loading the trucks with bricks, and their noses and cheeks under their eyes were covered with red brick-dust. They were singing. Ahead of them all walked Lipa singing in a thin voice, and breaking into trills as she gazed up at the sky, as if triumphant and ecstatic that the day, thank God, was over and she could rest. In the crowd was her mother, the day-labourer Praskovya, who was walking with a bundle in her arms and breathless as usual.

'Good evening, Makarych!' said Lipa, seeing Crutch. 'Good evening, my precious!'

'Good evening, Lipa dear,' cried Crutch, delighted. 'Sweet girls and women, love a rich carpenter! Ho-ho! My little children, little children.' (Crutch sobbed.) 'My dear little axes!'

Crutch and Yakov went on further and could still be heard talking. Then after them the crowd was met by old Tsybukin and there was a sudden hush. Lipa and Praskovya had lagged behind a little, and when the old man drew level with them Lipa bowed down low and said:

'Good evening, Grigory Petrovich!'

Her mother, too, bowed down. The old man stopped and, saying nothing, looked at them both; his lips were quivering and his eyes were full of tears. Lipa took out of her mother's bundle a piece of buckwheat pasty and gave it him. He accepted it and began eating.

The sun had completely set; its glow had died away even on the upper part of the road. It grew dark and cool. Lipa and Praskovya walked on, and for a long time kept crossing themselves.

The Bishop

I

The evening service was being celebrated on the eve of Palm Sunday at the old convent of St Peter. When they began distributing the willow-branch 'palms' it was nearly ten o'clock, the candles were burning dimly, the wicks needed snuffing; it was all in a sort of mist. In the twilight of the church the crowd swayed like the sea, and to Bishop Pyotr, who had been unwell for the last three days, it seemed that all the faces—old and young, male and female—were alike, that all who came up for a willow branch had the same expression in their eyes. In the mist he could not see the doors; the crowd kept moving and was apparently never-ending. The women's choir was singing, a nun was reading the prayers for the day.

How stifling, how hot it was! How long the service went on! Bishop Pyotr was tired. His breathing was laboured and rapid, his throat was parched, his shoulders ached with weariness, his legs were shaking. And it disturbed him unpleasantly when a holy fool uttered occasional shrieks in the gallery. And then all of a sudden, as in a dream or delirium, it seemed to the bishop as though his own mother Mariya Timofeyevna, whom he had not seen for nine years, or some old woman just like his mother, came up to him in the crowd, and, after taking a willow branch from him, walked away looking cheerfully at him all the while with a kind, joyful smile until she was lost in the crowd. And for some reason tears flowed down his face. There was peace in his heart, all was well, yet he kept gazing fixedly towards the left choir, where the prayers were being read, where in the dusk of evening you could not recognise anyone, and—he wept. Tears glistened on his face and on his beard. Now someone close at hand started weeping, then someone else further away, then others and still others, and gradually the church was filled with quiet weeping. But a little later, within five minutes, the nuns' choir was singing; no one was weeping and everything was as before.

The service ended soon afterwards. When the bishop climbed into his carriage to drive home, the cheerful, melodious chime of the heavy, costly bells was filling the whole garden in the moonlight. The white walls, the white crosses on the graves, the white birches and black

456

shadows, and the faraway moon in the sky directly over the convent, seemed now to be living their special life, incomprehensible, yet close to man. It was the beginning of April, and after the warm spring day it had turned cool; there was a faint touch of frost, and the breath of spring could be felt in the soft, chilly air. The road from the convent to the town was sandy, the horses had to go at a walking pace, and on both sides of the carriage in the bright, peaceful moonlight pilgrims trudged through this sand. And all were silent, sunk in thought; everything around was welcoming, youthful, so close, everything—trees and sky and even the moon, and one wanted to think that it would always be so.

At last the carriage drove into the town and rumbled along the main street. The shops were already shut, but at Yerakin's, the millionaire merchant's, they were testing the electric lighting, which flickered violently, and a crowd of people were gathered round. Then came wide, dark, deserted streets, one after another; then the high road outside the town, the open country, the fragrance of pines. And suddenly there arose before the bishop's eyes a white turreted wall, and behind it a tall belfry in the full moonlight, and beside it five large, shining, golden cupolas: this was the Pankratiyevsky Monastery, in which Bishop Pyotr lived. And here, too, high above the monastery, was the silent, pensive moon. The carriage drove in at the gate, crunching over the sand; here and there in the moonlight there were glimpses of dark monastic figures, and there was the sound of footsteps on the flagstones . . .

'You know, Your Eminence, your mamma arrived while you were away,' the lay brother informed the bishop as he entered his room.

'My mother? When did she come?'

'Before the evening service. She asked first where you were and then she went to the convent.'

'Then it was her I saw in the church, just now! Oh, Lord!'

And the bishop laughed with joy.

'She bade me tell Your Eminence,' the lay brother went on, 'that she would come tomorrow. She had a little girl with her—her grandchild, I suppose. They are staying at Ovsyannikov's inn.'

'What time is it now?'

'A little after eleven.'

'Oh, how vexing!'

The bishop sat for a little while in the parlour, pondering, and scarcely believing that it was so late. His arms and legs ached, the back of his head hurt. He was hot and uncomfortable. After resting he went into his

457

bedroom, and there, too, he sat for a while, still thinking of his mother; he could hear the lay brother going away, and Father Sisoy, a priest-monk, coughing the other side of the wall. The monastery clock struck a quarter.

The bishop changed his clothes and began reading the prayers before sleep. He read attentively those old, so familiar prayers, and at the same time thought about his mother. She had nine children and about forty grandchildren. At one time she had lived with her husband, the deacon, in a poor village; she had lived there a very long time from the age of seventeen to sixty. The bishop remembered her from early childhood, almost from the age of three, and—how he had loved her! Dear, precious, unforgettable childhood! Why does this time, which has gone for ever and can never return, why does it seem brighter, happier and richer than it actually was? When in his childhood or youth he had been ill, how tender and caring his mother had been! And now his prayers mingled with memories, which flared more and more brightly like a flame, and the prayers did not prevent him from thinking of his mother.

When he had finished his prayers he undressed and lay down, and at once, as soon as it was dark, there rose before his mind his late father, his mother, his native village of Lesopolye . . . The creak of wheels, the bleat of sheep, the church bells on clear summer mornings, gypsies under the window—oh, how sweet to think of this! He remembered the priest of Lesopolye, Father Simeon—mild, gentle, good-natured; he was a lean little man, while his son, a divinity student, was a huge fellow and talked in a roaring bass voice. The priest's son had once flown into a rage with the cook and scolded her: 'Ah, you ass of Jehudiel!', and Father Simeon, overhearing it, said not a word, and felt merely ashamed because he could not remember where any such ass was mentioned in the Bible. After him the priest at Lesopolye had been Father Demyan, who used to drink heavily, and at times drank till he saw green serpents, and was even nicknamed Demyan the Snakeseer. The schoolmaster at Lesopolye was Matvey Nikolaich, who had been a divinity student, a kind, quite intelligent man, but he, too, was a drunkard; he never beat the schoolchildren, but for some reason he always had hanging on his wall a bunch of birch-twigs, and below it an utterly meaningless inscription in Latin: '*Betula kinderbalsamica secuta.*' He had a shaggy black dog whom he called Syntax.

And the bishop laughed. Five miles from Lesopolye was the village of Obnino with a miracle-working icon. In the summer they used to carry this icon in procession throughout the neighbouring villages and ring the bells the whole day long, first in one village and then in another, and it used to seem to the bishop then that joy was quivering in the air, and he (in those days his name was Pavlusha) used to follow the icon, bareheaded and barefoot, with naïve faith, with a naïve smile, infinitely happy. In Obnino, he remembered now, there were always a lot of people, and the priest there, Father Aleksey, to save time during Mass, used to make his deaf nephew Ilarion read out the notes and the inscriptions on communion loaves 'for the health' of someone, or 'for the repose of the soul'. Ilarion used to read them, occasionally receiving a five- or ten-kopeck piece for his efforts, and only when he was grey and bald, when his life was over, he suddenly saw written on one of the pieces of paper: 'What a fool you are, Ilarion!' Until the age of at least fifteen Pavlusha was backward and a poor learner, so much so that they thought of taking him away from the church school and putting him into a shop; one day, going to the post at Obnino for letters, he had stared a long time at the post-office clerks and asked: 'Allow me to enquire, how do you receive your salary, every month or every day?'

The bishop crossed himself and turned over on the other side, trying to stop thinking and go to sleep.

'My mother has come,' he remembered and laughed.

The moon peeped in at the window, the floor was lit up, and shadows lay across it. A cricket chirred. Through the wall Father Sisoy was snoring in the next room, and his aged snore had a sound that suggested loneliness, like that of an orphan or even a homeless wanderer. Sisoy had once been housekeeper to the diocesan bishop, and was called now 'the former Father Housekeeper'; he was seventy years old, he lived in a monastery ten miles from the town and stayed sometimes in the town, too. He had come to the Pankratiyevsky Monastery three days before, and the bishop had kept him that he might talk to him at leisure about matters of business, about the arrangements here . . .

At half-past one they began ringing for matins. Father Sisoy could be heard coughing, muttering something in a discontented voice, then he got up and walked barefoot about the rooms.

'Father Sisoy!' the bishop called.

Sisoy went back to his room and a little later made his appearance in his boots, with a candle; he had his cassock over his underclothes and on his head was an old faded skull-cap.

'I can't sleep,' said the bishop, sitting up. 'I must be unwell. And what it is I don't know. I feel so hot!'

'You must have caught cold, Your Eminence. You should be rubbed with candle grease.' Sisoy stood a little and yawned. 'O Lord, forgive me, a sinner!'

'They had the electric lights on at Yerakin's today,' Sisoy added; 'I don't loike it!'

Father Sisoy was old, lean, bent, always dissatisfied with something, and his eyes were angry-looking and protruded like a crab's.

'I don't loike it,' he repeated, going away. 'I don't loike it! Bother it!'

II

Next day, Palm Sunday, the bishop conducted the service in the cathedral in the town, then he visited the diocesan bishop, visited a very sick old lady, the wife of some general, and at last drove home. After one o'clock he had dear guests dining with him—his old mother and his niece Katya, a child of about eight. All dinner-time the spring sunshine was streaming in at the windows, shining cheerfully on the white table-cloth and in Katya's red hair. Through the double frames they could hear the cawing of rooks and the singing of starlings in the garden.

'It is nine years since we met,' said the old lady. 'And when I looked at you in the monastery yesterday—good Lord! You've not changed a bit, except maybe you are thinner and your beard is a little longer. Holy Mother, Queen of Heaven! Yesterday at the evening service no one could help crying. I, too, as I looked at you, suddenly began crying, though I couldn't say why. His Holy Will be done!'

And in spite of the affectionate tone in which she said this, he could see she was constrained as though uncertain whether to address him formally or familiarly, to laugh or not, and as though she felt herself more a deacon's widow than his mother. And Katya gazed without blinking at her uncle, the bishop, as if trying to discover what sort of a person he was. Her hair sprang up from under the comb and the velvet ribbon and stood out like a halo; she had a turned-up nose and sly eyes. The child had broken a glass before sitting down to dinner, and now her grandmother, as she talked, moved away from Katya first a wine-glass and then a tumbler. The bishop listened to his mother and remembered how many, many years ago she used to take him and his brothers and sisters to relations whom she considered rich; in those days she went pleading with her children, but now it was with her grandchildren, and she had brought Katya . . .

'Your sister, Varenka, has four children,' she told him; 'Katya, here, is the eldest. And your brother-in-law Father Ivan fell sick, God knows of what, and died three days before the Assumption; and my poor Varenka is left a beggar.'

'And how is Nikanor getting on?' the bishop asked about his eldest brother.

'He is all right, thank God. Though it's nothing much, he has enough to live on, praise be to God. Only there is one thing: his son Nikolasha, my grandson, did not want to go into the Church; he has gone to the University to be a doctor. He thinks that's better; but who knows! His Holy Will be done!'

'Nikolasha cuts up dead people,' said Katya, spilling water over her knees.

'Sit still, child,' her grandmother observed calmly, and took the glass out of her hand. 'Say a prayer, and go on eating.'

'How long it is since we met!' said the bishop, and he tenderly stroked his mother's hand and shoulder; 'and I missed you abroad, Mother dear, I missed you dreadfully.'

'Thank you kindly.'

'I used to sit in the evenings at the open window, all alone; often there was music playing, and suddenly I used to be overcome with a longing for my native land and felt as though I would give up everything, just to be home and seeing you.'

His mother smiled, beamed, but at once she made a grave face and said: 'Thank you kindly.'

His mood suddenly changed. He looked at his mother and could not understand why she had that respectful, timid expression on her face and in her voice: what was it for? And he could not recognise her. He felt sad and vexed. And also his head ached just as it had the day before; his legs hurt dreadfully, and the fish seemed stale and tasteless; he felt thirsty all the time . . .

After dinner two rich ladies, landowners, arrived and sat for an hour and a half in silence with rigid countenances; the archimandrite, a silent, rather deaf man, came to see him about business. Then they began ringing for vespers; the sun set behind the wood and the day was over. When he returned from church, the bishop hurriedly said his prayers, climbed into bed, and wrapped himself up as warm as possible.

It was disagreeable to remember the fish he had eaten at dinner. The moonlight bothered him, and then he heard conversation. In an adjoining room, probably in the parlour, Father Sisoy was talking politics:

'The Japanese are at war now. They are fighting. The Japanese, my dear, are the same as the Montenegrins; they are the same race. They were under the Turkish yoke together.'

And then he heard the voice of Mariya Timofeyevna:

'So, having said our prayers and having drunk our tea, we went, you know, to Father Yegor at Novokatnoye, and so . . .'

And she kept on saying, 'having drunk our tea' or 'having had our tea', and it sounded as if the only thing she had done in her life was drink tea.

The bishop slowly, sluggishly, recalled the seminary, the academy. For some three years he had been Greek teacher in the seminary; by that time he could not read without spectacles. Then he became a monk, and was made second master. Then he defended his thesis for his degree. When he was thirty-two he was made rector of the seminary, and consecrated archimandrite, and then his life was so easy and pleasant; it seemed so long, so long, no end was in sight. But then he had fallen ill, grown very thin and almost went blind, and on doctors' advice he had had to give up everything and go abroad.

'And then what?' asked Sisoy in the next room.

'Then we drank tea . . .' answered Mariya Timofeyevna.

'Father, you've got a green beard!' said Katya suddenly in surprise, and she laughed.

The bishop remembered that Father Sisoy's grey beard really did have a tinge of green, and he laughed.

'God have mercy upon us, what a nuisance this child is!' said Sisoy in a loud, angry voice. 'Spoilt child! Sit still!'

The bishop remembered the perfectly new white church in which he had conducted the services while living abroad, he remembered the sound of the warm sea. His apartment had five light, lofty rooms, with a new desk in his study, and a library. He had read a great deal and often written. And he remembered how he had longed for his native land, how a blind beggar woman had played the guitar under his window every day and sung of love, and how, as he listened, he had always for some reason thought of the past. But eight years had passed and he had been called back to Russia, and now he was a suffragan bishop, and all the past had retreated to somewhere far away, into the mist, as if it were a dream . . .

Father Sisoy came into the bedroom with a candle.

'Oho!' he said, wondering, 'are you asleep already, Your Eminence?'

'What is it?'

'Why, it's still early, ten o'clock or less. I bought a candle today; I wanted to rub you with candle grease.'

'I have a temperature . . .' said the bishop, and he sat up. 'I really ought to try something. My head feels bad . . .'

Sisoy took off the bishop's shirt and began rubbing his chest and back with candle grease.

'That's the way . . . that's the way . . .' he said. 'Lord Jesus Christ . . . That's the way. I walked to the town today; I was at what's-his-name's—the archpriest Sidonsky's . . . I had tea with him . . . I don't loike him! Lord Jesus Christ . . . That's the way. I don't loike him!'

III

The diocesan bishop, a very fat old man, was ill with rheumatism or gout, and had been in bed for over a month. Bishop Pyotr visited him almost every day, and saw all who came to ask his help. And now, when he himself felt unwell, he was struck by the emptiness, the triviality of everything for which they asked and wept; he was vexed at their ignorance, their timidity; and all this useless pettiness oppressed him by its sheer mass, and it seemed to him that now he understood the diocesan bishop, who had once in his young days written 'Studies on Free Will', and now seemed to be all lost in trivialities, to have forgotten everything, never giving any thought to God. The bishop must have lost touch with Russian life while he was abroad; he did not find it easy; the peasants seemed coarse to him, the women who sought his help seemed dull and stupid, the seminarists and their teachers uncultivated and at times barbarous. And the documents coming in and going out were reckoned by tens of thousands; and what documents they were! The senior clergy in the whole diocese gave the priests, young and old, and even their wives and children, marks for their behaviour—a five, a four, and sometimes even as low as a three; and about this he had to talk, read and write serious reports. And there was positively not one minute free; his soul was troubled all day long, and the bishop felt at peace only when he was in church.

He could not get used, either, to the awe which, through no wish of his own, he inspired in people despite his quiet, modest disposition. All the people in the province seemed to him small, frightened, and guilty when he looked at them. Everyone was timid in his presence, even the old archpriests; everyone 'flopped' at his feet, and recently one old lady, a village priest's wife who had come to ask for help, was so overawed that she could not utter a single word, and went away empty-handed. And he, who could never in his sermons bring himself to speak ill of people, never reproached anyone because he felt so sorry for them, was moved to fury with the people who came to consult him, lost his temper and flung their petitions on the floor. The whole time he had been here, not one person had spoken to him sincerely, simply, in a human fashion; even his old mother seemed different, quite different! And why, he wondered, did she chatter away to Sisoy and laugh so much; while with him, her son, she was grave and usually silent and constrained, which did not suit her at all? The only person who behaved freely with him and said what he meant was old Sisoy, who had spent his whole life in the presence of bishops and had outlived eleven of them. And so the bishop was at ease with him, although, of course, Sisoy was a tedious and cantankerous man.

After the service on Tuesday, Bishop Pyotr was in the diocesan bishop's house receiving petitioners there; he grew excited and angry, and then drove home. He felt unwell, as before; he longed to be in bed, but he had hardly reached home when he was informed that Yerakin, the young merchant, who subscribed liberally to charities, had come to see him about a very important matter. The bishop had to receive him. Yerakin stayed about an hour, talked very loud, almost shouted, and it was difficult to understand what he said.

'God grant it may,' he said as he went away. 'Most essential! According to circumstances, Your Eminence! I trust it may!'

After him came the Mother Superior from a distant convent. And when she had gone they began ringing for vespers, and he had to go to church.

In the evening the monks sang harmoniously, with inspiration. A young priest-monk with a black beard conducted the service; and the bishop, hearing of the bridegroom who cometh at midnight and the mansion richly adorned, did not feel repentance for his sins, nor tribulation, but peace at heart and tranquillity. And he was carried back in thought to the distant past, to his childhood and youth, when, too, they used to sing of the bridegroom and of the mansion; and now this past seemed vivid, beautiful, joyful, such as in all likelihood it never had been. And perhaps, in the next world, in the life to come, we shall remember the distant past and our life here on earth with the same feeling. Who knows? The bishop was sitting near the altar. It was dark; tears flowed down his face. He reflected that he had achieved everything accessible to a man in his position, he was a believer, and yet not everything was clear, there was something still missing, he did not want to die; and it still seemed to him that he lacked something most important of which he had once vaguely dreamed, and that now in the present he was still disturbed by that same hope for the future which he had felt in childhood, at the academy and abroad.

'How wonderful their singing is today!' he thought, listening to the choir. 'How wonderful!'

IV

On Thursday he celebrated Mass in the cathedral; it was the Washing of Feet. When the service was over and the people were going home, it was sunny, warm, cheerful; water gurgled in the ditches, and the unceasing trilling of the larks, tender, invoking peace, rose from the fields outside the town. The trees had already awakened and smiled welcomingly, while above them the infinite, fathomless blue sky stretched into the distance, God alone knows how far.

On reaching home Bishop Pyotr drank some tea, then changed, lay down on his bed, and told the lay brother to close the shutters on the windows. The bedroom was darkened. But what weariness, what pain in his legs and back, a chill heavy pain, what a noise in his ears! He had not slept for a long time—for a very long time, so it seemed to him now, and some trifling detail which haunted his brain as soon as his eyes were closed prevented him from sleeping. As on the day before, sounds reached him from the adjoining rooms through the walls, voices, the jingle of glasses and teaspoons . . . Mariya Timofeyevna was cheerfully telling Father Sisoy some story with quaint turns of speech, while the latter answered in a grumpy, ill-humoured voice: 'Bother them! Not likely! What next!' And the bishop again felt vexed and then hurt that with other people his old mother behaved in a simple, ordinary way, while with him, her son, she was shy, spoke little, and did not say what she meant, and even, so it seemed to him, all this time she had tried in his presence to find an excuse to stand up, because she felt embarrassed to sit before him. And his father? Probably, if he had been alive, he would not have been able to utter a word in his son's presence . . .

Something fell on the floor in the adjoining room and broke; Katya must have dropped a cup or a saucer, for Father Sisoy suddenly spat and said angrily:

'What a regular nuisance this child is! Lord, forgive me, a sinner! We'll soon have nothing left!'

Then all was quiet, the only sounds came from outside. And when the bishop opened his eyes he saw Katya in his room, standing motionless, and looking at him. Her red hair, as usual, stood up from under the comb like a halo.

'Is that you, Katya?' he asked. 'Who is it downstairs who keeps opening and shutting the door?'

'I can't hear it,' answered Katya; and she listened.

'There, someone has just passed by.'

'But that was a noise in your stomach, Uncle dear!'

He laughed and stroked her hair.

'So you say Cousin Nikolasha cuts up dead people?' he asked after a pause.

'Yes, he is studying.'

'And is he kind?'

'Oh yes, he's kind. But he drinks vodka awfully.'

'And what did your father die of?'

'Papa was weak and very, very thin, and all at once his throat was bad. I was ill then, too, and brother Fedya; we all had bad throats. Papa died, Uncle dear, but we got better.'

Her chin began quivering, and tears came to her eyes and trickled down her cheeks.

'Your Eminence,' she said in a tiny voice, by now weeping bitterly, 'Uncle dear, Mummy and I are left very wretched . . . Give us a little money . . . do be so kind . . . Uncle darling! . . .'

He, too, was moved to tears, and for a long time was too upset to speak. Then he stroked her hair, patted her on the shoulder and said:

'All right, all right, my child. When Christ's bright Easter Sunday comes, we will talk it over . . . I will help you . . . I will help you . . .'

His mother came in quietly, timidly, and prayed before the icons. Noticing that he was awake, she asked:

'Won't you have a drop of soup?'

'No, thank you,' he answered, 'I'm not hungry.'

'You seem to be unwell, now I look at you. No wonder you fall ill! On your feet all day, all day . . . And, my goodness, it makes my heart ache even to look at you! Well, Holy Week isn't far off; then you will rest, please God, and then we will have a talk, too, but now I won't disturb you with my chatter. Come along, Katya dear; let His Eminence sleep a little.'

466

And he remembered how once very long ago, when he was a boy, she had spoken exactly like that, in the same playfully respectful tone, with a member of the senior clergy . . . Only from her extraordinarily kind eyes and the timid, anxious glance she stole at him as she went out of the room could one have guessed that this was his mother. He closed his eyes and seemed to be sleeping, but twice heard the clock strike and Father Sisoy coughing the other side of the wall. And once more his mother came in and looked timidly at him for a minute. He heard someone drive up to the front steps, in a coach or in a chaise. Suddenly a knock, the door slammed, and the lay brother came into the bedroom.

'Your Eminence!' he called out.

'What?'

'The horses are here; it's time for the Lord's Passion.'

'What time is it?'

'A quarter past seven.'

He dressed and drove to the cathedral. During all the twelve Gospel passages he had to stand in the middle of the church without moving, and the first Gospel, the longest and most beautiful, he read himself. A mood of confidence and courage came over him. This first Gospel, 'Now is the Son of man glorified,' he knew by heart; and as he read he raised his eyes from time to time, and saw on both sides a whole sea of lights and heard the splutter of candles, but, as in past years, he could not see the people, and it seemed that these were the same people who had been in those days, in his childhood and youth; that they would always be the same every year—and until such time as only God knows.

His father had been a deacon, his grandfather a priest, his great-grandfather a deacon, and his entire family, perhaps, from the days when Christianity was accepted in Russia, had belonged to the priesthood; and his love for Church services, for the priesthood, for the pealing of bells, was innate, profound, ineradicable. In church, especially when he himself was officiating, he felt active, cheerful, happy. So it was now. Only when the eighth Gospel had been read, he felt that his voice had grown weak, even his cough was inaudible. His head had begun to ache intensely, and he was troubled by a fear that he might fall down at any moment. And his legs were indeed quite numb, so that gradually he ceased to feel them and could not understand how or on what he was standing, and why he did not fall . . .

467

It was a quarter to twelve when the service was over. On reaching home, the bishop undressed and went to bed at once without even saying his prayers. He could not speak and it seemed to him that he could not have stood up. As he covered himself with the blanket he felt a sudden longing to go abroad, an unbearable longing! He felt that he would give up his life not to see these pitiful cheap shutters, these low ceilings, to escape this oppressive monastery smell. If only there were one person to whom he could talk and unburden his heart!

For a long while he heard footsteps in the next room, yet he could not recall whose they were. At last the door opened, and Sisoy came in with a candle and a teacup in his hands.

'Are you already in bed, Your Eminence?' he asked. 'And I've come to rub you with vodka and vinegar. A thorough rubbing does a great deal of good. Lord Jesus Christ . . . That's the way . . . that's the way . . . I've just been to our monastery . . . I don't loike it! I'm going away from here tomorrow, Your Eminence; I don't want to stay longer. Lord Jesus Christ . . . That's the way . . .'

Sisoy could never stay long in the same place, and it seemed to him that he had been a whole year in the Pankratiyevsky Monastery. Above all, listening to him, it was difficult to understand where his home was, whether he cared for anyone or anything, whether he believed in God . . . He himself did not know why he was a monk, and, indeed, he did not think about it, and the time when he had taken his vows had faded long ago from his memory; it was as if he had been born a monk.

'I'm going away tomorrow; I've had enough of it all!'

'I should like to talk to you . . . I just can't find the time,' said the bishop softly, with an effort. 'You see, I don't know anything or anybody here . . .'

'I'll stay till Sunday if you like; so be it, but I don't want to stay longer. I am sick of them!'

'I ought not to be a bishop,' said the bishop softly. 'I should have been a village priest, a sexton . . . or a simple monk . . . All this oppresses me . . . oppresses me . . .'

'What? Lord Jesus Christ . . . That's the way . . . Come, sleep well, Your Eminence! . . . It's no use! What next! Good night!'

The bishop did not sleep all night. And at about eight o'clock in the morning he began to haemorrhage from the bowels. The lay brother was frightened, and ran first to the archimandrite, then for the monastery doctor, Ivan Andreich, who lived in town. The doctor, a stout old man with a long grey beard, made a prolonged examination of the bishop, and kept shaking his head and frowning, then said:

'Do you know, Your Eminence, you have typhoid?'

After an hour or so of bleeding the bishop looked much thinner, paler, and wasted; his face was wrinkled, his eyes were large, and he appeared older, smaller, and it now seemed to him that he was thinner and weaker, more insignificant than everyone, that all the past had gone far, far away and there would be no repetition or continuation.

'How wonderful!' he thought. 'How wonderful!'

His old mother came. Seeing his wrinkled face and large eyes, she was frightened, she fell on her knees by the bed and began kissing his face, his shoulders, his hands. And to her, too, it seemed for some reason that he was thinner, weaker, and more insignificant than everyone, and she no longer remembered that he was a bishop, and she kissed him as if he were a child, very close and dear to her.

'Pavlusha, darling,' she said, 'my own one! . . . my darling son! . . . Why are you like this? Pavlusha, answer me!'

Katya, pale and severe, stood beside her, unable to understand what was happening to her uncle, why there was such suffering on her grandmother's face, why she was saying such sad and touching words. But he could no longer utter a word, he could understand nothing, and it appeared to him that he—now a simple, ordinary man—was striding across a field, quickly and cheerfully, tapping with his stick, and overhead was the broad, sunlit sky, and he was now as free as a bird, and could go wherever he liked!

'Pavlusha, my darling son, answer me!' the old woman was saying. 'What is happening to you? My own one!'

'Don't disturb His Eminence,' Sisoy said angrily, as he crossed the room. 'Let him sleep . . . What's the use . . . it's no good . . .'

Three doctors arrived, consulted together, and went away again. The day was long, remarkably long, then the night came on and passed slowly, slowly, and towards morning on Saturday the lay brother went in to the old mother who was lying on the sofa in the parlour, and asked her to go into the bedroom: the bishop had breathed his last.

Next day was Easter Sunday. There were forty-two churches and six monasteries in the town; the sonorous, joyful clang of the bells hung over the town from morning till night unceasingly, stirring the spring air; the birds were singing, the sun shone brightly. The big market square was noisy, swings were swaying, barrel organs were playing, an

469

accordion was screeching, drunken voices were shouting. In the afternoon there were trotting races down the main street—in short, there was good cheer, all was well, just as it had been the year before and would be, in all likelihood, in years to come.

A month later a new suffragan bishop was appointed, and no one recollected Bishop Pyotr any more. And then he was completely forgotten. And only the dead man's old mother, who now lived with her son-in-law the deacon in a remote little district town, when she went out at night to bring her cow in and met other women at the pasture, would begin talking of her children and her grandchildren, and told that she once had a son who was a bishop, and as she did so she spoke timidly, fearing they would not believe her . . .

And, indeed, not everyone did believe her.

Notes

Biographical Note

Anton Pavlovich Chekhov, the third son of a despotic shopkeeper and grandson of a serf, was born on 17 January 1860 in the south Russian port of Taganrog. After a grim provincial childhood, he studied medicine at Moscow University, qualifying as a doctor in June 1884. The first signs of his tuberculosis occurred in December 1884. For several years Chekhov combined twin professions, as doctor and writer.

For the most part, his life was outwardly uneventful. Despite persistent ill-health and the demands of writing, Chekhov supported his improvident family, treated peasants for their everyday ailments and at times of famine and cholera, planted trees, built schools, and donated books to the Taganrog library. In 1890, he undertook the unexpected and arduous journey across Siberia to the island of Sakhalin, where he conducted a detailed census of some 10,000 convicts and settlers.

A self-disciplined and private man, Chekhov lived on his estate in Melikhovo from 1892 to 1898, travelling to Western Europe (notably Italy and France) in 1891 and 1894. After suffering a massive lung haemorrhage in 1897, he was forced to spend his final years largely in Yalta or Nice. Chekhov married the actress Olga Knipper in 1901. Ravaged by tuberculosis, he died in the south German spa of Badenweiler on 2 July 1904.

For a survey of English-language biographies, see the Introduction to *Chekhov: A Life in Letters*, translated and edited by Gordon McVay (London: The Folio Society, 1994), pp. ix–xxii. Since then, two further biographies have appeared—Philip Callow's sympathetic, yet inessential *Chekhov: The Hidden Ground* (London: Constable, 1998) and Donald Rayfield's monumental, indispensable, but controversial *Anton Chekhov: A Life* (London: HarperCollins, 1997).

Textual Notes

In the notes below, the first publication of each story is indicated. In many instances, Chekhov revised his stories for subsequent editions.

All the translations in this Folio selection follow the definitive texts in A. P. Chekhov's *Polnoe sobranie sochinenii i pisem v tridtsati tomakh* [*Complete Collected Works and Letters in Thirty Volumes*], Moscow: 'Nauka', 1974–83 (works in eighteen volumes, letters in twelve volumes).

For the Folio edition, Constance Garnett's translations have been revised by Gordon McVay.

Where a story has been translated into English under various titles, some alternative versions are listed.

The Death of a Civil Servant [*Smert´ chinovnika*]

First published in the Petersburg comic weekly *Fragments* (or *Splinters*) [*Oskolki*], 2 July 1883, under the pseudonym A. Chekhonte. This was Chekhov's favourite pseudonym during his early years as a writer.

This translation first published in *Chekhov: The Early Stories, 1883–88*, translated by Patrick Miles and Harvey Pitcher, London: John Murray, 1982. The story is also known in English as 'Death of a Clerk', 'The Death of a Government Clerk', or 'The Death of an Official'.

Fat and Thin [*Tolstyi i tonkii*]

First published in *Fragments*, 1 October 1883.

This translation first published in *Chekhov: The Early Stories, 1883–88*, translated by Patrick Miles and Harvey Pitcher, London: John Murray, 1982.

The Huntsman [*Eger´*]

First published in the Petersburg daily newspaper *The Petersburg Gazette* [*Peterburgskaia gazeta*], 18 July 1885.

This translation first published in *Chekhov: The Early Stories, 1883–88*, translated by Patrick Miles and Harvey Pitcher, London: John Murray, 1982. This story is also known in English as 'The Hunter'.

'The Huntsman' was highly praised by the older writer, Dmitry Grigorovich, in his letter to Chekhov on 25 March 1886: '. . . I was struck by its distinct originality and, above all, by the remarkable truthfulness of its characterisation and nature descriptions.'

Sergeant Prishibeyev [*Unter Prishibeev*]

First published in *The Petersburg Gazette*, 5 October 1885.

This translation first published in *Chekhov: The Early Stories, 1883–88*, translated by Patrick Miles and Harvey Pitcher, London: John Murray, 1982.

Misery [*Toska*]

First published in *The Petersburg Gazette*, 27 January 1886.

This translation first published in *The Tales of Tchehov*, Vol. 9, *The School-mistress and Other Stories*, translated by Constance Garnett, London: Chatto & Windus, 1920. The story is also known in English as 'Despair', 'Grief', or 'Heart-ache'.

Easter Night [*Sviatoiu noch'iu*]

First published in the Petersburg daily newspaper *New Times* [*Novoe vremia*], 13 April 1886.

This translation first published in *Chekhov: The Early Stories, 1883–88*, translated by Patrick Miles and Harvey Pitcher, London: John Murray, 1982. The story is also known in English as 'Easter Eve'.

On 3 November 1888 Chekhov wrote to A. S. Suvorin, the editor of *New Times*, concerning the monk Nikolay in 'Easter Night': 'Merezhk[ovsky] calls my monk, the one who composed hymns of praise to God, a failure in his personal life. How is he a failure? God grant everyone a life like his: he believed in God, he had enough to eat, and he possessed creative talent . . . Dividing people into successes and failures means looking at human nature from a narrow and prejudiced angle . . . Are you a success or not? Am I? And Napoleon? And your Vasily? What's the criterion? One would need to be God to separate the successes accurately from the failures . . .' (Vasily was Suvorin's manservant.)

Romance with Double-Bass [*Roman s kontrabasom*]

First published in *Fragments*, 7 June 1886.

This translation first published in *Chekhov: The Early Stories, 1883–88*, translated by Patrick Miles and Harvey Pitcher, London: John Murray, 1982. The story is also known in English as 'Love Affair with a Double-Bass', 'A Romantic Adventure with a Contrabass', or 'Romance with a Double Bass'.

Vanka [*Van'ka*]

First published in *The Petersburg Gazette*, 25 December 1886, in the section 'Christmas Stories'.

This translation first published in *Chekhov: The Early Stories, 1883–88*, translated by Patrick Miles and Harvey Pitcher, London: John Murray, 1982.

The Reed-Pipe [*Svirel´*]

First published in *New Times*, 29 August 1887.

This translation first published in *Chekhov: The Early Stories, 1883–88*, translated by Patrick Miles and Harvey Pitcher, London: John Murray, 1982. The story is also known in English as 'Panpipes' or 'The Shepherd's Pipe'.

Boys [*Mal´chiki*]

First published in *The Petersburg Gazette*, 21 December 1887.

This translation first published in *Chekhov: The Comic Stories*, translated by Harvey Pitcher, London: André Deutsch, 1998. The story is also known in English as 'The Boys'.

Kashtanka [*Kashtanka*]

First published in *New Times*, 25 December 1887, under the title 'In Learned Society' [*V uchenom obshchestve*].

This translation first published in *Chekhov: The Comic Stories*, translated by Harvey Pitcher, London: André Deutsch, 1998.

A Lady's Story [*Rasskaz gospozhi NN*]

First published in *The Petersburg Gazette*, 25 December 1887.

This translation first published in The *Tales of Tchehov*, Vol. 9, *The Schoolmistress and Other Stories*, translated by Constance Garnett, London: Chatto & Windus, 1920. The story is also known in English as 'The Story of Miss N. N.' or 'Lady N—'s Story'.

No Comment [*Bez zaglaviia*]

First published in *New Times*, 1 January 1888.

This translation first published in *Chekhov: The Early Stories, 1883–88*, translated by Patrick Miles and Harvey Pitcher, London: John Murray, 1982. The story is also known in English as 'A Story without a Title'.

The Beauties [*Krasavitsy*]

First published in *New Times*, 21 September 1888.

This translation first published in *The Tales of Tchehov*, Vol. 9, *The Schoolmistress and Other Stories*, translated by Constance Garnett, London: Chatto & Windus, 1920. This story is also known in English as 'Beauties'.

A Dreary Story [*Skuchnaia istoriia*]

First published in the Petersburg monthly journal *The Northern Herald* [*Severnyi vestnik*], November 1889, No. 11.

This translation first published in *The Tales of Tchehov*, Vol. 5, *The Wife and Other Stories*, translated by Constance Garnett, London: Chatto & Windus, 1918. The story is also known in English as 'A Boring Story', 'A Tedious Story', or 'Dull Story'.

The dilemma of the protagonist (an old professor suffering from the lack of a linking 'general idea') reflects aspects of Chekhov's own unease and underlying aimlessness.

Chekhov had written to A. S. Suvorin on 24 or 25 November 1888: 'You and I love ordinary people—yet people love us [writers] because they regard us as out of the ordinary. For example, people shower me with invitations, I'm wined and dined everywhere like a general at a wedding . . . No one wants to love us as ordinary people . . .' This predicament ('No one wants to love us as ordinary people . . .') plagues the heroes of such works as 'A Dreary Story' and 'The Bishop'.

Gusev [*Gusev*]

First published in *New Times*, 25 December 1890, where it was dated 'Colombo, 12 November'.

This translation first published in *The Tales of Tchehov*, Vol. 6, *The Witch and Other Stories*, translated by Constance Garnett, London: Chatto & Windus, 1918.

Chekhov had written to Suvorin on 23 December 1890: 'Since the story was conceived on the island of Ceylon, you may, if you wish, add at the bottom, to impress the readers: "Colombo, 12 November". . .'

This was the first story published after Chekhov's return from the island of Sakhalin. The closing section of 'Gusev' is echoed in Chekhov's letter to Suvorin on 9 December 1890: 'On the way to Singapore two corpses were cast into the sea. When you see a dead man wrapped in sailcloth somersaulting into the water and remember that it's several miles down to the bottom, you become frightened and somehow begin to think that you too will die and be cast into the sea . . .'

The Grasshopper [*Poprygun'ia*]

First published in the Petersburg weekly *The North* [*Sever*], 5 and 12 January 1892.

This translation first published in *The Tales of Tchehov*, Vol. 5, *The Wife and Other Stories*, translated by Constance Garnett, London: Chatto & Windus,

1918. The story is also known in English as 'The Butterfly' or 'The Dragonfly'.

To some extent, the story is based on real figures and situations—the salon of S. P. Kuvshinnikova, the artist I. I. Levitan, and others.

In Exile [*V ssylke*]

First published in the Petersburg weekly *World Illustrated* [*Vsemirnaia illiustratsiia*], 9 May 1892.

This translation first published in *The Tales of Tchehov*, Vol. 9, *The Schoolmistress and Other Stories*, translated by Constance Garnett, London: Chatto & Windus, 1920.

The story reflects Chekhov's impressions of Siberia and Sakhalin in 1890.

Ward No. 6 [*Palata No. 6*]

First published in the Moscow monthly journal *Russian Thought* [*Russkaia mysl´*], November 1892, No. 11.

This translation first published in *The Tales of Tchehov*, Vol. 10, *The Horse-Stealers and Other Stories*, translated by Constance Garnett, London: Chatto & Windus, 1921.

With typical self-deprecation, Chekhov had written on 25 October 1892 to Vukol Lavrov, the publisher and editor of *Russian Thought*: '. . . I really should give a fresh coat of paint to my "Ward", as it reeks of the hospital and the morgue. I'm not an enthusiast for that type of story . . .'

'Ward No. 6' embodies many aspects of Chekhov's thought, about medicine, the Stoic philosophy of Marcus Aurelius, protest and resignation.

The Black Monk [*Chernyi monakh*]

First published in the Moscow monthly journal *The Artiste* [*Artist*], January 1894, No. 1.

This translation first published in *The Tales of Tchehov*, Vol. 3, *The Lady with the Dog and Other Stories*, translated by Constance Garnett, London: Chatto & Windus, 1917.

On 25 January 1894 Chekhov wrote to Suvorin: 'It seems to me that my mental health is quite normal. Admittedly, I have no particular desire to live, yet that's not really an illness but probably something transitional and natural. At all events, if an author depicts a character who is mentally ill, that does not mean that he himself is ill. I wrote "The Black Monk" in a mood of cold reflection, without experiencing any depressed thoughts. I simply felt like depicting delusions of grandeur. The monk who scuds across the field appeared to me in a dream, and, upon waking up in the morning, I told Misha about it. So you can tell Anna Ivanovna that, thank God, poor Anton Pavlovich has not yet taken leave of his senses, but simply tucks in to a good supper and as a result sees monks in his dreams . . .' (Misha was Chekhov's brother, Mikhail; Anna Ivanovna was Suvorin's wife.)

'The Black Monk' evinces Chekhov's interest in psychiatry, and his lifelong love of gardening.

Rothschild's Fiddle [*Skripka Rotshil'da*]

First published in the Moscow daily newspaper *The Russian Gazette* [*Russkie vedomosti*], 6 February 1894.

This translation first published in *The Tales of Tchehov*, Vol. 8, *The Chorus Girl and Other Stories*, translated by Constance Garnett, London: Chatto & Windus, 1920.

The Student [*Student*]

First published in *The Russian Gazette*, 15 April 1894, under the title 'In the Evening' [*Vecherom*].

This translation first published in the present collection. The story is also known in English as 'At Evening'.

In 'The Student', the narration of Peter's threefold denial of Jesus combines the language of everyday conversation with direct quotations from the Gospels (see especially Luke, chapter 22; also Matthew, chapter 26, Mark, chapter 14, and John, chapter 18).

According to the writer Ivan Bunin, Chekhov described 'The Student' as his favourite story, and a refutation of his alleged 'pessimism'. Bunin recalls Chekhov's words: 'How am I a moaner? How am I a "gloomy person", "cold-blooded", as the critics call me? How am I a "pessimist"? After all, of my own works "The Student" is my favourite story . . . And the word itself is repulsive: "pessimist" . . .' (I. A. Bunin, *O Chekhove* [*About Chekhov*], New York: 'Chekhov Publishing House', 1955, p. 57). Chekhov's brother, Ivan, claimed that Anton valued 'The Student' above all his other works, because he considered it the 'most polished' artistically.

The House with the Mezzanine [*Dom s mezoninom*]

First published in *Russian Thought*, April 1896, No. 4.

This translation first published in *The Tales of Tchehov*, Vol. 1, *The Darling and Other Stories*, translated by Constance Garnett, London: Chatto & Windus, 1916.

Constance Garnett took Chekhov's subtitle, 'An Artist's Story', as the title of her translation. For this Folio edition, Chekhov's original title has been reinstated—the 'house with the mezzanine' is an important leitmotiv in the story. Other translators have given the title as 'The Artist's Story', 'The House with an Attic', or 'The House with the Mansard'.

Concerning the central argument between Lida and the artist, it might be remarked that Doctor Chekhov himself treated the peasants and built schools, and yet he also recognised the limitations of such activity and the need for more fundamental or radical measures.

Peasants [*Muzhiki*]

First published in *Russian Thought*, April 1897, No. 4.

This translation first published in *The Tales of Tchehov*, Vol. 6, *The Witch and Other Stories*, translated by Constance Garnett, London: Chatto & Windus, 1918. The story is also known in English as 'Mouzhiks'.

Chekhov wrote 'Peasants' in Melikhovo, his estate outside Moscow, and Melikhovo characters and events are reflected in the work. With its uncompromising picture of the harshness of peasant life, the story provoked controversy. The censor S. Sokolov noted the 'excessively dark' depiction of the illiterate, ignorant, tax-burdened peasantry, where drunken peasants beat their wives with impunity. For its first publication, Sokolov accordingly removed a page from the story (which Chekhov reinstated in subsequent editions).

Ionych [*Ionych*]

First published in the Petersburg *Monthly Literary Supplements to the Journal 'The Cornfield'* [*Ezhemesiachnye literaturnye prilozheniia k zhurnalu 'Niva'*], September 1898, No. 9. *The Cornfield* [*Niva*] was an illustrated weekly.

This translation first published in *The Tales of Tchehov*, Vol. 3, *The Lady with the Dog and Other Stories*, translated by Constance Garnett, London: Chatto & Windus, 1917. The story is also known in English as 'Doctor Startsev'.

Encased [*Chelovek v futliare*]

First published in *Russian Thought*, July 1898, No. 7.

This translation first published in *Chekhov: The Comic Stories*, translated by Harvey Pitcher, London: André Deutsch, 1998. The story is also known in English as 'A Hard Case', 'A Man Encased', 'The Encased Man', '[The] Man in a Case', 'The Man in a Shell', or 'The Man who lived in a Shell'.

'Encased' is the first story in Chekhov's 'little trilogy', followed by 'Gooseberries' and 'About Love'. These three linked stories explore the theme of freedom and restriction.